Praise for *London Bridge*

“Reading this novel reminds us once more w
wielded the literary influence he did. Céline
preached exactly what he pleased, especially
everything in the so-called Establishment, w
was prophetic as he gave voice to a giddy, don t-give-a-damn nervousness that has proven to be, like it or not, one of the defining characteristics of the second half of the twentieth century.”
—Harvard Review

“Céline invents a verbal London fog of his own amid which his weirdos and nasties can please themselves, consecrated to a cult of mere energy, like surrealists who have read too much Bergson. Eliot’s and Céline’s London fogs are not that far apart. . . . In a way, Céline readies you for life as if you, the reader, were an intern in a raucous, blood-bathed trauma center.”—Paul West, *Boston Phoenix*

“Whatever you think of Céline’s politics, it’s hard to deny his position as an innovative, influential and still readable writer. . . . This is the hard-edged-world so perfectly suited to Céline’s slangy, propulsive language, filled with ellipses and exclamation marks. Céline at his most grizzly is also Céline at his most maniacally funny.”*—Publishers Weekly*

“Translator Di Bernardi has achieved a tour de force by providing an English equivalent of the underground’s unsavory grammar and by re-creating Céline’s *metro emotif* (the latter’s own terms): dislocated phrases separated by ellipses, effecting a constant firing of verbal energy.”*—Library Journal*

“*London Bridge* is without question the warmest and most benign of all Céline’s works, amusing, grotesque in places, tender for the most part, full of enthusiasm of youth.”—Melvin Thomas, *Louis-Ferdinand Céline*

“Driven by a merciless cynicism, Céline mocks man’s hopes, but conveys as much compassion as ridicule for the human condition. This fine translation captures Céline’s trademark slangy style, a breathlessly hysterical flood of invective, desire, and self-loathing, punctuated with ellipses.”*—Magill Book Reviews*

“It’s a rollicking rollercoaster ride of language, and readers must hold on tight.”—Michael Perkins

"His novels are verbal frescoes peopled with horrendous giants, paraplegics, and gnomes, and are filled with scenes of grotesque sex, dismemberment and murder. Highly recommended."—*Reader's Review*

"The exuberance and humor in the novel equal anything Céline's done."—Harvey Pekar, *Riverfront Times*

"In Céline, one encounters the pure writer—someone who can suspend inhibitions, shut himself off into his fantasies, and plunge headlong into writing. . . . This late addition serves to strengthen an oeuvre that should not be ignored."—*Booklist*

Books by Louis-Ferdinand Céline in English Translation

Journey to the End of the Night

Death on the Installment Plan

Castle to Castle

North

Rigadoon

Mea Culpa *and* The Life and Work of Semmelweiss

Guignol's Band

Conversations with Professor Y

Louis-Ferdinand
Céline

London Bridge

Guignol's Band II

translated from the French by
Dominic Di Bernardi

Dalkey Archive Press

Originally published as *Le Pont du Londres* (Gallimard, 1964); revised, expanded edition published as *Guignol's Band II* (Gallimard, 1988).

First edition, 1995
First paperback edition, 1999

Library of Congress Cataloguing-in-Publication Data
Céline, Louis-Ferdinand, 1894-1961.
[Pont de Londres. English]
London Bridge : Guignol's Band II / Louis-Ferdinand Céline; translated by Dominic Di Bernardi.
1. World War, 1914-1918—England—London—Fiction. 2. French—England—London—History—20th century—Fiction. I. Di Bernardi, Dominic. II. Title.
PQ2607.E834P613 1995 843'.912—dc20 94-25168
ISBN 1-56478-071-6 cl
ISBN 1-56478-175-5 pb

Publication of this translation was made possible in part by grants from the Illinois Arts Council, a state agency, and the National Endowment for the Arts, a federal agency.

Dalkey Archive Press
Illinois State University
Campus Box 4241
Normal, IL 61790-4241

Translator's Preface

London Bridge is a continuation of Céline's novel *Guignol's Band* (1944; English translation, 1954), for which a summary might be useful. In the middle of the First World War, twenty-two-year-old Ferdinand leaves the battlefields of France for the streets of London, following a lead provided by Raoul Farcy, a soldier whom he met in an army hospital, since executed by firing squad. Raoul is the nephew of Cascade, arguably the most powerful pimp in London. The milieu's favorite watering hole is Prospero Jim's pub, the Dingby. Here Cascade informs Ferdinand that all the pimps who are being called up are entrusting Cascade with their stables of prostitutes. Adding to his problems is Inspector Matthew from Scotland Yard, arch-nemesis of all the pimps.

During their session Angèle, Cascade's legal wife, is attacked by a jealous hooker. Ferdinand and a fellow crony, Borokrom, aka Boro, escort her to a hospital where a cohort, Clodovitz, is on staff. Upon returning to the Dingby, Cascade alerts Ferdinand and Boro that Matthew is on their tail. Boro tosses a bomb into the Dingby.

Ferdinand flees the wreckage and eventually lands at the Greenwich shop of Titus Van Claben, pawnbroker extraordinaire, who dresses up like a pasha and whose junk resembles an Oriental bazaar. Ferdinand discovers that Boro has already preceded him. He is dead drunk and starts a fight with Van Claben. Delphine arrives, an ex-English teacher forced to resign her post three times due to fights with her pupils. She is both mad about theater and literally mad. Although she is Van Claben's maid, she will allow herself to be called only "governess." Boro plays the piano and brawls with Van Claben. The latter, suffering from asthma, has an attack. Delphine goes out for Clodovitz, but quickly returns, claiming that she was attacked by "the Sky Magician." Furthermore, she claims this magician gave her "magic" cigarettes apparently laced with hashish. During the ensuing antics Van Claben takes out his sack of gold. Boro eats a few coins and, aided by Delphine, forces Van Claben to devour the remainder of the gold. Then in his attempts to get Van Claben to spit up the coins, Boro kills him. Ferdinand and Boro blame each other for the death; in turn Delphine accuses the pair.

The trio eventually takes the body to the cellar, but Boro locks in Ferdinand and Delphine and tosses in a bomb. The house burns to the ground, but the couple is saved by firemen. (The press calls the incident the "Greenwich Tragedy.") Boro shows up again and wants to haul Ferdinand back over to see Cascade. But Ferdinand jumps from a tube car and escapes.

In his wandering through London Ferdinand crosses paths with various hookers, including a woman nicknamed Curlers (French: Bigoudi) and the lesbians Finette and Fernande, and meets up with a character called Centipede (Mille-Pattes). The latter informs him that Boro has told Cascade that it was Ferdinand who threw the bomb in the Dingby. Centipede wants to take him to the Leicester pub to talk it out with Cascade. At the tube station, however, Ferdinand spies Matthew, thinks Centipede is setting him up, and pushes Centipede under an oncoming train.

Ferdinand is once again on the run, and winds up at the French Consulate, where he asks to sign up for the war. He is thrown out. In a delirium he sees all his Leicester pals dead at the front. Outside the Russian Consulate he meets up with Hervé Sosthène de Rodiencourt, an eccentric Frenchmen dressed in Chinese garb whose business card reads "Licensed mining prospector, explorer of the occult regions, experienced engineer." After Ferdinand fills in Sosthène on how and why he came to London, Sosthène announces that he has planned an expedition to Tibet and hires Ferdinand to take care of their horses. He gives Ferdinand an introductory talk on mystic lore, including the much-prized Tara-Tohé flower.

The next day Ferdinand shows up at Sosthène's. He is not in, but Ferdinand meets his wife Pépé, who flirts with him as well as with a milk delivery boy. Sosthène arrives back home and puts his wife in her place. Sosthène sees an ad in the *Times* placed by a colonel who is seeking volunteers to try out his gas masks, and the duo speed off to land the job.

In the course of part two Ferdinand also makes occasional references to another character named des Pereires. This is Courtial des Perieres, the eccentric inventor, who dominates the second half of Céline's *Death on the Installment Plan*.

The present translation is based on the fully revised text published in volume 3 of the Bibliothèque de la Pléiade edition of Céline's complete works (Gallimard, 1988). In 1964 a preliminary version of this text was published in France under the publisher's title *Le Pont de Londres*, based on the uncorrected, unrevised typescript, which Céline left in France before his flight to Germany and Denmark after the war. The revised Pléiade edition is the result of a compilation of several manuscripts, thus incorporating Céline's complete existing corrections and revisions. The Pléiade text faithfully transcribes Céline's manuscripts, which were never edited, much less copyedited, during his lifetime. It retains many idiosyncracies, including inconsistent spellings (e.g., London street and borough names, the Colonel's surname, Vedic demons) and English phrases that often are nonidiomatic when not ungrammatical. It is difficult to tell whether these many distortions were part of the author's aesthetic plan or merely the result of carelessness, the unsettled circumstances in which he wrote the novel, and/or lack of access to proper reference materials. Henri Godard, editor of the Pléiade edition, leans toward deliberate distortion on Céline's part, often giving correct spellings, quotations, and so forth only in the form of endnotes.

Since this translation of *London Bridge* is a trade edition aimed at the general reader, not a scholarly edition intended for the Céline specialist, the more obvious misspellings have been silently corrected. Other idiosyncracies have been allowed to stand: his Colonel O'Collogham probably should be spelled O'Callaghan, but that sort of tinkering has been avoided. His use of *Vegas* instead of *Vedas* is probably one of his deliberate distortions and thus has been retained, as have certain London street names that don't appear in any directory. For the scholarly debate surrounding Céline's geographical imprecisions, the interested reader can consult Jill Forbes's "Symbolique de l'espace: le 'Londres' célinien," *Actes du colloque de Paris*, 1976; Nicholas Hewitt's "Londres, capitale du XXième siècle," ibid., 1979; chap. 5 of Merlin Thomas's *Louis-Ferdinand Céline* (New Directions, 1979); and Peter Dun-woodie's "L'espace londonien: *Guignol's Band I & II*," *Australian Journal of French Studies* 2 (1982).

The doorway's already mobbed... Even though we'd raced over... so's the gate... so's the sidewalk... and every copy of the *Times* opened wide... Every last one of them is here about the want ad... A great-looking house... real posh... surrounded by a big garden... flower beds, roses, fantastic... some flunkey held the people back... urging patience.

"The Colonel is not ready!..." He shouted from the steps to keep them away.

Ah, hell! we didn't come here for this! Ah! waiting around isn't our style!...

Suddenly Sosthène explodes in a squeal over the crowd... "The Colonel! The Colonel! Quick! Quick! We're from the War Office... Emergency! Emergency!..."

He brandished his big roll of paper, unfurling it above the mob... like a banner!

"China! China!" he declared...

Naturally everybody cracks up... his chance to slip to the front...

"The fool! The fool!"

They think he's nuts.

I hurry after him, we're through the door, standing on the carpet, a magnificent vestibule! We give our shoes a good wipe... Huge paintings, antique tapestries... I'm an expert... It's a fantastic joint...

More servants crawl out of the woodwork... I bet they're here to kick us out!... Sosthène jumps down their throats... "War Office! Gas masks! Gas masks!"

He scowls, scares them, they keep staring, a little leery. They block the Chinaman's path. They circle around his Oriental robe for a look-see at his embroideries, especially the one covering his ass... He shows off his dragon... a beautiful blue and yellow fire-breathing beast! He's a smash!

"Speak English!" he says to me, "speak English!"

His plan is for me to start shooting my mouth off.

But no need... a very young girl... just a kid... but so pretty, a sweetheart!... fair-haired, a real charmer... Right away I'm all admiration... ah! ravishing!... ah! I'm knocked off my feet!... Ah! Love at first sight!... Ah! Those beautiful blue eyes!... That smile!... a real doll, I adore her!...

I shut my ears to the bullshitter beside me!... I've shut out everything, dead in my tracks, I'm speechless...

If only it wasn't for these crummy clothes!... I'm so ashamed... If only I'd had a quick shave... if only I wasn't in such big trouble... I'd come right out and tell her what she's doing to me... how wonderful it is... No! I wouldn't... I'd keep it all to myself just the way I am now... head-over-heels... drooling... miserable... Ah! I feel such joy!... I'm afraid to breathe!... Ah! she's so beautiful!...

The servants are puzzled... They were supposed to wait for their boss... They go off, leave us there... both standing in front of the little girl... we don't know which way to turn... How old is she? twelve... maybe thirteen, I'd say... anyway, that's my guess... and those calves!... short skirt... what grace... what superb legs... tanned, muscular, you name it!... she must be athletic... athletic girls always drive me crazy... That's just the way I picture fairies, in the same kind of short skirt!... And she's a fairy!... That creep Sosthène leering knowingly... sneaking winks at me... His sort shouldn't be allowed to look at her unless he's on his knees! stretched prostrate, begging her forgiveness!

"Uncle! Uncle!"... she even talks!... she's calling her uncle! What a voice! Pure crystal!... Ah! I'm hooked!

Sosthène gives me another wink, she catches him!... He'll ruin everything!

"It's OK! It's OK!..." he whispers back.

The jerk!

"The Colonel's coming!"

He's announced.

And here he comes.

"Virginia!... Virginia!..."

He walks up to us. He talks to his niece.

Ah! her name's Virginia... Such a pretty name, Virginia!

The Colonel's a fat pig, big and bloated, bursting at the seams, nothing like Colonel des Entrayes from my war days! With that big butt and tiny head, he looks like a cannonball in his dressing gown, with sharp beady eyes, and a scowl, actually a facial twitch constantly running back and forth across his nose from cheek to cheek, a rabbit wrinkle, he's always nibbling... He's bald... completely bald... He's got an eye that tears... just one... He keeps wiping it with a finger. He studies Sosthène. He looks at Virginia sternly.

"Why are they here?" he asks her. I can understand his English.

I jump right in.

"The War Office!" I declare very firmly.

Bold move!... I'll run the whole show!

I add: "The engineer only speaks French!..."

I point to Sosthène de Rodiencourt.

"Oh! Oh! But he's a Chinaman," he says with surprise.

That makes him laugh! He takes in the odd bird from head to toe. Sosthène unfolds his maps all around... his rolls of paper... he yanks out a steady stream of papers from his beautiful yellow robe... Ah! the Colonel's a tough one, but this is starting to distract him... He lets Sosthène jabber away, eggs him on with his gestures. He shows us into the living room like real guests. He leads the way... I'm afraid to take a seat... but then I dare... Such so-oothing armchairs! I slump down! Luscious monstrosities! Colossal sponges! Sopping up every drop of my exhaustion!...

Sosthène's still rattling away, dithering in the middle of the room, he didn't sit down, take a break, nothing... gesticulating, haranguing, spluttering... Now again he's brandishing his copy of the *Times*, the want ads...

"Do you understand me, Colonel! I tell you I'm just the man you're looking for! So you agree, yes? You can count on me one hundred percent! Me! Me!"

He's talking just about himself. Thumping his chest hard. He's afraid he's not getting through! Then he goes over to look out the window, shows the Colonel the crowd! all those people milling around down there... thronging the sidewalk... He won't have any more of that! no sir, won't hear another word! He won't put up with any competition!

"Ah! my dear Colonel, it's too bad! I'm telling you to your face! All those people have got to go! This situation's got to end!"

Ah, really he'd rather just leave!...

"I work alone or I leave! Come on, let's go!..."

He leads me away... A question of dignity!

Everybody's laughing, including the servants... holding him back by his basque...

"No! No! Sit down, sir!"

He's won... The guy's a riot!....

The Colonel wants to keep laughing, he makes him run away and back... pop his hat on and off... All this right in the living room... A real sideshow! Darling little Virginia is having as much fun as anyone, but she doesn't want Sosthène to make himself sick playing the buffoon!

"Sit down, sir! Sit down!"

Ah! But that's not what the Colonel wanted! he wanted the whole show with dressing gown, dragon, the works. Sosthène didn't catch on... he reeled off his life story while bopping along, bolting back and forth like some loony... his death-defying exploits in India, his unburied treasures... which slipped through his fingers... his raw deals with the Gem Company... and loads of other stuff... just like that while strutting around... his technical innovations, the veritable revolution in electromagnetic circuitry... the great debt science owed him... his special poison-gas detector calibrated to the millionth particle... all the patents he'd taken out since Berlin in 1902! everything he'd been chiseled out of...

"Drinks!" the Colonel orders.

A flunkey bustles off, comes back with an armload... an entire cellar of bottles, flasks, whiskey, cognac, champagne, sherry...

The Colonel pours himself a glass, then another, then another... He's drinking all by himself... And then another!...

"Baah!" he goes after each swig... The stuff packs a wallop.

He nestles back in his deep armchair, groans "Oooh!... Oooh!" over and over again... his belly's shaking... he's having a ball... he loves Sosthène... thinks he's really funny. Meanwhile I've been dying a thousand deaths, especially in front of the girl! Sosthène's still sneaking those looks at me. I wish the guy would shape up... No fucking way! He's on a roll!

"My dear Colonel, let me congratulate myself on being the perfect man to fit your bill!... I'm not afraid of coming right out with it! Lead us to the laboratory!... Just you wait and see!..."

Ah! ah! now the fun's really starting, and I mean the grand old rip-roaring variety! The Colonel's tickled pink. Slapping his thighs, crowing in delight. Out in the middle of the room Sosthène's still raring to go... running through his little act all over again... the flunkeys must be in a complete fog... he's just some loony, that's all! Every word out of his mouth is drowned in laughter... he's happy he's a hit... Great technique!... The Colonel offers him a drink... he doesn't want anything alcoholic... Soda water for him! plain soda water!

I go over to take a look into the street... the applicants are still milling around... Quite a mob... it keeps multiplying... more people constantly arriving... the ad hit its mark... they've all got the *Times* open over their heads!... It's raining now, a real downpour... Somebody's got to send them away, take charge... but the Colonel's not charging anywhere... He's still checking out Sosthène... I wonder if he understands French. He knocks back another glass of whiskey! Oooh!... His gasp echoes through the room. Each swig must scorch his mouth... But at least he hasn't kicked us out yet! That's the main thing! I'm sort of just twiddling my thumbs... Too bad Sosthène won't shut his mouth... keeps raising such hell... I wish I were a tiny mouse... and could hide here forever!...

And now the rain's coming down even harder!... Torrents lashing the windows... The job-hunters are soaked to the bone!... A rumble's mounting from the mob outside... gets to be disturbing... The Colonel's not bothered... He claps his hands... The lackeys bustle off, come back with more trays, set out a whole tableload of food... packed with eats, hors d'oeuvres!... what a terrific spread!... what mouthwatering goodies!... I'm drooling. Foaming at the mouth, in fact! My head's spinning... meat pies, anchovies! slices of ham! beef! Gorgonzola! whole heaps! Grub galore!... Ah! a wonderland of great pickings!... you can't imagine how it looked to my starving eyes! Mountains of butter!... Foothills, and soaring peaks! Ah! Everything's a blur! Ah! I'm seeing double! Triple! Before my eyes Sosthène starts swaying, shoots to the ceiling, stretched full height, for one second poises on tiptoe between heaven and earth... then whoosh! he swoops on the tray!... On all fours! Flat on his belly! Wolfing down, inhaling everything in sight!... a mastiff! growling like mad... Such a horrendous spectacle!... Got to find somewhere to hide!... The Colonel keeps his trap shut... tickled pink!... Anything but sore! He must have taken a shine to us! Fact is, the guy's elated!... Ah! he's never laughed so hard!... He leans down to help Sosthène stuff his face!... Shovels in whole platefuls of hors d'oeuvres! dumps them right into his mouth... And Sosthène just can't get enough... he asks for more... Ah! what a pretty sight this is in front of the girl!... My Chinaman's turned into a mad dog! greedy, lapping chow right from the rug! What an exhibition!...

Colonel O'Collogham offers me some chicken, but I'm not getting down on all fours!... on second thought, I'm famished... dizzy from hunger! About to collapse! But I don't give in! Won't touch a crumb! Not on my belly, on my butt, or on my feet! I don't want to eat ever again in front of my walking miracle, my fantasy! my soul! my dream!... I'm palpitating, quivering!... Nailed to the spot!... On fire!.... Dizzy with joy!... it was love at first sight. No, I'll never put food in my mouth again! I love her! I love her too much! How could I chew in front of her? Stuff my face like that other guy? The nerve of that pig!... So what, I'll die, tough luck!... I'd give my life for her!... die of hunger! but my goddess, my soul! she's inviting me to have a sandwich... or two... or three... how can I say no? she insists... smiles at me... I give in... helplessly... I give in!... Ah! she's got me beat!... I swallow it down!... bolt my food in turn!... The Colonel congratulates us... I'm excited, I've been beaten... We're devouring his four trays!... digging in with great gusto all around.

"Bravo, boys! Bravo!"

He's glad we've picked it clean... Ah! yes, now he's a real buddy! Let's do justice to his sandwiches! his leg of lamb! his caviar! his sweets, his bombe glacée! Magnificent tutti-frutti ice cream!... we inhale it!... But there's no contest, Sosthène's making the biggest pig of himself!... He's putting away at least a month's supply!... And whenever his jaws stop chomping he's right back to blabbing! Talking big! Dishing out his crazy stories!... he piles them on between mouthfuls... what a jerk! what crap!... nothing keeps him from yakking about how terrific he is! he lays it on thick... he's worked umpteen wonders!... Here comes another feat!... This invention, that invention!... his big spectroscopic mirror able to detect gaseous emissions... patented in Liverpool!

I think Sosthène's putting the Colonel to sleep... he's nodding back in his armchair... yawns quietly behind his hand... Ah! now I sneak a look at the little girl over there, that radiant mystery... Good God, she's beautiful!... What an angel!... What gentle grace!... And what darling mischievousness too!... I motion her slyly that I think Sosthène's talking too much!... I'm taking a risk... She answers back slyly... she's really very nice... "Let him go on!... Uncle's falling asleep!..." In fact her uncle was dozing off... Me too in the end, my eyes start blinking shut... I'm really done in!... Sosthène is still talking... I'd like to stay awake... Look at Virginia again... Never take my eyes off her!... adore her... but my lids won't stay open... my eyes heavy, burning... Ah! I mustn't seem very nice... nor fun to be around... nor even funny... I can't make her laugh like the other goof... I can't feel a thing except on the inside... The way my heart's pounding... I'm heavy... made of lead... lead over my eyes, filling my head... I'm pumped full of lead... Ah, I give up... I'm lead through and through... down to my bones... only my heart is light... pounding every which way... and that's just how I fall asleep, head in hands, elbows on knees... because I'm just too weak... I'd rather not drop off in front of the girl... but I give up... give up... Oh! please let me do anything but snore!... Virginia's standing right there in front of us!... How comfortable this living room is!... I'm only half dozing!... nodding off and on... I wish she wouldn't see me sleeping... I can still hear the other guy's bullshitting...

"Colonel sir... Colonel sir..."

He won't give it a rest!... his lousy voice lulls me... lulls me... I can't catch what he's saying.

We woke up the following morning around six... slumped back in the armchairs... everybody else had gone up to bed... They'd left us sleeping.

As soon as he heard the house stirring Sosthène started sniffing all around. He went down to the kitchen to boil some water. But he couldn't find any fixings for the coffee he wanted... he came back up to the living room, we polished off the eye of lamb and the meat pies... the leftovers...

Sosthène was raring to go... He went to wash up... another trip downstairs to the kitchen... This time he came back with an iron... He started pressing his dressing gown on the large dinner table... fussing over the pleats... at last he finds a flunkey... just passing through on his rounds...

"I'd like to see your Colonel again, Mr. O'Collogham! And make it snappy!... I'd like to have a word with him!..."

I had to act as translator. Nobody showed up.

We ran over to see whether any applicants were still waiting outside... They hadn't even gone home to bed! Or else they'd come back at the crack of dawn... Either way, they were pale as ghosts... we could see them a long way off, their sorry figures, heads still plastered with the *Times*... the rain hadn't let up... the footman was motioning to them that they were just wasting their time... They didn't give a damn, they weren't budging... We were motioning to them too... telling them to clear the hell out! They didn't understand... Meanwhile the Colonel is announced... He's on his way down to breakfast... In a bubbly mood... happy...

"Let me shake your hands!"

In a leaf-print dressing gown... well rested... he's in excellent spirits...

"Boys!... Boys!..." he claps his arms around us... cordial as could be... whisks us away... Ah! this can't wait!... we chug along... wind up back in the garden... between two groves... a small hidden shed, camouflaged with ivy... plus grass, weeds, rubbish, and twigs scattered all over the roof...

"Shh! Shh!" he goes... starts clearing his throat, but breaks into a coughing fit... he pops in a big candy drop... doesn't do any good, he keeps sucking, sucking...

"Did you sleep well?" he asks...

At last he's done hacking, we step inside the shed. He shuts the door carefully...

"Do you know about gases?" Another question.

"Oh! Yes! Yes!..."

We didn't want to miff him... Suddenly he stoops over.

"Right there!... There!..." he shouts...

He opens a forceful tap... and how it spews! spews!... psssst!... violently. Took us by total surprise, whew... Full blast right in our faces... Couldn't dash to the door fast enough... Quicker than when we got here!... What a fruitcake!... Racing off, we can hear him behind us... roaring with laughter, busting his gut! We zip around the lawn three times from sheer momentum!... coughing hacking... Ah! he really let us have it!... We flop down on the grass. Pooped... I had such an acrid taste in my throat I was afraid to take another breath... Small wonder that jerk had such a cough... The pair of us was coughing too! Sosthène even worse than me!... I puke up a gob of blood... I'm choking... All this hacking tearing me to pieces!... Ah! I've got my own bag of tricks! Look at that fresh gob! Hey, this is no joke!... Ah! I'm getting out of here... I shout over to Sosthène...

"You deal with this wiseguy's crap yourself! I'm fed up with his gas taps! Be seeing you! Love and kisses to blondie!..."

"Ah, don't do this to me!" he grabs me, absolutely beside himself... flings himself around my neck... kisses me...

"You'll kill me if you do that!"

He begs me... beseeches... with excuses, sweet talk... the Colonel was just kidding us, horsing around... a typical English prank, an eccentric's whim... The problem was I just didn't understand England... this was no big deal at all...

So in the end I let myself be bamboozled again. The Colonel comes looking for us, his estate is one big amusement park... he leads us farther off to another hut, another shanty, entirely camouflaged with ivy like the first... Ah! This time I'm watching my step, goddamn it!... The next trick he pulls will be his last!... I won't come back!... I peer in from outside... A real junk heap in there, motor belts, small dynamos, spilling all over the tables, a worse clutter on the floor... heaps of hammers, bit-braces, one big load of machine rubbish...

"Here's where I work, gentlemen!..." he announces, proud as a peacock... "Work! Work! I and my engineers!..."

Whatever, but today it stands empty... Engineers my foot... the place is deserted...

Again he stoops... Pssst! A yellow stream... he found another tap! Pssst! Blowing into our legs! Didn't have time to spot it... Ah! this moron's a genius when it comes to acting dumb... he goes into ecstasies, starts dancing around! hacking the whole time! hacking away!... Bouncing around, batty over his gag... He's got a special knack for this kind of crap! And he's running his legs off! Smug silly son of a bitch! I'd like to cram his gas taps down his throat!... I always run into these prize pranksters...

"Shut up, you dumb idiot!... That's our first experiment!..."

Sosthène latches onto me... he moans, he can see I'm about to clear the hell out, he puts on a sad face so I won't leave him high and dry.

"Ah! Our first?... that's a hot one, you fairy... Skip to the last, why don't you?... I'm going to drop dead coughing!..."

No kidding, I can't take anymore. I'm oozing blood, some yellow gunk, from all the holes in my head... from my nose, my ears... See ya!... What a big joke!

The Colonel's getting a big kick anyway, he doesn't give us a break, he's coughing, coughing like crazy, but having a blast... He leads us even farther off... Sniff! Sniff! Sniff!... He shows how to clear our systems out like it's still part of the joke... The trick is to blow out backwards!... such a reek and rasp in your throat... way down inside... a burning sensation... scorching you, worse and worse... I'm going to puke up my lungs!... Smmmuuff! Smmuuufff! No good! damn!... He's still sucking on his big licorice drop... I should have just left! the hell with Sosthène! They'd have worked out something between them!... But then there was the kid... If I blow this place... then I blow all my chances!... I'd never be able to set foot here again!... My rotten attitude makes her uncle sore... Ah! I forced myself to stay on... I kept coughing... coughing... sniffing... trying out his little trick, sniff! sniff! tagging along after him, I was a coward at heart... Now we're climbing stairs... one floor... two... this is the place... he plants us in front of the door.

"Wait!" he goes.

I'm sure he's going to pull the same thing again! ah! I'm positive! I let the jerk know what's on my mind. "Wait and see! This time he'll kill us!"

Ah! I feel jumpy, I want to get out of there.

"So, bye-bye, Sosthène, I'm beating it!..."

I can hear the crackpot through the door rummaging around his gear.

"Wait! Wait!" he shouts from way back inside.

He's scared we'll get away.

"Hear that?... He's getting the pipes ready!..."

I was sure, really sure...

"No! No! Wait a second!"

Fine! I wait, I let him talk me into it again... since I'm totally whacked, I take a little breather. Now the wall starts shaking... this hanging tapestry starts rising... higher and higher... up like a theater curtain... and who do I see before my eyes... center stage?... Our very own funny man!... in person, and all tarted up! hilarious! in dress uniform! epaulets! sabretache, the works!... A quick costume change. He wants to blow us away with his wealth... He's putting on the ritz now... A Colonel! shako! big sabre! just magnificent!... A gala performance!... frogs! boots! spurs!... tight-fitting khaki, red inner lining!... Ah! His head's out of this world!... A feathered shako no less!... A walking costume drama!... Could that be an English uniform? where did he dig up all that gold?... Ah! Sosthène in his yellow dressing gown looks pretty shabby compared to this! his little asshole dragon!... his mimosa trimmings! Man oh man! It really cracks me up!... He holds his pose an instant for our admiration... turns on his heels walks off struts back onto the small platform! The Colonel in fancy drag! What a knockout!...

He gives us no time to think... Bam! he pounces back on top of us!... He leads us off somewhere else again... not allowed to catch our breath!... down a short corridor... up one floor... a flight of stairs... up another... Whew! here we are!... in front of the attic. He shows us around... the "Hall of Experiments" as he dubs it... right under the rafters, it's enormous... a kind of misshapen hangar... I spot the experiments... another incredible pigsty!... everything you want, scrap metal, glassware... heaps of junk like over at Claben's... I keep running into messes, junk collectors, pack-rat setups... I'm sure he'll lock us in... That's his one big obsession! What's he going to come up with now?... where'd he stick the taps?... ah! I'm certain, I hunt for them along the walls... in the air... everywhere... along the floor...

"Shhh! Shhh!" He comes back acting real mysterious... everything's a big secret!... Anybody follow us?... he asks, grows worried... Then he leans over... calls... shouts down the stairs.

"Virginia!... Virginia!..."

Twice more... Nobody answers...

He turns back to us.

"She's shrewd!..."

So now we know.

He gobbles down his cough drop. He could tell a tale or two about Virginia... Oh, man! And how!... He listens... No! No! not a sound... He shuts the door very gently... creeps back to whisper his secret... practically right against our ears...

"Me! O'Collogham! Colonel! Royal Engineer!"

He gives a military salute.

"That's right! Thirty-two years of active duty! India! Here!... the Empire is in danger! Grave danger! Gas! Gas! Did you smell it, gentlemen?"

You better believe we smelled the gas.

"The devil! Gentlemen! Look, gentlemen! Sin! Lucifer! Sulphur! Did you smell? You understand me? So you've got to pray to God! And right now!..."

That's an order.

"Pray to God! And right now!..."

"Pray to God?..."

I just stand there like some ass.

He grabs my hands, pushes them together, he's going to make me say my prayers... He's dead serious...

"Right! Now, down on our knees!..."

He too kneels down, in dress uniform... All three of us on our knees... It's got to warm his cockles.

"Pray to God!" he yells... "Pray to God!..."

No choice but to obey.

All I know is the "Our Father"!... I recite it... Suddenly he sticks his face into mine... wants to double-check my devotion... gives me a hug... a kiss on the forehead... he stands up, genuinely delighted!...

"Oh! You understand!... Oh, you understand!... my dear, invincible! in... vin... cible!... allies! magnificent allies!... China! Frah-hance!... Stay on your knees!... I'll consecrate you!..."

This is a big-time event. Got to keep a straight face... he unsheathes his sword... hits me... with a tap on the shoulder... Presto!... We're consecrated!...

"England Rules the World!..." he squeals. He waits for us to take up the chorus.

"Hip! Hip! Hurray!..."

Gotcha!... we belt it out, and throw in a "Vive la France!" We're in the spirit! He's rejoicing!...

"Gentlemen!" he gives us a hug... "You've understood! The Boches are kaput! Gas! kaput!... Finished!..." He guffaws!...

Exuberant outbursts make me suspicious.

"Heads up!..." I shout over to Sosthène... this time I caught him in the act!... he dove under the workbench!... He's going to open another tap! No!... that's not it! A new trick! Oh, I got scared! He's lugging out two huge contraptions, masks sort of, wild gizmos with monster goggles... plus tubes, coils winding around every which way... little ones and big ones... a diving mask kind of thing... but even more freaky-looking... really incredible gear... got to weigh a ton... we lend him a hand, he couldn't manage on his own...

"Gentlemen! Safety first!"

You can see how proud he is... showing off his treasures.

"William the Conqueror 1917! Off to Berlin! To Berlin! Modern!... Modern!..." That's his grand announcement. He whisks off his shako... He's going to put on his contraption... His goal must be to head out for Berlin with it on... I won't stop him...

Ah! Just our luck, we came up with a real doozy! he gives us the rundown on his doodads... they're all different... mustn't mix them up... these here're valves!... Those over there too!... But those other ones aren't!... That one's a carboy!... the heaviest of the lot!... with a big lead tube... that other thingamajig with the so-called valves opens at the top... see that copper connecting panel that pulls down and seals off your eyes, plus the red and blue goggles... Now Sosthène's got to give it a go!... Come on, let him sniff in the valves!... He'll get a kick out of it!... We'll each get our turn, of course!... They start discussing technique... I watch them, they're getting on my nerves... Sosthène in his Chinese drag... the other guy in his operetta getup... They're firing each other up... I just stand back and think... I'm not involved... But they'd like to fill me in on the sniffing hookup anyway! Ah! I positively refuse to listen to a word! They want to suck me in... Aw! I'd like to tell them to take a flying fuck! The whole deal stinks, and that's that... The only thing that holds me back is Virginia... So my mind keeps working... working hard...

The Colonel's geared up, totally gung ho. He's got another idea... "All three of us! All three of us off to the war! War! Ouarr! Ouarr!..."

With him in that mask, don't forget...

Is this what he was getting at the whole time?... He wanted to roll back the Germans with his valve-equipped snout... Oh! he could be my guest... Damn! he's outdone himself this time! Just as I suspected!... I motion to Sosthène for us to scram... this time it's settled! End of the line! But forget it, they're bosom buddies! absolutely nuts about each other... they want to stay together forever... the instruments turn them on... Sosthène's not even looking at me anymore. They're going to throw a scare into the Germans!... They promise each other, swear up and down... They gobbledygook nonstop back and forth in broken French and English. They must be getting everything ass-backwards... In short, they adore each other. But there's no way you'll see me marching off... in some gas mask or shit mask... Ta-ta, lamebrain! The pair might as well go and get hitched... I'll forever hold my peace... Why don't they lug along his ancestor, Achille Rodiencourt?... Sosthène went on enough about him... First of all, I knew about helmets... I'd worn my share in battle... with thick plumes, brush, the works... I was thinking back... Those helmets in the Fourteenth Cuirassiers were a lot lighter than these... and they were the real thing too... Oh! Yowee! My head's still hard from wearing them... But now rigged out in those supposedly antigas toad eyes of theirs... what kind of crazy shit would they cook up next?... oh! life throws so much crap your way! And there was more to come... Plus with my fruitcake Colonel into the bargain... they were hitting it off fantastically!... They didn't give another second's thought... They were pouncing onto the equipment... Pulling apart, breaking everything up... Both on the same wavelength... smashing every single hookup to pieces... busting away with hammers!... screwdrivers!... they were popping pins... going full blast... ripping fragile membranes!... raging rummaging it's horrendous... like they're in the grip of a fever... But booming with laughter, and happy... as though the gadgetry had gone right to their heads! If I open my mouth they'll gang up on me... a frenzy of destruction! they don't give me another thought... they've got a vendetta against their junk... They lunge on top of it... Savages... one on each side!... Let 'er rip!... they grab the gorgeous masks... dash them against the wall! and then dive on top of the debris!... all I can see is a pair of butts! the embroidered Chink, and the scarlet-lined Colonel... flinging around all their doodads... chucking them up in the air!... Fistfuls at a time!... they come raining down... falling back... the nails... the Muscovy glass!... They must be high on gas... having one hell of a time!... crazy bastards!... Ah! they were turning my stomach... So long! I could have slipped out without any fanfare... They wouldn't even have noticed... All right then! Do it!... I start moving!... And then plop! I chicken out again! Can't get the girl out of my mind! I hesitate, all mixed up, unhappy... How am I going to tell her good-bye?... It'd sure look bad to slip off like some bum... after the way she was so nice... so generous, especially toward both of us... and we acted like such slugs, especially the other guy over there, the weirdo from China... Ah! I wanted to see her once more all the same... let her know before I left that I wasn't a loser... just have a word or two... and not just slink off like some slob, some yahoo, some brainless pig... True, she was just a girl, but she had the poise of a woman... You could see that in the way she gave orders... and made her presence felt... she was the mistress of a house made in heaven... Ah! I'd just wait for her, that's that!... my two whacked-out roughnecks would run out of steam soon enough, then conk out on top of their rubble... Even now they weren't whaling away quite as hard. Crazy fits don't last forever.

The situation dragged on for a while... they were having way too much fun together... they kept it up for another three hours at least, putting/pulling things together/apart, and then playing tricks on each other... they'd hide utensils... then make them reappear smack on each other's heads... openly thumbing their noses at each other... an absolute free-for-all! Monkeys cutting loose!

Sosthène had tucked up his shirt with diaper pins.

"The membrane from one calf embryo, gentlemen!"

The Colonel was demonstrating everything... his great invention, the one he'd clicked onto his belly, a stroke of genius! how he "houmiidified" the gases, the air and the nitrogen! dissolved them together through a slow dripping process! with the poisons! you really should have seen his setup! Sosthène stood there jaw to the floor... drank up every single word... mimicked every move...

All at once the Colonel shoots upright with a start... frozen motionless finger in the air...

"Piss! Piss!" he shouts... "My prostate!..."

With his eyes locked in a stare as though he were hearing voices!... Here we go again, another song and dance! Then he pokes around his underpants, sticks his finger in his butt... and dashes off, he's gone!...

Afterwards we got used to this, it came on him every now and then, especially after having worked himself up... and whenever it did, get out of the way, for Christ's sake! But this time around I was all too glad... I had to give Sosthène a piece of my mind. I was going to set him straight.

"Sosthène! Sosthène!" I grabbed him... "Sosthène! How much longer is this going to go on? Could you please tell me, huh? Do you have any idea, dear sir? Because you can count me out!... No way I'm going back to the war!... Just forget it!..."

Ah! I've gone and left him speechless... He looks at me, knocked for a loop.

"What? You were the one who used to talk about dying! About suicide! Despair! Now you're shaking in your boots?"

Ah! I've taken him aback.

"I thought you'd be happy!..." he throws at me, "that you'd jump at the chance!..."

Ah! his nasty dig rubs me the wrong way! I can't believe it, the guy's making fun of me!

"And what about you, Mr. Smooth Operator!" I snap back... "Magic, my balls! Still enchanted by your journey to India? Are you leaving or aren't you?... Maybe you'd better stick to one spot?... You old swindler con artist cuckold!..."

I let him have it...

I hit him with: "You old phony!... You old bullshitter!..."

I was out for blood.

"Oh, my, oh, my, oh, my!" he goes... "Oh! where are your manners!" He scowls... I've put him through the wringer.

"Where'd you learn to treat people that way?..." he asks me, very high and mighty.

"And what about you, you old con man!"

The situation was turning ugly... I repeated loud and clear: "I'm not going to go and get myself killed to save your ass!"

"How's that supposed to happen? You silly fool, can you just tell me how?

This is our lucky day! A break beyond our wildest dreams! Our one chance in a thousand! Don't you understand what we're dealing with?... We're about to rake in 1500 pounds!"

He's acting infuriated!

"Where'd you get 1500 pounds, huh?"

"But that's what the Colonel's offering us!"

"Ah! That's what he's offering us! So where is it? All right, fine, I'll take you at your word, I want some clothes right away! A suit, a brand new one! Those are my terms... quite reasonable... not a luxury... you've let me know often enough... 'Clothes make the man, my son, clothes make the man!'"

The truth is he'd rubbed my nose in it...

"Very well then! So's twelve pounds enough?"

I set my price, I wanted a peek at this supposed pile of dough, at least some hint it existed... Look, I'm not asking for the whole 1500! just twelve!... merely a small down payment!

"I'm off! For some duds! So I won't embarrass you!... I don't have a Chinese gown, milord!"

"Oh! you're in such a big hurry, so rude!..."

That's just his style, the slob!

"You're going to blow the whole deal! The Colonel's very favorably disposed toward us... But we can't be blunt! That'll scare him off! Simple as that! Plain as day!"

"Come on, let's go! A small advance! I can't stay in these stinking rags... Just look at me! I make a lousy impression! It's even awful inside the house!... Do you have any idea? You yourself spelled it out for me! You kept saying, 'Appearances, Ferdinand, appearances!' Just take a look at the young lady! What can be going through her mind?... Appearances! Two bums, that's who's landed on her doorstep! You in Chinese drag, me in rags! Ah! Not exactly charming!... I've been sleeping God knows where, you know it too! I'm not presentable anymore!"

"Ah! So you're interested in the young lady? I see! I see!"

"Butt out, shithead!"

"Ah! the little rascal's horny!"

"Horny!... Horny!... We'll see about that."

As if that's any of his business!...

"But what about the Oowhar Minister! War! Didn't you hear?"

He's back feeding me his line.

"He's put in his order! I swear to it!"

That was a lie! He was off on the same old bullshit! What I needed was my twelve pounds so I could deck myself out!... I didn't want to hear about anything except my demand, and right now! And no substitutes!...

"The Colonel's got ideas!..."

"Everybody's got ideas! Nobody gives a shit, you fucked-up old fart!..."

He was pissing me off!

"The world's lousy with ideas... I'm in this for my shoes, period! Plus my tweed suit!"

I kept hammering away! Twelve pounds! Twelve pounds!... An advance! A small advance!

I was a broken record.

"So the love bug bit you? You're hooked, Romeo?"

He was striking back, real proud of himself.

"Love, shit! My shoes matter more! I've got holes over my ass! Can't you get that through your head, you idiot?..."

"What're you going to do with this money?"

"Put some clothes on my back, master... A real fine-looking outfit! And do you proud! Dazzle you!"

"It's your fever talking, of course!... Your fever!"

He had an explanation for everything.

"I've had it with walking around in rags!"

"Well, I'll tell you what then, stop by my place, ask Pépé for a beautiful robe!... One of my very own!... Something real beautiful with flowers! I'll lend it to you!"

"One Chinaman's enough!..."

"Your big hurry is going to ruin it for us! It's real simple, I'm warning you... This is a bad move! absolutely reckless! You go and do this and you wreck all our chances in one swoop! Hold off until Monday... I'll have time... next week... I know! I'll talk to him tonight!... That's the best I can do... It's such a delicate matter in French! You want me to come out and hit him up just like that? Oh, no, no, no!"

He was sick.

"No way! No way! I'm not waiting. Go screw yourself! I'm clearing the hell out of here!"

Ah! I'm incorrigible!

He looks at me hard, rolling his eyes... my decision just floors him.

"Oh, yes! You'd better believe it! I'm pigheaded! Six pounds!... Six pounds I say, and right now!..."

I dropped my price. Six in cash.

"You can't cough up six pounds?"

Back to dickering, dragging his feet...

"Let's say tomorrow! Tomorrow morning!..."

"No way! No way! Right now or forget it!..."

He could see this was going all wrong. He turns his pockets inside out... his whole dressing gown... not one red cent!... his linings... zip...

I did some arithmetic! A decent suit?... That would come to at least three pounds... four pounds... a nice raincoat: twelve shillings!... and I wasn't going for an elegant look! Just something to see me through, something presentable... As for the footwear, we'd get back to that later...

"Yesterday you were so happy!..." He was surprised... "You had no complaints about anything whatsoever!"

"Yes, but today I've changed!..."

"Ah! My, oh, my! the youth of today, will you just look how capricious they are... how moody..."

He huffs, puffs, grumbles, gropes around his body... smacks his forehead... He's thinking... darts a glance at the ceiling... the shelf... the odds and ends... the long line of flasks... motions me...

"Hand me that one over there!... There, the big shiny one!..." I hand it to him. It's heavy.

"OK, scram! Get the hell out!"

He jams it down deep into my pocket.

"Well, what are you waiting for? Clear off, quick! You're set!..."

I look at him.

"Stop by Petticoat Lane. You know where the market is, right?"

I did.

"It's mercury for thermometers!... it'll bring you seven or eight pounds at least!... but now watch you don't get ripped off!... It's pure stuff!... Top quality!... be careful!"

Ah! he whispers in my ear... and he sends me off! I hadn't thought of this!...

"Come on, stop dreaming!..." he shoves me along... "You want to deck yourself out or don't you? You'll be a knockout in your raglan!"

And he shoves me out the door! Ah, pretty gutsy move all the same!

"A cheviot wool suit for Monsieur! Lady-killer!"

I pat the flask, can't make up my mind.

"Ah! You got to decide what you want..."

He hit the nail on the head! he's right. Now I'm the one hemming and hawing.

"Off you go! Damn! He's going to come back up!"

Ah! he's making up my mind for me, for Christ's sake!

"Bye!" I go... "So long! I'm out of here, got that? I won't be long!... Back in a flash!..." I had a suit picked out in my mind... one I'd seen in the shop windows... at the corner of Tottenham-Euston... a real beaut... beige check, the latest style back then... I had spotted it... I can see the thing... I was afraid it'd be gone...

I snapped up what I was after... I got back before six, absolutely dressed to kill... a real bargain... not where I thought in Tottenham... but at Süss's in the Strand, practically brand new... Did a good job fencing the mercury... Three pounds fifty exactly... it was worth the trouble... didn't run into any of the wrong people... handled the matter quickly... galloped from one tailor to another... couldn't rest easy out on the street, far from my friends this way... while I was gone they could be up to anything!... I bought the *Mirror* on the run... nothing more about Greenwich... Looked like they'd forgotten about us... Even so it didn't calm me any... Ah! pins and needles!... I didn't dawdle around the street corners... I was a handsome devil, true enough... One pound fifty, every last stitch included!.... genuine homespun Cheviot wool!... Just take a look at this clubman! Whoosh!... I race along!... Willesden!... There's the house, I spot it!... the gate... Not a single competitor at the door... not a soul... they got it through their skulls finally... I enter through the small entrance to the garden... here I am in the main vestibule... I clear the stairs... a lackey stops me... steers me toward the salon...

My first thought: "Disaster!..."

I barely sit myself down when another door opens... the Colonel and the little girl.... No need for small talk... I was sure!...

"Oh, there you are!..."

How happy they were to see me again... the pair quite amiable! He's sucking on his candy... a piece of nougat... he looks me up and down... He's taken off his gorgeous gold, back to everyday clothes.

"Oh, isn't he smart? Such elegance! What a young man!"

That was all.

But he ends with a point-blank question: "What about the mercury?"

So that's it!... I was sure!... He's attacking me! And at the same time, laughing... busting out.... Man, oh man, they're having a great time!... Ah! what a terrific trick! The girl, too... They're delighted, the pair of them... Easy to please!... Ah! right off, I'm sure as hell... Sosthène... Ah! the sly bastard! Let me lay eyes on him!...

Not hide nor hair of him, naturally...

I turn red... green... start humming... what are they going to do with me?... Am I going to ask their forgiveness, or what?... Throw myself at their feet!... beg!... the hell with this! Enough already! That's just too bad!

"Can I go?" I just come out and ask...

"Sit down! Sit down!"

Couldn't be kinder, more cordial... They won't hear of me leaving... They're getting too big a kick out of watching me... They don't look a bit mad... But that doesn't mean anything... the English are two-faced, every last one of them!... They'll put on a simpering show for you... But this was all a setup, I'd bet my life on it!... A trap, end of story!... And I'd walked right into it, dumb ass!... The police were going to turn up... Nabbed, Madame, caught red-handed! we could have a little fun with him... "Come clean, young man! Where'd you get that suit? Come on, out with it!... In the can, kid! Six months for this! Three months for that!" Not to mention my IOUs! Man, oh man, it wasn't hard to imagine! They were playing me for a sucker, and how!... Ah! their little plan went off without a hitch! I'd gotten screwed over... A lamb to the slaughter! An eleven-... twelve-month stretch!... Where could that other crook have got to? A sure bet he was up in the attic... What if I went on up to tell him a thing or two?... Or if I filled in this pair?... Now he's in civvies, the senile old fart!... Was he ever really a colonel? Maybe he was just a stoolie for the cops?... Ah, shit! I was hurting all over... Ah! more blabbing!... badgering!... gesturing!... smooth talking!... Ah! they were making my head spin, and that was that! Enough already! Enough was too much!... Let them go ahead and think anything they wanted!... "Give up! Give up! Stay in your seat"... That was the voice of reason... I was going to let them have their way with me, but then damn, I had second thoughts all the same... I'm not any dumber than they are!...

"So Matthew's on his way?"

I just come straight out and ask them. I know the score.

"Inspector Matthew?... Huh? The cop from the Yard?"

"Matthew? Matthew?" they don't understand me... don't have a clue!... That beats everything!...

"Tea? Tea?" they offer me instead.

"Come on, have some tea! For God's sake!..."

They really are lousy hypocrites... getting a kick out of seeing me squirm... a bungler, trapped and bound... Entertainment. That's just like these people... They're rich, they're British, and they're rotten swine... one and all, regardless of age or sex...

"OK, let's have some tea!... I'd love some..."

Since we're waiting for the police... I'll keep my cool too... don't want to be more jittery than they are!... When all's said and done what the fuck does it matter to me!... Let's go ahead then!... And keep going!... I don't really have anything much to lose!... Let's start the fun! The girl's babbling away... fluttering about... all around me! indescribably titillating... constantly hopping... what lovely muscles!... She conducts the conversation! And such a chatterbox! Bold for her age... talks to us about the movies... cricket... sports... contests!... all the while capering about... Nobody brings up my mercury anymore... The Colonel wipes his mouth... about to get up... His prostate again? No. He informs us it's something else... he's going to work... He leaves me and the darling to our private chat... Ah! such weird behavior... He goes off sucking on his candy... Ah! he's got a few surprises in him all the same... He excuses himself with great politeness... He is going upstairs to his experiments... To rejoin Sosthène with his masks... Good!... Very good!... Couldn't ask for better!

I'm calming down after all... since that's the thing to do around here!... Anyway you look at it I'm not risking a thing... Why should I knock myself out? They're not worried... I stay in my seat... have some more tea... it helps me keep my composure... the girl pours me a cup... Ah, how beautiful she is!... how wonderful! I just can't get over it... what a smile!... All this for me!... both of us here together!... Her uncle's one funny bird... I do some thinking... Ah! what a mischievous little imp... a tease, she must know what's going on... I want to bring up the mercury with her again... it's nagging me:.. bugging me... No way! She won't stay still... It's in her nature to keep moving... she even makes me dizzy, I have to admit... bouncing around, pirouetting like a pixie... all around me through the room... What lovely hair!... what gold!... what a doll!... Whenever I say something she looks at me... she's pretending like my situation is no big tragedy... but I'd like a big tragedy... I spot a twinkle of malice in her eyes!... I wish she'd keep on smiling forever... even at my stupidity... idiot that I am in this suit of mine! To think that was my only reason for going out!... I've made myself look ridiculous... plus the mercury into the bargain! really, what a rotten impression! A thief! I'm so ashamed... on tenterhooks... I blush... can't seem to get out a word... I listen to her... her twittering... English bird-talk... I don't catch everything... She speaks a bit quickly... English from the lips of little girls is whimsical, playful, mischievous... it bounces around too... tinkles... laughs over trifles... capers... flutters... What cheerfulness!... What bright reflections, first blue, then mauve... her eyes completely captivate me... Happens in a flash! I forget... can't see a thing anymore... she's just too nice to be around, a blossom! yes, a blossom... I breathe in... Bachelor's button!.... a bird I said... I prefer bird... never mind! I'm bewitched... Her eyes, bachelor buttons... a little girl... and that short skirt... Ah! she's just too attractive, damn it all! her blonde hair fanning out... when she hops, brightening the air... Ah! just too beautiful!... I'm going to faint... She's adorable!... Ah! I calm down!... The hell with this, tough!... I shouldn't... He's left us alone, the old crank!... And here the two of us are together!... Ah! I'm too comfortable in this armchair... I feel awfully damn good... I'm quivering! quivering... Ah! this little kid's so beautiful!... ah! how I adore her!... She makes my mouth water... How old is she? I'll ask her, just watch me!... On second thought, no, I'm too afraid!... I have some more tea... don't eat much... still careful not to go overboard... I remember the last time. It's horrible to be chewing with her looking on... to sit there chomping away, gulping down, under her beautiful, adorable eyes... I could never... I'd die first, ah!... a pang of politeness eating away at me... I lost my appetite, even if I were skinny as a rail, I still wouldn't have touched a crumb... I'd've gone to my grave with my pangs, so there!... all out of burning love for Virginia!... Did I get her name right—Virginia?... I've got to ask her, but do I dare?...

"Virginia?... It's Virginia?"

"Yes! Yes!..."

Ah! Too beautiful... everything is too beautiful! Her eyes! her smile! her thighs! I can see them when she jumps, those thighs of hers... she doesn't care... muscular down there, pink and tanned... her dress too short... Ah!

she's keeping me great company... or else just keeping an eye on me... Really got to keep that in mind... pack of hypocrites... but I don't feel like going... I'm caught!... And she's the one who caught me!... Ah! I'm afraid to move a muscle... Maybe she would have called for help if I did?... Some private little chat this is! I mind my p's and q's... I let myself be charmed, listen as she makes her very funny remarks, her wonderful little comments about everything... and nothing... I turn down the cookies... she's not happy... she scolds me... I'd gobble down the lot for just one of her smiles... every last cookie, the tray, the table... I'm already her prisoner... in the most beautiful prison in the world!... Ah, I'd stay right where I am and not ever move... I go: "Yes!... Yes!..."

I really do want everything she wants. She wants me to have more tea... I fill up, stuff myself... but she's the one who makes me stand up... walk over to the shutter... she wants to show me something... right there in the shutter... in the ivy... Ah! yes! I can see through the glimmer... the tiny eye of the sparrow... Ah! even he was on the lookout... tweet!... tweet!... you bet he sees her! now this is something really extraordinary! a big bold sparrow with ruffled feathers! just like her!... waiting... peering... gazing at us with his tiny round eye through the slit... itsy-bitsy eye in a pinhead... all black and glossy with his tweet! tweet! tweet!...

"He's waiting too..."

She lets me know... Just so I'd understand... so I'd be as patient as the sparrow. She laughs.

Curious how looking back after ages and ages, from practically the next century, I still think about that sparrow... She was the one who showed it to me... Whenever I see a shutter, a thatch of ivy, I always think about its tiny eye... Ah! when you come down to it you don't bring back much to remember from a whole lifetime made up of petty hassles, wild brawls, and promises—I mean not much pleasant... well, just a few measly scraps... life's not exactly crawling with such occasions... Everybody knows what I'm talking about... For me that little sparrow is something I'm always happy to remember... I want it to stay right where it is... it'll fly away once I'm dead and gone...

The kid was one clever cutie... chatting me up skillfully... psyched me out as sensitive, hooked... because I was all ears for her prattle... so then, she talks about her big dog, her spaniel... and here he comes... big paunch... coughing, trotting like the Colonel... like her uncle... The animal's hopelessly clumsy, pretty old already, wheezing, drooling, she does his thinking for him, it's wonderful how she thinks and speaks in her dog's place... for him... and he's as glad as could be about it... wagging his tail... it's goofy but magical... I'd like to understand the spaniel, the bird, plus her just like that... ah! plus every animal... horses too, for Christ's sake... I'd like to carry her off with me... a fairy... What joyful power. It's joy. I'm bowled over... so happy there right next to her... I fawn all over her!... It puts knots in my chest when she stares at me... makes me go all tickly inside... to hear her English, so lively, so whimsical, a twittering garland in the air... full of secrets, rascally... Ah I had no idea... that dog's a mischief-maker!... Ah! I ask to hear more!... for her to keep telling me stories about Slam, that clumsy creature... ah! give me more!... it's absolutely delightful! absolutely divine!... No kidding, she's a real live fairy! much more than a child!... the dog understands her too... they're both talking about me, about my suit, my behavior... he answers with his tail, he beats, paws the carpet... It's true... You can see they're in tune about everything... She must understand me too... Ah! all of a sudden it's another world!... Now she wants to take a stroll... we stroll around the table... it's the Garden of Earthly Delights... with the old spaniel... a nice threesome all in tune... I'm walking in a dream... she guides me by the hand... she leads our way into wonderland... from one little word to the next... about a lump of sugar... the pâté on her plate... the swallow due to arrive... Ah! such magical theatrics... Ah! how I love this stuff!... Ah! how I love her!... we're taking a stroll to fairyland!... And open your eyes, we're here!... the whole salon all around is an enchanted fairy world!... I didn't know... she teaches me... Ah! how I adore her!... everything's about to come alive... start talking... laughing... the big fat cushion and the old fleabag... plus the armchair!... the teapot with its long neck!... the entire household going all out!... every body and thing in on the act.... dancing in its own way... miracle theatrics... the big, three-legged pedestal table... crosses the room with its potbellied swagger... almost like Boro... all this from one little word to the next, one little word from my fairy... and I understand everything! no more need for chat... One smile makes me understand!... And the enormous chandelier in the air... the immense candle-studded crinoline petticoat!... Dripping crystal tears... trickling all over!... An enormous scale... real fancy-shmancy!... Ah! this is all just so weird! My eyes are playing tricks!... I see all the candles! the wicks! I'm drenched in tears!... chandelier tears! A big tomcat leaps on me... up from the cellar madly meowing... all velvety soft and warm... Meow! Meow!... he ni-nibbles... ni-nibbles... he's got his own chamber music... and then in my ear, because he's a confidant too!... We understand each other right off... Ah! I'm not myself anymore... Ah! I can see into my heart!... into my own heart... solid red... Ah! I purr along with my meow cat... Ni-nibble!... Ni-ni-nibble!... absorbed just like him! He sharpens his claws on my shoulders... Ah! how pleased Virginia is! Such a wonderful way to act!... Pretty Virginia!... I'm blissed out! simple as that!... it sort of just snuck up on me all by itself... just with one of her smiles!... she's really behaving like a darling... outdoing herself.... I ni-nibble... ni-nibble! I am her heart!... my heart... her heart!... Ah! I'm talking gibberish... I adore her like mad!... A peak of delight just the way things are...

I just need to shut my eyes now... drop off... very gently... Nibb-bble! nibb-bble!... nibb-bble!... drooling... defenseless in ecstasy under her spell... about time too! I've been all aches and pains for months... in my head... my hip... now I don't feel a thing anymore... just a gentle warmth... I let go... let them go ahead and execute me!... If they dare! If they dare! In a word I'm lulled, lulled... I forget... But somebody throws a rock at me!... it hits me right in the side... I jump with a start... shoot to my feet!... What a rude awakening!... The bad guys are here! I sit back down... If they're keen on it, who cares! I'll give myself up to the hangman... Her eyes!... her hair!... A little girl! before anything else! Ah I'd kiss her in full knowledge of what I was doing before I go to the gallows... before the final end!... Ah! the wonderful enchantress! With open eyes... but careful! watch out, for Christ's sake!... all of a sudden I'm choking... just been stabbed... by jealousy! Maybe she's the Colonel's daughter? And not his niece, by some chance?... maybe his mistress?... his baby doll?... Ah! the question nags at me... Still more lies?... his mistress?... who knows what else?... A dirty old man?... I see red! I'm burning up with jealousy! A raging inferno! I ask her savagely...

"Is he your father? The Colonel?..."

Ah! Learn the whole story! Pronto!

"Oh! No! Not my father! My uncle!"

What a beast I am! Such questions!

"My father's no more!..."

Her fragile so graceful face... her small pointed chin starts quivering, quivering, in tears... Oh! I've distressed her!... Clod! moron! Ah! the spell is broken... Ah! I've hurt her!... ah! what sorrow!... I ask her to forgive me!... I'm sorry!... I collapse!... I'm going to die if she cries... I come right out and tell her!... make threats... Ah! she's got to forgive me!... she gives a little shrug... I want her to pity me... dog that I am, me too!... a dog! That's all I am! A filthy dog!...

"I'm a dog! A dog!"

I bark!... bark!... I'm showing her that I love her... that I adore her!... she thinks I'm full of horseplay, even so... I gesture... bark, behave like a beaten beast... run around under the furniture on all fours until my head hurts like hell:.. It's all a little too physical for the likes of me... I've got this buzzing, and I mean through my whole head... plus the whistling... my head's throbbing... all my chimes are ringing... my cauldron's bubbling.... I'm thundering... boiling over... rolling around on my belly!... moaning... writhing on the cushions!... I want her to forgive me, I'm unworthy, unworthy... I'm simmering over with love... that's a fact!... Ah! I'm in raptures!... true raptures!... I want her to understand me!... Maybe she's still too young?... Maybe I'll wind up scaring her?... by flailing around this way?... And I bang my bad arm... it sends such a pain shooting through me I let out a howl, and I wasn't fooling!... I mess up my suit, my handsome brand-new suit. What a big waste!

"Virginia!... Virginia!..." I plead... "This happiness is too... too great!..."

I ask her to forgive me once more... ten times more... a hundred... I climb up into her lap... I'm going to let her hear my most tender prayer... I want to adore her until I die... That's what's in my heart!... and even more!... Death's nothing... just a sigh!... But I'm sighing up a storm... I'm talking worship here, a hundred times more intense!... That's just the way I am!... She laughs over seeing me so hot and bothered... wrinkling crumpling my whole suit jacket... She scolds me... Ah! I'm such a kick even so, despite everything... A one-man circus... She's sitting there right in front of my face... nestled back in the armchair... laughing... legs crossed... those lovely thighs of hers... ah! I'm so ashamed!... ah! I adore her!... she's wearing short blue socks... Ah! she's really just a little girl... ah! yet another danger! ah! but I adore her!... Why have we been left alone together?... Why didn't her uncle come back?... Maybe this is another trap?... My suspicions are back... A stab of doubt... of sharp fear!

"Matthew! Matthew!"

I'm sure!... Ah! I don't find them funny anymore... I get to my feet... quivering! Ah! I'm shaking in my boots again... obsessed by that cop!...

"Sorry! Sorry, Mademoiselle! You're too beautiful! Too wonderful... I'm going to die with my heart on fire!... Fire here!... Fire!... Right here!..."

I show her my heart... She touches my chest!... Ah! the way I make this child laugh... She still doesn't know me!... In the end she makes me sore!... I'm going to sink my teeth into her!... Ah! I can't think straight anymore!... I look at her legs, those firm, muscular, wonderful pink legs down there... long... tan... I'm going to kiss those thighs!... I'm afraid! What if she sends me packing?... If she called to her uncle for help?... What a dirty pig I am!... Ah! I could gobble her down whole... ah! I adore her!... All or nothing!...

She's unfazed, doesn't take me seriously... she just wants to talk about the movies... on and on about the movies now... she goes to see them on Regent Street!... Haven't I seen *The Mysteries*?... Mysteries... Ah! mysteries? Ah! she's grating on my nerves... teasing me with perverse glee... Mysteries! Mysteries! I could tell her about a few mysteries that don't turn up in movies no way no how... the dirty little brat's so frivolous with these mysteries of hers!... *The Mysteries of New York* seems to be the title... Oh, brother, *The Mysteries of New York*! I could tell her about a few mysteries all right that are just around the corner! horrible and tragic mysteries beyond any stretch of her imagination... cruel little girl!... and how terribly unhappy I am... Me, unhappy?... I surprise her. Ah! she's poking fun!... with a beatific smile... she's too young! she disgusts me!... I give her such a laugh... So I strike back!... in a flash! Enough!... Of these flirty games... I bawl her out, the dirty little snot-nose! She makes me run through my list of insults... That's how unhappy I am!... it's all her fault, it's not my arm... I own up, I'm war-torn...

Maybe she caught a glimpse of my arm? Of the state I'm suffering in? I peel away my clothes on purpose, show her... She touches... gives a little "Ah! Ah!"... and that's the end of that!... she's not exactly surprised... And what about my head, she get a look at that?... my ear?... Doesn't scare her!... Maybe she doesn't believe me?... these scars are the genuine article... maybe she thinks it's all a scam? Like with her uncle? And Sosthène? That this was all one big costume party... She's got eyes all the same... what's she think, it's some magic trick?... Ah! hell, she's pissing me off all over again! Ah! so she wants to see atrocities?... The movies are doing a real number on her... Blood's what they need to have in them, mademoiselle... Now she's looking at somebody who can tell a story or two about battle atrocities!... how the blood oozes all over the place! So, listen up, darling!... Me, live and in person, the one and only!... Plus the hail of bullets, such fun and games... the hell of combat! bellies splitting open! slapping shut! heads blowing apart! guts everywhere!... gurgling!... Ah! those slap-bang massacres! That'll give her something to shudder about!... So listen up, honey!... Slaughter fests so red, so thick, they coat every square inch of the ground with a sludge, flooding the furrows with mashed flesh and bone, hillocks and hills! and overflowing ravines full of cadavers that still have a spark of life in them, still sighing! and the cannons rolling over them! Caught up in a charge! oh yes, no exaggeration!... whirlwinds, you heard me!... And then the transport vehicles! and then the whole cavalry trampling over them!... over and over again! banners unfurled and whipping in the wind... and such an incredible din... a roar filling heaven and earth! Ten! Twenty! One hundred thunderclaps! I imitate the screams from the carnage for her... the groans, the howls!... doesn't make any impression... leaves her cold, doesn't even look like she's entertained... Doesn't she think I'm the world's greatest hero?... Ah! damn it now, this takes the wind out of me! The most fantastic combat-scarred soldier ever?... And here I am shouting myself hoarse!... Spitting, foaming... I charged too, Christ Almighty!... Badada... dee... I show her! at the head of the toughest squadrons!... the fiercest!... the most ferocious!... I outdo myself!... It's got nothing to do with the crap in the movies, got to admit after all!... all these wacky goings-on give her the jitters! Ah! how about this one!... An earthquake when the division rushes into battle! This is the big time! At the Batteries! Come on, you old nag!... Breaches!... Bullets flying like crazy!... the whirlwind of the cavalries!... Bats out of hell!...

The whole thing gives her a big laugh!... Ah! little dummy!... she just doesn't get it! I collapsed, that's a fact!... plopped back into my armchair!... really shook up... wiped out... A waste of breath!... such nastiness!... the spell was broken!... I should have spared myself the trouble...

Later on in life you come to terms... deal with everything... make do, stop your singing... you ramble on... then drop to a whisper... then fall silent... But when you're young that's damn tough! You need bigger than life! Blow-outs! marching bands! and whoops, look out! Ka-boom! Thunder and lightening!... you've got high standards!... Truth is death!... I gave Truth a good run for her money as long as I had it in me... flirted with her, feasted her, flung her around in a little jig, put fresh life into her time and time again!... Decked her out in bows, made her juices flow in farandoles that went on and on... Alas! how well I know that a moment comes when it all falls apart, gives way, gives out... how well I know a day comes when your hand drops, drops back alongside your body... A gesture I've seen thousands and thousands of times... the shadow... the last strangled breath... And all the lies have been spoken! all the announcements sent out, the three knocks are going to ring out somewhere else!... to signal the start of other comedies!... Get me, you slobbering brat? Look at me!... Now it's my turn to entertain you, sing you a ditty, "This little piggy!"... No, better yet, give me three fingers!... now we'll hear the adventures of the fourth!... the wiliest... the smallest... the most famous... your little pinky... the one that goes wee-wee-wee all the way home!... Back then I had big ideas about myself... I aimed to create terrific fireworks when the mood hit me!... sometimes I fizzled!... got to come clean, admit it... with Virginia, zero... she didn't want anything to do with mysteries, she thought listening to me was a kick, kind of funny, nothing more... she didn't take me seriously... I was just some Frenchman after all, no doubt... she was English... Romantic is how I wanted her to see me, not as some phony clown, some sideshow comic like Sosthène... I tried showing her everything, my arm, the hole in my head, my scars, the long ones, the short ones, even made her feel my skull, but I didn't scare her, not one bit!... Ah! callous! and in a way I found surprising in such a young girl!... A cynic deep down!... Ah! slowly it dawned on me!... I was the one under her spell, swooning! in raptures, her victim!... Ah! I stroke her hair! Never mind!... I run my hand through her curls, so thick, so deep!... Ah! the electricity of her soul! I tell her about it! I fall into a swoon! Feel her full charge in my fingers! Ready to put my hand between her legs!... Down there I'd have hold of her soul! I tell her as much, beg her!... Can't get her soul off my mind... A cute, spiffy pixie, standing right there in front of me, so bright and so bitchy!... Ah! I'm ready to explode!... Can't take any more!... I admired her magic... let myself be bewitched... want her to admire me... to love me truly madly deeply!... I launch back into my adventure saga!... Ah! I'm not through by a long shot!... There's the one about how I rescued the captain! I want her to know everything! my extraordinary valor!... dragging him by his hair across the entire battlefield... and he wasn't some Goldilocks like her! no! no! jet black! short and spiky stuff, like on a horse! between thick swarms of hot lead, literal clouds of smoke and bullets! the bombs falling so fast and thick the sky went dark... over both of us, the captain and me... I mimicked the gunfire for her, did my rendition of the whistles and blasts... Even after this she didn't give a hoot! I was ludicrous! Wasting my breath!... And I was really going at it too!... flailing my arms around so much it hurt!... But I just stayed put! Didn't touch her! A flop!... Didn't make her tremble, shudder, beg for mercy, apologize a thousand times over! Cry for help! Throw herself in my arms! Ah! my beautiful girl! Ah! have pity! Rotten slut!... True, she was a teaser... maybe worked for the cops into the bargain, a stoolie, simple as that!... Which would explain her sly come-hithers... her thighs... this way she was behaving... in short, just what kind of joint had I stumbled into?.... cutest little darling in the world!... so I amuse her, do I! What an act! she's putting one over on me! Turning on the charm for the cops!... Ah! You're a pretty one, Mademoiselle! A real charmer, my balls! Ah! the little birdies! I'll keep you lingering! She's just waiting for the cops, end of story! The kid was in on it! Of course! Little Miss Innocent playing me for a sucker! she must be having fun!... And big jerk that I am, jumping around... it's really true, a life of vice starts right in the cradle! Ah! a sudden thought! Those cops are taking their time getting here! If you ask me... they must be dawdling over at Matthew's... He's going to show up with them... I'm sure as hell... Even so I ask her: "Matthew?... Matthew?..." I'm dead serious.

She doesn't get it...

"Don't get it?... Don't get it?... What a smooth operator!..."

Ah! it's damn awful how treacherous this is... bottomless pits of dirty tricks... Come on, got to give her a kiss still and all before I leave... it's been eating at me for an hour... got to take the chance... it'll be over... she was no better than Finette... when you really came down to it, all said and done... Two-of-a-kind no-good two-timing sluts!... but this one here, is she ever precocious! Geez, what a nasty business all the same! I felt like letting out a howl... I wanted to be certain despite everything... one more go-around... I wanted to ask a question... to put my mind at rest... But she's the one who launches into me.

"You're just like the movies!" That's what she's come up with! "You're sad! and then you're happy!..."

That's the impression my pantomime made... pretty unflattering... at present she was sure... I was like the movies! Like the movies or nothing!...

Ah! I had no comeback for that! I could leave!... But how could I go back to being all alone?... No can do now... Right away I was frightened... I couldn't live without her anymore... ah! what a scary thought! cripes! Never mind! I'll stay right where I am, won't budge... sorrow nails me to the spot... stand here glued down dumbfounded... without a clue... ridiculous!... all I could see now were her eyes!... How would I manage out in the world? I'd bang into everything... And what about the others? The two goofballs?... The thought set me off again! what the hell could they be doing? were they ever coming down?... What catastrophe were they concocting up there under the rafters?... What a pair of first-class nitwits!... I had time to think about them even so in my helpless confusion... Ah! there was a surprise in store!... Some big deal in the works! Rats! I shake a leg! I force myself... Hey! I'll bawl her out! She's been rubbing me the wrong way long enough! I'm going to terrify her, for Christ's sake!

"You don't have a care in the world!...," I go to her, "not a care in the world, little birdbrain! Don't you know? I'm going to kill myself tonight!..."

Now that was a stroke of genius.

"You?... You?... You?..."

She refuses to believe me... I can see the merry twinkle in her eyes... What I wouldn't do to blow away Little Lambykins! I rack my brain again... give up... nothing I do works with her... How I'd love to make her moan, writhe, roll around, wail through her tears, the little bitch! Ah! so you're waiting for the cops!... The thought's back on my mind... I'll give those cops a show! Me! I'll knock off Sosthène! Do you hear me? Rotten clown! Crook! Stoolie! Smash him! Wouldn't that outdo anything in the movies? Plus her uncle at the same time... hell, yes!... while we're at it! Dirty little bungling Colonel! A wholesale slaughter! Buckets of blood! So much for the young miss! A massacre right in the salon... I'll fill the room... with puddles!... pools!... streams!... she wants a real-life movie! I promise her my own death, she giggles... well then, she's going to see something else! she's going to see a threesome die! A tensome! A dozen! the servants along with us. A mass murder! Like at Prospero's... like at Claben's!... and then I'll torch the place!... She'll see real good whether I dreamed or not!... they'll all see real good whether I'm kidding! Ah! I'm going to kiss her... before things get cooking!... she doesn't want to, forget it, she ducks away, plays Hide and Seek!.... I can't do anything right!... Heaven in her eyes!... little spinning top!... Ah! she's so beautiful a miracle!... I forget everything just looking at her!... Ah! I'm losing my mind! my memory! Ah! I drop to my knees!... Gladly she takes my head on her lap!... Ah! dear wonderful creature!... Ah! the mushy words that come back to mind!... I'm melting under her touch! Melting... I ask her to forgive me! again! The day'll come when I cut out my tongue!... I roll around at her feet... the others'll see me... She's laughing again... Ah! how cruel she is!... Here come those confounded servants! you're never left in peace for long... they're bringing the table settings, it's almost dinnertime... scurrying back and forth, opening doors... I catch the aroma from the kitchen... my nose knows! It's leg of lamb... definitely... I sniff... can't control myself... Shame!... How hungry I am!... Still hungry!... yes!... Before dying, before suicide! the wholesale slaughters! Yes! Yes! Ah! the horror! Dirty little pig! I admit it! I'm rumbling with hunger... ravenous with pangs.

"Will you stay with us?"

She's inviting me. She's poking fun... I should leave... And so what about the mercury?... Forgotten... I forget about everything!... I'm going to see her uncle again! Sosthène! the whole family round the table! As though nothing were wrong!... Zero self-esteem left!... My pride flares up! The hussy's laughing!... She can see I'm suffering... from shame and hunger!... And here I never wanted to eat again!... Had absolutely sworn not to!... from the kitchen more whiffs of lamb reach our noses... definitely leg of lamb... I'd vowed to die! or at least run away!... But I'm already so tired... my head's buzzing... from hunger!... I'm staying put, never mind... so I can croak? fill my tummy?... I'm pulled both ways! so I can tarnish my oh so very tragic love?... She'll never understand me!... She's callow!... A darling... a fairy... but frivolous, a babe in the woods, flighty... she has me all wrong!... So should I bump her off then? Christ! she should make herself scarce!... love her unto death?... I'm raving... I crack myself up!... I'll kill her some other time!... So, chow down then! Come on, dig in! My appetite makes my head spin! the aroma reaching us... through the door... permeating... penetrating... I breathe in!... start drooling... Star-crossed love!... It's really tough!... Having a hard time holding back!... the leg of lamb!... I don't look at anything anymore... waiting for the roast... don't give a damn about the others... Let them show up!... the knives are moving around... the settings... the crystalware... goblets next... the champagne!... all stands ready!... the hors d'oeuvres... and sprays of roses!... Say, this is a real celebration!... All this expense for little old us?... Ah! wait now, what's that flask? Smack in the middle? the mercury!... my mercury! They're throwing it a party! They're throwing me a party! A flask like the other! a spitting image!... I recognize it!... as a centerpiece!... smack in the middle, sitting among the roses... they're going to throw a party for my mercury!... all in the family a chummy get-together! Ah! what a zinger! a real inspiration!... Ah! the perfect touch!... Ah! right on target! I understand I'm being invited!... that they're counting on me!... oh God! they're about to walk in... the whole crew... A spark of self-respect! Scram, Ferdinand!... I look at the lovely child!... She sort of smiles at me... Am I leaving? staying? I blush... stammer... show the girl the flask!... right there on top of the flowers smack in the center.

"Oh! how funny it is!..."

I don't find it one bit funny... you can see it's not her doing... Strange ways of having fun around here...

"Don't pay any mind!... Don't pay any mind!..."

That's all she can come up with... for me to take it as some sort of childish prank... I'm a despicable coward!... I'm all for surrendering... I'm going to hang around here a little while... I blush, but don't budge... doddering... spineless... until the cops come!... and then they can haul me off!... the plot's been hatched of course!... planned out!... they're all in cahoots!... I'm convinced deep down... this business with the mercury is the dot on the i, the crowning touch!... the mercury on the table! the flask! the movies!... Come and get it, Monsieur!... You bet I won't forget Sosthène!... That stinking carcass!... The pimp was in on the con!... And I keep my eyes on the little darling standing in front of me! She's a royal pain in my ass... I feel a burst of energy... So what about it, you little cock-teaser!... Cutie pie! what's the name of the game you're playing with us?... with the cats? the birds?... all the funny faces... the whole song and dance?... What're you after?... with our play-acting... smoke screen... ruses... What if I pulled your panties down?... And spanked the hell out of you?... shameless hussy... what would you say about a little number like that?... we're not talking little birdies! Your uncle's got it right! Punishment on the spot! Ah! I'm feeling down in the dumps! So many things to decide! Can't make up my mind!... about any damn thing!... threats at every turn!... wherever I'm drawn?... the proof?... that leg of lamb's just about here!... I can smell it!... the full rich aroma coming in!... tantalizing!... coming up from the kitchen... the butlers bustling around... all this bustling makes my head spin... I sink back down in my armchair! Close my eyes...

"Well, well, so here you are!..."

Sosthène walks onto the scene, very jovial...

"Ah! so it's you, you son of a bitch!... you just wait!"

Ah! he shakes me out of my stupor... ah! that bastard, I'll wipe the floor with him!

"You dare show your face, slimeball?"

I collar him.

"Come, come now! what a temper!..."

He shoves me away with one hand.

"Mademoiselle, excuse him!..."

He's ashamed for me! He's apologizing for me!... The rules of behavior!

"You dirty bastard! You hear me, scumbag?..."

I don't want to drop it! I'm spiteful!

"I'll show you what I got in store for you!..."

"Come, come now! Let's calm down!... in front of this child!..."

He begs me to respect her ears... extends his arm... leads me away... Ah! it's the same old crap like with Boro!... They're all one big pack of hypocrites!...

Dinner's on the table! Here comes the Colonel! And the twit! They've both changed clothes... in overalls, high rubber boots... the Chinese and operetta drag over and done with... both down to business... experiments all the way! Scientists on the job! Next to that I don't exist anymore... even with my three pounds six! Right off I lash out... grab his attention!

"You're a pretty sight, Sosthène! Have you been stealing, too?"

Pow, take that!

"Not as much as you, you snappy dresser!"

He was expecting my dig. We whisper friendly cracks to each other... don't let each other be... the girl can't hear anything... the Colonel neither... he doesn't say a word... I watch him between his mouthfuls... he just keeps smiling straight ahead... his mind's not on us... He's a man wrapped up in his thoughts!... Every now and then he grumbles, "Hum! Hum!" then he helps himself to another big slice... ham, lamb... everything!... He's got a hearty appetite... And there's plenty to go around... you should see this spread!... I whisper to Sosthène again: "I'll make you pig out, you dirty bastard!... I'll give you a taste of the upper crust, you hear me, milord?... I'll make you eat shit!..."

He was really making me mad.

And the mercury flask sitting there right in front of our faces smack among the flowers, it was there for a reason!... The joke was on me!... to see the sort of face I'd pull... Ah, they were wasting their time!... I didn't give an inch, goddamn it, not an inch!

"So tell me," I go and whisper up against his ear again, "so tell me, you lousy creep, whether the others are coming... your buddies... your cop pals, you know who I mean?... You sack of shit!... oh well, I won't be leaving by myself! cop! I'm warning you in advance, cop!..."

"Shhh! Shhh! Now stop it, you scoundrel!"

He's offended... he finds me impossible!...

"What a way to act!"

He's complaining... Ah! I'm pushing him over the edge! My behavior's way out of line!...

"Be careful! Come on now! Shape up! You're not back in the barracks! You're making noise with your mouth! Not everything at the same time! Cut up your meat!"

I was behaving poorly, that's a fact, I was really worked up... it was his fault... the girl watched us whispering... fortunately the uncle wasn't watching anything... he just kept staring into space... eating in a trance... swallowing everything without looking... as in a dream... the celery... a big sardine... then a huge hunk of roquefort... And then some candy... a handful... he started the meal over again, backwards... beginning with the fruit... and the racket he was making, oh man! chomping like a dog!... ten times worse than me!...

"Well, well! You're not laughing, Sosthène?"

Nope! Not one bit!... Right there right across from him... Wasn't that funny? Wasn't it? Well? Wasn't it? Now there's an asslicker for you!

Ah! I wasn't going to start up again bitching bickering, pissing myself off! For what? It was pointless... It turns my stomach, but I just let it go, never mind, the hell with it! I'm all bickered out already... here we go then, a smile for all around!... that's it, I'm a dumb jerk just like them, and calm, I act polite and proper, of course, I'm everything you want!... Are those cops coming? They can show up anytime!... I'll be waiting for them here, they'll find me polite and proper! at my nice little family dinner, with the mercury in the center of the table... the flowers... the smiles...

We'd barely had a chance to close our eyes... to snooze off at last in the armchairs... Nobody'd sent us packing... That was already a plus... and here Sosthène goes and wakes me up.

"My friend, no more loafing now! You're going to have to make yourself useful!..."

The first words out of his mouth... bullying... Right off the bat he gives himself a promotion! He's the one making me toe the line... passing on his "directives"...

"Pop over to Rotherhithe! Go up and see Pépé! Tell her I'm feeling pretty good, I'm satisfied with the Colonel, and that she should bide her time like a good girl and not eat too much chocolate! And not get into too much trouble!... Or mess around with the catafalque! She knows what I mean!"

He whispers to me: "Achille..." I understand... the mummy...

"And tell her to give you my pipes!... Ah! plus let her know in no uncertain terms that if she doesn't stay quiet she'll never see me again!... Make sure and tell her not to buy anything... or run up any bills for me!... Tell her I just may be stopping by to see her soon... if she behaves! OK! There you go! Right!... That's everything you'll need to say... Ah! plus the most important thing of all! You'll have to drop by the Ministry!"

He gives my suit the once-over...

"Now you're dressed properly!... Ah! Do watch what you say."

He studied me...

"You'll do... mind your manners!... Get off at Whitehall... that's a number 42 bus... you'll see the buildings right away... it's not hard... all the ministries in a row... on both sides of the avenue... you'll need to find ours... they all look alike... So watch out!... the War Secretary... Just ask for directions... the Department of Inventions... You walk into the building, ask for the Special Office for the gas mask competition, the rules, times, dates, and bring me back the sheet of instructions... And don't lose it!... They say they've changed everything!... that they've moved up the trials... Hurry up! Be back before dark!... Don't loiter around Rotherhithe... Don't come back soused! Run your errand right!... Off with you now, and mind what you say! Don't give out our address!... Ah! nobody gets any addresses! Never an address! Especially not Pépé!..."

"Count on me, Monsieur Sosthène! You won't find many who can keep their lips buttoned like me!..."

His advice was irritating the hell out of me...

The Colonel lent an ear, approving every last detail... nodding... bam! all at once, he jumps to his feet... Look out! like last time when he felt a piss coming on...

"England! England rules the Gas!"

He's off again, howling... not his prostate anymore... he sits down again... end of show... drops back into his stupor, staring straight out into space. His niece fusses over him.

"Uncle!... Uncle!..." she murmurs very sweetly... full of affection...

But Sosthène's raring to go! He cuts short this little family scene! He wants to see some legwork, some action!

"Down to work!..." he shouts... "Down to work!..."

And he catches Uncle by his arm, grabs hold, leads him off... Ah! how awful to see characters like him in action! thugs of his type! Such brass! Such arrogance!... He's the big shot now! I can't stand it... Sure, I could pick up and leave, drop the whole thing... That's all he deserves! I think it over... Ah! and over... Can't shake the thought... But what about the girl then?... the girl?... drop her cold, leave her for the birdie, hand her to the bozo... no way!... Just let that sleazebag try and make me clear the hell out!... Ah! forget it! I'd kill him first!... But what if I took her with me, kidnapped her! Ah! that would be wonderful!... heroic and sublime!... Ah! I'll ask her... I want her consent... I'm enthused... ah! fired up! my happiness is in sight!...

"Mademoiselle!... Mademoiselle!..."

I walk up to tell her right away... I stammer... stutter... lost my nerve... ah! rather give it a little more thought...

"I'm leaving!..." I announce... "I'm leaving! I'll be back!..."

They're sort of surprised even so... me going off so obediently... following orders without any lip...

Now I'm outside, on the sidewalk... the avenue... hobbling a little but at a good clip, delighted, head-over-heels with happiness... She's an angel! She was a real live talisman from heaven, a little girl like that! an idol of radiant beauty!... and her magic should save me for sure!... I was lucky in love!... And if the war ended pretty soon, maybe we could get married?... settle down... Ah! my mind was running with the idea... spinning it out farther and farther... I pictured a hearts-and-flowers fantasy, a miracle... I'd be off the hook one way or another... some way some how... rolling in dough I can't tell you how!... drowning in moolah... everything would work out miraculously... Swept along by my thoughts, my mirages, steaming hot, bubbling away, I couldn't see where I was walking anymore, blind to the streets, the passersby, the bus! Completely swept away by passion! faith! joy! I sleepwalk my way into Rotherhithe... find the street... the house... land smack at the right address... and up the stairs! four at a time! one door!... another... I take a whiff... This is the place!...

"Pépé! Pépé!" I call out... "Pépé Rodiencourt!..."

I knock... pound... This is taking forever!... go back to knocking... I can hear voices inside... Nobody's in any hurry to open up! Finally somebody gets to the door... It's her!... Hair spilling over her face... she's spitting, wheezing, all smeared with lipstick... she's just walked off a battlefield!...

hitching up her petticoat... her dressing gown, the flaps of her rags... Ah! what a pretty sight!

"Madame," I go to her... "Madame!... Your husband's got a big message for you!..."

"Ah! So that good-for-nothing's sent you? Quick, give me his address!... where's he holed up?..."

She gets her wits back in a snap.

"Madame!... Madame!... That's impossible!..."

With that she flies off the handle.

"I can see what's going on! I can see what's going on! He wants to drive me to my grave with a broken heart!"

And she starts blubbering, sobbing something awful... Writhing in pain against the door... And here I came to patch things up between the pair...

"Madame! Madame! Please! don't get angry! It's just that, you know, it's a secret!"

Ah! hell! why'd I go and say that!... She starts bellowing ten times louder...

"He wants to drive me to my grave! I get it now!... He wants to see me dead!... I know that crook!"

She reeks of booze, and how, blowing it right into my face...

Just then, "Tuhwheep! Tuhwheep! Tuhwheep!"... A voice calling me. A man's voice from back somewhere behind her... can't see the guy.

She's making like she can't hear a thing... A drunk's voice... "Tuhwheep! Tuhwheep!"... starting again...

Ah! just wait a second... Tuhwheep! Tuhwheep!... it rings a bell!... reminds me of something... I'd like a look at the joker...

"Who's back there?..."

"Oh! A friend!..."

No chance she quits her blubbering through all this...

"Your friend have a name?"

"Nelson..."

"Nelson who?" I ask... "Nelson the painter? Trafalgar Nelson?..."

I can see my questions are bugging the hell out of her... but she's got me real curious... I want answers... repeat my question... she positions herself crosswise... blocking the door... I want to pass... She pulls the door shut behind her until it's just open a crack... on her guard now... All right! I'm not budging... We're locked eyeball-to-eyeball... She's one sly little slut...

You'd better believe I knew Nelson! if he was the chromo clown... the open-air artist... doing his thing right on the steps of the National Gallery... a nasty customer if you ask my opinion... deformed like Centipede, just as ornery, crippled from birth, and a spiteful, rotten snitch... everybody at the Leicester was wary of him... Despite his short leg he could really tear along at an unbelievable clip... he circled sidewise like a crab around his sketches...

a real live spinning top on the sidewalk... fidgeting nonstop pirouetting... without letup... giving the rundown to all the dainty dames about the Pyramids, Niagara Falls.... plus every monument the world over... all for his clientele... the Eiffel Tower, the Crystal Palace! Plus a square-rigged six-master and the waterfalls of the Epsom River... plus a Roman orgy scene with eighteen women in peplums...

Couldn't argue with his facts... He put his work on display all over London, in trains, in Charing, in Chelsea, but his main gallery was on the flagstones of Trafalgar Square just under the monument... that's where you could usually find him between the pigeons and the basin... which is how he got nicknamed Nelson... From the very first that swindler had turned my stomach... he advertised himself as a wounded vet... a total sham! "Ex-serviceman" his sign read... absolutely bogus!... He was born a cripple, period... Couldn't fail to disgust me since I had credentials, and real ones at that... He didn't scrape by just on his art, by being a sidewalk hack, he had other irons in the fire. At the museum exit the ladies often stop for a break and to admire the beautiful view, leaving their things behind on a bench, unbelievable how ditzy they are, especially the young ones... Nelson kept himself busy, on the alert, eyes always peeled... his specialty of sorts was handbags... not that he swiped them, he just subtracted his modest fee, a couple of shillings, with his light fingers, and nobody was any the wiser... I wouldn't have trusted him. But he really came into his own when the fog rolled in, blanketing all London in one swoop smack in the middle of the afternoon... like a feather comforter settling over the traffic... He had no peer when it came to guiding people back to their hotels... often in groups of ten, or twenty, all in single file... people left stranded in the thick of the fog, stricken and petrified... Have to give credit where credit's due, he was a virtuoso in the department of rescuing tourists... Whenever the clouds dropped smack in the middle of a stroll his dough came rolling in... The whole Empire passes through Trafalgar Square... inevitably... one day sooner or later, all the dominions roving around, gawkers from three continents... When the mist blows in from the river, and the gusts kick up hard, the whole square is smothered, blotted solid white in a blink, the confusion's just out of this world, people can't see the shoes on their feet, need to be led back to their places like blindmen... Sweeping down the broad stretch of Whitehall Road the fog blankets the whole city in five seconds flat... anytime from October on you could be avalanched in white... And that's when business boomed! the fever nicknamed Nelson on his tiny pegs, bolting after tourists, little misses missing in the mist... he'd catch them groping their way into the gas lamps... collect the dodderers, the distraught or alarmed, those strollers wobbly on their feet, hobbling along every which way only to crash into each other... He'd assemble/hail his whole crew, rallying, chugging around from one group to another, leading them all by the hand and then at his cry

"Tuhwheep! Tuhwheep!" just like that to the next tube station and even right to their door if they were still afraid... As soon as the world went white, and you couldn't see to save your life, he'd let out his "Tuhwheep! Tuhwheep!" his foghorn in every direction... he'd make himself useful, got to admit that, loads of people were grateful to him, it's no joke when traffic stops dead, you could find yourself going around in circles for hours on end when the fog's so thick everybody's afraid to put a foot forward and the city grinds to a halt, even the small taxis, even the horse-drawn cabs, it's a disaster on the Strand, and the coaches desert the streets, the whole crowd stumbles down the sidewalks, knocking into the walls... The Tuhwheep! Tuhwheep! hunchback had a nose for threading his way through fog, a special knack for finding his bearings through the thick gauzy layers, by dead reckoning, like a navigator, never a second-guess or a zigzag, even those times it was so thick it smothered the Bengal lights, the soldering flares roaring at theater exits, raging forges, but no matter, you couldn't make them out anymore, the fog conquers all! It feels like the entire mist is going to seize hold of the city. Nobody but Nelson could find his bearings in such weather... No matter whereabouts in London, whatever the lost soul, whatever the destination, he never landed at the wrong address, in the wrong square, the wrong dead end, he could have spotted a ghost from one mist hidden in another... And yet London streets are real killers, a fuck-you layout, their street numbers all cockeyed and ass-backwards... Yet never once did he get fouled up, he'd hit the bull's-eye every time, the doorbell, Gentlemen, there you see! The missus is home! and with a "Tuhwheep! Tuhwheep!" he'd charge off to scrounge up new clients. He'd bring in five, six pounds easy just like that in one afternoon... From the peristyle he'd draw his whole pack of wanderers: "Tuhwheep! Tuhwheep! Any direction! Follow me!" He'd lead them off just as he found them, people of every stripe to all corners of London, skinny misses, fat slobs, characters from Afghanistan, Peru, China, Panama, plus plain old ordinary folk from the country... gatherings of those struck dumb, alarmed by the sudden fogs. He'd sort of use the confusion to his advantage, the fact helpless people would blank out about their belongings... Even given that he didn't get out of hand... As a guide, beyond reproach! he'd bring them all into home port, to the exact address! He'd really up his take on days the fog rolled in. He'd stash away his chromos at the first wisp of cotton stuffing... Actually he had a great location for his racket, his kind of place, Trafalgar Square, it's a real circus, a genuine rendezvous for the clouds... the mists come pouring in from every direction in thick cushions, gigantic whirls... the customers had every reason in the world to fly into a panic, especially since it's slimy and slippery. He had to walk them across the street hand in hand, plus keep crying "Tuhwheep! Tuhwheep!" over and over again, single-filing along the shop windows... "Lady, watch your step!"... He was a born joker, with a great sense of humor... always horsing around to set people's minds at ease... All that on top of his "Tuhwheep! Tuhwheep!"

Ah! it all comes back once I start thinking... Ah! it's him! I guessed right! that face of his! I did hear him, I wasn't dreaming! right in front of Pépé it was all coming back to me... The oddball in person!

"Pépé!" I go, "Nelson's here! You've got to let me see him!"

I'm sure he's a stoolie... I want to look him square in the eye...

"No," she answers back, "you're not coming in!..."

"But I know your visitor!"

She moans again but so loud, acting like a Little Miss Innocent offended by the likes of me.

"You know him?" she asks.

"Sure do! Tuhwheep! Tuhwheep! Right! Sure do!... Tuhwheep! Tuhwheep!" I call him just like that...

"Tuhwheep! Tuhwheep!" he answers me back from inside.

"You're not going to talk about anything?..."

Now she's the one who's scared.

"No! No! That's a promise... But how he'd wind up here?"

"He was looking for you..." she whispers... selling him out already...

"How he'd find you?"

Yet another riddle.

So, anyway, at least I enter, walk inside, find him on the bed.

"Tuhwheep! Tuhwheep!" he greets me raised glass in hand, tickled pink, sprawled out. He's made himself at home...

"Hi! Tuhwheep! Tuhwheep! You're sloshed, how's it going?"

I light into him, he disgusts me.

"You can see for yourself, pal!... You can see for yourself!"

He doesn't get sore.

"What the hell are you doing around here?"

I'm finding out a few things.

"Having a good time, wouldn't you say? Don't you have eyes? I'm having a good time! Plus I'm looking for you, you brat! Tuhwheep! Tuhwheep! old pal! Ah! how glad I am to find you!"

He wants to get up and give me a hug.

"Why're you so happy?"

"Cause you're going to give me my two pounds!"

"Two pounds of what?"

"For me to keep my trap shut!"

We needed to hash this out.

He rearranged himself on the bed. He breaks into a serenade:

Hello, my beautiful stranger!
Hello! Hello!

Then he flops back down, stretches out.

"A drink! A drink, darling!"

He's placing an order. They're on the best of terms, I can see that right away... She comes back with a bottle... Rum... she pours... for my benefit she acts like this really bothers her... putting on airs... then he grabs her... sits her down... oh! man, what a tramp! he starts feeling her up, turning her upside down... she protests...

"Tuhwheep! Tuhwheep! Quit it now!" she squeals.

He kisses her... they tumble back together. Such guffaws!

"Darling! Darling! I love you!"

She warms up to him... digs out the flask from under the bedstead... they serve each other, and they're not stingy either!... using the same glass to drink to my good health!... the floor's all scattered with rose leaves, petals, sprinkled down from the baskets... She pulled the same trick on him! Ah! I know how she works! The come-on! her little scam with the photos!... so it's working like a charm, not one false move, and I show up right for the grand finale!... Pépé's one of a kind! He slips me an obscene comment, along the lines of whether I wouldn't say he was hung like a horse. And his father was a groom at the racetracks at Maisons-Lafitte!... Now that's a laugh! Absolutely hysterical! The pair of them doubling over with laughter!... she needs to forget all her woes!... and right then the memory hits her again hard... and she's back blubbering something horrible...

"Shut up! Shut up!" he cuts her off... won't have any tears around him! He starts cuddling back on her lap... they're hugging again!... Ah! Jesus! enough already! I'd like to have a chat with him! I tug him by the feet!...

"Who's looking for me, huh? Out with it, Nelson!"

Seeing as how he's in a good mood now... Maybe he'll feel like flapping his gums!

"Hold on, bub! Just wait! I'm going to tell you..."

He's all eager to tell me about it. He lifts Pépé back onto his lap...

"There you go! There you go!"

Big loud burps, he feels better...

"Here goes! Here goes!" he starts telling me... "So then, Angèle shows up this one night, his old lady Angèle! you know her! Madame Cascade to be more precise!... she nabs me right in the middle of one of my performances... chalk in hand, can you picture it!... a mob scene... and she starts yapping at me!... She goes: 'Not a minute to lose! Nelson! Nelson! Big emergency!' That's a quote. 'Cascade's asking for you! Quick, get yourself over to the Leicester! Shake a leg, move it!...' You know me, right, obliging, helpful and quick, despite being the invalid I am... but all the same this was a disaster... I had people crammed in on top of my doodles! tourists, respectable types!... In fact I was just finishing an Eiffel Tower... she insists... begs... I give in... drop everything... Very good! You know Cascade! Always ready to go off the deep end! I don't want any hard feelings! Don't want to rub him the wrong way for anything in the world!... I owe him too many favors... Plus you know that I never lose one cent with Cascade!... But his old lady's another story!... First things first, so I ask Angèle: 'So this is for your husband, right? Not you?' 'It's for him, at two pounds an hour!' Ah! I was hooked! 'It's a very tricky manhunt...' Oh! as soon as I hear that I'm ready to go! I'm always interested in hunts!... So you can see how it happened!... Oh! Oh! Oh!..."

And he's laughing again at the memory of how this had fallen into his hands... how he had snapped into action... and Angèle, and hustle, hustle, hustle! And then he and Pépé are back billing and cooing... I witness their little romance blossom into sloppy kisses and tiny squeals... they don't notice me anymore...

"Come on! Come on!..." I pull them apart... "Come on! Out with it then, you lousy creep!"

"Here goes! Here goes! As I was telling you, she's saying to me: 'Cascade's in on this! it'll be worth more than your finger paintings... Get a move on!...' I race over... here I am... you get what I'm saying... Soon as I get there he lights into me: 'My dear Nelson! What about the Chinaman! Have you seen the Chinaman on that Trafalgar Square of yours? Did you catch a glimpse of him? The Chinaman! The Chinaman in his dressing gown?' That's how he lays into me. I laugh. 'Chinaman... Chinaman... it depends!... there're lots of Chinamen around...' I'd seen loads... no exaggeration... Chinamen of all shapes and stripes! I don't know whether he was one of them! whole battalions in front of my pictures! Little ones big ones in-between ones... 'You'll have to be more precise!... A Chinaman's not some seven-day wonder!' So he starts filling in the details... In a nutshell his Chinaman's a phony... according to what I could make out... in reality he was a Frenchman, camouflaged in a gown... a wild getup... green gown with a yellow dragon over his ass... a guy in disguise, incognito... he gave me a quick sketch... the way he talked... his mannerisms... his face... I know the fellow! Tuhwheep! Tuhwheep! Ah! the weirdo!... Always clinging to his umbrella... plus that frock of his stuffed with rolls of paper... always on the move... strutting all over the center of town practically, but especially out around Dover... Bond Street... 'Tuhwheep! Tuhwheep! Got it!... I'll catch him for you in no time!...' 'He's always tomcatting around girls... hurting them... pinches their bottoms till they bleed!...' Say! That rings a bell!... a sex pervert!... Finette'd mentioned him... A Chinaman, right... Just hold on one second, I'm trying to remember!... Ah! Then all at once it comes back to me!... She'd even spotted him with you!... You can see what I'm getting at... 'He some fairy?' I ask... I meant you... I could see he was looking for you too... 'No, he's not the type,' he answers back... 'the whole business is fishy, a con in the works!...' Ah! so that was bad news then... I understood that he was hot and bothered. That you and this Chinaman were pulling some rotten trick on him... that you'd left his digs with a few schemes in your head... 'A little squirt I'd picked up off the street!... who didn't pan out... and is double-crossing me now! Catch that Chink! You're the eagle eye! get your ass moving! I got to have him! And the kid too!' 'All right! All right! No problem, Cascade!...' No bargaining with that guy, I know the way he operates... I tear out of there!... He doesn't like hemming and hawing!..."

I thought he told a good story... opened up a few new angles for me... he was really rolling. Whoops! Another break in the action... Knocking, ringing... Pépé leaps out of bed, runs, it's the milkman, she charges from the bed, leaving us to ourselves!

"Well? Well?" I prod him, "out with it Tuhwheep! Tuhwheep! keep it rolling, damn it! How'd you land here? How'd you find this place to shack up, this dame?"

"Hey, watch your tongue, sonny boy! You think I don't have connections?"

Ah! I insulted him.

"My boy, a Chinaman's not hard to dig up! Especially a phony! Get me?... The world's not exactly crawling with them!... Why, I'd have found him all by myself disguised as a mouse turd! A no-Chink Chinaman! In the Lord Mayor's ass hairs!... Ah! so you see, take it from me!"

Hard-nosed!... that says it... hard-nosed!...

"You don't know how I get, you little ass, once my mind's made up!..."

He eyed me with a look of such pity. A real swellhead when it came to scrounging up any old character at all from the streets of London just as he pleases. A more eagle eye than anybody around.

"You see! Didn't even put in one full day!... and Tuhwheep! Tuhwheep! the fox gets in the henhouse!... I'll haul in the handsome couple! Granted, I had it easy! There wasn't a wisp of fog... ideal weather! Right! But even if the cotton stuffing came down over all the twelve districts just like that, a fog thick as pea soup spilling all over, I'd have still brought them back... Not a damn bit of difference! When I set out looking for something I find it! Remember that, loafer! That's one sure thing you can't deny!"

And he spits onto the stove off a ways! Splat! a huge gob... sizzling and popping!

"That's the way it is, pal!..."

So proud of himself he's roaring! Taking me in from on high, from the edge of his bed, the filthy stuck-up cripple! Pépé's outside on the landing, oblivious to us... clucking away, lovey-doveying with the little delivery boy in the door frame... the young milkman... we could hear their smooching! She wasn't wasting a second... Our gab session must have got to her... Love the one you're with, that was her style... I understood the lady. Tuhwheep! Tuhwheep! is treating me to another go-around, he absolutely insists on showing me, another tale of his amazing stunts, he could see me smiling...

"I'm the one! Understand, you little dope! I'm not blowing my own trumpet when I tell you I'm the greatest pilot in London! The ones out on the river don't exist! get that through your head, little bird! I'm Nelson, king of the fog! Tuhwheep! Tuhwheep! I scare away the pigeons! Just get a look at this! Boom! Boom!"

He was pretending to raise his rifle... then firing through the fanlight... at all the imaginary pigeons... I had to admire him for all his accomplishments... including this one!

"So, what've you decided?"

I'd had it with all his posturings.

"Oh well, it's all over! I found you!"

"What'd you find, dick-head? You found some old hag to booze up, his broken-down old bag Pépé!... But the Chinaman couldn't give a fuck about you... So you can take that from me, sucker!"

I was going to take that lousy show-off down a peg or two... Despite the rest, he turned my stomach... Now it was my turn to have some fun...

"Hey, now! Hey, you little twit! You watch your mouth!"

He wasn't expecting this, he's ready for a fight...

"OK, enough, Tuhwheep! Tuhwheep! I'm just kidding..."

I didn't want to make him mad right off the bat, that would have killed my chances to find out more. He goes back on the attack.

"So, you're going to see Cascade, right? Ah! You just got to! Absolutely! If I let him know I found you and then you didn't want to come see that hell-raiser! Ah! you don't know what you're in for!..."

"And what if you don't breathe a word?"

"Then he'll say: 'Nelson's a double-crosser! No way he can turn up empty-handed! All of a sudden Nelson turns out to be a bumbler! Ha! Since when?!'"

"Don't you want to do me a little favor? You know I'm up shit creek..."

I'm testing him out.

"Just knock it off now! Poor jerk! Try and get serious... What's the big risk if you just drop by and see him, talk things over man-to-man?... Cascade's not some sword-swallower... He just wants to understand you!... He proved it to you! As a friend! So it's just that he doesn't want to be double-crossed... He knows London a little better than you do!... He knows where things can lead!"

"Yes! But you see, it's like this, I don't want to see him... I'm involved in something right now... I'll explain... an angle!..."

"Ah! Ah! So you're working on some angle!"

Old eagle eye's snapped back with a good answer! I've confessed! I'm not denying it at all! On the contrary!

"Sure am! Sure am!" I lay it on thick... "A deal, Nelson, see, like this!"

I show him the bag... act out the plan... pounds and pounds galore!

"Ah! Tuhwheep! Tuhwheep! So now you see the whole picture!"
I want him to drool over it.
"You just can't imagine!"
He nods... looks at me funny... wonders whether I'm playing him for some total chump...
"No! No!" I insist... "Look! Like that!"
I act it all out again... the big bags... hand over fist... Ah! he puts on a face, doesn't believe a word...
"A deal? A deal? Excuse me, snot-nose! It's not in the bag yet! I've got more going with Cascade than a lot of hot air! I never go hungry with him! He pays off down to the last red cent, my friend! Five pounds! Ten pounds! I show up! Everything's OK! Then off I go! Never a word! So long! See you next time! Now there's a job for you! This deal right here is worth, let's see, at least ten pounds for the way I found you..."
He was telling me to put up or shut up... holding a door open for me...
"Yes, but Tuhwheep! Tuhwheep! you're getting ahead of yourself, you're not paying attention to a single thing I'm telling you... you just got dough on your mind... but what I'm talking about isn't just about a pile of cash... a big caper like this!"
I start acting it all out for him again!...
"Anyway, that ten pounds of yours sort of makes me smile! Chicken feed... Oh, brother!... It cracks me up... if it was just about loot I wouldn't have even mentioned it... but there's a whole lot more at stake! Just listen to this..."
I move close to his ear...
"It's also an affair of honor!"
With that he gives me a look, rolling his eyes... So then I whisper into his canal...
"Military secret!"
Ah! he wasn't expecting that one. He's nailed on his ass... shocked.
"I can't breathe another word! Do what you want now!"
He was rocking on the edge of the bed, back and forth, he couldn't believe it.
"You're putting one over on me, snot-nose! You really think I'm an idiot!..."
"No, I don't! I really don't! Not you, Tuhwheep! Tuhwheep! A big waste of time with you! You've got an eagle eye! Come with me if you have any doubts!"
What more could I say!...
"And I'm telling you that you're trying to pull a fast one!"
He was hanging back.
"No, I'm not!"
He remained leery. I cut him to the quick.

"This deal'll win the war! There, now do you get it? Now do you maybe understand how serious it is? Do you want the Allies to win? Or don't you give a shit? Or doesn't it matter to you?"

He sat there with his jaw in his lap.

And I didn't mince my words.

"Now, Tuhwheep! Tuhwheep! you've got all the info. Do what you want! If you sabotage this, that's your business. I've filled you in, and that's that... Do whatever you think is right!"

That's how I came at him. Ah! my words riled him! He glanced down, then up... that's how upset he was with my mysterious mumbo jumbo. He was afraid to look me in the eye... Torn up inside, and pretty violently at that.

"What an idiot you are! Because that's already happened! Because the war's good and won! What the hell does this have to do with it! England won the war! And France too, goddamn it!"

Then he has second thoughts.

"Ah well, come to think of it! Fuck France!"

He's mad.

"Ah! You see, Tuhwheep! Tuhwheep! you're talking bullshit! You don't have any idea what you're saying anymore."

"What idea? What is it?"

"That it's all up to you, Tuhwheep! Tuhwheep! It's plain and simple! Clear as a bell!"

"Up to me how?"

He wouldn't drop the idea.

I run through it all over again.

"Tuhwheep! Tuhwheep! you're just like a woman! You can't keep from spinning crap! I'm on to an amazing deal... I want to clue you in as a pal... But you keep shooting your mouth off! Never mind! The deal's blown!"

"Never mind about what?"

"The secret, what else? The secret for winning the war! Jesus fucking Christ! I'm not going to stand here and talk myself hoarse! You're going to spill the whole thing at Cascade's! Easy enough for you to talk! Monsieur, come and get it! we're going to lose this one... that's the way wars are lost... just takes one asshole like you..."

"We are so winning it, you snot-nose!"

He won't give in one iota.

"How're we winning it? With your dick, huh?... tell me, pal!"

I'm sticking it to him. His blood's really starting to boil.

I kept hammering away.

"Not the way you're going at it, you walking disaster!"

Ah! he couldn't keep to the bed anymore... climbing the walls in his anger! Ah! You bet I was having one terrific time!...

"We'll win it!... It's all sewn up!"

He yelled the words in his pigheaded rage.

"Ah! Don't think so!..."

I wouldn't back down.

"Long live England! Hurrah for England! Fuck the French!" he hollered again even louder.

With that he grabs the rum, knocks back a swig, just like that, bottoms up... glug-glug-glug... then he's back to his act... he wants to show me what he's made of, the way he shoots pigeons... his imaginary creatures... through the fanlight... Boom! Boom! He's working himself up this way. He sees pigeons surrounding me like we're out on the esplanade of his square. And then he breaks into his big song. He's determined to keep his pecker up in the face of my bullshit!...

"Hurrah for England! Vic... tor... ious! Rious!... and Glori... ous!"

He bucks up his confidence this way... He starts over two, three times... He feels a lot better, perky, in tip-top shape!... Let's go!... He's going to give me my chance!... It's nagging at him all the same...

"Snot-nose! Snot-nose! Start talking!..."

I run through the entire business once more, how we're going to win the war thanks to this marvelous invention... never mentioning exactly which...

He thinks it over.

"Good! Good! OK, right! So you're sure then? A military secret?..."

"Yes! Yes!"

I blurt it out. I'm positive. He buys it.

"Good! Now you're going to tell me everything, right? I won't repeat a word, I swear!"

He blurts it out too.

"Shh! Shh! Shh!"

At this point I squelch him. And what about Pépé and the kid!... Can't he see them out there on the landing? They've got ears, right?... This Nelson's one dumb-ass blabbermouth!

"I've said too much," I say to him.

Ah! now that pisses him off!... I whet his curiosity, then cut him off! He was dying to start shooting his mouth off like some old busybody... He looks at me unhappy as hell... takes another swig of booze, a glassful, straight from the fifth... empties his lungs... right into my face... gives me a wink... I've whacked him out... he doesn't understand anything anymore...

"Your story's a load of crap!"

So he concludes.

"All right then, come and see! Let's go!..."

I can't do better than that.

"Let's go where?"

"To see Kitchener. You mean you don't know about him?"

"Who's this Kitchener?"

"Over at the War Office!"

"You're going to join up?"

"Course not, you idiot! To see the minister! He's the minister!"

"You going to tell him?"

"Not everything! Not everything!"

"Ah! Ah! Well, how about that now!"

I made an impression with this latest. He's really bowled over by how discreet I am...

"You're a sly one, kiddo! You're sly! A real riot! You chiseler you!..."

He takes aim at my side too... right there point-blank... like with the pigeons... and Boom! Boom! he sets his sights right on my heart. I joke with him.

"Come over to the ministry, you'll see!"

I twist his arm, beg him.

"I can't offer you more than that! I'll show you Kitchener in person!"

"So you're a spy, are you? A spy? You never told me!"

All of a sudden he gets it into his head that I'm a spy, or something... he looks at me... Ah! he can't get over it! I've got to clear my name.

"Course not, dummy! It's for the invention!... Didn't you get anything? It's personal!... It's for the minister!"

"Did you go and invent gunpowder or something?"

"Better than that, Tuhwheep! Tuhwheep! A thousand times better!... Ah! Just wait till you see! You've got no idea!... Come along with me!... What more can I tell you?..."

"Ah! but then after that, you'll tell me everything?"

"You'll see for yourself! Promise!..."

He tumbles, topples down off the sack. Plonks himself back on his screwed-up pegs. He's a bundle of energy now.

"Well then, let's hit the road!... I'm leaving with you!..."

"OK then, we're off!"

Let's move it!... Don't want any second thoughts. Pépé's still standing in the doorway with the kid, all lovey-dovey... She wants him to go back inside, he doesn't want to!... they're squabbling over whose fault...

"Oh!" she goes, "you taking off?..."

She's real surprised.

"Out of the way! We'll be back!..."

We push her aside, and quick!... Ah! I forgot the old man's pipes! He specifically reminded me to bring them... Never mind, I'll come back! I was in too big a rush!... Ah! I got a kick out of my fine hoax! The nipper didn't suspect a thing... I had a nice little plan in store for him... once outside I'd ditch him... I had it all worked out... The time it took for him to find us again would at least give us a little break... two or three days... a short breather...

had to ditch him, and how... ah! but no violence... had to come up with some ploy... So we're off on our way. We reached Aldgate right at the tram intersection... He starts wobbling... stops... and then he's back to his bullshit again...

"Get lost, kiddo, you're conning me!" he lashes out! "Minister shminister! This is one big setup! I'm heading back!"

"Ah! look here, you rotten bastard, keep moving!"

I pull him, push him. Can't let him slip through my fingers, fucking hell!...

"Don't make a scene in the street, you hear me!..."

Ah! I'm in a pissy mood. He grumbles, starts walking again. We cross back over the Strand. We can still see his chalk strokes on the asphalt... his Crystal Palace... his Eiffel Tower... They held fast despite all the rain... Colors still bright and vivid... He's puffed up over his job.

"You see, kiddo! you see! it's not junk!"

Quite right, I congratulate him.

Ah! here we are in front of Whitehall... the long buildings... we look around... keep looking... find the War Office. I stop him under the street lamp.

"You wait for me here, Tuhwheep! Tuhwheep! Just stand here and wait! Stay put! Don't you move!"

Ah! what a drag in his opinion... He'd like to come along too. I insist.

"You wait for me here, and no questions!... I won't be a minute up there... I'll come down and get you... Got to let them know there's two of us! Make sure you don't leave!..."

He wants to come along anyway, he protests... I shut my ears, get cracking... Head first through the revolving door... hustle down the hallways!... charging along!... Here's the stairway!... Up in a flash! The doorman stops me!...

"Inventions, please..."

I beat him to the question...

"Inventions? Room 72!"

Hustle! Hustle! I run smack into somebody! I chicken out! Make up for lost time! Off again! Seventy-two! Bam bam! I knock! "Enter!" comes the answer... Here at last! Walls desk signs everywhere... and posters colors "GAS MASK TRIALS"... Don't have to strain your brain to understand... This is the place, all right!... The bearded doorman hands me a flier... the contest rules... I understand pronto... Gas Mask Trials... They'll be held at Willesden... all the details...

"Thank you! Thank you!"

Now, back on my way! Whoosh! So long! Down the other side! What if Tuhwheep! Tuhwheep! followed me?... And I land smack into him! Oh man, you should have seen me tearing along, ripping down the stairs!... I'm setting the carpet on fire! I race in the opposite direction... it must come out on St. James Park... I spot the trees way at the other end of the hallways... I'm just racing like hell!... doors, doors, endless doors!... charging along another stretch... two flights... scrambling down the whole way... like a whirlwind I hit the turnstile... come out the other end! I did it! here are the trees!... ah! I take a breath! whew! nobody!... the bastard! I screwed that dumb fuck but good! Flitter around, you stinking gimp! Ah! the eagle eye! old fart! what a riot!... Bye-bye, butterfly!... A number 17 bus! I jump on board!... I'd give anything to pop back to the Strand just for a peek at his face! Ah! the sucker! the jerk! I'm enjoying the thought!... I'm having a blast in the breeze up on this double-decker... I breathe in let it out!... Ah! the nasty stoolie... Mustn't run into him again... Cause he's a tough vindictive SOB.... Man, that character was mule-headed as hell!

"Master," I say to him, "things are looking bad!... our days of peace and quiet are just about over... Nelson's on our trail... That dressing gown of yours is not exactly helping the situation... They can spot you anywhere... it'd be a good idea to take it off..."

"Who's this Nelson? Never heard of him!..."

I give him the lowdown about what a two-bit hustler he is...

"Ah! The people you know! You keep such classy company!"

Then I tell him all about my visit... how I found Pépé... of course I skip a few details... I give him the big picture... about how she was feeling... pretty good, actually... plus about the crowd she had over... cheery Tuhwheep! Tuhwheep! in person!... plus my adventure! how I got out of my jam... how I'd ditched that creep!... oh! but this wasn't over yet!... the guy was a tough customer! a leech! oh no, we hadn't seen the last of him... my big news didn't make much of an impression on Sosthène... He just took it all in with a blank look in his eyes... What was his beef with me now?... He had this look... I'd run his errand for him... the instructions, everything... and had come back right on time... he had gotten his damn details! the trial site... the factory... you name it! The event was set for early June... that gives us a good amount of time to play with... he could monkey around all he wanted!... Ah! I'd forgotten his pipes!... Not that he mentioned them... He just sulked at me... Finally I'd had enough...

"Hey," I lash out at him, "are you listening to me? I'm not talking to the walls!"

I wanted an update on the contract. That's what interested me.

"Did the crank make up his mind?" I ask, "or didn't he? What'd he tell you? He forking over our advance or not?..."

Still in the clouds. I give him a shake...

"Ad... ad... advance?" he stammers.

"That's right, you screw-up! Our advance!"

Wouldn't want him to be the only one to be making a mint!...

"But... But you don't need anything!... You've got great-looking clothes! You're got up like a prince! a lo... lord!..."

Ah! this fairy's a sneak! I'm sure!

He helped himself, I could smell him a mile off!...

I give it to him straight...

"Sosthène, I'm going to let you in on something... Your number's just about up... I'm repeating myself to death... Tuhwheep! Tuhwheep's on our trail... Everybody knows who you are, you cheap chintzy Chink! All of London knows you! Wait till Nelson blows in with his gang of jokers! You'll feel sorry then! I'm just letting you know!... I'm sort of familiar with what these people are all about! Still wet behind the ears though I may be! It's a bad situation, master, a disaster! It looks like no big deal... I don't want to work you all up, but you might land in jail... I feel it in my bones!"

I'm the tough guy now.

"Jail?... Jail?..."

Ah! That knocked the wind out of him... Ah! the words that come out of my mouth! "Jail" woke him up... pisses him off, he insults me... says I want to hand him over to the most bloodthirsty cutthroats! that's the sort of person I am!... and I'm jeopardizing him on purpose... I'm the mastermind behind his kidnapping...

"How am I mixed up with that kind of scum, just tell me? Let me hear it! You little smart-ass! Come on! Spell it out for me, why don't you!"

"You mean me, dear sir? You mean, how come I know them? A conspiracy of fate! the war!... the horrors... the quick getaways... the dreadful circumstances!... Ah! if only I could be someplace else!... In hell! Yes, that's right, in hell!"

Why pull any punches, after all... I've got my own problems! and a whole lot worse!

"You'd promised me China, Sosthène! Tibet, mister! The Sunda Islands!... Marvelous and magical plants! What happened to it all? Huh? I'm asking you now... Sham! Shaam! Shaam! and Tam Shaam! Hot air! A bunch of bull!"

I was rubbing his nose in his lies!... He had shit on his face, real embarrassed, sniggering, half-laughing... But the look I shot him meant business... I was going to do something violent again... with just a single hand I was choking him... my left... his duck windpipe... Dishonesty can knock the sense out of you!... and from a Chinaman of his sort! it makes you fly off the handle... now he's back chuckling... I completely lose it! Twist away!

Ah! wonder of wonders! right then a brightening glow floods us, hits my eyes, dazzles me... fills my head... my heart!... A glow... a rising sun!... We were in the vestibule, right in front of the dining room... I was waiting for the dinner gong... It was her!... Right there before me!... Yes, her!... her divine smile!... She had just walked into the room... I hadn't noticed her... Magic! I adore her!... Ah! I'm trembling! She's just walked in!... my Virginia!... My heart's beating harder! harder!... It's her... in all her glory! Her adorable little face!... I stammer, stutter!... Don't know what I'm doing anymore... just stand there shaking!... shaking from fear under her gaze... What eyes! Heaven itself!... tiles from the vault of heaven... I'm lost, dazed and confused... No! the glint in her eyes!... Ah! what if I lost her for just one single day!... I'm afraid to risk it, any way any how... I'd like to give the whole world a kiss! including Sosthène! him too! out of joy! over the miracle! All my anger's out the window, gone poof under her spell... all my nasty digs!... I'm cured, juiced up, in seventh heaven! I'm dancing hopping around... can't feel my trepan anymore, the pain in my head... Just allow me another look at her, my treasure... Ah! a good thing she came back... I was about to commit another crime... Saved by her smile, her little sugarpuss... My guardian angel, my adored darling... her pleated plaid dress... her pretty thighs... such quivering muscles down there... firm, pink, matt...

Oh, my God! what's happening now?... "Dinner time! Dinner time!" I was looking at her legs... They're just too fantastic, beyond fantastic... She's sculpted in light, pink, fresh and insolent... And if she ever tries running away! I'll reach out and grab her! Ah! I'll have to catch her... right around her knees... that's where I'll close my fist, give her just a tiny little nibble... Oh! such things I'm planning!

"Come on! Chow time!" The other one's prodding me! Mr. No Manners... He's exultant, wriggling around... he had a pretty good scare a minute back! saw my nasty side... Now that's all in the past! The gong sounds! Here we go again, back to pigging out, stuffing our faces till we're ready to explode... What a miserable mess! I shouldn't ever eat again!... I should live on her light alone, the beauty of my adorable love... that goes without saying... on the halo of her hair... I loved her too much...

"Come on, let's go!"

Talk about being in a hurry! Even the girl thinks I'm a slowpoke... she too wants to get to the table... And I who adore her light, just standing there paralyzed in admiration... She smiles at me... I gaze upon my goddess... She swishes ahead of me...

"Let's go! Get moving!" she says...

"Do you want to eat everything ice cold? Don't you want any soup?"

That's Sosthène, his heartfelt cry... Ah! the villain!

Ah! To live on nothing but kindness.... burning love... illumination... Maybe just one piece of fruit... her kiss... or on one small word at mealtime!... That's all!... with a darling delicacy!... let her come out and tell me now "I love you!"... But she's too young, too sensitive!... Ah! the swine, that ugly snout of his... he's shoving me!...

"Time to eat! Time to eat! The Colonel's waiting for you!..."

He leaps ahead, dives forward... pounces on the tablecloth, on the dishes... Digs right in... springs on the artichokes...

"I'm a vegetarian," he blurts out, fooling around of course...

He chomps down like a jackass with every tooth in his mouth... making a racket... gnawing down three heads one after the other... And then he digs into the ham... just like that, ham-handedly... Tears right into it! An ogre!... And amazingly, he's not big as a house!... He's a skinny thing, a twig... But you should see those jaws in action!... a scrawny ogre with a bottomless gut!... A hurricane on the hors d'oeuvres... The way he eats would make your face go red... He's making me so ashamed I don't even dare look at Virginia anymore... He pours himself some claret... the Colonel says grace... their personal way of praying... Sosthène drops his eyes... communes with himself like when he's chewing something soft... "ever and ever"... their "Our Father"...

Even so, after this big blowout, instead of falling asleep, and the guy was all tuckered out too, still I kept him from dozing off, really hauled him over the coals something fierce... he sort of obeyed me... he lit into the Colonel who also had a full belly, nodding gently, burping... saying that this couldn't go on any longer, a decision had to be made... with both of us there working on the masks, part of the family in a way, we should be sleeping in the workshop... and no beating around the bush!... this bright idea of catching our forty winks in town was one huge waste of time!... it took away from our research! The Colonel had to take all this into consideration!... Sure, we had the salon, but that was a makeshift deal... snoozing on the sofas... that was OK for a couple-three days... but sleeping in the laboratory, now there was a real solution... always on the job, so to speak! we wouldn't need much... just a few cushions, a straw mat... Ah! now I thought he had a stroke of inspiration there!... gutsy, when you came down to it... but what if the other character took it wrong... told us to fuck off?... No way!... He welcomes the idea with open arms... Oh! such a terrific brainstorm!... it enchants him... He's tickled to death... "Yes! Yes! Certainly!..." and signals the servants!... for them to put us up... settle us in... and do a much better job than in the salon! we scurry along, climb stairs, here we are on the third floor... A splendid bedroom with two beds... Excuse me let me rephrase that... The lap of luxury!... silk everywhere!... brocaded curtains!... gigantic eiderdowns!... double carpets... just incredible!... in the same house as my idol!... ah! what fantastic luck! under her very own roof!... my sweetheart!... my dream! It boggles my mind!... It's impossible!... Both of us reach out... run our fingers over... it's real, all right... not some fake scenery!... and heated, cushy-comfy, the works... Hell, yes! and what a spread, what eats, what a first-rate production! They do give a shit about us!

"Hey!" I shout over to Sosthène, "don't you think this here is our magic plant?... we've already got where we're going?... Seriously, I mean..."

He sits down... doesn't answer a word!... gives the mattress a bounce... a perfect spring... a wool blanket so soft it's unbelievable... total comfort... Ah! really gets to you! You just sink into the surroundings... His heart's melting, I can tell... He nods gently, leans forward, with a faraway look... his eyes well... one tear runs down... he keeps glancing out the window...

"What's wrong with you?" I go... "What's wrong? Don't you like it here?..."

He's overwhelmed... more than he can bear... He's all choked up...

"My poor boy!... My poor boy!..."

He sobs, dissolves in tears.

"What's the problem, man? What's the problem?..."

He's worrying me.

"I can't tell you... I just can't!..."

"Can too!... Can too! Give it a try!"

"We're at a dead end, my poor child!... A dead end!..."

A dead end?... That's all I can catch from his words...

"Why?... Why a dead end?..."

I want specifics!...

He's collapsed, crumbling, he's lost all his nerve, he's a wreck!... He sits there, an empty shell, lost in a dream... Then he starts back up with his sob story...

"My puh... puhoor child!... We... We don't know where we're going!"

Give me a break! With that he splutters, blubbers, shakes so hard he's rattling the whole bed, the posts and frame are clattering... He's falling apart, a miserable mess... Ah! well isn't this just great!... He doesn't know where we're going anymore! Just terrific! Wonderful!...

"Tibet's where we're headed, pops!... Tibet! Where else?... We've said so a hundred times!... Now we've got it good!... As soon as we pocket that little allowance! that goddamn advance! we beat it the hell out of here!"

I was wired.

"Oh! Oh! my child!... oh! my child!... If only you knew!" That's all he can say... If only you knew!...

"Only knew what?"

He crumbles back into hot tears!... His heart broken beyond repair. He gets up. Throws himself around my neck... kisses me... drenches me in his tears!... I play along...

"The masks!... the ma... masks, my child!..."

Ah! now we have it! the masks! that's the snag! ah! just as I suspected... he moans... sniffles... sobs...

"So what about the masks?"

"Not up to snuff, my boy!... Not up to snuff!"

"But you'll get there!..." I reassure him... "You've still got lots of time!... Almost a whole month ahead of you!..."

He starts sniffling harder than ever!... I didn't reassure him... We're in a real jam!... He's chickening out, throwing in the towel!... My Tibet's gone and forgotten!... The plans, mysteries—into the drink... He won't hear any more about them... Curtains on the big act! The stinking stooge's shitting in his pants! no more talk about running off!... got to come up with a new angle! But the cops are going to turn up in full force! That's what's in store for us!... I can feel it! I give us less than a month! Here in a flash!

"And so? So?..." I blister him... "So you're dropping it right here!... what good's bawling going to do you?... You're going to go see the Colonel! because I understand the man! go over and tell him off right in the middle of his work! his endeavors! cranks are bad news! they're capable of anything!... Man, oh man! You better believe it! off to court!... watch and see how he starts bitching and moaning!... Ah! you'll have brought this on yourself! He won't think twice!"

I don't show him any mercy... I rub his face in his disgrace...

"I don't know if I'll be able to, Ferdinand!..."

"Able to do what?..."

"Put it on!... Put it on!..."

He shows me the mask on his head. He goes through the motions, the whole production... He's convulsed with fear, clacking his teeth, a big song and dance... in the throes of an honest-to-goodness breakdown, scared shitless... going to pieces, his eyes rolling back in his skull, locked white... he sits back down... Ah! a sorry sight...

"Bu... Bu... Bu..." his hands latch onto me... he's drowning, giving up the ghost at the mere mention of the experiments.

I push him back down on the bed, prop him up with a big bolster...

"OK, man! you shouldn't call it quits... There's still time!... a solid month!"

I'm trying to get him to stop shaking...

"There's still time..." I insist... and then I laugh at the feather mask... how very becoming it is...

"Isn't all this gear great... isn't this great shit? a great discovery?"

I sort of fish for info... couldn't say myself... I ask questions.

"Yes, it is!... It is!... I think so!... Maybe..."

Not exactly enthusiastic...

He's getting cold feet again... Really not convinced!... He asks me what I think myself... Now isn't that a killer!

"Do you think the Colonel's an oddball too?..."

"An oddball?... An oddball?... Depends on the day!... Inventors are always oddballs! If you'd have met des Pereires you'd know for yourself! But look at us, you're telling me we're normal?"

I want him to laugh, to realize... that it's really no big deal... that his mind was playing tricks on him... he had a sick spell... which was going to pass...

I tell him: "Come on now! You're running yourself down!... You're not yourself anymore... you're tearing yourself apart inside!... And the fact is you don't have a single good reason!... You didn't even read the directions... You're working yourself up over nothing... Take a look! Get the info first! Take a look!"

I show him the flier, the note... Spell out the words... we look at it together... He wouldn't understand anything on his own... He's thick as a brick when it comes to English... The contest rules are clearly set out... Pretty strict, must say!... "Each Inventor at the same time wearing his respective gas mask, in a single blockhouse, two gas canisters in a row! arsines, followed by the mystery gas... on July 8th at 9:00 A.M. sharp at the Wickman, Kers and Strong plants... Upper Bethnal Green." On the following day two more gases, another round of trials, two minutes each. The entire proceedings under official supervision with "the blockhouse hermetically sealed in armor plating," these last words underlined no less. And then the panel of judges: an admiral, two generals, three engineers, two doctors, three chemists, a veterinarian. Really quite a serious business...

The program seemed planned down to the last detail. The range of premiums and prizes. In case of slight asphyxiation, a small premium of twenty-five pounds. In cases of rather grave illness, forty pounds fifty. In cases of death, one hundred pounds for the widow, thirty for each orphan... but as for the inventor who sails through with flying colors, winning every single trial, well, what treats were in store for him!... what great glory, millions! shitloads!... A huge immediate order!... One hundred thousand masks a month!... Who needs Tibet anymore!... A terrific grand prize! An out-of-this-world jackpot!...

I tried firing him up over that...

"Ah! You see! Take a look! This is big-time stuff!... Learn a few things!... Get a move on!"

It didn't light his fire... He sat in his deep funk, letting out long-winded sighs... a beaten dog...

"Ah! shit!... You're hopeless!..."

He was bringing me down!... I didn't need this... blubbering hard enough to break your heart in two!... I was sick and tired of the guy... What could I do?... I grab him again by the shoulders, give him a little shake...

"Well?... Well?... You through yet?..."

My shaking lulls him, rock-a-bye baby... He keels over, plops back on the sack, conks out... like a log... tenderly... Right off he starts snoring! Will my luck ever end?

I sit down opposite... stare at him... Fatigue's catching up with me too...

torpor... Feel my eyelids growing heavy... the bedroom's just too comfortable... we've been barreling around for days!... running and running!...

Ah! the old fart! really, come on! he'd better hold out!... this is our once-in-a-lifetime shot!... he'd better not alienate the Colonel! Ah! I'm going to give him a lecture! He's just got to listen to me, goddamn it! I sit up, get to my feet, go wobbly... I've lost the strength too... First off, my arm's killing me!... then there's my head, twice its size, enormous... Made of lead it's so heavy... Plus there's the bed, it's just too soft, too treacherous to even sit on... overpowering... overpadded... I count the flowers on the wallpaper, the cretonne... on the ceiling... I sprawl out like this other guy!... In the end I flop back, stop fighting, I surrender... my eyes're killing me... my eyelids... my head... yes! my headgear! my mask!... the whole damn mess!... everything!... Doing the beddy-bye jig!... all over the cretonne, dancing all over the walls... shepherds and shepherdesses... loads of sheep everywhere... sheep dancing away... little boats... little lambs... their fleece so soft... the surf... waves and surf! The other jerk snoring away beside me, ah! I can hear him all the same!... this bed's all feathery... a cloud!... a cloud for my bones!... shepherdesses... my eyes turning red!... there's music for sure... our eyes like burning coals... a pair of solid blue, Virginia's... shepherdesses and reclining ladies... close your eyes beddy-bye... won't work...

The next day's a whole lot worse... he didn't want to get out of bed at all... He was on strike... He didn't want to go up into the gadget room under the rafters... He didn't want to ever set eyes on it again, not the masks not the Colonel not anything... total panic... I reasoned with him, met him head on... We had the nicest chat... Naturally he didn't want to die! Everybody feels the same on that score!... Especially not by being gassed to death... "It's not humane..." His very words... Wouldn't exactly have been my cup of tea either!... Battle wounds're bad enough, no fun and games, but at least you're out in the open!... you're not exposed to shameful stenchosities, racked by rat-poisonous fumes... Gave you something to think about... no argument there!... and even a man whose mind was made up could keep weighing the pros and cons just a little... I understood his reluctance... A person could be totally brainless and still prefer to do some things rather than others, be put off by certain daredevil stunts... He wasn't too hot about this business of swallowing gas... Plus the Colonel's masks didn't strike him as up to snuff... an additional risk... It all added up... I know that even I, who was pretty savvy about the dangers of war, who had gone headfirst into the slaughter, and still was in a bad way, a gimp with a limp, who had suffered his share when it came to gases—despite everything, the mere thought made my skin crawl!... I could understand him hemming and hawing... You'd never catch me trying to pull off something like this!... I'm no yellow belly, mind you! It's just that

I was staying away from O'Collogham's crapola... I'd warned Sosthène! I wasn't squealing on anybody! I knew all about inventors!... They usually started out not asking anything of me! All I'd have to do is carry out their procedures, run their errands, do business in town... I wouldn't see any cash in hand either!... He's the one who'd be rolling in dough when it was all over!... If he survived!... Those were the cold hard facts!... If he came through safe and sound! I'd be showing up for act two, for the caravan to Tibet!... the hunt for the flower he'd mentioned, the Tara-Tohé magic deal!... Think through what's at stake... He can't go screwing up, for crying out loud!... He had to keep his claws on our little rascal... Meanwhile I could see what was coming... I'd be laying low for a little... I had a turn coming to me!...

"You've charged the front lines, dear Sosthène," I pointed out to him... "The feats of bravery are all yours now, my dear professor! Now it's up to you to save England! France! The United States! So make your Colonel happy! He treats you nice... like an equal!..."

I was talking about mine, about my own version of the Colonel... the incredible centaur General des Entrayes... You better believe I made my fellow happy!... in the Fourteenth Cuirassiers heart and soul!... You'd better believe I followed him everywhere!... Right into the cannon's mouth!... without a second's hesitation!... and he only had to do just like me... wars need heroes... in short he'd re-enlisted in the special gas mask brigade of research scientists! This was news to him! I was opening his eyes to the fine points of the situation...

But my horsing around didn't particularly crack him up, his face froze in a sly, gloomy scowl, he was giving me this funny look, nasty, pigheaded, mumbling under his breath... He wanted an end to all this commotion... wanted everything around him to stop dead... His situation was going from bad to worse... What if he really went out on strike!... I was getting jittery!... I looked back at him sitting beside me on the bed, I'd nestled right up close... Maybe I had come on a little too strong?... especially right after waking up!... The guy was still all sticky-eyed... maybe I'd got him up out of the wrong side of the bed... I was laying the blame on myself... There's a knock... the butler... full-course breakfast... Come in, my friend!... heaps of pastries, whole platefuls, sponge cakes, éclairs, jams, sandwiches, soft-boiled eggs... Ah! this perks my man up, presto! his eyes are twinkling!... His mouth starts watering... drooling/gurgles at the sheer sight!... such a lavish spread of goodies!... All his sorrow's a thing of the past!... He wants the whole tray on his bed... He snaps into action with the slices of bread... You'd think he missed dinner... He whips up marvelous concoctions, triple-deckers of butter and jam... Of course he slops up everything, covers his chops and the sheets, acting like the crudball he is!... I mention this to him... He'll have the servants turning up their noses at us... That makes old pork-face laugh...

He's on top of the world stuffing his face just like he's doing... he's getting off... hopping, wriggling, because it's just so awfully good!... scrumptious!... This sets his mind back bubbling with ideas!... A whole slew popping up at the same time... Ah! he scratches his head... He's got it!

"Hear ye! Young man!... Young man!..." he calls me... "A brainstorm!... A brainstorm!... A bolt of inspiration! Give me your hand... Here! Here!... I can see where it is!..."

"Where, what's where?"

Damn it! Ah! Fuck! ah! it's slipped away!... The idea's gone... Hell!...

"No! No! No! Wait! Yes, I know! Yes!... In the big trunk!... No! in the chest of drawers! No, under my wife's dressing table!..."

He changes his mind again... Ah! his receptors are on the blink... Sort of fuzzy as visions go... He's still discombobulated... panting, huffing and puffing... an incredibly wrenching ordeal, heartbreaking, the sheer hell he's putting himself through... the strain... He tries for a repeat vision, a revision... Squeezing his head harder than ever!... Genuine self-torture... I didn't have a clue what he was after...

"The *Vega*, for heaven's sake!... The *Vega in Verse*..." Ah! I'd lost him there!... "Come on now, you rascal!... It was left behind in Rotherhithe!... Don't you remember? At Pépé's, where else! The big book!... Don't you understand anything?... Didn't you see it?..."

Ah! so that was the big deal?... I'll be damned!... He was back to his bullshit!... All fired back up over the *Vega*... of the Hindus... the opportunities it opened up for you... an unforgivable oversight... he was spluttering right into my face, whipped up into such a lather... seething to set eyes on his *Vega* again...

"Come on now!... Honestly! wake up!..." Now he was the one on my case... "*The Book of Signs!* The *Vega*, young man!..."

His insults started flying the more excited he grew.

"You birdbrain! You idiot! can't you get it through your thick skull!... we wouldn't last two minutes in the poison gases!..."

What's this "we" business?... Why wouldn't "we" last?... The gas is all for him!...

"Don't include me! Not for one second! Can you hear me: not for one single second, got that, pops!"

I see him turn white... mere mention of the gas, fear grips him...

"You're scared shitless, Sosthène!..."

That's one thing I'd bet my life on!

Ah! shitless!... Ah! poor devil!... What did I just say?... He's fit to be tied!...

"And what about the cyanide, what do you think about that?... and the arsines?... and the arsols?..."

In a raging fury, and how, just look at him go... over my harmless little comment!... Ah! he knows every variety... all the terrors of the atmosphere... the gasmares...

"And don't forget about the perols!..." he goes on... "And the xylenes!..."

He carries on this way for a quarter of an hour!... He lists the thousand and one painful deaths... every single thing a person can drop dead from after sniffing... Actually, the choice is frightening. I laugh, can't help myself, I feel like a total jerk... He keeps heaping it on... I hit a raw nerve, and he's going to work me over good...

"Your guts just like that, down there, look!..." He points to them... "Look! your confounded guts!..."

He's got it in for me, something personal!... Little rat!... Dirty cockroach!... He squashes hunks of meat pie in the serving tray...

"Your eyes!... Your sweet, pretty eyes!..."

He shows me what they'd look like infected... two shriveled prunes... turdified by the gas...

"And you'll croak along with... smoked!..."

He wants to kill my appetite... Ah I'm still having a good time... He'll never scare me...

"So, you finished, Sosthène?... Kaput? Kaput?..."

I'm screwing around with him.

"Finished? Finished?"

Ah! he's getting a second wind... Just what do I take him for, huh? some lily-liver, do I?... ah! the last thing on my mind! what an idea!... His dander's up, he's fighting back... Enough tears!... Enough ranting and raving!... I'm the sorry sight now, scared shitless!... I'm the pitiful wreck!... He refuses to accept the situation, jibbing at my remarks... He's going to give me a pep talk!...

"Ah! damn stupid bugger! Do you have faith?" he asks.

"Faith in what?"

What's he getting at? He sighs, and with that he shrugs...

"Ah! If only you'd come sooner!..." Ah! how sorry he feels... "You'd have had time to learn!... to do a little spelling... s!... p!... ell!..."

"To spell?... To spell?..." Another of his bright ideas? What will he think up next?...

"Before, I was in the hospital, Monsieur Sosthène!... having my poor wounds tended to! Before the war I was still wet behind the ears!... Maybe that doesn't mean anything to you!... in the silk trade... earning twenty-five, thirty-five francs a month... and after that, a brigadier in the sixteenth regiment, at your good service!... Monsieur Rub-a-Dub-Dub!... I never had any call for spelling!..."

"Come, come now!... Show some get-up-and-go!"

I'm irritating him again... He thinks I'm ill-mannered... He pouts... Ah! not so fast with the pout!... sweetie!... Ah! do I ever hate that damn pouting puss of his! That crummy scarecrow!...

"Go on and make a face!... Be my guest!... I'm going to tell you again!... You've got to get one thing absolutely straight!... You're the one involved in the experiments, Mr. Marmalade!... Not me!... Let me repeat!... Not me!... I'm not in the running, and don't you forget it!... End of discussion!... I've told you a thousand times!... *Vega* or no *Vega*, faith or no faith... Turd! You listen to me good! I don't lie to anybody!... Make sure you're crystal clear on that point!..."

Blunt and up front!...

"You're impossible!" he answers, "You're in love!"

Just throws it into my face, wham, just like that!

"Ah! you stupid old bastard! and so what of it?"

"Passion makes a man impossible!"

"In love, bull! you old fool!... Mind your own business!"

I bring him back to the subject in no time flat!

"I've signed on for the trip, the Chinese treasure hunt! and that's it! nothing else included! and not for any of your harebrained whims!... I'll gladly climb onto your nags, slap your junk together, trot along, run all sorts of risks... but I'm not sniffing any of your crap!... I've had four operations, and nobody's going to put me under again!... I'm no good for experiments..."

He looks me up and down... really I break the guy's heart!... I tell it to him straight... I sort of egg him on in his lies...

"And so what about your *Vega*? as if somebody gives a damn..."

He grabs my hands...

"Are you my friend?..."

It's got him going again...

"Why, of course, how could you even ask, Sosthène!..."

"Can I really place my trust in you?..."

"Ah! when it comes to that, go right ahead!..."

He squeezes my paws even harder, grinding away, he's taken them over, trembling along with...

"My child!... Not a minute to waste!... Hurry up! Hop to it!"

He did it now... he pulled one over on me! he's going to have me running around!

"Go back to Rotherhithe, I beseech you! I beg you! Rummage in every corner! Give Pépé a good shake so she'll find it!... Turn the whole place upside down if you have to!... Don't come back without the *Vega*! Without the *Vega* we're sunk!"

This knocks the wind out of him so badly he's panting... it's the end of the world!... He sends me off... The *Vega* or death! Or it all comes crashing down!

"I won't be coming along," he bows out, "can't leave the Colonel!... You do understand, right?"

"Oh! Certainly, goes without saying..."

He looks me deep in the eyes... throws some sort of hypnotic spell over me to send me on my errand!... Ah! the slick greaseball! He enunciates each word clearly...

"Look hard for the *Vega*!... You! Will! Find! It!... The ***Vega in Verse***... Don't forget the *Verse* part!"

Ah! And then right away he bursts out laughing! poking fun at himself! Man, oh man! he thumps his chest, his head, that poor head of his!...

"Where was my mind at, my boy?"

Ah! he just can't forgive himself!

"Go on! Be quick! Hurry up!"

Wheezing like mad he starts whispering again...

"No dawdling!... Give my love to Pépé! I love her!... I adore her!... She knows it... Ah! but no address! don't forget, no address!... She'd be at the door in five minutes flat!"

"And what about Nelson? Nelson?..."

Ah! I was a pain in the neck with my Nelson...

"Just handle him, for Christ's sake! You're making my head spin with this Nelson of yours!... We've all got our own worries!..."

Easy for him to talk, the fathead, he didn't know Tuhwheep! Tuhwheep! It was a piece of cake for him! In the first place, the whole thing was a crock!... Mr. Marmalade was setting me up for a swindle!... I could see his con coming a mile away... Keep right on talking, dear old pops!... I'm not any dumber than you, you bullshit artist! You'll get yours! I didn't bat an eye, I kept a straight face... was even raring to go...

"Very good! Very good! I'm off and running! Jumping!... I'll do everything to a T, Monsieur de la Chine!"

I throw some clothes on my back! Presto! He thinks I'm one hell of an eager beaver all of a sudden! wouldn't know it was the same man! We've got to get a move on, fast... I drag him along... We run smack into the Colonel, he'd just finished his breakfast, cheery, whistling, a happy bird... he's all soft and cozy, bundled up, wearing a dressing gown covered with large checks and leaf designs, a genuine chickadee... roly-poly, perfumed, his beady pig eyes darting around... He looks us up and down sardonically... still finds us funny... He's all scrubbed, pink, smiling... With gleaming dome...

"Hello! Hello! Gentlemen! Good day! Glorious weather!"

In excellent spirits... It's true the weather was glorious. With that he turns on his heels... leaves us... ascends with dignity one step at a time...

Right then Sosthène feels real awful.

"Go on! Go on! My dear child!... Hurry up! Please!..."

"I'm going! I'm going! my dear master!..."

Ah! my mind's on the girl... I wish I could have said something to her... even a short good-bye... Nothing doing! Ah! he won't have it!... he shoves me... insults me, here we go again! Don't forget, no dawdling along the way!... got to be back with the book in a flash! Ah! the damned *Vega*!

"All right already! All right! Monsieur Sosthène!"

Just so he stops bugging me! I zip off! catch the tram, passing just that second!... Plock! Plock! Plock! Shaking!... Rattling along!... Here's my stop! Rotherhithe! Everybody off!... the house... up the stairs! ding-dong! Is this going to be another big production? And here's my gal...

"Ah! Hello there, young man! Ah! so it's you again?..."

I was already in hot water.

"Sure, it's me, Madame Sosthène. Your husband has an important message for you, he sends you lots and lots of love... and says not to worry your head over anything!... Here's fifteen shillings to cover your week... Try to make it last!... and use your head before you do anything!... So there's his advice... plus, he says not to diddle around with Achille, the fellow in the box... One of these days your husband will be by!... He'll come and pick him up... He's never been busier in his life... Ah! plus the *Vega*, the *Vega in Verse*! That's the real reason I came! I've got to bring it back with me pronto!"

I unload on her in one breath...

"Ah! can you believe that buffoon?... Ah! the no-good snake!"

Right before my eyes I see her face get this mean look...

"Just wait and see! Ah! take that message back with you! Ah! you're a fine one! you too!... you dirty little bastard!... You've got a lot to be proud of!... You show up to clean out a woman who's got no one in the world!... That's your game!... Just as lowdown as that rat of yours!... And to think you're helping him, you rascal you! Ah! go right ahead and team up!... The pair of you against a poor weak woman!... Ah! he's deserting me, the thief!... Thief! Thief! You just wait! Robber! You heard me! You heard me! Thief! Crook! Pervert! Dirty old man! Thug! He's made off with everything! The big phony!... My youth!... My life!..."

Her hair hurricaning over her face. She's spluttering over me just like her old man. The pair really heated up once they started sounding off... Plus with that accent of hers, that rolling Mediterranean singsong.

"*Butta itza nota overra!...skirta-chasa!... He wanna maka me die dirta poora like a rat!...* dirt poor in this filthy rat trap! He wants to see me at death's door! Ah! the clod, the kook!... but he can just forget about strangling me!... You're hearing it right from these lips, didn't know did you, he's been trying to strangle me for the past twenty-five years!... The dumb dope finally reaches the point where she won't take no more! you hear me, the dope don't take no more! Enough! Enough!... I'm free!..."

She's cracking up something awful!... I'm here at just the right moment... She's writhing around, twisting her arms back...,yakking my ear off... trying to get me on her side... shaking her jungle mane!... I try to bring her back to the subject... I want to get out of here.

"It's for the *Vega in Verse*..." I venture...

"*Vega*!... *Vega*! Fuck the *Vega*!..."

That was her answer... She'd gone totally berserk... boiling... she won't let me leave!

"Ah! so he thinks I'm finished, the old cuckold!... goose! old goat! You tell him that his Pépé... his Pépé's starting a new life! And as for his old tricks! Out the window, buster! A new life! Over from scratch! Yes! She's starting over!... and with no dead bodies! Not his! not Achille's! Right! You get me?"

He can just take his Achille out of here! She heaves an enormous sigh, arms up in the air! And she starts laughing! hooting like crazy! ah! he's out of her life! This is a grand occasion! She's so glad! Such joy! What happiness!... A new life! OK! I'm happy for her... "Ha! Ha! Ha!" I'm having a laugh too... she's not so nasty after all... I join in with her mood... shout "Yeah! Yeah!..." that tickles her... she lets me step into her shambles... Ah! I'm going to hunt up my book, quick! quick! and then I'm out of here!

"The book! The book! Ah, you little tough guy, that's bugging you again! Listen to me first! Listen up! That man's a bully, get me? A tyrant! You spread the word around!"

She's off again about Sosthène!

Ah! But it's over, over and done with! Whew! Whew! And another whew! She snorts like a seal, another conniption fit, she's ripping away the bonds she abhors!... acting the whole ordeal out for me, really gives me quite a show... I keep my comments to myself, mum's the word... My silence drives her up the wall.

Ah! she's going to dig up that book of mine since I'm so keen on it! After that, we'll be able to chat!... She calls out the kid from in back... who sort of lends her a hand... here he comes... it's the dairy punk... the delivery guy from last time... he's returned... Pépé's a man-eater!... her sweetheart's kind of embarrassed... he was back in the kitchen... she hitches up her nightgown pretty high, doesn't want to get it dirty... we've got to turn this pigsty upside down!... the *Vega*, the magic book, was buried, so she says, under the hugest trunks... we barely touch a finger to the heap, give a little shake, and we trigger a hurricane of crap... lose sight of each other groping around blindly... Here comes a chest crashing down, wicker baskets in its wake... we've got to open the skylight... everything's tumbling scattering, cheap junk, props all over the place, grass skirts, Chinese dressing gowns like the old geezer's, splendid specimens, stoles... of every shape, size and color... must be worth a bundle... the kid's hacking, spitting, giggling... Now it turns into fun and games... he deserves some big fat smooches... Spirits are running high again... Ah! all together now! Heave-ho!... Goose egg!... Isn't that the one? That packet there with the string, does she see it?... Nope, another dud! The hell with this, she's selling off everything! "Name your price! Take your pick, it's auction time! It'll cost you nothing! A whole life up for grabs!

Sweetie, go open the window!" Pépé's offering the whole lot! she hollers out her pitch... laughing hysterically... everything must go, gentlemen, we're moving!... There's one more chest to turn over... Whomp! it damn near crushes our legs! I'm wondering whether she's playing us all for jerks.

"Madame," I venture, "Madame, now you're sure it's in that corner?"

"Ah! corner! corner! that corner! How am I'm supposed to know? Is Monsieur in a hurry or something?"

"It's not me who's in any hurry, it's Sosthène!"

"Ah! the mangy coyote's in a hurry, is he? ah! you can all fuck off! In a hurry! In a hurry! And so what about me, huh? Thirty years I've been waiting around for him! He'll wait his turn, that fathead of yours! You just wait and see! In a hurry!"

I fired her back up... she's bitching and hissing down in her trunks... fed up with scrounging around... she sits up on her knees, in a better position to spout off about Sosthène right to my face...

"You hear: a bloodsucker! That's what your dumb friend is!"

So ticked off she chokes on her words again... then she nabs the kid as he's passing, and myum! myum! myum! plasters his cute puss... the lady's always red-hot and ready... Now they're really going at it...

I look around, inspect the digs... the junk heap was bigger the other day... I can see some stuff has already disappeared...

"So you're moving, Madame?"

Is that any of my business?

Her quick comeback.

"And what about you, my fine little birdie! Why don't you tell me your story? You want to know everything! Where do you call home, huh? Where's your little nest?"

I couldn't come up with an answer.

"Nya-nya-nya-nya-nya!..."

She's driving me crazy.

"Ah! Madame! Please now! Slip me the book and I'll beat it! I'll be taking it off your hands!"

"So that voracious beast of yours is waiting for you, right? Worrying himself sick? Eating his heart out? The cannibal..." She hoots with laughter... "Ah! the dirty pig! Aren't you ashamed?... Feeding me a line like that?... Come on now, it just can't be! You're not that stupid, my little man! Thick as a brick, are you? thick as a brick?... Just mosey on over here and let me take a little look at you!"

But she winds up walking over to me... rubbing up against me, fondling...

"Come join us!..." she invites me, with a lewd wink and a flick of her tit... she shows me her big black nipples... on purpose...

"Ah! the pipes! Madame!" I shout! Fact is, it comes back to me in a flash...

"Jackass!" she snaps back violently.

I made her sore... turned her off because I'm so slow to catch on... She just keeps nodding...

"Don't you know he's going to put a hex on you, you runt! So you came back from the war, big deal! You're still one dumb son of a bitch! You still don't know him!... He'll make you lose everything, understand?... your years... your life!... He'll screw you! He'll drain you dry!... That's what your professor's all about! Ah! Go ahead and stick by him if you want!"

In a word, she was jealous.

"Ah! I'm through with him! Through, got it? Ah! life, my darlings! Life!..."

With that she grabs me again, then the other guy, the kid! smooching, fussing over the pair of us... she wants to cuddle us both at once... and then she's back whining...

"A slave! you hear me! a slave!... his plaything! he hit me, he beat me black and blue!"

She can't get over it, she rubs her eyes, bewildered she's still here!... after such ghoulish tortures! like some refugee from another world!... she's awakening from some nightmare!... A Sosthène-mare!... ah! the thought of it all, too much for the gal... all the crap she had to put up with!... here we go, another flood of tears drenching her face... her mascara running plus her lipstick... what a pitiful godawful face... I was about to leave, I'd had it... she grabs me, plasters me with smooches, the kid too...

"Come on, since you're so keen on it!"

She's going to pick up the hunt again... Heave ho! all three of us buckle down... Still got lots of trunks left! They haven't moved out everything yet!

"So who's helping you move? You taking away everything?"

I keep asking my same old questions.

"You'll see soon enough!"

Pretty wary!

Need to clear some space!... we'll have a better chance... now we're hauling the biggest ones out into the hallway, the chests on the large sofa...

"Won't you ever be back again, Madame?"

"Ah! so what kind of future would you wish on me, huh? To be found behind some trunk? Haven't I made enough sacrifices? lost enough of my youthful bloom? that I'm starting to look like his mummy Achille! That's what he wants, Achille Norbert! That's what Sosthène needs! Of course he's a monster! Maybe that's news to you? Out for himself and nobody else! They don't come any crummier!... The world waiting on his whim!... Of course he wants to murder me!... he's itching to... Ah! but he's got another thing coming to him, my fine sir! You be sure and tell him... Finished! it's finished!... Finished! Pépé's leaving tonight! she's free! free as the wind! Isn't that right, my sweetie! Sweetie!..."

She grabs the kid again... hugs, licks, nibbles him... the trunks sit right where we left them...

Ah! the silly cunt!

"OK fine! I'll look through them myself!..."

I pounce on the pile, lift lids... stirring up volcanoes of dust!... I sneeze... choke...

"It's not here!... It's not here!..."

The dumb old bag's razzing me! Tickled to see me rummaging around for nothing...

"He'll never find out where I stuck it! Nyah-nyah-nyah-nyah-nyah!..."

"And what about the pipes, you slut?" I demand.

"Ah! the pipes!... the pipes! ah! can't forget about them!..."

The pipes are even a bigger riot!... they're both playing me for a sucker...

The thought whips me up even more! I want the big book!

This gives her an idea for a dirty trick...

"I'm keeping the book, you're not laying a hand on it!... So that hypocrite of yours wants it, huh? He wants to pick me clean! Ah, the bloodsucker! Well, the hell with you! I'd rather croak first! When I think of all the stuff he's messed up for me! Ah! no, no, you'd never believe it! the kid! the kid! look, on his head!..."

She swears to me on his innocent head...

"That bumbling boob of yours snatches people's souls! he snatches their souls! You can tell him I said so... today I could have been a maharanee! a maharanee, did you hear me? that was my future... You don't know what a maharanee is? It's bigger than a princess, it's like a queen!... If only I hadn't been just some meal ticket, hadn't listened to that dumb rotten prick! that geek! that worm! that fly-swallower! Crying over the past is a big waste, that's for sure!..."

She's dumbstruck... something just dawns on her...

"Now you just listen to me, you little punk!" More conniptions... "I married him, get me, officially! lawyers! courts! the works! Don't let that bloodsucker back there tell you any different!... It's absolutely true! A maharanee, that's what his wife could have been! And that maharajah... He would have built me a temple in lapis lazuli! in jade if that's what I wanted!... He'd already given the orders! Ah! don't have any comeback for that one, do you?... Sosthène! Sosthène! goddamn you!"

Her anger flared back up... she swoops on the kid again in her raging sorrow!... blubbers on him, wraps him in her arms, lovey-doveys... Her fury had a tender touch.

"Who's carrying off your junk?"

Back to my question.

"Nelson, that's who! Happy now?"

She sticks out her tongue at me. It wasn't any great surprise... I'd figured it out... Still and all he worked fast... already part of the family!...

"He'll be back any minute! You can get the hell out!"

Nobody was holding me back.

"Wait!" I go... "Just hold on a single second! First let me find my book... you're going to cart it off I'm sure!"

Ah! she really gets off on that idea... lets me rummage around all by myself... doesn't even want the kid to lend me a hand...

"Tsk! Tsk! Tsk!" they go to me.

She spins a little "tsk! tsk!" ditty to rub it in good.

"Buenitas! Buenitas! Whoop! Yippee!"

And I'm supposed to wriggle my ass to the beat! swing it, oh yeah, baby... she's laughing so hard her hair's falling into her mouth... I ignore the whole show, keep poking around... I'm tossing through the heaps...

"It's not inside there, Madame?"

I'm talking serious. Now I've come to empty the biggest chest...

"Pssh! Pssh! Pssh!..."

She drives me into a rage.

"Nya-nya-nya-nya-nya!"

I've got to let her put a blindfold on me... then she'll tell me whether I'm hot or cold... if I don't she won't lift one little finger to help me... it's a crazy whim, an impulse... Ah! now the kid thinks I'm a laugh-riot... she's still a little girl herself... I grope around... Ah! I'm such a stitch! I stumble... "This one? This one?" I ask... I dive into the pile... topple over everything, rummaging... Don't give a damn whose feet I step on... "No! No! No!" Cold as ice!... Backtrack with my arms flung wide right into the junk pile... blind as a bat... Up to my ears in props... and rose petals! I kick up billows and billows of them!... A big laugh for them!... I'm so fed up I'm going to wreck everything! I knock over three baskets in one swoop!

"Ah! he's hot! he's hot!" she squeals.

I yank off my blindfold, I look, a big zero... just some crummy old basket... tied with string, which I undo, lift the lid... a dummy's inside...

"This is it?"

They're holding their sides, howling like idiots!

"Ah! real funny! So what about it? Hell, this isn't any book!..."

I look, touch, it's a skeleton, bones, hands, skull, in the ceremonial duds of a marquis at court.

"So what about it?" I go, "what about it?"

Ah! the glorious assholes! Some big joke! I join in the laughter, watch me! Hardy! Har! Har! Ah! sly devils! Ah! clever as hell they are! Something's written on the lid... in red... a sign... I bend over... "Achille Norbert"... Ah! I get it now! Ah! clear as day! Astounding! Ah! No kidding! Brilliant! I join in the laughter... Hardy! Har! Har! just like them! ah! how extraordinary! Ah! silly galoots!

"So," I go, "a dead body with stockings shoes the works! never seen anything like that?"

Ah! they're working on me!

"It's so hilarious! so fantastic! Doesn't take much to impress you!"

True, he was nicely spiffed up, with polished shoes no less, crimson satin breeches, a tail coat with silver lapels... gold earrings, precious jewels... dressed to kill! a blue baldric, a dress sword... waistcoat with florets... Ah! ah! she's looking at me, I've made her sore, didn't fall over on my ass... I've already seen corpses, you old hag, you dingbat! Think I was born yesterday!

"So this is Sosthène's granddad?"

He'd talked enough about him...

"He doesn't bite, you know! he doesn't bite!"

She decided to play Miss Smarty Pants... smile her way out of this!... Ah! you little phoney!...

"No, he doesn't bite! No, he doesn't bite! the proof is that I'm taking him with me. This stiff belongs to Sosthène!"

Ah! Fucked her there! she drops the act, absolutely refuses! she's attached to this puppet of hers!

"You're not taking it anywhere, you dumb brute!..." She's going through the roof! "So, you want everything! You just listen here, I paid a small fortune for that! Just take a look at that little pirate! He's even uglier than the monkey who owns him! Go on! Beat it!"

"Where you going to move it to?"

I make a point of being nosy, just to be a pain in her ass.

"None of your business, you impolite jerk!"

"Oh, come on, it belongs to Sosthène! since it's his old man! got to bring it back to him! ah! no two ways about it! it's all been worked out!"

I'm not fooling around, I'm cocksure!

Her reaction? She jams herself across the doorway, yanks me back by my shirttails, really hooks into me, she won't have me laying a finger on anything... I brush her aside, chuck her out of the way, knock her to the floor... How she squawks! blows up! And I battle back more determined than ever! I want her marionette, the carcass, the skull and bones! with tricorn hat! and feather! ah! I want the works! not a single stitch left behind!... His walking cane, even... a long tapering stick topped with a knob! the whole scarecrow! The finger bones tied to the knob, the whole shebang off and away! One really nice piece of work!

"I'm not leaving without my Achille!"

I boom out the news. We're going to have to fight this out! The broad's still flat on her ass, can't believe her ears...

"It's a beautiful piece, indeed, Madame, it's one hell of a piece!"

I'm having some fun. I show her the choppers...

"Don't find teeth everyday in such great shape, Jesus no! Ah! I know my corpses! I've seen hundreds! thousands! They're my special hobby! Achille's a big shot, you know! He's a big shot! You can see that right off... he's a VIP!... And such a handsome devil with those big peepers of his! Just get a load of them!"

Huge holes, no kidding. Genuine chasms that once were his eyes... and the bony parts, spick and span! actually bright and shiny... under his tricorn, his bone-dome's gleaming... sort of like the Colonel's, but yellow, bright lemon... the embroidery work's moth-eaten... but nothing that can't be fixed...

"Ah! About time I got here! when I think you were going to give it away!..."

Ah! I worked fast... the string... quickly... one knot here... one there... nobody'd notice me in the street... it looked like a sort of large flat basket... but awkward to lug around... how happy the Colonel'd be! I could see him even now! Maybe he'd deck it out in his uniform... he liked fancy drag... Maybe he'd stick on his big mask?... his sort were capable of anything... Ah! how delighted I was going to make the pair of them! What a nice new toy, my little pet!

"Good-bye, Madame. Take care of yourself!"

I hoist the basket onto my shoulder. Up, and off we go!

She throws herself around my neck, pleads with me.

"Don't be mean, boy! Don't be mean!"

She whines in English...

"Don't be so awful! I'll tell you everything! You'll get your book!"

A fine idea! A meeting of the minds! Ah! now she's talking sensible!

"That's right, honey bun! Go get it for me!"

I kept my clutches on my prey, ready to make a trade, or forget it... it'd be better for us to work something out... And so what if she were going to raise hell!... chase me down into the street! hysterical! Since her mummy was so important to her!... At least I'd bring back the *Vega*...

She zips off, dashes into the kitchen. I hear her knocking around the pots and pans... ah! so that was her hiding place... I ought to have looked there a long time ago!... She pops right back... Oh! brother, what a whopper!... heavy as two big Britannicas... She has a hell of a time lugging it over... It's heavier than the strawman, even with his weapons, his wig! I crack open the mysterious book somewhere in the middle... to make sure there's no funny business!... It's the *Vega*, all right, no mistake... I recognize the fancy decorations... plus the label *Vega in Verse* in flaming letters... the crocodile insets... mammoth binding... worth a bundle to be sure if only pound for pound, plus the pictures... all hand-drawn illustrations... a superb job... She was gawking through the pages along with me... like she'd never seen it before... warriors on horseback... tiger hunts, manhunts... watercolors in two-page spreads... gold and blue elephants... winged dragons... a Barbary ape etched in mother-of-pearl relief... chimeras in flames and dancing girls!... more dances, dances galore!... bayadères and young boys... bright double-page pastels... Incredibly fragile!... an entire ballet in miniature... Flying through the air... delicately intricate flourishes with a fly's ball's eye for detail! really mind-boggling to see every speck of dust and ass hair in place... and then more ballerinas, the "swallow" variety... sea monsters breathing fire... a gigantic one-of-a-kind piece of work... plus this entire text in hieroglyphics highlighted with gold and red illustrations... plus more figurines lizards sunflowers tulips... weaving around huge parades of trooping devils with corkscrew tails... on the flip side another dance of two three-headed monsters writhing around... page after page after page of masks... all the spellcasting grimaces...

"Well well, my darling, quite a show, huh?"

"I never looked very closely at it before."

It's true, it was eye-dazzling... it wasn't beautiful but it was rich... made your head dance/go blurry, it bewitched you, that's a fact!

"Say, kid, leave it with me!"

Here she goes with her second thoughts! Ah! it's a crying shame! She yanks it out of my hands, clutches it to her body... It's downright stinking dishonest! It was all agreed I'd be taking it! She offers me Achille Norbert again...

"Ah! you really don't know what you want!"

"Take him! Take him! Leave me the *Vega*!"

She begs me, turns the faucets back on... Just like a woman... I stand my ground, I keep the book... don't give a damn about her blubbering... Doesn't she want to sell it to me? If it was for me she'd sell... She must have a collector in mind...

"What will you do with it?" I ask.

Button-lipped. And what about the other fellow there, Achille in his breeches, maybe she wants to sell him too? Maybe Nelson's mixed up in this deal? Ah! Very possible... They're capable of anything...

"And what about Achille here, what will you do with him?"

She simpers, back to her smarty pants act.

"Out with it, you tramp, what've you got in mind?"

If they take the mummy to the public market over on Petticoat, it'll make the papers for sure... and then one thing will lead to another... Ah! the bitch's got big ideas!

"Give me a little hint what you're cooking up!"

I've had it! I want to get this over with! I grab her by the throat... she giggles, thinks I'm fooling around...

"Will you talk, you pain in the ass!"

Ah! The rough stuff turns her on... She wants me to fool around with her some...

"He's going to fix him up with a new pair of eyes! electric light bulb eyes! there, now you know, happy? Give me a kiss, you nosy little boy..."

I don't quite get it.
"What kind of eyes? Achille?"
"Eyes that light up, dumb shit! for his number!"
Ah! I'm slow to catch on!
"Where's he going to do his number?"
"Oh, this sort of thing's been going on forever, you stupid slob! Were you born yesterday?"

She gives me the lowdown on how they were going to work the gimmick... There was this guy in Vancouver who collected everything he wanted, a skeleton just like Achille, but in pharaoh drag... the catch is that it's bogus, a phony... plaster bones, fake costume, you name it!... The mummy'd come out with pronouncements about the present, the future through this gramophone in his belly, a super ventriloquist... plus the eyeballs: flashing blue, red, depending on the answer... "The Fun of the Past" it was called... But now Achille was another story! with his papers, costume, the works, absolutely authentic! irrefutable! nobility, jewels... Americans were tired of cheap fakes... Sosthène would have gotten this off the ground if he'd had a little time... but he was always on the move... starting everything finishing nothing... he'd only got as far as the sign... she goes to the kitchen... comes back and shows me...

HERCULE ACHILLE DE RODIENCOURT
COMMANDER IN CHIEF OF THE KING'S ARTILLERY
MARSHAL OF FRANCE
MARQUIS OF APREMONT
SENESCHAL D'EPÔNE
COMMANDER OF THE ORDER OF THE CROSS OF SAINT-LOUIS

In short, it was a cinch. Nelson showed up just at the right time, he was hauling in a treasure, it would make a magnificent sideshow attraction, that I realized, with its blazing eyes, the record player, the voice from the next life, the laughter from beyond the grave... she gave me her rendition of the laugh... it was all worked out... Couldn't help but feel glad, one terrific setup... yet even so while filling me in she feels a prick of doubt... wonders whether it wouldn't be for the best if she took the book back, all things considered! Ah! such brass! Ah! damn! Ah! Enough already! I'm as patient as a man can be but there are limits! I've got the *Vegas* and I'm keeping them!

"Sosthène's asking for them, they're his! It's understandable! Anyway, I'll tell you what, this is the best I can do—if he wants, he'll trade with you! As for me I'm getting the hell out of here! So long!"
No lies or tough talk...
"Got to go, Pépé! Good-bye! Stay cool!"
I race back down the two flights with my load under my arm. She didn't

have a chance to get out a peep, I'd already put some distance between us! Up onto the bus! Change to another! I'm really moving! Chug down a stretch, I'm back! Ah! I get in, drenched in sweat...

The old clown was watching for me at the window.

"You have it? You have it?" Waving his arms around... couldn't he see my package? Too small for him, or what?

"Bring it up right away! Watch out! Don't let anybody lay a finger on it! hide it under the bed."

Right off the bat he starts with the orders! I'll shut his trap for him.

"Hey, you clown, show some manners! Better be a little careful who you're talking to!..."

Always need to put him in his place!

"Maybe you'd like to hear some news?"

He didn't ask for any.

"Well, sir, this is hot off the press! You can hop to it! Hurry on over and fetch your darling little girl! It's high time! Right this second she's walking away with Achille!... Or rather she's going to put him to work! with Nelson no less! That very Nelson I was telling you about the other day... you know, the one you weren't afraid of! They're going to rig him out for the fairs, a tell-the-future robot... lamps for eyes, the works... phonograph in his belly... the future the stars... were you in the know? It was your own personal plan, so I hear... plus the sign... they've already got their contract... all the big fairs throughout the Midwest... plus, they simply adore each other! A new life! Which is what she wanted me to tell you all along, plus a load of other stuff! I think they're taking the kid along... he's part of the act... you know, the little milkman..."

Ah! now this really is new news! I keep watching his kisser...

"Pretty interesting, don't you think?"

He doesn't bat an eye, buries himself in the book, sticks his nose way in, starts coughing... Got to start over again from the top, Christ Almighty!

"They're going to make him sing, I'm telling you... Make the most incredible crap come out of his mouth... He's going to make America laugh! 'The Fun of the Past,' that's what it's called... How about that! Original!"

He still refuses to answer me.

"She's going to start her life over," I yell at him, "and Pépé's message to you is go to hell!"

He couldn't give a damn! I'd put him through hell! Ah! I lay it on a little thicker, off the top of my head, make it up as I go along...

"Shush! Shush! That's enough, you whippersnapper! You do pick great times!"

My timing's wrong, that's the only reason he's miffed!

"Go on! Go on! so take the book upstairs!"

"Take it up yourself, you big wimp, it shouldn't be too much of a strain!..."

If I don't put my foot down, he'll have me polishing his shoes!

Pépé was right... he flips his wig over petty crap... And the guy can grate on you something awful... I'd seen him in action ever since we arrived, he'd changed from top to bottom... All because of the atmosphere around there, the servants, the rugs, the bells, all the fancy-shmancy... He'd forgotten how to piss. Even his screwed-up woman back here, with her temple, her opals, her madly in love maharajahs—where'd she pick up those loony fantasies of hers? Doesn't take much to get your head all hot and spinning, like a compass out of whack... A small compliment, an itsy-bitsy breeze, and watch out, oh man, you set sail!

Cast off! Hold tight! No stopping now!

You could hear them hammering away, it sounded like they were trashing everything... Sosthène and the Colonel must have been letting loose on their masks, calibrating them with stupendous might... an incredible clash-clanging... an earthshaking racket... really a din so awful it couldn't be for real... Even so it scared the hell out of me... Jumping into my clothes, I race down, reach the salon. The girl was there, right near the piano, my adorable darling, even cuter than the day before... Ah! she's so beautiful! such an angel! I can't think of anything else... I can't hear the ruckus anymore... Can't hear anything but her... nothing but her pretty words... "Good morning, sir!"... Ah! I can still see her now... her short yellow dress in Liberty fabric... a daffodil, a corolla... so shorty short... her legs her thighs... that mocking face... her eyes... plus she's frisky as ever... slippery... always on the move... ah! the little minx!

I can breathe!... No, I can't!... at the mere sight of her... forget how to breathe... Ah! this is too much!... I love her too much right away... I'm not myself anymore!... I give out! No! I bounce back to life!... My eyes are playing tricks on me... Ah! her hair! A golden glow! A feast! Blonde, the feast of her hair... Blonde her curls!... Blonde my joy!... Blonde my prayer!... Blonde at play!... Blonde my fairy!... Blonde, and how!... Ah! how I love her!... Ah! my mind goes blank!... I just stand there in front of her!... It's me!... Yes, it's me!... Ah! I'm so happy by her side!... Dazzled! I pull myself out of it! Cling to the piano!... I'd like to kiss her, touch her thighs... In a flash I blot out the whole world!... nothing left but her beautiful eyes, her laugh... She's in fits over me, oh geez... my galoot look... I'm red-faced myself, what a warrior! who doesn't know which way to turn... I'm going to bark with happiness!... the blondeness! the gold of her hair!... Her beautiful sky blue eyes!... here we go again!... Her smile! Ah! worries, wounds, gloomy thoughts, they all vanish! into thin air! up and away! with the miracle of her hair! at this very instant dimming disappearing! Blondeness! Blondeness! shimmers... I'm beside myself with joy!... in marvels of delight!... Never mind! Never mind! I'll take a stab! I flutter all around her! A feather! Lighter than air! pirouetting! all around my idol!... how happy I am! And then, plop! I collapse at her feet... in doggy delight!... I want to lick her all over, I lap! spring around again, gamboling! yipping!... taking a little nibble at her fingers... her fingers of light... Grrrrr!... Grrrr!... I growl!... Roar in sheer pleasure!... She's laughing!... laughing!... what a good time she's having!... I totally lose my mind, somersaulting like crazy, leaping, darting around, galloping again around the furniture, along the rugs! all goofy because I love her so much... I slam smack into the big armchair, the enormous one... ricochet high into the air, glide! a bird I am now soaring along! Ker-boom, I crash! Spread-eagled... smashing everything! What a racket! I give her a laugh, she's wriggling giggling my angel... going to pee her panties I'm such a riot!... I can see her fanny through them... taut wriggling... she's laughing, laughing... never mind, I adore her!... her laughter peals... how cruel she is!... I love her anyway, and ten times more than that!... I can see all her thighs, I roll around on the floor... I can see her fanny!... my knees hurt so bad... I feel like I've been shot!... That makes the heartless girl laugh... she laughs at everything! merciless! Go ahead, laugh! Laugh! little bitch!... I'm going to gobble your thighs! I can't hold back anymore! I roll around at her feet... I kiss her little shoes... the tips... and then her socks... and then her leg the taut flesh down there so pink and tanned... her muscles laughing too, quivering... the downy blush of life... ah! laugh, laugh, little girl! my goddess! I'm going to sink my teeth in you raw!... You just watch me! A spring of vibrant happiness gushes from her laugh... spurts cascades in the air all around us!... Ah! I'm a dog down to my bones now!... Ah! how I adore her!... She pets the top of my head!... she calms me down so nicely... her hand runs through my hair!... Ah! I want to die on the spot for her!... my fever flares back up!... I don't ever want to leave her!... I growl!.... I roar even louder... she pets me... sort of brushes back my mane!... she's poking fun a little... impish darling!... what an angel... what kindness on her part... I want to howl in adoration... roar like a lion full of love!... I'm shaking in fervor... in fright!... afraid she'll leave me alone an instant... her gentle hand sets me at ease.

"What is your name?" she asks.

"Ferdinand."

She gets a kick out of me.

My whole life for her!... my whole death!... everything she wants and more!... I kiss her knees... the fabric of her dress!... She sort of pushes me away... Ah! what sorrow!... what heartbreak!... I apologize... then start over again! I lift her whole skirt up real high! I bite right into her bare thighs!... Myum! Myum! Myum!... I could eat her all up!... devour her!... Raw and right now!... I adore her too much!...

She pushes me away... all ready to laugh... but I'm too rough. How old can she be, when you get down to it? Around twelve or thirteen... Ah! what a pig I am!

"So, don't you have anything to do?"

"Oh, yes, lots! Listen to me... I beg you! Don't laugh!... I love you!..."

"Stop it now! Don't be silly! What if the servants... if my uncle spotted you?... You don't know my uncle!"

Hands off! Hands off! She's used to being pawed. She's not raising that much of a squawk... Ah! say now, wait a minute! just wait! ah! come to think of it! there must be others who paw her! My suspicions flare up... I'm burning with doubt... ripped to pieces...

"Does your uncle do that to you, too? Does he, huh?"

I grab her thighs again, finger them hard, pinch them... she's got to come clean... I'm gasping... with anger... I've stopped breathing, I'm hurting myself... Ah! how blind! what a chump! thick as a brick! and I didn't have an inkling!

"He loves you, doesn't he? He also kisses you the way I do?"

I want to kiss her on the mouth, she dodges me at every turn, wriggling around... I want to know the whole story! every last detail!... I grab her, hold her tight... she's laughing... laughing... Come on! the details! and I don't mean tomorrow!... Must say I'm working myself up with all this carrying on... plus I'm so unhappy... everything comes at once! enough to put you six feet under!... I'm ready to take off the kid gloves... start beating her! I want to find out everything, every single detail!... I kiss her... Oh! the monster! her uncle's a shifty two-face, you can bet your life on that! A dirty old man, a hypocrite! with his masks and his dumb blah-blah-blah! he's a monster, he's got to pack his bags and scram! Either him or me! One or the other! End of discussion! I don't have any time to lose! I can't wait! I'm sincere, simple as that! and I'm suffering!

"I'm going to kill him. I don't want him kissing you anymore!" I announce to her in French and English... and I don't want her laughing! she does anyway... busts out loudly... I'm not concocting anything, this is definitely definite... that old son of a bitch is laying his hands on her... plus what else is he doing besides? Tell me, you wily devil! And not just that he does "things"! Tell me everything! She doesn't want to tell me anything, she giggles, wriggles... ah! my little honey buns! you're pushing me too far! ah! my slick cagey chickadee! ah! the hussy! I'm sure she loves the old guy deep down... she goes nuts when he paws her... Ah! I get so jealous I could howl with tears...

"You like it, don't you? you like it?"

Does she even understand me? She won't hold still, waving her arms around, going "Bzz! Bzz! Bzz!" at me. She's ribbing me, this dumb galoot with his ludicrous barking! Must be how she sees me... And so what about you! you cunning depraved little bitch!... that's how I see her... If I'm ornery obnoxious it's all her fault... All she needs do is give me an answer! Ah! then I won't be able to bawl her out anymore... I run out of steam, I babble rave start crying again... all my anger peters away... I've lost heart... I'm washed out... I collapse... throw myself at her feet once more... Here we go for another round... Once more I beg her forgiveness a thousand times... what a fine way to act... rolling around the rug! I beg her, for pity's sake!... I grovel!... I plead with her... I don't know which way to turn anymore!

"Mademoiselle, I'm unspeakable!... You're just a child! Virginia, I'm asking your forgiveness... I've taken advantage of your youth!... Ah! I'm fit to be hanged! I'm the monster! Virginia! Please! Please! You're going to understand me! You're so very young so very darling... I'm suffocating with a secret! I'm on fire and my wounds are killing me!"

Play it up, pour it on thick! I want to see a flood of tears... she's got to hear about all my woes, big and small... and all the threats, everything hanging over my head... plus all the hard knocks I've been through... she listens, she's nice, but it doesn't bring her around... I even think she's sort of poking fun at me... a twinkle of mischievousness... kids this young are callow... I start my whole story over from the top, all my battle mishaps... naturally I stretch the truth a little... it would have done the trick pretty well, hooked her... but now it's the other pair drowning me out... the madhouse Vulcans upstairs... whaling away so hard it sounds like they're pounding the walls to dust... their pandemonium's terrifying... they must be heaving everything into the forge to guess from the din they're making... no way she can be listening to me...

All my efforts down the drain...

"How about if we step out for a moment? Please be so kind, Mademoiselle! I'll tell you everything... Not here..."

She's a kid but, even so, such poise already! such bearing, such boldly sculpted thighs! I can see her now, she still dazzles me... That's where you judge what the animal's made of, in the tuning fork of the crotch... the way it vibrates against the ground with each stride... the music of the body... the irresistible music...

She leads the way, runs ahead, I step as quickly as I can... We're in the garden... a child, a little girl, a dream... what graceful strides! what impishness in her smallest gestures... Ah! I'm completely bewitched! a creature lost between heaven and earth... Muddy cruddy I adore you!... I slither wallow! Down in my ooze I cherish you!

Whatever can I be thinking in the end? how can I be kidding myself this way? What kind of sap am I acting like? What sort of sucker? Ah! I get a hold of myself! In a flash! So she doesn't give a damn! That Little Miss Fidget! Just wait till you see what a sly old fox I can be! What, drop dead over something like this! Ah! make no mistake! just the opposite, I want to live! To live ten times! A hundred times! a thousand times over! one happy fella! For your beautiful gaze! under your beautiful eyes, my asshole! Ten, a hundred lifetimes, and a lucky devil! in order to worship you all the more, my spellbinding charmer! But all my thrashing around scares her off... all this teeter-tottering so close to the deep end...

Ah! I want to be tortured to death!... Please, stab a knife through my heart!... quivering!... throbbing! bleeding all for you!... I want my suffering to be excruciating!... go ahead, trample on my heart for your own personal kick!... my martyrdom!... I want to be drawn and quartered under your eyes!... damned!... begging for mercy, putty in your hands!... On second thought, no! not when you really come down to it! hell, no! too much stupid crap over such a rotten kid like her! a kid who doesn't give a damn, I'm not that blind! she's having fun, that's all, she's fanning the flames... What love! My adorable fairy, no less! What is she doing running away? Abandoning me? well then, it's all over, I sink down, my heart breaks, I disappear... Dumb hick! clumsy ox! Clod! you're going to scare her! Will you ease up a little on your adoration! Ah! Cross my heart! I'll stop scaring her!... And yet I really ought to tell her the whole story... she's got to listen to me!... all my secrets... all the dirty details... beware, little girl!... I've got some terrible confessions to make.... mysteries that go on and on!... Ah! meaning that I'm the one who starts trembling because I'm going to let the cat out of the bag... Buffoon! dithering and shaking in your boots worse in this garden of sweet affection than in the gales of Flanders... under the barrage of squalling shrapnel... ah! see how a person can tremble, my beauty!... how my heart dances in my chest!... shaking me up all over, head legs eyes... so badly I don't know what the hell I'm seeing or doing anymore!... I don't know how to get a grip on myself anymore!... everything all around gives way, I'm staggering... my heart bolts off! gallops! races! a dizzying blur closes in around me... stabbing chills zigzag through me, I'm shivering... my beloved's gaze clouds over... I blank out... ah! but I was holding her by the arm! Whatever was I thinking! here she is, my dearest darling!... very delicately... and such laughter!... and here I'd barely grazed her... totally tongue-tied with devotion... We were walking from one lane to the other, me woozy with happiness, fervor, fear... the small birds flittering past made us giddy with their chirps... high with spring fever... all the daffodils on the lawn were dancing in the breeze... There's the pristine picture... Springtime in London is a fragile business, the damp sun laughs through its tears... the peach trees in blossom blaze pink... a bunny over there in the grass... escapes, dashes off!... Virginia charges after it, catches, lifts it in her arms, kisses it... carries it away with her... ah! I'm jealous!... all at once, awful! murderous! I'm jealous of everything! of the sky! her uncle! the lawn! the bunny! the air wafting through her hair!... she's barely listening to me... she can't hear me anymore... I'd like her to give me a kiss too!... All the tender loving care goes to the bunny! Ah! hell! This kid's working on my nerves with her precious fussing! snot-nose! Got to sit down first chance... I'm completely pooped, all done in... She's wearing me out with her pranks! My ear's acting up again, buzzing away! and what whistling! what drumming! exploding jets of steam! a factory at full blast! All the pots and pans in my head rattling away! I'm a raging hurricane and I can't hear a thing... I'm in a bad way because of my ear... not to mention my arm! and my ribs!... the child's clueless!... after holding out for two-three hours I'm done in, done in... I lag behind the rest of the world... I lag behind... hang on as best I can... no act either, not a put-on, I'm drained to the last drop, and that's that... I collapse... plop! I look like I'm bitching and moaning... Ah! I'd love to run!... I can't even lift a finger... Come on, let's go... over there... the bench under the trees!... I whine splutter!... Virginia, honey! Virginia by my side! Ah! I hold her back because otherwise she'd take off!... There's a nip in the air... the damp breeze sends a chill through us... I want to shelter her from the gust, can't have her shivering! I want to lend her my jacket... she's got to accept, goddamn it!... The shirt off my back for her... I'll shiver for her... the breeze is treacherous!... I want to warm her up with my heat... Ah! but she refuses! she won't hear another word about it!... she wants to shiver in her blouse... I'll warm her up anyway, goddamn it! I palm her two small tits, hold them, so hard so pointy, it's true she's cold... she wriggles around but nicely... her clear cheerful ringing laughter puts me on top of the world... there I sit in sheer delight beaming with joy... ah! how darling she is... a sweetheart! I thought some awful things that's all!... I'm dreadful, an ornery old turd... now she's laughing at me... everything's all right! I'm even cured... hardier than ever!... I'm in heaven!... Bursting with happiness... never mind! never mind! I'm flying out of whack! wherever I look I see nothing but blue... I can see the angels!... I see the good Lord on his cloud... a thick enormous cloud... he wishes me well too!... He, Virginia and I, an affectionate threesome! I'm back loving her, kiss her most of all... I give them both a great big smooch... ah! this is no ordinary celebration... I dance with her, with him... and now the angels!... they farandole after each other from one cloud to the next... we all love each other... the whirling makes me woozy... I keep rising higher, traveling further... it's like back in the Greenwich... here we go, it's starting all over again!... it's not Delphine anymore, or Claben... now it's the Big Guy over there on his cloud... not Boro anymore, but the Man in the White Beard... They're going to start playing their atrocious tricks on me again!... giving me hallucinations!... got to get away! farther away farther away... got to take off!... I'm beating it, kid! I clear out dodging through the banks of mist... soaring along at top speed... Ah! but I spin around... sail along upside down... snarl myself up! somersaulting! tailspinning!... I'm going down! I try grabbing out... hold onto your hat! I yell my shout catches in my throat... Virginia! Virginia! Help me! Ah! a close call! by a hair! I was off on one of my dizzy spells...

I'd blacked out... Good thing she was there... she hadn't abandoned me...

on the same bench... in the same garden... Ah! I could see it all again!.... I was prone to fainting fits... she realized this... she'd seen me close my eyes... I didn't let go of her hand! ah! no way! not for one second... Right away I go back to my old tune... still pretty sick from my dizzy spell... back to bending her ear about how she's got to understand me... know every last detail of my ordeal...

"Virginia, I've committed crimes... I was forced to!... I shouldn't be telling you, of all people! I'm going to scare you... it's also my head that's to blame... you saw with your own eyes what a bad way I'm in, right?... I can murder again in the same exact way... Aren't you scared?... My folks aren't like this! Ah! It doesn't run in the family... it's because of the war!" I explained to her... "Ah! If only you knew them... especially my mother! and don't forget my father! Have I ever given them a load of heartache! Ah! don't think I'm not remorseful!..."

It all came spewing out... She had kind eyes for me but was totally in the dark... I ran back through the whole song-and-dance in English... from first word to last... same result... she didn't catch on... what I was trying to say meant nothing to her, the poor dear... nothing to a darling little girl like her... She understood that this was the stuff of adventure movies, horrible stuff... but I just wasn't a scary sort of guy... she couldn't see me as one of life's tragic victims...

"Why remorse?"

What a question!

"Well, what about me robbing your uncle! your good uncle, so good to us both! whose mercury I swiped! isn't that ghastly? Isn't that frightful?... And plus lots and lots of other stuff... a thousand times more criminal!..."

I paint a wildly black picture of myself... it didn't disturb her.

"But so what did you actually do?"

Ah! dumb kid! I'd best keep my mouth shut. She definitely doesn't understand a single word. And what if I pumped her for some info about the masks... Maybe she's more in the know?...

"The masks, Virginia?... your uncle?... does he believe in them? does he, deep down, just between us?... or is it one big joke?"

"Oh, you know Uncle! He's one for having a good time!... he always likes inventions!"

She doesn't know any more than that... what interests her is her bunny... sitting on her lap, nibbling... nibbling its own muzzle, what looks to be its tiny nose... its little nib of a nose quivering like crazy... She imitates it, down to a T... she wants me to do it too... Ah! she's unbearable!... she doesn't listen to anything... I've got to pop the big question... go on, for Christ's sake!

"Virginia! Virginia! for crying out loud! do you want to marry me? I love you!..."

I'm dumbfounded... I blurted it out in one breath... didn't even recognize my own voice... goes to show how off the top of my head it was... I sit there staring wide-eyed... She doesn't answer a word... keeps up her little game... Ah! I've got to take another shot at it!

"Virginia! Virginia! I adore you!"

I take her hand firmly... then right before our eyes something extraordinary happens, a marvelous wonder there in front of us... Or rather in the stretch between us and the trees... My memory's picture perfect... it all happened like on some stage... Enter Happiness! literally blazing, brightening... Never saw anything like it! an enormous bush of fire! and what flames of radiance! green, shot through with pink, shimmering... with a few blossoms of yellow-blue light sprinkled in the branches... The whole bush of fire is throbbing... like me... I'm throbbing in rhythm with the roses... and now other fragrances reach us... a sort of petal essence tickling our noses... full of sweetness charm... the sweetest rose scent wafts past intoxicates us... what ecstasy! in raptures... gaga... dazed... totally beside ourselves with happiness!... Ah! but dark clouds are about to roll in... I can spot them in the distance... I'm shivering... No! No! I'm fascinated by the fire's burning glow, its heat... I squint into it!... Before the cold settles in I want to burn up in the heart of the blazing miracle... I leap headlong inside, flail around, the flames envelop me, sweep me off, up among them, with the tenderest touch, wildly whirling! I'm fire!... my whole being is light!... Myself miracle!... I can't hear anything anymore!... I'm rising!... Moving through the skies!... Ah! this is too much!... I'm a bird!... Twirling about!... A firebird!... who knows what!... it's hard to resist!... I howl with pleasure... I saw happiness before my eyes in the Colonel's garden!... so I swear!... I saw the bush consumed by flames!... I'm repeating myself!... don't you think I know that!... cause of my supernatural excitement!... Plus I don't understand anything anymore!... I reach forward a couple of inches with my right hand... I dare... I run the risk... I touch graze... the fingers of my fairy child!... of my rose, my marvelous darling!... Virginia!... I barely brush her... I lost my nerve!... Everywhere all around us... now crackling... a thousand fluttering sparks... graceful streamers of fire circling all around the trees!... it's a festival... a festival of the skies... from one branch to another... trembling... joyful glittering daisies with open corollas... flaming camellias... blazing wisterias... bouquets rocking between bursts of music... the fairy chorus... the immense murmuring of their voices... the secret of the spells and smiles... The fire festival is in full swing!... the height of happiness!... Ah! I sat there so flabbergasted so dumbfounded, so paralyzed with love that I was afraid to take another breath... happy deep in my blood... I could hear it whipping around inside me, throbbing through my arteries... my blood in full celebration... throbbing... throbbing... my heart swelling... I'm on fire... all in flames, me too!... dancing through space!... I cling to my capricious girl, my little devil, my darling, my torment, my life! I don't want her to get away from me!

"Virginia, my sweetheart!..." I beg her... "Virginia! Virginia! Please! I beseech you, my little sweetheart!... my little sweetheart!..."

She's an absolute sweetheart, that's the truth! my own heart for the two of us!... she's beating right here in my fingers!... Ah! now I have a firm grip on her... I squeeze her right up against my chest... How I'm grabbing onto her! I'll never let go! I'm happy!... The garden is closed forever!... Forevermore we're locked inside together!... prisoners amid the lilacs, the roses!... the enchanted bushes hold us in their power!... hold us back! Ah! such grand happiness!... Fragrances! More and more fragrances!...

"Virginia! Virginia!... my baby doll!... my dream!..."

I want to rock her to sleep!... until she closes her big eyes!... sweet child, sweet child, this is happiness!... it's right here!... let's go beddy-bye! beddy-bye! I give her a few pecks... KEE-RRRASH! all hell breaks loose again! what a godawful din! exploding over us! Coming from upstairs, from under the rafters... one hundred thousand out-of-tune old pianos pounded in a frenzy! there they go, they're back at it! None other than our very own gorillas! the hideous racket!... crashing grinding hammering against the windows! whoosh! a spray of shards over the garden... ah! my poor ears! My head's mashed up! Oh, the clanking metal! They're twice as loud, hell-bent! Virginia's scared! I kiss her! I coddle her! I massage her, pat her thighs, throw myself at her knees... but the infernal ruckus sweeps down on us from way up! earsplitting! from the roof, the skylights, a gang of hell-raising demons!... up above flying in tantrums... they're moving out... it shakes me up too, infects me, rattles my nerves... I'm at loose ends... it wouldn't have taken half as much... they piss me off again, I go totally berserk... I roar, yell twice as loud... hitch up Virginia's skirt, attack her! overpower her! bite right into her thighs! Ah! the divine treasures of flesh! light! light! I'm fuming myself! It's those two! Those two! They're what's feeding my fire! they just don't quit! Slam bang clang! They're pushing me over the edge! Driving me into a red-hot fury! Trashing everything! You bet there's some huge discovery at the bottom of this! some earthshaking find! to explain such a bashing binge!... I lick Virginia, lap her up! all over! her legs... her belly... that's the truth! she laughs... laughs! she fidgets around giggles... I suck at her thighs! This is over the line! she gets scared! squeals! tenses up! Why's she afraid? I ask her... I don't want her to be scared!... Easy does it there, my darling... Easy does it... She's afraid of me, afraid I'll growl... her big doggy of love! My sweetheart! My little sweetheart... I'm going to gobble you up! swallow you down! alive! I'm going to devour you!

"What is it, you devil? What is it?"

She pushes me away with a laugh... so she thinks I'm a devil... I've got it now!

"Ah! What is it! Wait! Just wait! I like you an awful lot!"

I explain that she shouldn't grow frightened... I was just fooling around with my myum-myums... pretending to eat her... even though she's good enough to eat, and that's a fact... I sort of ease her mind, I cuddle her... Kaboom! Kaboom! Their crashing and banging! Our beasts are back at it again upstairs! They nip my song and dance in the bud... It starts all over again... the godawful racket! at full blast! they've flown back into their fit! twice as wild! They're going to demolish the whole shack... you can see the roof, the way it's wobbling... the windows are buckling... the birds zooming away... It's a hell-raisers' holocaust... they're starting to smash everything to smithereens!... they must be pounding their masks to a pulp... grinding down the workshop to dust... shaking the place to its foundations... unbelievable!... you can't hear yourself think anymore out here in the garden... chunks of tiles, the hammered glass, shards of zinc come hailing down on our heads... Ah! the juiced-up sonsabitches! the lousy creeps! They sure as hell must have been drinking like fish, in private... a real pair of hypocrites behind closed doors... You can bet your life they're half-crocked, loopy with liquor... unless it's the gas again?... unless they flipped into a stark-raving rage after a sniff of that stinking crap?... It was just their style... but they've outdone themselves this time! Ah! those jokers smashing everything to bits! I can see them from here... I can picture the scene... wrecking the whole damn joint!... busting up every single thing in sight!... Nothing'll be left the way they're whaling away!... echoing up to clouds! What a juicy scandal this'll stir up!... the racket spilling over the whole grounds and street... nature and the cops!... they've driven the angels away!... a nice start... drowned out the voices from heaven, extinguished the magic of the lights, the pink and blue candelabras... what a terrific success... a lot to be proud about!... the seraphim have vanished, their enchanted procession... and they'd been heading right for us, I saw them in their sumptuous velvets, their festive diadems... advancing in our direction, descending step by step from the clouds to whisper their secrets in our ears... Our happiness was all in the works! These first glimpses were wonderful! And those loony slobs made it all disappear into thin air!... And they weren't about to call it quits any time soon! They wouldn't let up until they trashed every single piece of equipment! damn right! An enormous echo rumbling inside, like a slew of cauldrons bubbling away inside some volcano ready to blow its top! Ah! each and every crash was awful... I was afraid to move I was so ashamed... afraid to look at Virginia anymore... all my gushing cut short... Maybe they were brawling amid the wreckage? Maybe they weren't just whomping away on the cauldrons?... But on each other, a duel to the death? They had it in them... Sosthène was for sure the one who'd thrown down the gauntlet at the other nutcase... I was certain! ah! I knew him... I felt like burrowing underground in shame... and just when my sweet nothings were in full swing... in the heat of our tender heart-to-heart... such no-good jackals! ah! you can't even breathe with such bastards around... I need some air!...

But it didn't dim the kid's spirits... on the contrary she thought they were funny, she laughed good-heartedly.

Under the impact of their horrendous whacks the house shook split apart... everywhere the windows burst the roof flew off in pieces... More than any man could take! Ah! I'd reached my limit! I start running! Fleeing! I ditch the kid! Beat it straight out of there... Then break into a gallop, charge along!... two-three times around the house!... I hurt myself the way I'm overworking my leg! Tough shit, zoom! into the air, Christ Almighty! Pour it on! Pour it on!... literally off the handle! lift off... actually rocket from bush to bush... pursued by their hell-raising din... "Dumb shit!" I shout, spurring myself on... "you'll never set foot again in this filthy dump! Never again, it's your curse! They don't give a good goddamn about you! The news is all over! You pathetic chump! Not a second to waste! Off like a shot! All together now! Sosthène, the screwball, and the kid! You didn't see a thing, private! What a journey! Yeah, right, are they ever tossing a slap-up party for you, best wishes, Jesus, what clever bastards! Get cracking! Never set eyes on them again! Especially not on her! The little kiddie-poo! she's a slick customer! pint-sized sorceress! She'll have you going back into battle, she'll bamboozle you into eternal rest! she'll work things out with her uncle, the whole plot's already hatched!... Ah! you're no match for them, you candy ass!" That's what I dish out to myself... to snap out of it give myself some backbone! Escape! Vamoose! But even so I couldn't leave without a few words first... a little piece of my mind for that bratty bitch... budding butcher, just open your eyes!... a little taste of the tone I'll take... I'll tell her how she'd taken advantage... nah, that would be too easy!... Could be I'd been seeing things, I could really get worked up at times... everybody's saddled with their own weaknesses... but as far as taking advantage goes, that's a whole other story! she's not going to get out of it so easy!... ah! damned little slut!

In just such a gamboling rage I plotted my revenge out loud... Veer! storm ahead! Tear across the lawn!... legs churning like mad... even the crippled one the gimp peg! in the fiery rush of my fury a sharp right and zoom! pirouette! I can't stop myself!... Those two jokers are in a red-hot fit... So help me they're rattling me pretty bad! I'm swept along by their racket... like they're pounding on a hundred anvils with all their might... Goddamned drums and thunder from hell! I bolt off, barreling, a cannonball! right down the center path! Quick buck with my butt! Zoom! Bye-bye baby! I land right smack on the front steps... Whew! I'm back inside the building, the large vestibule... Ah! I huff and puff, take a breather, sniff... I look all over for my Virginia... She's disappeared again! Where'd that little tramp get to! Impudent snot-nose! man, am I mad! I catch a whiff of her perfume... a peppery carnation fragrance, her shock of hair... I gallop across the rug... run knock the maid right off her feet... she shrieks loudly... I'm trembling like a mutt who's just lost his mistress! panting! sweating blood!... frothing at the mouth... off my rocker, I lift myself up, bolt off on my trick leg... crash on my ass, topple backwards... my head's ringing, I slump down... my kid's nowhere to be found!... not in the salon! not in the garden! maybe in the bedroom?... "Ah! Come on, slow down, buddy! Just take a look at yourself in a mirror! You're going to scare her again! Don't show up looking like such a shitty mess! And right in her room no less! You filthy lummox! You really ought to clean yourself up a little! Your suit's already gone to the dogs!" I bawl myself out, fret, calm down while sitting there... Maybe I really will find her again after all! She's not lost... Maybe I've just got to think it through... hash over all that's happened... it'll be good for me... I ought to put to use this quiet moment I have to myself... Ah! Kaboom! fucking hell! The thunder crashes twice as loud! Another clanging cyclone is ripping loose upstairs! their session's not over! Our two experts are still in the heat of their toil!... Busting their butts with all their scrap-metal might! The party's rolling full blast! I'd thought they'd already destroyed each other... and bang! and boom! and wham-bam-bong! not only haven't they pooped out yet, they're going stronger!... Nothing must be spared! They slam away in a full-metal frenzy... the rage of the cyclopes!... Nothing can stand in their way... The racket shakes the eyes in your head... rattles your sockets... the whole building's jumping giggling, all the furniture too, the enormous chest of drawers, the chandelier's swinging itself loose along with its thousand crystals, all tinkling, the sound of music! The big chest I'm sitting on spins left right all around, lifting me, launching me! I hang on... Ah! it's like a bombardment! That's what their violence is like! A quaking volcano! They erupt in another furious binge!... The walls are cracking right before my eyes... They sure mustn't realize their own strength anymore... they're going to bring the whole joint down... they're like pneumatic drills... Arms as powerful as some sort of Creusot!... Ah! they scare me to death!... I step out onto the perron, look around... at that very second a red rocket... an awful blast from the roof... a stream of sparks!... it's the anvil crashing through the joists! everything's shooting flying crackling up in flames!... Ah! it's terrifying!... plus loads and loads more flames! the comet's ass... yellow! blue! orange! a full peacock's tail!... whirling through the skies, the anvil and its tail!... Ah! now's no time to be gawking in admiration... It's going to come to an awful end... What sort of experiments could they be conducting?... No time to think about that now!

"Virginia! Virginia!" I call out to her.

"Hello! Hello!"

"Show your face, kid!"

I couldn't see her! she was there... standing right in front of my nose! Ah! happiness! she was playing Hide and Seek with the bunny among the trees...

"Let's go, hurry! my little girl!"

I lead her away! Can't hang around this joint! Horrible things are going to happen... I'm starting to grow used to the routine... I don't want to be one of the usual suspects again... the bunny scampers off on its own way... with a wee squeak...

Just what I thought... They'd unsealed a carboy of absolutely special gas which had made them sick, go ape shit after the first sniff... shot right to their brains... like two animals smoked from their lairs caged exploding in a howling snapping frenzy!... butting their heads into whatever they saw!... human monsters into battle!... a horrible fit!... the first whiff's the worst, and then after that it's just like being soused!... in fact, the entire carboy was Ferocious 92... with a touch of something extra, a small sealed glass flask, Ferocious concentrate... the methylomethyl gas superdistilled to fifteen times normal density, nothing else in the world could come close to its brain-killing punch... took no more than a millionth of a dose!... The discoverer was still flabbergasted by his find... in total shock, some high school botany teacher in Dorchester who devoted just a few hours a week to his experiments. In short, one idle moment he'd set out treating yperite with methane salts, then supercompressed it through filigree glass until it was so dense that... well! a piece the size of a thimble weighed a ton!... That gives you a small hint of its intensity. Our two intrepid scientists sniffed the whole thing at one go, one ton per nostril! Flash reaction! So quickly that they'd charged at each other, purple, red with rage, and went at it, first whaling away at each other with their fists and then with whatever implements lying around they could lay their hands on, all the equipment in the joint, horrendously ransacked... the Colonel, so full of misgivings, afraid of getting hoodwinked, dubious about the reports, so suspicious about Ferocious, well, he had had his proof now! two three hundred punches' worth right in his kisser, that's how savagely the other guy went after him!... just one small catch though, those two precious masks of theirs, with valves and feathers, were totally knocked out of shape... into smithereens... the workshop left in an awful shambles, the roof kissing the floor, not a single floor tile left, not one retort, every device reduced to slag, ground down, plastered against the floor... A revolting spectacle... out-and-out kill-crazy mania... the way they'd slugged the hell out of each was totally outrageous, demented, truly mind-boggling... without knowing why or how... mangling carving they left sweeping slashes across each other's faces from the tips of the noses to the napes of their necks, skin, flesh, tearing off everything! stabbing with scissors, trying-planes, slicing away bloody shreds, using graters to hack away huge hunks of ear. They came out of their fit all cruddy, staggering like crazy, icky trickling, pop-eyed, they'd frightened everybody, two scarecrows!... even their dogs turned tail, and the servants were even worse, shrieking, the cook blacked out... they could already see all fingers pointing at them for having hatched some sort of plot to murder their masters... Ah! it was a bad scene! They wanted to inform the police, bring the whole story to light straightaway to keep tongues from wagging... The Colonel nixed the idea, he'd come back to his senses, regained his composure, his cocksureness, and even that pisser's tick of his, hollering out of the blue with absolutely no warning "England rules the gasses!" his right arm shooting high into the air, rigid at attention! and always at the most off-the-wall moments, and then following it up with a triple chorus of "Hip! Hip! Hurray!" Black and blue all over, crown covered with gashes, mouth solid red with clots of blood, Sosthène didn't let himself be outdone... he echoed the Colonel and put his whole heart into it... "Hip! Hip! Hurray!" at the top of his lungs three times in a row!... Not a hint of hard feelings between them over that furious scrap, on the contrary it looked like it had brought them even closer, better buddies than before... they had to have a toast, celebrate this right away... at least three flasks of whiskey. Sosthène, who normally never touched the stuff, became unhinged. The Colonel raised his glass five or six times to the health of that jolly good fellow Sosthène... "The gallant Frenchman," he called him... then to King George V! and then to the great magnificent Joffre! A perfect formula for working yourself up... Then to the great Sarah Bernhardt! and then to King Peter of Serbia! then to the Lady of the Camellias!... Nobody was left out! And quite naturally it turned out that he and Sosthène were all agreed to start everything all over again, their entire experiment from first step to last!... they were tickled pink over devastating the heap of gear, all the filters, the Muscovy glass, the sheet iron in their Furious fit, they felt they'd done one bang-up job! plus, Christ Almighty! damn useful too! what a clean sweep! now they were going to start back over, and with completely new methods! hardly recognizable processes, much more clever patents whose tricky details boggled the imagination with their cleverness! ah, fucking hell, and even me over here, things I couldn't even begin to conceive, poor dumb shit that I was!... and they pissed themselves in hysterics over my astonishment, went into a perverse rollicking laugh-riot over the prospect of the earthshaking discoveries, the wonders... In short, the homicidal Ferocious gasses had taught them a big lesson they'd never forget. In the end there was no denying it... The colossal clobbering had worked to wake them up, shake them out of their moronic self-confidence... Tempered them, yes it did, braced them body and soul! They were all raring to go! They went back to the drawing board... their masks weren't up to sniff or snuff, they had their proof, all the equipment had to be restocked and with less than four weeks until the contest!... an all-but-impossible challenge! Not a minute to waste! They whacked each other with affectionate slaps that could have flattened an ox, the Colonel especially packed an incredible wallop... the way a little runt like him could send Sosthène flying three or four yards away into the walls... reeling at each blow... All in all the really amazing part was that they didn't kill each other while they were at it... the thought was definitely running through my mind as I watched... All the extras must have been what saved them, all the padding soldered to their masks, their high bristle-top crests, the whole cockeyed contraption, the Greek-like high visor, Medusas and Gorgons, Peloponnesian warriors... that's what had really absorbed the blows, spared their foreheads, got to admit... but they needed to start back over again! Ah, absolutely in the same style! Embellishments! Embellishments! Even for the inlet and pneumatic valves, down to the last detail guilloched, outlined, bordered in pure silver... Embellishments! Embellishments! The Colonel demanded flash everywhere... Mustn't remove a single item, not a single feather, not a single plume... I had to go out and buy a boa, with splendid plumage, for seven guineas, the finishing touch for his crownpiece, this little factory on his head...

"Looks are everything!"

That was his motto... engineering with style!

"Smart! Smart! we'll be smart!" Stuck to his guns on that score... "We'll be smart!"

To hear him tell it, appearances were half the contest. First priority, impress the judges, make the panelists go ape... next came technique, the marvels of his soft valves, his reversible piping...

"Smart and efficient!... and different!"

"Different" meant in the English sense... eccentric... irresistible... the situation was looking up!... Since they'd destroyed everything in their invigorating rage, cleaned out the whole floor, left the laboratory in shambles, I was going to have a chance for a good time, bop around town! The whole shebang fell on my shoulders—reassembling all the equipment, dashing out for hardware, coupling rings, crystalware, everything they'd smashed, bashed, trashed...

Had to race over to Soho, Tottenham, over to Bromley for the piping, the valves, to highly specialized factories, way out past Chislehurst, where they calibrated Muscovy glass to a filigree thinness, for all of London and the dominions! And, no kidding, I really had to keep my eyes open! and not be off by a single microcon, hair's breadth, one breath, one eyelash! The Muscovy glass was incredibly important for protecting the eyes!... I had to dig up even more mind-boggling doodads, tungsten filters, magnetic needles, ruby dust, they'd incinerated everything... When they saw me back fishing around, the suppliers would jump at the bait!... I had to keep mum about what was going on... yet somehow spark their interest, get the job done and not forget anything!... the Colonel stuck to his guns on that point, he wanted nothing but gorgeous finery.

"Gas masks! Gas birds!"

That was his idea... Especially since the Ferocious business. Sosthène was with him one hundred percent.

We gave it some thought... Resupplying all that junk added up to one hell of tab... he was going to feel it in his wallet, especially with the skyrocketing prices, the stock market crisis... Ah! I could see I was going to have to run myself ragged... they studied the matter... I'd need two or three weeks at least... especially for the small manufacturers stuck way out in the middle of nowhere... I'd get around on foot and by bus, no fun for me... by taxi for the sheet metal and the retorts, ever so fragile.

If I charged around from morning to night, like some chicken with its head cut off, maybe I'd manage to do the job in two... three weeks... we came up with a rough figure, I mean just for the basics...

The prospect of running errands all over the place made me think of Nelson, the champion gofer!... Now there was somebody who knew his London! No way he wasn't hot on our heels at this exact moment... Ever since I'd fucked him over, he must have been hell-bent on seeing me again... I'd be smart not to run right smack into him while out and about... Lucky thing London's one hell of a huge place, a total chaos!... unless I get all screwed up... and wander back through Trafalgar Square... tickled by the risk... We talked money a little more, a rough guess about the cost of replacing everything... all they'd massacred/pulverized in their rage, couldn't say exactly, but in the vicinity of seven-eight hundred pounds... that was a nice piece of change in those days... And I'd be pocketing my small cut... Plus we wouldn't even be dealing with the roof, a good fifteen yards of which had been blown apart, all the tiles sent flying off into pieces... they'd burst open the laths whacking away with their winches and pickax handles... And even worse... hacking away at the walls with mine pickets... Another flick of the fingers and the whole place would come tumbling down around our ears!... Ferocious 86 was no gas to kid around with... It taught you who was boss... Sosthène applied medicinal brandy-soaked compresses over all his lumps and bruises... his head was covered with them... I opened the faucet... we were in the pantry... running water was all that was left... he whined anyway...

"I feel rotten, son... Just rotten..."

He complained pretty loudly... and then in a damburst of tears... he never wanted to see the Colonel again...

"Quit beefing! You're back to singing that old song! And so how we're supposed to put beef in our bellies, jerk?"

Actually, that was the question... To beef or not to beef...

"Ah! You got it easy, you do! You're having a ball! plain as day you're not the one doing any of the sniffing!"

With that he starts hacking, choking, to make me feel good and ashamed...

"If other people kick off you couldn't care less, you're in the dark! I'm going to tell you a thing or two, you little dummy... No! I'll save it for tonight!..."

A nasty sort, the kind of guy who makes your life hell... Ah! he turned my stomach... This was no place for a shouting match, we'd just sat down to eat, had to hurry up and finish, the Colonel was eager... Even so a word to Virginia just in passing... "I adore you... I love you..." Grace... then down the hatch in five seconds flat... back upstairs on the double... Sosthène leads the way... hobbling pitifully... blubbering with each step up... busted up a lot worse than me, a hundred times worse!... he can't walk anymore, he crawls... once he gets upstairs he plops on the bed collapses...

"No! my friend! No!..." he exclaims.

The only words he can muster! "No! No! No!..." He refuses to return to his post... Ah! what a disaster!... what a crybaby!...

I know the whole story! Our little game is over! just one big bad-luck screw-up...

"Come on!" I give him a shake, "Up we go, pops! You're going to get sick! The only thing for you to do is throw in the towel! Simple as that! And get the hell out of here! I won't hold it against you! Can't take any more, huh? It's over! So, just drop the whole thing!"

"Me, drop the whole thing? Just drop it? Where'd you pick up an idea like that, you whippersnapper? Ah! little liar!"

I hit a nerve, he jumps to his feet, mad as hell...

"Snake in the grass! Slug!" he calls me... "Dishonest rat! Fink!"

He heaps me with insults. A sudden outburst.

"Did I ever tell you I'd had it? Just listen to this slimeball! For crying out loud, who does he take me for! A chicken like him? Ferdinand Yellow Belly!"

He sniggers, the big windbag... He's a different person... splitting his sides hysterical over the nerve of me... my accusations of cowardice are an absolute riot...

"Me? Scared away from the gas, you little squirt?... I dare you to repeat it! Look at me!"

He's swaggering, throwing out his chest...

"Mr. Lives Dangerously, kid! That's my name!"

He pushes out his scrawny chest...

"I'm not looking for any alibis! I'm not putting on any wounded veteran act! If I've got to sniff, I sniff for Ferdinand! If suffer, then suffer I will! If I've got to die for Ferdinand, then die I will! Sosthène reporting here! So there! My two cents!"

Nice spiel, he really showed me! I'd worked him back up. He couldn't hold still...

"Excuse me! Professor! Excuse me!"

I slinked around, stammering excuses... but he wouldn't have anything to do with my apology... he kept hammering away about my foolishness...

"You have no fine points, Ferdinand! Not a single one! Oafish clumsy klutzy... Apeman Ferdinand! That says it all!"

He was pouring it on...

"Smooth out your rough edges, for Christ's sake! Pick up a few fine points! Learn a few things! Make an effort! Try at least! Try! Take a look at how I live... Try and understand... Appreciate! Don't devastate! You're seeing me here in the thick of battle... I'm battling! Battling! That's that! Knocked for a little loop, that's a fact... but I haven't fallen to pieces over that!... Don't jump to conclusions!... I'm outgoing by nature... Admire! Take a page out of my book! Keep your complaints to yourself! Idiotic trash!... You're spreading the worst sort of sleaze! you'll be my ruin! my downfall! Hey, everybody, gather round! What a gossip-monger! Blabbing from the rooftops! Sosthène's finished! End of story! Drop the curtain! Funny old bird! So watch your mouth, my boy!"

He swells his lungs, sniffles... avalanche of sighs... a slew of insinuations... Ah! the big act! what a creep!... the old con artist doesn't have an honest bone in his body... I let him shoot his mouth off... He's playing on my vanity... trying to fire me up with the thought of amazing feats... I can see where he's going... back to the hero routine! with me sniffing Ferocious gas... he was dead set on the idea! Yoo-hoo, sweetheart!... I know your game! Right away I bust his bubble...

"The masks, Monsieur de Sosthène, are for your ugly kisser, not mine!... You're the technical engineer!... I don't know the first thing about them! You're the one bursting with confidence, Mr. Genius! The Colonel swears by you! I've been totally disgraced! You know the score! I'm not worthy to set foot in your kitchen again, I'm a swindler, Monsieur Sosthène! I swiped the mercury! Keep that in mind! Just imagine! Your boss doesn't want to set eyes on me again! Quite understandable! Lay a finger on his masks? Don't even think about it! I'm a good-for-nothing bum! What would they say at the War Office?"

I had a good point there... I wasn't fit to be seen in any way shape or form... he really had to grant me that... a reprobate, a roughneck, a cutthroat... All wrapped up in one, standing right before him... a thousand times worse than him... I practically brought tears to his eyes over my situation... I'd hit the right note, used just the right words... as a result we buried the hatchet... I'd run myself down lower than slime... He became very levelheaded again... even agreed at last that absolutely from this point on we ought to get along, arguing was plain silly... we ought to join forces, goddamn it, the pair of us against the world, tooth and nail!.... right then and there we swore an oath on our invincible pact... Friends unto death!... we were going to battle dangers... whatever they were, hand in hand... ah! but his first, they were more serious... we agreed on that point... he had to prepare for the trials... real death-defying feats!... the masks, the Colonel, the gasses, the works!... I'd brought back the instructions, the deadline, even the site... a little less than a month to go...

"You'll have just enough time, Sosthène..."

And I meant it, too! I didn't want him to spread himself too thin... I wanted him to pull himself together... I'd see to the errands on my own... his job was the knowledge and know-how... plus the magic too, of course... if he wanted to protect himself, not drop dead after the fatal whiffs... that's what his method amounted to... he'd bragged about it often enough to me... he had to make himself amenable to the spells, the Vegic vibrations... attract the divine graces... otherwise he'd drop dead for sure... the masks would work like sieves... He'd kick off from the rat poison... he needed his own personal magic! Zero confidence in the Colonel... those contraptions of his slapped together with shoddy spare parts, or lying in pieces... Those were the depressing facts of the matter... Ah! but he'd better not duck out of it! I knew this old con man of mine! a cunning con artist who lied with every breath... and a smooth talker into the bargain... he won't throw in the towel, the dirty pimp... he was really hoping that in the long run I'd let myself be won around... that I'd have a little snort or two... help him, just to see what happens... Oh yeah, watch me, precious! I gave him a hard look, I held the whip hand...

"So what about the *Vega*?" I start browbeating him... Ah! I'm indignant... So the *Vega* doesn't matter anymore? He owed me an explanation... "You couldn't sing its praises high enough!..." He made me bring that crummy book to him! "And I stole it for you from your wife! A fat lot of good that was! I steal everything for you!" I make him ashamed again... "Now you don't want it anymore?"

"Yes, I do! I do!" he mumbles...

He's spineless... I dive under the bed... bring the object out in the open... all twenty-five pounds... I realize I went through a lot of trouble on his account... What heft! What volume!

"Here you go!" I say... "Here you go!"

I crack the book open smack in the middle... we look... right in the dance part... he stands there stunned...

"So doesn't it turn you on anymore, you softheaded geezer?"

"Who's a softhead? Who's a softhead?"

Ah! he immediately perks up... a bundle of energy again... But now he's fretting and fussing... doesn't want to go back to cavorting with the situation as it stands... He needs the proper setting... first we got to draw the drapes, shut the windows, the blinds, every damn thing... And then seal up the cracks... absolutely airtight... and I've got to dig up some candles for him... harebrained touches... we're still keeping the light bulbs on... completely masked though, practically gray... The maniac! the louse!... And still more...

now he needs to slip into a new costume... back into his Chinese drag, apparently it's an absolute must... otherwise forget about any magic... I'm included too, he lays out the plan for me... finally I catch on... I sort of have a clue... how my role is to play accompaniment... his is the dancing of the magic... I'm on drums... I rap the bed board click!... click!... click!... varying in time with his grimaces... up tempo up up, then more slowly... with each new contortion... my fun's just starting!... This is only the beginning!... supposedly in imitation of the dancing figures, the splashy drawings of the *Vega*... he looks, I look, we get all mixed up... he wants a da... da... dah!... dah! That's the hardest... with some sizzle! some crackle!... in short a wildman's beat... actually, we don't have any drumsticks... just two knife handles... I've got to give it all I got!... and with my arm, the pain kicks in once I pass my limit... he couldn't care less, though! What he wants from me is a driving, jumping beat... So I grab the toothbrushes, they'll move faster actually... I click-clack even harder, no mistake about that! and then even faster with two spoons... It might have been big fun if my arm hadn't been hurting... plus he didn't really make it clear where I was supposed to jump in... exactly at what little leg twirl?... and where I should lighten up at what little smile? There were smiles in the *Vega*, the Buddha figures... all explained in the sacred characters of the big fat book... he gave me the rundown on each image... deciphering as we turned the pages... Forward, Oriental Studies!... Mostly he talked a load of gibberish.... You just had to keep your eyes open and watch when you came down to it... and then imitate wherever possible!... Ah! they were such pretty illustrations! all the dance positions, costumes, facial expressions, sabers, on figurines, individuals, Brahmins in every state of convulsion... the whole crew wiggling their bellies, arms, legs, feet in the air!... one foot on top of the other... grimaces and broad grins, monster leers... later on we'd make ourselves up just like them down to the last detail... in full color... from head to toe... went without saying... the perfect illusion!... Sosthène didn't want any close tries!... pigheaded on that point, a maniac... I screwed up a lot... "Magic Rituals" was its title... I had trouble catching on... I was supposed to provide a subtle accompaniment... jump in the middle of the music of the spirits... my bop! bop! click! click! fantastic!... at bottom it was real kids' stuff... He'd lift one foot then the other... bop! bop! click! click!... He'd turn his arm around like this bop! bop! click! click!... He'd make a scary face, eyes popping... Wham! Wham! Bang! Bing! my part... he'd contort his hands around facing palm out behind his neck... he forced his elbows into a cross... took a real effort... rocking throwing around his whole butt... at the same time giving his thighs a twirl... and me going Bang! Bang! Bim! Bam! Bang! Bim! Boom!... Nice job! Whew! he collapsed out of breath... a breather! time for the prophetic proverb... I repeat the saying... It was for putting you in the right frame of mind... supposedly... according to him... he shook himself off just a little and whee! off on another round!... still madly panting... another mystical bout... just like in the book... he put himself through hell, spared himself nothing... swinging his torso back and forth shoulders shaking down to his fingertips... castanets-in-your-hands style... the whole number punctuated by my bop! bop!... very faint hushed crackling... almost inaudible... drawn out with finesse... bang! bang! bang!... "The Skota for Inner Peace"... that's the term in the Hindu text... and this was still just an intro, the initiation into the Mysteries!... now we were about to start the real show!... I wouldn't believe my eyes when I saw what was coming next! the ceremony! He made sure to tell me to hang tough, keep my head on straight... we were about to launch into the Incantation! the meat of the matter, the heart of the ballet!... He was the celebrant, the magus! Ah! wait until I feasted my eyes on this little show-stopper of his! First, he had to hitch up his gown so nothing'd hamper his spirited kicks, his fervent flights... the whole number was clearly explained illustrated in precise detail... he wouldn't scrimp by one fraction of a hair... the full treatment was in order, the complete muscle-crunching workout... he plants himself in the far corners to get a running start... gathering steam with a few caprioles and rebounding, plop! smack in the middle of the room!... an awesome impact from such a scrawny crow like him! rattling the frames off the walls... I'd never have believed he was so heavy!... something supernatural... the deafening din of a ceiling reduced to dust... of water crashing out of a wash basin... of an earthquake!... a thunderbolt! No two ways about it, he's magic all right... His gown hitched up... I shout to him from my bed...

"You're magic, old boy! You're magic!"

I want to make him feel good!... can't help myself... Ah! plus I'm having a blast... he can't hear anything... walks out of the corner... hands hooked like handles over his head... the sacred garland... with mincing not so very graceful steps, almost on tiptoe, simpering... timid odalisque... he wiggles his hips at me, gives me a wink... I look at him funny... scare him off... he comes back at me fit to be tied arrogant... frowns at me, threatens, shows me the drawing... he's sore, he's really got the facial expression down pat!... the dragonlike thing on the page, I've got to hand it to him there... just needs the flames shooting from his jaws... he sniffles for that effect, coughs... he'll breathe fire for sure any day he picks!... Had to see him exerting himself, busting his gut... at first glance you'd never think he had it in him, such a puny, washed out sorry-ass runt like him, but you had to see him now all revved up! a whirlwind! making your head spin! and on top of everything else, a bully! I'm always off the beat!... he chews me out, pesters the hell out of me... he's everywhere at once... my hands can't keep up... always lagging behind... the scar at my wrist cuts me off... he doesn't give a damn, constantly popping around, I've got to give it more juice, no ifs ands or buts, keep click-clacking away like mad... he's whipped up into a breakneck tizzy, going at it on all sides... an amazing mime show... he depicts two monsters at once as in the book illustration... now locked in an all-out battle!... right in his own body! he hollers for me not to just sit there like some dumb jerk, I've got my job cut out for me!... got to click-clack, fucking hell!... this is the big climax! his grand moment!... one dragon on his ass it seems, the other smack on his chest... about to pounce on each other's tusks, a duel to the death!... all taking place right inside Sosthène, in his body itself... he buckles over in convulsions twisting turning like crazy... rolls across the carpet, heaves EEEYAAHs and EEEYOAHs, monster roars... A one-man battle, both monsters going at it tooth and nail... their limbs knotted... it's hideous... inside his tiny body... he jams twists himself up in the doorway... if the door opens he'll be torn limb from limb... it's a dragon free-for-all... he prys himself loose, crawls under the table, groaning, wriggling... he moans, spits, bends backwards and sinks his teeth into his legs, draws blood, waging a fearsome battle against himself... he's going to devour himself completely... dragons in a fray... even worse than Ferocious... all his bones are cracking... he's gobbling himself up... watching him is sheer hell... My click-clacking's not doing the trick for him, I've got to match his violence... I need to beat time with my hands... rap out at top speed... I'm going to demolish what's left of my arm... the great dragon bashing... got to fire the monsters up for the carnage... plus holler EEEYAAH! EEEYAAAH! every time he rolls across the carpet... he demands it, chews me out, feeds my flames... I get caught up in the game, this was bound to happen... I outyell him!... But he wants to remind me who's running the show... "This is still just a rehearsal!" he shouts while shooting past. He throws cold water on me... So what's the real thing going to be like! He's so inflamed, so fanatical, he barely has time to leap, stop in the middle of the room, take a look at his model in the big book and whoosh! sail up in entrechats! another little jig! I go at it twice as hard! "Keep it up! Keep it up!" he badgers me...

Ah! what a despot! what arrogance! Torture inflames him!. he's totally in thrall to the dragons! their claws gouge his guts... This would be impossible without magic... make no mistake about that... I whip myself, give it what I got... I'm still slowpoking behind anyway... handicapped by my arm... stabbing with howling pain... I'm yanking too hard on my stitches... it's not that my heart isn't in it... can't even see my hands anymore they're moving so fast... my click-clacking so hot and crackling the copper's smoking... the whole bed is glowing red... The bones in my arms, hands, my nerves, are on fire too... shocks, bolts mashing up my shoulder... My slaving away juices up the jerk... he loves suffering.... martyrdom's the only thing that turns him on!...

"Great going, my little cherubim!" he bawls over at me...

My whole hand on fire because I was playing my two little sticks so hard... faster and faster! Hell-bent!... In a lather, wiggling like mad... whirling around even more nutso than he is... the genuine sacred dance, make no mistake! Here we go! the big shake and quake!

"We've got it! We've got it!" I exclaim... I'm already getting off...

"We've got it, Sosthène!" I shout...

"No, we don't, you dumb bastard!" he jumps down my throat... "You need moonlight for that!"

Moonlight? Ah! the baboon! he's tearing me apart! All the trouble I went through! He'll pay for this! He's been killing us over some practice session! I'm ready to drop dead from exhaustion! Ah! the slimeball! I choke on my words, I've had just about enough! Ah! Goâ! Bullshit! My limbs are drained, numb! He handed me a line! He'll cross over into the Armoid all on his own, the conqueror of the Arkiosaurs, monsters! No more butt-bumping for me! I'm pooped! the mites can have their way with me! the ferociousness of body and soul! He can go take a flying fuck all by himself too! ah! but he's got something else in mind!

"The mites? what mites? If you stop now you die! a victim of a savagely unleashed fury! The atom strikes us dead!"

Ah! now I'm in another stew! what's he cooked up this time? What am I mixed up in? In what magic vibrations? "The dragons'll swallow you up if you stop drumming!" What a fine fix! Out-and-out blackmail! I'm forced back into his silly-ass routine...

"You're in the fourth power!" he shouts at me, shooting past...

A fat lot of good that does me! I've got to start up again! I'm seeing everything double triple quadruple!... I could see Sosthène with thirty-six heads and a slew of dragon tails all around, sticky icky, with broad scales, a total mishmash, a cyclone of flesh and bone in the middle of the room, wound into an enormous ball, a seething pulp from which waves of drool shot out, scorching ceiling-high streams... all quivering convulsing the entire throbbing mass, the whole tangle of knots, banging ricocheting off the walls... and frightening curses that exploded nonstop... monster roars... and Sosthène's own sharp voice coming out of the slimy gob, the knot of intertwining tentacles... I remained flat on my ass before the sight... no slacking off! he'd warned me... If I'd petered out I'd bring on the cosmic hurricane! No way out of it! If I stopped my click-clacking the mites would snatch us away! That was the real horror... we'd wind up zapped vaporized! the risk was tremendous... The book spelled it all out... the rituals, the necessary precautions, the sacred body gestures... Sosthène had it all at his fingertips... For the moment at any rate I could barely catch a glimpse of him in the heart of the furious fuming tangle... just a couple of heads here and there... then came the moment when it all unwound... collapsed in a heap... crumbled down to the carpet... the whole raging hulk... the monsters wheezing like forges... tired too probably... then they lost their scales, their finery, their immense fins... their mother-of-pearl wing-things... the entire mess melted away before my eyes... went up in a little puff of smoke... nobody but Sosthène left standing after the dust settled, the battle, the lone survivor of the chaos, naked as the day he was born, pale and ashen... I shout over to him:

"Get what you were after?"

"Let's go!" he snaps out. "Back to work!"

He hunches in lotus position... feels his head with his fingers... incredibly deep in thought... meditating, muttering... filling his head with inspiration... this new bout would be with the devils... a brand new story! a brand new rhythm, a new approach... with a whole new set of rules... We'd put on a charmer, a genteel perky jig, a bouncy step... had to turn the demons on... seduce them by winking wildly... right off at the outset... impishly bewitch them... with some butt-bumps thrown in to be sure... but all in a frisky playful tone, none of that slinky sultry stuff, with coarse spells, and monster free-for-alls... Ah! no way!... a different deal!... now we were talking one hundred percent refined... he explained that according to the text the trick was to amuse the evil spirits, to turn their heads with some spicy banter, and then do them in when their minds were elsewhere... jump at the chance... to lure them in with high jinks... once they were rollicking and rocking with wild laughter, totally distracted, then I'd step into the trance... that was my cue! I'd sneak behind their heads and whack them unconscious one after the other... hard with my baton across their mouths! and whack! whack! Game's over! I'd take advantage once they were pissing themselves with laughter... and let them have it!... Ah! damn clever! For the time being I was just going through the motions, naturally... and bop! bop! had to keep hopping, and how!... I really put myself out! according to the book I had to massacre a dozen demons... right on the spot one after the other... He acted out the magic gesture for me... The way I was supposed to swing downward...

"You're looking at a man who did the bamboo dance for fourteen years! Imagine you're Prince Gorlor... You knock them out with all your might!"

He gave me a demonstration of his style, such great panache! and what a show-off!

"I used to fly through the air, you better believe it!... My feet didn't touch the ground!"

The comparisons... mean and bitchy!... In the meantime he couldn't stand up straight...

"Bingbangboom! You old asshole!"

I sit him down... so exhausted his knees are like jelly... he's doing the shakes to my beat... I give myself a little show... His entire body's streaming with sweat... I sit down beside him... the joint's absolutely sealed... sweaty/steamy, stifling... he can't stop flapping his trap, whispering hoarsely, hacking like crazy... he's back on the Prince business... the way I should land my blows... And all his spouting about stuff, his great successes, his mind goes back to the old days... between 1898 and 1915... the Miracle Man of the Pacific!... No stopping him...

"Heaven's Own Pépé, that's what they called her... judge for yourself!... In her blue-lamé white dress... I can still see her now! You can't even begin to imagine!... A full-size Brahmin orchestra! the entire band of the Deltas! Three Burmese fakirs on cymbals! plus thirteen black flute players from Ceylon! A once-in-a-lifetime ensemble! It wasn't just a musical number anymore, it was a grand mystical enchantment! an orgy of magic vibrations! It made all the papers from Cyprus to Capetown! Fourteen column stories, my little dimwit! from Suez to Tokyo! You ought to have seen my Pépé hovering over the demons! You wouldn't believe it's the same woman today! carried away by the vibrations, swaddled up in the spell, transported, she sailed through the air with the greatest ease, a bird! that's how beautiful the music was!... whirlwinds of mites, my friend! That's what lifted her! invisible mites! Just to show you how special it was! You've got a long way to go, you poor tadpole! a storm of flutes so captivating you forgot where you were! You took off into the air, that's a fact! the audience too! we often had to run and pull them back down... found them all over the place, in all the theater loges... Now that was enchantment, I'm telling you... not the sort of show that bores the crap out of you!"

Recalling his glory days snapped him back on his feet, miraculously, his juices flowed faster with each passing second...

"We'll never see such days again!..."

The memories give him quite a turn... now he starts with the shake-snorting pawing the ground... just like that, stark naked... he wants to do his rendition of Pépé for me... he really wants me to get it through my head how she floated through space, the grace of her sky blue veils... her arms fluttering in triple time... "The Waltz of the Spiritual Rays"!... the grand hypnotic translation!... so I can savor the quality... And all this a dozen yards off the ground! keep that in mind! Without a net!... no props of any kind... except for the incantory emanations! and the bewitching music! Heaven's Own Pépé!

"Go try and do that over at the Empire or even at the London Hippodrome with the jungle bunnies we have nowadays! Won't you look pretty! The only thing they understand is quick razzle-dazzle! tenors with no balls, show girls with spring-action asses... legs everywhere! whizz! boom! boom! Full spotlights! I'm sending over my mummies! Jazz them up for me! What are their music halls like? They turn your stomach, that's what! I'm telling you straight out! When they start giving you their Oriental Fantasy numbers, it's too disgraceful for words! Their crummy junky souks, the trashy Ethiopian crap they rig up for you! Couldn't get any worse, I'm telling you!... all the buggers from the Arden docks decked out in ridiculous getups, that's what their mirages are about!... and they throw it at you in gala performances! this sort of crap is killing off the carnivals like the one they used to have in Neuilly! That's no joke! Hey, I'm all for that! a smash success! a stampede for seats... Everybody's happy! they applaud, clapping till their hands break! You should see them! You call that an audience! There are no audiences anymore! And so what am I supposed to do about it, you swindler? Come on! Let's go! back to the grindstone! I've broken my back for peanuts! Twenty-two years straight! get that, son? Audiences just like shit! They're thickheads, and that's that! I'm not going to drop dead in grief over it... Ah! no, that's not for me!... Actually you're pretty thickheaded yourself!..."

He eyed me suspiciously...

"You're thick, you know, you numbskull! I give my all and you don't give a damn! You act like you're here for the show... Plus maybe it tuckers you out..."

He was flat out provoking me, acting like a smart-ass now... It was incredible in a sense... just a minute back he had one foot in the grave... Ah! goddamned prick!

"Come on! Come on! Let's see your stuff!..."

I'm tantalizing him, I want to see him drop dead!...

"Come on, you clown, start wiggling!"

Here we go again, back in action, only this time around with a new approach... All my idea soundwise... Actually I wasn't doing too bad a job banging away... I'd already worked up a nice, steady shower of click-clacks... very graceful... he couldn't top that himself... I held my own with real skill... Ditto for the dirtball!... and in spite of my trick arm, my bum leg, I was terrifically nimble, I spread from my click-clacking over to the demons... there and back knocking them cold! all ten and whoosh! they'd never laid eyes on me!... I poured myself into it... the real grind was the shouting-in-anger part... "Tshoooh! Tshoooh!"—those were my lines... an enraged she-cat... and at the same time he was supposed take a few swipes at me with claws, and then hop back into his jig... I wouldn't have won any prizes, I admit, I spit out everything ass-backwards... for a start I was frazzled pooped...

"From the top!" I sigh...

We'd been knocking ourselves out for hours... time to wrap up... He damn sure had the devil up his butt, that asshole monkey over there, and in spite of his age, the clobbering he took, you name it... even with his mouth bashed out of whack, nose swollen, eyes inflamed, he was raising hell all the same, the gorilla! And I had to keep hustling!... He pushed me to the limit...

"You're a damn fanatic! shut up!"

He gives me the rundown anyway, dead set...

"Take a look! A good look, brat!"

There he goes whipping out his pictures, opening the book back up, spelling out the details again, without skipping over a thing... it's fabulous... this gives him another brainstorm... ah! a real whopper!

"You've got to be able to remember the words... recite them to me as we go along... just a single sentence... in rhythm... just as I strike up... with my leg..."

"Ah! you're off your rocker, you flake!"

So I was supposed to pick up Hindi on the fly!... I gave it a try... No go... Mangled the pronunciation, choked on the words... I'm pissed! Did he take me for some idiot!

"We all have our own special talents, Monsieur Sosthène... take your English, for example, not so great, is it? Let's just hear one of your *thou's* and give us both a laugh! Now in my case, you see, my stumbling block's Hindi! Imagine that!"

I said it, so there! I drop the subject, don't move a muscle, I gaze around at the disasters, our bedroom looks like a cyclone hit it... Lucky there was a carpet, our entire place was covered wall-to-wall... it cushioned the leaps... By now we'd have broken our ankles with our beastie bounds... Only the armoire got messed up... whacked right in the mirror, a good third in smithereens...

"That's for good luck, right, you mongoloid?" I check with him...

I wanted to have a laugh... Ah! but he doesn't even crack a smile! He takes it all the wrong way...

"It's easy to be silly, my little birdbrain! Obviously I look funny! You think I don't realize that? And you think your own idiocy's not a real crime? That you're not flirting with calamities, jinxing our innocent activities by carrying on this way like some imbecile!..."

Crude talk, a bolt from the blue!

"Tsk! Tsk!" I answer, "And so your hands are spotless or something?"

"Shut up!"

He's terrorizing me.

"You wouldn't be so dissolute, you'd have other things beside high jinks on your mind, your horny sex-maniac business, if maybe you'd lend me a little hand... you're not just some young war veteran wounded before his time... you've also got filthy senses!..."

That's his big insight... On that note he levels his stare at me, looks me over hard...

"Filthy senses?... look who's talking, honey!..."

Ah! I'm going to take him down to size!... the guy's gone a little too far!

I hold off, want to catch my breath...

"We're celebrating a mass!..." The same old song... back to that... "You've never understood that!" My sour grapes gave him grief... "You've been working against me all the way!..." He was letting the tears flow... "You're the saboteur of my mystic vibrations! You're worthless to me!... You're thicker than a thousand bricks! A mass for the Spirits of Goâ, the Sars of the Third Trial! I've explained it to you a thousand times! What a waste of breath! I'm so weak! You've just got sex on your mind! Debauchery! A depraved birdbrain!... That's what heaven sent me!"

Ah! I drive him to total despair... he's shaking his head in hopelessness... he's got one more thing to say to me... one last sigh...

"When I think that I put clothes on his back!"

Ah! that riles me back up!... He's crossed the line! Ah! the balls on that bum! Clothes on my back! Ah! the words stick in my craw! he's vicious as hell! a two-faced sack of shit! He's going to throw that suit back in my face?... the mercury? all that jazz! He's putting me on with his lousy crap... I stand there like a jerk... He doesn't back off, he keeps piling it on, keeps up his little falsetto number, spouting off at me stark naked...

"Of course you're completely clueless! You'd swallow any load of nonsense! not hard! An easy mark! You're like the British public! any old act enchants you! Gullible as they come... One example! the way that little vixen of yours carries on!..."

Phooey! Phooey! Phooey! What's he getting at?... What's he trying to dig up, the old goat? Ah! I don't want to hear it! I cut him short! Start screeching like a peacock!... he looks at me...

"Come on, let's go, pops! No foot-dragging! I need to make lightning progress!... I admire you! I worship you! we mustn't waste a second... Quick, teach me your little guy!"

I draw him back into his act... He's not so ornery when he's hopping around.

Good! he agrees, all right, but I need to strip naked, otherwise we can't hop around anymore! Those are the basics for esoterics!

"Come on! Come on! No little tricks! Take off those filthy trousers! Your gear's ridiculous! Wear your soul on your skin, young man! You're shutting off your whole soul! Forms, my friend! Every form! God exists in forms! Show off all your forms! Stark naked! Let's breathe!"

Yet another demand! He was really turning out to be a despot!... He sort of had a point though... we were practically smothering to death... Even with me stripped down to nothing... nothing but my undershorts... I take them off... but being in the buff or not won't improve my click-clacking... I snap back at him right away... my real problem was my drumsticks... I needed the thin orchestra kind... the real things... not these snapped-off toothbrush jobs... I would have put out a whole lot better sound...

"That can wait!" he remarks, "You're always ready to spend money!..."

OK, damn it, OK, three raps! He opens with a few warm-up moves... we run through the whole devil number again... the seduction... the serenade... the showering rhythm... Ah! he's really hitting his stride... he sways/shimmies his rump... casting a spell over the evil souls... I can see all the hairs on his carrot-ass... on the undersides of his arms too... He's off again on tiptoe... arms in a garland... It's time for his rocking trance... he's hypnotizing those demons... I'm working my hands like mad... twice as fast on my sticks... my part... I show those Luciferians a great time... I titillate them, give them quivers... put them into one hell of a good mood... they've got to be perfectly primed... then I slip into the dance... following the etiquette of esoterica... charm all the way supposedly... And I come on stage in turn... Now I need to show I can pack a wallop... Gwendor the Magnificent! The Sar! Nimbleness! twelve flicks! twelve heads while shooting past!... to take advantage of the emanations from the spell... while bewitched by Sosthène... my click-clacks filling their heads... zoom! I knock them unconscious! ah! my jokers! I barely need to graze them... they vanish into thin air, and how! such is my radiance, my power of hypnosis! Wham! Bam! Whoosh! The invincible kid! I must have looked like a lightening bolt, no joke! all twelve in a row! I hit the jackpot! top prize for seduction! wiping out the merry minions from hell... and zoom! back to my sticks... Not a single wasted breath! Full steam ahead for the Apotheosis! I was whipping along, my whole body vibrating! Yet it wasn't enough for him!

"More pizzazz, kid! More pizzazz! You're getting mixed up!..."

Never satisfied!

"It's a smash success, not just some nice try!"

And this with the instruments I was using! He was worked/whipped/fired up like a whole shitload of devils on the loose... And I was hot on his heels, a whirlwind! a carcass swept through the atmosphere, whisssh! This was the grand moment, had to admit... he was supposed to take off over our heads fueled by his fiery spirits, a spinning top a cannonball of bone... right at the very second I was knocking them out!... his sheer speed whipping him up... literally sucked up propelled through midair by the incredibly intense whirl... It was really awesome!... an unbridled dervish a whirligig of vibrations... I spurred him on with my click-clacks... the crackling hail from my sticks... plus my mouth noises too! Tshoooh! Tshoooh!... a she-cat in a fury... and then I do my "madly spinning top" effect Brrrmmm! the trembling roaring thundering whir zz! zz! zz! zz! he pulled away from the carpet, spurted up off the floor driven by fervor, by "mystical displacement"... theoretically during a real session he would be bashing through the ceiling! In a gyrating flight! would shoot to the zenith on his whirlwind magic... the mind-boggling moment... the Grand Crossing was its name... the leap between worlds... He barged into another dimension... he explained it well... it was all in the hieroglyphics... I had to believe him... Then once he mastered the law of gravity there'd be no stopping him, he could do anything he wanted! He was very sure... the mystic jackpot, the great bull's-eye in the sky... All prizes would be his for the taking!... His presence would go undetected, he'd vanish whenever he wished... he became an enchanter of the whirl, transformed into a soul of dance and chance... with one gesture he'd disappear... you wouldn't see him anymore! why, in a word, he'd be one of the spirits himself! That was really something... It was worth a try... especially in our situation... And he wouldn't have had to be scared of anything ever again! not gasses, not cops, not anything... he could do anything he wanted... nobody would be able to lay a finger on him anymore, no elements, no power... He would be invulnerability incarnate, the Sar of the emanations... Endowed with extraordinary powers... He would be the one who regulated the compasses from the moment he was "admitted," "recognized by the emanations"... Ah! when you came down to it the guy really impressed me!... I did my best to help him, that's a fact!... I whipped up a storm of click-clacks so powerful I broke my toothbrush ends... played passionately, with all my heart... I didn't cheat him any way any how... my sound effects weren't so hot though... I couldn't do the whizzing top... zz! zz!... I made some rasping noises... he was right about me... We took it from the top fourteen times... he was pigheaded on that point... just one little false step could throw off the whole shebang... Success was all in the nuances... He'd never be able to shoot up, bash into the ceiling, outdo everything, zoom to his zenith! with my z! z! z!... he'd never metaphysicalize himself! I had to knock off my rasping!... stubborn... a mule!... ah! Taratoist my balls! I reminded him of his pet obsession... the Brahmanic multicolors! Tara-Tohé, our emblem...

"We'll try everything! The miracle-working rose, pops!"

This time around we'd go out looking for it! to the very ends of the earth, Christ Almighty! to the highest reaches of heaven if need be! We'd shrink before nothing! That was agreed! But first things first, he had to win!... survive the ordeal of the roguish Sar! We were going at it! Let 'er rip! Kee-rist! Now was no time for slacking off!...

"Come on, whoosh, up into the air, pops!"

He had to take it from the very top.

"Shake that fanny! The fifteenth jolt!"

In the end I frazzled my nerves, too! If only he'd start out just from the place we messed up! And quit his sighing! Knock off the mumbo jumbo! He was possessed, true enough... he'd go back to the top over every picayune flub... one tick of my stick... But I was in charge now!

"Come on, pops, shake those legs!"

Ah! I want him to drop dead!... The way the sweat's pouring off him is hard on my eyes! the blood, the grimy trickle... stripping his hairs away... one foot in the air he's already shot his wad, he wobbles, collapses... Ah! you finally did it, you old wreck! He won't be busting my ass anymore! He's stretched out on his side, panting, deeply hoarsely like a seal...

"Drop dead, pops!" I snap, a dainty note!

His tongue's hanging out, lapping, licking the carpet.

"Ah! you can see for yourself, pops! now what you need is sleep..."

I don't want him to wind himself back up. He was the type... I'd have bashed in his big fat face for him if he even tried...

After such thrills and chills... such savage free-for-alls, Ferocious gas, etc.... and to top it off, the dance of the demons... I was shattered real bad... thrown into such turmoil that my feelings slipped out of control... I was afraid of everything... of losing everything... ah! I adore you I love you! my little sacred charm! I was hallucinating with love, wild with passion... seething too madly for my wounds, my whacked-out head... Ah! I adore you I love you!... I just kept repeating the words... in a fresh rage of obsession... over my happiness above all else!... Ah! I wanted to kiss her! harder! give her a nice little bite! hurt her, goddamn it!... I would have done everything tried every trick in the book to make her adore me a little too... "Yes, Ferdinand! Yes! You're the one for me!... You and only you!... nobody but you!" ah! I'd just come out and rape her! bet your life on that! at the slightest squawk! the least little "oh, no"! I'd been hanging around here pretty long for her... she was supposed to be coming down those stairs... my patience wouldn't hold out forever!... in fact we were supposed to go out, run around, dash about on our errands... the resupplies: all on my shoulders! everything that had been trashed and smashed!... One small problem: no way would I be allowed to do it on my own, not a chance, forget it... Virginia had to tag along with me everywhere for everything! her good uncle's orders... couldn't trust me... my name was mud because of the mercury business... everybody considered me shiftless, irresponsible... Virginia was the levelheaded responsible one... conscientious... her job was to keep an eye on me... she was supposed to follow me wherever I went... Three cheers for my chaperon! That suited me just terrific! I'd be lugging around the stuff! And so clear the way! Heads up, supply heap coming through! She'd do her young maiden number... and her share of the work even! London was still pretty much unknown territory for me... as a team we'd never get lost!... At any rate that dear name of hers was wonderful—Virginia... I'd call her constantly... so that she'd stick to me like glue! I'd be in charge of our stroll... ah! no, I'd be smarter to obey her every order, thrilled delighted... I'd snap into action... I'd never be mean ever again... my guardian angel! my joy! my soul!... meanwhile she was taking her good time... not even close to coming down... had no inkling of the mad dash ahead of us, all the stampeding around we'd have to do!... Her voice, at last... her light footfall... Here she is! wonderful love of my life! my incredible creature!... even more adorable, more darling, more radiant with joy and charm and smiles than the other night... What night? Last night? Which morning? Can't remember. The sight of her standing there like that dazes me... in a flash everything blurs blazes up... The look in her eyes makes me crazy with happiness!... I love her too much, that's why! She's laughing. She's laughing... I'm dead in my tracks, looking back at her, I've left the world of the living... is she poking fun at me?... No. She's laughing just for the fun of it... I spring back to life!... I die ten times a second... What joy! I'm floating on air! In seventh heaven!...

"Ferdinand! Ferdinand!"

Angel voice, I'm at your heels! Here I am! The dream sweeps me away...

"Let's go, Ferdinand!"

I drop back to earth... What could I have been thinking of again? The staircase is there... the girl calling me... nothing more... And how about my worries! my messes! They're swarming and churning around inside my head, grabbing me by the neck, choking me, whole heaps and slews of them... a fierce load of snakes... tying me up, squeezing hard, they'll never let me out of this alive... my worries are working my brain over... crazy figments of my imagination, bigger than life... Ah but I can see, I can see things!... mustn't move a muscle... There's Centipede climbing off the subway tracks! Just what I figured, I could have told you!... Son of a bitch acrobat! Looks like he's been reduced to a pulp!... another one of his tricks! He's hit the ground on purpose to put one over on me! So he's mashed to a pulp, good news! He'll always be the same rotten bastard! I'm reduced to a pulp too! every last inch!... sheer torture, my whole bag of bones gouging deep into my skull! and he's so shitty-looking now! oozing from every pore! And he expects me to kiss him looking like that? Just push my whole face right in it? That's going a bit too far! And the filthy creep comes closer! All my fingers are sticky! I show them to Virginia who looks down at me from the stairs! Look, my poor fingers! what kind of bum would do a low-down thing like that!... ah! naturally, she's looking right at me... still smiling... she's not the one with the sticky fingers! Plus the others into the bargain!... the kid doesn't catch the slightest glimpse of them... And they're standing right beside her too... she's laughing like an idiot... poking fun at my face... I've got lots of reasons to make faces... and there's Nelson, another guy she doesn't know... he shot past like lightning! seven steps at a time! got to dash after that one... plus the others, the rest of the gang! I recognize them one and all, I keep my wits... Some cruel customers!... Van Claben's there, without his cough!... he's determined... a tiger! about to tear me in two, heart still beating... I yowl from the shock! it happens just behind Virginia's back... EEEYAAAH! I shout... See myself struggling. Another round like with Goâ... only this time the demon's my old pal... he coughs in my belly, sneezes inside me... knocks around my innards... Ah! I knew this was coming! Once I saw Centipede come onto the scene... but my ears tell me it's Boro... I hear the thundering racket of his piano... he's playing with eighteen hands... I'm burning up with fever of course... the worst part is I'm paralyzed on my feet... I'll never be able to stretch out again... my one chance is to stand and take it... ah! go ahead, laugh, you little scamp... if only you could see what I hear: the splintering keyboards from the La Vaillance pub... "The Waltz of the Roses"... I'm going to join in the singing... I do my damnedest... No go... I'm choking... wobbling, feel myself blacking out... ought to signal somebody for help... I'm blind to the world... Virginia! Virginia, my sweet! I know she's there... I collapse... Sit up, use every ounce of my energy... just so she hasn't disappeared... my spinning head my queasy belly... stars dancing before my eyes... I squeeze them shut... can still see anyway... red on white! Colonel des Entrayes! Standing in his saddle! at the sight of him my heart sweeps me away... my very own heart! I need to clamp down onto my chair I'm throbbing with so much emotion... I'm back in the war... Look at me! The charge, the strength! Ah! can't give any ground! I'm a hero! He too! but I'd rather test it out on the floor... I slip down off my chair... stretch out gallop along even so... I can see my Colonel under fire again, my beloved chief! Sitting bolt upright in his saddle! Saber bared to the sunlight! I blink shed tears! I squeal out how beautiful it is, writhing on the ground! I roar along with him: "Take heart!" I recognize his shout... The commander of the armed cavalry squadron... we thunder swiftly into the fray... I'm drenched in horse slaver... My teeth sink into the carpet bit in my mouth... the advancing tides of the brigades... Ah! now the abyss yawns wide... the whole horde swoops down... I'd like to prop myself up a little... where can the Twelfth have disappeared to? The Flanders field stretches endlessly around me... where can my buddies have gone? where can they be engaged? In what still raging battle? Maybe they've found my arm? And what about Raoul, who was executed by firing squad? And what about the others? All the others? I'm completely in the dark... I'm stretched flat on the ground, that's that... the girl must be around here somewhere... Centipede is really the one I'm nervous about... His dirty work's the dirtiest, his tricks the most treacherous/criminal... he'd finish me off right here on the floor... where can he have popped to now? with all his evil schemes?... I can't get that stinking bum out of my mind! I should have shoved him harder back when, that's my big regret... Ah! my memory's playing tricks... my mind's a total blank... she's the one who dazed me... that kid's giving me hallucinations... she's got me all confused, my soul's in turmoil... my mind... you name it! and it hits me that I'm flat on the floor I'm out of it... I can hear the angels! I can hear the trumpets! it might look like I'm having fun! their silver trumpets! My head spinning just a little... I can see the stars... I can see Saturn... I can see des Pereires' Milky Way! I can see my divine Virginia... smack in the middle of the constellations... circled with stars! standing right there on the stairway! I'm growling and drooling! Ready to howl with happiness!... ah! never been gladder in my life!... and then I'm ripped apart again... snap awake... Racked with all my pains... the dream is over, now it's back to the nightmare... pains from all sides... shooting in like trains from every direction... their whistles echoing in my ears... they're roaring in my head... I don't want to know anything anymore, damn it to fucking hell!... I'm giving out! I cling to the bannister... Another burst of brightness dazzles me... Ah! it's Virginia she's there... ah! it's my honeybuns all right! Ah! I wasn't cracked in the head... in the flesh and smiling! Ah! as alive as could be! Ah! I'm quaking with joy! ah! but what an awful fright! All over a little hitch... let's go, you little devil! hit the road! I've got to regain the upper hand... She got a little scared too... I kind of blacked out... Maybe I'm a tad oversensitive... it's all because of my head... I sort of give her a rough idea of all my woes... in my broken English... explain how life's hard knocks, the heebie-jeebies take their toll... war's no picnic... the memory of all the ups-and-downs... Let's go! we're off, kiddo! enough with this looniness... I've pulled myself back together... Maybe not quite a hundred percent... moving forward in a fog... I rub my eyes... I had a dream, I passed out... They mentioned it in my medical report when I was discharged... "lacuna cerebra"... my poor old bean... mustn't scare this kid... I joke around, trot along beside her... Come on, let's head for the bus! no more messing around, time's passing... A bus every twelve minutes... Running's a nice idea but I trip... can't see the houses all that well, or the sidewalks, or the people... I stumble again, fall, pick myself back up... I'm all excited because I love her too much... that's my craziness... can't even see the bus anymore, it passes, we let it go by... happy-go-lucky scatterbrain... Ah! here comes another, we catch this one!... a leap, two hops, we're in our seats... I step on the conductor... his feet... he shouts over to me... "Where you headed?" he asks... The Marble Arch! that's where! then we'll see... The roads from Marble Arch lead everywhere! we cross underneath... "Sur le pont d'Avignon" I sing to the kid, tell her that's where we're crossing... she doesn't know the song... I don't give a hoot about the bus, about the people listening to us... they all can sort of figure out what a live wire I am... And the darling little kid mustn't be in the dark on that score either! or take me for some quitter just because of a little dizzy spell! Ah! Goddamn it! I keep yapping away in the bus... it's a pretty long trip... and I just don't let up... and then I ask her who's her favorite, her uncle? Or me? Or Sosthène? Or other people she knows? I ask whether she has any boyfriends! Right to the point! No beating around the bush... she really doesn't understand my question... the bus is making too much racket... I don't want to holler too loudly either. She's just a kid, that's why... but that does nothing for my jealousy... and I'm really getting bent out of shape! No point in me needling... I'll just wind up annoying her, that's all... I change the subject... First we'll drop by Stream's! Upper Lime Lane! for all the accessories!... I talk to her as we bump along... maybe we'd find our ostrich feathers there... the Hellenic crests! the junky doodads! And then like bats out of hell right over to Gospel! on bus 124! A good hour-long trip... we'll cover the entire neighborhood on foot! the metal suppliers are there, the small cauldrons, the suction valves... the tow padding too... No way we'd come up with everything... I could see that from here... I'd told Sosthène last night... "So you'll go back, it'll be a nice outing for you!" He'd take care of that... the kid wasn't worrying herself sick either... she could see we'd be gallivanting from one store to the next... a real workout!... she'd have brought back everything from the moment she was out and about... no matter what the gizmo what the strange contraption thingamajig... just to see her old uncle's expression! Money flying out the window! She didn't take anything seriously! Everything was a joke to that brazen brat! especially if we came up empty-handed, if the item no longer existed!... and I put on a face... well, she got a real kick out of that! this was all just one big lark for her... and if I'd really hollered at her she'd have cut out, end of story... that wasn't possible... clip-clopping along from door to door we did a pretty good job even so... we lucked out at the Gospel Co.... practically right out of the starting gate two cauldrons, a burette and a bellows... plus two skeins of tow padding and all our large rods with coupling rings! the complete array! A terrific break!... the whole lot bought cash on the barrel! the kid had the dough! but oh my aching bones! what a load! I had to take a break every twenty yards! well, it didn't matter! some days are worse than others! And this was one hell of a job! But the Colonel would be in for a treat! He'd have no reason to curse me anymore! I'd be bringing him home something! They could get right back to the carnage if they took a whiff of gas... plus we didn't spend all that much... we still had at least a hundred pounds left... give or take a few... we'd managed quite well... we were making for the chemists... we still had a few things to pick up over there... the list was still long... then straight to Soho for the druggists... the pretty green, blue, yellow chemicals, the zinc chloride, the aluminum oxide, the putties... the sulphur gum lacs... ah! but keep watching your step... Soho's a risky neck of the woods!... all the working girls from the Leicester had their sleepless peepers peeled... Mimi... Fauvette... Ninon... Margot... their prime hunting ground... and every last one a sleaze-monger... Ah! I was flirting with danger!... I was aware of that... I ought to have sent Sosthène... I could kick myself! But I was intrigued, hell yes, even so! I was dying for another peek at my old haunts, especially the faces, the gawky struts, the old gang of girls, the pimps... just to see how it all would look... This was on my mind as we bumped along... sitting there on the double-decker... 112 Oxford... I looked down on the streaming crowd, the getups... the flowing traffic, people... hookers stand out in a crowd... you can spot their kind a mile away... I mean, at least back in those days, because of their outfits, their gaudy garish frills... the corners where they take turns, where they flap their lips... always in groups of two or three... so we're heading up to the "National"... the bus bumping along... in front of St. Martin-in-the-Fields... I think I spot Nenette... Bunny Eyes... but I didn't see a single pimp the whole trip long, and do I ever know what they look like!... it was extraordinary... things were no different on Edgware Road... Dott Street... Shaftesbury... more women... packed with streetwalkers, but not a single man... it was mind-boggling, I thought it out... a raid sweeps the streets clean... But this situation's here a real puzzle, a brainteaser... I make a mental note to look into this... They haven't all bumped each other off!... just now we're passing through

Trafalgar Square... I think: let's get off and see Nelson... it was a risky notion, I grant you... I knew the guy was a stoolie... well, when you want to know the story... I spot my man on the asphalt... the artist at his post... posing over his chromos giving his spiel... right in the middle of one of his spiels... I point him out to Virginia from a distance... the Eiffel Tower! the Pyramids!... "Gentlemen, the tallest tower in the world..." He'd colored the whole works on the asphalt... I could hear his loud mouth... I didn't want to get too close... I was still testing the waters... Maybe it was pretty reckless... but Virginia was the bold one, she wanted us to march right up for a chat... she didn't understand why I was carrying on... I was grating on her nerves with my Hide and Seek act... I talked myself hoarse explaining the risks I was running, but it didn't do any good... one more word and she'd have bawled me out... didn't give a damn about my run-ins... she got a kick out of the chromos, and since I knew the artist... right then I jump out of my skin... I spot somebody watching us...

"Come on, off we go, you pain in the ass! About-face..."

We run away... I think I saw some kind of straitlaced sort... somebody from the Yard... we keep up the pace a little while... stop for a breather... I'm pooped with my bundle... I'm positive he was the fuzz... he was walking his beat in front of the National Gallery... I fill the kid in about my fear... the news thrills her! what marvelous fun! she wants me to point out some others... she'd like the whole square to be crawling with them... every last inch... under the doors... detectives hot on my heels... ah, I've become interesting... and don't forget the hoodlums... she's got to have some of those, and famous ones at that... I'm supposed to pick them out in the crowd... I must know scads and scads considering how spooked I am, my big secrets!... Plus she doesn't give a damn about me... Come on, let's go, Ferdinand! She's calling on my services... This'll teach me to shoot my mouth off to a little girl... The little snot-nose's already working on a few ideas... wondering whether this wasn't some sort of Frenchmen's game, lying in wait for each other on street corners... just like in Nick Carter!... or in *The Mysteries of New York*? she's not one bit scared off... I'm the yellow belly with the jitters... she slipped ahead of me anyway... or shot ahead is more like it... dashing this way and that... her short pleated skirt fluttering up... what sturdy muscular thighs! little devil! my creeps meant big laughs for us... one catch: I was really losing steam... I was the packass in this little routine, with my enormous cargo, a whole factoryload of gear!... and she kept me talking too, I had to spin out/concoct yarns... she was a real bully, that pain in the ass... endless adventures till I was blue in the face... why was I being shadowed like that? how many crimes had I committed?... I added a few to the list to hold her interest... otherwise she'd have cleared the hell off, ditched me... you could bet on that... heartless... once she'd escaped I'd never set eyes on her again... Keeping her hooked with my heebie-jeebies was a real song and dance...

We might have gone over to sit in the church nearby, St. Martin's... or in the National Gallery... or walk back up to the Leicester... or the square where Curlers hung out... the weather was wonderful, delightful... that last suggestion was reckless... off the deep end!... just a stone's throw from the clink... and yet I was dying for a little gander at their ugly mugs, their dirty behind-the-scenes deals... the pimps going in and out... the shifty surroundings of the hole in the wall... maybe they were under surveillance!... and it smelled like a setup? It's settled! I can't stand it anymore, I'll take my chances! my curiosity gets the better of me! I charge ahead... I station myself a stone's throw from the sidewalk... right under the tree in front of the statue... I shush the kid, tell her not to move a muscle... from there we had a great view of the bronze Shakespeare... we could check out all the action, not miss a single thing on the sidewalk... The little ploys of the ladies in full swing... and one by one I recognized them... by the way they went at it, snapping up their tricks... Little Sweetheart... Gertrude... Finette... Mireille, Gendremer's old lady in her plum dress... the whole crew in action!... I recognized each and every one... and they were doing great business, pirouetting around, snagging Tommies by the armload... whole armies at a time, hot and horny! Non-stop! This was the right time of day! Five o'clock! A few hours of leave!... wave after wave of privates... streaming in from all four corners... stampeding toward happiness.... Business at full blast!... Hortense over there giving her line... Maryse... Réséda... Ninette too, a ball of fire... plus two-three others... the girls working by the hour... the little gang without a worry in the world, babbling blabbering... laughing their asses off... As far as the fuzz goes, nothing to report!... This corner of the Empire bar is a hangout for stoolies, absolutely safe as far as I could tell... Just Bobby Rooster, as he was called, the district's flatfoot, taking up space... in front of Lyon's... a harmless guy... a friend... In short, business was booming, terrific, going great guns... Cascade might have been glad, considering he owned practically the whole stable... what's it add up to by now? Twenty-five girls? I made a rough count... naturally, it got me dreaming... the girl could see clearly... I couldn't spell it all out for her... not for her young ears... she was just a kid, even though she was quick-witted, mischievous, you name it, precocious of course, but still not streetwise... it wasn't possible... the more I kept mum the more intrigued she grew... she wanted to know what was going on between the ladies and the strollers... all those servicemen out on the town, what was with all their little spats?... Just why was I so interested in what was going on over there, sitting here gawking away?... what were those ladies' names? Where'd I know them from? I told her they were French ladies who were meeting their godsons... wartime was always like this... the ladies were decked out pretty flashy for godmothers... they really stood out against the khaki... those rainbow-flaring frills... they caught your eye... ten twenty chiffon butterflies fluttering from one sidewalk to the other... Business pennants... most of all the hectic flurry... the starting gun goes off at five... and such great gusto!... such a crush! an incredible mob!... smiles all around! Fatso Godard in front of the Queen pub, in his gray derby, green spats, beautiful carnation, he also was keeping his eye on the rumpus... Fatso Godard, one greedy son of a bitch... as far as I knew he ran a good dozen hustlers between Tottenham and the Cecil pub! a sharp cookie!... A whole lot worse than Cascade when it came to money... He didn't cut you a break on a single penny... I'd heard he was supposed to join up, go off to war pronto... So what the hell was he still doing in this neck of the woods spying on his tramps? He ought to have been hauled off by now, so why wasn't he? I was going to cross the street and ask him, pull his leg... on second thought it's pretty chancy... I thought it over, and kept cover... I think that he's just following his usual routine, a slave to habit, that's all... and he'd still be there keeping tabs, spying on his bitches until his train blew its whistle pulling out of the station... Lots of pimps are like that... I was afraid he'd spot me, that he'd also come over to shoot the breeze... Wasn't the time for that... I huddle farther back... Most of all I don't want the girl showing herself... Right at that instant all hell breaks loose... The whole scene a total madhouse... the ladies clear the hell out, scattering in all directions, ditching their soldier boys... pandemonium... I watch the cop on the corner everybody knows about... I can see his helmet in the distance... a ballbuster probably... one-eyed Pedro the accordion player on lookout at the corner of the Bragance pub, he's the guy who tips the gang off... he picks up his gizmo starts it mooing, that's the signal, he rips into a rendition of "A Long Way to Tipperary"... at the first note the ladies race/bound off... scrambling every which way to the tune... shooting off in all directions... lighter than air, taking wing... the police van shows up for a raid... that's what the panic's all about... switching sidewalks... switching feet... How they zip past sting, those dragonflies!... A quadrille on the asphalt!... A genuine street ballet! go to it! here comes the next cop onto the scene... passes real peaceful-like through the bustle... calf eyes... it's OK... doesn't bat an eyelid... he's a cop, right... but this is all just for show, going through the motions, nothing more... respect for the uniform... Virginia wants me to tell her... wants to know what's rattling me... Why're all the people running away? what're they shouting to each other?... most of all she wants to know their names... how about that lady?... and the other one?... I try to remember them all... they're just too many... hell, are there ever!... there's Flora... Raymonde... Ginette... Bobichon... Dream Fly... Glass Ass... true, I kind of know them all... they all spent time at the Pension... But I spot somebody over there who just slays me, none other than Arnold, oh brother! out for a stroll! Mr. Great Smoocher in person... On the sidewalk across the street, in fact chatting with the fuzz... I thought he'd left weeks ago!... had to report to Dunkirk according to the word out on the street... he was sporting a boater... another change of outfit... the pimps in those days wouldn't be caught dead in anything but gray derbies...

"Let's go, enough!" I shatter the spell, "now we've got to get a move on, kid!..." I'm talking to my girl, my little vixen... "Enough loafing! We're a team, child! Let's get on with our errands! Or else you'll see what your uncle does! Whizz! Whizz! The whip!"

I show her...

Ah! but she doesn't want to obey! she wants us to stay right where we are and keep looking... she's having too much fun!... she's just knee high to a grasshopper!... She doesn't want to pull herself away from the banter... the ladies' little games... She wants me to tell new stories... about the big secrets and all that... where those people live... whether Curlers is with the ladies?... in short, umpteen no-no questions...

"Come on," I go, "let's start walking! I'll start talking when we get farther away..."

What a girl she was! Curious as a cat!... she drove you nuts in the end! I'm all for sitting back for a short break... the weather was absolutely enchanting... A rare event in these parts... mustn't miss it all... Leicester's a pleasant spot... not heaven on earth but even so an oasis of green smack in the middle of traffic, as it were, right at the spot vehicles cram in on each other in hair-raising bottlenecks, and the racket is deafening, all the buses crisscrossing... plus the mob, horses, bikes, the Piccadilly whirlpool... we're satisfied with our patch of grass and the birds... My adorable Virginia was a fairy charming the sparrows, practically the second we sat down... they landed in small flocks... for a little crust of bread they flitted about... perched on her hand pecked... the boys next door in the St. Augustine boarding school also showed up cheeping, but they were pillagers, spending their recess throwing rocks and yanking pigtails... the girls at the school were almost as young as Virginia... maybe not so savvy... but in any case their skirts were just as short!... People filled the benches all around... no empty seats in the oasis!... Recess for all ages! secretaries snacking... moms with tots bouncing in baby carriages... and little dirty old men, Peeping Toms pretending to read their newspapers... three-four Tommies and secretaries dozing against the bandstand... Virginia wouldn't give me any rest, I'd hooked her too badly on my big secrets... she refused to have anything to do with me if I stopped talking to her... she fidgeted on the bench... her pretty golden thighs so muscular... people were looking at her, no helping that!... she got noticed real easy... a bitch from hell if I put up any fight... I can't win, I've got to keep talking! make stories up if I have to! for her this whole business was some wildly wacky adventure... And she was demanding! a little bully! her imagination fired her up... in the end she was riding me too hard!

"I give up! I give up!" I said... "Virginia!"

I begged for mercy... at first she didn't really believe me, I'd been making such a pathetic effort... she razzed me pretty hard... I'd be smart to change the subject... move on to something a little more serious... not one bit imaginary!... and it worked like a charm... Didn't her uncle every now and then ever bring up the masks?... I was sort of fishing around... just to see what I'd come up with... Sosthène was a great guy but he was kidding himself... in my opinion he wouldn't last against the gas... and it'd probably be a total fiasco... plus the risks were very high... I wasn't going to bring up the *Vegas*, the Goâ dances, our fourth dimension... the poor darling would have got scared... or run away... or walked off laughing hysterically!... It wasn't worth the trouble!... I didn't press the point about her uncle, about how I thought he was off his rocker... his crafty pet crazes... his pranks with his gas taps... Walking and talking at the same time was running me off my feet... we sat down in a corner of Lambeth Square... I kept my thoughts to myself... I sat there on the bench muttering, talking to myself... Truth is, I was wiped out... this happened to me more and more often... Psst! Psst! Psst! somebody goes right into my ear... I jump... turn around... It's Curlers! Canard's old lady!

"Well, well," she goes, "look at you, fathead! you into raising babies now?"

"Me?"

I don't get it.

"What about her?"

She points to the kid... lifts her dress... True, her short skirt came up almost to her thighs... she'd gotten big... well-built, muscular, golden, you name it...

Couldn't help but catch your eye... it had caught Curlers'... I cut her off.

"And so what about Canard?" I said.

She's surprised.

"He's at the front!... didn't you know? The guy's been there a week already! Would you ever have believed it? A good-for-nothing deadbeat, wasn't he, no kidding! Rolling out of bed at five in the afternoon!... didn't show any more get up and go for shooting craps in the bars either... he had a cushy deal with me, you better believe it!... good-natured, no trouble or anything... a fucking pansy if you ask me! plus with his varicocele... he was declared unfit three times!..."

She showed me what Canard's equipment looked like, using both hands to give an idea how swollen up he was... big as a cauliflower...

"The major rejected him three times! 'Stay, my good man! Stay here! Wait your turn!' That's how he put it... 'The war's not over!' Damn it to hell! Damn it! My man couldn't take it any more!... He was dying to see the other guys scrambling for cover! Tatave! Gigot! François! Old Bean! More than he could take! He couldn't stay put! He'd have ripped off his fat dong with his teeth! I'm telling you, he was a raving lunatic... fiddling with it night and day... he made the swelling worse... big surprise... he couldn't get his pants on anymore... it blew up as big as a cantaloupe... in the end he was a real pain in the ass... 'Beat it!' I go... 'Beat it, you dumb scumbag! You're pigheaded, tough shit, to hell with you!' I wasn't the only one he was driving crazy... He suckered them down at the Consulate. 'Get out!' they told him. 'Get out! We never want to set eyes on you again! Here's your ticket for Boulogne... Good riddance! Ta-ta! Moron!' Now you know I'm not some tough bitch without a heart... I had a sick father at one time and all that... I know what taking care of a man means... I don't have a special thing for knives but I came this close to cutting off his dong, just to have some fucking peace and quiet!... And not one kind word out of his mouth, mind you... not one friendly word down at the station... Ah! a big fat zero!... Shit! he scrambled out of here like a pig... grunting, listen up, like this... 'Hrrunk! Hrrung!' a real animal... off to the slaughterhouse, the pigheaded bastard! I couldn't dig up any way out for him! He didn't even say good-bye to us... 'I'm late, Curlers! I'm late!' That's all he was able to yap back at me... even on the platform, believe it or not! Charing Cross... Granted, he's nuts! his great cause! France! The fatherland and blah blah blah... Baloney!... And so what about us then, isn't England where we're earning our living! And a pretty good one at that!... You can take it from me!... I'm raking it in, and how! He could stay with me! I earned his living for him, the shit! And I didn't start yesterday either, that's no joke!... I've got a good position, take it from me... Do I know these Rare Beefs or don't I? You just have to take a little look around... they're all in cahoots! Take a guess how big the crowd is. Less than one in a hundred's leaving! I'm on easy street. What are they waiting for? They're just waiting... So why shouldn't he wait too? Why's he got to act like some big asshole?... Nobody's rushing him out the door... those tricks of mine aren't in any rush! I see them day in day out... Doesn't he know the customers?... So what's the big idea? Dumber than the hicks from up north back home, shit, and that's really saying something! Just look at the way these Englishmen are eating their hearts out! Just take one glance at their cars on some Saturday! Cricket! Cricket! Carloads of tricks! Crammed full, collapsing with players!... The only thing on their minds is fun and games... And they're dead serious about them, no kidding, you can take my word for it... Wouldn't they make good cannon fodder?... It just turns my stomach... they're waiting... they're in no hurry, of course... And their dongs didn't get like that!... I'd show him all the time! I'd show him! they'd all come passing through there... the Marble Arch... and shitloads, no joke! You ought to see the mob!... I kept harping at him... 'Just take a look and tell me whether they're eating their hearts out!... When they go, you chump, that's when you go!...' I'd make him feel ashamed... The fuck with him! Champ nutcase... Going off to war, that's all he wanted to hear! So now he's off, goddamn it to hell! And didn't even say good-bye, you hear me!..."

On that note she started stewing... Ah! the way that cad of hers just upped and left stuck in her craw...

Curlers was a splashy dame... dolled up in every color of the rainbow and then some... blue white yellow... I couldn't tear my eyes away from her!... she was right up O'Collogham's alley!... with that solid gold handbag! a cockatoo!... she too thought looks came first... rigged out like an hysteric... you could see her from Marble Arch, she caught your eye as far away as Soho... you could spot her for miles around... she didn't walk the streets alone... she always had a mob on her ass. Endless dickering... pipsqueaks and old farts... at least five-six broads under each door hashing things out haggling... and often around the clock... and every last one, mean rotten windbags... And here I was walking right into their clutches!... where was my head at? Geez, were they going to have some real fun cooking my goose with my jailbait!... blab the news all over town... Ah! you dirty sucker! I was so furious I could have rammed my head against the tree... And if I asked them to keep a lid on it the situation would be a thousand times worse... once I asked her to keep her lips buttoned... she'd race off to trash me!...

"You stopping by the Leicester?" she asks, acting innocent.

"Come off it! You know I can't!..."

She's a fucking pain, the sly bitch! She doesn't press... switches the subject... She takes an interest in the girl... gives her the eye, a smile...

"Well, Miss, how you doing?" she asks, sugary-sweet cajoling...

I glance over at Curlers' face, one big mess of wrinkles and cream... She's an old bag all over except in her eyes... ah! they're on fire!... She has an animal effect on me, those things happen to you when you're young... It doesn't bother the girl at all... they're both laughing together... The old bag imitates a kitten for her... comes out with a few "meow-meows"... her English isn't so hot... baby talk... All at once she gets this bright idea, a wild hankering... She rivets Virginia with her stare, grabs my arm.

"Say, what if I took the girl?"

A stroke of genius!... She plops down beside the kid... touches her rubs up against her... the way those black eyes of hers are sparkling through her pancake makeup... All three of us take up the bench... I already mentioned where it was... on the right under the Shakespeare statue in the square...

"How do you do, Miss Darling?"

Here she goes plunging full steam into English... she even makes herself laugh good and hard... and what a laugh! it gets to me... something awful, that laughter... she sounds worse than a cow, with a real weird moo... they probably hear her down at the Leicester... Ah! she's a real monster... ah! just my luck!... She starts up again, "How? How?"... just can't get those "How"s right... When she sucks in her breath she chokes... she starts in again anyway... she's just like Sosthène... on fighting terms with English...

"How! How! How!"

Virginia shows her... and how they laugh! like lunatics!

"I speak English, just listen! You're telling me she speaks well! My precious sweetheart! Miss Teacher!"

Real enthusiastic in that husky voice.

And now, a few liberties. She takes her arm...

"My goodness, she's so beautiful! she's so beautiful!"

Just comes right out with it, real worked up... she slips her hand under the kid's dress, gropes around, appraises...

"Ah! how about that! how about that!"

Such nutty nerve to come right out and act this way in broad daylight on the bench... she sniffles stutters... I needed to find some rock to crawl under...

"Ah! you know, your miss is a real sweetie pie!..."

She's fidgeting she can't sit still.

"So, you're going to let her shack up with me, you big lug?"

She's serious. Talking strictly business. The deal's on the table.

"She couldn't be any worse a turd than Canard!... Couldn't be worse!..."

She's already got plans.

"I'll lock your little pet up!... I'll lock her up till she gets used to it... Isn't that right, my little honey bunny!"

Another big smooch.

"I'll send you off to war, just look at those gorgeous thighs!"

On that she bends down, nibbles her. The kid lets out a squeal... sort of soft... I can't stand in the way, she'd throw a fit. She'd roll around on the ground.

"So you'll let her shack up with me, OK Ferdinand? So, let's hear what you want for her!"

The people beside us are eavesdropping, lucky they don't catch on.

"The British've got gorgeous thighs, don't they, my little honey!"

She feels her up/pinches her... the child giggles... Here we go again... her whole greedy face creased in a smile...

"So your daddy plays soccer? huh, I betcha he does! You can't take that away from them: they've got gorgeous legs! So take a good look, why don't you, since it's all wasted on you! You'll never understand women! You're like Fathead the pimp, that's right, you're a lamebrain!"

Now she's dumping on me... thinks I'm a jerk and a lummox, dumb as they come! and while she was at it, thick as a brick to boot!... I'm going to introduce her to Sosthène... a chip off the old block when it comes to tact... she's one incredible pig. She raises the kid's skirt... feels her up, those gorgeous golden thighs... the girl doesn't put up a fight, treats the whole thing as a game. But Curlers has got some brass carrying on this way in front of everybody... it's sheer lunacy... playing Blindman's Bluff right out in the open... All her bird of paradise feathers are bouncing around, her headdress is teetering... she's fiery red with excitement. Her face powder's melting off...

"She's got muscles, no kidding! She's got muscles!... And look at that pretty little puss!... Ah! Ferdinand I'm whisking her off your hands!"

She doesn't even ask for my two cents anymore... I laugh her off.

"Knock it off, Curlers, you're bugging me! You're not going to win this time!"

"Bugging you! Bugging you! I'll show you, you little shit!"

Ah! she takes it wrong, gets sore... straightens her headdress, looks me up and down hard... I thought the girl was going to help me out, work out of her jam, defend herself... Ah! no way, she didn't put up a fight, chuckling/sniggering away, and that's that... the other broad's slipping under her skirt, this was really getting disgusting. If I manhandled the kid, dragged her out of the square, she'd have raised hell. The stinking bitch was totally clear on that score... Curlers I mean... It was too risky. So she really went at it!... took advantage of the situation... the pair were really cooking, that's a fact... I don't mean kid's stuff either... Ah! it knocked me out!... The old bag was no holds barred with those roaming hands... the kiddy and the biddy!... in the bright sunshine!... I'd never have believed it! my baby doll! my sweetheart!... they were cooking!... I was young, still wet behind the ears... I'd no real idea what people could be like... they were tickling each other... two vixens... What kind of dope did I look like?... And the people all around us on the benches!... What a performance! they didn't worry their heads over such piddling stuff... two spirited little girls letting their hair down...

"So you're handing her over to me, fathead?"

She had a one-track mind... up for sale!... she was stuck on the idea...

"How old's she?"

"Twelve and a half years old!"

I wanted to throw a scare into her.

"Ah! Twelve and a half years old!"

She's even happier now!... She smacks her own thighs!...

"Ah! you don't say, where'd you dig the kid up?"

She's practically on the point of turning the tables and accusing me!... Actually we were attracting stares... Couldn't find a goddamn hole to hide in... maybe she was a little high too... whiffs of ether... hovering around her feathers... I didn't want to cross her... she would have taken even more liberties... enough was enough... I couldn't figure out what to do... I motioned to Virginia that I wanted her to go... she's mystified... acting all surprised... huh, why?... frisky kittenish... with that old sow! Neither one of them gave a good goddamn about me!... even the old gal was goading me...

"Ferdinand! Ferdinand! the cops! Well, I'll be! Get a load of that! The fuzz feasting their eyes!"

And that was a fact! A mob! bobbies at the gates eating us up with their stares! I hadn't noticed them! but they'd sure as hell noticed us! It's a damn crime! Now she was razzing the pigs! And me in my situation!... the kid got a kick out of it too... they were both sticking out their tongues!... What kind of dope do I look like? Ah! such defiance, shit! I couldn't get over the kid... depraved at the drop of a hat. I was looking for a break in the action so that they'd move along on their separate ways... get together someplace else... I'm humming hawing hustling even hugging the bewitching witch. I promise we'll meet up with her that very night at the Empire no later than eleven... in the standing gallery, downstairs... So help me I swear!... She blasts her ether breath right in my face. She makes it a date! A-OK by her... we'd have a ball together... I promised her everything she wanted, just to get her off my back... rotten bitch! I was scared she'd start squawking her head off... I think she snorted some dope, plus doing the ether.

"You're pure! You're pure!" she muttered. She wouldn't let go of Virginia... squeezed her against her heart... love pecks galore... Finally she releases her... we parted company... she shakes my hand... goes pale... so pale... white as a ghost... a Pierrot... her eyes wide... she gets up, walks straight off... stiff as a board... a robot... she ditches us... crosses the square... slowly disappears... Happy flying! You old bird!

All her feathers floating behind her... her yellow-blue boas... she struts just like that in front of the cops... marching like a soldier... one two... one two... fires a salute... They don't say a word... now she's gone. We both linger on the bench... "Just you wait, kiddo," I say to myself, "I'll be biding my time! I'll show you what kinky's all about! Cutie pie, you deserve a good beating! Now that the old witch is gone, wait and see what I do to your fanny!" Ah! I'd snapped back to myself!... I couldn't let myself breathe a word in front of her, but how I make up for it now! I make her feel good and ashamed! Let her hear a thing or two... I dot every i. Tell her that woman's a piece of shit, a washed-up hellcat... a gross grungy old junkie! an ugly witch, a pig! That it's horrendous for a young girl to be hanging around with such women... I want to give her comeuppance, not quit until she starts crying... I want to see her tears... She's completely dry-eyed... listens to me with her pug nose up in the air, straightening her dress... stuck-up... shutting me out! So cool and collected! Nothing rattles her... she thinks I'm boring, crude... sulking at me... now if that isn't a pisser!... and she's barely out of the cradle!... I'm not going to go over it all again, I don't have the time... we've wasted two hours at least...

"Come on, brat, let's hit the road, damn it! We'll be out here forever! Let's go, little lady! We've got some shopping to do!"

Heave ho! I hoist up my cargo... the whole shebang plop! on my shoulders! what an incredible load! Now we've got to get a move on... we're off... I hit the ground running... this little hellcat's really something! defying me, putting on a face... the more I thought about it while walking along the more worked up I got... she was traipsing beside... totally oblivious... as though nothing had happened... what a disgusting blow to my personal pride, that behavior of hers back there... still and all she was just a girl... and I already loved her like crazy... my adored Virginia... my pure one my precious my dream, messing with that tramp... my little girl my sweetheart... and here I was afraid to kiss her!... but with that out-and-out dirty two-bit whore... Oh man! I was rattling all my gear, banging into the shop windows... pretty shook up, you better believe it... I was seeing stars... I tried clinging to the shop fronts I was so wobbly on my feet... boiling mad... the dirty brazen slut... my head was spinning, I could see her ugly mug everywhere, her war paint her eyes, that Curlers, her filthy leers... I also saw sleazy scenes, awful fantasies reflected all down the shop windows... All at once I could see the pair together right there... the kiddie and the biddie... awesome! got me hard as a rock... oh yeah! I was hot and horny!...

That's when I nabbed the kid, held her arm because I wanted her to cough up an answer.

"Didn't you think she was revolting? horrible? disgusting? stinky?"

I wanted to know... at every street corner... I held her back, I didn't want her to take off... I wanted an answer... and don't spare the details!... My mouth was dry as cotton I'd worked myself into such a state... They were sucking the life out of me, this burning desire this vice this jealousy... everything... It was more than I could take in my condition... my brain like oatmeal... it was too much... too cruel... those monsters!... I looked at the kid pressed against me... I just couldn't accept the idea... she was looking up at me too, traipsing along... not bothered in the least, mocking... she sure as hell didn't give a damn about me... she did whatever looked good in her eyes... her lovely blue laughing eyes... Now she was acting innocent... couldn't understand me anymore... just a happy-go-lucky little girl... with a frisky little fanny... her tightly pleated skirt... she was really pushing me over the edge!... she was skipping along real close to me... absolutely oblivious about everything that had gone on... and there I was brokenhearted, stuttering and hiccuping... Oh yeah! I saw the pair all over the sidewalk... the lampposts... among the passersby... That's how terrifically confused shook up I was because my heart hurt like hell... and all because of that old dike!... I was groping forward with my doodads my junkload... lugging and lagging... couldn't see clearly... all I could make out were sleazy visions... Curlers... the girl before my eyes... Ah! what an horrendous number that did on me... drove me into one of those jealous fits... seeing the way those two were gobbling each other up!... and me underneath them both, lapping like mad... sinking my teeth into her thighs... the visions tripped me up in my tracks... I had to sit down... right there on the curb... I could see them tearing away at each other... a genuine slaughter fest... wolfing me down too, they were so totally crazed... that's what I was seeing... climbed back on my feet... started to zigzag forward... Ah! a pretty sight I made in the street!... I sort of realized it at the time... I had a shred of wits about me... I forced myself to keep moving... the sort of raging jealousy that attacks/ravages you/sinks its blade into your skull and stirs it up all hot and bubbly... sure was one hell of a torture... and I was hee-hawing like a jackass... Christ Almighty what a joke!... the kid took me for some clown having a laugh with her... And I was asking her to forgive me...

"My little Virginia, my little Virginia!... Don't leave me! I beg you! I'll never yell at you again! Tell me you love me just a little... that it's not just Curlers who's caught your eye! Tell me I matter just a little to you!..."

Ah! I wasn't yet down for the count, I acted real sweet, the rough stuff was getting me nowhere. I wanted to be in on the party too... my visions totally obsessed me! Damn! This jealousy! I had the shakes... Ah! I bleated/pleaded with her... for her not to run away, to forgive me! I'd never say another word to her!... not one single word, not one single sigh! I wouldn't bug her anymore! I'd carry my bundle like a good little boy. Honest! And then, damn, it started right up again... I was back to my questions. I was dragging my bum leg after those crazy visions... I glance over at her cute little puss... and wham! my blood's back to boiling, you bet!... I wanted a fuller picture than before... more and more details! Hell-bent for those big secrets... it was too much for my poor wreck of a body, and certainly for my head, my filthy third degree sent my fever sky-high... my kooky questions... she kept mum... she could hear me mumbling... she kept mum, skipping along beside me very frisky impish... she must have thought I was off my nut... I was afraid to push her to the limit, my adorable Virginia, my Madonna, my fairy... I kept hobbling forward with my sack of junk, really busting my butt... wheezing... she kept me hooked with her smiles... I was one deadbeat old rascal... I felt like sacking out right there on the sidewalk. Now was no time... Ah! have to hand it to these British girls!... so spruce and trim so waifish so blonde... and heaven in their eyes... the kinkiness of angels... with a touch of devil mixed in... a touch of devil, sure as hell... a devil down to her fingernails she was... a devil I was just crazy about!...

We reach Buckingham Street... Right there, as we pass a doorway I want to drag her inside, give her a kiss... it was a dark nook... I want to give her a little hug, she fights me off, wriggling like a fish... I kiss her tickle her... force her into a cranny... geez, the way she starts screaming!... Whoah! do me a favor and pipe down! Pipe down! how thrilled I am... so scared she was going to get away from me!... I sort of hurt her... pinched her, I wanted to know the whole story... I wanted to punish her... for Curlers, for all that jazz back there!... I wanted her to confess... that she was one kinky little kid... I had to take a hard line!... Ah! I loved her so much!... little bitch!... even worse than before even stronger... it was sheer hell... a poison scorching me inside and out ever since Curlers... my pants were on fire... I was racked with all sorts of excruciating spasms, thigh cramps that set me howling... I was barking in the doorway... slobbering her with kisses, and with my left hand, my strong one, feeling up her little body, her belly, her little bottom so hard and taut... a baby animal!... a bouncy little ass!... quivering! I clamped onto it, squeezed it, kneaded it, I'd have pressed out every last drop of juice... every last drop of her wily ways, the little hellcat!... every last drop of blood of flesh... and then, goddamn it! I started to come... I was coming... and I let go of everything!... staggered around... braying... flailing!... I latch onto her! Crunch! Sink my teeth into her! right into her neck... and whap! she belts me! A real zinger! The viper! what strength! I'm knocked for a loop... now was that nice?... and whap! I belt her back!... Fair's fair! I catch her in both arms squeeze hard... grind her against me... mash her with one of those big sloppy smooches right there against the wall... lap her up... she starts turning to jelly, I feel her wobbling... her head crooks backward... I prop her up straight try to bring her around... give her a shake talk to her she stammers... I rub her kiss her... she comes to... starts breathing again... This happened on Buckingham Street as I said... a fainting spell... just past Wickham Gate, past the fresh produce market... but back in those days it was empty. I'm not going to bog my story down in details again... "Come on, kid!..." I head back on our way... I had to cut it short... before we drew a crowd... "Let's go, my child!" I mean business... this time she follows me... no more skipping back and forth, no more frolicking... I guess I'd really shaken her up... she could have spit nails, had about as much as she could take, darting me dirty looks at the intersections... I thought she was going to cut out. But still we couldn't drag our feet anymore. I stepped up our pace, though!... I was hauling a whole scrap heap on my shoulders, a jumble of odds and ends... a horrendous burden... ah! I was sweating worse than a pig with every new mile... I even stopped looking at the little snot-nose... whatever happens will happen! but now she comes up close gives me a kiss... she's the one making a pass at me. She wants to lend me a hand, and right now... she acts nice as could be... back in her good mood, time to make up!... carry the sack between us... each on one end... I'm real happy!... The sack teeters crash! she drops her end... it spills out over my feet! I yowl! it goes rolling all over the road... now I've got to leap and lunge after everything! all the small coupling rings in the gutter!... Ah! what a kick Virginia's getting out of this! me pouncing after all the gear... getting under everybody's feet!... under all the passersby! What a terrific trick! She got her revenge!... Worked like a charm!... I keep my mouth shut... gather up my goulash... I'll see to her later... the little horror'll get what she deserves!... I make myself a promise... I sure as hell don't want any more of her help... let her stay pissed off! That's the way I'd rather have it... I was stopping everywhere to catch my breath... practically at every corner... naturally this slowed us down some... we finally reach Wardour... between Wardour and Guilford, way back when during my first weeks in London, I'd spotted a hotchpotch of shops that were really like museums of travel souvenirs, curios, world maps, chromos, antiques from all corners of the world, prints of sailing ships, compasses, mounted fish, albatrosses... heaps of miscellaneous junk like I'd never seen before... between Wardour and Guilford Street... Plus it was a pleasant spot, no mob to fight, nice and enclosed, with connecting walkways... It put a dry roof over your head where you could wait out downpours... And give your shoes a break... It reminded me of the kind of passages we have back in Paris, but loads more fun, cozier too, not crawling with riffraff, a sewer for the great unwashed like ours... nothing but shops dealing in colonial goods, in the foreign, the exotic... I'd dropped by often, always brought back for one or another reason... I'd already spent a good amount of time lingering around here... in front of practically every shop window! Ah! this was the kind of place where you could let your mind wander, get a feel for different countries, at least in a certain way... the one catch is that it sort of wears you out, it's tiring and depressing... the world is full of so many places! Tibet's not the only country out there! your mind ends up racing... reeling... there's too much to see! All that exotic junk winds up going to your head, offers you too many different windows... in the end it makes you world-weary, woeful... poor crummy cockroach, the likes of you will never get to see anything, with your pathetic screwed-up feet... Shitty rinky-dink bug... you'll never go anywhere! Plus I was incredibly greedy... I felt like cleaning out the whole shop, the back room, piling every last thing in the window on top of my cargo of hardware, so maybe that bum Sosthène could teach me a thing or two, give me a real sort of education, not just his constant Hindu crap... He had the chance to put all his knowledge to work. I bet that ugly sucker knows his stuff... otherwise, what was the point in being such a tough guy, somebody who had been around the block a few times... I bet anything he was feeding me a line! I'd have shown him the butterflies in their little boxes, the star maps... I was sure he'd be stumped... he didn't know the first thing about astronomy, des Pereires knew a hell of a lot more... my lousy grade-school diploma didn't open up any horizons for me... I'd have liked to learn about the world... but he'd have poured on the snake oil again... tough, I'd just have to deal with it... I was lecturing Virginia... while working our way from one window to the next... at least twenty weird stores all in a row... botanical curios from around the world... plus a four-eyed monster bat with sixteen paws... a flesh-eating plant... an astrolabe... a "feather head" iguana, the last of its kind in the world, as pretty a sight as Curlers... I point it out to the girl, it gave her a good laugh... Ah! I was sure happy too... I was making my impression after all!... explorers' maps of Africa... the polar bears of the Arctic Circle, I was chewing her ear off about them, the seals, the woolly mammoths... packing the ice fields... I concocted stories for her! the only problem was that my brain was working overtime, I really lost track of what I was saying, I was going at it too hard, lost my steam... the kid was treating me like a dumb-ass clown, she kept firing questions at me... I couldn't really tell what I was looking at anymore... everything was whirling in front of me, the island savages, the iguana, the astrolabe... like a merry-go-round in my head... my heart pounding... another dizzy spell... I get two-three a day... I catch myself against the window... wind up sitting on top of my bundle, my junk pile... my mind's spinning... everything's spinning!... I hold my head in my hands... I can see it all again... the painted savages in their masks... dancing in a circle around me... plus des Pereires among them, poor old des Pereires collapsed in a heap in his wheelbarrow... I don't know why... the feeling of faintness was bringing my memories back... fluttering heartaches, butterflies of muted music... I can still sort of hear... it's my heart... and now blazing red I can see it! my jealousy's flaring up!... I ought to move but I can't anymore... got to keep an eye on the girl in case she beats it!... Ah! it's just awful how weak I am... collapsed in a heap against the shop window... and everything stirs up my memories my strength... got to keep an eye on the girl... so who's really been violating her?... her uncle? the Colonel? Sosthène?... which colonel? I can't remember... I've got a colonel too!... a real one, you bet! not some jerk! des Entrayes! Fucking Christ Almighty! the Sixteenth heavy artillery! I'm all discombobulated! I puke right there against the shop window! It just happens! Tough luck about the *Vegas*! Don't know which end is up anymore... And that sly devil Nelson! and the astrolabe! And Curlers, that old painted sow! I'll show you where I'll stick them! Plus Matthew, that dyed-in-the-wool pig from the Yard! his eyes whirling me around... never off me?... where am I going to stick them? a merry-go-round humming in my brain... roaring like hell inside my head... dazing me badly I wobble on my feet... I'll never make it through this. They were a gang of geeks... geeks! I'm positive they put their paws all over her!... in any case her uncle sure did! No mistake on that score! She wasn't new at this game! I'd seen her with Curlers... if she'd just been some kid, I mean genuinely innocent, she'd have run away screaming! but no fucking way, what delight! I sure got an eyeful! And they'd sure had one hell of a time, two turtledoves in bliss! two lowlife tarts smack in the center of the square! a little girl! not even a speck of shame of decency! the snot-nosed slut! driving me up the wall with that cheap tramp! that creepy old bag! they put me through hell in a hurry, no buts about it! I can't keep still! I climb to my feet. I want to charge straight out of here! I'm seething inside! damn, my head! tough shit! I force myself! I'm really obsessed! I've got to get away! to react! Come on, off we go, Virginia, we're out of here! Can't let her go! I drag her by the hand! Brazen snot-nosed little vixen! I said get a move on! let's hit the road! that dirty louse Sosthène! Hypocrite! He's looking for the devil! Well, I've got him right inside! Day and night writhing in my skull! He's just got to grab him and carry him off! No sweat! The devil's moving all through me, I've got him in my guts, in my leg! in my brain! and in my heart! and the kid beside me is a devil from head to toe!

we've all gone to the devil, goddamn it! Crummy Sosthène with his magic crew! And then there's Curlers! she's got the *Vegas* beat with her hundred thousand grimaces, a one-woman show!... she casts her spell and sucks the life out of you! Whoah, things are bad, my legs like jelly... can't move forward... forced back on my butt... dizzy with anger... my mind back on that bastard Sosthène... and then Matthew... two fine specimens!... and then there's my jealousy beside me, I'm clasping her by the hand... cocky little bitch from hell... fairy princess of my heart... my well-knit kinky little treasure... what you going to do with her, moron? my mind slips its tracks soars off with me in tow... I lose control... I'm straightjacket material... I am aware of that much all the same... this is totally insane... the fairy princess of my heart, so mischievous... what a depraved nymphet... with Curlers, that toad!... some fairy tale that was back there... I was moaning panting on my pile, my gear... collapsed like a beaten mutt against the store front... what a pretty sight!... she could clearly see I was done in, the hussy was totally aware... she could have lent me a hand a little... People were looking at us. It was quitting time... Crowds were passing... Heads up for the cops! What if they haul me in like some bum?... some wreck zonked out on a public sidewalk... On your feet, you mongrel! I buck myself up. Bust my gut! Nose to the grindstone, punk... I pour it on. We weren't too far from Gingolf's, paint and putty... I'd lots of provisions to stock up on there... Gingolf & Co., I can see the store... I keep going... walk right by. I was caught up in my thoughts. Sleepwalking... straight ahead... holding Virginia by the hand... absolutely determined she stay with me... I wanted to keep her by my side once and for all! That's where my mind was at. Even if it came down to locking her up... While walking briskly, I gave this idea some thought... I needed to stash her away in safekeeping like a jewel... no more traipsing about for her... like the Crown Jewels in the Tower of London!... that was my hot idea!... nobody would ever set eyes on her again!... I'd drink her up with my eyes all by myself... as much as I wanted!... an impregnable fortress... with dungeons loopholes... giant drawbridges!... and boiling oil for Curlers, her dirty creepy pork-face! always standing ready over the doorway! the fire always hot! right on her chops! so that she'd never come back for more! old sow!

"I'll lock you away!" I said to her... I promised she'd be happy... "I'll lock you up in my tower!"

"Where's your tower?"

She wasn't fazed.

"In my big castle, you little ninny! You'll be nice and cozy! In my fortress, my pretty one! You'll be nice and warm!"

She was giving me a sarcastic look... she kept trotting along, the little goat... and then she started to skip... not one bit upset... "Cuckoo!" she said to me, "Cuckoo!" sticking her finger to my temple... she kept skipping... and I kept walking... the nutcase!

"Yes, my precious treasure... behind triple locks! And another triple set on top of that! That's the way it'll be!"

"Kii! kii!" she started giggling... Ah! great start... the more I hammered away the funnier I got!... I felt like crying... the darling... flower of my dream... what a precocious kid, damn! Ah! It bowled me over... little British girls of this sort with their sturdy calves and all, who would raise holy hell at the drop of a hat... start a riot screaming and shouting over nothing... over some itty-bitty liberty... and this from a girl who makes a public spectacle of herself with a rotten old battle-ax, a sex-crazed granny... Ah! what an absolute hoot!... Just wait and see what I've got up my sleeve, brat! Asshole craziness!

"Cuckoo!" she kept going at me, "Cuckoo!" Actually I was sort of funny, walking and talking... a raging pig tortured to pieces... she could see me all in a dither, fretting away, racked with worry... but she just didn't care, she just didn't. I was showing her the best time she'd ever had... I was her weepy-eyed nitwit. She was clueless... Come on, keep moving, funny guy! lug along your torments with your bundle! Let's go, shake a leg! Klutz! Keep moving, crackbrain... We covered a nice distance even so... we were almost back where we started out that morning... right at the French bookstore... Ah! I was done in, I had to break for a minute. And this time I wasn't kidding... I was at the end of my rope... I set down my bundle... Got to keep the girl amused... I'm forever scared she'll take off... we do a little window shopping... the picture books the children's comics... just right for her age... Virginia reads French well... Plus there are dirty books... which interest her, I've got to say... She'll take *Suzette's Week*... We step inside the store... Scads and scads more books... especially adventure stories... the trek of two orphans to the North Pole... plus color engravings, complete collections of airplanes, turbine-powered cycles, race cars... Every sort of gas-driven invention... It took me back to the past... at least seven years... eight years... I was counting... that long already! how time flies! des Pereires... his inventions... his great favorite... and then the wheelbarrow... damn, those really were the good old days!... screwed-up old clown! And what about this new guy? Mr. Jig, Sosthène! how would we say good-bye?... I already had memories... war piles them up for you... I looked at the girl... the kid... She didn't have an inkling... I talked to her about the pretty pictures... just right for her age... I told her all about the globe-shaped ones... I sure knew a thing or two about them!... the manager was real easygoing, we were allowed to turn the whole place upside down, all his collections... he'd let you linger for hours on end while the rain came pouring down... he'd never bitch... he hardly ever left his cashier's office, he kept tabs on the scene from way on high, I can still see him now... his pince-nez!... hopelessly nearsighted, lived in a cloud, celluloid choke collar, your change with a smile... the only drawback was that you could smell him coming, a pungent reek, the taste of the period, a stink of stale sweat. It took World War I to wipe out people's stink, I mean their B.O. I wonder what this new war's going to wipe out? Tooth decay? bad breath? just another two or three cataclysms and we'll be all set! Back to wearing peplums and the reign of the great god Pan! Paradise Regained!... But four-eyes hadn't gone off to the war yet! so why's he unfit for service looking so stiff and starchy? how was he disabled? Didn't really look so old, after all... I never asked him any questions... I didn't want to come across like the cops... he had just a few strands of hair... a small grafted-on-looking mustache... sort of like des Pereires. It was as though he'd been appointed here... they might as well stuff him right away, not another soul would be cast in his mold, no others of his ilk would be sent over from France or anywhere else... in short, he was already a thing of the past, part of a collection, frozen in time at the end of an era... he was a walking museum... whenever I'd pass I'd stop in to see him... I used to wear the same soft collar as he did, the same celluloid collar... bow tie... but he was still at his post... I'd left it all behind... I was the one adventuring through his collections... and well, I've got to admit, some adventures they were too! ships down through the ages... a really mind-boggling array... from every century under every flag... from draggers to ocean liners, clippers, cargo and passenger steamers, frigates, galleons and corvettes... every vessel that had ever plowed the waves in all oceans and climes, sky blue mirrors, sheets of slate, storm-tossed waves!... I was so tempted to buy something, a big change from tracking down cotton padding... replacing cast iron... Ah! I felt like snapping up a ship or two, a collection, a real assortment, I'd've plastered my walls with them, covered the Colonel's stairwell, plus the bedroom I shared with Sosthène, a whim a craze on a sudden impulse, a couple-three magnificent three-masters for instance, and how about five or six passenger and cargo steamers?...

"Bet you don't!" the kid challenges me.

"Bet I do! I'll go for it! Give me a dozen!"

The most beautiful color prints, plus another dozen on top of that! with yards, sails, clouds, storms! puffed up parrots! hurricanes gusting through halyards! I don't scrimp on anything. I give it a whirl to the tune of forty-seven pounds! Pince-nez can't believe his eyes even when I fork over forty-seven bills... He'd never sold me a thing... It made for a pretty hefty roll added to all my hardware my cast iron... Plus I was the one busting his ass!... Finally I got over my urge... Now was no time to go back on my word... Of course it would be plain wrong... running through the Colonel's dough! We just didn't know when to stop!... I said so to the girl... she was as much to blame as me... she was the one who dared me... it came down to the same thing, just as irresponsible... but she wanted to hear stories... so I talk about some more battles, the other pictures in the shops. I already mentioned where it was: Wardour Street... a stone's throw from the Palladium... Pince-nez had loads of other absolutely gorgeous old maps... famous battles,

Lépante, thundering galleys... plus sea monsters!... whales with hair-raising nostrils... raging in the waves... ramming frigates! The caravels of the Armada whipped by an Atlantic squall fierce enough to split the ocean wide open, exploding with seaspray and gunpowder... awesome subjects!... plus an entire shelf of atlases, with all the long course routes charted out... the emerald distances: Pernambuco 3,000 miles... Yokohama 10,100 miles... Tahiti 14,000 miles... plus other remote spots scattered around the globe... to the very ends of the earth... to the opposite poles, and beyond... the only problem was choosing...

"Come on, Virginia, pick something!"

True, this was her big chance. Absolutely whatever she wished! the Coral Sea! The Caribbean! some island out there, something teeny-weeny?... a sea speck? perfect for a little girl like her... The mere thought excited me... I wanted to wow Pince-nez! Wanted him to really register the kind of guy he was dealing with! a globe-trotter with the best of them! I even set out my conditions for him! My voice booming through his shop. I want an island with trees, but sheltered from the elements! with a triple barrier of reefs! And no hassles! no worries about where our next meal was coming from... all you can eat falling off the trees... Maybe he's heard about someplace like that? bananas pineapples guinea pigs... plus an ideal climate, a genuine Garden of Eden, that's what I need... after all, I've just got back from the war! oh yeah, plus a pleasant cheerful atmosphere... I want to put these rotten migraines behind me, I want amusement... flying fish everywhere, parrots that sing on key. I want to laugh myself back to health with Virginia, my little creature... Ah! it's enchanting, no two ways about it... the pain gone from my arm, and from my head most of all... that's the most godawful part! an end to the whistling in my ears... no more gas contests, no more Colonel! no more creepy Matthew!... no more nightmares day and night!... Ah! the easy life in the Caribbean! I could see it already! No more geeks on my ass! India's out of the picture! Pépé too! Ah! my enthusiasm was carrying me away. Pince-nez didn't get it at all... he was giving me sheep eyes... Come on, let's leave, all three of us! It was bighearted of me! I was offering him a once-in-a-lifetime deal!... a generous gesture... it'd do him a world of good... I'd take him away to the tropics... I wasn't jealous about him... he'd get out of his office... Ah! he wouldn't hear of that... right away he put his foot down... "What do you take me for?" he asked, real down in the mouth... That's how it was...

Well OK then, we'll go by ourselves! ah, just understand I'm not going to be held up! Tough luck for Pince-nez! Let's hit the road, my little Virginia! You'll grow big and beautiful out there! in the Tragacanth Seas! I'd already come up with a name! The Lazuli Ocean! Let's get going, kid!... and whoosh, I drag her off by the hand! my roll of pictures! my sack of junk! the cast iron odds and ends! she was starting to get the hang of me, to catch on that I was a quick-to-act, determined kind of guy, well at least when I wasn't hurting too bad... This time around, the hell with my pain! I was seething, that's a fact. We'd charged off at a gallop... I was whinnying with enthusiasm. The antipodes on my ass! I forced my leg into action! My sack up on my shoulder clinking away! a deafening racket! I barreled through the mob!... ah! what a cushy life we'd live out there! Ah! I didn't want anybody slowing me down! People were cursing me up and down as I flew along! I ran at least twenty off their feet! mowed them down as I raced past... all down Oxford Street... Regent... Virginia was having a blast... galloping beside me... all along Selfridges department store... Marble Arch... we'd shaken up quite a crowd! Ah! Enthusiasm's a scary thing! What if we bumped into Matthew? Ah! the thought was running through my mind... The kid was clueless... Getting all fired up is fine and dandy! Danger! Big scenes! Whoosh, I'm tearing along so fast I'm forced to sit down. Heads up! Look out! Look out! I get back to my feet... scared of being followed... What if the cops were on our tails?... I keep pouring it on... another avenue... I cross... Hyde Park... I charge ahead... great, a stone post, whew! The trees over there, better yet... need time to think... what's gotten into us? dragging all this goddamn crap around! I dump the lot! Crash! right on the ground... a bench... I really need some time to think... the kid wouldn't have helped me... she's out only for herself... I'd really been barreling around too much... I'm heaving wheezing hoarsely... ah! a perfect moment to collect my thoughts... take advantage of a break in the action... nobody at our heels... no Nelson no Matthew no nobody... it's one chance in a million! so I've really got to concoct some plan... running away sounds awfully good but it's expensive... and we can't take Sosthène along! Ah! First things first! Ah! No way! To hell with the dirty chiseler! I never want to lay eyes on him again, not for all the gold in the world! the dirty old dog-face! He'll jinx me for sure! Let him go off himself to dig up his demons! plus his ancestors while he's at it! it's all just a bunch of depressing mumbo jumbo!! and then there's sex-crazed Pépé with her jade temples! Oh! I'm telling you, I wanted to put all that stuff behind me! The whole crew can all go and get embalmed! We were off to the other side of the world! my gamine my sweetheart my bird! she'd be my totem! my salvation! we'd have the Tragacanth Sea all to ourselves! All for just us two! Virginia! Let's hoist our flags! Anchors fucking away! Two years! Ten years if we need to! All our worries overboard! Southward bound! Someplace where no-body'll know us anymore! Whoah! hold on! I see a cop! Come on, let's beat it! Let's get to those other trees over there, honey! the curving lane... I'm so exuberant I'm a changed man... still fired up!... but with a brand-new charge!... of speed of hope!... I can't feel my legs under me! we take a shortcut... I whisk across the grass... carrying my fairy along by the hand... my cherished one in tow... Whew! we made it! Christ, I got so scared!... of what? Can't really say... at least a moment's breather!... just a false alarm... But London's crawling with cops... I've got my work cut out for me!... still, I need a break, damn! got to catch my breath... farther off over there is Speakers' Corner, on the other side of the grove, you can hear their big traps... we could creep a little closer... open-air speechifiers... a good dozen yapping away... we can hear bits and pieces of their spiels... the crowd has no use for them... "Haw! Haw!" the listeners are going... we can tell how the talkers are struggling from their faces... sticking up over the crowd... they're perched on something... And are they ever screaming their lungs out! the crowd answers back, razzes them... they're not taken seriously... "Haw! Haw!" the mob's in stitches... just like Virginia with me, the people ragging, putting them down... the speakers flailing/flapping their arms around... angry prophets, curses floating on the wind...

"I say the rich must pay!" the guy's pouring it on so hard he's red with anger, from far off you can see his color changing... he passes around a hat for donations... scarlet with rage... He wants all the rich to pay up... he's out for blood... chokes on his own message... the crowd's hoo-haaing... guffawing... "Hah! Hooh! Hooh!" the echoing laughter... mounts into a whopping roar...

"Christus is at war! We bleed with him!" quavers somebody I can't see down past all the hats... on another podium... an old lady's voice... Christ is at war! She's bleeding with him! or so she claims... she squeals out shrilly that we must pray... and right then and there! tough to please... the crowd isn't laughing so much with her... Now it's starting to rain! a sudden shower... umbrellas snap open... It doesn't cool off the Christian lady, she's imploring/quivering in the water... we must sing Hymn 304 for her! she does a solo... begs/implores heaven for an end to the war... It's coming down in buckets... Virginia wants us to leave, duck under an umbrella too. I don't want to be on the move... The place is lousy with cops... mobs bring them out every time... she's shivering in her short skirt her drenched blouse... I hug her in my arms... I untie the package, take out the tarpaulin, spread it over our heads... presto! we're more comfortable! Is it ever coming down! but it doesn't cramp the haranguers' style... their big mouths boom through the downpour...

"Women of Britain, win the war!"

She's a shrill-voiced soapboxer... squealing in such a high pitch it sets your teeth on edge, and they're already chattering from the cold... This dame'll win the war with the suffragettes... I'm all for that! Great idea! There's something for everybody here, hogwash for every hog, swarms of people bawling out from every corner... more cloudbursts! look at it coming down! raging torrents... all the way at the other end, practically out in the street, another yawper plugging away... we can hear him even at this distance, his voice carries... we can't miss his scarlet top hat, he's gesticulating writhing bellowing...

"Accordions for the Army!" That's his cry... Dead set on it. When it comes for R & R for soldiers, the accordion can't be beat! He yells out his message... and breaks into a little ditty... a jig a cakewalk... dancing at the same time... a day without bread... shuffling on his skinny pegs... he sings... serenades, hollers... an eccentric philanthropist... "Accordions for the Army!" Ting! gg! Ding! dg! dg! jigging on his soapbox... he couldn't care less about the cyclones!... he's beyond all that! doing his fantastic number, having a ball! Nobody donates jack shit... Accordions? Just him playing! Hopping around, going all out! the big lanky galoot! I'm hopping around too, working like hell, and nobody's donating jack to me! It's all the same to Virginia! I'm hopping! hopping!

"I love you, don't I, Virginia?" I ask her jokingly... "I love you! I love you! I do everything for you and you don't do a thing!"

I gaze into her beautiful dreamy eyes... my darling sweetheart my dear soul... she's not in a real great mood, sort of sulky... I hug her, hold on for dear life, take advantage of the situation... both of us hunkered for cover under my tarpaulin... since she can't exactly run off in her dripping wet short skirt... I smother her with hugs, suck the water from the tip of her little nose... I lick her lap her like a dog all over her dear cute little face... ah! am I horny, flaming with passion and joy over having her huddled up against me... ah! I couldn't give a hoot about the rain and the torrential downpour and my arm hurting me so bad, as long as she stays pressed against me so cute quivering and smiling... but where'd the other thugs get to?... What about it, you fiendish gamine, maybe her mind's on them too?... ah! I'm positive it is... little miss innocent, kinky to the core, that's for certain!... Another panic attack... here I go, my mind's off again!... wandering for sure cause I'm not all that wacko... A pang of jealousy. So where'd Nelson disappear to? and what about Matthew? And Cascade? And big Angela? Ah! I'd like to see them... they're going to swipe the girl from me for sure... they've already got a plan... I check out the gardens all around us... nope, don't see a soul...

"Do you see anybody, Virginia?"

No, nobody... Just look how guileless she is, wrapped in my arms, chilled to the bone from the cold the showers and from love... poor little birdie!... No! No! No! That's not what she is, the little bitch! my mind's running away from me again! she's a brazen brat, that's what she is! a little slut, I saw her in action! with Curlers! Gusts of rain lash me right in the head, torrents of icy water, it cools me off. She was just so goddamned impudent! I can still see that angel of mine... I'm seething, I see her with that other woman... Ah! unbelievable insolence from such a pretty little girl... and those thighs of hers too, can't forget those thighs... I feel them against me... I should marry her! then nobody'll steal her from me ever again... I should marry her right away.

"You're coming with me, Virginia? To travel across the seas?"

I ask her the question. That's the right idea, I've got to marry her! I repeat...

"Will you come and travel across the seas?"

I invite her to join my journey.

"Swim! Swim!" she answers... kidding me along... I talked about oceans... I don't want her poking fun. I lay down the law.

"You'll stay with me forever!"

She shows me the rain the downpour... I must be funny again...

"You'll come, Virginia?"

I keep pressing... I cling like a leech!... What a prospect! What an ideal! Together for life! For starters, I've got a good grip on her, I cuddle her... very tenderly against my shoulder... the rain keeps coming down... one of those sudden heavy showers... the sun'll break through any minute now... I boost her confidence, caress her... she shivers soaked to the bone... I kiss her again, whisper into her hair... nibble her ear... she lets out wild squeals... I feel like biting her even harder. Curlers went at her shamelessly... and for all the world to see! right in the middle of traffic... without a soul around... I caress her little neck... so graceful, so sensitive... velvet, satin, glazed with rain... I'd just need to give it a squeeze... with my left hand, the strong one! I could choke the life right out of her, cheep!... a thrush... I'd hold her quivering body in my hands... I caress I suck her little beak... Ah! the rotting old carcass! She pops back into my mind! Curlers, that tramp! Lousy bitch! I could gobble up her little sweetie all by myself! I'll teach her how to laugh! little nymphet! I'll wolf her down! Curlers won't get a single morsel! With my own eyes I watched them kissing full on the mouth! in full view on the square... at high noon! frightening, isn't it? considering they'd just met one minute before!... talk about witchcraft! I'm seeing visions of wild orgies... this whole downpour won't be enough to cool me down... I can still see that vampire!... she'd have bled the life out of my little girl! Curlers was one to do it!... she pawed her until I went berserk!... playing to the crowd! What if Matthew had seen those goings-on right in the heart of the city! Seen that I was putting on girlie shows!... He'd have staged a bust to end all busts, oh momma! The whole pretty lot of us slapped behind bars! But still I just kept at it! Dangers or no dangers, I didn't give a damn! genuine visions from hell that blotted everything out of my mind... flare-ups that set me howling more horribly than I could take in my condition... I had to kidnap her, no mistake about that... twisted/tortured with love. Purity? What a crock! Hot and horny!... it took balls, simple as that! I was ashamed, and then wanted her something awful... I hashed it over a little more... a prick of conscience... maybe I'd gotten it all wrong?... in a word, it'd all been some hallucination... maybe she'd gotten raped?... taken advantage of by that fat filthy bitch? victimized by horrible pressure tactics? Goddamned street slut... It took next to nothing for me to go over the edge! since I was already fever-stricken, my brain hammered to pieces, a poor sicko... Whatever the case, I had to put an end to this! Let's go, up on our feet! I just had to keep my focus... and stay on track... ah! I need to think this thing through!... especially now that I'm in charge... An island would be better, I think... something tiny, for instance, well protected by reefs, with lots of sunshine, not some head-clogging factory, or brain-soaking swamp like this rotten son of a bitching England of theirs! ah! that's my number one priority... sunshine practically every day, so I'll be cured of my aches and pains... no more winter! eternal springtime! and such places do exist! In the tropics, of course! I shout loud enough for her to hear... which she didn't, because the rain was drumming down so hard—plus there'd be flowers! giant convolvulus that would completely cover our little hut! and flocks of lyrebirds and hummingbirds so tiny that they'd do battle with ladybugs... She had no inkling... I keep teaching her new things... about all the goings-on in dream climates... a perpetual wonderland... full of never ending delights... goodies for all comers... everything she adores she'd find there... butterflies big as two hands, the kind that light up so bright you wouldn't need lamps after dark... you'd have their soft glows... plus flying fish... seals that tag after you like dogs... and just for laughs, swarms of acrobatic niggers peopling the forests the branches, squawking cavorting way up in the crests... gnomish creatures, monsters... but what about our bellowers over there? It suddenly comes back to me... we can't hear them anymore... The meetings in the downpour? I can't see the contortionist anymore. They've got no staying power... look at us, we held out... I kept my honey nice and warm... and we really got dumped on!... but what time is it?... what could I have been thinking of?

"Aren't you hungry, Virginia?"

Look at her, she's dying of hunger and cold! I'm nuts myself, my mind's running away with me! my mouth's running off! Christ Almighty, it's time to go! It must be at least seven! eight o'clock! On your feet, dear little birdie, let's hit the road! I give myself a shake, buck up on my legs... so numb they don't even feel the cold... the kid stays glued to the spot, curled tightly on the bench...

"Virginia, get up, my honey..."

She's so pale she scares me... she's staring off into the distance on the other side of the lawns...

"Did you catch your death?" I ask her point-blank... poor little face... "What do you see, Virginia? Your face so drawn and those big eyes?..."

Nothing's out there on the lawns... just more rain... puddles... long tatters of fog drifting along... I take a look too, peer hard... don't spot a thing... not a blessed thing... ah! wait a sec, some guy's over there... a shape heading down from the end of the lane... toward us... like a stroller... he skirts the lawn... then treads across the grass... ah! it's really true, somebody is out there... just like that all alone heading toward us... the mist dancing around him... he comes closer... freezes... starts walking again... stepping slowly... sleepwalking... very calmly... another step, then another... he's disappeared... cloaked by a gust of rain... it's coming down hard again and you can't see a thing... the girl just sits there flabbergasted...

"Don't be silly, Virginia! Virginia!"

She can't hear me... her eyes growing wider and wider... and then "Aaah! Aaah!" what a scream she lets out! then keels over, plop! she's blacked out... all in a second... I catch her... sit her up... she opens her eyes... the man is standing right in front of us... I hadn't seen him... she's staring hard at him... it was really no joke... a dizzy spell... but now she's come out of it, fluttering her eyelids, smiling... that's no ordinary character... standing there... right in front of us... he moved quickly... I saw him way out in the fog... now we make three... I look at the man... he doesn't seem embarrassed... I think he's talking to the kid... I can't be sure, my head's starting to buzz all of a sudden, like something's slicing right through it... now it's me who almost plops over... where'd this weirdo blow in from?... he's friendly as could be now... talking in French then English... I miss most everything and give up... I realize I'm sitting there with a dumb look on my face, I didn't get scared, just queasy... I can't explain what he's doing to me, it's a funny sensation... he's talking funny too, in a quavering voice... planted before us, and not budging an inch... the kid chatting away, actually kind of talkative I think... I don't understand what they're saying... bewildered, I blather on... muttering under my breath... I don't know what's happening to me. He really was a damn strange customer!... what's he after?... ah! just amazing how he's pulled the rug out from under me... he's bothering me more and more... I'd like to look at him but I'm leery... by contrast the girl grows animated... they're talking nonsense to each other, I listen in... now she's laughing uncontrollably... from the word go, they hit it off wonderfully... Christ, he's a funny bird! no ordinary character... and with one hell of a nerve! bosom buddies just like that... not a minute gone to waste!... ah! it's scary, just like with Curlers when you come down to it!... squares and parks will be the death of me!... I'd like to get a good look at this buzzard... have a man-to-man with him... nothing doing, I don't have the strength... he's got me pinned down hard... right away a queasiness... feels like a ton of bricks... in my head my limbs... I can hear his obnoxious voice... like a goat's trill, that's it, a falsetto... sort of like Sosthène's... ah! I've got to get a look at him! I force myself to look at the guy... the fact is he's ugly as sin... of course the kid doesn't think so to tell from the way she's smiling at him... she practically can't take her eyes off him... Geez, she's fascinated! ah! I stare hard at him... while I'm thinking he says something to me... I recognize him... then I don't... I'm not sure... he gives me this queasy feeling... it's him... no, it's not!... he's standing right there in the downpour... doesn't seem to notice, even though it's coming down like cats and dogs... and he's got no protection!... both of us are still under the tarpaulin... the hard rain's splattering off it...

"Well?" he asks me, "don't you have a clue, Ferdinand?"

He's talking to me... How does he know my name? I stammer, can't get out an answer... where'd this guy come from? I think hard... What wind did this funambulist blow in on? with the kid things're going great... the pair couldn't care less about me... that's how I see it... I stammer/splutter... Truth is, the guy's really given me a bad shock... he offers me his hand... I could holler, refuse it... even so I force myself! and shake firmly... his hand's hard... made of metal... and cold too... like ice... iron... He's not trembling like me, he's a rock... I look him square in the face... and then at his getup the out-of-joint bag of bones of that ugly baboon!... I don't try to hide it, I look him up and down... dressed in his black rags, every inch tattered... his hand's freezing my whole arm now... I start shaking, feel the whole side of my body go cold... he's a weird customer...

"What's going on?" I say. "What's going on?"

I just blurt out the question... can't hold my tongue... I can hear my voice but don't recognize it... I can't keep my lips buttoned... my voice sounds ugly... comes out real odd... changed like his... a dead tone, all messed up... what the hell am I doing with a voice like that? I repeat in a whisper, "What's going on?" I force myself... the words parch my throat, I can't breathe... don't I sound cute!... with my nanny goat trill!... I eyeball that lousy bum real hard... he just holds his ground, twanging/quavering... I can't catch what he's saying... he's nodding his head, talking... I look at that noggin of his... and then his whole person, his jacket, his vest, his tatters... then his trousers... just some castoff... hadn't noticed it before... hitched crookedly across his belly... his vest sloppily stitched together... just like that from rags... completely rain-soaked... but he doesn't scare me! up on my feet just as tall too! I can speak my mind and not worry... I go face-to-face with this buffoon! Stand just as stiff upright... I was smiling too I imagine...

He starts in with his questions again.

"Well, Ferdinand?"

He wants me to start talking more than anything. He pulls his hand back, offers it again... putting on airs... Maybe he'd like me to get lost?... leave the girl to him? They've all got the same obsession...

"No! No! No!" I go... That's the only word I can get out...

He holds out his hand again.

"Centipede," he announces, "Centipede!"

He introduces himself... with a bow!...

"Centipede, don't you know me? don't you remember? Centipede?"

He keeps pressing.

"So, you're back?" I go. "You're back?"

I stand up to him... hold my ground... face to face... even so I stutter... "You! You! You!" I can't stop... he creaks grimly... that's his laugh...

"You can see for yourself... you can see..." he answers...

I had a sneaking suspicion just now... but I'd told myself I was seeing things...

"Virginia?... Virginia?" He points to her with his finger... How can he know her?... he never met her... doesn't even surprise the kid... not the least bit dumbstruck... they chat away, understand each other, so it seems to me... I look at the pair... then at the grass, the sand, the puddles... if I could I'd disappear... I try to put on a good face... not a soul in the park all around us... ah! this beats all!... I'm in for it now!... what a freak coincidence! I'd looked hard at him too, that's a fact... his jacket his torn rags... his tattered duds his ugly face... a subway train ran over him!... ah! my heart's in my boots!...

"So, you're back?" I creak out. "You're back?"

Now I've got his voice... I'm shaking like a leaf, you better believe it... and me with my heart already out of whack, now racing along at a gallop... now my whole body's pounding... thump! thump! thump! thump! my butt's pounding, my asshole, I feel like screaming... ah! my throat's closing up... choking me off, tightening like a vise... I'm not about to ask him any questions! I try to act like nothing's up, push my fear into the background, force myself... for starters, we should have beat it before he showed up... that's obvious... the kid was cold... we should have looked for a restaurant... ah! got to toss this idea out, rattle him... I'm rattled too, damn it! now this funambulist's throwing a monkey wrench into the situation... It'd be a relief to start moving again, and get out of the open, the fog, the rain... "So, you clown," I'm going to say to him, "you ever eat now and then?..." That'll embarrass him but good! maybe he doesn't eat like other people anymore? Now that he's started looking like a funambulist? No ordinary character... Just watch me floor this creep!

"You! You! You!" I cluck out for starters... whining... my voice hits a high note, nothing comes out... they can't help but laugh... they jump at the chance... I'm a sensitive soul, feel uncomfortable... Virginia breaks the ice...

"Shall we go to lunch?" she proposes.

She's shivering too, from not from fear or fright that's for sure, she took a shine to Centipede right off the bat, in a flash she was his best friend... the same rigmarole like with Curlers... give her a touch of the new and unusual, and bingo! she's under your spell... she's wild about the idea, can't sit still, doesn't look at me anymore...

"Come on, let's go then! Let's go!" I recover a wisp of my voice, and squeak out... they mimic/make fun of me...

"Let's go!" they repeat in a rasp, "let's go!"

They're talking in a trill just like me now... right then Ba-room! Ba-room! Big Ben strikes six... the boom bouncing through the fog, you had to hear the reverberation... what an echo! it shook the air... lunch is long gone, Jesus! It's a lot later than that!... we've wasted hours... Ah! each stroke bongs

Centipede full force, ba-room! he sways staggers... it looks like the echo's hurting him, it sends him lurching, rattles his whole body, every last inch of his bag of bones... as though he were going to fall over with each ba-room... ah! isn't this a real kick now... I'm not the only funnyman around... the dumb bastard's hilarious too! what a scowl on his face! each ba-room sends him staggering off like a drunk... the chimes go on forever... he shuts his eyes feeling queasy... ah! what a pretty sight!... the crazy little girl's tickled to death... ah! we're getting a great show... little imps! The bongs come galloping in through the fog, from far off, from Big Ben, belting him right to his body, banging him off balance... he tries to catch himself, bucks bolt upright, creaks sniggers... it's all a big game... he's trying to take the whole business as a joke... Ah! I've about had it with this clown!... one more boom and I'm over the edge... on a sudden impulse, I snap out at him, can't hold back anymore...

"So, it's you?" I go... I'll show him what for! I touch my hand... don't say another word... just stand there like an ass... glued to the spot... ah! this feeling of emptiness... as though I've been sucked inward... forced down on my ass, my mind a muddle... I sit down... stop looking at him... I've gone and hurt myself again!... I pushed myself way beyond my strength... really overdid it... Let the filthy freak go ahead and snigger! he's just like Delphine's boyfriend that night with the cigarettes when Claben was so sick, the guy wheedled his way around her and everything... I'd wised up a little!.... This was the guy who'd fallen on the train tracks... after showing up with his two cents to put in. Ah! he'll be in for some trouble if it's up to me, just let him keep talking! he wouldn't be making any undertaker-love to me! I'd nip that in the bud, and how! succubi were tearing me limb from limb!

All the same, the little effort I'd just made did me in... I practically passed out... Ah! he was a mean rat, hair-raising, you name it... but Virginia didn't see it my way... she thought the fellow was the life of the party, comical and charming, a real treat... they were thumbing their noses at each other... chime time was over... he was standing up straight on his own two legs, he'd stopped swaying... she was still set on lunch.

"Chop! Chop! Chop!" she reminds us... ravenous... "Time to eat, gentlemen! Let's go!"

Everything gave her a terrific kick... the rain, the awful downpour, and even this silly ass! what a pal! and me down in the dumps! everything made her bust out laughing, maybe me most of all with my hangdog look... she'd splatter us with mud at every puddle... whoah, look out! splash! smack in the middle!

"Dinner! Dinner! Come and get it!"

Since they were so keen on the idea we raced along! I didn't want to lag behind... but for starters, which restaurant? where were we going to take old goat-throat? Could it be she hadn't gotten a good look at him? could it be she didn't realize?... The guy still knocked the wind out of me... so what effect would he have in public? maybe I'd have felt hungry if he wasn't around... but here with that reek... I'm sure it was coming from him. I let them get ahead of me a few steps... she was capering down the lane, showing off her thighs, coming onto him, geez! the little cockteaser! he picks up on this real fast... loves her act, starts laying it on! sweet-talking!

"Little miss! little corolla!" he calls out to her... in his trill... "You're our rose in the rain... you're just as radiant! leave us to the cold! the frost! hee! hee! hee!" With that he creaks out his snigger, an horrendous screak... rubbing all his bones together...

"I'll keep the cold all to myself!" So he declares... "The cold! The frost! hee! hee! hee!"

He's ecstatic capering around... the kid keeps skipping along, dancing all around... what a pain in the neck! letting that filthy bastard whisper sweet nothings to her... I'm getting a whiff of the guy, oh am I ever!... she adores her walking corpse! she flipped over him right away just like with that old sow this afternoon... same old story, give her something overripe and she's in bliss... she could keep this smelly pig all to herself! I can hear him clearly I come up from behind... he's clanking in every part, this perfect gentleman... making as much racket with his bones as I with my whole load of gear up on my shoulders... Clank! Clip! Clop! Clank! his entire skeleton's rattling with every jolt... plus that reek's not my imagination... I inch closer, sneak a sidewise glance... it's him, no it's not... he's sure got Centipede's mug... I wouldn't swear to it... but with that glow under his skin... that's the word for it, a glow... especially when we're walking under trees... in the shade he casts a sort of reflection, gives off a yellowish light... no ordinary sight... his whole head glows, his hands too... doesn't the kid notice too?... it's coming from him... from under his skin... headwise he's a glowworm... I'm right on that score, positive, I'm not going to ask him... he'd just dish me back some crap, he'd act arrogant... have an easy time, he'd mortify me, make me wish I were six feet under... I think before opening my trap... clank! cling! clang! clank! arrogant, the works... tagging close behind's good enough, he'd just snap back that it's all my fault his holes his reek his rags... that I'd pushed him under the train cars... where he died from his injuries, torn to pieces alive... which is why he's talking like a nanny goat now... I shouldn't have knocked him off the platform in the first place, he'd tell me... he's freezing cold and it's my fault... everything's my fault... he'll end his days talking in a trill, throwing out this huge glow all around him... ah! the more I think about it the more it fascinates me... I feel drawn by his spell... I'm like the kid when all's said and done... I give him a sniff, a listen... clank! cling! clang! clank! I'm the mutt on his trail... I give him another glance, another listen to his noisy bones... I'm slaving to keep pace under my load, struggling along, my cargo my sack of junk... limping... no problem, I'm right on their asses! they don't give me a second thought... he's going to paw her in a little while... they're already arm in arm... walking toward the gate with me behind... ah! it's him all right... it's him and none other an absolute fact... when I recognize him my heart starts pounding, this isn't just some farce, just some nightmare... Ah! I'll keep tagging behind them anyway... I'm under one hell of a load in my sack, lugging around the new supplies, and still not raising as much racket as this guy! I could feel sorry for myself, I'm suffering horrendously, my bones are aching too... My leg my arm my whole body's killing me... I'm limping I'm reeling rolling... but I'll never make as much noise as he does... his noise goes to my head, right to my head... but I'm not giving off any glow... they chat while trotting along, bantering, flirting, I can hear the whole thing... they move a little ways ahead, I catch up... another effort... I barge right between them on purpose... I can act cocky too! I want her to give me an arm, too... I want her to prop me up more than she's doing for him... I lean into her on purpose... I go sort of fuzzy, I trip... my whole kit and caboodle comes crashing down... right on our feet! Whoah! What a scowl! he's got to hoist it back up for me... I'm pressed right up against him, I breathe him in... Jesus, he reeks, no bull! he's decomposing in knockout whiffs... the pretty boy smells like a sewer in his rags! I say so right out loud! "You stink!" Doesn't the kid notice? I want her to catch a whiff so she'll realize!... he lets her sniff... I want him to disgust her... he stands still, glued to the spot so we can sniff to our heart's content... her nose must be plugged up but good! she doesn't smell a blessed thing!

"He stinks! He stinks!" I shout, yell real loud, holler into the sky. I want to cause a scene! I'm sick and tired! but there's not a soul around us, it's absolutely deserted... just the three of us in the rain plus the lawns plus the fog... I insulted him up and down, big deal, he's laughing... well in his own way, that croak of his... they're both making fun of me... this guy's a real strange one, hell, I'm not making any of this up!... where he'd come from? what's he up to? I'm through stalling, I blurt it out... right to her face pow! I pop the question... you just got to open your eyes and take a look at him! so I ask her... Doesn't the kid realize?... can't she see the guy? Can't she see what he's all about, what a screwy customer he is? And they're the ones who split their sides, who get a kick! they think I'm a scream, absolutely hysterical! How convenient this way! How very convenient! Laughing like hyenas... I won't pull a thing out of them of course... they're chuckling!... I'm busting my gut killing myself all for nothing!...

"Come on, let's go! Hit the road, you rotten bastards!"

That's how I wrap it up! one turns my stomach as much as the other! I tag behind, whacked out, I quit bitching, damn! Even so, right before Bishopsgate, another fit, another outburst of anger comes over me... right on our way out.

"Listen up, Centipede, you listen up, creep!"

With these words I corner him, block his path...
"Enough's enough! Scram!"
I want him to clear off and leave us alone... He doesn't answer, looks at me, and just places his hand on my arm, his hand meaning his pathetic excuse for a hand, a little stump of bone... that's all it takes, wham! I don't exist anymore. It's like I've been cleaned out inside... I stutter. Ah! how funny, how sidesplitting! I'm always the butt of their jokes!... the pair are jumping with joy... I feel like bumping them off! both of them! and dumping my load! the crap! I'd bring back jack shit to the old man! He'd get it right up his ass! just one more thing swiped! can somebody tell me where these two giddyheads are headed? now they're leading the way... I really don't feel like eating! I've lost my appetite! They should just go ahead and eat each other since each other's what they want! That little floozy, and that stinkpot! Go ahead, wham! get it on together! Right now! why don't they just start fucking, goddamn it! why not tie the knot, fucking Christ! they're two of a kind! I get nasty! I explode!
"Tie the knot," I holler at them! "Then go hang yourselves!"
I want to raise a hair-raising ruckus! I want to stir up the mob... and I don't pick and choose my words! I want the whole world to know! I yell at them from behind... far behind... they move quickly, now they're ditching me... I want them both to tie the knot right away! then I want to see them hang!
"Hang," I said! "Hang, fucking hell! now that's something! Hanged! Can you hear me, you stinking son of a bitch?..."
That'll draw a mob for sure!... "Hang," such a splendid word, I think! Ah! he heard me, he's turning around!
"Hang! Hang!" I holler... "You hear me: hang!"
He mustn't like it... he's heading back... I stand my ground and wait for him... we're right in front of a shop... people are gathering... putting on these looks... they must be thinking: two cutthroats, some underworld scrap... I can see we're not stirring up any warm feelings...
"Hang!" I shout at them. "Hang! You cockeyed idiots!"
They just gawk with their mouths open... they don't understand me, they're Englishmen... Centipede trills out a few words, chats them up, sets their minds at ease, points to my head, says I'm hurting, my brain's going bumpety-bump... but there's no danger whatsoever... I'm not a nasty sort...
"Hang! And hang! I'll hang every last one of you!" I holler again...
Now it's my turn for some fun... he takes my arm, leads me off... doesn't want a scene... I hoist my huge pouch my gear back up, and we're off again... with me between him and the girl!... ha! made it this time! I'm walking between, hobbling along, force them to take it slow and easy... Ah! it's not the people back there who scare me!... I'm sure about that!... it's Matthew! he's the only one who scares me! the guy who'll hang me... I tell them just be-

tween us, explain the whole story... I'm not afraid of anything Centipede can do to me, poor shitty stiff! Smelly specter! Ah! no way! I treat him like mud... he clink-clatters, creaks, casts me his bogus glow! I laugh it off! Matthew's the guy I dread! he's the worst jackal in the operation! he'll catch every last one of those pimps! and make short work of them if I know him... he's got the eye he's hungry got the taste for blood... he'll put them away no sweat! he'll be worse than a court-martial, more rotten than the war, more of a hell-bent bloodthirsty bastard than their whole war machine! Nobody needs to join up! He'll do all the work! He'll clean up the underworld single-handedly! lousy loudmouthed greedyguts! ah! I was right on the money... I had such a bad feeling about it... The Strand would be swept clean!... it's their business, damn it, after all! they thumb their noses at the beast! And old stinkpot won't be able to do a damn thing about that! Ah! I gave him an earful... He keeps listening while walking along... they'll find out what a real cop is all about! malicious English double-crosser, a Scotland Yard champ... but one cop who doesn't know me! who doesn't really know what makes me tick! I explain the whole thing to the pair, pour out my heart... they just can't run off and ditch me again!... they've got to hear the whole story!... all just one big misunderstanding, I spell it out... I surprise Matthew, I exasperate him!... I drive him berserk, into a boiling rage... he can't figure out my way of walking and talking, my gimp gimmicks, he thinks it's all an act, and I grate on his nerves... I'm number one on his shit list, he'd pack me off on any slave ship, any meat wagon, on whatever just to get rid of me, he'd string me up himself just to put an end to it all, he had zero use for me. That's the fix I found myself in after all my noble efforts!... my very existence rubs him the wrong way... all a disastrous misunderstanding, he ought to have met my parents, the very souls of loyalty, upstanding as could be, noses to the grindstone... Then he'd realize how I'd been born and bred!... I can see him over there coming to his realizations... the fine style of the Passage... my parents' lively shop... the pathetic creep'll be bowled over! A completely different class of customer than his usual fare!... especially the ladies! nothing but baronesses from high society! sophisticates from the upper crust! such distinction, such charm, you name it! plus the perfumes, the veils, the batistes and Chantilly lace!... the stupid oaf'll get all tangled up in them! it'll be a change of scene from his riffraff! I can see him, imagine the whole thing, what a kick! I can't help myself!... I can see him tangled up in the lace! gives me a fit of laughter, I'm so wound up! Ah! he'd look a sight in batiste! dirty jerk-off fuzz, I can see him! he'll give everybody a good laugh over there! Ah! I sit down I'm out of steam, it's too much for me... I'm working my head too hard... getting carried away again... There, good, I'm resting... sitting on my big sack right in the middle of the sidewalk... it bugs the other guy, he stoops, creaks, asks what's my problem.

"Hey, you look tired! Don't you want to take the underground?"

Underground? the underground? ah! I jump back... Ah! he's singing that song again! The underground?... the nerve of this guy!

"Pansy! Murderer!" I call him. "Murderer!" I yell it! shout it! I wish the people around would pounce on top of him and drag him away! They don't lay a finger on him, they just stand in a circle. I'm the only one they find unusual, they pat my head my cheeks... the other guy keeps smiling, thumbing his nose at me, jaws locked in a snarling grin... he's jerking me around for all the world to see... his own special scowl... then he takes my hand, squeezes it hard, relentlessly, I stand up like a good boy, follow him, he leads me out of the crowd nice and quiet, I fall in with his slow steady trudge... the kid's skipping along ahead... the crowd's walking a few feet behind... we form a procession of sorts... passing one street then another... I see where he's headed!... the restaurant... it's called the Corridor... it's full of candle rings, candelabras, a ritzy joint... I'd never have dared walk through the door... now it's his turn to pull one over on me... he read my mind... the superperceptive rotten bastard!

"Let's go in," he says, cocksure, barging right inside, high and mighty... my heart's in my boots... Ah! nothing'll rattle him, the darling! The waiters scurry to his side... the maître d' gives him a deep bow... they're awaiting his orders... the people outside are the ones who're really floored, they'd no idea we were so chic... they press their noses against the windowpanes, they see the respect we command... we're seated in a snap... cushions armchairs the works, we settle into the cushy surroundings... I think we've really got the best table... flowers, roses galore, a gorgeous centerpiece... were they expecting us?... but it's not just the flowers spreading their fragrance, once I'm in my seat I catch a powerful whiff... coming from underneath!... I knew it'd kill my appetite!... a musty funky sickly stink... I'd love to ask them to open the windows... it's going to get awfully stuffy in here... it smells like wax plus something else... obviously it doesn't bother him... nor the kid, not at all... I'm not going to start sulking again... it's a smell of wax, end of story... even so, the little kid's onto something, wriggling her nostrils... like a bunny... sniffing all around... no, not the people at the next table... uh-uh, can't be! it's a real peculiar odor, a stench I'm familiar with... He sees us sniffing... it puts him in a terrific mood... he starts winking at me knowingly... Ah! he's doing his stuff!... My appetite's back, you better believe it... I glance down at the menu, but the smell comes up in my face! I take another whiff, it's real revolting, thickening beneath us, he must be stirring things around under the tablecloth, his body remnants... I really don't get any of this... it's still him, his stench! I'd bet my life!... ah! I'm going to let him know, oh hell, he should just leave! I pinch my nostrils between two fingers... right in front of his face so he'll get the message... not very subtle... we're sitting right across from each other!...

"No! No! No! No!" he protests, "No! No!"

Ah! he's going too far! I'll whisper to him... I lean over the table, looking down I have a good view... right into his ear... all green stuck to his neck, with shreds of flesh missing... plus this kind of gunk oozing down... shreds of pink and yellow skin... ah! how incredibly gross!...

"You putrid carcass!" I whisper, "You putrid carcass!" I just blurt it out... straight into his ear...

"Right you are! Right you are!"

He's not bent out of shape, look at him laughing harder than ever! he thinks I'm an amazing joker... he screaks, that laugh of his... his jaws clench grind... teeth clacking together... an old grandfather clock in his mouth... his way of enjoying a joke... he agrees, he's in ecstasy... rasps out his bone-racket on purpose... stops trying to cover it up, he's a stiff and that's that! Real fast I plop back into my seat... quick, got to change the subject... I'm going to order... but he beats me to it! quavering out to the whole room... everybody has to lend an ear... he insists... that's his style, good cheer for one and all... my remark threw him in a fit... he's literally exulting... ordering over the hors d'oeuvres, the big pedestal table loaded with grub... an unbelievable spread... olives and caviar in a sauce, stuffed herring with mayonnaise, and pineapple with tomatoes... he gives me a hard stare, watches my expression... maybe I feel like puking? I hold back, fight the urge, stare back at him over the olives, right into his big eye sockets, he's riveting me I'm riveting him back... there's a glimmer deep in his eyes... a sort of phosphorescence... followed by a faint sparkle, and then the show's over... the guy's got it all, he's out of this world... just like Achille Norbert, the mummy they're going to stick in some sideshow... Nelson and Pépé I mean! Not Sosthène! That other clown! Ah! I mustn't get them all mixed up! In the end they put my head in a whirl, battling inside my brain! mustn't get muddled! I give him another hard stare over the hors d'oeuvres plates... he won't scare me, I don't lower my eyes... so it's him, huh? Big deal! So what? Hell, I'm fed up! I settle back down clam up... what else am I supposed to say to that ugly creep? apologize maybe? Ah! fuck no! I'd rather fling him under the train again! Hardened murderer that I am! I'd love seeing him all mashed up again, end of story! And I want him to know, right here and now! I want him to be real clear! And not go thinking that I'm waffling! not any more than he is, the lousy shit! Go on! Do it! I'll chew him out! No, in a little while... in a little while... it'd be smart of me to hold off a little... he uses the chance to stink up the place... put a sparkle in his pupils...

"Glowworm!" I shout at him, "Glowworm!..."

He points to the caviar...

"Won't you have some?"

Acting like nothing's up... the little girl totally out of it... all she thinks of is her appetite, picking a little here a little there... licking her chops... a kid through and through... he recommends the shrimp to her... they practically fight over them... ah! what a ploy!... carrying on like he's an expert, then a scatterbrain, like he doesn't know anything! he looks at the menu upside down... another fit of giggles... I'm going to put a lid on this...

"You're crazy, aren't you, Centipede!"

That's what I dish out at him, in a harsh no-nonsense voice... I want to rattle the son of a bitch!... No more hush-hush in his ear!... I psych myself up...

"Ah!" he answers... sweetly suspicious... "Think so? Think so, young man!"

He takes it as a compliment... about how snazzy he looks tonight... and then he moves right along, places his order, delighted! in a very loud trill on purpose! so that everybody at the surrounding tables can listen in... and I'm sniffing him, sniffing away, can't stop... his reek from under the table packs a wallop!... it can knock you on your ass!

"Centipede! Centipede!"

I pour it on... I want that walking boneyard to catch on... Ah! All right already! his mind's miles away, he's big-mouthing off to the room at large, I'm not going to steal his thunder... he's ranting against the movies... the hottest films... dope straight from the horse's mouth... attracting glances attention... drawing all eyes on us how awful... everybody freezes forks in midair... he's about to get in the way of the waiters working himself up gesticulating... plus gleaming deep in his eyes... a striking performance... And so he wraps up a tirade about the actors who are all the rage...

"They're all ghosts! Hee! Hee! Hee! They're all ghosts!..."

He thinks that's the wittiest remark in the world, he wants us all to join in with his hee! hee! hee!, but he's just feeding these folks a line all the same... they think he's an outrageous eccentric... they're all ears... they've stopped swallowing... his success goes to his head! he's on top of the world, fired up, the freak! His racket and that trill are horrendous, his whole bag of bones clinking wriggling... and this reek in the restaurant!... the guy's got diarrhea of the mouth... bursting with more information than anybody around. He spins his yarns, and he knows what from! dumbfounding his audience... the dirtiest dirt... the pig's so snoopy! about the most famous stars... flipping back and forth between English and French... Mr. International!... about Max Linder... Pearl White! about Judex! Suzanne Grandais: he knows how to keep his public hooked... and don't forget about the music hall theaters! the stage actors the clever wags... dirt on Basil Hallam, Ethel... he's especially enthused about Basil! the star attraction of the Strand Revue... Basil the charming lisper... the way Centipede belts out all those choruses... you just had to hear... the way he lisps the lyrics in his quavering trill...

I'm Gilbert the Filbert!
The Prince of the nuts!

He did a perfect impersonation... and everybody had to pick up the chorus! he beats time with his knife... and then he moves on to Ethel, with her mannish voice... here he's a riot, he goes all out... Ethel Levy in her operetta...

Watch your step! Watch your step!
She's an adventure!...

The customers repeat the lyrics mumbling... Damn! that ticks him off! Shh! enough! everybody just knock it off... Quiet! He has something important to say... he wants to tell me in secret... no, both of us, Virginia too!... we need to lean close to his mouth... This gets really gross again... he wants to whisper right up against our ears.

"Listen," he goes to me, "Listen to me good! Gloria Day mean anything to you? No! No! Not her!" he changes his mind... "No, she's not the one! nope! Goddamn it, not her!"

What a big boo-boo! He bops his skull bonk! bonk! bonk! with his knife handle, the way I did on the bed frame... His head sounds hollow... but this gets his brain working... jogs loose the facts... eloquently...

"Gaby Deslys! Ladies and gentlemen! Gaby Deslys! That's the woman!..."

He addresses the entire restaurant.

"Listen closely! I'm announcing that she's dead! Harry Pilcer's dancer! dear sweet ravishing soul... she passed away this very morning... hee! hee! hee! Do you all hear me? I saw her pass away..."

The diners trade puzzled glances... they can't figure out what all this has to do with the hors d'oeuvres...

"But it's true! It is!" he insists... and bursts out laughing, absolutely delighted. "Isn't that right, Ferdinand! Ghosts! nothing but ghosts, Ferdinand!"

He calls on me in front of everyone, takes me to witness... I'm his crony... I can't blow him off he'd get sore... he'd go berserk, it'd be an ugly scene... he has a spooky laugh, that's all... Gaby Deslys was a big celebrity... they just can't believe the announcement.

"Ghosts! Ghosts!" He was back to that tune, glad he was shaking them up so badly they didn't know whether they were coming or going...

"Isn't that right, Ferdinand? Isn't it? nothing but ghosts!"

Ah! I wasn't going to tell him no!

"Certainly, Centipede! certainly! you're dead right!"

I sort of wanted to change the subject.

"The soup!" I call out. "The soup!"

A gutsy move... as though I were hungry!

"Ah! why, as a matter of fact, yes indeed!"

Damn dizzy fool! He remembers... He gives his skull another good bonk, it snaps him into a whole new frame of mind.

"Garçon! Ober! Waiter! Hash-slinger! Kellner, schnell! schnell!"

He calls them in all languages... he wants the whole crew at the same time... such a practical joker! and so young!

"For starters, bring us a chicken! a nice chicken in a cream sauce! Make sure you don't forget the cream!"

He gives me a mischievous wink.

"Ah! Cream's so wonderful! You'll see, my little friends! You'll lick your chops! You still hungry, darling? what about you, clown?"

"Sort of...," I answer.

"What about having some crab? Caviar? Quenelles maybe?" He suggests everything...

He wants to turn my stomach, he knows what he's up to with his stink... He's starting to grate on my nerves again.

"So, you're in the money, Mr. Centipede?" I remark to him in a very loud voice.

"Oh, in the money... the money?... That's one way of putting it! it comes and it goes, that's all... I keep the cash circulating!... I inherit I spend... you see, I inherit every day, get me?"

He's completely unflappable. He gives me details... like it's no big deal...

"Every minute I've got something rolling in, get me? Small fortunes here and there... hee! hee! hee! a little from all over the place! when all's said and done it really adds up! It never stops! I've got plenty!"

What a funny setup! He split his sides at the very thought... the way the dough came into his hands... just kept coming and coming... the kid didn't understand a word he was saying, she just laughed along with him... she must have thought she was at some puppet show... and he had them rolling in the aisles!... a babe in the woods! He repeated how he understood everything...

"It keeps rolling in... rolling in!" he's all worked up wriggling around! "Hard cash! Hee! Hee! Open around the clock, ladies and gentlemen! Corner House! around the clock! Day and night."

Honest, what a clown! A real scream! "Day and night," he repeats, he came up with that one himself... like Lyon's, the big pub over in Leicester! One hell of a prankster, honest! Who let this guy out in the street? He casts a glow all around his head, given off by his clothes... a glitter deep in his eyes, his mystical way. Achille won't go over any better than this character! It dawns on me while I sit looking at him... the mummy poster... even with the light bulbs, the works... they could go all out slapping his remains back together... but they wouldn't come up with anything more extraordinary... they should have picked this guy here... I'd gladly have wrapped him up with a bow for them... The people around us are catching his whiff even so... starting to grow concerned... They look at me, my heart's in my boots... they're wondering where that swampy stink could be coming from... they pick up their plates with both hands, push their noses in their steaks and sniff... ah! all of a sudden they're hilarious... I start laughing hysterically, can't stop... now all three of us are yukking it up... all those people sniffing like crazy. The old funambulist isn't worried. "Hard cash!" he squeals, he thinks that's a real hot one... The kid's hooked all the same.

"Isn't he funny? Don't you think so?"

"He kills me," I answer.

That triggers more hysterical laughter from him. But he's miffed that I'm putting up a fight, not puking in my plate. Only Virginia doesn't smell a thing, doesn't notice the foul stink... it's extraordinary... she's delighted and that's that... she adores the restaurant, all these people... the music... this is a lark! and with her uncle waiting for us back at the house!... the party's in full swing... Her turned-up snub nose quivers, I can see she's about to pop a question... a kitten's curiosity.

"Have you known him long?"

She just comes out and asks Centipede... brazen of her I think... talking about me...

"Forever, dear girl! Nobody knows him better than I do!"

And that really sets him off! What a lucky break!

"Oh brother, do we ever know each other! You better believe it, miss! Just ask him and see... He can throw one hell of a tantrum! He flares up, flies into flaming fits, boils over! I know you, don't I, you powder keg!"

He follows that by flashing grins that grind his choppers down to stumps... castanets rattling through his head... and then from down under, a rotting corpse reek that could knock out a battalion... the others in the room are still sniffing, digging into their steaks, they're totally oblivious...

He wants an ovation, that's a fact! This funambulist's one hell of a ham!

"Little girl, I know a few tricks you don't see every day! I'm not just blowing my own horn either! the funniest routines on stage! I know what I'm talking about! The most sidesplitting sideshow antics!"

He gives me a wink naturally... He saw I was thinking about Achille... he could read it on my face... ah! I hate being an open book!...

"Yep!" he keeps hammering away, "without blowing my own horn! not your usual numbers! I picked them up way back when!"

He follows that by heaving one of those sad break-your-heart sighs, an enormous huff out his nose... sounds like a big burp... and what a stink! horrendous... I barely grab hold of myself, I was about to black out... he nearly got me that time, the pig!...

"It was another world!" he goes on... lost in a dream... incredibly wistful... he winks...

"In America?" the kid asks... it makes America pop into her head.

"No, no, miss... in Paris..."

"Paris! Paris!" She fidgets... she really wants to see Paris too... first off, she wants to go everywhere... and then she suddenly becomes sad... starts mumbling... she's been to Paris it seems to me... with her uncle... now she's talking as in a dream... not your usual mood!... she's also waxing nostalgic... ah! where'd she pick this up?... she's mimicking Centipede! "Often, often in Paris..." she's mumbling like that... incredibly sad... "with my aunt, my uncle, everything... dear little auntie, dear little uncle!... dresses hat lace... all for my aunt... dresses! dresses! me too, you know! dresses!" A coquette's nostalgia at her age!... she's awfully sad and then real cheerful... from one second to the next... and then she sobs...

"You didn't know my auntie?" she asks me, just like that, awfully innocent awfully grief-stricken... as though everybody knew everybody else... Another example of that crummy stiff's work! He's positively breaking the kid's heart.

Even foxier than he aims to be!

"I know everybody, miss!"

"Everybody? What about your mother, you creep?"

Bam! I shut his trap on the spot...

"Ever catch a glimpse of my guts once or twice before?"

He snaps back angrily... I see his hands drop, rummaging around his rags. He's going to dig out his crap. I'm about to retch, I'm beaten... I clam up, swallow my tongue... but I've made him sore, he's stopped glowing, stopped grinding his teeth, stopped everything, he was just plopped there drably in his seat... stubbornly... the rotten old grouch... stopped giving off his glow... sulking... the goddamned kid's back at it again... she absolutely wants to know...

"But my aunt's dead, sir... she was so nice... nice..."

What a conversation...

I jab her with my knee, she doesn't catch on.

"She's dead, you know, sir..."

She repeats. He snaps around to face her.

"Nobody killed your aunt, did they?"

Real terrific impression on the people around us...

The kid's eyes pop wide open, she doesn't know what the words mean anymore... she repeats "killed her... killed her..." she looks around the room... at the people...

He leans over, asks her bluntly, "She didn't have an accident?"

Then he starts creaking, rattling, raising such a racket from his bag of bones, the glasses, plates, that I think he's going to send the whole lot crashing to the floor... what a ruckus, rocked by his giddy fit...

"Ah! how funny it is! ah! can't you see?" he trills so shrilly that it scrapes and rattles the windows.

"An accident! An accident! I don't believe in accidents!"

The way he's carrying on... squealing... such a disgraceful spectacle... I glance over at the manager, he's standing there in his tails... Why not show this guy the door?... Is he under his spell too? Can't he smell the stink? It looks like he holds Centipede in high regard, with respect, studying him from a distance... This can't go on.

"He's a skeleton!" I shout over at him loud and clear... I made no bones about it... He acts like he didn't hear a word... the poor little kid is shattered... what a lout!... her cute distressed face... completely bowled over she gazes at that monster... we're in a jam! but if the cops showed up it'd go from bad to worse... what a twisted situation... I sit back down, listen to his bullshit... Geez, he's bewitching everybody! nobody dares utter a word... it's an extraordinary spell... even so the funambulist's bubble has burst! his question about the aunt was plain dumb! what the hell did that have to do with anything?... murder! murder! that's all he can yap about... all for my benefit! I saw him coming! Let him go right on creaking out that laugh of his... I could give a good goddamn about the hints he was dropping! I was a hardened murderer, and totally upfront about it! flaunting my medals, honors, you name it! so watch out, poor knucklebones! Great idea for him to keep shooting his mouth off, bullshitting like that, like there's no tomorrow, because just another word or two and he'll be twisting her around his little finger, and swipe her away from me with his mystico-hocus-pocus... in the end she sees everything though his eyes... at her age the ghostly and supernatural cast a glamorous charm, lucky thing he screwed up badly, and dropped a brick, wham!... ah! she couldn't get over her aunt, she was grief-stricken, the poor little dear!... so cheery just a minute before!... ah! he'd won, the dead meat! the skeleton! but what a gaffe! and he still wanted to pick up where he left off, but had no idea what tack to take... he was sort of aware of what he'd done, tried to make up for it... he didn't mean that, he meant something else! He was wallowing in his quicksand, sinking fast with his fits of teeth-screaking laughter... ah! he was working himself up to a feverish pitch-black... poor pathetic slob! suddenly he lights up inside, all his skin starts glowing... he wants to recapture his razzle-dazzle... he can't just sit still... he's got to be the center of attention... she's shut her eyes and ears to him... all she can do now is let the tears roll down her cheeks... ah! what a terrific twist!... what a fiasco! and am I ever jumping for joy inside... but I'm not casting any glow... not rattling around as much either, I hope... Mr. Joker from the Beyond! Tail between his legs now... forgotten how to place an order... now the waiters are making up for it, really pouring on the service... bringing everything... three salad bowls of celery... plus a pedestal table of roasted fowl... I wish they'd ease up a little, give me a breather... well, so to speak... I couldn't catch my breath in that reek... three more big platefuls of cold meat... everything comes in threes... cold cuts and blood... three gravy boats full... plus three more bowls of a green-yellow juice... I feel like I'm going to be sick... he's eyeing me.

"For the members of the family!"

He lashes out, creaking laughter... witty barbs are his specialty... he repeats his remark... I keep a lid on my anger, I'm stoical... the manager's watching us... but I've got this taste of something in my mouth... something extraordinary, frightening!... I snatch a piece of bread and start chewing chewing... and don't stop, I don't want to puke! The girl doesn't want to overdo it with her sulking... seeing my hearty appetite she takes a little taste too, picking at all the plates... I keep stuffing myself with bread... and what about him? I'd like to see how he'll manage to chomp away... he just watches us eat that's all...

"Aren't you eating?" I shout at him, "Monsieur Eau de Cat Piss?"

"Oh, I don't need to, you know... just a little daisy... by the root..."

Another ironic jab... he'll never change... But as for booze, Christ Almighty! break out the bottles, let's tie one on! for starters, some wine! Banyuls! the kid's got to drown her grief! he has to undo the harm he did! he pours her a glass... we pour ourselves one... she pours us one... and more wines, redder and redder... nothing too pricey, he said... she's talking, talking up a storm, the kid's tipsy! Yackety yak!... it didn't take long... going on about how we're leaving for America... the price of the trip, the maps... the fake passports we'd have... she tells all, got to treat the guy... mentions how I'll drop my name Ferdinand... This is a genuine deposition. Ah! foxy half-crocked kid! I jab her with my knee under the table, does no good... just blah-blah-blah-blah!... she wants to be the center of attention, in a flash she's an idiot... plus she's playing to the entire room... she has to have everybody's ears, she's just like the other stinkpot! I could wring both their necks! everything for the whole world to hear... English words French words... This is just what he was waiting for, sweetie!... it's a real lucky break! and is he ever ecstatic! he's regained the upper hand.

"This is just what I've been waiting for! This is just what I've been waiting for!" He screaks very loudly. "Great going! Great going, Ferdinand!" He's behind me all the way one hundred percent... the people are interested too, they're getting a kick out of our conversation... now nothing will make the little hell-raiser shut her trap! And the crap she can come out with! Ah! we're creating a real sensation... nobody'll forget we've been here... it would be pretty funny in a way if it weren't for that putrid reek... but it doesn't seem to bother anybody, the only person it bugs is me... the customers are chattering away, guffawing... they let gibes fly at us... Ah! nothing kills their appetite... I'm the only one who can't stomach a bite... Centipede doesn't hold any grudge at all against me... Even though I just put him in his place a second back... we've never been better buddies...

"Damned Ferdinand!" he keeps calling me... and following up with one of those wallops to the back! what a horrendous hand... a whole lot harder than mine... really nothing but bone! I feel like screaming at each thwack... but I don't let out a peep...

He wants to make a toast...

"To the young couple! Hip! hip!" He invites the room to join in.

"Hip! hip! hurrah!" they answer in chorus.

They pig out worse than before... the whole restaurant's noisy as a trough... oh! but our swindler looks different now, I mean his glow, he's flickered out... Oh! a question! he smacks his skull, the bone echoes like a bell.

"What about your uncle, is he in the know?"

This is what worries him all of a sudden... For starters, where's he know her uncle from? He's never laid eyes on him... The kid's unconcerned, she's goofing around, shooting pieces of bread all over the room... she's totally out of control, it's the wine, the little lush!...

"Uncle! Uncle! he doesn't care!"

She pours some bubbly, just for herself.

"You'll need a lot of sterlings!"

He's back on that, it's nagging him.

"Hoards of money! hoards of money!"

He screaks it out again so shrilly, so sharply and shrilly that the waiters freeze in their tracks...

"I'm trembling for you!" he squeals, "I'm trembling for the pair of you!"

And he's off again clanking/crunching/clinking louder than ever before... his whole bag of bones... a racket like a hundred sticks rattling around in a box... at the same time it's funny... some diners are laughing...

"I can see you're getting off to a bad start, my children!"

He's still moaning over us.

The people are moaning along with him, they mimic his shrill whining... He heaves a sigh, they sigh...

"The Pacific's far away! It's far! It costs a fortune! at least five hundred pounds, my darlings! the boat! the boats! the soup!"

Ah! he's really bullshitting now... I won't allow it! I shut his trap.

"It's cheaper than Tibet, come on now!"

He's not going to get away pulling any crap! I've got the figures in my pocket!

Tibet! Tibet! what fuse did I light with that word! ah! he jumps up in his seat! such an outcry!

"Tibet!" he squeals. "Tibet, Tibet! Will you listen to that!"

Every part of him's shaking, giggling, wriggling... all his joints are cracking, his head's joggling around, with every shout he springs three feet into the air... such suffering, what an horrendous sight... ah! what did I say with that one simple word, Tibet!

And then, surprise, he pitch-blacks into me, pinching me, roughing me up! He thinks I'm a scream! sidesplitting! he wants us to howl together, and to bring down the roof too! to rabble-rouse our audience! What a live wire! he gives me one of his bone-shattering thwacks! his hands meaner than clubs. I'll never be able to walk again if he keeps whacking me this way!... I yank myself up by the arms, change seats... ah! that makes him laugh even harder... just despicable how he's kicking up one hell of a stench with all his jiggling and pirouetting... that foul reek of his is ghastly... he wallops me real hard on my back... all in fun! I don't hem and haw, just belt him back... he raises his arm to hit me, baring the hole under his sleeve... the cavity, the flesh, the rotting shreds... he's coming all unraveled inside... you can get a good look there... plus his ribs!

"I'm going to let you have it!" I shout, "you rotten bastard! I'm going to knock some sense into you, you putrid piece of shit! I don't give a damn about any scenes, you hear me?"

Ah! I'm furious! I think his odor's to blame more than anything... and nobody else smells a thing!

"You lousy bastard!" I light into him, "get your rags up out of that chair! You ham! You slimeball! Let them see where you crawled out from! I'm not some little girl, you filthy turd!"

That's the tack I took.

"Tibet! Tibet!" I keep repeating. "Tibet's exactly what you heard!"

I want him to know!

"So it bugs you, does it, you asshole? You scumbag?"

And then I look him right between the eyes, stare hard right into his sockets... I want to see if he'll strike back... ah! he's tr... tri... trilling for a second... doesn't know what's happening... surprised by the attack... But he snaps back quickly, that piece of grave dropping! At the top of his lungs he belts out! Let'er rip!

And through the holes in the roof
The sun shone down upon us
And in passing flashed to all
A bright little smile... smile... smile

It's a quatrain from the Second Empire!... he whispers it in my ear... followed by another couplet! and then two!... and then he's back on his pet subject... our trip, what else! our damned trip! ah! it's eating away at him!...

"It costs an arm and a leg, Ferdinand! An absolute arm and a leg! that's what it adds up to!..."

He's emphatic on that point.

"Do you have five hundred pounds, Ferdinand? Huh, do you? You little bugger?"

I've got no answer for that. He caught me off guard.

"Well, you can't leave then! Nothing's more expensive than ships! plus the dishes! plus the rest of your ménage! Can't do without dishes on the other side of the world! And a skiff for trips across the waves!"

Little cabin boy, sail on!
Little cradle, little skiff,
For trips across the waves!

His voice scratches screaks screws up... pure hell on the ears... and he wants everybody to join in... conducting with a fork...

Ah! what a birdbrain! he whacks his skull, maybe to knock loose another bright idea? No, something that slipped his mind!

"What thoughtlessness, my sweethearts! Why, the cradle is life!"

And he's off on a lullaby, mushy at present, a nanny.

Beddy-bye, my cuddly little buddy!

Followed by a big swig of bubbly!

Time for your milkie!

Clever move! Ah! so fine and dandy he is, the blithering idiot stiff! cooing to the angels! A delight to see him so carefree!

And he has a few other funny tricks up his sleeve! a big announcement!

"But I've got a cradle, you little scamp!" He's talking to Virginia.

"Cwadle! Cwadle!" he's lisping, nonstop... "Cwadle!" Now he's in a frenzy of exultation... Over the idea of his "cwadle"... I try to put a stop to it... he reeks something fierce when he starts fidgeting around...

"Enough! enough!" I order him. I try to think up a reason... "You're going to hurt yourself!"

"Ah! Hurt! Hurt! Just listen to him!" He points me out to the audience. "The nerve of the guy! Ladies and gentlemen! The nerve of him!"

No chance for me now but to swallow my words.

The girl's found some great consolation, she's dishing herself out some strawberries and cream, with mounds of sugar... he drowns it all in champagne... a concoction that goes right to your head!... and she's already tipsy! they're having a ball! the little hell-raiser!... now she wants grapes... he's got to go dig up some! he rises, crosses the entire room with that robotlike tread of his... his walk makes the people laugh... he's doing a famous routine... mimicking Buster Keaton... the disturbing comic back in those days... He returns to his seat, full of himself... the kid stammers, she can't stop...

"What's 'ménage'?" she asks him... the word he used a while back... she didn't understand 'ménage': "'Ménage'... 'ménage'? 'Ménage'? What is it?"

"'Ménage'? But come, come! home sweet home! darling, dearest Virginia!"

Ah! how fine and dandy! such perfect timing! He's peeling her grapes... The pair are as thick as thieves... each as bouncy as the other... it's a champagne romance! a duet of bubbly laughter... his, a shrill hoarse rattle... hers, a rippling warble... she's fidgeting around on her little fanny in delight, wildly mischievous... I look real smart... he's shaking/jittering his whole bag of bones, constantly laughing at his own dumb jokes... I look like even more of a jerk-off dummy just sitting there like a lump, grouchy, maybe I ought to start fidgeting around too, carrying on, snappy and wisecracking? Toss out a few digs! But he shuts me up, shoots straight up in his seat, raises his glass to our health. He's going to make a toast... while at the same time his whole head's ringed with a glow, glittering like fireflies...

"Spare a few coins!" he shouts... "A few coins for the kids! Money, money for the lovebirds!"

But it was just a trick! a hoax! he was loaded with dough, so he bends down and whispers in my ear.

"Money, you bet, buddy, loads and loads! all these people around here don't have a clue what it's like! numbskulls! numbskulls! chumps!" He flicks them away with a wave... "They're nobodies!"

And he starts jiggling again, so worked up he sets the whole table rattling... he's getting a crazy kick out of all this... and the kid's right behind...

"Strawberries, Ferdinand! Strawberries!" she offers me... she doesn't know what she's saying...

Wham! it's all over, onto something new! he doesn't want to stay another second! we're clearing out, and fast!

"Check! Check!" he commands. And make it snappy! I hardly touched a thing, I couldn't get that stink out of my mouth... the girl did us all justice... I glance at the check, what a whopper!... with both arms he digs deep down in his rags over his belly... right against it... he brings out a big bundle of bills from the cavity deep inside... pounds sterling... digs back down, rummages around... now comes back up with fistfuls of wadded dollars... he tosses the whole pile on the table...

"I'm loaded," he squeals, "I'm loaded! I'm fat, my children, though I don't look it!"

He fills two plates with sterlings, a jumble of bills, Banque de France francs... all damp and icky/sticky...

"And now for some gold!" he announces.

All heads turn at the word... he's hoodwinking everybody, that's obvious... you had to see his magic act... the way his hair lights up, well, his excuse for hair, that sort of bristle... teeming inside, swarming, maggots of light... his putrid phosphorescence... I had my jaw in my lap I confess... he keeps yanking out fistfuls of gold... brutally turning himself inside out... coming up with another plateful, then another... Can you beat that! small heaps of louis d'or... and the waiters' eyes big as the plates! now that's prestidigitation!... a black magician! and these gold mines for a tip! genuine louis in teeter-tottering piles... it's dirty money for sure! he can afford to be generous! where he'd dig up that Klondike? all from his trousers? clever bastard, what an operator!

"You're more fun than a barrel of monkeys!"

That's what the child tells him. He's a hit! He's never been in more brilliant form! or jiggled so much! and it still isn't enough! she razzes him! sss! sss! he's got to come up with some more treasures... hunting around real deep... he works himself into a fury digging like a dog in the roots of a tree... he comes back up with everything... more cash more sterlings... more twenty-franc pieces... he flings them all up to the ceiling... and now his tour de force: he tilts his hideous kisser in the air and snags the louis on their way down... swallows them... then he fetches them back from his trousers... with both arms rooting inside... shows his whole body's hollow... shows everybody he's walking openwork... what an extraordinary stunt! the child's tipsy, she doesn't realize, she's red, crimson... what terrific work! she's carrying on something disgraceful... her skirt hitched way up... exposing all her thighs... she props her feet on the wall seat... they're both going ape...

"I'll call you Punch!"

"Mr. Gollywog, if you please!"

"No, I'll call you Lord Centipede!"

That's the way they banter back and forth. A shower of gold! A shower of gold! and such laughter! The customers are crawling after the riches, I see them on all fours pecking away! Now they're attacking me... I mean, my two cocky friends... Because I'm putting on a face, I'm a party pooper, that's how they think I'm acting... some jealous bum.

"Look at Ferdinand!"

I don't look well, naturally, but I'm not about to split my sides, go into stitches over such shit, such crapola from some putrid cutthroat, a freak on the loose from some graveyard! ah! dirty son of a bitch! That guy really riles me... and turns my stomach! I'm ready to black out from the stink, that's what I think about his cleverness! and I'm fighting back! fighting hard! Doesn't the kid smell anything?

"Don't you smell anything, little girl? Take a whiff, for Christ's sake!"

Ah! she can really make me as mad as hell, that depraved piece of jailbait, that bitch! she absolutely infuriates me... she doesn't pick up a single hint... she's sloshed, simple as that... I'm such a killjoy, me, a killjoy! That's what they keep repeating... She can go right ahead and get it on with the bag of bones, get plugged by Lord Maggot since she's so nuts about him! All women are sluts from the day they're born.

"So let's get going then! And shake a leg!"

I'm sick to death of their harebrained whims. I've laughed enough for the time being. I think I've had plenty to drink too, when all's said... I needed a few, and of the bubbly... to help me beat the stink... I'm not used to liquor... in any case I have a good view of those thighs... Virginia's, I mean... like a young boy's, strong, muscular, pink, solid, that about does it. So maybe I'm drunk, but I'm levelheaded... I'm not some sex fiend... wonderful thighs, I'm telling you, magnificent specimens... but the little girl's nasty... a sly minx from the day she was born, it's in her blood... and debauchery turns her on... the monstrous whambams... that's what it's all about! that's the snag! I saw it all with my own eyes, her and Curlers! the sideshow! I've really had an eyeful today! An experience of hitting rock bottom! thighs like that... ten... twelve years old... Curlers is fifty... a good guess! with a solid gray, hairy ass! Ah! what a fine home sweet home... home sweet whores! depraved and cunning!

"I'll call you Gollywog!"

I heard that! Maggot's worst promises! Virginia, my sweetheart, she's the heartbreaking angel in the flesh, Cupid with his arrow ripping apart my guts... these aren't war wounds, but far more agonizing tortures... and I don't want to see the rest, goddamn it! his complete bag of magic tricks! First off, let's blow this joint! He stinks too much indoors and he's thrown away enough louis d'or. Me, a killjoy? What damned nerve! I'm the happy-go-luckiest of the gang! Just wait and see, my little errand girl! My limbs've been pumped full of lead but I'm still the funniest guy of the bunch! You can't have a good time without a few drinks! Me, jealous? You won't get any fight from me! Whoever wants to, come and get my tramp! I'm suffering, I'm an open wound, that's a fact! plus my agony saps the strength from my injured limbs... but I'll laugh last some other time! during some other fireworks display! some other war that'll reduce the world to ashes! That'll last and last and go nowhere for centuries on end! ah! I won't act shy then! At the first shot I'll be general! Now I'm feeling pretty crummy, still up to my antics but without much pizzazz, I couldn't even throw a tantrum... I'd only be able to manage a little nibble out of my sassy brazen vixen, from under her little checkered skirt... with my own eyes I watched the way Curlers sunk her teeth in, and she didn't act shy... a little fling in broad daylight and in full view of everybody in the square... both wriggling around, getting a big bang... another second or two and she would have made off with my little devil... right in the middle of Leicester, and that's no lie! the girl's skirt hitched all the way up!... and me cuckolded in the bright sunshine... checkered skirt... they were positively wild about each other... so shameless, fast and loose they set your mind on fire... and I was like a sleepwalker! and those raw visions kept flaring up at the drop of a hat... I felt like screaming! Ah! I had to quit thinking...

"Come on! What the hell're we doing?"

I get up. Enough already! Let's leave! I start heading out.

"What're you hashing over in there, Mr. Millionaire?" That's the line I take with him... "Endless!..." I want to show I don't give a damn about guys like him.

The fact is he doesn't want to move a muscle. Slowly he sips his coffee...

I'm sure I'm smelling like a corpse too on account of being so up close pressed together... constantly rubbing up against him... I sniff sniff, they're the ones poking fun at me... they must think I'm some bumpkin who jumps at every boo... they glance at each other, sort of uncomfortable... I don't give a damn, I'm determined. He's aware who he's dealing with.

"So, you both leaving?"

He's back on the attack.

"To the ends of the earth, Frère Jacques!"

Can't let him get it into his head that I'm going to chicken out! I'm more determined than ever, and how! He wants to wear me down with remorse, knock me over with sighs! ah! poor daisy! He's going to find out how tough I can be! The old glowworm's underestimating me! I'll do anything to save my vixen! anything to rescue her from this evil spell, from the skullduggeries of the catacombs! ah! Trickster from the crypt! Just step outside and get lost! And leave us alone, you glorified bag of bones! Outside, I said! I'm willing and loyal! I want my idol all to myself! I want to ravish her! kidnap her! take her away with me! rescue her from temptation! I'll kill whoever stands in my way! whether he glows in the dark or not! Goddamn asshole! To the ends of the earth I said! I'm burning up with excitement! And it's not the wine, it's the thought, the feeling, the hot rush of indignation, of love!

"Didn't we both promise we're leaving? Didn't we, Virginia?"

She's got to come out and speak her mind, the flighty thing! Oh youth, youth, what a headache! Innocence, what a load of crap! Never too young to put me in my grave! I want her to promise this very instant! I beg her implore her... we've got to settle this once and for all... plus she should dump the creep herself... and not in ten years but pronto! let him go shine somewhere else! Let him go dig up Nelson and Pépé, and Achille while he's at it! They'd make one hell of an act! Ah! the glowworm stiff! There's the door! No luck! He's stinking us up, that's what he's doing, he's making us sick!

"Tell him, Virginia! You tell him yourself! Yank him off! Send him packing! Tell him what we think!"

I say it loudly on purpose so he'll hear me...

"I'll crush you," he snaps back, "I'll crush you!"

He picks up some huge strawberries and smashes them on his plate... little red blobs...

Ah! let him drop his hints, he doesn't stand a chance!

"You're just a lousy bastard!" I shout.

"Oh, Ferdinand, what's bugging you? Come, come. Cool off! Show some self-control!... Cool off! Cool off!" he creaks trills... "You really want to cool off, Ferdinand?"

And that sets him off again, he's tickled to death. I didn't rub him the wrong way... on the contrary, he's never been more full of piss and vinegar... full of plans... and dirty innuendos.

"I ran into you, my darlings, and I'll never let you go! You just wait and see my wonderful present! Promise! I swear! A treasure, my angels! Say you'll accept!"

And damn if he doesn't start glowing... phosphorescing for all he's worth... his rags his head his hands... and plus he's back wriggling and jiggling... a transport of delight! and the stink it kicks up, funky knockout...

"The most wonderful trip on earth! That's my present, my pets! Yes, on earth, and I'm an expert! on earth up and down and all around! It'll be a treat! No more underground, Ferdinand! No more underground ever again in your whole life! I'll rescue you from all undergrounds!"

Geez, that's a hot one! Funny enough for a solid five minutes of bone-cracking chuckles, every limb going like a castanet.

"Just ships from now on, honey! cabins padded in silk! cabins! No fuss and bother at night! You'll come into love, little one!"

A little couplet for a laugh.

I've got good tobacco
In my tobacco box...

Christ! he's so sneaky! couldn't be more pleased with himself... hands out cigars all around, now he's rooting around under the table... the table moves/jerks... he's tickling Virginia's thighs... she lets out little squeals, but doesn't move away... he even tries to give her a little smack in fun! He's happy as hell! I look real bright plopped there, some old grouch... he's back to nosing around... rooting at random underneath... he grabs my leg... I bend down take a look it's her he's hunting for... she's doing her kittenish number, giggling, exactly like in the square... revolting sleaze...

"Come on! let's get a move on!" I order, my mind made up.

"A move on! A move on! Always in such a rush!"

"Where we moving anyway?"

"Outside! Outside!"

My big obsession.

"But Ferdinand, let's be serious..." He creaks gnashes sadly in reproach... "I melt away outside, I suffer! In the heat! the light! even now I don't feel so good... everything makes me melt away! You're heartless, Ferdinand! a damp spot's what I need, I do! Cellars! Down in the gloom! Can never go deep enough down into the gloom!"

He calls over a bellboy.

"Three Benedictines, waiter!"

Now he doesn't want to leave anymore, he's putting down roots.

"Enough lights! Enough bustle! Solider in no one's pay, be quiet!" That's the tone he takes with me. "Down, hothead! Now listen to the voice of your master!"

So much for his calming approach.

Ah! always ready for a laugh! I lose my temper! no! nix that! it's better to get going!

"Let's hit the road!" I'm back to my old song...

"Very well, as you like, terrific!"

He's screaking/gnashing shriller than ever, quivering, throwing a fit... tripping on his tongue he's working himself up so badly...

"I... I'm the biggest holder of out-of-this-world passions!"

He rises a little from his seat to say this. Fine, let him shoot his mouth off, just so he gets it out of his system! Now he's waving his long dry arm through the air... I think to myself: Get ready, another speech... he's calling the room to attention... But he drops his arm and Ka-zoom! thunder! I look around, don't want to be taken in again... my head back to its old tricks, hearing things... not this time... there's a blaze, all the walls are rumbling... tongues of flame shooting from one wall to the next... Ah! you should hear the people howling! No, I'm not alone!... the dump's on fire... and then a red cloud... the whole restaurant's going up in flames... an explosion a storm... and whoosh! the dishes... the women are the worst... "The zeppelins!" they're bawling, "the zeppelins!"... I stop looking around. I charge straight ahead... forgetting my sweetheart... In a flash I totally lose control... Shit, explosions are a real jinx with me! A big botch like back at Ben's! The noise goes right through my head... Fly straight, soul of mine! Fly straight! Lucky there's not a big crowd, just a bevy of gourmets. "A zeppelin bomb! A zeppelin bomb!" They're charging for the door, yelling... ah! it turns into a total screw-up anyway... a savage crush... Ah! here we are all together again! Damn, I keep my cool now!... Virginia Centipede... The kid's disheveled... he's shooting sparks from everywhere... a prize practical joker... the prankster behind all this... the diners think it's a bomb... that's what they're squawking! they're sure... "Zeppelin! Zeppelin!" We can't move forward a single inch, crushed against the door... ah! but Centipede snaps into action... thins himself to a slat right before our eyes... works himself into a jellylike leaf... his whole bag of bones... a mere wisp... in such guise he slips between the door crack... phenomenal... a glittering jelly... painlessly he passed through... and outside!... he's in the darkness... out on the street... but the rest of us are getting squashed... I can hear him laughing outside... at last we meet up with him... his laughter my guide... like a jackal's... ah! how happy the girl is!... she flings herself around his neck... I grope my way up to them... she's as titillated as he is...

"Let's get going! We're off!"

I'm in bad shape, limping, bitching and moaning, I've lost all my junk... forgot it on the wall bench... and I'm not going back for it! I can also see the police won't be far behind, that we're going to waltz right into an ambush... Come on, let's go! get a move on! I'd like to take advantage of the dark, the fact our whereabouts are still unknown... but he's not one bit worried... he's frolicking and twirling about, gamboling among the clusters of people... playing Hide and Seek... a piece of cake with that glow of his... the kid chases him... They pitch-black into me for being such a grouch.

"Look at Ferdinand! Look at him!"

"Aren't you having fun, Ferdinand? Aren't you having fun, hero of death?"

What can I come back with?

"Let's go, this way!" he decides. All of a sudden, a dictator! Plus his atrocious stink... ah! hell! I'm dumping it all! No! I'm sticking with it...

"I'm right behind you, Froggy!" I shout. I've put up with this rotten bastard long enough!... I can't go giving him the idea he always comes up the winner! I tag after him through the night... he trills/quavers while skirting the shops... I can hear him... I can... he keeps it up... They won't lose me, they can bet on that! I'm dogging their footsteps, I'm right on their tails... I can hear him clattering, his hyena laughter... the way he's frolicking around!

"Ravishing beauty! Heaven! Treasure!" That's what he's spouting... that con artist! such antics! not one iota of shame... even worse than Boro!... No consideration whatsoever!... I keep running into monsters!... After all those glorious fiascos not a single atom of embarrassment over anything... he's flirting/goofing around... and with a child at that...

"Ravishing beauty! Heaven! Treasure!" he keeps warbling... He glances back my way a moment...

"So, buddy, can you hear me? Mr. Sourpuss!..." he hollers over at me from far away in the darkness... he wants me to kick up my heels too... hurry along, catch up with them... out of breath... "You're going to get a nice present, little brother!" he grabs my hand, squeezes it, shakes it real hard... he's hurting me like hell with his bones, I'm about to howl!... but I don't... we keep chugging along... he slips something into my hand... I can't see what it is in the dark... something hot... dead sickening, but I don't bat an eye... from inside his body his underpants... I can sense him rooting around... feels like a tube, a sausage... soft round... maybe he wants to see me swoon... black out? beg for mercy? ah! poor little birdie! you don't stand a chance!

"Ghost!" I shout, "You're rotten! This is your rot!"

I come out and nail him... tit for tat... Ah! hee! hee! let him go right ahead and snigger! He's got nothing to show for all his trouble!

"You clown, you're a dirty son of a bitch!" That's what I dish out through the darkness and the night... through his stink, through everything! He doesn't discombobulate me anymore. He's given me his best shot! Now I'll follow him to the ends of the earth, I couldn't give a fuck about him...

He quickens his pace... we're not out on a stroll... I don't give in an inch... when crossing streets his whole body starts shooting out will-o'-the-wisps... all over from his tatters... pretty handy for seeing our way...

"Tweet-Tweet Club!" he croaks... "The Tweet-Tweet Club!"

That must be where he's taking us... a nightclub, some sort of dive... he's going to treat us! such extravagance! that's what he promised at the start! A night out on the town!

"Whoopee! Whoopee! Tweet-Tweet Club! Tweet-Tweet Club!" he croaks over and over nonstop!... He wants to wow us with anticipation, con us with the head-spinning thrills to come... But the stinking bastard won't get rid of me so fast! I know he's mumbling down into his torso... just pretending to be a pal... he wants the girl all to himself... another of his bloodsucker's tricks... hatching some rotten deal to turn me in for cash, one damn dirty double-cross! ah! his supersavage revenge... I can feel it, I can just feel it... and I'm keeping my eyes peeled... he'll walk away with zip! that's what I think... and keep on thinking... and then think about my bundle my crazy hardware, it brought me good luck up on my back, I shouldn't have ditched it!... what a dumb move...

He kept on squealing, the scamp the life of the party!

"Nightclub, children! Nightclub!" The whole time capering around... I have trouble keeping up with him... he's farandoling all over the damn place... back to being the bounciest of the bunch... the street is pitch-black dark... the air-raid warnings have been sounding nonstop... following one after another for the past month... This war has got to be just about wrapping up... that whole situation's back on my mind again... we wouldn't have been able to see more than a yard or two in front of our faces if it wasn't for his will-o'-the-wisps, plus his stink, got to be honest... I do wonder what the passersby must be saying... They must think we're playing some sort of game, striking little matches... Nelson was a different sort, he rallied a crowd with his shouting, kept them in tow... Every enchanter has his own special magic... But now it's still not enough, the pair are so happy/excited they want me to hop along with them! leap like a goat and do a jig on my twinkletoes! what do they have in mind? that I should be running people off their feet?... ah! I'm in no mood, you little kook! I'm tagging along that's enough... But that duo's doing farandoles... I can't believe I went and forgot my bundle!... At least one person around here has his mind on his responsibilities.

"Come on, children!"

He's dead set... Even though it takes an awful lot to surprise me anymore, this walking corpse of a crook is pushing things a bit too far in his own way... now he's clicking his fingers... castanets really truly... reminds me of Carmen on stage... he plays well, got to admit... a hailstorm!... he's a genuine artist too... got what it takes, in short... a shame he's a little tattered around the edges... The rotten SOB would bring down the house! but I wish he were anywhere but here... meantime he orders us around... we're never moving fast enough for him...

"Come on, *enfants de la patrie!*"

We've got to shake a leg... he throws out his glow every ten steps... more or less... and stink bombs practically with every jerk of his body... clattering rattling... a real delight! He's all I can hear in the street... most of all his gnashing joints... plus his braying... words sort of... So awful beside him walking along... like some old basket he is, full of junk jewelry, knocking around like crazy... I was raising a racket too back when I still had my sack! Why'd I ditch it? It brought me luck... To lighten my load, goddamn it!

"To the ends of the earth, you gangrened creep!" I'm talking to him... it's all his fault, the filthy putrid dank sickly smelling tomb-dweller! He hooked us real good. No way to undo his spell! Tweet-Tweet! and make it snappy! The word has been spoken! We don't have what it takes to fight back... he keeps plugging away with his sales pitch-black... I can hear his falsetto... *The Depths of the Earth!* is what he's dishing out to the little shit ass... *Enchanted Caves!* he's promising her wonders... I don't want to miss the festivities! I'll be there too! I'll be a part of everything!... I hurry along pick up my pace... he chugs even faster wants to ditch me... reeks twice as awful... so let him, he's not going to make me puke... he won't leave me behind... I'm keeping up... my tongue's hanging out, I confess... they're running me ragged... I listen to the ruckus we're raising as we scurry along, what a racket echoing along the walls... just can't be all our doing! sounds like the sidewalk's swarming with a scuttling mob... I call "Virginia! Virginia!" In the end I grow worried... For a moment now she's stopped talking, doesn't answer... just keeps moving, moving... running along with us, nothing more... seems she can't even hear me...

"Hello! Hello!" I call out again... So fine and dandy to be running our heads off this way!... Come on, we haven't lost all our marbles just yet... plus where's he leading us?... This is one of his fishy whims... Delphine did some running too... I'm a believer in runs of bad luck. If a person knows how to read life he'd see the same scenery keeps recurring, and that for each one of us a secret exists... Life keeps going through the trouble of repeating it, her riddle I mean, so that the rattlebrains will open their eyes wide, take a good look and get the message... Ah! but I wasn't some rattlebrain! I could see how he was mucking up the whole works! blasting it all back into our faces! and that he'd wrap up his performance with a real killer... we would have asked for it too, bungling suckers that we were, we deserved everything we got... This would have been the perfect time to skip out, give him the slip... not a split second to lose... break the evil spell in one snap! For Delphine, it was some little gnome who jumped on her back from the top of the tunnel... but for us, our disaster was right here, our smelly crook having a blast bowling us over... he'd stopped digging up bits of his guts, we were moving too swiftly. We took Standwell Road at a fast clip... we were chugging too hard for cripples! Then Briars... Then Clapham... I recognized the street corners... but starting from Acton Vale, what a hell of a mess! nothing but winding detours, it looked like he was losing us... a labyrinth of dead ends... he was treating us to a great stroll... The night was dark, turning blacker and blacker... I kept my eyes glued on the sky, the silhouettes of the small chimneys... It was gray up there... the moon... the clouds blowing in from the distance, from the river... where's the wind coming from? where?... My leg hurts... I catch up to Virginia, squeeze her hand... "Virginia! Virginia!" I call out, but she doesn't answer... she keeps going and going, nothing more... If pooping me out is what they're up to, it's not going to work! I'm determined about that! he can go ahead and reek all he wants, a stench ten times worse! I'm dead set, beyond death! I tell him in a whisper as we race along! He couldn't give a good goddamn!... He keeps galloping, and we do too! Clink kuh deeg klack! What a racket! He can reek a whole lot worse, that's one sure thing! we'll see! and smell! He's going to lose us in the mazes... This is no ordinary neighborhood... Ah! even so we hear something... a siren far off... the river, a boat... maybe another air-raid warning? some zeppelin flying overhead? I don't want to talk to the jangling wreck! I don't want to hear his quavering crapola! I'd rather chug along with my trap shut, I don't know where we're going, big deal! he's leading the way, simple as that!...

The piece of shit lights into me.

"You'll never find your way!" he croaks. He's really rubbing it in! I was waiting for that crack!

"No," I answer, "my angel! Of course, my pet! keep going!" I dish it back! same kind of wisecracking! tit for tat! He's nowhere near intimidating me! Those signals surely mean the docks... Maybe he's going to dump us in the drink? leave us for the rats, that's what's out there... I know all about the banks of the port, the crab-ridden silt... no, he's not heading in that direction... I make a joke out of the situation...

"Keep at it, Artemisia!"

That makes the kid burst out laughing...

"Lord Centipede! Centipede!" she calls him, "Where's your Tweet-Tweet?"

"This way, darling!"

Always sweet as honey with her... Could it be we're just about there?... he slows up, glances around, feels his way in the dark... knocks on a few shop fronts... it's a side street no different from ten others, twenty others... maybe a thousand like this in the dark... I can't figure out what he's up to... he stops in his tracks, pounds/rattles doors... raps with a knocker... Nobody answers... we cool our heels... out in the rain... a hard steady downpour... and this door that won't open up... ah! somebody's there! the door cracks open, stream of light... Whoah! we all barge right in... I grab the kid by the arm, look out! Ah! I'm not staying outside, I charge ahead! can't see a thing, blinded right away... terrible lighting, and what a blare, what a deafening noise! Plus it's hot as hell, like a furnace! Hits you as soon as you step in from the street... This big ruckus makes you see stars! Especially the cymbals... they've got a big bass drum! you cannonball inside the club barrel down... down down all the way to the bottom... Ah! can't see a goddamn thing... just hear this hubbub... plus there's this fragrance in the air, something real special, reminds me of a powerful verbena... it packs a heady wallop... ah! the corpse stink is gone!... we keep scrambling downward... land smack in the middle of a party, the more the merrier!

"Whoopee!" I shout. I'd be able to see them all if the light were different... everything's a yellow haze... but you better believe I can hear them, that yammering through the music... plus the laughter, great big guffaws... they must be rolling on the floor back there... maybe they think we're funny?... stumbling in like this from the sidewalk, tripping all over them... a fresh crop of entertainers! but this must be some big private affair, huh?... I stagger down the steps... down... down... it's an orgy! That's what I think... Whoah, time to do an about-face! A 180 right out of here! I'm thinking about Virginia! Got to make sure the clothes don't start coming off! I know something's brewing! I can smell it!

"Let's turn around and get out of here!" I shout... Nobody answers... I still can't make out the faces, just a sea a swarm... a sure bet our funambulist, our rotten mastermind cooked up the whole thing... He's handing us over to a mob of hell-raisers!... He hatched the whole deal! But with a ka-Boom! and a klang! they're cutting loose... Not a second to think... a storm of drums cymbals. They're hammering away even harder than those two screwy engineers of ours... It sounds like I'm hearing them again back in the garret! My typical run of luck, I was positive! my run of rotten luck! I can't shake the old feeling... right there in the club amid the seething orgy... and then the others start yelling... "Tweet! Tweet!" in chorus to the beat... which is just what he had been on about... the Tweet-Tweet Club! What a thrill!

"Help!" I call. "Virginia!"

I dash down another couple-three steps... they're screaming in delight... Do our faces look funny, or what?... Ah! I'm starting to see a little better... we're in a long tunnel shimmering with lights... revolving mirrors everywhere... plus the dancers in back revolving around each other, socialites I think... couples and then long snaking lines... everybody singing and bawling in chorus... or squawking's more like it... we lady-killers showed up just in time! ah! all at once I spot the nigger... pitch-black in the light... I see his mouth, gaping wide open, his big teeth... he's a big shot, overlooking the sea of dancers!... he's calling out to me no less!

"Shut up," I yell back, "crocodile trap!"

Some hilarious comeback. Presto, he's bellowing, swiveling his hips, going into absolute convulsions. Ah! if only Sosthène were here for this! they'd make a perfect team... this has got his Hindu trances beat! This guy knows how to work his drums! his sticks move so dizzying fast you lose track! and then, with the limberest limbs, he flips them to the ceiling, they whiz back into his hands, snap! like they're on rubber bands!... quite a performance... he can zap a fly at twenty yards!... and zip! pop them back into his fist! Centipede is watching him, gawking like a jerk... It's a tremendous routine, Centipede couldn't even come close! Can't resist calling over to the snazzy gigolo!...

"So, what've you got to say about that, Bony? See that fly?" I want to rile him in broad public...

Nobody's listening to me... For starters I've lost track of Centipede... he's melted into the melee with the kid on his arm. It's the Tweet-Tweeters who're bellowing and shouting... swarming all over the dance floor. No mistake about it. This is one hell of a big party... Ah! but there's our skeleton again! I glimpse him in the mirrors! carrying on like a weirdo too... going head-to-head with the nigger... he won't let himself be outdone...

"Hey! Jelly-belly!..."

Amazing, but you can't see his glow anymore... it disappears into the dazzle... just his head and rags left, he's floating in his tatters... his dome pure bone, period... they must think it's a mask, a crank's crazy idea... plus they're too busy... bumping/grinding into each other, rumbaing their bellies red-hot until the whole tunnel is braying and neighing... Not your ordinary delight... the crowd's grunting/roaring in glee... they're much too busy... they mustn't even smell the stink, the reek he's giving off... the fragrance in the tunnel overpowers everything, like a huge blast of verbena... it would make you black out too the way it goes right to your head... anyway the scuzzball's swallowed up... I have a clear look at the dancers now, one enormous vat of bliss... everybody all wriggly/giggly squealing... my eyes are adjusting... and Ba-boom! from the big bass drum, a blast that sends the whole mob, the joyful swarm flying up into the air... with each whack they leap three feet off the floor... the whole scene a riot of black and bright... satin dresses sequins... and the way everybody's hopping hooting... it's seething down here, people dancing in threesomes, tensomes, twentysomes! wait, what am I saying! in packs of a thousand, Christ Almighty! squealing away, and the big drum that keeps stirring them around, and the trombone, raging! raucous, raising hell! And "Tweet-Tweet" everybody sings in chorus, hollering out the words! Centipede can really let it rip! Nobody's bothering him! Did he skip off with the kid? I can't spot her blonde hair anymore! Here we go again! Maybe he hid her somewhere... Doesn't matter too much right at the moment... he's putting on his act, amazing his audience! He wants to outshine the nigger... He walks up a few steps... he's going to take a flying leap right into the hoopla smack onto the heads of the Tweet-Tweeters! There he goes! Into the shaft! His whole body bounces all the way up to the ceiling! his whole body! not just a limb or two! Boing! Right into a mirror! zapping flies can't even compare! his whole body in one bounce! pretty astounding, got to admit... even this jaded crowd is impressed... they let out a group "ahhh!"... Our slimeball has gotten his revenge... Their poor spook's been creamed... yes, but where's Virginia?... I'm not going to go hollering her name, hear it echoing all over the place, it'll just be good for a laugh, nothing more... they're wowed by Centipede, all hot watching him... true, he's out of this world, fluttering everywhere at once... lighter than air, totally weightless... floating, a bundle of rags above the audience... a genuine freak, a literal flake hovering in the air, drifting/swaying however he likes... gives people a pat, grazing their heads, hanging straight down from the ceiling like a spider... unreeling himself above them as if along a thread... and whoosh! a gust, and he escapes! That's how he sails around!... He's the life of the party in rags and bones! Boggles the mind, got to admit, how the guy keeps his balance, the way he whisks through empty air... What an eyeful for the fired up Tweet-Tweeters! Squawking down on the dance floor of their tunnel... in wild amazement, in excitement... "More! More!"... now he's done it, he was their idol! they're clamoring for him to top himself! somersaults genuine showstoppers... right in midair... he went through some rigadoon moves, capering like a crazy spider... way above their heads... another twirl a waltz... and then he returned, swaying above grazing the crowd... head down feet mirrorward, a genuine fly scurrying through the air... his old rags fluttering about... such admiration it stirred! oh! such gasps!... so much so that a few women dancers felt sick... just because they were guffawing so much with delight!... big puddles of piss everywhere... the way he stuck to the walls was truly phenomenal, clambering straight up vertical, flitting about comically, plus with his head upside down, and all to the beat! of the blasting blare! too sidesplitting even for the niggers... they couldn't even play their instruments anymore... slayed with hysterics... crumpling into a heap on the floor, and the dancers along with them trying to catch their breath... that's what Centipede could do to people!... Shooting backward straight up to the ceiling! Never seen such a performer! From up there he goes flying into the walls! shoots back to sway over the heads in the crowd... packs a phenomenal power, soaring around without strings anymore! ah! he's captivating the entire audience... the flying skeleton!... I'd love for Sosthène to see him! Sosthène with his get-a-load-of-me-now trance-dances! his Pépé! his granddad in a box! He'd pick up a trick or two! Ah! the poor slob and his China! he'd have a look at a real head-spinning performance! at what virtuoso magic's all about, genuine gravity-defying feats! that clown with his slithering costume antics! Ah, the poor chump! I might hate Centipede as much as I wanted, but he never failed to bowl me over... a truly wonderful performer... three times ten times twirling between the walls and the big chandelier... a pirouette, skim the crowd, with a rap on the drum he rebounds! goes into his act all by himself in midair! a frantic insect! whirling and twirling to the music!

Nobody in the joint's dancing but him!... all heads tilted up... they've stopped in their tracks fascinated... ah! I grab a hand... somebody standing against the wall... it's my darling! what joy! I love her!... "Is that you, Virginia?..." There in the sea of dumb gawkers... What a miracle! Geez, she's trembling like a leaf... so nervous she's stuttering... latched onto me and clinging... It's Crazy Legs up there who's scaring her!... She points to him.

"Well," I go, "so what? He's just a circus clown!" I want to put her mind at rest... he's swaying right above the jazz band above the niggers... back and forth... hanging from sheer nothing! that special touch which makes him the miracle man...

"Isn't he wonderful?" she asks, fascinated as well... she's stammering... and he's hovering up above lighter than air...

"He's a pathetic gagster, come on, you damn little cretin! he's playing tricks with your eyes!"

She's a pain in my damn neck carrying on about this rotten show-off, this scumbag prankster, joker, this piece of human shit! "Human"'s way too polite, that's giving him too much credit! I tell it to her straight, rip into her.

"He's using trick mirrors, can't you see?"

She opens her mouth, nothing comes out, she's dumbfounded, period! Ah! I can't figure out what kind of number he did on them! They're gaga standing in their piss... it's that old beyond-the-catacombs glamour... they're looking at that crazy thing up above convulsing its way through the air... it astounds them, they're rocking back and forth purring in astonishment... Now he's back attacking the drum... a few rolls and then on to the piano!... he all-fours it across the keys... a racket in octaves! a horrendous grinding din that sends your eyes rolling and punishes your earlobes! ah! the ravager! the fiend! And he's tickled pink! he woke up the whacked-out crowd, got to admit... they burst out in acclaim, howling... he pays his respects from on high, from the chandelier... perched triumphant... these ovations inspire him all the more... he whisks off again into the air... endless somersaults between ceiling and floor... never touching the ground... his spirits flying high with his virtuoso brilliance! ah! we've got ourselves one terrific little pal! we can be proud of the way he carries on!... the kid's standing there with her mouth open, it's real simple, gaping up toward the ceiling, her mind a blank... it's the dirty bastard's hypnotic spell... he's the only person left in the world, that coon that clown that decaying creep... didn't she smell the stench he spread through the street a little while back? And what about the restaurant! during the mussels, the endives, the quails?... didn't she smell anything? and out in the street, didn't she see what he slipped me from his guts? Wasn't it something foul? didn't it turn her stomach to see what he was made of? that rotten bag of bones that crooked unsavory thug? I shouted to him above the roar so she could hear me and get it through her head... and snap out of her stupor. Now he was a one-man band, a cacophony all to himself... beating on all the drums, plucking all the strings, blowing on all the brass, into every instrument as he flew past! suspended in the air acrobatically! Three fingers on the piano and plllinng! he runs through all the scales! a mighty ripple... and all this with his head upside down... he nabs the drum while whizzing past! carries it off! sways with it through space... you've never seen such dexterity in your life... a miracle-worker working on nothing at all!... keeping up his sway he sucks on a flute, starts playing! a genuine little hummingbird in the air... he tosses the flute into the cymbals! Tllling! What a funny guy! the audience is stomping in excitement! It does a number on the kid, first she's crying, then laughing, she's nuts... "Oh! Whoa-oh oh oh oh!" she goes, caterwauling, she's a different person... He's doing a jazz routine now, solo... he drops to the stage with the niggers... smack into the bass drum he cannonballs his full load, bones, rags, the works!... and Boing! he bounces all the way to the other end of the room... comes flying back into the bass with a tremendous bone-clatter... sounds like he's blowing apart, scattering in smithereens... endless ovations... they adulate him fanatically... a genuine rage rattling them, they're slamming into each other... They want to catch Centipede, he's just too fascinating... They raise their three hundred arms into the air... and catch nothing at all!... nothing but smoke... he's just a spinning top over their heads... whirling so fast so fast as he rotates he sings, the air zinging over their heads... a head-spinning living top... that describes him... he turns into pure speed momentum like a huge cannonball of blue light... and then even faster! faster still! and clang! he's crashed into the bass drum... and comes out the other side like through a cloud... a ray of pink light... here he comes... shooting back out handsome as ever! the big blue cannonball has stopped dead... there he is, firmly planted, right in his element in charge up on the drum... his finger in the air above everybody... his long finger of bone... he's got something impressive to show us... up on the drum he cuts quite a figure... it looks like he's stretched a few inches, I mean along the whole length of his carcass, his bones... a literal scarecrow... plus that head of his... his death's head... Doesn't that rub these nut cases the wrong way? Can't they see what kind of phony they're dealing with? And on top of everything he shouts out to them...

"Ladies!" he twangs out... "Ladies! Gentlemen! we are here to present you Virginia, the virgin beauty! and Ferdinand, her jealous lover!"

He follows that with a long drum roll played by himself... peppering out a dense barrage on drumsticks, fingers, even his long toes get into the act... shoeless on all fours... a whirlwind on the drum... the whole room's rattling! rattling... Then he plants himself back on his feet, frozen, bolt upright... looks the audience up and down... seems like he's spied me... spotted me back at the other end of the mirrors... I can't catch every word he's saying... he's shooting his mouth off in that famous quaver of his... the people aren't paying him any mind... they're wailing out, they don't want to hear another word... they're doing donkeys, pigs, dogs... they rush the stage... they're going to grab hold of Virginia... and he's the guy who pointed her out to us, the monster funambulist! now they've got it in for me too, they all want to lay their paws on me anyway they can... That's it, they're holding me now, shaking/yanking me by my trousers... is this some kind of sickness? what's wrong with them? are they wackos? is this some drunken frenzy? "Tweet-Tweet!" they all cheep... that's their refrain... they chant it with every shake... maybe this is going to turn into a hunt?... a slapbang sacrifice... and they're going to spit-roast, then chow us down?... meantime they're getting all entangled/ fouled up in each other, maybe this is the dance of the victims? dancing in foursomes! sixsomes! eight-somes! by the dozen! It's one hell of a mess... a screaming tumult in every corner... the whole mob's back on the move... Virginia and I are snatched up lifted carried off... it's a dizzying whirl... a farandole, no mistake about that... jiggly-wriggly... humpy-bumpy... and shouting their lungs out! The whole joint, mirrors, piano, lamps rattling and rocking... plus the walls!... all too much for a place like this... the crowd's too revved up, full of too many frenzied fun-lovers, any minute now the roof's going to come crashing down... we'll all be buried alive... That's what I think deep down... all hell's broken loose! just as I'd suspected... the whole band's caterwauling... they've revved their racket back up... possessed, shouting "Tweet-Tweet!" what a squawk!... they holler/shout themselves hoarse from every corner... between the trumpets the drums... a wild crazy shimmyshaking without letup... Centipede grabs a flute while whizzing past, still flying high, plus a sax, blows into it, sends up one of those wails! a sour squawk, a nightmarish desecration... pure hell on the ears... followed by another damburst meow... it grates on the Tweet-Tweeters' nerves... they wail twice as loud/hard... in pain, they embrace each other, cuddling, swaying in rhythm the whole time, noisily sucking each other's mouth, let me spell it out for you, it's an orgy... simply appalling behavior... smacking each other with kisses so hard they're wearing themselves to a frazzle... I can see how they're bleeding, frothing at noses and ears... and eye sockets... genuine bloodsucker cruelties... they hit it off horrifyingly well... keyed up all the way, glued belly to belly, their bodies intertwine, and bump by bump melt into a mob... if the music breaks off, even for a second, they scream for blood... they can't stand it!... "Murderer! Bloodsucker!" they yell... they're ready to tear the whole damn joint to pieces... they want their pleasure before anything else! The niggers don't want to hear another word... they're scared, bellyaching... What a huge mess in store!... I can see disaster heading right our way... Lucky thing it was just a petty sulking fit... they strike their ruckus back up... full brass, strings and trombones!... ah! this great aaah! of relief... bad blood had them ready to slit each other's throat... the whole party's back in full swing... just two-three couples poop out/collapse/swoon away under foot... all the wild dancers tread on top of them, trampling/

crushing barking with delight... The big Tweet-Tweet dance party's really cooking now... pure mass hysteria, literally, the whole mob whooping it up crazier and crazier... the entire tunnel's seething, especially in the far corners the crowd's on fire... genuine fiends in all four corners... and the fun's just starting!... they're preparing one last assault... the rowdiest characters, I mean... they're sniffing us out over there... I can see them gathering in a huddle... I keep my eye on them in the corner... sniffing out Virginia and me... there's something special going on, nobody's fooling me, nothing surprises me anymore, this is some ploy... they're hatching the nastiest sorts of plots... the meanest dirtiest... I'm ready for anything and everything! where'd our scumbag disappear? our bony crony, our high-flying acrobat? I can't spot him anymore... but he's around here somewhere for sure... he's in hiding, ducked for cover, but he's the mastermind of the crew... I'm ready for the lewd devils... and here comes ten four a dozen stampeding, about to shoot out of the mob... they work free, fling themselves forward, they're on top of us!... can't withstand their impact... Virginia and I are snatched up lifted carried off worked over by ten... twenty... a hundred gentle hands... feeling us up pulling us apart... pitching us... high into the air... catching smothering us in hugs... at least a half dozen women wrap me in their arms, rub up against me shamelessly... I should take a harder stand, lay down the law... but might is on their side... my Virginia, my darling, my sweet kid, my little devil, where are you?... ah! the sneaky bitches are tearing me to pieces... See you soon, Virginia, my fairy child... on the other side of the cyclone! But in what condition, twenty thousand tears later! I ought to rip off my gloves howl rend these creatures to shreds... Brazen rapists smothering, tackling me six at a time... I've never felt anything like this before in my life! what they're doing to me is positively disgusting!... They're numbing me with kisses, heavy-duty hickeys that suck the breath right out of me... they twist/turn me upside down... head to floor... yank off my undershorts... revolting maenad antics!... with lip-to-lip action that makes me scream!... they'll never get me hot and bothered! let them give it their best shot, crush/swallow me up in their crazy clutches, get under their skin, I'll never be their little sweetheart, never swoon for them!... faithful in my fervor, first and foremost! Against any and everybody, fucking hell! They dump me in a small cubbyhole, now they're ten against one... and I call them every name in the book! cocksuckers! she-donkeys! gargoyles! They make me jump up onto their laps... nothing I say makes them mad!... just as I am, underpants down. I can see myself in the mirrors... my sorry-looking puss... I can see their expressions too, the she-devils! Their hair flying like wild in the storm! They're in heat, in a frenzy, red-hot and ready! I'll defend myself with fervor! With Virginia's memory! all and everything for her adored little face! The whores want me to take a swig of something... another trap!... some witches' brew! "First some chicken! Chicken! Caviar!" I push aside their dirty glass!... a last-ditch move... magnificently cool and collected! I'll take a swig only when my mouth's full... then spew the whole mess out, blah! right in their dirty god-damned painted faces!

"Virginia! Virginia! Help!"

My cry of agony.

Ah! fucking hell! Nobody can hear, everybody's laughing. The din's too deafening... my ravaging harpies couldn't give a good goddamn... they turn over, on top of me now, just like that, with their bodies upside down... push their crotches right up over my nose... I'm lodged in their pink smothering thighs, steeped in the incense, the aroma of ass, the fragrances... waves... of heat that could set you nibbling and gobbling for centuries on end, asses made in heaven, the blonde tufts of angels, oh how like slices of ham cured in Paradise, you can stuff your face with piping hot Eternity... I go at it... I go at it... nibbling away... chubby cheeks here... her hot butt... I'm going to swallow suck down everything in sight... I'm drooling drooling away... an ogre of love! I'm ravenous... fuck Virginia! I want every last one of these bitches from hell... I change my tune in a flash... In the tangle of interlaced flesh, between thighs I spot her in the mirror... it's her, the slut! my tramp... way at the end... between the wall and the piano... my little dove's no wallflower... she's mobbed all over too! Ah! I can make her out... I have a real good look... a huge crush of men on her belly... tails coats suits... white hair... a melee on top of her too... every inch of her swarming with a wriggling mass... going at her frontwards and backwards, pawing and mashing her... her short skirt flung in the air... just like my trousers... she's having her fling! ah! she gives us a good laugh... and she joins in the laughter too, the saucy little vixen! in leaps and bounds she escapes their clutches! they catch her again knock her back over... a furious feel-up fest... I can't even hear her screams... the racket's too loud... the Tweet-Tweeters and the trumpets... blowing howling something fierce! Keep on yelling, cutie pie! scream! they're going to make mincemeat out of her! a grand hurricane of passions! sweeping swirling through... at least three fun-lovers straddling me... I'm not going to be able to restrain myself much longer despite everything... I'm muffled in hugs, satiny skins, wild tender burning kisses, wrapped tight in the fiery humping frenzy of twenty-five she-devils who'll never loosen their clutches... they overpower me, flesh and blood furies, she-gluttons for pleasure... they'll suck the soul right out of me... they knock me back over force me to the floor, remount my mouth my nose, I've got to give them head, that's a fact... if I put up a fight they'll slit my throat... with a superhuman effort I yank free... spring to my feet back to life, I can breathe... I can still see Virginia! her little face in the mirrors... her cute adorable little mug!... but I can't spot her dear body... swallowed up, my dove, my sweetheart, my adored child, under this disgusting jumble, this enraged heap... They're at least twenty guys on top of her, suits, tuxes, tailcoats, grunting groaning floundering out... such things just can't be! those greedy lunatics are going to strip the flesh right off her bones! they're roaring after her thighs, stupendously wonderful golden and amber fruits! after her lusty little treasures, her mischievous titties, fidgety fanny, marble and flesh and rose... Everything is up for grabs with those pigs... they're wallowing in her swamping her... Jesus, they too adore her! they want her whole and burning hot... a cowshed bliss exploding with mighty moos... multiplying ecstasies... they're dragging her through the mud something dreadful... this agony's too intense for me, I wail beneath my crazed bitches, I wail... They're dumping champagne down my throat, whole bottles at a time... I'm choking suffocating... ah! the damned tricky devils! I disentangle myself all the same, pop back to my feet, keel over at once, collapse to the floor... their potion's what did me in... the no-good sluts gloat in triumph!... I shrink to the floor under their lapping tongues... they want to strip me stark naked now... in every corner, full swing, fever pitch, the whole damn dive's exploding in frenzy... wailing, wriggling in rhythm to the chorus now... farandole/gamboling in all directions, steamy stew of sex... the party's at full blast...

Tweet-Tweet Mister!
Tweet-Tweet Sister!
Yippee Master!
Quack! Quack! Quack!

Pretty monotonous stuff... but the tunnel's whipped into a fury! The mob's tweet-tweeting, bellowing with gusto... unleashed, beside itself... they straddle each other in flying leaps and yank out hair by the handfuls... they're hurting each other, making each other scream, dropping in heaps on the dance floor... piles of drunkards, come-slicked, puking... fuck fever bubbling away... heaps of socialites tangled in all different directions tongues lolling... the hard boom-boom of the band beats/throbs through the sea of dancers, and the music sort of like fluffs up the omelette, the whole flesh-mess sprawling groaning... like a whopping soufflé big as the dance floor, swelling up ballooning gigantically high until it pops and drops... all thanks to the music... which gives you some small idea of the drunkenness the intensity! the trumpet blasts through the joint so stridently you can hear the air ripping, all the mirrors rattling... that's just how it happens.

Everywhere a simmering sea of passions... they want to turn us into criminals... I too howl in chorus... I can't decide what to do—low like a cow like them? Do a pig? A laughing hyena? I'd rather be an eagle so I could fly away with my darling... I bray like a jackass, I'm muffled in hugs, they're all over me, hot cold soft scratchy... a thousand fingers running over my shorts... decimating me with caresses... every time I jump back I turn the bitches on... but if I balk they'll rip my balls off... How can I fight back? The spell can't be broken... Either I surrender or they tear me to pieces... The Tweet-Tweeters howl in my honor.

"Damn him! Damn him!" Easy to see what they think of me... I'm damned! What gall!

I'll snap back loud and clear. They'll get a taste of my anger... But they're not waiting for my comeback... now they're crawling free of the piles, out from their filthy tangles, climb to their feet in a rage, and leap back into the fray, crazed loons scrambling to attack each other! I look for Centipede in the turmoil. Can't see him anymore... Where can Mr. Amazing have gotten to?... Nothing to see on the dance floor... just one big indistinguishable blob... even my bacchant bitches ditch me and dive into this mob hot for a fight!... the guys immediately pounce on them, pull their dresses up over their heads... it all makes for a rip-roaring great time! The high spirits of fiends! this is really and truly a witches' sabbath after all, I had it wrong... Straddling each other, that's their latest flash... never-before-seen pirouettes I've got to say, one standing, the other scissoring through the air head upside down... I think they want to imitate Centipede... he fired their imaginations... where is Mr. Corpse-Out-on-the-Town? I can't see that filthy bone anymore... I'm sure he'll pop up again, sure he's preparing some showstopper, a sensation, a spectacular finale... I still can't see him... the mad dogs are out there in the swarming sea roaring and raging worse than before... little more than wild lunatics... chomping each other down to nothing... I'm still hunting for my Centipede... Ah! this beats by a mile his run-in back in the underground... the victim's got more than he bargained for! Impossible to spot him... The raving crazies are all squawking in chorus, finishing off the women now... pushing/knocking them over on the floor... ripping off their dresses, stomping on top of them... looks like they're aiming to squeeze out every last drop... Squishsquash the weaker sex. Feet pulled together hopping popping around... Their adorable bodies in the nude... Free rein to every instinct... No sparing the rod... That's how they are... my harpies from hell are snatched away too, wind up ravaged, they get beaten up like the rest of the women... They shriek in agony! Ah! But their turn has to come... Beauty spurts out all over the floor, oozing in puddles... a stupendous drubbing... the gentlemen triumphant... Ah! I'm glad as hell... I take a breath, it's hot and stuffy in here. If I could just grab hold of my honey, my charming love... She's still in their clutches over there... "Tweet-Tweet!" they scream down on the floor, the decimated darlings... Ah! Jesus Christ Almighty, I'm snorting and shaking myself, flailing out, whinnying into action too, I don't want to waste away, some do-nothing bum... let's go! I want to rub out somebody too... those show-offs really went too far... quick, grab a curl a tit! I knock the cockiness right out of them! for starters let me poke out an eye! let me rip the treachery right out of them! I'm not fooling around! A sure thing they dumped that potion down my throat! Everybody all around's in stitches over me. They can see how I'm trying to disentangle myself and leap into the whirling fray of bodies! the way I'm busting my gut... in a flash the women pounce on me... red lionesses chomping away... they want to punish me for pulling free... this time for sure all hope gone... I'm the plaything of these Messalinas... their teeth rip off bits of my privates... I'm outmatched... Evil incarnate triumphant... I lose one shred two then three... I'm flat out woozy dead weight... losing every last drop of strength... another spasm, one more hiccup... Quack! Quack! I'm kicking the bucket, going under... What kind of hell did we land in? What kind of whorehouse did that vampire that hood lead us into? my arm already failing so badly goes totally kaput... I can't even prop myself up on my elbow anymore... can't lift myself off the floor... I can still remember Virginia, I beg her, implore her... ah! there she is, waving to me, she's not terrified, the party girl, not worried sick, the saucy miss, with her bare ass sticking up in the air... I can see her in the mirrors... sitting right on the men's laps... I can watch her wriggling and fidgeting around! she's not acting like the orgy's the end of the world, but just some hilarious acrobat antics... what a disgrace! I roar/bark... and then she starts kissing all the men around her, first come first serve! go to it, sweetie! she has a whole procession on her tail... first a Gypsy, then a nigger, then a bearded guy, then an athlete, then—hold on here—a little old lady in a bonnet, with a pince-nez and ear trumpet... they both give each other a whoop and a wink to show they've got the same thing on their minds... and then leap to it... straddling each other every which way. Ah! what a terrific routine, I don't miss a trick, can't be mistaken, she's giving the whole crew a real big treat without even trying, that dear little pupil of mine... The old gal especially is raising hell, she wants to sink her teeth all over the girl's fanny... she loses her glasses... Ah! this is sheer torture I howl... my happiness is out there... I'm shaking... my burning love my soul... I'm stammering in fury... my bacchant bitches knock me back to the floor... flip me over so I can't see anything... start massaging me ferociously, twisting every part of my body... I can't even howl in pain anymore... I just topple helplessly into their clutches... all the same I can still hear her voice, she's totally spontaneous by nature, bursting with youth, youthful spirits... the greedy hogs are in hog heaven, the old biddy's the craziest of the bunch... people pick her off the floor stand her back on her feet... this time they want her to start singing... they threaten her with a big shellacking, eighty hands spanking her ass! I can see she's putting up a fight, crying, hugging her breasts... then she gives in and drops her arms... and now her voice goes up... positively the voice of an angel, that's a fact... sweet, crystalline, smooth, velvety, you name it... But it's the old coarse chorus:

Tweet-Tweet's the way to be

the fiery refrain of this lair...

No sort of muck's too good for my dove!... Ah! I'll never spring back to life!... A horn explodes with an incredible blast! a thundering scream! off-key, hell!... It's a signal... Hubbub... the couples/groups pestering each other for a clue...

"Clear the dance floor!" the niggers roar, charging into the heap... "Clear off!..."

A fire hose trickles, gushes, explodes!... Ah! a clean sweep! A waterspout right up their asses! Whoah, look out! the floor's empty!... the mob melts away!... the rumbling of a big trunk... a bellhop pops out of the wings... carrying a huge deck of cards, gigantic playing cards taller than he is... up on his back... he deals out the entire deck on the floor... another bellboy brings on a roulette wheel... "Les jeux sont faits!..." All at once this triggers a mad rush!... All the Tweet-Tweeters want to play, pronto! An instant brawl... Nobody wants to wait one second... right off they start working each other over... They beat each other's brains out to lay their hands on the cards... the bellhops carry off two massacre victims... the champagne corks pop... and the bubbly comes flooding... "Les jeux sont faits!..." Centipede assumes his position... ensconced as croupier!... Ah! so our invisible man's back!... Still green and gray!... He sets right down to work! Brandishes the rake!... He's inviting me!... wants me to come up close!... He gnashes out above the melee!...

"Lookee here, Ferdinand! Riches!..."

Just a little bit closer... All bets are down!... Ah! I can't move a goddamn muscle!... The crazy bitches have ganged up on me! I'm sprawled lifeless under their caresses!... my last ounce of energy trickles out of me... the perfumed creatures strip me bare... my distress goes to their heads... they abuse my body something terrible, my scars, most of all my arm... which they twist... and tug... I howl but don't give in... I'm not crazy about any of these lewd maniacs... I hate every single last one... I adore only Virginia! the farther away she gets, the more I worship her!... I can see her out there, kittenish, panting, being hugged, sniffed, licked, lapped, she's writhing and swooning down to the carpet... way over there at the other end of the mirrors... With socialites piled on top of her again... they're moaning in delight... I could kill every last one of them!... By writhing and twisting my body out of whack I manage to budge an inch or two! I slither! slither! slither my way up to my Virginia... to reach her... and rescue her from those swine!... The bellhop calls out the winning number... I hold back a second... twelve... twelve... I cross the dance floor, all the numbers are written in chalk... I slither!... keep slithering!... six... three... nine... All bets are down again!... Centipede is the guy who sends the balls rolling... I have a full view of the son of a bitch!... He's huddled under the piano... hunkered down in his stink... glowing like crazy at the start of each game... at each new spin of the wheel... nine! nine!... He sniggers... swindles... everybody... raking in all their jewels... He quacks... quacks... quacks... like a duck... his kind of humor!... His rake whisks across the floor... he skims away everything, it's truly an awful scene... Now he's raking in their souls... The souls also bet the works... the Tweet-Tweeters! The whole dance floor's mobbed with souls... rolling around... they're sort of like hearts... but totally pale see-through... You can tell they're incredibly fragile!... I look at him in all his horror, this Centipede from hell!... Ah! he deserved what happened to him down in the underground!... Ah! Jesus fucking right he did!... I see him at work... Ah! not an ounce of remorse!... All my own remorse vanishes into thin air! Every last wisp! Ah! I'm over it!... I feel like throwing him right back under the train! Ah! I'd go right to it!... Just let him come back again! I'd snicker just like him!... Haw! Haw!... I start slithering again!... I cut across the battling bodies again!... the sex-crazed swarm! I'm going to howl... and wail, me too!... I'm slithering along... When all at once the drum... rolls... rolls... bass beats... pounding... pounding... closing in... from somewhere up above... from the top of the stairs... Brr... Brr... Brr... the orgy grinds to a halt... the music breaks off... the partiers freeze in their tracks... struck dumb just like that... motionless... the drummer comes down... taking his own good time... Brr... Brr... Brr... He's coming down toward us one step at a time... down from the street... We can see him now... a tall scrawny guy... we can see his whole body now... Brr!... Brr!... Brr!... He's solemn on the job... with each step downward... Brr!... Brr!... He's beating out a call-to-arms!... He holds his head stiff... draws nearer and nearer... real close past... I can see his cap... "Cemetery" in silver letters on oilskin... He keeps coming down... A uniformed guard... Long frock coat yellow baldric... he's some sort of official... a big shot... you can tell by that great big long beard... he keeps coming down this way... walks past... heads for the piano... at a slow steady pace... Centipede crams himself underneath!... rolls his whole bag of bones up into a ball! shriveling away!... Shrinking down into a small heap... He's so scared it's disgusting!... Reduced to little more than the sound of faintly rattling twigs!... Ah! his acrobat days are over!... high up in midair... no more fluttering through the atmosphere!... He's huddling under the stool... trying to slip down under the floor... ripping up some boards... digging down, hollowing his hole... like a dog!... and whining horribly... right in front of the caretaker with his drum!... The caretaker walks closer to him. Touches him with the end of his stick... Centipede jumps, and gnashes his teeth something scary... and then it's all over... finished... Centipede bounds out from under the piano, he's yelping like good little doggie. Hopping around his master... Pouncing on his big shoes... licking... lapping the soles... couldn't be more affectionate... Now the caretaker heading back up the way he came, one step at a time... his face remained blank through the whole scene... He didn't utter a single peep!... Just keeps beating out his drum roll, period!... after each step up! Boom!... Boom!... With the drumbeat he lures Centipede along behind him... boom!... boom!... boom!... Centipede sticks to him like glue!... tagging along at his heels under the spell!... sniffing around on all fours!... At each step he lets out a small yelp... as though whining in pain. Nobody dares go close up to them... All the socialites are frozen in their tracks!... they took in the scene, just like that, dumbstruck, jaws wide!... Centipede and the cemetery caretaker keep slowly climbing the stairs... brr! brr! brr!... they vanish into the night!... through the door that opens all by itself!... Ah! the socialites weren't in a mood to party anymore!... They just stood there totally sheepish... Ah! feeling pretty shabby!... Mystified about what to say or do next!... Ah! damn! now if you ask me, I thought it was one hell of a good deal for Mr. Beard to have yanked that filthy gloomy heap of bones up and out of here!... so putrid and crappy and everything!... Ah! I'll shove him right the hell back under the hard metal if I catch him at his old mischief again!... playing tricks on people who were minding their own business... Ah! he got off easy! Ah! I'll just come right out and say it!... That stinking creep was a big pain in the ass! with his little glittering routine and all that crap... his hazy glow! Ah! the amazing incubus... I hope the caretaker was planning to bury him in a way he'd stay buried this time around... in the Hole of Eternity! the real thing!... throw him down in with the maggots for laughs!... The rotting louse with his harebrained whims!... There would be some whirlwind fireworks!... If I ever again catch the little imp ghosting around dance joints!... Ah! I'd be pulling the pranks next time!... Ah! The bearded caretaker made me feel a whole lot better! Order was re-established! Ah! I felt completely invincible! re-charged! trembling! a brand-new man! made of steel, you better believe it!... Ah! my spirits do a flip-flop!... I pump myself back up in a flash!... in a bound!... I tell the frisky bitches to piss off! Send the lewd ladies flying to the floor... disentangle myself... and charge ahead!... With just one leap I'm on the stairs... While whizzing past I nab Virginia... She's about to go rolling across the dance floor... Ah! I pounce on her... Ah! I'm going to take it out on the little monster!... I drag her up to the doormat... She's sobbing something awful... pleading with me!... Punishment! that's what I shout... Punishment!... And that gets the Tweet-Tweeters back in their party spirit!... Mr. Cemetery hit them pretty hard... I'm dragging Virginia by the hair...

"Kill her! Kill her!..." they cheer me on. They force my hand... No need!... I let her have it!... think a second, and wham!... wham!... a good walloping!... Ah! This makes the mob delirious!... happier than ever! They give me an ovation... fan my flames!...

"Bravo, young deer!..." That's what they nickname me... I trample the darling girl a little... jump up and down lightly on her tummy... two or three times just like that... Ah! what wild unleashed fury... They tear off their clothes! fly into convulsions... fling themselves into the attack... ransack each other... ripped-off trousers sail through the air... Such an awful sight!... Their asses gushing blood... and their ears!... and their eyes!... a seething eruption of mass rage of strangleholds... Even the niggers wound up getting the willies... They clambered onto the big chandelier... hovering above the free-for-all... hanging like that in midair and singing:

Tweet-Tweet! Madame!
I say!
Tweet-Tweet! Madame!
Weep and play!

And then their huge shout... "Fikedee-ee-ee-ee!" piercing through everything. Ah! the revelers seethe with renewed fury... hurl themselves back on top of each other!... They meld in the horrible heat... the fusion of fanatical feasters... the vat frothing with embraces... You can hear their enormous pleasure... roaring then bursting into laughter!... Smothering in assholes!... They don't give a hoot about me anymore... they're totally absorbed! I'm going to make my escape... slip through... that's what I tell myself! Up on my own two feet! Whew! I nab Virginia... drag her off... force her to bound up on all fours... the stairway's clear!... I push my legs to the limit!... ply my pain... plus everything!... I jostle past the bellhop... plow open the door! Whew! Fresh air! And a pitch-black street!... It's pouring, cats and dogs... torrents... can't hang around here!... Let's get moving! We jump into the puddles... Now it's just the two of us, me and my sweetie!... Ah! her licking's far from over! I made a promise... and I'm going to keep it!... I stop in a doorway... sheltered from the rain... a whole lot cozier here!... she's drenched... in tatters... she's not listening to me anymore... puking... I keep her from falling... hold her head up...

"Leave me alone!" she shouts at me, once she's through puking...

Ah! the goddamned nerve of the girl!... Ah! it's a crime!... To say such a thing to me after I rescued her from the monsters!.... after I turn heaven and earth topsy-turvy!... to save her from the demons!... ah! the spiteful little minx!... The rotten bitch!... Whack! I give it to her good!... send her reeling!... She sprawls flat and blubbers!... I lift her up... all the way, so she's even with my face... and give her a kiss! Ah! I adore her!... I hug her!... Ah! I love the kid too much!...

"Don't cry!" I beg her!... "my little sweetie pie! I'm a monster!... Yes, I'm the most horrible monster!... more horrible than anything!... forgive me, darling!..."

I stammer out the words in English... hug her against me!... she's shivering!... I warm her, rub her, kiss her! She's not affectionate... or even nice!... She's angry... I beat her! Yeah, but the truth is, I saw what I saw!... And I didn't miss a trick!... I caught every dreadful detail! the way she let herself be fondled!... plastered... felt up and down!... Ah! And how! by the horde! Little Miss Goody Two Shoes!... Ah! the little hussy! Ah! I still can't get over it!!... Ah! Never in my life! Just can't be! Ah! This sets my blood back boiling! Ah!

And how! A dream!... Ah! they're back before my eyes! each and every one!... that stampede... that wild spree!... Ah! I sink my teeth into her neck!... I bite her!... she wants to break free, she shouts... I clamp down onto her loins, her butt!... just the way she is standing up against the wall... This way I keep a good grip on her... Ah! she just can't run away!... The rain coming down in buckets... the drainpipe's flooding over, spraying out... right on us... our heads... Not a soul passing by... She wants to go... I don't... I keep her braced... against the gutter... I talk into her curls, suck her hair... the rain... I want her to tell me... tell me everything...

"Centipede, darling?... Centipede... do you love Centipede?... Little one!..."

I want her to tell me she loves Centipede!...

"Little tramp... little two-face!... Ah! I'll find out everything!" I don't want her conning me!...

"Nympho!..." I yell... "Slut!..."

Ah! the mere thought's sheer torture!... the way she got everybody off... Ah! it's all too crazy... too incredible!... So intense! I bite her... nibble away... jam her back up against the wall!

"What about Curlers? You love her too, don't you?... You love her a lot more than me, don't you, huh?... You'd like her to take you away with her, huh, huh? Say it... let me hear you say it!..."

I beg her... implore her!... I knead her!... Right there under the gutter spray!... Ah! it's tearing me to pieces!... that she won't give me an answer... Ah! are we ever getting soaked!... to the bone!... it's coming down in torrents... pitchforks... a sweeping flood!... We're prisoners of the downpour!... the wind's whipping the rain under the archway!

"Don't you? Huh?" I shout!... "That's what you'd like, isn't it, huh? You want me to give you to Centipede, huh? You'd kiss him too, huh? Plus Curlers? You'd eat out Curlers, right, huh? The two of you together, right, huh?... which one you love more? Tell me, dear! Tell me! Tell me! Sweetheart!... Tell me, little darling I adore!..."

And I give her a good shake!... squeeze her hard!... and sink my teeth deep into her!...

"Ferdinand!... Ferdinand!..." she answers me real sweetly... she's real affectionate... real loving!... her breath... her angel breath in my mouth... She gives me her mouth... "My precious!..." She's the one who kisses me... I take her lips... "My baby doll!... My life!..." Ah! I adore her too much! I lift her... pick her off the ground... little darling I adore too much!... Ah! this face so cool and moist!... how I kiss her... suck her!... "My queen! My sweetheart!"... Standing there in the night!... "My little honey! My little fairy!"... Ah! but what about her looniness a little while back? Ah! how about the Tweet-Tweeters?... and the old bats?... Ah! I'm goddamn sizzling all over again... Ah! the fiery driving rain, fuck it all! Ah! I squint into the darkness!... I'd like to see her eyes!... how she's lying!... her mouth!... her face!... her so soft and darling face!... drenched!... right here... laughing under my mouth... I lick her all over! I'm losing my head!... She's behaving better now... back to her old self... cruel... nasty... mischievous... her nastiness has lost some of its edge, just because I'm cradling her in my arms... Oh! she's going to leave!... escape! Ah! she's going to run away and never come back!... Into the darkness of the night!... just like that... laughing at me!... A scamp... an imp!... an angel... "My little angel!..."

"Virginia!... Virginia!..." I call her name... "Virginia!..." She stirs a tiny bit... lets out a teensy little giggle... It's true!... Ah! she's laughing!... poking fun!... Ah! the brazen little brat!... She's a rotten kid... starting to fidget around!... Ah! she's all better now!... a whole lot better!... she wants to escape from me right away... I hold her back... kiss her!... "Little bitch!" she's wriggling around! I touch her little breast!... I want to suck it too!... her dress is gone!... all torn in tatters... she's wrestling hard!...

"Pancake!" I shout... "I'll flatten you like a pancake!... Make a move and find out!..."

She starts kicking me... I'm an animal, whack!... Not a soul around!... At first she whimpers... then wails... I keep her hopping I'm so strong!... "Hop! Hop! Little goat!" I'm totally batty!... I feel she's just about done in... with each whack she groans... My hand's hot!... hot where it hits!... "My angel!..." I kiss her... she turns away from me... I shake her... shake her!... I hug her too hard... she snags my ear in her teeth... and bites down! Ah! I howl! the bitch!... I plaster her against the wall!... I'm going to beat this little viper's brains out!... I ram my knee between her thighs... there. "You won't be moving anymore!" I brace her against the wall... she keeps wrestling... wriggling! squealing! I lean down hard... flatten her back down... I've got a good grip on her!... I'm all whipped up... even worse than before!... her carcass is done in!... in the raw done in!... the raw! Ah! I'm shouting!... shouting! I can hear the whole street... shouting along with me... but not a soul around... just me!... it's nothing... just the darkness!... the echoes!... Good news!... it's horrible!... not a soul! Ah! I bite her again... my grip firm... I adore her!... I suck her bare shoulder... her darling dripping wet shoulder... Ah! I jump up and down!... Pumping!... I do it all doggie-style... a rain-drenched pup... in the full spray from the gutter!... soaking us... running out between us... I ram!... ram!... with all I got!... my whole body against her... Ah! I'm in pain all over!... Yanking all my parts out of whack.... my own strength knocking me to pieces...

"Honey buns! Honey buns!..." I call her. "Sorry! Sorry!..." I shake her... bite her!... suck her!... Ah! it's my hot love!... my blood!... my lightning passion!... I'm all revved up! revved up full blast!... I'm going to bust her up!... crush her alive!... can't stop myself anymore!... I hammer my whole body into hers!... crush her... I'm out of control... I ram! I ram!... and talk... got to bellow... bellow... "You'll do everything to her!... You'll do everything to her!..." I can feel her kissing me!... sucking at my lips... she's a sweetheart!... I plough into her!... Ramming away!... Killing her!... Killing her!... That's the truth!... The truth!... I ought to know! Even harder now!... Faster!... Got to be worse!... until we tear each other limb from limb!...

"Virginia!... Virginia!..."

She's flagging... giving out!... totally limp!... she's stopped kissing!... I stand her back up... hold her against the wall!... take her in my arms again!... I can't see anything... can't see her face!... I grope for her nose... in the downpour!... her eyes!... her mouth!... I'm going to carry her!... I sit her down against the wall!... Ah! it's awful!... frightening!... What's happening to me?... What have I done?... I throw some water on top of her... sprinkle her... with lots of water... from the gutter...

"Virginia!... Virginia!..." I gave her a few light pats on the cheeks... Ah! she's coming round!... Ah! happy day! thank God!... This is just great! She's starting to talk a little... a few words!...

"Virginia!... Virginia!..." I call her name again... she's in the buff!... not wearing a stitch... her whole dress ripped to shreds... I pass her my jacket... slip her arms through the sleeves... get her moving again... all with the gentlest touch...

"Let's go, Virginia! Come on!..."

I'm thinking about the house... the Colonel... Sosthène... Ah! the errands! the appurtenances!... the goddamned gear!... where the hell did I leave it all?... Ah! at the Corridor... Ah! my wits were coming back!... the Corridor... Jesus fucking Christ!... Ah! what a botched job!... Ah! I remember clear as a bell now!... Fat lot of good it does me!... Can't see a goddamn thing!... I'm trying to figure things out just like that in the pitch-dark... where the hell can we be?... Not the faintest glimmer anywhere... surely some calm quiet neighborhood... with little houses that all look alike... row upon row... did a bus just pass? at the end of one street or another?...

"Must have been a bus..." I say to Virginia... that would be a nice break... Ah! but we couldn't take it!... I didn't think about that!... dressed in rags and tatters as we are!... especially with the girl without a stitch on!... in nothing but my jacket... it'd never work... the conductor would have us arrested!... we've just got to keep scurrying along!... keep cracking before the sun comes up!... and find our way!... in the darkness... and not ask the policemen anything... I was regaining my presence of mind!... helps you sort clear through all the bull... that's out there waiting to trip you back up!... you're saved!... you stop talking crap!... Presto, my plan... Plain common sense!...

"Kid!" I say... "Listen to Big Ben!"

We stop so we can hear better...

Five o'clock!

"There!" I say... "No problem! Let's go, honey pie!..."

I didn't know where we were going... but I wanted to use the echo as my guide... Once we found Westminster we'd be home free!... So I take the girl by the hand and head out of this place! We had to escape from this neighborhood, worm through the maze of narrow streets... zigzagging into each other.... We were stumbling all over in the dark... At last an avenue... one I recognized... Acton Road, then Long Avenue... Ah! the situation's looking up!... This is just great!...

"Quick! Quick!..." This is our road!... we're happy!... Even so we still had one hell of a stretch to cover... another good hour at least... Luckily it's almost stopped raining... but it's cold... I step up our pace... the only thing on my mind is getting home!... the kid's not complaining... just wondering where we are... is there still a long way to go?... the poor little angel's skipping to keep up... I have long legs... and we're not out here for our pleasure, of course!... Now it's straight ahead!... Edgware Road... then Orchard Scrubbs... the small park... finally Dwilk Commons... farther along we reach Willesden... the avenue... the large trees!... Ah! now we got to keep our eyes peeled... Can't just race along the way we are, whoosh!... There's home, over there!... I can see the house... the facade... the surroundings!... Totally deserted!... just the milkman... his ramshackle cart... the garden door's open... zip!... we both slip through... back inside... it's still dark!... nobody spotted us...

"Hey!" he goes to me... "Hey, come on, what's the story!... The old man's in a nasty mood!"

That's how he wakes me up.

"His niece told him you lost everything!"

As soon as I got in I collapsed in a heap just as I was, plop!... He shook me awake to give me the news... He wanted an answer...

"Who said that? Who?..." I wasn't following... I was still half asleep...

"His niece, for God's sake!... Well! Out with the story!... Let me hear it!..."

"Is he fuming?"

"Ah! just what you'd expect!..."

"Is he ornery?"

"He beat her."

"Shit! With what?"

"His riding crop!..."

"Oh, no!...."

Nice way to wake up... he's dumping some outrageous news on me...

"I think he's jealous..."

"Of who?"

"You, of course, you bum!... not me!..."

Even Sosthène had noticed! Just terrific!...

"Our only chance now is to beat it!..."

I jumped to that conclusion.

"Ah! don't even think about it! He already did. He said that if we ran off he'd notify the police!... He'd have us hauled in!... He said he had our contracts... that we'd been paid... boarded... bedded... and that our signatures meant something!... So that's that!... that's what he said... He laid it all out for me!... that he would do whatever he had to do!... that the contest was right around the corner... and that we mustn't back out!... that he couldn't replace us now!... it was too late!... we had to try out the masks... that was the whole reason we were hired. Not for goofing off!..."

"We! We! We! You mean you, just you!... Not me!... So just get that straight!... I didn't promise anything about any masks!... I said I'd run the errands, one thing, period!... Just the odds-and-ends stuff!... I'm a wounded veteran, I've already been run plenty ragged!... You're not looking at some engineer here!... That's you, Monsieur de Rodiencourt!... You're the guy pocketing all the gold! You're the spoiled big shot expert..."

"You call what you did running errands? What errand'd you run on the niece?"

"None of your business."

"Yes, right, but it's her uncle's!"

"So what?..."

"Well then, you can tell him yourself... You'll sort it all out with him..."

"Great, I'll see him right away..."

"He's not here... He's stepped out..."

"Where to?"

"The manufacturers... to try to find everything you lost!... everything you screwed up!... He went with his niece, he said he'd return with everything... He doesn't trust anybody anymore..."

"What a riot!..."

"So where'd you supposedly lose everything?"

He was curious.

"She said you went nuts in the afternoon around Wapping... and you went down into a club... forcing her along... that you'd wanted her to have fun... made her drink champagne!... and you busted all the packages... dumped everything with the niggers... the whole load... all the implements, all the feathers, the doodads... just like that in one loony impulse! she said you were an awful sight!"

I kept my trap shut... and my ears open.

Was that all he had to say?

No big deal...

"And then her uncle really started walloping her!... Ah! I mean it too! A one-man gauntlet!... I could hear it from upstairs!... Ah! my sweetheart my fanny! Ah! wish I could've seen it!... 'Un-cle! Un-cle!' she screamed... and she wasn't joking!... you bet! a real licking... He was whacking away! I heard it with my own ears!... 'Help! Help!' what a racket!... You didn't hear a thing!... You were snoring away! People must have been able to hear it out on the street!"

Ah! I was floored...

"Her uncle's a tough customer, huh? Tough, huh?..."

That's all I could get out.

"But she's already a big girl! and strong for her age... don't you think so?... She must be fourteen if she's a day!"

He wasn't sure.

"So, what the hell you going to do?"

He was asking me.

Then he lets fly another crack.

"So did it shoot right to your head?... Your teeny drop of bubbly! Since you never touch the stuff!..."

"Fuck off!..." I snap back. "Fuck off!..."

I wasn't going to draw any pictures for him.

"Where'd you say they went?"

I didn't catch every word.

"To the manufacturers, you idiot!..."

And then he fills me in... from the top...

"You should have seen the Colonel then!... He charges into her bedroom, look out... going after the kid!... he drags her out of the sack! Stark naked!... Orders the servants upstairs... the whole staff!... every last one!... the kitchen help... the whole crew... the butlers... the little downstairs maids... in their caps!... those from the linen room!... everybody in the bedroom!... the whole household... and he spanked her in front of them all!... Talk about a workout!... Apparently this wasn't the first time!... when she was small... and had disobeyed him... the butler told me the story... the guy in tails... the one who speaks French... Her uncle obeys her every wish, but she's not allowed to stray from the straight and narrow... if she does, the gauntlet!... and no holding back, I'm telling you! make no mistake about it!... She gets a good tanning!... But apparently these days ever since she's all grown up, he's sick and tired of his niece... he doesn't want to lay eyes on her! He's going to send for his little nephew... and dump the girl... The guy lives by whim!... He's going to ship her off to boarding school right after the holidays... the butler knows the family... He's been with them for twenty years!... He doesn't think she's his real niece!... just some girl they adopted, well not him... his wife... In short, a real big mess!"

"You know a thing or two, Sosthène! That butler of yours can yak up a storm!..."

"He likes talking French... it's been ten years since he had the chance...

just the Colonel's wife used to speak it... the lady of the house... she died in an odd way too... ever hear the story?"

"Not letting any moss grow under your feet, Sosthène!.. What else do you know?..."

"Ah! yes! the little girl's supposed to be sole heir."

"Wow, he's really spoiling the kid!... Really!..."

"Well, yes, but just hold on, things are up in the air, because he's going to adopt the nephew... the little boy!... six years old..."

"You mean he's not going to adopt you, you chump? You big mouth? He's not going to use the strap on you? Maybe that's what you're both into now!... You've already had knock-down drag-outs!"

I didn't understand.

"It's just a matter of time!... Just a matter of time!..."

Couldn't resist the joke.

"Whatever, Sosthène, but listen to me! I hate the guy's guts! I'm going to give him a few real nice strokes, you watch! Take my word! Since he likes the rough stuff!..."

"He can't stand your guts either!... Get that straight!..."

"So why's he keeping us around?"

"Maybe so he can bump us off!"

Ah! real funny!...

"It wouldn't really surprise me!... that's right up his alley!..."

And then he brings up the spanky session again. Ah! our boss was some creep!... What a kook the Colonel was! His niece in front of all the lackeys that way!...

Ah! Sosthène went back to the beating... The riding crop!... Let's go to it!... Ah! it was eating away at him... Why hadn't the Colonel called Sosthène in, too?...

"It turns you on too, you disgusting pig!..."

He didn't give a damn about my feelings...

"You're a rotten son of a bitch Chink!... You're a perfect match, you should shack up together!... I'll pimp out the pair of you!..."

Nothing could burst the bubble of his vanity... a waste of breath.

"So, did my name ever come up?"

I wanted to have some idea even so.

"Ah! Never! I swear! Not once!"

Real sincere.

"He doesn't want to give me the boot?"

"What're you saying! No, no way! No, no!..."

"You should know, you're in cahoots!..."

"No, Ferdinand!... No, I swear!... 'You came here together...' That's the line he took... 'And you'll leave together... together!... Ah! together!... I want to test out the masks!... to perform every test!... I hired you to see this through to the end!...' Those are his exact words!..."

Ah! he was back to that tune... I could see what he was up to... the double-cross!...

"Well let's get one thing straight, Sosthène!... Count me the hell out! I'm just here to run errands!... And don't you forget it, Monsieur Sosthène!... just the errands!... I'm not sniffing a damn thing... I already said so... I'm a wheezing wreck, got that? it hurts me!..." Ah! I didn't want him getting any ideas... start the wheels turning in that brain of his...

"No masks!... No masks, Monsieur Sosthène!..."

"You only think about yourself... so easy..."

Always the same comeback... Over the slightest little things, mean and bitchy.

The next morning my adored one was pale, that's a fact... a sorry little hang-dog look... At lunchtime I was afraid to give her a glance!... well, I snuck a little peek!...

Despite everything, I still had her there... I was happy to be in her dear presence... But what a state she was in!... Her poor eyes!... her poor little face!... A pitiful sight!...

He was there too, the brute, the Colonel, her tamer-trainer uncle... They'd returned at noon... They must have moved like lightning... from one section of the city to the other... I knew the route, even by taxi they set a real record!... But they didn't bring back everything! Deliveries were to follow... the Colonel was growing antsy... if it was up to him, he'd already have been out and back, a new buying spree... He was still pretty wound up... he turned my stomach... He was whistling... rocking back and forth... popping his monocle in and out... a flick of the finger, snap!... a flex of his eyebrow!... I didn't want to open my mouth, I was pissed off... but situation too tense!... I kept my trap shut!... He would have taken it out on my honey pie!... But let him make just one crack... Ah! I'll sock him hard right on the jaw... goes without saying... it looked like his guard was up... The flunkies brought around the platters... I had them dish out my food... couldn't do it myself on account of my arm... I was in too much agony... especially after yesterday... Another attack... and another... Sheer torture just to move it!... I studied her uncle out of the corner of my eye... He was really a repulsive freak!... a crafty walking catastrophe!... an unpredictable crank!... I knew him inside out!... I hated his guts!... But Sosthène made the best of him, for his money the Colonel was one funny guy... interesting to work with! Everyone has the right to an opinion.

But that thrashing he dished out to the girl really stuck in my craw!... Probably stuck in hers too!... How she must have hated the lot of us! Me included!... I was responsible!... The culprit! Why did I drag her along?...

But I was clueless!... Nobody brought up the subject, not a peep about it since we'd been back, except for Sosthène with the butler... the flunkies who'd seen everything, serving with impeccable style, you'd never suspect a thing from their behavior... Luckily... Even so, despite everything, on second thought, they might have felt pretty uncomfortable... Well, I didn't know for a fact! Maybe they got a kick out of the whole thing?... And they and Sosthène were birds of a feather?... out-and-out perverts!... Once you start flying in the face of decent behavior, right away your life's in the greatest danger!... You lose your nerve... your footing... ker-plop!... in over your head! A person's got to stick to the good old proprieties, always and everywhere, that's what I say! once you start playing fast and loose, you stop giving a fuck about anybody or anything!... you don't know which end is up!... You forget the way life's supposed to happen... once you let out all the stops there are no more surprises!... reasonable social rules are there for a purpose! once you flout and confuse them... you're headed for disaster!... When I was a kid back in the Passage, my mom constantly preached about keeping my nose clean... I can still hear her voice ringing in my ears... "First you steal an egg, then a cow, then you end up murdering your mother!..." She didn't mince her words... I repeated them now in my helpless confusion... That was a warm-up exercise... They were perverts... I had a more or less clear picture of the situation... but I got fouled up in the details!... I had a hard time sorting out what's true from what's not! I didn't have much experience in the ways of the world... I was a little wet behind the ears... the trickery of people in refined circles... plus the type of man her uncle was... his English eccentricities... that had a lot to do with it.... a hell of a lot... at such an awful moment when the war... social conditions had turned the whole world topsy-turvy... morals were out the window... customs too... everybody said so, including Cascade... Once you start talking crap it takes one hell of an effort not to lose touch completely... you've got to hang tough!... through the mazes and mirages... I didn't want to say another word... The Tweet-Tweeters, when all was said and done... after some thought... maybe they weren't so incredible!... Maybe it was just a cheerful little night-spot! lively lovely liberated, end of story!... a weird crazy nightclub... nothing more... Maybe O'Collogham was one of the crew?... a dedicated honorary club member?... What if I popped the question? I didn't know... I just had my hunches about everything!... maybe he also walked down those steps to have himself a blast?... and he knew Centipede? his smell... his rags... and together they used to treat themselves to one hell of a good time... real screams, the pair of them... maybe I was the unlucky one weighed down by some sort of rotten gloom?... I was some dopey down-in-the-mouth weirdo?... a killjoy pain-in-the-butt sourpuss? a sorry-assed grouchy gimp? a whiny wet blanket? a pathetic party pooper?...

Ah! I could really bring people down in the dumps!

Maybe I was spitting in the wind?...

I sort of kept my eye on the Colonel... my old trusty sidelong glance... He started twitching something awful... practically ripping out his underarm dress shields... clawing himself mercilessly... rip!... rip!... like that! plus a scowl at the same time!... He rattled the place settings, all the doodads the tablecloth... sent everything flying into the sauces, his monocle, the spoons, even the corkscrew after one horrible spasm... he was having a fit... And then he turned all nice and pleasant again... in a snap... smiling all around... his attack over... lasted just a second... I blushed at each mishap... thinking about the little one... my eyes on her... I turned red as a beet... it was really unbearable... with all that had happened... I couldn't take any more... I got up again... stepped out in the hall... paced up and down... wandering this way... and that... going... coming back.... walking off my embarrassment... While strolling around aimlessly I stumbled upon Sosthène and the Colonel by surprise... their little plot... they were sneaking each other rascally little winks... I caught them at it in the mirrors... They thought they were so cunning... bastards!... They were setting up some nice little job for me... Ah! I was brought up short! there was no mistake!... I saw through their scheme!... But I'm not as dumb as I look... Whenever I'm cornered and look like a goner I let my animal instincts take over and fight tooth and nail to the bitter end, incredibly ferocious... hyped up!... I dig my heels in and go at it... I come out swinging something awful!... Nobody'd better count me out!... You crazy jerks, I'll make you piss blood!... my mind was made up!... even if the bastards showed up twelve dozen strong, and a hundred thousand times slicker... I'd make them gobble down their load of shit... crawling on all fours!... streaming in their tears!... That's the way the world works! the cry from the heart! The iron law!...

Your guess what happens next.

OK then, great! Great!... My mind's made up! I concentrate, become two-faced!... He who laughs last laughs loudest! They sent me off on my errands, run right down the list, pronto, in a snap, flitting between buses, charging ahead, running like mad, whipping my bum leg along, not a single second gone to waste... I'm a new person. I've become a different young man, I'm not myself anymore, diligent, punctual, neat and tidy. Beyond reproach.

Virginia doesn't come with me anymore. Our gallivanting days are over.

I see her only at mealtimes at the other end of the table, we trade a couple-three friendly words... That's all!... As though nothing had happened. The dignified face people slap on existence is ugly as sin. The Colonel's eyeing me sidewise, we both have our guard up. Cat and mouse. Sosthène's all put out because I'm in no mood to chat.

When we go up to hit the hay, he's full of stories, I keep mum, snore, he can go fuck off... His monologue's a flop.

In the afternoon if my shopping takes me into Rotherhithe I go up and see Pépé, I always find her in the same condition, tipsy or all but, and still very much in love.

"Where's Sosthène?"

It's eating away at her.

"He was my cross! He owes me paradise... he's a monster, young man!... A monster!..."

I bring her five shillings six every week for her expenses. I don't give her the Willesden address... that'd be the end of everything. I don't run into Nelson anymore... nor the young milkman. Thus time goes by... one week... then two... then three... Of course I couldn't call them pleasant... they're full of suspicion and worry... even so we've got a place to stay... food on the table... but no goofing off... noses to the grindstone in short... both of us... Sosthène works at the gadgets... and sensible me runs the errands... no more scenes... no more carrying-on... He worked long into the night up under the rafters... I turned in around ten... He had a late bite with the Colonel... came up to bed around midnight. One night I was snoring away!... And here he comes excited as hell shaking my bed... beside himself... I've got to listen to him!

"Do you know?..." he says to me, "or don't you? The trials are in a week!"

"Ah! Good news!..." I answer. "So, you happy?"

"Happy!... Ah! happy's not the word!..."

My cockiness takes his breath away... He thinks I'm an outright monster.

"You'd send me off to my death? Doesn't mean a thing to you, does it, of course..."

"Ah! I'm not sending you off any goddamn where!"

"Ah! you're not sending me off any goddamn where!... Now the gentleman's acting cynical!... And what if I kick the bucket... would it suit you just fine? You wouldn't give a damn, would you?... Not a goddamn? Ever since you got back from your bender, you've hardly said a word to me!... Come on, admit it!... hardly a word!... You treat me worse than a dog!... I don't exist anymore!... But I'm the one taking all the risks, Mr. Romeo!... While you're throwing yourself into a life of vice, Mr. Romance! You'd be tickled pink to see me croak!... you'd have peace and quiet at last!... you're not much for other people's opinions, Mr. Romeo! You're hearing it from my own lips!..."

Ah! he was going a little too far!...

I snap back: "But think of my situation, Mr. Pain-and-Suffering... think about me, I nearly kicked off myself! You no good dirty tongue-tied freak! You weren't in my shoes! Go on, get the hell out of here! Out! Beat it! I'm not the certified engineer! You are! Leave me the hell alone!"

I was straight frank and up front... I dotted my i's.

"Yes, but," he retorts, "You're real happy with the loot. You don't let anybody have a taste of your stash. Isn't that right, my little hickey! And your cock's had a grand old time too! And now you're gussied up like a prince!"

He was really dishing out the insults!...

"Ah! Mr. Asshole Sosthène, you're pushing it! You're way the hell out of line! I'm going to put you back in your place!..."

"Well, just take a look at this delicate lad! And so what about the little girl, my wonderful young man? A child! nice going! A sex maniac for all ages! Or I don't know what I'm talking about! Who needs to be an engineer, Mr. Migraine! You're an early bloomer!..."

That's the line he takes with me.

I have visions of knocking him on his ass... and then I calm down... I'd prefer to keep on talking... I really wanted to ask about the girl... it was a little more serious all the same!... like why she totally clammed up?... And whether it was on her uncle's orders?...

"Does she talk to you?"

"No, my little laddie! Not a single word! Ah! you know, her fanny's still smarting! 'Goodness me! That uncle of mine!'... She doesn't want him to go back to that! And the whizz! whizz! the switch! such a severe disciplinarian! How it whizzed through the air! Oh my goodness! My ass! You should know about that, having been in the cavalry!..."

It really turned him on something incredible! Thinking back on the circumstances! How they were all in the audience... the flunkies... all the servants!...

"Ah! the flunkies too, no less!..."

He was sorry not to have been a part of the scene!...

"Shut up! Christ!..." I cut him off... "Shut up!..."

He was starting to wear on my nerves.

"Shut up, Sosthène... You're a big show-off! I'm going to let you in on something... You're too funny for your own good!... I've known a lot of funny guys in my time! some real jokers, absolute laugh-riots! And they all came to a horrible end! I'm telling you this as a friend!... ease up!..."

"Me?" he snickers at me, "me, too funny? Ah! you're going too far there, Ferdinand! What do you take me for?"

He's getting all worked up now.

"But you've got to laugh, goddamn it!... You're bursting with health! Good spirits! And so tell me then! Whizz! Whizz!... What if Uncle gave you a go? like that right on your own butt! Wouldn't it make you laugh? You know you'd be splitting your sides! show me how you'd act!..."

He did an imitation with his ass...

"You're a dimwit, Sosthène! You're a dimwit!... a dim-witted moron!"

"Me, dim-witted? Me, dim-witted?..."

Ah! he looks at me... hard... he's floored... me calling him a dimwit!...

"Me, dim-witted?... Me, you snot-nose!..."

Ah! He won't hear a word about dimwits!... Ah! he lashes back something horrible!

"A metaphysical guy like me?... Did you get that? Metaphysical!"

Ah! floored... I struck a raw nerve!...

"That's what you'll never understand, my little bungling shit-assed brat! Metaphysical!... metaphysical!..." Couldn't get a word out from the shock... crazy with anger!

"You ju! ju! just li-listen to me go-good! instead of following your instincts... thief! looter! lout!..."

Ah! he didn't consider himself to be dim-witted in any way shape or form... Ah! that stuck in his craw!

"Metaphysical! Etherian!... So there, you little jerk, now you know what I am!"

"If I were in your shoes, Mr. Sosthène, I wouldn't lose my temper... I wouldn't start preaching to anybody... I wouldn't act so conspicuous!..."

"Conspicuous! Ah! conspicuous!... Ah! That's just too rich! Will you just listen to this snot-nose! And what about you, you dirty little roughneck, you mean you haven't been acting conspicuous! Ah! you want to know the whole story! Ah! you want me to fill you in! Ah! you make me lose my temper! Well now, I'm going to give you a little piece of information! Here's what's going to happen to you! You're going to get sacked! kicked right the hell out the door! you little ingrate! you little rat! right out in the street! you dirty little pig!... right into the gutter you crawled out of..."

He was boiling mad at me...

"You're jealous, Mr. Sosthène... You don't know what's coming out of your mouth!..." I answer real calmly... "But since you're such a blabbermouth... one little secret deserves another! I'll let you in on something too, Monsieur de Rodiencourt... if you get me sacked... well then, you'll be hanged! Monsieur le marquis de Sosthène! You unmitigated son of a bitch!..."

Ah! Got him there, tit for tat!

"Hanged! Yes, dear master!" I rub it in... "Hanged! You heard me!... Hanged!... and that's the least of it! Hanged high! And I guarantee you! Oh yes! High! That's what's in store for you!..."

"You're yelling like a stuck pig, Monsieur Squealer!... We're guests here!"

"What I said's not sinking in, you're a dimwit, Monsieur de Sosthène! Let me run it past you one more time! I've already told you... You're the one forcing me to yell!..."

"This isn't our place... and you're acting like a swine!... Like a bum!... It's obvious you were born in a whorehouse!..."

That did it! Wham, I pounced on the jerk, didn't have far to go, his nose was in my face...

"A whorehouse! A whorehouse! Ah! just hold on one second! I'll show you what a whorehouse looks like!"

"Ah!" he hollers... bellows... "Murderer! There's the murderer!..." like that, his finger pointing in the air... "WATCH OUT! LOOK! LOOK! LOOK!"

Ah! he turns my stomach... he takes the heart out of me! I wash my hands of him! Shit!... I flop back on the bed... I could reduce him to a pulp and he'd be just as totally vomitous!... It wouldn't do a damn bit of good!... He's a son of a bitch, end of story!... I roll over face to wall!

"I want to get some shut-eye!" I shout... "You hear me! I want to get some shut-eye, you bastard!..."

If I can, that is...

"Quiet! Lights out!" I bark.

I'd had enough!...

OK! Fine!... a second goes by... I hear him blubbering quietly... sobbing into his bolster...

"How long you gonna keep that up?..."

Long... his wheels keep spinning... I know... the circus in his head!... I don't give a damn... he's making me drowsy... wah... wah... wah... on that note he sends me beddy-bye!...

The thought of more hassles worried me stiff... I beat it for the whole day... right after breakfast... I was off and running! Heading into the City, to Holborn, and then especially to Clerkenwell! for all the nice little chemical ingredients, the chlorine, the sulfur. I stopped by Pépé's, she was still the funniest gal of the gang! She filled my ear with some real dirt about Sosthène... about the time they were traveling acrobats in Australia and the Midwest, about his mining flimflam in Capetown, the crap he pulled in India, his so-called prospecting. According to what I thought I could make out about his run-ins and bum deals, his name was mud throughout the entire southern hemisphere, he must have had at least twenty search warrants on his ass!... Setting foot in that neck of the woods again was out of the question! Sosthène could bend over backwards to deny it, but Pépé wasn't throwing any bull about the clink, time behind bars, she had seen the whole rigmarole up close!...

"You can't imagine, darling!"... (she always called me darling) "what those judges in Bombay are like! they're vultures! genuine vultures! Worse than the judges in Rangoon! Jungle hyenas? They're lambs compared to the judges in Rangoon! They'd tear you straight to pieces!... with your heart still beating!... And honey, those prisons of theirs! Just the thought, oh sweetheart! I feel sick!... the stink!... my precious!... the stink! mass graves! ten, a hundred prisoners to a single pit! living and dead left to rot! all squashed together! You can't imagine!... Ah! the judges in Burma!"

She shuddered in fear at the mere memory!...

"Ah! if only he had loved me!"

She started up that old song on cue!... The one about Sosthène... It really threw her into a blue funk!... I dropped her a kind word, then flew out of there. Another afternoon, I passed by Prospero's pub, well, the place where it used to stand anyway... nothing but rubble... ashes... a picket fence... that's all that was left of the Cruise pub... I ask around for some news... from the neighbors... the other pub farther down the block... Nobody'd seen Prospero again... I had some dealings in that neck of the woods, a little farther off over in Wapping, at the Gordon Well factory... carburized carboys... The traffic's crazy out this way, a steady stream of goods toward the docks... Basically it keeps right on rolling!... a perpetual hubbub... the vehicles pour between the walls of the buildings tall as cliffs... A roar echoes inside... crashing, thumping, bumping... shaft horses... drays, heavy lorries pulling up to the holds, the edge of the water, all part of the scenery, the river itself like a stage, brightly lit, whipped by the wind, and your dreams carry you away... I can see it now... I'm starting to go mushy... So I asked all around... I'd really have liked to see Prospero again all the same, despite everything, have a peek at how the old guy was getting along these days!... and that joint of his built out over the water... anyway so what'd I turn up?... Just the fact his whole place had gone under, and up in flames!... Nothing left from his joint, the two-story Cruise pub, but the piles! plus bits and pieces of everything in the sludge!... At ebb tide the river bared it... the debris... all rotting away in front of the Dundee Docks... I'm telling it like it is...

Ah! but to get back to my story...

My strolling days were over, that's a fact!... every now and then I'd just sneak in a small detour!... between two factories!... I wasn't parading around with thick wads of dough in my pockets... Just a couple-three pounds for what I needed to buy, and always absolutely alone!... never again with Virginia!... I had time to read the papers this way hopping from one bench to the next!... There were scads left scattered all over the place... Greenwich wasn't in the news anymore, our nasty business... not a single word mentioned... not a single allusion, zip... True, lots of other stuff, more exciting mysteries were going on in this great big world! even for London... some real killers... so there was no end of things to read!... A corpse found under a subway car, a nurse down in a sewer stabbed with this terrifically long knife!... an infant dangling in midair... from a telegraph wire... plus the big offensives revving up in Flanders!... the plan was to drive forward all the way to Berlin... plus the capture of Salonika due any day now!... endless excitement!... at least eight "EXTRAS" every day!... This gives you some idea what a jumping time it was... But not one word about our calamity!... You would have thought that Claben had never existed... Delphine neither!... It was outrageous!... A dream!... It really gave me the willies!... Yet I hadn't dreamed the whole thing!... Those scrapes were all too damned real! horrible and threatening!... The proof was the way I was shaking... jittering at the mere thought!... Sure I'd got a breather, but so what, big deal! The ups and downs of the war!... kept people kind of fascinated... cause the tide would turn our way any day now!... it just put off the final day of reckoning!... "Boomerang, sir... Boomerang!..." Greenwich'll pop back in the news some day... Ah! I was ready to bet my life on it!... I carried my load of junk and worries from one district to the next... I looked for crowded spots... streets thick with traffic... where I could vanish in a snap... melt suddenly into the mob... I took a good look around... the number of wounded was on the upswing, the squares and esplanades were crawling with them... the war was starting to take a real toll... From every country... of all stripes... strutting around... in roving packs... squadrons!... mobbing the sidewalks, hobbling, thumping along, twisted out of shape, arms in slings, crutches everywhere. The Zeelands especially looked the most messed up to me, lots of them around in little wheelchairs!...

No more scenes back at the house... not a single word!... model behavior!... I'd roll in around so-called mealtimes, go beddy-bye right after!... Sosthène worked day and night! I could hear him up under their rafters rattling around all their scrap metal... filing, cutting... when I woke up they'd still be banging away!... they were still whacking away at the sheet metal!... feverishly preparing for the day of the so-called big contest... I thought they were going to flip into their old routine at any moment!... fly into one of their awful conniptions... and tear the whole joint down around our ears again!... in a fit of frenzy!... knock each other off right on top of the rubble!... It'd take just one puff, just another whiff of their gas... their nastiest concoction... their "Ferocious"... and they'd be back to their old crimes!... they slacked off only at the first light of day, pooping over dead asleep! right in the middle of their gewgaws!... But they didn't laze around with the wind knocked out of them!... Just a couple of hours of shut-eye, back on their feet, bam, quick, to the table!... Touchy situation, oh yeah... a real tough time... I could see Virginia's poor face, her sad little expression... she'd have really liked to talk with me. Ah! I was on my guard... She scared me too much... Yes, honest! It wasn't just my yellow streak... I kept looking at her uncle, at Sosthène... the window... anywhere... at anybody... to avoid her glance... she gave me the creeps sort of... ever since our night out with the Tweet-Tweeters... Could it be just a fever?... one of my harebrained hallucinations?... a fit?... Maybe I'd imagined the whole thing?... and nothing had really happened?... Back at the Dingby neither!... and what about the rest?... my eyes playing furious tricks!... they'd just come over me like that... It was real possible!.... with all the awful shocks I'd experienced... everything my head had been through!... fractures, concussions, trepanation... Maybe they were just dizzy spells?... Ever since my operations I'd had my share!... horrible bouts!... my mind would start wandering... I'd fly out of whack at the drop of a hat! I didn't want to dig too deep for the reasons... Too dangerous!... More than I could handle!... My head was my heel, Achilles' I mean!... well, wasn't that just tough shit!... Stay on your toes!... Poor little darling!... she scared the hell out of me, that's all there is to it! End of story!... She was wearing me out!

We had dinner at eight on the dot, everybody gathered around the table... The touchiest moment of all!... I hardly ate a thing... I was losing weight apparently right before their eyes... in a truly extraordinary way!...

"Your bones are showing, Ferdinand! Eat, my friend! Eat!..."

The Colonel wanted me to eat... he cared a lot about my figure!... He adjusted his monocle for a better look...

"Your bones! Your bones!... fantastic!..."

Was that any of his business?

Nothing fantastic about me! He was the queer customer!... the weird bird! I'd never been so sensible... I'd grown old, body and soul! That's what'd happened to me!... I didn't want to have any more adventures!... or misadventures... or whatever the hell you want to call them!... Ah! no! no kidding, you can keep them all!... Right off I told them straight to their faces!... so that they'd be informed once and for all!... And they could take off for the moon! the Cyclades! the Sunda Islands!... Happy sailing! Good riddance!... Have a nice trip!... with masks on or off! by dirigible! by underground! on all fours! by trolley! by omnibus! I couldn't have given a royal fuck! I was no part of their travel plans... they could count me out completely! Totally calm and sensible! The new me!... "Your bones are showing through, Ferdinand!" So I had to pack on a few pounds!... The word from him!... No more worrying myself sick, no more misunderstandings!... nothing but kindness... a quiet recovery... so I could just sit back and wait for peacetime to roll around, the bright future!... My life would be made once the war was over!... That's right, a piece of cake!... I could already picture myself in a first-class setup!... some small concern... hustling something or other that would jump off the shelves!... Ah! no more heavy stuff! no more bulky crap!... my backbreaking days were over!... I'd had it with humping around tons of junk!... No, from now on, nothing but featherweight articles... wristwatches for instance... which as a matter of fact were just starting to come in!... With my 80 percent disabled veteran's pension, if I watched my pennies, I'd be living in the lap of luxury!... Just had to let it fall slowly and surely into my hands... and not rock the boat! not act cocky, but be a nice boy, pleasant even... Enough with the hard knocks... Sure or not, I'd had it up to my eyeballs... Good luck! Good riddance! Fly away, darling floozies and clowns!... slick rascals, old scarecrows! Life's too complicated as it is! Beat it, sluts! You too, virgins! Blow out of here, cyclones! To hell with you freaks!... Leicester! Van Claben! Tweet-Tweet Club! Enough anarchy!... Clear off, dumb clowns! I didn't want to work up my mind anymore!... or my body!... or anything at all!... Patience!... Patience! and a totally cool head!... Meantime, I had to make a living... keep slogging away... holding out!... Matthew was hanging around outside.... Ah! You could bet on that... maybe here too?... Probably!... Her uncle must be cooking up something!... even more two-faced than his other schemes!... not to mention his fetish for his riding crop! I saw right through that guy's game with us... playing cat and mouse... He kept watching us... plotting... must have been having a ball these past days!... must have been stretching out his pleasure... One fine morning he'd rat on us just like that! to the cops!... Ah! I knew what he was up to!... But what if the pair dropped dead in their gas masks... Ah! that'd be a different story!... that'd be just fantastic in my book!... Maybe I'd even inherit a little something... I'd rob them blind before taking off!... A slew of plans was popping in and out of my head during our lunches while I babbled on about this and that... what a bunch of worthless creeps!... selfish pricks, period!... the kid too, when you came down to it... each out for himself!... The trials were around the corner... the famous contest of theirs was almost here... It sent shivers down the spine of Mr. Chinaman Sosthène... Most of the time the cat had his tongue... he mumbled only a word or two to the Colonel... He looked down in the dumps... every meal we sat there at the table with our two gloomy mugs. Luckily the Colonel came through with flying colors... a one-man conversation, kept up a sparkling patter, perpetual witticisms, endless riddles... little cock-and-bull stories!... Danger breathing down his neck really brought out the joker in him, goofier than ever, constantly firing off quips and conundrums... luckily he forgot everything... from one minute to the next... He'd keep repeating the same ones:

My first one's a little birdie!
My second's a big ministerrr
Ministerrr! Ah! Careful! Look out!
Look outteee! Careful!...

Complete nonsense... Even so we had to find it funny!... Ah! don't look for trouble!... don't rub him the wrong way!... Ah! careful!... laugh, and from the belly while you're at it!... Sosthène had to force himself!... explode in his big guffaw... anything less and the Colonel'd be miffed. Ah! right away he'd put on a face... And then it was celery time... "Celery, my first... I crunch into my second, etc." Finally, by way of wrap-up, he'd turn serious: spread wide the big pages of his *Times* and start reading... muttering over the articles... skimming over the hard news... didn't really interest him, he jumped right to the ads... Sports... Holiday rentals... he read them in his low grumble... didn't press the matter... while working himself up... the highlight of the event was the obits... When he reached this section, he'd adopt a new voice and tone... turned solemn... the notices in their black borders... deaths... he reviewed the list... the long columns labeled "Military Deaths..." "Death in Action..." he announced gravely.

"Major John W. Wallory! 214th Rifles Brigade!"

He runs through his mind, comes up blank...

"Don't know him!"

Sharp salute, heels click under the table.

"Captain Dan Charles Lescot! King's Own Artillery... Don't know him!..."

Salute. Heels.

"Lieutenant Lawrence M. Burck, Gibraltar Pioneer D.C.O. Oh! Knew his father at Sandhurst! No! Nigeria! Good man! Good man!..."

And so on right down the columns... the names of the dead going on and on... all his former friends, their sons, cousins... everybody he'd known... And all those he didn't... scattered in every corner of the globe... from Ascot, to posts in the middle of nowhere!... from the backwaters of the Bermudas to the Hebrides!... everywhere in the service and stripes of the Seventh Royal Engineers.

When it was all over and done with, when he'd run through the whole tragic list... he proposed a toast to the king... So everybody up on your feet and join in, the kid too! Raise your glasses!...

"Gentlemen! Ladies! Long live the King! And our gracious Queen Mary! And long live our General Haig! And long live your Joffre! Long live France! Rule Britannia!..."

Glasses filled all around... Talk about an entente cordiale!...

We finished up with actors... another big toast for that crowd!... to the glory of the glories of the theater world!... to his personal memories!

"Long live our Helen Terry! our glorious Keats! Bravo for Sarah Bernhardt! Long live Camille!..."

Then we were free to go.

I didn't act very curious. I asked next to nothing about how the experiments were going... like whether the masks were working smoothly? or whether everything had been patched up?... Or whether they were sniffing correctly?... At any rate they'd stopped cursing each other out!... that was already a big improvement!... I didn't hear them hollering at each other anymore!... just a lot of awful hammering... and streams of pressurized gas that came shooting out above the lawns, often all the way into the street... they had their breakfasts brought up to the lab... everything they put in their mouths was laced with Ferocious!... So they wouldn't need to lose a single minute by coming down! they were in the full throes of creation, that's how

I sized up the situation... but I didn't ask for any details! any secrets!... The days went by, period!... I snored away the nights... or pretended to...

I didn't want Sosthène to talk to me... when he'd come back down after midnight... not a peep... or a single sigh... I was absolutely determined... my way of buying time!... that was the only thing on my mind!... I'd had enough of wacky projects... I wanted to make it to the end of the war without getting hanged or arrested!... that was my supreme ambition!... I didn't even look at Virginia anymore... not even when we were both at the table... I kept looking straight ahead... I'd just peek a little out the window... whenever she'd be walking through the gardens... She couldn't see me... As it was I had a hell of a time with my buzzing ears, my throbbing arm, not to mention Matthew! and Claben! And the Leicester!... and my one-track mind about that crowd!... plus my obsession with not sleeping ever again, and the Consulate, and Centipede! I wasn't going to let some all-consuming love do me in a second time!... Ah! no way, just hold on one second! If I dragged that poor little girl into some wild and crazy scrapes... other calamities would be sure to follow! My dick had gotten me into enough jams like this one!... These days I was scared of my shadow!... Nobody ever died of a broken heart!... but if you fuck up you've got hell to pay!... horrendous consequences... kidnapping a young girl... etc.

In England they'd throw you right behind bars!

Buy some time... that was my one and only obsession!... To make it to the end of the war without getting hanged or arrested... just a few days' time... one more!... one less!... I was counting them!... to escape from this hellhole!... Everything else will fall right in place by itself!... No more mushiness!... no more recklessness!... keep my nose clean, act sensible... No more complications in my life!... I was really sucked dry... Kidnapping that innocent girl again... getting the Colonel on my ass, high morals, the courts!... the birdies out in the garden who lost their little girlfriend... I couldn't get away from it!... Sure bet this was all plotted out beforehand... Was I falling back into the trap?... Ah! no way, uh-uh! Older and wiser! overnight!... especially since my bout of delirium... that night at the Tweet-Tweet Club... It all came back to me something godawful! the mere thought! spooked the hell out of me... The memory gave me the shakes! I could flip out all over again... You bet the others were keeping their eyes on me... the old geezer and Sosthène... they were dying to catch me red-handed... That's just the way this place operated... Ah! I was more and more suspicious!... Had to be I was funny in the head... inside, I mean, my notions, my gray matter... Ah! I knew the score... I saw blurry, and such pain... The hospital crew must have been gawking during my operation... must have left something inside... a small splinter... a metal sliver... right behind my ear... that's where it hurt worst!... I could feel the splinter whenever I laid my head down to sleep... if I concentrated hard... It whistled and ached like hell!... My mind wasn't playing tricks, this was real, excruciating agony, I'm telling it to you straight... got nothing to do with being excitable!... All you need is a little bitty taste to find out just what great joy it is to be some poor son of a bitch, a wanted man, battered by his own body, without a soul alive who gives a damn about you... including my idol, Virginia, with all her lovey-dovey ways, basically she just had one thing on her brain, her pussy, getting her jollies, wasn't her fault!... Wasn't anybody's, all of us crazy to live life to the fullest, give it everything we got, and today not tomorrow, nobody has a single second to waste, on your feet or on your back, that's the law of the world... There's no room for lame ducks... can't let them be a drag on our delights!... They're just left with their imaginations, with beating their meat for all they're worth, hunkering down, keeping a low profile...

I was flat on my back, wide awake, my mind spinning... And here comes Sosthène barging in! It must have been just about midnight! he shakes me... wants to have a talk!... I play deaf!... dead!... He rocks my mattress, insists.

"Tweet!" he goes to me... "Your ears working? Tweet!"

He pinches my nose... my butt...

Goddamn him!...

"You asleep?" he asks...

"You can see for yourself, idiot!"

He flicks on the lights.

In a total dither.

"You've got to listen to me!... You've just got to!... This can't go on!..."

"What can't go on, what?..."

"You've got to help me!... You've got to!..."

"What's gotten into you?"

"So you don't want the *Vegas* anymore?"

"The *Vegas*?"

Slipped my mind!...

"You woke me up for that?..."

"But the *Vegas* are a matter of life and death! Mr. Devil-May-Care! Including your own measly little life!... If that doesn't matter to you!... There's nothing more serious than the *Vegas*!... It's worth being woken up over!..."

"Oh, come on, you're exaggerating!"

"Exaggerating my ass! Do you understand that we go up against the competition on the fifteenth of this month? In two weeks?... two weeks!... that's all!... Do you feel ready?..."

"Ready for what?"

"Ready for the gasses, for Christ's sake!... Not for an audience with the pope! Not to go butterfly-catching!..."

"Ah! So you're back to that, are you, Sosthène?"

Ah! That jolts me awake! The brass of the guy!...

"That's your business!... I've got nothing to do with any gas!... So you just hold your horses!..."

I balk at the suggestion!...

"Of course! Got it! Mr. Not-My-Problem! Mr. Hard-on! Mr. Sweet Nothings..."

"Hard-on! Hard-on!... But not for you!"

"Mr. Homewrecker!... Mr. Bewitches-Young-Virgins!"

"Me!... Me!... Ah! I can't believe this!... what nerve!"

That bastard was infuriating me! All hell was going to break loose again any second now!...

"That's right! Mr. Scumbag!" That's what he called me... "You don't even have the guts!..."

Ah! now that got under my skin!... what was he really driving at anyway?...

"What're you after, Sosthène?"

"I want to find the flower!..."

"Whose flower?"

He comes up close... whispers: "You know which one, the Tara-Tohé..."

Ah! I lost him there... this flower he's mentioned... oh yeah, Tibet!... Slipped my mind!...

"The Tara-Tohé?" Ah! I shouted out... "You wake me up over that, you faggot?"

"I've got the right to defend myself!"

"So go and look for it... and don't be a pain in the ass to anybody!"

I had as much as I could take of his silly crap!...

He bursts into tears.

"My old pal!..." He breaks down sobbing... "Don't let me down, old pal!... I'll never make it all alone!... If I don't get that magic charm I'm a dead man!... You won't do this to me!... You won't!... think about my wife! think about Pépé! I care for her, you know!... You know her!... She's a good old gal!... She loves me too!... Doesn't treat me like shit!... How ungrateful you are at your age!..."

"But what do you want?"

"I don't want to drop dead like some fly! I want to defend myself! You understand? I want to defend myself!... I believe in the Tara-Tohé!"

"What do you believe?"

"Just what I said, for crying out loud!... What you read!... Come on, damn it, you read it along with me!... Don't you remember anything at all?... Your poor head!... Of course you're in foreign territory!... But give me a break! Didn't you look at the book? the pictures!... you're just being stubborn, right?... No, hostile!... So you don't want to help me? I can see you're hostile!... You hid the book from me, didn't you?... Where'd you hide it now? Where'd you stash it?..."

Right away he starts getting wild ideas... spouting his crap! picking a fight. He's back to his old song and dance...

"I believe in it, I do!... You hear me?... I'm a believer in the Tara-Tohé..."

He was professing his faith to me!... his eyes whirling like mad in his sockets!...

"I believe in it!... Where'd you stash the book?"

His damn *Vega* was right under the bed!... My memory was still working! Way at the other end of the carpet... I had to cram my whole body under the bed... and yank the book out... more fucking bullshit!

"Do you want it real bad?..." I ask him... "Huh, do you?"

"Ah! You want to know whether I want it badly? Ah! how about that! Ah! whether I want it badly?..."

I was stark naked!... I'm busting my butt, groping around, crawling, I've got it!... What a huge monster this book is!... thick as a couple-three telephone directories at least!... I lug the tome up... on top of the bed we crack it open... to the page with the incantations... presto it starts dancing before my eyes!... swarming with colors!... people!... too many!... too bright!... My head's in a whirl!... I rub my eyes!... I start feeling sleepy!... Shit!... I want to take a snooze!... To hell with his book!... I stretch out!... Ah! he'll have none of that! He badgers me!...

"Let's go now! Where'd you put the drumsticks? Come on! Forget already?..."

He wants me back on the job right away!... He can't hold still...

"Let's go! Back to our dance, and I mean now!..."

Ah! he's possessed!... he's making my head spin!...

"Ah! What do you want? Shit! I'm sleeping!..."

Can't hear me... The birdbrain's fixated on his plan!...

"I'm telling you you're going to start playing and right now!..."

On top of everything else he's bossing me around.

He meant I should pick up my table setting... fork and knife... the ones I drummed with our last go-around... like this tap! tap! tap! against my bed, the copper posts... my part... I'd stashed them in the closet... so the maid wouldn't spot them...

He doesn't have a second to waste... he strips... stands stark naked... just like that, ready for dancing!... His whole body matted with red hair, especially his belly...

"Aren't you wearing a few strands on your head?" I joke.

The fact he was as bald as an egg... Simple observation...

"You're not funny, Mr. Kiss-and-Run! Not just anybody can go bald!... To go bald you need to have ideas!... Ah! and that excludes you!..."

He flipped through the pages... looking for an example of his dance...

"Ah! here's the Sohukoôl! All laid out for us!..."

He cries out... happy as could be... filling me in!...

"Sohukoôl's the caged demon... the one obsessed with traveling around... the 'cooped up demon,' that's just what we need!... We're going to have to break him out!... That's the task before us, my young lad!"

I got a good look at his caged demon... huddled up behind the bars... that's exactly what the illustration depicted... Sohukoôl was one ugly sucker... nicely drawn... gaudily colored... one bored-to-death devil... splashed yellow, green and blue, with a tail that stuck way out... an enormous blue and yellow tail... reaching to the other side of the page... to really emphasize the gloominess!... a horrible scowl!... his mouth pushed up into his eyes... twisted all out of shape... contorted!... because of his supreme ennui!... Sosthène underscored the point for me!... Nobody could suffer from boredom worse than the caged demon, Sohukoôl!... So read the caption... and we were supposed to break him loose with our incantations... shimmying around... a dance frenzy the book called it... And then afterward from that moment on, in gratitude the demon would be our servant for life!... the demon Sohukoôl!... He'd travel with us everywhere... at our beck and call!... He'd fight for us to the end of time!... He'd fuck up all the other devils... all those who'd come to bust our balls on the magic route to Tibet!... who'd want to snatch away the flower! the Tara-Tohé... all the devils for starters, then all the bandits!... and the high plateaus of Tibet were teeming with bandits!... the Himalayas are number one when it comes to thugs!... in the foothills... It was just like that!... No buts about it!... Sosthène was firmly convinced!... And the proof of his conviction was that he'd woken me up... and that he really meant business!...

"So, OK now, let's rehearse!..."

Had to make every minute count!

"He's caged up!... Do you get the full picture? Surrounded by bandits!... bandits and demons!... By now you've been concentrating!... Sheer determination!... Exerting yourself to the fullest... The emanation's already flowing into you... You're about to burst... Your mind's on what you're going to do!... the battle you're about to wage! Right off you recognize Sohukoôl... The one with the yellow tuft!... Look!..."

He had to stick my nose up close!... into the drawing... In short I had to work myself up into a hallucination!... And make sure not to mix up tufts!... Oh, look out, hell to pay if I bopped Sohukoôl unconscious instead of some other devil!...

"Ah! You be careful! Make sure you recognize him!... And make sure it's him! And nobody else!... He's got seven fingers on his left hand... the other devils just got five like everybody else!..."

Simple as that, it'd be a real snap for me now!... Let's hit it, on with the music!...

"You see! Sharp raps!..."

He showed me how with the fork click click clack!... like that on the copper frame...

"A syncopated beat, got me? Syncopated!... Don't start playing any old way! You're in a crouch!... Then you rise to your feet!... First you bow! You salute me!... every twenty clicks! clacks!... You're doing me homage!... that's what it's called... homage!..."

At the same time he's looking at the picture so we'll both understand!...

"You see? I do a right twist, follow with my neck, my head! Blink two, three times!... Are you catching on? Click! Click! Clack!... Both together!... I fire myself up! get all hot and bothered! and then I launch into the adagio!... on point, theoretically... And you rap out the beat!... clack! clack! click!... I do a few déboulés... a few more!... You see me coming!... around the would-be cage... the demon... inside... Sohukoôl... I've got to hold my arms like this..."

He showed me how the arms were in the illustration... crooked in half-circles... above his head... very graceful...

"That's the way I do my déboulés... Let's rehearse!..."

He starts going through the motions... stops short.

"Ah! Pépé! my friend!... if you could have seen her on point!... Ah! for sheer charm, nobody else could even compare... A fairy dancing on point... a sylphid! Ah! I can't hold a candle to her!... What ambience! Let's go, my friend, clack! clack! clack!..."

Memories...

I start rap-tapping... rap-tapping away... drumming hard the way he wants! along the entire copper frame!... from top to bottom... He quivers, wiggles... but in the same spot... A far cry from the drawing... Ah! a far cry from its fiery passion!...

"Yoo-hoo!" I protest... "You're cheating, you bum!"

I'm starting to catch on fast!... the guy cracks me up... he's just wriggling his belly a little... that's not what he's supposed to be doing!... I'm an expert!...

"What about putting some oomph into it?... You said oomph was the secret!..."

I want to see him slaving away!...

"You'll never catch that joker of yours! You're going to make that demon sick to his stomach! He's going to be thinking: 'That slob!... that pimp!'..."

I want him to bust a gut!... beat his brains out! I want my money's worth since he's gone and woken me up!... Right away he starts percolating... putting himself through the wringer! He stamps his heels... hops around... he's off!... gives me the eye... blinks... sails above the floor!... honest-to-God leaps... he's starting to look like the book... But hasn't quite broken into a farandole!... the real whirlwind Sohukoôl-style!... Ah, no, he's got a long way to go!... He's sweating so hard the drops pour off as he pirouettes... stark naked his body's working like a sprinkler!... He's huffing and puffing a little... runs through his routine again... But I've got to mute the light... mask it with my undershorts!... cause it's much too raw for the Spirit!... much too violent!... Still no good, nothing comes of it!... Shit! he's pooping out!...

"Enough already with Sohukoôl!... Geez, I've had it!..."

He's throwing in the towel... stopping dead... panting!...

"I'll never catch him... He's too damn dumb! I can't feel him anymore! shit! I can't feel him!... Scram, you dirty bastard!"

He boots him out bluntly just like that!...

And then collapses in a heap.

A flop... had to face the fact!... even so we can't just roll over and die!... We got off track... that's all!...

"Find the Goâ page! Now there's a Sar for you!... the genuine article!... with real magic powers!"

He's revving up again.

"I used to make him appear whenever I wanted... Sar of the Third Ordeal! You hear me, Curlylocks? the Third... We're talking about a powerful demon here! Sohukoôl doesn't like London!... I can see what's behind this!... I don't want to say too much... Got to bring back Goâ, that's all there is to it!... I almost had him a while ago... Now Goâ's the sort who can hold up in London... he likes a damp climate!... the other's a dry spirit!... I've always said so!... I could have guessed what would happen!..."

We start riffling back through the *Vegas* again... We find the three pages... the Ritual and then the Offerings!... There're at least two hours' worth of gesticulations!... if you follow the illustrations...

"You rap-tap!... Rap-tap!... Remember?... And I work my heels... Daa! Dum! Dum! and then you chime in, four times!... Plunk! Let's go, hit it! With some pizzazz!... I'll be right on top of you!... Daa! Dum! Dum!..."

He starts working himself back up into his trance... he's a true believer!... Now he's off again!... Dancing in a peplos... my sheet... twisting himself up in it... whipping it off into the air... catching it... dashing after it... revving up for takeoff!... his feet leave the floor... up, up and away! Wham!... slams right into the mirror... standing in his way!... the whole joint rocks!... and a hundred thousand shards... cascading down!... Ah! that face of his!... He looks like a real jerk now!... One hundred thousand pieces!...

"And so?" I ask... "Done yet?..."

"This means ten years of bad luck!..." His only comment... Don't have to be a genius to know that!...

"Yes! So, what about going to bed?"

I thought this was going to do the trick!... that we'd already wrecked enough things! Ah! but no way!...

"End on this note?... hell no!..."

"Come on now, you don't know when to quit!... the whole mirror's in smithereens! Ah! just hold on! You're not going to fool me a second time!... Ah! you're a monster!... Take it from me!..."

"Come, come now, none of that, you weakling!..."

The guy's a real bully, that's a fact... treating me like some kid!... He's a tyrant, a despot no less!... He starts badgering me!...

"Keep up the pace!... and put some life into it!... Be steadfast in the face of adversity!... Didn't anybody ever tell you that before?"

And here we go with his pirouettes and catlike leaps... the dumb clown's really cutting loose!... He's everywhere at once... doing his déboulés from the beds over to the windows! leaps over the sofa... pirouette! the text calls for fff! fff! fff!... marked in tiny hieroglyphics... meaning fast... I'm starting to catch on... carrying through on my fork... then my spoon... And he's going wild in the middle of the room... wriggling around his belly hairs... dancing... trancing... Plus his little sighs... he snuggles up in a ball... kittenish... sensuous... and then springs back up on his feet!... another round!... Mimicking fright... I'm going to run him ragged, to his last breath!... I don't spare him a single fff! fff! fff!... I want to see him whirl it all out!... and give me the eye at the same time!... otherwise I'll quit, and take it over again from the top!... that's what the text says to do!... I'm the stronger one now! a slave driver!... I keep him moving!... shake him up!... bam! bam! boom!... I keep him hopping!... I want to see some fire!... He's got to outdo himself!... both with his eyelids and his pelvis!... plus his quivering head... Ah! I'm a stickler... a real ballbuster!... "Everything to the letter!... Everything to the letter!..." He has to play out the whole page for me... And I won't be cheated!!... not out of one single illustration!... I want it all!... I want to see him keel over!... He's still performing but his knees are turning to jelly, arms flailing around as he hops! I've gone and drained him dry, shit!... He's got to say he's sorry!... It must be three in the morning!... The bongs echoing in the distance! Big Ben out there in the night!...

"Come on, get a move on!... I'm still holding up... Show some vim!... Put some pizzazz into it! Ah! I'll need to get out a whip... lazy son of a bitch!"

That's what I dish out to him... Now I'm the one spurring him on! For starters the pages are full of whips... every drawing's got loads... plus pikes, hooks!... enough to tear an entire regiment to pieces. All by way of example for me, I say! the rods of the *Vegas*!... lashes of every shape and size!... I alert him!... He's in a sweat... squealing... like a stuck pig... Ah! but he won't give up!... He's a tough old bird, no quitter! But I'll make him say he's sorry!... By the time we finish he'll be mine!...

I've got the music down now... all the clip! clack! clack!... I perform each and every last one of them!... like a swarm of locusts on my copper frame!... steady pingping drizzle!... But he wants to screw me up too... complicate my life... now he wants me to make tongue sounds... ah! he's getting fancy!... he wants me to gurgle in syncopation!... that's how the spirits of the dance like it!... apparently it gets them all excited!... makes them shine their brightest!... One more thing to worry about!

"OK! OK! OK!..." No bickering!... He's the one who wears me out when all's said and done... He had the upper hand... the last word... next time I'll act sick!... He can go and wake up the Colonel to play his rattles... that's what I thought of that belly dance and gurgling of his...

"Ferdinand!... You just watch me pour it on!..."

He wanted me to whoop it up... go wild with the rhythm! He outdid himself whirling around!... I couldn't even see him anymore he was moving so fast!... And whoosh! up into the air! There he goes!... The hairy typhoon!... Ah! I was doomed to keep running into the most godawful screwballs!... Now he was Terpsichore in person! Lucky me!... King of Transcendent Dances!...

I'm shot... I yawn... He curses me out...

"So you giving me the sack? You lousing me up? The gentleman's just packing up and taking off!... And then what happens to me? The gentleman doesn't give a damn! Couldn't care less!... The gentleman is clearing out!... Mr. Sex-Crazy Big Mouth!... Who's on the job?... nobody!... you're taking a powder!... Oh yeah, sure, you'll get it all, all for yourself, the girlie and the meal ticket! You'll get everything I've been telling you about!... And meanwhile your benefactor will've kicked the bucket! That sucker Sosthène won't be bugging you anymore!... You'll be feasting on huge legs of lamb!... All just for you!..."

Ah! So he was my benefactor, was he!... Ah! the guy cracked me up!... One moment of doubt from me and he bares his claws, flings unfair accusations... Goddamned ornery bastard!...

We had to take it over again from the very top... the Goâ dance was turning out to be a total no-magic bust!... The sweat was pouring off him!... his old bag of bones was clattering!... he was wheezing, shaking everything on his body he could shake!... No good... It did as much magic-wise as marmalade!... just turned him into a bitchy loon! Big fat zero... He wouldn't call it quits.

"Hold on, let me take a look..."

He grabs the book... I yawn... it was striking four o'clock!

Another bright idea!... Another!...

"Hmm... What I need is rhythm twenty-seven, the Pandah Voûlii. Ah! now that's really something!... from the Khorostene Temple!... Ah! Wait till you get a load of that one!... I make my entrance from down under... Can you picture it?... My face covered in soot... completely blackened... At first you don't recognize me!... You beat out your fright on the copper frame... your crazed terror!... a nonstop staccato panic! The storm of fear!... I come toward you... I want to strangle you!... So right away you kiss me!... You clap your hands! You're happy!... I grant your prayer!... You've been praying for twelve moons!... I've come to bump you off... naturally!... You couldn't ask for more... You think I'm consenting... that I've come to grant your prayer!... A comic routine!... Go fuck yourself, Jack!... Look, it's all right here on the page!..." He shows me the book again... "Here, drawing twenty-seven... You can see the pauses, the grimaces!... The stances... the various wiles... Take a good look!... You see... I refuse your sacrifice!... I scorn your body!... I don't want your hide!... your smell!... I don't want your soul either!... Just look and see how much I despise you!..."

That's just what figure twenty-seven was about all right... Clear as day!...

"That's when it gets good!... You shimmy around... work yourself into a lather!... You want to breathe me in! You want me to take you come what may! I am the Spirit of the Khorostene Temple! I just want what's good for you!... But not your body! We act out the whole thing! I dance all around your body!... I fascinate you... but find you unclean!... twelve pirouettes as the moon turns from left to right... a ploy... all the way to the washstand... circling around the entire temple supposedly... You're crying because I don't want to sacrifice you!... You're rolling on the ground!... Pleading with me!... You offer me your neck!... Look, like this..."

He shows me.

"You call Wandôr to the rescue!... the demon-bird!... to make me jealous!... and you accompany me in sextuple time!... Ah! never forget your music!... You've got to keep belting it out with your fork!... bop! bop! bip! bip!... And then your spoon... clack! clack! clack!... and then three gurgles... glug-lug-lug!... Go ahead! You start out nervous and then you turn lovey-dovey!... lovey-dovey for Wandôr!... Wandôr shows up from the other side!... You weren't expecting that!... Surprise!"

The whole description was printed in red in the *Vega*... All the Sanskrit characters... He spelled them out for me word by word!... He mustn't have been able to read very well!... The illuminations were beautiful!... The Wandôr-bird was breathing fire!... Its blue and green wings spanned two huge pages, top to bottom... the fantastical bird...

"I'll teach you Sanskrit, you greenhorn!... it'll be a lot easier that way."

"And how, Monsieur Sosthène!"

He translated for me as he went along!...

I was supposed to tie myself into knots... some pretty tricky business... but of absolutely utmost importance!... Ah! he really hammered away about that, I had to switch from friendly to imploring to sensuous!... Let's hear it on drums!... He snuck onto the scene from the hallway... a Wandôr wanna-be... on the tips of his wings! hunkered down... crafty... to create the total effect!... rolled up in the rug... He was supposed to surprise me... So I went "Oh! Oh! Oh!" in surprise!... Right then I unleashed the storm... in full swing exploding away on the bars!... the box springs... the chair! and just look at that guy go!... he's taking off... maneuvering all around the beds!... the devil incarnate... just like in the engravings!... He scowls at me... We stand nose to nose... Ah! this is a riot!... I bust out laughing!... My mistake! He gets pissed off... we've got to take it from the top!... My fault!... He goes back out onto the hallway!... this time around he works up some real momentum! a terrific bound!... he takes off! With one wingbeat he sails across the beds... and crashes down ker-boom!... a ton of bricks!... on his back!... what a racket!... And he doesn't even weigh that much! the whole joint trembles... He's howling in pain!... Squawking! He hurt himself real bad this time!... I think he might have broken his back!...

"Ah! Ah!" he goes!... "I've got him!... I've got him!... Ferdinand! He's mine!..."

He gloats in triumph!

"What do you have?"

"I feel him!... I feel him!..."

He's contorting... and recontorting all over the carpet!... jerking around his arms... his legs!... his hairy belly quivering like crazy!... sucked in and then puffed out!... swelling up... he sighs!... a goatskin! bagpipes!... then he's off again!...

"I've got him!... I've got him!..."

He's having a fit...

"I feel him!... I feel him!..."

He's drooling... foaming at the mouth... groaning... barking... a dog!... then he moans some more!...

"I've got him!... He's mine, Ferdinand!..."

And such sweat and strain... an awful struggle!... As though locking horns with himself!... braced in hand-to-hand combat!... in a superhuman convulsion!... right in the middle of the room... as though his arms were clutched around a giant!... Ah! just awesome!...

"I've got him!... He's mine!..."

He's shouting at me!... Squawking!...

Ah! scary stuff!

"Go to it! go to it!"

I cheer him on.

"Lie down on the bed," I advise.

Seems to me a more comfortable spot for waging his agonizing struggle...

"Get into bed, will you!... Into bed!..."

"No, stupid asshole..." he answers... "This is Goâ!..." Boiling over furious he rages in a life-or-death struggle!... hand-to-hand around himself!...

Ah! Goâ! now that's a surprise... We weren't expecting him! he's not the one we'd invoked!... Great ferocious Goâ! What a colossal screw-up!... I understood his amazement!... his increased fury!... We were expecting Wandôr... Wandôr the devil-bird!... not Goâ!... Ah! no confusing those two!... We'd been expecting Goâ back at the last contortion... And now he shows up on the scene... after we'd given up on him! Ah! what a dirty trick! Ah! no-good bastard!... And with such a ferocious grasp! a real bone-crusher!... I could see it with my own eyes!... those deadly strangleholds!...

"I'm telling you it's him!... Goâ!" he bellowed over to me from the thick of the fray... his knock-down drag-out with the monster!... he got bowled over on his ass, rolling around the carpet, drooling, one foot in the grave... wheezing like crazy!... That's just how it was!... I stood there taking it all in, dumbstruck in terror!... I couldn't help him!... He was battling a presence, a symbolic body!... Nothing to do!... "The Sar of the Third Power!..." he stammers out through his drool...

"He's all over me!... He's all over me!... He's coming inside me, Ferdinand!... He's coming inside!..."

It's all one big horrendous herky-jerky spectacle of mystic fury down there on the carpet... as though he were bucking in convulsions against himself... right in Goâ's clutches!...

"He's coming inside me!... He's coming inside me!..."

Now he was growling on the carpet like a dog, dead tired, worn out, beaten to within an inch of his life!...

He was fainting away in agony... stark naked... flat on his back...

"He's heavy, Ferdinand!... So heavy!..."

That's what he was moaning...

Goâ was on top of him, mystically speaking... and crushing him under his horrendous weight! I wanted Sosthène to get to his feet... I tried to give him a hand... and yank back... heave ho! again and again!... No good!... He was too heavy apparently... pinned to the floor that way... under the demon...

"Ah! Fuck this shit!... You're screwed now!..."

"This is no joke, moron!..." he insults me...

He was choking in anger... and then got the hiccups!...

Shit! This was funny stuff!

"You're a scream!..."

I start braying hee-haw hee-haw like a jackass... I can't stop!... What a sight he was wheezing away down there! belly in the air in the buff! red hair! Just amazing! My God!...

What a performance!...

He couldn't move a muscle... pinned down under the tremendous load!...

"I'm dead beat!... I'm turning in!" I announce.

I was glad it was over!... I was up to my eyeteeth with acrobatics!... He could go ahead and croak with that belly of his sticking up in the air!...

Ah! was I ever wrong!... It was far from over!... He starts shaking like crazy all over again... His whole body's racked with spasms... from top to bottom!... still flat on his back!... Writhing!... Flying out of whack... eyes turning back in his head... rolling on himself... flailing... it's the falling sickness!... I lean over him...

"Where's it hurt?" I ask.

In the end he was a royal pain in my ass.

"I'm happy!..." he moans... "I'm happy!... It's Goâ!... It's Goâ!... I've got him!..."

The old fool.

"Where at, sweetie?... Where you got him?"

I wanted to laugh.

"In the trunk of my body, dummy!... Inside me!..."

I step closer... bend down over him, right up against his hair... stick my nose right on top of him... I want a glimpse of Goâ under those bones!... Who knows, maybe you can see something!... I can't see a single thing!... He just kept on wiggling harder and harder... more and more wildly...

"So, you're OK?" I conclude... I absolutely didn't want any bickering... "Great then!... It's a success, Sosthène! Bravo! Bravo! my dear master!..."

He's racked by another convulsion, real horrendous... ten times stronger than the last! It looks like I threw a few logs onto the fire!... just with my innocent little compliment... He's wriggling... and writhing his body incredibly out of shape, bending backward until his head meets his heels and he loops into a perfect O... and still bent backwards he clenches his feet in his mouth... starts gnawing his heels!... It's awful!... You can't imagine how extraordinarily supple he is, the way he continues to contort his body... I let out a whoop of enthusiasm... I want to give him a kiss... He's biting his toes... and then with a heave of his back he flips around on his feet!... That's the way he is!... and what an expression on his mug!... what a smile!... what ecstasy!... He's in bliss!...

"My dear boy!... My dear boy!..." he calls me... Total bliss!...

And then he confides in a whisper: "He's still not used to it... Shh! Shh!... most of all, don't bump into me!... I've got him in my belly!... Be careful!..."

He's warning me.

"The least little goof-up!... one wrong word... one careless word! whoosh!... he'll fly off!... the least little jolt!... He'll be up and away, and it's over!... We'll have lost him!..."

Ah! pretty serious stuff...

"I've got him in my belly!... I'm breaking him in!..."

That's the latest!... the reason why he's tiptoeing around on eggshells!... Ah! great, really terrific!... This is perfect!... The best thing would be for us to call it a night... the pantomine has gone on long enough! Ah! Time for intermission! A little snooze!

"Beddy-bye, Goâ!..." I coo.

He takes it the wrong way.

"So don't you believe in him?... Do you? Just come right out and say it!..."

His dander's up again.

Ah! fuck it all!

"No, you don't believe in him!... No, you're making fun of me!"

Ah! He couldn't stand for my doubting Thomas routine!... He wanted faith!...

"Yes, I do! I do! I believe!... You're completely right!... But I'm sleepy! Do you understand?"

Ah! he jumps back... starts sounding off... chewing me out again.

"Sleepy! Sleepy!... Will you just listen to that!... Ah! that good-for-nothing bastard! and me standing here with Goâ in my belly!... It does me one hell of a lot of good to hear that!... You just listen to what I've got to tell you!... You don't deserve anything!... And me standing here with Goâ in my trunk!... all over my body!"

He thumped his scrawny torso, and then his thighs and his butt... He sounded hollow!

"Here! Here! Hear it?"

"Yes! Yes! You're right, Sosthène!..."

I wasn't going to start bickering... I was falling asleep where I sat... He came over to egg me on, spouting crap right in my face...

"I already had him once in Benares! You hear that? I already had him once!"

He was shouting at the top of his lungs... I had to listen.

"I already had him for two weeks!... I know what you can do with him!... hand me the phone!... You can do everything!... You hear me!... You're incarnate!... You've got the power! The third!... You hear me!... The third!"

Another fresh idea!... He wanted to give me proof of his Goâ! Ah! I couldn't wiggle out of this one! No way!

"I know him! I'm telling you! I know him! He's possessing me!... I'm possessing him!..."

He started pacing back and forth, holding his belly in both hands... from the door to the window... he just wouldn't call it a night, Christ Almighty!... all simmering and seething with enthusiasm!...

I go: "You're gonna catch cold!"

He was stark naked and in a sweat.

"Hand me the phone! Hand me the phone!..."

His one big obsession. I hand him the phone.

"Who's the toughest guy in London?" he asks me point-blank.

He catches me up short.

"Who you scared of most?"

I just stand there like a jerk.

"Just wait till you get a load of this number!..."

"Whatcha you gonna do?" I ask.

"Never mind!... It's not me talking!... It's Goâ... It's him inside me!"

He thwacks himself on his forehead, his belly, his sides... He's showing me he's not himself anymore... That he's one hundred percent Goâ, through and through! he's possessed... And then he bows toward the window... And solemnly too!... Real solemnly!... keeps going lower!... a big deep bow...

"Spirits of the Night!" he intones.

He throws the window wide open... He's going to catch his death!

Another two... three greetings!

"Goâ! Goâ!..." he's shivering... talking to himself... muttering a prayer!... Takes a deep breath! Prostrates himself butt up in the air...

"Goâ! Goâ!..." he calls out just like that imploringly.... How scrawny he is!... all skin and bones!... I can see his backside! his pointy ass!... he runs through his acrobatic routine all over again... a good ten... fifteen times more!... genuflections!

Homage to Goâ!...

OK! that'll do... He's back up on his feet! primed! radiant! raring to go!... All energized with emanations and faith!... The faith of the Brahmins!

"Get me the phone! You loafer, let's go!... Hand me the ear trumpet!"

Now he's cocksure... there's trouble brewing!

"Did you come up with the name of your big bad wolf?" he asks me.

He's itching for action.

I can't imagine who he thinks he can be scaring... especially over the phone this way.

"I'll put the curse of Moûrvidiâs on him!... You heard what I said!... It's the worst curse of all!... it hunts you down wherever you are!... So who is it you want me to take on? You still haven't given me a name yet! Wait till you see what his ugly mug'll look like in a week! Ah! whooh, look out! I'm telling you! You've never seen anything like the curse of Moûrvidiâs!"

I can see he wants to pull one over on me, get me going on the idea.

"Call up the French Consul! Now there's one lousy creep for you!"

True, that guy pissed me off, goddamn it! ever since I dropped by his office! and he had me bounced out on the street! Ah! the bastard!... Ah! I'd've got one terrific kick if a log came crashing down on his damn face!... some huge sucker, wham!... Ah! let me see some of that magic!... let it tear him limb from limb, fucking hell! the French Consul!

"Hand me the phone book, you little devil! You wait and see what I do to that chump of yours! I'm going to fix him real good! Wait and see how you find your French Consul in a week! You've got no idea how bad a curse can get! The very one I'm throwing on him!... through Goâ! But got to strike while the iron's hot! Come on, let's go! Goâ's emanations! He goes on the fritz over next to nothing!"

We both look for the number... riffling through the phone book...

"Bedford!... French Consul!... Bedford Square!... Ah! Here it is! Tottenham 48-486!"

"Dial it up!... Ask for him!"

He couldn't manage himself.

"Four! Eight! Four..."

I help out.

Consulate on the line!... I hand him the ear trumpet...

"I want to talk to the French Consul! In person!"

High and mighty, no ifs, ands, or buts.

The person on the other end starts spluttering...

"What's it about?"

Ah! he flies into a fury. Ah! He won't stand for this! He grabs the phone away.

"You hear me! The French Consul!"

"Sir, the Consul's in bed!" comes their reply.

"In bed!... In bed!... Go wake him up quick! The president's on the line!... You hear me, the president! This is Raymond Poincaré! So get your ass in gear! Shake a leg!"

That's the way he carries on.

Ah! Decisive as hell! No mistake on that score!...

They start scurrying at the other end of the line... sounds of a switchboard being plugged and unplugged... voices talking over each other.... Ah! Got it!... Consul on the line!

"Hello! Hello! French Consul!..."

"Hello! Hello! Is that you, Monsieur le Consul? President Poincaré on the line!... You wait and see..." he whispers to me... "Just wait and see!..."

He gives me a wink... shows me he's confident!...

"Hello! Hello! Is that you, Monsieur le Consul? Ah! very well, thank you! This is President Poincaré!... I've got one thing to tell you.... Shit! Shit! Shit! You're nothing but a dirty rotten son of a bitch! And Goâ's going to make you croak!... Yessiree!..."

Bang! he hangs up!... Ah! you bet he's thrilled to death!... jubilant! kicking up his heels! jumping and shimmying with joy... in the raw just like that and completely off his rocker... all around the carpet... doing his Brahmin victory jig!

That's how he is!

"You hear that? Did you? I really gave it to him good... Three 'shits' will do the trick! Just imagine!... His curse'll last for eighty years! That's the minimum when you're working with Goâ, between eighty and ninety years!... Just imagine what a number I did on him... He'll never break it!... That's a Benares job for you!"

He's juiced up like crazy! Over this telephone success of his!... He prances around in a circle again... does his saraband of victory!... without a weary bone in his body now! He's really tripping the light fantastic!...

"Three shits! Three shits!" he gloats. "Ah! my boy!... Ah! my boy!... Can't you come up with anybody else? Some other rotten bastard? So we can knock him for a loop! Go on, hurry up! We don't have a minute to lose!"

Clearly the guy's all whipped up, in the throes of his trance as Prince of the Emanations!...

"Hey, he's scratching my bone! He's scratching my bone! Feel my hip right here! That's the real true sign! Ah! Ah! the absolute best! We got to pray a little more!... Hold on! Hold on!"

He prostrates himself again... Bow... another five or six times!... to the Spirits of the Night! with the ritual bleat "Goâ! Goâ!"... Ah! that did the trick!... He's all set for another round! Leaps to his feet! All right!...

"Are we ready?"

"Hit it! click! click! clack! I'm throwing a terrific curse!..."

He's tipping me off...

"A whammy that'll knock the breath out of him!... that'll make him throw himself under a tram! That's the magic I'll send his way! Come on, join your magic to mine!..."

He's advising me. That's how cocksure he is!... Ah! the guy floors me... but who knows, maybe he's onto something after all? Maybe he's got influence?... Like the people who hold seances?... Ah! it really makes me wonder... He sure as hell looks like he's convinced!... Big-time magic's such a swindle!... A scam for charlatans and their cohorts!... A Robert Houdin racket!... But still and all, maybe he really is conjuring?... screwing people up long-distance?... it really had me stumped! Ah! I try and come up with a name! What the hell!...

"Nelson! what about Nelson? There's a stinking scumbag for you!"

Seeing as he wanted a son of a bitch.

"Ah! That guy, yeah... Ah! That guy!"

I'd forgotten about him.

But Nelson doesn't have a phone!... Skip to somebody else!...

"What about Matthew? the copper! Now there's a name for you... A lousy bum!... Fuck, do your stuff!... Bump him off... Ah! Man, if you could get that guy! Throw a curse on him!... Go ahead, like this!..."

Ah! look out!... I gave him a little demonstration myself... I throw a whopper!... I suggested Matthew!... Ah! I couldn't stand the sight of that guy!... Ah! you'd better believe it!... He was hands down the sneakiest of the bunch!... the biggest snake in the gang!... any way you looked at him!...

"Get me Scotland Yard! Pass me the guy on the line! Ah! come on, what are you waiting for?... we've got to do it before dawn!... After the sun's up the magic goes kabloeey! it peters out! Goâ!... After dark's the only time!... He's a night spirit!..."

Matthew was over in Whitehall!... A Whitehall exchange!... I knew it by heart... 0! 1! 0! 0! 1!...

We reach them on the first ring...

"Hello? Hello? Scotland Yard?... Whitehall!... 0! 1! 0! 0! 1! Got it."

"Hello, Miss! Please! It's urgent! Urgent! Chief Inspector Matthew! Very urgent! Matthew Donald!"

Discombobulation like last time!... They need to track him down in the department!... Ah! not there!... Yes, he is too!... No, he's not!... Their zzz-pop-crackling racket... Deafening!... That switchboard of theirs makes a hash of everything... Ah! the oafs! They'll need to ring him up at home and check whether he's there!... Maybe he's home and in bed!...

"Call him up! A special emergency! Special! Wake him up right away! And make it snappy!..."

Acting high and mighty becomes a habit fast... I was even turning into Goâ myself!... in no time flat I was talking in the magic voice...

"Special!... Special!..."

They had to call him at home.

"Special! Special! About a crime!..."

I really cracked the whip... and no crapola!...

Ah! His home phone... Brrring!... Brrring!... An answer! Presto, he's on the line!...

"Hello! Hello!..."

We listen to our separate ear trumpets... that's Matthew all right!... That's his voice!...

"Your turn!" I go to Sosthène... "Your turn!"

He was the demon after all!...

"Shit! Shit! Shit!..." he hollers into the gizmo... But so fast!... Much too fast!... He slams the receiver down!... Running for cover!...

"You mean that's it?" I ask.

"Ah! so what do you want!... The curse's on him!" he answers me just like that...

But I couldn't see how... no way!... I wasn't buying it!...

"You scared of Matthew, Sosthène?..." Ah! I accuse him to his face. Ah! I lower the boom on him!... He woke me up!...

"Scared?... Ah! scared!... Ah! you damn little pest!... Goâ's not scared of anything!... Get that through your thick skull, snot-nose!... Not anything!..."

He's ticked off!

"Go on, quick! Another name!..."

He's badgering me... wants me to toss him another victim... Ah! I'm thinking... Ah! I draw a blank!...

But then: "Ah! what about your pals down at the Leicester?... Don't you want to add those hooligans to the list? You could shake them up a little!... It won't do any harm!... spook them a little!... They're just a bunch of lazy bums!..."

"Ah! No! Not those guys!..."

He doesn't want anything to do with them!... He doesn't want me to wake up Cascade!...

"You scared of him too?"

Just what I figured!...

"No! But they're small-fry... they wouldn't count for the magic spells...

We need fat cats... big shots... not a pack of cheap hoods!..."

"So think of somebody yourself, Mr. Picky-Picky!..."

"What about the lord mayor?"

Now there's a name that lights his fire... what a stroke of genius!...

"Did you ever see him in his wig? In his golden coach? He's a big shot!... I'll reduce him to smithereens, and how! As soon as Goâ gets down to work! I want him to collapse in his coach as soon as he sets foot inside! That's my wish! Yessiree! Wham! Let's go! Up and at 'em, come on with me!..."

I'm with him all the way.

"Now get him on the phone!..."

"At this hour? You out of your mind?"

"Go ahead! Listen to me! Say you're King Alfonso of Spain! Announce that Alfonso is on the line!"

In a way it's not too harebrained!...

I dial City 7-124, the number's in the phone book... The operator tries to connect me.

"Hello! Hello! The lord mayor, please. The king of Spain here! Alfonso!"

Just asking for him cracked me up!

It surprises them at the other end of the line... leads into yet another wild tizzy!...

"Hello! Hello! King of Spain here! Esta you, Mayor? Yes? Yes? Yes?"

"Yes! Yes! Yes!" they answer.

"Well then, shit!... shit!... and shit!... Goâ says to kiss his ass! which means you'll be croaking any time now!..."

With that, bang! hard! we hang up!...

"You hear that? That's a group curse! An anathema! The anathema of the avalanches! The major grand power! The absolute worst curse in the world!... Hear how I threw that one?... Did you see me in action?... He's in for it now!... You can take it from me!..." Ah! so proud of himself!...

This Sosthène de Rodiencourt, Old Red Fuzz, is incredibly diabolical!... I'd never have guessed just how much!... This curse-throwing business has him on top of the world!... Gamboling around in his omnipotence!... doing a Benares farandole!... all around the beds, the goof!...

"I've got to warm him up!..." he shouts to me while bouncing around... still going on about Goâ!... "The cold temperature's bad for him!... It freezes him up... demagnetizes him! He loses three-quarters of his strength!... That's a fact! Let's go, hit it with that fork!" He was throwing me back on the job! Back to my table settings and my click! click! click!... in a steady barrage... nice and steady... He does his saraband and then a pirouette! a glissade! another pirouette! just like that all around the carpet!... Ah! the tyrant, make no mistake... just like on page 81... the entire red, gold, and blue watercolor drawing!... But he's got no props!... neither shield nor breastplate!... No grimacing mask! Just his birthday suit! with me on drums... click! click! click! clack! clack! clack! he's giving his all! getting all worked up... He slams into the armoire... wham!... Too psyched up! He collapses!... Plop! Full body flop!... Takes a few sniffs... bucks up!... And he's off again!... He rears up... like a circus pony!... Ah! it's wonderful! What a comeback!... This belongs in a horse show!... absolutely! a first-class riding school!...

"Go to it! Go to it!" he eggs me on.

He's the one who's pepping me up... chewing me out!... He's flying high! Whirling around!... Spinning so fast I can't see his legs anymore!... he's not even touching the ground!...

"Go to it! Make the most of it! he's ours! Got a firmer hold on him than back in Benares!"

He shouts that out to me in mid-gallop!... then he slows down... halts! Stretches out on the carpet!...

"Feel me! Feel me here!..." he goes.

He means on his stomach!... his belly button!...

"There! You feel that? The knot?..."

Goâ was under his belly button!... right in the hollow of his stomach!... something hard... Sosthène wanted me to grope down deep!... press my whole hand all the way down... my left hand, my strong steady hand... and feel around.

Seeing how scrawny he was, you hit bottom right away, touched his other side, his backbone!...

"Listen, now, this is big time! You loafer! Listen! I've got the Goâ cramp!... This is the ultimate! You better believe we've won favor!... Take a look!... Turn to the page!" Got to crack back open the *Vega*!

He stays flat on the floor, wheezing!...

"What page where?"

"The king's page!"

Couldn't find it.

"Concentrate! Lord in Heaven... Concentrate!"

"To do what?"

"Get Buckingham Palace on the line!"

"Won't get it."

Ah! He sighs!... I'm putting a damper on him... He remains flat on his back with his cramp in his belly!...

"Ah! you know, you're mucking up everything for me!..."

What a thing to say! It was really out of line! After the way I'd gone all out for him.

I just didn't see any miracle, and that was that!... It wasn't my fault! he had nobody to point a finger at but himself!

Sure as hell made him sore... He was still after something!...

"You want me to change the face of things?"

He was talking bigger and bigger!...

He wanted a trance to top all trances! Make me drop dead in admiration! He's shooting for the moon.

"So, evil curses aren't enough for you? You need cataclysms? The gentleman wants another Great Flood?"

Mr. Claptrap really cracked me up! I could barely stand on my own two legs, I was so wiped out... and him flat on the floor with that big knot in his belly!... And now he's talking catacylsms!

"Ah! you know what?" I say to him... "You're full of bullshit!"

I just can't keep it in... I've had it!

"You red hairy ass! You're up shit's creek, Goâ!..."

I'm having a ball... I need to!...

"Watch your mouth! kid... Watch your mouth!..."

Ah! he's threatening me... I'm in for a performance now.

He peeks toward the door to check whether anybody can really hear him. He motions me to stoop down close... wants to say something in my ear... He grabs my head... and whispers...

"I'm going to stage a battle of the gods! They'll all mix it up together!"

He lets go of my head... I stand up! Ah! I don't get it!... Something fantastic as usual! I open my eyes wide... and wait!

"So what's going to happen?..."

He motions me to stoop close again... and he'll spell it all out for me!... I can't stop giggling!... he gets mad!... I bust out laughing right in his face!... He spits in mine... Seriously miffed... in his eyes I'm one hopeless moron!

Ah! what's he got to gripe about? I did everything! Called up everybody, the lord mayor!... the Consul!... the pope!... Now he wants to phone up the Good Lord in person! He's a pain in the ass with his Goâ! He's bullying me!... I'm a real sucker!... it's true... for putting up with this all!...

"Fuck off!... the pair of you, you and your Goâ!..." That's what I hit him with all of a sudden! What I want is for him to leave me the hell alone!... and for the two of us to turn in! And for him to let me catch a few winks! Enough is enough!...

"Yes, it is! It is!..." he keeps harping away... "It's rare for a person to keep hold of Goâ! It's a miracle, you damn no-good oaf! You're lousing up everything! You're botching it all up!..."

He's pointing the finger at me again!... He stands back up on the carpet... He takes up his position at the other end of the room.

"So you want me to do the seven signs?" he announces... "So I'll do the seven signs!..."

He cuts loose.

We're in for another big show!...

He starts waving his two arms... signaling through the air!... and zigzagging... then runs through it a second time with his back to me! facing the opposite direction... more zigzags...

"Don't move," he shouts over... "This is the Sar of the Third Power!... The overthrow of all religions!..."

He's shouting at the top of his lungs!... Waste of breath... I hear him loud and clear!

"Fine! Fine!" I shout back!... "I get you!..."

"Look at me!" he goes!... "Take a real good look!... Don't move!... Take a good look! Don't you see anything around my head?"

He kept waving his arms around, standing stark naked in front of the window.

"Take a good look at me!"

I opened my eyes as wide as possible! Didn't see anything around his head.

"Concentrate! Concentrate! For God's sake! You're going to see the halo, I'm telling you!..."

"Ah!" I answer... "Enough already! Get the hell out of here!"

"Nothing's there? Nothing? What kind of jerk do you take me for?..."

The mouth on that guy!...

Ah! what do I have to do to shut his trap? Ah! he's really pissing me off!...

"Ah! OK, time to hit the hay!"

My riot act.

"To do what? What was that?..."

He won't hear any of it... He wants to concentrate till he drops!... He wants me to see his halo!... I go ape!

"So what're you saying, you don't want us to go to bed?"

"I'm slaving away for a lout! a boor! I'm reducing my life to cinders!"

That's what he fires back!...

"I'm floating, you get that, moron? I'm floating on my magical emanations! Can't you see me floating? Look!"

Ah! I quit looking at him! Ah! let him rip himself to pieces! go at it hammer and tongs until he breaks himself in two, the asshole!... He's chugging around the room!... The dance of the magic emanations!... That's what he's wailing over at me... I shut my ears! Ah! he can go and take a flying leap! the crummy crackpot... the fucker! I don't give a damn!... I quit looking at him... and even hearing him! I don't give a damn! I hit the sack like a ton of bricks!

Here we are back in the workshop. I could see their glorious gear, those masks, masks galore... All over the place, small ones, big ones, incredible jobs both in size and appearance. There were the flops, the winners, misshapen messes, camouflage masks, some with valves, with tubes, with ropes, all the Colonel's brainstorms, every variety, dimension, a carnival of hardware... Helmets and masks from every epoch, updated for chemical warfare. Made out of cardboard, copper, nickel, for every conceivable danger. Weapons and toys! all the headgear for hell, the trek to the depths of the abyss! Three gigantic diving suits for deep-sea pressure. An entire armoireful of small Henry II-style toques done up with feathers, plus tulle net veils by way of gas filters, quite smart-looking. The Colonel thought of everything. One goddamn unholy mess! I always run into slobs! The workbenches disappeared under five or six layers of tools of every size and type. Sosthène was rooting around at the bottom, hunting around for a little screwdriver, and setting off avalanches in his wake! The whole heap of trash came crashing down BA-DA-BOOM! spilling all the way to the stairs! Torrents of tangled metal! And the wrangles that broke out between them!

"Mr. Sosthène! You are a skunk! You lose everything!"

They traded some harsh words, raked each other over the coals because of the mess. Apparently I was going to restore order. I was supposed to hang up everything on little nails driven into the rafters, all the instruments scattered around, clear off the workbenches, the oven, the dormer windows. Lucky me, I had it made now!... My arrival meant order!... I was going to make myself useful!

"You know, young man, we are lost! Lost! Lost! And this gentleman is a swine!"

Over the large door to the workshop, way up high, were written in red the words: *Sniff and die!* Colonel O'Collogham pointed out the motto to me, tickled pink, laughing up a storm... he really got a kick out of it!... He was having a good chuckle all by himself!... "Hee! Hee!... Sniff and die!..." This was his hyena streak, his way of spooking us. Then he went back to work, shook a carboy, two carboys, dripped out some liquid, took a whiff, laughed hard... As for Sosthène, he was roaming around, filing down pieces, adjusting the pins on a huge fire red mask with nickel copper mounting, equipped with huge mica goggles, plus right at the crown, a can ingeniously rigged in place! with adjustable straps that buckled under your arms and then looped around your waist, really a very graceful effect, plus a dozen tube coils with thin piping that unfurled toward the back in a plume two or three yards high, a great fantastical touch! In short, a sort of customized dressed-to-kill version of the Eiffel Tower, one you could wear around on your head!... To hear them tell it, from a strictly technical viewpoint it was a miraculous feat of skill!... providing nearly one hundred percent antigas protection... A considerable, indisputable advance, with huge implications... Universal filtration...

Sosthène, who fancied himself well-informed on the subject, judged this model the best of the bunch. Although cumbersome, if not outright excruciating because the thing wasn't padded, it was still rational and reliable, the little head-factory, the "antigas washer" held in place by a dozen straps. Even so it wasn't foolproof... a leak could spring somewhere... not to mention any unpredictable twists... Unpredictable twists upset Sosthène, they actually threw him into a pretty bad funk... He'd go hours without saying a word!... and the trials were getting closer... Preparations were being made over at Wickers Strong... "Have your gases delivered!..." It was going to be held in some sorts of blockhouses... we already had the specifics...

For himself the Colonel had picked out a so-called "tow snout" canvas model, soaked in three absolutely neutralizing solutions whose formulae he would divulge only after the trials, and then to no one but to the king in person... This device for experts in the field transformed the most toxic gases, the most diabolical instant-death poisons into harmless fumes by combining them with ozone, hence making them actually good for your system by your fifteenth or twentieth lungful, on top of the fact they were regulated by an automatic air clip that responded to the density of the cloud and the nature of your physical effort, with such and such an amount for cyclists, another for swimmers, another for pedestrians, an air pump control calibrated to the millimeter, obviously the ideal system, the dream machine sought by every engineer since the Air Pump Convention held in Amsterdam in March 1909.

The gentlemen out in Wickers were going to be flabbergasted! The Colonel was bringing them not just one, but twenty solutions to the problem of millidoses! his protocol proved it! Just think of it!

Ah! but watch out!... Caution! he'd take his full battery out of wraps only as an absolute final last resort! His second contest mask was more in the domino style, equipped with faceted goggles, protruding snout, and netted padding... the entire mask mounted on muslin that pulled down over the head and hugged the face, topped with three feathers! ostrich plumes, Prince of Wales-style! His ever-present preoccupation with elegance. High fashion science!... This piece of gear was finished, absolutely polished and perfected, but the heavy mask, Sosthène's, the copper diving suit, was still giving them lots of worries. They had to send it back to the forge to make it a little more airtight, and then pop it back into the fire again for at least another two solid hours so that they could stick on the valves... a godawful headache... And it was all Sosthène's fault! He was always to blame!... Apparently he was having trouble breathing, and he'd been told a hundred thousand times that he was supposed to count two beats between breaths and not gulp air in one go like some animal! Every time he hiccupped he unhooked the whole contraption! And then the entire suit had to be readjusted! More excuses for chewing each other out! The pair were really pissed!

"Hey!" he shouted over to me, "just take a look at this catastrophe!..." and he let out an awful yell to let off some steam, a howl that went like this: "Yee-oowoh! Yee-oowoh!" The Colonel was going too far! He didn't understand anything.

"What's that, Monsieur de Rodiencourt? What's that?"

"Nosing! Nosing!"

What a fit the Colonel threw over Sosthène's mangled "nothings"! He gives him a real tongue-lashing!

"I'm going to teach you, Monsieur Sosthène! Repeat after me! Listen! Thing! Thing! Thing!"

"General, sir! It's not worth the bother, I'm killing my tongue, beating myself up over nothing... Maybe someday I'll be able to cope with the Tower of London, the pointed tower, the Watch-Out Tower! But I'll never be able to cope with the little zigzag you do inside your mouth!... You need to have a different kind of tongue!... As far back as 1893, back in Chandernagor, I lost £235 on a bet that I could do it... And I really kept at it!... It was in the canteen of the Indian Medical Service... I kept it up for five hours straight!... My wife and I were guests... What a hoopla!... The Thousand and One Nights! Ah! people in those parts really know how to treat a guest!... now there's flair for you, dear Colonel! The Indian Medical Service!... But as for your zigzag action, Colonel, you can go and stick it right up your ass!..."

It went on like that the whole afternoon, the pair taking turns chewing each other out... missing most of their own insults because of the horrendous racket, the hammering on sheet metal, carboys overturning, tumbling around... scrap metal in motion!...

Around five Virginia would come up with tea and sandwiches. Her uncle used to call her through the dormer window. She had to wait for the exact moment down in the garden...

She wasn't allowed to go out anymore, our city errands were a thing of the past. The only exception was the garden with her dog and birds!... The fact is she was cut off from the world... a state of affairs dating back to the Tweet-Tweet to-do! Ah! it was no joke!... Ah! I had my tail between my legs!... Ah! I felt real sorry! It scared me whenever she talked to me, if only to say hello! I wished I could be living out in the sticks somewhere! Everything spooked me!

The poor darling looked so sad, pale as death. Wish I could have kissed her but I couldn't... I felt I was the culprit behind everything!... felt guilty as hell! So how could I console her? I was powerless!... Without the strength or the money!... I was sick, and out of whack... Discombobulated!... Hallucinating!... My fever had carried me away... My ever so trusting, beloved little girl!... What harm I'd done her!... Dragging her along with me into a topsy-turvy whirl of the senses!... A dance of delirium!... Ah! some nice guy I turned out to be!... Couldn't tell true from false! And I'd kept my eyes peeled too!... I'd had wild impulses before... this wasn't my first episode!... but never so violent... Ever since my stay in the hospital... ever since Hazebrouck I'd had episodes... I sort of would go on the blink... But this time I'd totally surrendered! went to pieces, flew apart in a loony fury right off my rocker! Ah! and now I couldn't find all my missing parts! Ah! such a crazy foul-up!... So sad, so waifish, so unhappy, my little sweetheart!... Ah! I was torturing myself, worrying myself sick!... But if I had ever said to her: "Miss! Please don't worry!" Well, presto, she'd think I was the worst sort of lout! a heartless cad! and gutless to boot! doing nothing but making fun of her!...

That's the situation I was in.

My poor adored little waif was so sad, so heartbroken... and a second before so fresh and frisky, so impish!... Ah! my little joke!... Ah! I'd distressed her!... killed her happy-go-lucky spirit!... All it took was a word or two at the table!... and she changed into the most mournful little girl in the world... That's what I did to her... And it all went on right under the eyes of the servants, that pack of shameful wretches... cunning... slippery... always ready with a yes!... first-class bastards!... And they'd seen her thrashing! It must have been sheer torture for her to be stuck under their noses that way... target of attention for all those pigs!... Why didn't she try to run away?... what a bold drastic move that would have been!... And what a good lesson for the lackeys!... Ah! the realization hit me!... Really would have been one hell of a solution! Some gamine she'd have been then!... Ah! I would have admired her if she'd pulled something like that!... Ah! it would have put a nice big smile on my face!... Truth is, it would have settled the whole situation!... I loved her a lot, to be sure... maybe even more than that... more dearly than before that damned night, my tender adorable idol... but I was afraid to approach her anymore, or show her any attention! not even the least little bit!... She scared me!... At mealtimes, especially dinner, I gazed off into space, to the side, under the table, out the window, anywhere to avoid seeing her dear face!... I'd put on all sorts of fronts, followed the conversation with such passionate attention my eyes popped from my skull and sweat trickled down my face... I went into ecstasies over the dumbest claptrap Sosthène could come out with, I looked like I believed in all his babble about India... I even applauded... Every now and then the Colonel would dart me a nasty glance! but he didn't give me the boot... that was the main thing!... then dessert right after... a quick bite, I excused myself... dead tired... and went up to bed... with no jaw-flapping!... I was wary of the way one thing leads to another during those after dinner heart-to-hearts... wary the kid might have something to tell me... Ah! and that would be that!... Oh! no way!... Oh! no risk of that... Ah! She brought me bad luck!... It'd make her uncle sore all over again!... the prickly old bird!... she just didn't realize!... she was reckless... too naive!... I had to be careful for both of us!... for both of us!... no missteps!... Night and day I was on my guard!... I leapt into the sack... sleep! or pretend to!... Going to sleep was a real workout... That's no bull!... Sheer hell! because of the whistling in my ears... plus my nightmares... noises... catastrophes... sorts of trapdoors... I tripped and tumbled to the bottom!... I'd wake up!... with a start! flames everywhere! like back in Claben's cellar!... enveloping me, sweeping me away... Just like that in my nightmare!... I hung on for dear life, and howled to bring the roof down!... Then fall back to sleep... wham! and keep on falling... back into the clutches... of frogs, this time!... fire frogs!... and then the dragon gulping them down! a fantastical icky creature all green and belching fire!... like the one on Sosthène's gown! but this one was gigantic, the real McCoy! in a raging fury!... He gobbled up the frogs as he flew past!... the fire frogs! And then with a pounce he was hurtling toward me!... started attacking!... He chomped down hard, KERRRUNCH!... sank in his teeth!... right down into my bum arm!... I let out a yell!...

Was Sosthène ever pissed!...

"Are you going to get some sleep, jerk?..."

Ah! Wish I could have!... He called me every name in the book... Ten times in a row the same nightmare played itself out before the horror faded... and let me catch a few winks despite everything!... And I do mean a few!... just an hour or two!... maximum!... Honest, as roommates go, I was a pain, I'd be the first to admit it, what with my jumping awake, my nightmares, my screaming my head off, it mustn't have been much fun for Sosthène... Plus my little girl who was finishing me off... driving me crazy with grief, and that sad little face... She was totally clueless, naive naturally, but self-centered... just a child!... she didn't understand my concerns... she complicated everything... it'd have been best for her to leave... take off on her own... run away... Ah! I felt sure!... it would have settled the whole situation... That's what was running through my mind as I lay there awake!... lying awake in bed turns a man brutal... if not vindictive... merciless... A man trying to get some sleep is a monster, all he's looking for is a nice warm womb, a child's happiness, the entire earth just one big tummy for his head, he wants to crawl back inside all comfy cozy.

They came up with yet another way to postpone the trials... for two weeks!... their new announcement... They'd never make up their minds!... That's what I thought. If the other gas mask contestants were as batty as our crew, we were in for some fireworks!... they must have caught wind of this on Downing Street! The big reason they kept constantly bumping back the date!... they were hoping to wear everybody down... to put off the inventors... but there wasn't a man alive who could discourage the Colonel... I'd bet my life on that... I was the lucky one in this deal... acted however I wanted without a damn thing left to do... all my errands run... finished... not a single reason to bop around town... I could just sit back and read the papers... which I did... each and every one... with an eye out... for any small item... any little reminder... anything... about our "Greenwich tragedy"... Ah! not a whisper!... not a single syllable... as though nothing had ever happened!... The cops must have been cooking up something, that was my sneaking suspicion... Ah! I was on pins and needles!... Some plot was afoot... Had to be!...

Meanwhile I did fuck all, and Sosthène watched me doing fuck all... It really pissed him off something fierce... Nose to the grindstone, that's the way he wanted to see me... His broken record!... He wanted me to march upstairs and whack my fingers... hammering, filing, wire drawing, slaving away at the machinery!... he wanted me to follow along and learn some chemistry!... take a few whiffs of their carboys!... Ah! I was ready for him! Always the same tune! Ah! I blow my top!...

"Cut it out! Remember what you said! You're nuts! Didn't you yourself tell me that it was over? that the war had wrapped up? well, at least for all practical purposes!... and that you had turned the whole world on its head!... that it was just a matter of time, a few hours!... The first shall be last... with Goâ running the show?... Ah! You're not going to deny it, are you?... I didn't make up any of this!... You're not going to say it was a bunch of bull? Out with it, right now!..."

Ah! Caught him with his pants down... Ah! I wasn't going to let that fairy wiggle out of this one!...

"Come on, you bullshit artist!... You liar!... You lousy scum!..." I raked him over the coals!...

"Didn't you swear to me honest to God so help me? You fed me your line and your rigmarole?... Don't you remember any of it? how you swore on Pépé?... how you screwed up the whole works! the war and all the rest of it!... Remember the telephone? My drumsticks? How you even shit right on the Good Lord Himself?... You said so yourself! An end to all our misfortunes!... it'd just be a matter of days, you said!... so what am I going to learn by sniffing your gewgaws?... You just came right out and told me!... The masks are a waste of time!... I've already whiffed your cigarettes!... I keep running into these puff-puff setups like at Claben's!... I'm a stove!... Is that what you want, Choubersky?"

Ah! I thought he wound up throwing a hex on me!... that goddamned chicken-shit magician!... He was casting some sort of suffocating curse on me!... The nitwit! the dick! Ah! I was turning mean and nasty! he kept me in his sights... with his sidelong glances... It really put him out to see me wise up, all at once turn so suspicious about their little ploys.

"I'm in the dark," I repeated... "I'm in the dark!..."

He muttered into his goatee... Too scared I'd smash his face in if he tried arguing back...

"Come on! Open your mouth! Start blabbing! Let's hear it!..." I was riding him hard... "Why'd you feed me a line?... You made me go nights without sleep! Hopping after your ghosts! Now you want me to kill myself!... Just come out and say it right now... You're a bloodsucker!... Shit, come on! I'm waiting!..."

Ah! that brought him to a boil... frothing over... percolating like crazy... then he finally blew his lid... hiccupping... spluttering!...

"Sss-see here, Ferdinand! See here!... It's me who's saving your whole life! And I still am!... Don't you realize?... The Colonel's got one thing on his mind—slapping you behind bars! Think he's blind or something? He keeps his mouth shut... But those are two different things!... He takes it out on me!... Tells me you're not a damn bit of good around here!... except to abuse a person's trust!... you're lazy... good-for-nothing!... a thief!... I tell him we should feel sorry for you... I do answer him back!... I calm him down as best I can!... I tell him you're a victim of your war wounds... that you're just a pathetic big mouth with a few screws loose!... some blockhead cripple!... It barely holds him back!... He's dying to finger you to the fuzz!... Ah! you know, I've got to pour it on!... give it all I got!... Fight hard!... You better believe you're an ungrateful bum!..."

Well now, Colonel Shithouse O'Collogham sure took his time to figure out what I thought about him! the damned dirty asshole, the cuckolded piece of shit! That's what I felt about the guy! Damned dirty scuzzball!... along with Sosthène, what a perfect combo!... Such a grand revelation! ah! what a stinking crew!... Ah! I'll be damned! So the big secret's out!... why couldn't the Colonel just tell it to me straight?... Shithouse O'Collogham!... since he had me right here, mug to mug! and was pitching into me... the scumbag!... because of his fanny-whipped niece and all that jazz!... Skeletons in the closet? He'd better watch out I don't go shooting my mouth off! Jesus!... And tell about a few other things besides!... So much for my two fine feathered friends!... So that was what was keeping them busy... up there in the scrap metal shack... putting my ass through the wringer... dragging me through the mud!... instead of working as they should!... I could see it all from here!... I ought to make myself useful again, give them a kick by smashing what was left of my fingers! between the hammers, the anvils! Ah! some balls!... A big joke!... But they meant business!... backed up with threats!... Ah! I was all too well aware of that!... I had to dream up some plan!... Run for my life! and scram out of there!... so that I wouldn't defile their domestic bliss with my vile presence one single second longer!... I had to clear off, and on the sly, you bet!... my good-for-nothing bum presence!... Ah! the prize bastards!... "No loafing!" Those were the Colonel's words!... And that went for his niece too!... No quarter! Ah! one big happy family!... they had her climbing up to the rafters too! and getting down to some serious housework!... Everybody had to make themselves useful!... Work away in double-quick time! Triple-quick time!... That was the big watchword of the day!... A tenfold increase!... By order of Lord Curzon... the grand edict of King George!... Plastered on all the walls! on gigantic posters! Everything for Victory! "Increase your efforts tenfold!..." You can tell Mr. George and Lord Curzon didn't have a pair of hands like mine... not to mention a head!... Ah! my only choice was to get the hell out of there, blow this hellhole. They wouldn't quit till I dropped dead!... But once out on the street my troubles wouldn't be over... the pigs on my ass!... Taking off was a fine and dandy idea!... But where would my next meal come from?... I was in no condition to earn my keep!... was I supposed to bust my butt on the docks? It'd be smarter for me to bide my time!... and put on a contrite look, and all that crap!... string them along like down at the War Office!... drag out the situation... pull one over on the jerks... go into my "I don't get it" act... Her uncle would have liked me to run away!... Ah! that's for sure!... for me to get lost like a nice boy!... and keep my trap shut!... He mustn't have been keen on big stinks!... or on me shooting my mouth off about his whip!... Ah! no way, forget it, he'd have preferred me to slink away with my tail between my legs... hush-hush!... just pack my bags and split!... And what if I kidnapped the little darling?... That'd give him something to cough about!... But out in the world I'd need to make ends meet! And it'd be a whole lot tougher if there were two of us!... Love, determination... it takes more than that! the most sensible course of action... the best of bad alternatives is to hang on to my meal ticket, fuck it all!... And not buckle under, goddamn it!... tough it out!... Bring on lunch, I'm ready for you! Right here and now!... Sitting right across from them!... Not a sincere bone in my body!... And then I'll charge up the stairs to the junk heap... do a knockout job for them!... bang and rattle those pots and pans!... keep faking them out!... And I'll show some spirit, Christ Almighty!... no more bellyaching!... Lord George and Mr. King and old Curzon had it easy!... their much ballyhooed work!... Triple time!... They weren't the ones working their fingers to the bone!...

I kept telling myself: let's just take it easy, gain some time, snap back to health... Wait out the winter, the chilly season... Then the toughest part will be over... even without believing Sosthène's rot, maybe this fucking war might actually end sooner than people thought!... Why not?... When hope's in your heart you bullshit on the bright side... I'll vamoose in the spring... Full steam ahead for Australia!... I had set my sights on Australia.... There were gigantic posters all over Haymarket Square... Calling for young men down under... resolute... enterprising!... Here you go! I'm your man! Gotcha!... My bag of bones would go on the mend down under... I could picture myself just like the guy up there in the ad... the terrific-looking cowboy riding high on his spurs... proudly he showed Australia, a mouth-watering countryside of rich, lush greenery... dazzling in the sunshine!... dappled with tulips and roses!... "Come live with us" it said on the poster... "Come live with us happily ever after!" Now that's what I call an invite! One I intended to take up! And I mean all by my lonesome absolutely for sure! "After the war, come with us!" Now you're talking!... Right away! Why not? Ah! the idea sounded better and better to me!... Ah! my brain was working overtime! That was the single chance in the future I could see for myself!...

One fine morning I'd pack my trunk... and just slip away on the qt!... Ah! that was my gung-ho plan... that's all I had left to keep my spirits up... to steel myself against the hard knocks... Hang in there!... Fight back against misfortune! Confront danger head on! Steadfast in the face of adversity!... I would go up to the rafters, hammer in nails, all in the name of order! My carefree days were a thing of the past!... Order—you were looking at him! the girl too!... She'd hand me the hammer! I'd smash my thumbs!... Even more order after that!... Like Delphine's system back at Claben's... An open space in the middle of the room... with valleys all around, all the gewgaws stacked up, the crap pushed out of the way in heaps... the old man kept a wary eye on me, he could see the big change, my enthusiasm, the way I poured it on, so different from the person he knew! Hunkering down to work! Ah! he thought there was something funny about me!... He kept trying to catch me and the girl by surprise... He'd pop up in the storeroom, the one where we washed and put away the crystalware, the flasks, the pipettes... the kid rinsed, I dried... All of a sudden he'd be standing there in the doorway... catching big fat nothing by surprise... Let him drop in all he wanted!... not the slightest little gesture!... not a word... He was real cagey!... Oh man, was he ever!... The lousy bastard!... He'd have just loved for me to do something like that!... the ornery jealous scumbag... would've loved to catch me feeling her up... red-handed!... That would have made his day!... He'd have been in seventh heaven!... He'd have turned me over to the fuzz!... You better believe it!... The brainless filthy-mouthed bum! The sex-crazy bastard with his thing for little girls! No way to avoid the cat-o'-nine-tails! They wouldn't miss their chance down at police court! Ah! what a terrific motive! The Colonel's very own niece! Ah! just let me show up at the right time acting like some little punk! Ah! would I ever be in for a dose of morality! Ah! I'd pay for everything! They'd skin me alive! Christ, and how! in less than five! than two! than zero seconds flat!... Phew! a fiasco!... Ah! got to keep my eyes peeled at all times! Ah! wary as hell! A regular old bristling porcupine, that's me, real simple! Ah! let him drop in as much as he wanted! Pop up right out of the woodwork, etc. That's how he'd find me!... Not three words out of my mouth... not even two to the girl!... I acted like I didn't know her anymore!... even when we were alone together, all the way back in the workshop... I pretended not to see her... an uptight fathead!... I could hear her heaving sighs... Ah! no funny business! no soft spots! thick-skinned, hardheaded, dead set!... While pottering away I couldn't get Australia off my mind!... I'd go "Huhmm-Huhmm...." whenever she spoke to me... just a grumble... I couldn't understand a word out of her mouth anymore... But my mind was running like wild... storms raging inside... topsy-turvy, a total wreck, migraines, my temples exploding... I was ready to start wailing in remorse, bursting with reproaches, memories, words... all the stuff blaring through my head... the golden rules of the Leicester gang... all of which I'd broken... the lines those pimps used to spout... all running back through my bean... all their big no-nos... Tried and true wisdom!... "Don't go hunting pussy in families! nothing but headaches from start to finish! Stick to pubs for your skirt-chasing! Bars with broads! No screwing unless you're out on a bender! Don't go looking for bad luck!" Acting too big for your britches will do a guy in! And that's just what happened to me! Too big for my britches! And I'd gotten my comeuppance! because where did I go sticking my nose? Ah! I can't believe I did something that dumb! A society kid! Ah! smart thinking! I got just what I damn well deserved! Ah! their words were all coming back to me! Ah! I shouldn't have stuck my finger in the pie! The pimps at the Leicester were right, my lady-killer act just sucked me down deeper!... I'd never get out now!... Me of all people, who's not hot to trot, at least not for sex, not really, I'll come right out and admit it. Where was my fucking head at, snatching the niece away from Mr. Forty Lashes! Uncle Fetish!... Ah! you can't get any dumber!... Goddamn it to hell!... Saving my own neck, just mine! Now there's a plan of action! And not let myself get suckered in again!... She was heartbroken!... Tough! It was a mistake! Ah! I wouldn't bring it up anymore! She could heave her sighs all by her lonesome! I had my own headaches too, and a thousand times worse!... not some piddling chicken-shit disappointments!... My softhearted days were over!... I'd get the life whipped out of me! With the police whip! The cat-o'-nine-tails! You're history, screwy eyes! A damn dumb mistake! Totally cracked, you poor bastard! Even now I couldn't even shut my eyes anymore with all my big time worries! So, little girl, go ahead, keep whining! Ah! I puked it all back up! it got me so down in the end I felt like cracking her across the face with all her blubbering!... over there rinsing out the implements!... Ah! I couldn't stand her anymore! She sniffled out her tears!... Boo-hoo-hoo! go ahead and pout, you filthy brat!... I was sick and tired of my destiny!... I was getting like Sosthène!... My destiny, yech!... I had to get myself a new one! Swipe a destiny! Something new, Christ Almighty!... My old deadbeat destiny could go and get fucked! My bullshit destiny! To hell with it! Now what I wanted was something nice and cushy! something comfy cozy, a piece of cake! Thanks to hanging out with wizards I was starting to pick up a thing or two! to feel a few mystical vibes myself! Ah! I was starting to become the perfect man for the job! The star you're born under means everything, as they say! The star of the English is world-renown! I'd have liked one just like theirs... I saw lots of Englishmen... I didn't know how they managed to catch that star of theirs... make it shine on them so comfy cozy... whether they cast their spells with some belly dance like Sosthène!... whatever, it worked!... I saw English lads loafing about all over the place... lots my age... who had unbelievably cushy lives!... Those English lads... cricket... rowing... soccer... toys... and gussied up like princes and tarts, their minds all on their complexions and flirting over bridge... so you can see what was working on my brain... jealousy... maybe I was in a bad mood, obsessed!... but wherever I looked I saw people who had it easy... of course there were soldiers!... I didn't give a damn about them! I'd have liked to see them kick off one and all!... For my money, even the soldiers were born under a lucky star!... coddled little darling destinies!... Considering what I was forced to do!... to live through some pretty raw deals! Shit! it was all because of my rotten luck! Destiny matters! On that score, Sosthène saw as good as gold! I needed to find some way to change my zodiac sign! Taurus! Any old thing, and fast! I needed to arm myself with esoteric weapons! this immediately fired me all up!... Being bored shitless for endless eternity gave me some big insights... just standing there rinsing out glassware, I thought about my fate!... with my nose in the tub... plunging in the pipettes, the test tubes... splattering around... going about things the wrong way!... splashing water all over the place... wasn't too dexterous... but I was serious on the job, no kidding!... Didn't lift my nose from the grindstone! all wrapped up, all business... no clowning around!... The kid was on edge, hovering around me... coming... going... she'd have liked to talk to me... Didn't matter!... "Hummhumm... Huhmmum!..." I was just some uncouth, klutzy sourpuss splashing around in my dirty water... without a naughty thought in my head!... grub... beddy-bye... and that's that! I chewed over my plan... said prayers sort of for my destiny to change... Ah! the idea haunted me... At night that's all I could think about... a wild man... twisting and turning in my bed... since I still had such a hell of a time sleeping because of my ears, the sprays of steam... Ah! You better believe me when I say I suffered!... I didn't do any belly dances like Sosthène, the Brahmin bump and grind of the Three Graces!... I thought it was goofy... but I mumbled burning oaths to turn my luck around... maybe such things existed?... maybe some good wind will blow my way before all my awful troubles snuff the life right out of me?... I wish my stars would get a move on!... This wasn't some heavy-duty spell, but still it would get me out of my jam in one terrific way!... I wasn't so very big for my britches, I wasn't the one who wanted to topple Christ himself after all!... I didn't want the pope to die! I just wanted some little way out, some escape hatch... for the bogeyman to quit bogeying me body and soul! For everybody to leave me the hell alone... Just grab my suitcase and Australia here I come! To shake the jinx of my existence! That's not asking for the moon!... my new life would be a cinch, no ifs ands or buts, I'd just had to stay on my toes, keep nimble... and not lug packages around!... Ah! I knew the score! dump my baby doll!... make like lightning... a mad dash!... with no cargo on my ass!... Set sail!... Shake off the rotten crew!... Claben and his cohorts!... Spazzed-out Sosthène!... That Fuzz Fatale, Matthew! Ah! I had visions of myself breathing free and easy once and for all!... A happy-go-lucky fellow! On easy street! Ah! my imagination was really running away with me!... I beat everybody else to bed!... I would get all fired up even in my sleep!... I hallucinated through the buzzing in my brain. Ah! It was one hell of a job! I'll admit that!... You got to work up a full head of steam... I'd leave the table before dessert... With apologies... my headache... Wasn't just an excuse... I'd reached my limit, I'd had it... I didn't want to be whacked out anymore... just wanted to chew the cud... hit the hay... and meditate... just like that nestled deep in my pillow, all by my lonesome!... Sosthène lingered late downstairs... He kept the old man company... Sosthène, a guy who supposedly stuck to H_2O, champion of the mystic vibes!... He'd forgotten his vows!... They'd both turn in late, burping, laughing, loaded to the gills... cherry brandy, whiskey, gin fizzes... and champagne... Bip!... Bop!... I could hear the corks popping!... their discussions were upbeat... Sosthène was learning English... learning "Victory!... Victory!..." how to belt it out like that... I didn't disturb them... drinking themselves under the table, stewing in their cat piss... nice way for them to wile away the time... and forget all about me... The girl must have been in her room... As for me, thoughts of the future were giving me the shakes!... The whole bed was rattling my nerves were so frayed... with intense, burning apprehension! How was I going to escape from these two goofballs? I thought hard on my pillow through all the buzzing, the whistling steam, the whole shebang exploding in my head, roaring, hissing... a hell-raising racket!... My cracked head!... Ah! that din!... Ah! did I ever work my ass off trying to get some shut-eye!...

One night... knock! knock! knock!... I hear a rap... I'm not dreaming... somebody's at the door!... I don't answer... Sosthène still wasn't in bed... So I open my ears... knock! knock! knock!... dead silence from me... I wanted whomever to think I was asleep... maybe it was a servant!... Maybe I was wanted downstairs... because the lushes got some wild hair up their ass!...

"Ferdinand!... Ferdinand!..."

It was Virginia...

I leap out of bed.

"Coming!... Coming!..."

I dash to the door... crack it open.

"Come down to the garden..." she whimpers to me... like that, real nervous... panting... "Right now!... Right now!... I've got to talk to you!..."

Oh! Boy oh boy oh boy! here we go again!... A calamity!... As sure as I'm standing here!...

"What?... What?..."

I stammer... trip up on my tongue... I want to know... I ask... and ask again... what a mess!... what is it now? She made up her mind just like that... a fit of boldness... she comes up to see me while her uncle's downstairs getting stewed... Ah! some cheek girls have! when you don't want to talk to them anymore they're the ones who get your tongue wagging again! she wants to take me down to the garden... dead set on the idea!... and this very second!... I've got to hop to it... and here I was not bothering anybody...

already in dreamland... Where'd she want to drag me off to? lead me astray one more time? Taking advantage of her uncle being half-crocked!... Ah! the double-crosser! Rotten from the day she was born!... Where're we headed, to the movies?... out dancing?... I wasn't one bit thrilled!... She was a savvy little vixen, and how!... diabolical... Ah! just get a load of her!... the devil in her flesh!... Monsieur Sosthène, you can just forget it... you're clueless... this little demon... standing here with me... Ah! you can just forget about your incantations!... I was starting to give way... Ah! I felt the spell working... sucking my willpower... Ah! the driving force of youth!... Ah! I fell prey, an easy mark to the little scamp... why not return to the Tweet-Tweet Club? Holy cow, what a kid!...

I throw on some clothes... obediently... I'd go anywhere she's got a mind to go!... But that didn't mean I wanted her in my bedroom... to walk right in... with me in the buff!...

"Go down!... Go down!... I'm coming!..."

She goes down ahead of me... I hurry... Ready to go!... Here I am!... We're together in the garden... At first I can't make her out in the darkness... she takes my hand... leads me all the way to the back... across the lawn... toward the ivy-covered wall...

"Ferdinand!... Ferdinand!..." like that up against my ear... whispering... worried... her voice sounds different!...

I held her against me... couldn't see her face.

"Ferdinand!... Ferdinand!..." she repeated... "Ferdinand!..."

"Ferdinand what?..." I ask her, even so... "Ferdinand what?"

She really had me guessing.

"Oh, Ferdinand!... Oh, Ferdinand!..." that's all she could get out... the words stuck in her throat.

"Well?... Well?..." I give her a little shake.

True... I was totally mystified... these charades of hers... what was she trying to get at?...

"Well? Well?..."

I press her... Good Lord!... for her to tell me what's on her mind!... She kisses me, still without a word... I don't understand what she's after... I kiss her back...

"Darling!..." I go to her... "My little darling!..." I hug her against me... I think that's what she wants... for me to coddle her while standing here this way... but it's pretty foolhardy... I'm aware of that... Ah! I shouldn't be doing this... what if this was another big tease?... a trap being set for me?... some hex? something to turn me back into a sex-crazed nutcase?... what if she really wasn't all weepy-eyed?... but just waiting, nothing more?... waiting for me to make a dumb move?... Ah! I wish she'd talk... but she's crying... crying... without saying a word... sobbing right up against my shoulder... standing there in the darkness... Nice mess I'm in!... Normally she's not a crybaby... Ah! she's getting to me...

"Virginia!... Virginia!..."

I beg her... coax her...

"Dear, what is it?..."

I was at a total loss. I wound up imagining things... that her uncle had caught her again... beat the hell out of her... something she was scared to come out with.

"Did your uncle whip you? Did he?"

"Oh no!... No!..."

Wrong guess!...

"Then what is it?"

Ah! her blubbering was starting to bug me. And wham, all at once, I don't know how, a light in my head snaps on!... Ah! fucking hell!... It dawns on me!... Never occurred to me before!... Hell!... Holy shit!... but!... but!... but!... Ah! but I've got it now!... Ah! I'd like to get a look at her face! Ah! you bet I would!... it's too damn dark!...

I pop the question point-blank: "You're having a baby?..." I ask... "A baby?... Virginia? A baby?..."

She goes, "Yes! Yes!"... nodding... into my shoulder.

Oh! Jesus! whoaah!... What'd she say?... I just had to go and ask!... Oh! I'm floored!... I gasp!... Can't believe my ears!... Knees like jelly... woozy... what a blow!... I'm choking... strangling... you bet I'm trembling... stammering...

"You... you... you sure?... Sure?"

"Yes!... Yes!..."

Dead sure.

Ah! can't be!... Can it? Why, sure can!...

We're swaying together on our feet... I'm rocking back and forth... don't know where I am anymore... the little miss... Oh! Christ!... Ah! I just can't believe it!... Ah! it's too much to take!... Ah! I'm a wreck! I'm biting my tongue... no, I'm rocking back and forth... cradling her as she stands there leaning against me... who knows where I am anymore!... can't believe it... the shock... my mind's a blank...

"You sure?... You sure?..." I keep repeating... just like that through the darkness... the only words I can manage to get out... "You sure?... You sure?..."

"I think... I think..." A sad little voice... a quaver... reedy... wasn't like her to talk in a quaver... impish and naughty was more her style... not all quivery...

I wanted this to be really sure!... and not just the jitters... what if she herself didn't know the whole story yet? And maybe was just imagining it all!... because of things she'd overheard... and got wrong... a scared little kid... just a girl!... with her head in a whirl... she was young... just how young struck me right then and there... and real little... Ah! hell! at that age!... Which was how old?... What was her age exactly?... Ah! Geez... That's right!... getting knocked up as a kid!... what if she died?... maybe it's fatal?... What did I know?... I'd never given it a second's thought!... Ah! that'd be the final blow!... the consequences scared me so bad my whole head started hammering!... I was trembling... even as I kept standing there with her rocking back and forth!... My temples were throbbing!... Ah! I shouldn't have!... shouldn't have!... with her short skirt... so short... I ought to have known... her calves... her thighs... Ah! but I didn't!... Ah! I had sex on the brain! Clear she was way too young!... the slammer for you, you son of a bitch!... the slammer!... the gallows... the slammer!... a rope around your neck!... snap!... end of story!... That's what happens when you mess around with jailbait!... Ah! the question was tearing me apart... Ah! hell! was it me?... was it her?... Ah! I didn't know which end was up anymore!... I was all mixed up... in a total fog... the whole time rocking back and forth in the darkness... with her against me... I squeezed hard... Nobody could see us... there was nothing to see... it was pitch-dark... Terrific!... My whole head one holy mess on top of the whistling steam in my brain! Ah! If it weren't for bad luck I wouldn't have any luck at all... me!... me!...

"How old are you?"

"Fourteen..."

"Fourteen!..."

Ah! I'll be damned!... such a mess... plus it's all true... it wasn't some dream!... I held her weeping in my arms... still rocking back and forth!... with her... it was nice outside... a gorgeous night... the sky thick with stars!... Ah! seems like yesterday... out there on the lawn! Ah! I felt like a heel!... what a rotten stroke of luck!... I still couldn't believe it!... she was blubbering... blubbering... she broke down in tears, sobs... Ah! it was all gone!... such gloom and doom!... she was always in such good spirits, bouncy, always off on one whim or another!... skipping... and running... and jumping... you couldn't keep hold of her... a pixie! Ah! all gone!... Her days as a little scamp were over... a holy terror!... Ah! Geez! crying her heart out!... like a doll smashed to pieces... without a hope in the world!... sobbing hard!... her fresh young body against mine!... Ah! I kiss her!... I kiss her!... but first... how'd she find out?... Ah! yes, by the way? Just how exactly?... Maybe it's only in her mind?... A guess?... just something she imagined... just something she overheard on the subject? Nothing more?... And she worked herself all up!... into a dither!... spooked!... by the bogeyman?... Ah! easy to understand at her age!... she was throwing a scare into me too... with kid gloves I pried a few words out of her... but she wouldn't quit her bawling... Ah! it was the end of the world!...

"Who told you, darling?"

"The doctor..."

"Doctor... You've been to the doctor's?... When?"

"Last night..."

She went to the doctor's last night?... Was this some new lie?... She wasn't a big fibber... did she go by herself?... a strong possibility... Ah! that's all I needed!... Ah! no mistake there!... Just my lucky night! I hit the jackpot!... Ah! I'm on a streak!... the grand prize!... Ah! I just stand there rocking... in place... the brat blubbering against me... I didn't know which end was up... Too much stinking crap was coming down on me! Ah! Fuck all this goddamn shit!... when it rains it pours, hell!... Give it all you got, little sister!... I can't do a thing about it!... Shout your mouth off, stammer, you dummy! Answer! It's too much! Too much! inside my head! KA-BOOM!... KA-BOOM!... and KA-BOOM! A nonstop bombardment... Everything crashing down on my damn head! Too many calamities coming my way!... I kiss her... kiss her...

"Dear!... Dear!... Dear!..." is what I say to her... incredibly shaken... upset... I felt like bawling too... I couldn't be hard on her... that would have gotten me nowhere... All from our night in the Tweet-Tweet Club!... Ah! I had my tail between my legs!... If she had gone to see a doctor... and he'd told her... then it was for sure!... Which doctor?... I'll ask her later... after she quits crying... Ah! how dark it was out in the garden... Had to be... Better this way... Just wish I could've seen her expression... her little face in front of me... and check whether it was true... Ah! but all I could do was keep rocking back and forth!... I held her tight in my arms... Ah! you horny rascal!... you naughty old geezer! Ah! I was starting to imagine what'd be next... you fuck little girls!... you appalling pig!... you perverted monster!... fucking a child!... Knocked up, mister!... Knocked up, sex maniac! Ah! You're a fine one!... You damned bum!... You crazy loon! Sex maniac! Frenchman! But no, not loony! Ladies and gentlemen! I see stars! I got a crazy cock, that's all! Crazy! you nasty boy! you cutthroat! You crook! Hang him high! Ah! I kept kissing her!... consoling her... still standing out there on the lawn... the pair of us... together!...

"Little darling!" I kept saying... real soft and easy... "Little honey!..."

Ah! what a fine mess!... Ah! I felt like a skunk! yiiyiipee!... she was kissing me back... kissing me back!... she held me by the neck like that!... Ah! we were both in a real jam!... you could bet on that!... But still she had to get it through her head, we weren't talking little girl's stuff anymore!... she had to listen... because I had something serious to talk to her about... so no crying... or hopping around... or running away... time to act sensible!... time for us to put our heads together...

"Virginia!... Virginia, sweetie.... My little pussywussy!..."

I couldn't spell it all out... I kept kissing her... she stopped crying! Ah! we could hear the birds... that just had to be a nightingale... I made her listen! "Nightingale!..." I knew she liked birds... I make her start crying again!... she was coddling me... cradling my big head in her arms... talking in a hush...

"Dear Ferdinand!... Ferdinand!..." like that earnestly...

I thought she was scared of the dark...

"Poor little one!... little one!... little one!" I replied... It's true she was little... well-knit, tough as nails... but little... compared to me anyway, I mean!... big for her age... Ah! damn it to hell!.. pregnant... everything I'd been saying... What a crummy break... What a dumb stinking jinx!... If I didn't have rotten luck I wouldn't have any luck at all!... "Little one!" I kept saying to her... Cradling her too just like that... we were cradling each other... "Little one"... out there on the lawn... in the dark... I hugged her against me, standing there... not too hard... I'm careful!... what about her belly? the thought hits me... maybe I might hurt her...

"Honey buns!" I say... "Let's sit down..."

I sit down with her on the bench... kiss her... lovey-dovey her... things are better now... she's not sobbing so hard... and then wham! another burst of tears!... she's crying her eyes out!... This all happened in the dark... I was clean out of things to do or say... I'd run through all my graceful touches!...

"Hear the birds!... Hear the birds..." I try the bird business again... That's all I could come up with... "Honey buns!... Honey buns!..." The words sounded soft and sweet to her... helped wipe away her sorrow... I tried to think of something... I knew what she was going through... Ah! she was really and truly upset... Ah! I wanted to console her... she could see real clear that it broke my heart too... I didn't know how to say it in English... that it broke my heart... I was so fond of her... that's it!... I was so fond of her... so little and cradled against my shoulder!...

"You sure?..." Ah! I blurted out the same question again. Ah! damn!... Ah! Phooey! Ah! it did matter! Ah! I was shaking!... all this crap dumped on my head!... at the same time!... just couldn't be!...

"You sure?"

"Yes!... Yes!..."

Just like that she told me "yes... yes..." nodding... against my arm... sobbing her heart out!... Ah! she was rattling me!... Ah! I couldn't take any more!...

"Then I won't go!..."

I made up my mind then and there... couldn't do better than that...

"I'll never leave!..." I swear to her. "I'll never leave you!... Ah! I swear... I swear!..." I wanted her to quit crying... I swear again...

She asked nothing of me...

Always!... Never!...

She kept up her crying though...

She wouldn't quit... Ah! her whole world was ending!... Ah! I knew what was happening! My stinking lousy loose morals!... Ah! it was her age!... Ah! it'd never occurred to me... I was young too... that's a fact... you can't think of everything... the snowballing excitement, the booze, the lights down in the club... the hell-raising bingbangboom! craziness!... the whole mess from the Tweet-Tweet Club!... that all takes its toll!... But what about now?... Ah! my mind's made up! Ah! I'm in earnest, my decision's final... I swear to her again... and now she's got to go to bed... it's late!... real late... out here on the bench... it's chilly... the nightingale kept right on singing... it was a brisk but clear night...

"Go to bed, dear!... go to bed... We'll see tomorrow..."

She mustn't catch cold... tomorrow we'd see... she was already shivering like mad... wasn't wearing a coat... just her little dress... I left her at the foot of the stairs... mustn't be seen together... She acted very sensibly... she was all too aware... I was ordering her around for her own good...

"Tomorrow, little one!... Tomorrow!..."

Promptly she obeyed... sweet and earnest!... I lingered in the garden... in the darkness... for a nice spell... and then I went back upstairs, up to bed, pretended to be asleep... Ah! Didn't get much sleep!... Too many things running through my head... I couldn't even hear myself buzzing anymore...

Oh, yeah! Terrific! Sure thing! A new leaf! On your toes! Raring to go! Backbone... then you think it over... firm resolve... a heart of steel... standing tall!... and then you start wondering... real great, all doubt behind you... sworn up and down... absolutely positively... there in my arms... and yet... poor little bird, so trusting... I go mushy... ah! no funny business! I give myself a good shake... whip myself back into shape... my mind's a muddle... I'm trembling all over... with horror... zeal... Put some heart into it! Buck up!... wham, and throw yourself body and soul into the fray? Face the dangers?... Ah! I swear up and down on my medal!... if I lose my nerve they can kill me... That's settled! Not a single step backwards! Stubborn as a mule!... And what if I'd disappeared, like some thug making his getaway! A fine how-do-you-do! An answer to the prayers of those bastards! By sticking it out this way I was throwing oil on the flames, a dishonest bum like me... Her uncle's blood started boiling at the mere sight of me... if I disappeared life would be so much easier... everything would all work out... little good-for-nothing cradle-robber... slimy little delinquent... Sure enough! Sure enough!... A hardened criminal back on the lam... the stinking whimpering weasel... yellow-bellied Romeo... French vermin, polluting hearth and hospitality! Sly little snot-nose chicken big phony! Randy French devil! Hot crotch! Polluting England! Take that! This guy's got what he deserves! her uncle's revenge, treating a rotten-to-the-core bum this way... the girl might come out of it with just a couple-three rounds with the riding crop... Whoopee! Another go at that little fanny!... Because I was the ugly customer... Once I was out of his sight he'd forgive her... He'd keep her under his roof... that was the main thing... Little by little it'd all be forgotten... except for her bundle of joy naturally... it'd be popping out when the weather turned nice... by my count it was due sometime in April... the key was for me to scram, no mistake about it... I'd clear out of the way... And then they'd all come together as a family... Up we go then, hop to it, no pussyfooting around! you got to show some guts whichever direction you take... whether you attack or cut and run... I told myself: you're not responsible... and then I'd start eating myself up all the same... harrowed trembling... what a disgrace!... this constant waffling... let's say I insist on staying put... confronting the old geezer, the law, the cops... well, sort of anyway? a faithful awesome romantic hero? What would happen to us?

One big bust!...

I cave in splutter chicken out... Paralyzed with fear again... I'll never be able to go through with it!... I start ticking off the problems imagining... running over it all in my mind again... Scared myself to death!... I'm going off the deep end just thinking about it... me and her off somewhere together... in her condition... knocked up and all that... whoosh, I whisk her away!... dump the whole crazy joint the grub her uncle the works! Take-charge heroics!... long live freedom! An outdoors girl! The streets and the asphalt belong to us! We'll live on love alone! A family in the gutter! Ah! what a pretty picture we'd make! especially given her condition!... She'd feel hungry, queasy... and then hungry again!... grub's a bitch... doesn't grow in the street... sure, we could always panhandle... pass around the hat... It was one way to get by... just think, a beggar's duet!... her voice and mine would be magic!... cheese it, the cops!... so, like I'm supposed to turn into a solid hard-working guy? a breadwinner for my family?... my clothes looked like shit!... at the first teeny-tiny question I'd have the cops on my ass... any way you looked at it, an awful situation... how was she supposed to deliver her baby?... and in how many months exactly was she due?... I did another count... I'd gotten it all screwed up... December?... no! in the spring... I'd been talking out of my ass... that'd be better... in springtime we'd have a smooth time of it... summertime too, we could mosey around... sit awhile in one park then another... what if she had it in a garden?... we could live outdoors... but what if the baby is due in September?... I did another count... in that case, one big bust... fog rain bone-chilling cold... We'd have to go to one of their Salvation Army shelters, and they'd never let us in... her being underage plus knocked up and all... they'd spot us in a snap... and finger us to the cops... The second you take a cold hard look at life your mind starts spinning with all the troubles out there... how endless they are... you've got to keep your mind off things... My main problem was that I didn't have a job... plus having a girl stuck on my back who was knocked up into the bargain!... and no job!... reckless living, that was my whole story! My mother could see it all coming! And where it was all leading! I could still hear her very own words... "A young man without a job... idleness, the devil's workshop... crawling from one gutter to the next... a life of crime!... Sex maniac corrupter of little girls... just like Soleilland!... Hauled into court..." My poor mother! My poor father too... my poor uncle! Poor everybody!... the disaster of dishonor!... And what if I racked my brains? how would that improve the situation any? What if I drain myself down to the last drop? Can you imagine? I'm putting two and two together now... rehashing the past... I can see the kid again... laughing her head off at the drop of a hat... constantly frolicking... pirouettes!... a little antelope... a pixie wherever she goes... she straddles the banister... and whee! zips to the bottom!... I shout after her! she thumbs her nose... I'm the gimp dragging his bum leg... Games are a thing of the past with me... plus I'm not the one who's knocked up, for Christ's sake!... I scold her... she kisses me... that's just the way she is... in a short skirt... her sinewy calves... so pretty... Her elastic muscles!... with a golden tan!... divine, sassy!... and there I am, my scars stabbing me with pain... in my arm... my thigh... my shoulder... I'm a wreck, for sure... a first-class provider, a real family man!... not to mention my migraines! The bullet lodged behind my ear... I've got tons of excuses... I saw stars... at the drop of a hat... plus the people... the things... Matthew closing in on my ass out of nowhere... a scary creep and I can see him right there!... Matthew, my cop! And his whole pig crew... I was never off his mind for one second, my health was his only concern... He wouldn't let me go to the dogs... I could see his face and eyebrows... his steely gaze... his pearl gray bowler... He just stood there, looking me over from head to toe... ah! the rotten son of a bitch... He was dead sure casting a hex on me... taking advantage of the fact I was on my last legs... spooking me with his terror tactics... I could see him lurking in every doorway... Didn't need any Brahmins to tell me that... didn't need to screw around with trances... shimmying and bringing down the roof!... Wherever I looked I could see Matthew... he showed up all alone... hollering at me, and a whole lot more... calling me every name in the book... every last curse to vent his disgust... he said he had the most awful punishments in store for me... The cold sweat was pouring off me... that horrible pig held me hypnotized, no lie... He popped up in the pitch-black all dressed in red, then in yellow and green... Those were his colors... and then he melted back into the murk... He threw such a scare into me I could barely stand on my own two feet. It was worse than the trance of the Brahmins... I had to prop myself up to keep from falling over... that gives you some idea what an unholy mess I was... And all because I was honest, and stuck by my guns... and wouldn't budge an inch... I'd sworn to the kid... Your heart's always the thing that does you in... it keeps beating, beating, and it carries you away... Parading around through the streets with my jailbait in broad public, you'd better believe I would be looking for trouble!... wherever Matthew'd send me, nobody'd be in the mood for excuses!... I wouldn't be spared the cat-o'-nine-tails... the gentle touch! Imagine what a blessing!... they'd never set eyes on me again! The penitentiary and all that! Talk to me about love! Ah! I was back to zero, everything topsy-turvy... my heart giving out... just imagining it all again... it was crummy, no mistake there... whether I was for or against... Don't press the point!... Don't be stubborn!... another side to the coin... another pang of conscience... another face to put on the situation... Make your escape and that's that!... Save your ass! What's left of it! Don't complicate your life! What you got left of it! Clear the hell out, cut and run! Hard heads get broken... This was pretty shitty and disgusting of me... But still a pretty sensible approach... a real solution... My gallantry had been my downfall... My pigheadedness, my loyal heart... Beat it, bravery, away with you, shithead!... an indecent washed-up old wreck in the prime of life... What a lovely sight!... Savior of unwed mothers! Break yourself in two! Ah! I'm going to break for it and run... I've had it! and then my qualms douse my fire again... You reek, you little pig! Hit the road, you piece of shit! My self-esteem speaking there... You deadbeat gigolo! Those were Sosthène's words... you slippery little devil, he called me... He didn't put his education to much use... One more con artist in my life!... He sabotaged my chances... led me smack into an ambush with his Hindustani trances... Ah! those evil curses had my blood boiling... I wouldn't give a rat's turd for that Mongol! and his spells... because now I'd be stuck in this jam forever! I was bewitched for sure! He'd got me all balled up in his mystic influences... My body was crawling with them... and my head... the action of my heart... I could positively feel it... my heartbeat wasn't normal even for a feverish wreck like me... whose nerves were shot... Irresponsible was just the right word, but if I went and opened my mouth to Matthew he'd show me what irresponsible was all about! just wait and see, buster! The noose! The noose! His obsession... the whole scenario kept running through my head... absolutely just the way I'm telling it... with Matthew, the gallows, the works... In Franco-English and Javanese... in a furious blast of words... Cascade's voice cutting through the din... hoarse, reproachful... ah! my luck would never end!... when I heard that my head started spinning... I grabbed hold of the table... a swelling din... sounds like women jabbering... a whole bevy... more reproaches... Why don't you marry her?... That's what they dish out at me... Ah! now that's true, what a wonderful idea!... ah! I light up! Jump for joy! Ah! I'm one happy fellow! That's right! A terrific plan! I'll up and marry her! What a kick! That solves everything! The British way, Christ Almighty! I'm getting married! Pronto! Watch how fast! Four shillings sixpence! At the Registrar! Sign on the dotted line, young sir! Well, go ahead and have a kiss! Hurray! Fifteen minutes from start to finish! And it's done! License and love pecks! Her uncle in seventh heaven! I worship you, my wonderful new son-in-law! Bosom buddies! Ah! I could see the whole scene! my heart's fluttering with exultation! Hope Sunshine Love! I caught a fresh glimpse of happiness the way I did out in the garden the other night... a regular burning bush a real live fairy tale!... for the pair of us whisked up into heaven! Burning with love blah blah blahbeatific! And blah blah BLAM, the whole thing comes collapsing/crashing down!... A cloud, everything grows dark and murky... I'm racked by doubts again... I'm back spluttering, pussyfooting around... No way in hell will her uncle allow it!... That's the first thing! He'd curse us in his crazed rage! He'd turn us over to the police... And this hare-brained scheme of mine would be put to rest!... Ah! Optimism is such a fool's paradise! A sucker's mirror! When you take a cold hard look at life you don't see any silver linings... So I switched back to my gloom... While washing the gear I ranted/yapped to myself... shouting a few plain truths into my ears... I couldn't even see what I was working on I was so worked up... And so behind! I ought to have rinsed right away... sped up my chores... left the stuff to drain, and then zip! onto something else! lugged the whole mess back over to Sosthène! back here under the rafters... I ought to have gone for fresh water... a regular cesspool!... Ah! but I was too out of it... too wrapped up in my pros and cons... thinking so hard I couldn't see straight anymore... all of a sudden I made up my mind! I'm going to have a nice little chat with those jokers! They've got to quit persecuting me! There's a mother and child involved now!... I'm the father! Goddamn it!... But I change my mind... My guts run in the opposite direction! a flash of inspiration! They're going to be floored!... What if I tear myself away from my heart's desire?... I change my mind again!... No! I'm going to tear her away from those scoundrels, those old jealous maniac pigs! And call this wild and loose living quits! a sudden fit of morality!... But then fuck, forget it! I'll dump the whole works! I'll take off to the ends of the earth... I'm going to save my own ass, just mine!... Every man for himself! Ditch mommy and the brat! I'll make a beeline right out of here! Rip my heart in two, that's for sure! So much the better, goddamn it! No more mercy! That's the line I'll take with myself! I'm giving you a blow-by-blow description of what a horrendous stew I was in... The mere memory makes me sick all over again... I can still see myself shaking over my tub... stammering out my pros and cons... I'm worthless... all fouled up/befuddled... chewing things over groaning so loud that they wound up hearing me... The kid came over to see what was what... "Hello, Ferdinand!" I make her laugh... scold her a little... she bursts into giggles... ah! how witty!... And what if I'd cut and run? How amusing would you find that, my little pet? I ask her jokingly... her cute smile... I surprise/disconcert her... no! I could never go away!... It hits me right then and there... I scoop her up in my arms kiss her rock her above my dirty glassware... it's those beautiful eyes most of all so bright so blue so mocking... with that faint gray twinkle... nobody would ever have dreamed she was knocked up... her mauve eyes, well sort of, when the light was low... like the sea's shifting reflections... I hugged her whole body in my arms... and now she's starting to cry... she cried often because of me... I hadn't made her happy... Poor kid, damn it, all the same! I was acting like a slimy creep!... I'm sorry! I'm sorry! my precious darling!... if I ever behaved dirty!... down at the Tweet-Tweet Club, what a performance! I'd turned into such an incredible monster at a snap of the fingers! a little kid, an innocent girl... And now she had this other crew... She never got a break. These days she had her uncle, Old Fancy Dress! plus the other character, daffy Sosthène!, and they were all competing for top prize... it's the magnetism of youth... the early blush of beauty... They don't let up on my precious... I'd catch them hiding wherever I looked... spying... sniffing out my angel... they were monsters of jealousy... but I really had no right to talk... I'd shown up here moaning/wheezing, a sorry-looking mess... All covered with scars, and then boom, flipped out!... Ah, a real oddball... a character who betrayed people's trust... Ah! up to his neck in trouble, up the creek! a lot of right I had to talk!... So confused I was reeling, seeing stars!... my pounding heart about to explode. Plus the insults... "Swine! Swine!" they kept calling me... the whole joint echoed... "Swine!" So get it up, hanged man! That was Cascade... one voice! two voices! a hundred voices! a dozen! Nowhere to hide... What panic! my legs wobbly in fear... jerking my mitts around in the dirty water so bad I kept spilling everything all over the place... suds, dishes!... they were threatening me with some pretty scary stuff... I've had it! I start yelling back... in my falsetto... I can hear my voice... help! help! Doesn't sound like me... I'm beside myself with terror. So I've given you a little picture of my condition... You bet I'm in a quandary!... Well, then, I'll just kidnap the girl! I've got pluck, goddamn it! Go to it! It was a wonderful idea. It fires me all up... nothing'll change my mind! And KEE-RASH! I think it over. How long will it last?... They'd catch us in no time... me with my limp and her with her short skirt... What fun and games it'd be for the Vice Squad then... they'd drag us back by our ears... And bingo! they'd slap my pretty face behind bars! The kid would be thrown to some nuns!... To the Reverend R.M.C.I. Finette, Fatso's old lady, was always going on about the Reverend R.M.C.I.s. She'd done a two-month stretch with the R.M.C.I. because of some slipup... They thought she was British because of her phony papers. The memory stuck with her, she'd used to taste the whip if she even looked at them the wrong way. A House of Correction, they called it, with psalms and prayers and pea soup. Virginia would land there to get corrected for dead sure. Whoever, nuns or her uncle, they all used a big stick. Just thinking about it spooked me. And one more time, all because of me! Even today still, I'm ashamed, after so many years, some hard-hitting, ferocious years, when I was just about at the end of my rope... I still wonder whether I could make up my mind... I mean back at the time, whether I was torturing myself... my poor brain was in such a state... And she thought I was silly! How *kind* of her! heartless little bitch! Amazing what smiles can hide all the same! She made me go off my rocker again! I'd started slamming around my glassware again! If I'd had two brain cells I'd have dropped that broad! Bye-bye, kiddo, my darling, my walking disaster! And no crap! Selfish, you bet! She'd have laughed like crazy then! Can't you just see how I'm bending over backwards? Killing myself for one of her titters! It's sickening! The hell with this, there's still time! Go on, beat it! I was pissed at myself for being such a dumb sucker! Come on, pack your bags and scram! Wake up! But I was too scared, I felt so sad, such shame... ah! I grab a bottle by the neck, sent it flying up against the ceiling! smithereens! she darts me a real funny glance... "Ooh! Oooh!" she goes... but I don't scare her at all anymore... she's hopping in place, having a good time... laughing harder... I'm the clown, that's clear as a bell... "Go away! Go away! Little bitch!... I've had enough of your cackling!" It drives me mad! I want her to get the hell out of here! I want to chew things over at my own convenience... or put myself through hell if I choose... She's fidgeting around, the devil in her flesh... You just wait for Matthew to come knocking, you little terror! he'll put the lid on your impish tricks! Just as I think of that dirty cop he pops up in front of my eyes! Smack in front of me, the pig, awful... out for blood... Right above the sink the guy was... swaying back and forth cackling... I was hallucinating... presto. His whole noggin tick-tocking... like a clock pendulum... literally the genuine article... wink of an eye I'm under his spell... can't react, too mind-boggling... You think I might have a good laugh, but no go either... I just stand there wiped out friendly, he talks I answer... he's mumbling... some mirage/trick... he obsesses/haunts me... unawares I conjure him up... he'd have me clambering onto the gallows with one quick wink... I went soft during those sessions with Sosthène... I'm really wise to that now... sensitized by the fakirs... That's the reason for my big obsession... I caught it during the performances... Another nice bonus!... Just what I needed, with this head of mine... I'm brainstorming myself to death!... it's all that bastard Sosthène's fault again! But Matthew's my own personal incubus... he hexes/ hypnotizes me... I've snagged his astral body... When I shut my eyes it gets worse... his grip tightens... I tried rubbing my fists in my eye, but no good... got to latch on to something... I fall... I can hear cannonfire... roaring from every corner... the horrors of war wherever I look... just perfect... it's that pair of goons whaling away at the other end of the workshop... pounding the anvil... I can feel every whack in my head... I realize I'm completely delirious... they're fanning the flames at the same time... I can see the massacres the lancers... I can see a whole smoking battlefield! Hindquarters charging! Masses of them! And all topsy-turvy, good God! horses by the thousand riding men! such reckless daring! And here comes Claben and his Greenwich crew, the whole awful mess on his back! Galloping hard, charging, sweeping down like a torrent! Nothing's impossible! I'm galloping too, Jesus fucking Christ! They're going to raze the Greenwich pub to the ground! I can see them swarming over it. I roll across the ground, duck for cover, I'm in battle fury, but still!... They're over there in the heart of the inferno...

charging straight in... the thumping heartbeat... I can see this huge heart throbbing... I'm going to catch fire too... Whoosh! a torrent smashes me against the ground! It's water! I'm drowning! Firemen! My tub spilling over... Two guys dunking me! Just like the guys over at the Greenwich! I clink glasses, down my drink, glug-glug... but it's a trap! they're twisting and turning me, working over my privates! in my scuzzy water! And then they hang me by the feet! From the branches! of the plane trees! I'm in a nightmare, the mob screaming at me... it's a fact! I'm under a spell... I sway and piss on the whole mob... They start bitching... the water's running off me... Perverter of families! Murderer! Vampire!... that's what I hear... I'd like to disappear down into some bottomless pit... turn into a mouse, a roach, Christ, anything—a turd. No can do, I'm myself... I bump against the branches... flatten my body against the trunk... the walls... Ah! I'm the victim of some ploy... blood fever... the ghosts are assaulting me... yanking my feet from above... along with all the Goâs and that other bum, Sosthène, plus Matthew and the rest of the crew... Some balls they have, gives me a laugh anyway! That does me good and it breaks the spell... I fall shivering on my side... I've had some kind of mind-boggling fit but now the fog's lifting... I'm not drunk... I huddle belly to the wall... My mind's made up! I've been to hell and back! All right, I'm going to marry her!... No more shilly-shallying! Sold! I'll see through the farce! Four shillings six! I'll force her hand! Now there's a man for you! bold move!... at the Registry! we'll play out our joke all sure and proper! No waffling! once we're hitched, look out, Scotland Yard! I'll drop off the kid at Curlers'! she'd be a sister for her, an object of devotion... She'll keep her safe for me during the storm... I'll head north to Edinburgh! for six months or a year... a breather... when the armistice is signed I'll head back... that'll give them a chance to find something new to talk about... Cascade'll fix me up with some phony papers... Then we'll move in together... I'll get a job... it would be a piece of cake... everything for Virginia! our family!... Cascade was the only man who could fix me up... we'd have to bury the hatchet... I didn't trust Boro... he was a snake a hothead... So that's how I sized up my prospects, lying there huddled against the wall... Ah! no kidding, I'd been through the mill, now I could see clear... I start to buck back up, feel all raring to go... it all comes crashing down! Got the willies all over again... Back to the drawing board!... all jittery! legs and arms jerking around, clattering, clinking... In my tub, I scrub away work up suds!... I'm a martyr to my scrupulous sense of duty... I'm going through sheer hell... just like my dad... tortured the same way... always talked to me in a pop-eyed rage... It was his scrupulousness that drove him bonkers too... he'd tear himself to pieces over trifles... over some put-down, one wrong word, a crooked glance from one of the neighbors, and oh brother, did we ever have neighbors! Count 'em, 140 all down the Passage... you better believe he was a nutcase... And I was just like him a chip off the old block... plus all the hard knocks I'd lived through!... I'd plenty of reasons to get riled!... and what another fix I was in now!... ah! I'd never get out! shit! I'm so worked up I break a jar... knock it to the floor!... try catching it... slip myself smash a bowl... clinkclinkcrash! I make more of a racket all on my own than the three of them put together over at their forge... They were firing me up after all, damn it! They were making my head spin driving me to crime... Nobody was listening to me! Tough! So what am I waiting for? Come on, let's start slaughtering! Slaughtering away! Ripping the whole place apart, goddamn it! Crummy equipment! Beat-up junk metal! wham! and bam! I want to see it sailing through the air! Let's wreck the place, Christ Almighty! A cyclone sweeping across the floor! I whip it along! Freedom! Bring it all down! Crush the whole shebang to bits! Smash 'em up good! Smithereens! Fire dancing before my eye—they're playing tricks! No—Flames, I see flames! For real, pools of fire all around! my tub's in flames! It's the Greenwich pub! and everything's trickling spilling over! a red-hot crackling blaze! I shout, I'm in pain, I cry out for help! Put me out, somebody! Pick me up with a pair of tongs!... I wish the pair would dash over! ah! what a real battle it'll be! I want them to realize what's going down! feel the full impact of the nightmare! see the conflagration we'll be living in! I'm sure they're feeling the girl up!... Turning a deaf ear now... Ah! I smell a rat... they're having their dirty way with her!... Sure are!... Cocks of the walk!... I should pounce over!... knock the combo to the floor! But I just stand there like a dumb jerk... Matthew! Matthew! He's the one paralyzing me... He's the one! with that steely stare! He's swiping my power... just horrible the hallucinations he's throwing my way... he's climbing the walls... scowling/winking at me... running back through his routine... It scares me... my bowels start acting up... I writhe... it's the fright, violent spasms... no time to think... Plop! I shit out my whole system!... you can't imagine the pain... my undershorts heavy as lead!... full of crap!... sticking all over me... can't even turn around anymore... I'm planted in my pie... Hope they don't launch an attack, me stuck this way!... I shouldn't have shouted so loudly... I'd never be able to defend myself... lucky they're caught up in something else... busy smashing up their forge... whacking away twice as furiously... they're going through one hell of a lot of trouble... they don't know what's what anymore... deaf to the world... ah! this would be a great time for me to snap into action... rush over and snatch the girl... the thought works me up... I shit my pants again... I dump a mean load a regular flood... I'm slopped to the spot... both my head and belly are an unholy mess... It grosses me out I dig in my heels who cares!... I've got to show my stuff! I brace myself against the shelf ready to charge into the fray! the hell with all this hemming and hawing! They've all got it in for me, what's their big problem? The end the means! I'll kidnap the brat, oh yes I will! We'll croak on the ragged edge! Honor's what matters! Under the rain, out on the street, goddamn it! I'm absolutely dead set! just as she is! with that belly of hers! baby on the way! you name it! ah! I'm hopping in place! they're whacking away twice as hard firing me all up! I'm churning up the wreckage, working up my steam! Fucking trouble's on the way! I'm going to put an end to this! my undershorts are slamming against me... roping me to the spot... I dumped too big a load, I weigh a ton... the crack of my ass is tight and sticky... I'll strip myself with a good yank!... watch and see the power I pack! No more Mr. Lazybones! I draw myself in under my plaster sheath... you just wait, sweetie! Everybody's going to see who they've been messing with!... My blast-off will amaze the world! Ah! every dog has its day! I spot them way in the back hunched over their forge! they're so red they look ready to explode! hideous hacking hopped up... I'm going to wipe them out too... they'll be a pushover... I'm going to snatch away the little girl... just wait, assholes! I'm about to pop my cork, that's a fact... No more waffling an unleashed hurricane I'll pound the whole damn joint to smithereens... No ifs ands or buts, Christ Almighty! I'm going to cream those tough guys!... Just wait, anvils! This is war! I'm a scary customer! The kid drank with them! That's the secret of the spell! just wait and see how I work, my little vixen! I'm all eager! wriggling and jiggling! all fours churning away! furious sinews! I paw the ground snort caracole! I pry my whole body free! yank off my seat with my fired-up arms and thighs! All my strength's back! And I'm one hell of a lot more powerful, like a horse! "A" horse, what am I saying, Christ Almighty! More like four put together! I send sparks flying against the walls I'm pawing up a spray! Got my bottom completely unstuck, the whole icky muck! ah! it was cramping my style got all the room I need now! you've never seen me at the top of my form! This crazy fiery wreck is going to pull out all the stops! the brain-geek! in a terrific fit!... It's war battle fury and horsies!... Make way for the cavalry!... A charge, now there's something you've got to see!... Not everybody's noticed about me... But Finette caught on right away... "You're cracked just like my brother! something hit you in the head!..." That really happened, no lie. "He stares at me just like you!" she mimicked my basket case way of dropping my jaw... "Except he can't go out by himself he falls over in the street..." She'd never seen me fall over... sometimes I did worse... Truth is, Finette, Fatso's wife, had a sharp eye... still she didn't see everything... her words came back to me clear as a bell... I could hear her talking to me... You wait and see also, my little hussy! She'd never seen me hit the ground at full horsepower! She hadn't seen anything yet... how impressive I could be on all fours! All right, so I was messed up just like her brother... but he didn't have my strength! my powerful charge!... I could have cleared twenty obstacles with three colonels on my back! on my saddlecloth! That's just the way I'm talking! Possessed, that's the word, with the fiery passions of magical power! That's what had me seething! Possessed by the Fourth Sphere! Where thunder lives! I felt like shouting it over to Sosthène! The old fucker couldn't hear me! I felt like yelling it to Matthew but it was absolutely the same story! "To the slammer, pal! To the slammer!" That's all he kept repeating... Bum! Scumbag! Those are the kinds of animals I had to deal with! Ah! I had to wipe out the whole bunch! Just let me get my hands on them! ah! it was all too true too cruel! I was seeing the light... I'd never be free with Matthew around... Doubts swept me again... I let loose another load... Flat on my ass I shit myself. I stretch out, almost fainted... that's where scruples land you... just had to entertain one for a split second... and now this rising stink... all my gunk stuck to my seat... just so they don't notice anything... I take a whiff... another... I ought to take off my pants... What the hell! What the hell! ah! freedom!... whatever it takes to pull out of this!... I yank off the whole mess my whole seat! peel off the tatters... my suspenders!... It still stinks! I'll never be free!... I holler: it's not me! it's not me! Now they come running over... I scrunch up into a ball wedge myself against the tambour frame... I don't want anybody to see me... "Go away! Go away!" I order them off... they won't let me be... they probe me feel me up and down... especially O'Collogham who catches a good whiff of me... hunts for my undershorts... rummaging under the tub... I'd stashed them... I just lie there curled up like a gun dog... I don't want to stand up looking indecent... "Go away! Go away!"... but they don't. I feel I'm really going to boil over this time... Dirty pigheaded brazen bastards! I'm such a scary customer over in my corner... raw rude scrunched... that they back off stammer... Ah! I'll show those two SOBs where to get off! I'll give them a taste of what real vengeance is like!... I take advantage of the breather... grab a rag off the floor... wipe my ass feel better... I can hear the girl singing way in the back... now that's nerve!... I'm going to snatch her away from those sharks!... I stamp my feet, raise hell... Her voice fills the workshop... a children's ditty...

Busy... busy... busy bee!...

Ah! I'm not going to bide my time forever... just wait, my darling honey-bee!... when I spy her I hit the floor... she's putting away some small utensils... skipping and prancing... I get a good look at her... flitting among the closets! everywhere at once! ah! my busy bee!... No more tummy aches, no more dizzy spells!... ah! now that and forth... I can see them... scheming... this all has got to end!... have to put my pants back on... I'd like a little chat with them too! just a word or two with those out-and-out perverts, and then I'd kidnap the girl! Just snatch her away! and trot her over to Curlers'... "trot," what am I saying—gallop! Ah! my mind's made up! but my butt's too cruddy! They take advantage of it... they're grinding iron crushing the forge! You should hear their fury!... That's not going to keep me from zigzagging past! But first I've got to scrub myself clean! Ah! that's the big snag! I'm sticky so godawful sticky... I can't show up in front of them looking like this! I squat back down coil my body into a ball... From twenty yards off they barrage me with their gas... attack sprays!... ah! you just wait and see, clowns!... Now they're adjusting their masks! It's the big tryout! Here we go, they want to suffocate me!... The girl is adjusting the masks on their heads... ah! some tough customers they'll make on the battlefield!... hacking... about time for me to butt in!... Crouched behind the autoclave I keep my eyes peeled... wind myself tight... I can see their little game I don't miss a trick... in a cloud Sosthène and the kid... To adjust his mask she climbed onto a chair for a better reach... her thighs... her strong lovely calves... He's getting a good whiff of her... right up close to his nose... ah! I'm keeping tabs... he sticks a finger in her, works it around... that's the way he is... feeling her up... feeling... and whackwhack-whack! on her fanny!... and that makes her laugh... they both sneeze and start over... ah! the girl's a little monster too, an unholy terror! ah! such sleaze! you had to see them carrying on... the little cockteaser shaking and wiggling her ass around... and me stuck there fretting my heart out!... Crazy bastard!... the sight of that pair! the sassy vixen! And me there covered with shit... ah! heartbroken I flatten out hunker down farther... I'm completely useless, powerless... he draws her into the other corner... I can't see a thing now... they're hidden by the billows... a thick acrid steam... inside they're sneezing and coughing... her uncle's whacking away at the anvil with all his might... Bang! Bang!... Sosthène ought to lend a hand... it's an awesome racket... the jolts wiggle and quiver me from head to toe... I jump out from behind the autoclave, as is, in the raw! Devil-may-care! "Man your horses! Horseshoes almighty!" I bellow, "now you're going to see some action! To your horses! Bing! Bang! Bam! You're going to learn a thing or two! Man your horses! Into the hail of bullets! Bang! Boom! I'm all ready! Climb right on! And let me take off! My horseman for an empire!" I have a fire in my belly! I've got to do something, my four paws are burning for action! I'm stamping around like crazy! Whipping my tail, digging my hooves, snorting! My blood's surging up from my balls, a rush that throws me in a spin, swelling my whole head top to bottom! I'll show these oafs! My guts are flip-flopping around inside, lashing me... I stand rear face forward! whoops ah! here I go! Belly up! All four hooves in the air! Slipped out from under me! What can you do, battle is battle! They're defying me! Hell! Hell! Look at those three! those hundred mouths of fire! If only I can stand I'll get out of this jam! I'm glued down again... my butt-crack's sticking... where're my undershorts?... they can see me!... my fiery nostrils!... I'm wailing in the fray. They dig down, fire another blast of their dense gas!... Let me at those swindlers! I'm greased lightning!... Tough luck! I've taken on new form! you damned freaks! Turn your cannons! A powerful new form! And with the colonel on my back!... He climbed onto my vest... me down on all fours... on all fours! and stark naked except for the vest... Let me at those squadrons of abductors! My love is unwavering!... A fanfare of trumpets!... I'm quivering... The great moment has arrived! The charge! Pull out all the stops! Let me run your horse to death!... Right off, the Colonel's voice... my own colonel, des Entrayes, my commanding officer! he mounts me in his breastplate! ah! he's a first-class cavalryman! he weighs two hundred pounds! one hell of a lot of guts! And the squadrons follow right behind! at his command! And what stupendous leather lungs on that guy! his voice booms above the cannonade... the other pack of crackerjacks are bombarding us with blasts of gas... Ah! they're totally possessed too... Ah! now ringing out from every corner... treacherous chimes, battering bells!... clang out your chorus, you horseshoed rascals! And let his tremendous voice strike a vibrant chord that will shake heaven to its foundation! Let the stars fall into my eyes! His tremendous voice snuffs all in its path! One mighty booming roar! The mere echo panics me! I whinny! race ahead twice as fast! The coon's plowing his spurs into me! Rending my sides! "Chaaarge! Chaaarge!" Nothing blocks his path... And it's amazing to see the way the brigade tears along! Tra-lay-ree-day-ra!... we hurtle upon them like greased lightning... The hypocrites are holed up way far at the other end of the joint! The pair of them, my kidnapper monsters! All three of them—the Englishman, Sosthène, plus my two-timing treasure! Why, it looks like they're turning tail to me! Ah! an outrage! They're not going to flee before the charge, are they? Hell for leather, greased lightning, we're not advancing even two... three... four yards!... Their spell's knocking the power out of our thighs... Yet des Entrayes defies them, standing up in his stirrups... which, by definition, are yours truly's!... arched on my saddle... He's magnificent, naturally!...

He thunders along just as he did back in Flanders... Here comes his grand feat!... Squadrons in open order! Chaaarge! What an earthquake! Four paws! You should hear them! Sixteen! Thirty-two! Christ Almighty, I'm shaking and panting... it's all so awesome... my mane's glistening, my ass too! with fiery spirit, and furiously!... one hundred thousand sparks!... a bat out of hell!! a whirlwind! I'm flying off! Take heart! I don't even feel my colonel anymore his lard ass his breastplate nothing! I send it all flying! glasses dishes along for the ride! all my implements! The hot H_2O the tub spills over! all the dikes burst flood the loft! the four squadrons are squish-squashing around! Bangboomcrash! I skid/sprawl flat out. He's digging in his spurs as he barrels along, my wild savage! hopping back on the rebound! ah! he's fiery horrifying! he'd gallop me to death! I rear up wrestle back! Everything sweeps me along! The cohort carries us away! And six! and nine! thirteen squadrons! blindly we go tumbling... collapsing... a complete fiasco on the staircase... my colonel's ballooned into a huge hulk... his mouth booming... his cry echoing... I clamp the bit in my teeth... I want to eat up the distance... I'm all horse body and soul! I fly into the line of fire! That's a fact! The cyclone whips me along... Trumpets shittershatter the windows... The great headlong sweep of the fourteen brigades! into the big black abyss at breakbit speed! the Fourteenth Heavy Cavalry... and the Fifteenth! des

Entrayes bears down on my neck, buries his boot in me, cuts into my sides. His spurs are huge sons of bitches! Just like him! He's putting me through the wringer! My storm of strength! I want to keel over in the heat of vengeance! Hell for leather! JEEEZUS KEE-RIST! "I'm coming! My angel!" I yell out to her! "Dirty bitch, here I am!" I think about what she's in for! Oh! that little fanny of hers! The fourteen thousand ramrods of revenge! but we're still moving in place suspended in midair! We haven't gained an inch! I'll be damned! and the three of them over there pawing each other... going "myum-myum"!... I can hear them... their tongues... their rapaciousness... Plus they're back smashing the equipment... They're keyed up all the way... splintering screwing up... All our chances're slipping through our fingers... we'll never get there in time! I'm dripping with sweat bathed in lather... we haven't covered twenty or a hundred yards... The plain swells sway under our hooves... melts away rises back up when we charge... it's always the same... a battle that comes in waves... a cosmogonic challenge... the landscape is haunted... I'm initiated into the magic spells! Sosthène didn't miss a thing!... I'm going to wipe the floor with him like with everybody else! Ah! I take off break away from the platoon!... I've gained three lengths at least!... I'm brushing against Sosthène, that's a fact! I sniff him next to his snout... crashbangboom! All fouled up! Tangled up in my reins! One hoof! both feet! everything! I'm tied up in knots! Thrashing around!... With a kick that could knock through the scenery I break free!... I zip out into the hallway!... The whole horde's on my tail, in tow! The entire squadron, all eight brigades swerve into the walls!... greased lightning! a whirlwind! "Chaaarge!" I'm on my last leg! And still des Entrayes keeps on bellowing... The horrible beast is stabbing right through me! Christ! I bellow louder than ever, me, his little old horsey! High-nettled and how! his rotten spurs hack savagely at my balls! More than I can bear! I plough into the platoon beside us! I knock down a wall... Now they catch me by all four hooves bind and hang me up... they shackle my paws... What sort of slimeballs are they? I wonder... Bing! Bang! Bam! I bust through all my bonds!... and back off I go at a gallop... bolting, bolting along!... I took three four strides... I'm drenched, all in a lather... galloping like crazy... in a whirlwind... I gained five six seven yards at least... almost at the other end of the workshop, touching the door, the anvil! now it's payback time! the echoing trumpets shatter the air all around... let them break you, send you reeling wriggling against the walls!... this is all-out war! I'm going to trash the entire hellhole! I want to reach my rotten creeps! They've ducked behind the carboys!... The cannon blasts the shells whoosh past, knocking us off course! that gives you some idea of the awful intensity! my des Entrayes has kept right on howling! Digs his feet way down, standing in his stirrups! He wants us to outdo ourselves, pour on ten times the juice! I'm ready to dump the clumsy dolt! I'm at the end of my rope! The wild maniac clutches me... he's read my mind! his two iron boots! with one buck of my awesome rump I'm off, careening, a miracle of flight! I glide above the explosions! Ah! there's still some life in me yet, goddamn it to hell! I pull back good and hard! he wobbles... grabs hold of my mane! He's tough as nails, a bloodsucker! I charge again I'm going to chuck him! Take heart! The brute breaks his fall!... And then breaks me hurtles me headlong!... Hell's bells into the hurricane!... Crashbangboombam! we send all the dishes to the floor... the stools... the whole works go flying!... Lucky thing, thank God, I'm not wearing undershorts!... I'm a war horse no joke... a bare ass... bare flesh and sinews!... and powerfully ridden! Look at me charge! along with the Seventeenth Heavy boot to boot... thirty-five hundred cavalry men!... plus mass formations! Hearts lather whipping along in the gust!... look at us bolting, ploughing forward! Ba! Da! Da! Boom! we all sweep ahead! at breakneck speed! The ground thundering! everybody yelling! des Entrayes in his gold crepe saddle! Just like him! *Te Deum!* Everything between heaven and earth is roaring and wheezing! a vast panting panorama! Fourteen divisions! I can see the standards!... whipping in the wind! Ah! Sosthène's ugly mug is under the table! Ah! peek-a-boo I see you! a flash glimpse! I'm a maniac on lightning hooves! I'll drive him out into the broad daylight! I'll make him bare his little scheme! The horde sweeps me along! You can go hang! the thundering cavalcade roars! a hundred thousand churning legs sweep us along! And on top of it all, the wicked cannonfire! It's too much! the ground goes soft wavy slips out from under... and now rises comes crashing down... all along the horizon the sight turns your stomach... hills made of molasses... melting away when you reach them... hills that hold up nothing... under the weight of the charge they buckle/cave in... It makes me puke! the whole sight's disgusting... The long walls pucker crease crack... the entire work-shop's breaking apart crumbling to pieces, it's all going to capsize with us along! Oh! des Entrayes, we're plunging into the abyss! It's right there! a big black gaping hole! sucking the whirlwind inside!... we're soaring through empty air! propelled by our damned momentum! the sixteen squadrons with the whole horde on our asses!... Des Entrayes, Colonel sir, listen to that godawful roar! the stampede of madmen! I churn the black air with my feet! It all slips out from under! charging into the abyss... the entrails of the black pit! Des Entrayes! ah! when I hit bottom I want to laugh... I paw the ground, wriggle, burst out laughing... Just like me! Horse or no horse! Entrails! Des Entrayes! What a rich gleeful word! Oh! man, Jesus Christ, that's one funny name! Des Entrayes! One man, two names! I'm hysterical! I swerve this way and that, backtrack! I laugh horse-style rearing on my hind legs! I paw the ground, whinny through my fiery nostrils! But whoah now, the other guy pops back up in the saddle! He thrashes me, savages my sides! He won't have me laughing! In mid-gallop I collapse in pain! ah! the torturer! the horde, the twenty-five squadrons caracole over my head and ribs... I'm worked over, mangled, a gaping wound!... "Take heart!" they all cry out in chorus... the

Colonel clears off! his grip slips from my pummel! He goes sailing into the abyss, that's a fact! I bucked my ass with monster force and threw him! It was inevitable! That word, railing, derailing reason! Entrails! Des Entrayes! That name, Christ Almighty! They'll kill me with loony laughter! my nostrils on fire!... ah! the abyss is swallowing us because we've been laughing too hard! the entire charge, the brigade all in a heap, plus the pack of bozos! And victory's within our grasp! Wham! Phew! I can't breathe! I'm being doused! an icy stream!... Ah! I snort, fight back, break through! Three people grab hold of me! A dozen! Twenty-five! I'm crawling with people... They wrestle me to the ground... it's a tub! what a treacherous attack! death by drowning! Bushwhacked! the Greenwich business all over again! The whole bag of tricks from those shit-heads! The firemen are back! Doing their number on me! Blinding me with their awful sprays... Flattening me full thrust... maniacs settling a score... who else can it be but O'Collogham... He's the brains who cooked up the whole thing with the other crook... took advantage of my headache... my injury-sapped body... they made me breathe their gas!... in their devil's workshop in the loft... ah! they're bucking me back up now... they're scared... they missed their target! their idea was for me to drop dead!... they're still at it, Christ Almighty! The proof is they're dousing me again! I'm going to rip your guts open with my four hooves! my lightning blow! they're giving me the business, calling me "kid"... now that really sucks! Smart asses! they're pinning my chest to the floor... "You shouldn't have done that, Ferdinand!"... that's the line they're feeding me... a lecture! They're plastered over my face!... they don't want me to look them in the eyes! Sure, naturally! Naturally! I react... writhe and untwist! They hammer away at me with fist and foot... I feel every blow... my spell's been broken... I'm not a horse anymore... this bag of bones is all mine... just lying here, a sorry shambles... I'm howling I hurt so bad... They grab me by the ankles... send me into pirouettes, push down against my body on purpose... I'm so limp they fly into a rage... Now they hold me at each end and start swinging me like a hammock... "He should've slipped on his mask... he wouldn't be sick..." Their same old put-down... "It's this stupid shithead's own fault!..." I couldn't come back with a word... they just went and tossed me against the wall like a dead weight... the little girl watched their goings-on. Sosthène had his say: "His bullshit'll be the death of him this time!" He kept harping on the idea that I was pigheaded. "Up and at 'em, my fighters!" I boom, and bop up on my feet... with a buck of my butt. Now that's anger! Sheer rage brought me back to life... I'm going to slaughter those slimeballs! I let them know about it... Don't they look just awful! Eyes popping wincing they're wailing... yeah, right, it's their turn to be scared! "Listen up, tough guys!" I yell at them, "I'm going to take back my sweetheart, my idol! Give me back my fairy child, you bastards!" They're shaking in their boots!... "Ah! diabolical schemes, that's the last time you'll take advantage of my condition!"

My mind was made up, I was gung ho, the works! Sick to death of my dizzy spells! my scaresparrows!... there was going to be a big change around here... I was going to teach that pack of swindlers a lesson! plus that hare-brained kid! "Just wait and see, Tibet and gang! It won't be any 'Fourth Sphere' of soft creamy vibrations! Watch out, you weasels!" There, I let them have it this time, they're quaking at the knees... they can see I'm stewing... they stammer, don't know what to expect next... Ah! they've got their tails between their legs!... Not really the best spot to be in!... They snap into action start showering me with attention... Ah! careful now, cannibals! I'm a be-gentle-this-is-my-wedding-night kind of guy! I want soft caresses kid gloves... They're sly bastards!... "I'm not Claben!" I warn them... "When I'm a hundred percent again, I'll bounce you down all twelve stairs!... jackals at my boot heels! monsters! swine!..." They slave away... I think they're under my thumb I treat them like crap... They've still got a long way to go!... I want them to massage me around my heart... That's where the pain is worse and worse... when I think about her I get so damned jealous! over such a dirty little tramp! "So where'd she get to? Hey, can anybody tell me?" Vanished again? I can't see hide nor hair of her... I raise my head a real strain... Vanished... "Where'd you stick her?..." I'll wipe the floor with them!... I'll break every bone in their bodies... with a crowbar like over at Ben Tackett's... they're all in cahoots!... So I'll be teaching them a good lesson! I'll set their dirty mugs right down on the anvil! And I'll do a little engineering on them myself! Hammer out a few masks! I make them a big promise! In my own way! Tra-la-la boom! and Bang! and Bang! the girl along with them! Stuck up bitch! my foxy fairy! I want to beat the impishness right out of her! And that's spoken right from the heart! My bout with des Entrayes brought me back to reality, my prize prancer! I blew my cork! That's the main thing! Strength and blood! I've got to get better! "Massage me, you weasels, but easy does it!" They've got to pay for their infamies! I want to see their tears! In addition to returning my idol! I won't budge an inch on that score!... I'm going to put my expertise into play!... "Listen up, scumbags!" I warn them, "I'm a fair kind of guy... I'm going to wallop you back once for every punch you threw!..." I can already see a hammer hovering... up above in midair...

"Darling! Darling!..." somebody's calling me... Why, it's my darling!... my angel! my angel! my sweetheart! The air I breathe!... I want a look at her! I want a breath of air!... I open my eyes wide, such a strain... What a dazzling sight! I answer: "Virginia!... Virginia!..." Everything's blotted from my mind! it's her! her hand! her little hand!... I blink... what a glow! Her dear face... little blonde ringlets... ah! a gauzy shimmer... she leans down... how kind she is!... her little hand brushes across my forehead...

Ah! I feel a whole lot better... I'm a new man... In a snap the other two catch on that she's casting a spell over me, brought me back from the dead... they can see the effect she's having on me... her bewitching kindness... that's the feeling... all my reproaches fly right out the window... I adore her, that's all there is. Her presence my life!... I keep sitting stay real still... back against the wall... recovering my wits... How mindful she is of everything... she doesn't want me to move... it's an honest-to-goodness miracle it's real simple... Just setting my eyes on her was enough... to cure me... I'm frozen to the spot in bliss... Even so I keep track of my two jokers... They've also started to act real courteous... They want to carry me upstairs, up to the landing up to my bedroom... I accept help, no more... give my arm to my darling girl... That's how I remember it... and yet I felt uneasy... I was fumbling through my mind... thinking hard... calm and cool again... I hadn't touched any booze... not a drop... I'd flipped out in one flash... just like back at the Tweet-Tweet Club... "Geez, enough already! Stop thinking about it, hell!" Ah! she's so ravishing/magical!... I can see her again, my little marvel! Just her... She still blinds me! I'm knocked out, trembling and moaning over how beautiful she is... I'm one happy doggie... She laughs smiles lets me bliss out... If she went away my life would be over... I'd die presto...

"Darling... Darling," I call her just like that real softly... I don't feel self-conscious in front of those two bums anymore... the wily uncle and that other weasel... Let them think whatever they want! They've got to face up to what love's all about! They escort me upstairs... I'm happy this is a joy... I feel like I'm being transported upwards upon a cloud... I stretch out on the bed... "My pet! My pet!" I call her... I want her to stay with me... I'd like her to sleep with me... But they won't have that!... They pull her away... but they're not brutal or cocky... just matter-of-fact because what I want is so off-the-wall...

"See here, Ferdinand! Virginia's just a little girl!..."

Sosthène's the creep who delivers that one! Well, the hell with it, I'm in no mood for a fight... just so she'll stay by my bedside... all I see is her, her pale blue eyes... the color of the sea... a blue mist upon her face... upon her pink and blonde face... I can see her soul!... I tell those other two stinkers about this! incredibly enthusiastic!... I wanted to cover her with kisses! And so what I shout is: "I'd like to eat and drink her!"

"Ah! he's really impossible!"

Right off the pigs get huffy! they're going to start throwing those scenes of theirs all over again!... But I'm in raptures anyway, damn it! Am I dreaming? Nope, this isn't a dream!... I feel her little heart under her dress... right here I probe keep probing... and her tiny tittie real pointy... and then the other... ah! how glad and happy I am! Her uncle can go ahead and scowl all he wants! I just won't look at that slob!... Let him croak from jealousy! I'm right here feeling her up... these are our two hearts in my hands... red hot in my grubby mitts... ah! hers mine I'm pawing them!... I'm hot all over! a gentle pulsing heat... flushing my whole body my belly my throat... thump! thump! affectionately and all that jazz... ah! how good how delicious... I'd like to catch some sleep... I need to... ought to... but what if she took advantage of me sleeping?... To run away?... no, her heart's right here! ah! little birdie... right in my hand it is, in my hand! "I love you! I love you!..." I close my eyes trustfully... I see hot and red... I'd like her to keep talking to me... to say a kind word or two... she's mum... she laughs real softly... I tickle her... kidding around... those other two better stay right where they are...

I was so preoccupied that I almost asked Sosthène for a bit of advice. I dropped a stray comment about life's difficulties in front of him... how a person pays for his moments of folly... how out of sorts her uncle looked... it was dumb to tucker himself out so much... his niece didn't look so hot either... This didn't get me much by way of an answer.

All Sosthène thought about was himself, his personal worries. Meanwhile he ate like a horse but didn't put on an ounce. Sosthène was just like me, he had a thing for jam... voracious, and how, especially orange marmalade, he stuffed himself sick. Every morning we were served a full-course breakfast in bed. We were living high on the hog! on easy street! Buttered toast, chocolate, you name it... plus haddock, sardines, and fruit. A shame it was coming to an end, sure, it couldn't last forever, but it still was crummy... Sosthène was wasting away despite chowing down for all he was worth. In the beginning he'd put on a few pounds, but now he was dropping them all. These days he was getting the runs eight-ten times in a row. The guy wouldn't quit... day and night... he'd wake me up with a start... charging off to the toilet, leaving the door open behind him...

In the end I chewed him out.

"We're dying here, shit! You don't give a damn!"

"Oh, and you do, you big dumb jerk!"

He dishes it back, mad as hell...

"You don't give a damn where I go! I'm taking a shit! Yeah, a shit! Got no choice! There's a load on my mind, mister! You know where I'm going to be enjoying myself in just one more week? Huh, my darling dickhead? The gentleman's preoccupied with his home life! The gentleman's only thought is setting up house!..."

"You've got the shits over the trials?"

I pop the question.

He doesn't answer, no, no way! he dashes out to the toilet, comes back, sits down, we chat.

"Tomorrow!" he goes to me. "Tomorrow we'll go!"

Just like that, determined.

"We'll go where?"

"We'll go test out the strength!"

"So you're sick for real then?"

"Ah! I beg you, you little crook, for once in your life, be loyal to me!... Don't you go forgetting you're not alone! That I'm the one who dug up the Colonel, our bread and butter!"

He was making a scene...

"Thanks to me, you stuffed your face! Look how happy you are today and I'm the one behind it, so come on, be a sport!"

"What do you want?"

"I want to see how things work at present... I've got it nailed down. I can still feel it..."

"You sure?"

"Positive!"

"But you're afraid anyway?"

"I've got the jitters... that doesn't mean I'm scared... I've even got an idea... a real beaut!... but I'm not telling you... you'll see soon enough!... Your mouth's too big... you'll go blab everything to your little pet!... Come on, we're leaving right now..."

Ah! He was catching me off guard... It was sort of a joke... His approach was to lure me out gallivanting... That was my soft spot... But I kept thinking about Virginia... It wasn't so awful... we'd be back in an hour, just enough time to pop out and back... to try out the experiment... get a little look at his power...

It was a deal.

"But look, I'm talking about leaving on the double! Right smack in the middle of our stumbling blocks!"

Sosthène was all in a quiver at the prospect.

"Ah! What you're going to see'll knock your socks off, buster! Ah! You can't say I didn't warn you!... You just need to bring your spoon and napkin ring... and look, you go like this with them... clack! clack! clack! You get cracking! Work up a good rhythm for me... I leap into the traffic... But you make sure you're up real close so I can hear you!..."

"OK, let's go, we're off!..."

We throw some clothes on, he rolls up his Chinese gown, a small bundle under his arm, and we're out the door.

It was still pretty much dark. We go down tiptoe, but when we hit the street we pick up the pace... jump onto the first tram... Dawn was breaking... a bone-chilling fog... It was October... we were shivering...

"Where you going?" I ask again...

"Can't tell you!... It's all in the surprise... You'll be running the show for me!... It's really got to grab you! No surprise, no shock! no magic emanation!... The spirits won't come!"

"Ah!"

I was still sort of suspicious...

"You'll do that for the gases too!... You get it? The rhythm! the enveloping action of the vibrations... everything depends on that!"

"You still got Goâ?"

Just checking.

"Do I still have him? Ah! well, you just wait and see, kiddo! I'll open your eyes! And how! that cosmic influx! Ho! Ho! Ho!"

So cocksure! The tram was packed. With rat-racers, commuters heading down toward Ludgate, clerks, "Harrows," pale faces, a scrawny down-in-the-mouth crew all piled on top of each other, the men having a little smoke... scraping off clots of fog from their newspapers. Early morning is a crummy time... The London trams stink like ship holds... journeys to the ends of the earth! to the Far East, rough times, because of the pipes, the tobacco... honied... with a hint of sandalwood.

Maybe the employees on the tram are thinking about this too, sardined, bunched up, bumping along like crazy, banging into each other, at track switches, street corners, piling out in a rush, limping along their way from Highgate to Shepherd's Bush, the whole suburban belt undulating, the long rows of bungalows, the single file of small garden patches, geraniums behind their fences, real spick-and-span, flower cages about as cheerful as thousands upon thousands of cemetery plots on All Saints' Day... The sky's to blame because in this part of the world it's always gloomy between sunrise and noon.

We were picking up mobs everywhere, at every stop they came dashing, wheezing, already dead beat from the grind even before starting, ladies, gentlemen, worried about the time, groping ghosts bristling with apologies...

"Beg your pardon!"

I was thinking about Pépé as we traveled along.

"Aren't we going to see her?" I ask.

It's been a week since he'd gone over... She must be sort of wondering...

"Everybody wonders, young man! Everybody! That's what life's all about! Wondering!... I'm wondering too..."

I drop the subject.

He was a cad. I knew that already...

We reach Shepherd's Bush, black and blue from all the knocking around! Everybody gets off! A mad rush, charging to the underground! Into the abyss! Everybody disappears! Dashing down the stairs!

Ah! I'm not too crazy about those murky depths! I had my reasons! I suggest taking the bus.

"Where do you want to go?"

Not a peep.

He's a walking secret. I go into my pigheaded routine. I dig in my heels.

"Do as you like, I'm staying put! My underground days are over!"

He gives in, we board a double-decker heading toward the center of town, number 61. The fresh cannon fodder route. We ride, roll along toward Charing Cross, where trains leave for the son of a bitch front.

It was now daylight. The place was crawling with footsloggers, slews of khaki-backs jamming the streets, the whole Strand, reinforcements, troops headed for the front, trainloads for Flanders, rolling into battle, plus hookers already on the job, at every intersection from Waterloo Bridge, I could see them from the upper deck of the bus, I recognized them one after the other, Cascade's girls, Gencive's, Jérôme's, plus Ginette, and Curlers in front of the Spark, the big pub at the corner of Winham Road.

He gives me a shake, lets me know we'll be getting off at Villiers Street.

"I'll tell you the whole story! You betcha!"

OK by me.

We go back to the Chinese dive, the place where we first met, which leads out to the tunnel in the middle of the slope. Just like the other time, the player piano is blasting away, along with trumpets, tambourines, and girandoles that light up at every crash of the cymbals. A thundering racket through the joint...

He shouts over at me: "I'm going to slip on my gown."

He dashes to the head. Abracadabra, he's back, all decked out in Chinese drag, saffron-powdered face, with makeup, pigtails, buskins, the works...

I tell him: "Fancy fancy! Bravo! Show me your dragon!"

He turns his butt around and shows me, red and green, breathing fire, a magnificent embroidery. The waitresses came over and admired it, running their fingers over the genuine silk.

"So you happy now?"

He was creating his little sensation, all the lushes at the counter staggered over for a look-see at his rear, and to scratch the dragon. The butt of some terrific jokes...

With the waitresses we downed three glasses of brandy on top of the tea and cookies.

"Where'd you dig up the pocket money?"

His answer: "Hmmpf!"

Dead broke, we were off... It was already a miracle.

"How you going to handle the others? You don't have much time left. Just an hour. Whatcha gonna do?"

"You got guts?" he answers.

"Loaded with guts! From top to toe!"

"Well, you're in for something special."

"You know, you've been making me the same promise forever, it's about time you give me my treat! Let me have a look at your big secret! So where you going to knock me out with wonders?"

I was still a touch suspicious about what the jerk would be up to out on the street, riling the mob, blocking traffic, that was his way of cajoling, of seducing the Spirits and Goâ, of compelling their magic emanations to obey his spell... It was one extraordinary job. He was revving up right before my eyes, by the third brandy he was going strong, snapped back to life on the spot. He was wriggling his shoulders, vibrating from top to bottom. He couldn't stay put in the bar. The customers were having a field day. They didn't give a shit about us, I felt uncomfortable.

I ask him: "You feel strong?"

"Go ahead, let's hear a little something on the fork."

So right away I play him clack clack clack... The accompaniment he'd told me about... our makeshift system...

"Didn't you bring the napkin ring?"

Beefing right from the get-go.

It didn't come out very loud on wood, actually sounded like castanets...

"Will you remember?"

"Course I will!..."

We were going to get arrested, I could see it coming, no two ways about it. But if I'd gone off right then and there, left this character high and dry with his gown, my napkin ring, his song and dance, his fakir craze, maybe he wouldn't ever have gone back either, never returned to Willesden, and that meant throwing in the towel, poor Virginia all by her lonesome with her uncle and his whims, which would make for one weird little setup, one incredibly bumpy ride, plus the family riding crop.

No way in the world.

Ah! hell, I'd see this through to the end! even if I got all fucked up, tough shit!

"Let's go!" I say to him, "pal, we'll give it a try! but shake a leg! we've got one hour, no more! So what the hell are you going to do? Don't you think it'd be better for us to go back? Do you have any idea how we left everything? Nothing's put away in the loft! All the implements are thrown around! Ah! he'll raise hell, you bet! The Colonel must be seething! Ah! I can hear him from here! And you bet the kid's in for a whacking! You know I've got that right..."

"Go fuck her then, damn it, scram!... Since you don't want to lend me a hand!"

"I do, I really do, but get a move on, why don't you? You're hemming and hawing! You leaving? You staying put?..."

He studied the customers, then glanced at the traffic outside, the gawkers on Villiers Street.

"Give me ten minutes!" he finally announces, his mind made up. "Button your lip and do what I tell you."

"OK! Things are all right then, I'm all ears, but try to get us back by eleven!"

"We have to get cracking, right?"

"You better believe it!"

He still hadn't spelled out what he'd planned... Was he going to dance in public? Pass the hat?...

I ask him point-blank.

He looks at me, nods his head like that...

"Oh!" he goes... "You don't see the big picture, you don't have a clue about the trials..."

He pays up... leaves... I follow on his heels... they applaud us on our way out... It must have been 10:30... At the other end of the Strand there was already a load of cops... On our way past I notice—just about on schedule—the changing of the guard at Whitehall.

Again I repeat: "Hurry up, I don't know what you want to do, but I don't want to be recognized by the gals in the Square, by all Cascade's streetwalkers, it'd be all for the best if I wasn't."

So, of course, he beelines in that direction, we cross Trafalgar Square, its whole length and breadth, we pass three yards from Nelson, luckily he doesn't raise his head, he's all wrapped up in his sketching... But Sosthène stuck out like a sore thumb, the people, the privates escorted him along with the idea he was in a stunt costume, hawking for recruits, about to climb on a soapbox and give a speech, especially behind the National Gallery which in those days, along with Hyde Park, was the spot for open-air gab fests...

He keeps on walking, no rest stops. We cross in front of the Empire pub, right at the corner. Yikes! I'm a wreck, Leicester Street... I tell myself he's crazy, got it in his head to walk right into Cascade's and show off his beautiful gown. Wrong. He keeps on walking, we've just reached the edge of Piccadilly Circus, setting foot on the sidewalk right in front of the theater, the place where the cars have a hell of a time circling around and the traffic's a nightmare, you measure your progress in inches! All roads lead back to the Circus, Regent Street especially, and Tottenham Court Road (by way of Shaftesbury Avenue). The police are stationed in their booth just to the right of the Eros. The heart of the Empire, as they say...

I can see Sosthène pulling up short, I was following four or five yards behind so people wouldn't think we were together.

He shouts over to me: "This is the place!"

He plants himself on the spot, starts rocking, wobbling, kind of seesawing at the edge of the traffic, right out in the open...

I think to myself: he's had enough, he's going to throw himself under a bus! in his gown, the works! Just my luck! He's pulling a suicide on me!... He made me come out here on purpose for this!... Depressed and scared shitless! He wants a witness.

I take a few more steps back from the sidewalk. I post myself under the theater marquee between the newspaper hawkers. He waves me toward him...

Hi there!

He shouts: "Come on over! I don't bite!..."

I walk up to him.

"Now, Ferdinand, show a little spunk! You're going to see the grand challenge! Get your drumsticks going! Stay in perfect rhythm with me, follow me up close so I can hear you... Clack away, and then give me beads... droplets... ping... ping... ping... And keep looking at me!... Don't take your eyes off me! I'll show you Goâ's strength! I'm going to turn back traffic! I'm going to wipe out the police! You think I'm shitting you?"

A pretty tall order.

"Nah, you're not shitting me!"

It was a challenge pure and simple. He steps down off the sidewalk, walks out into the street. The cop in the middle of the intersection can see him coming, blows his whistle, waves him back. The others stop short at the whistle—the buses, trucks, carts. Sosthène raises one mitt, then the other, in a dancing pose, takes another three-four steps, raises the long train of his gown, remains planted right in front of the cars, and brings everything to a halt. He folds his arms. They're hollering something horrible, you can hear the angry yelling all the way over on Oxford Street. An explosion of honking and shouting. He's blocking all of Piccadilly Circus, every lane, they're squawking away at him from every angle. He stays glued to the spot, heroically. Then he starts chewing them out. "Beefsteaks!" he christens them: "Quiet! England, shut up! Goâ's the mightiest of all! U-turn!"

He wants to make them turn around.

"Come on out here and see me!" he hollers over at me. "Come on out here!"

He's grown excited, works himself up, yells in a fit, takes off his little jacket, wants to sock them with a genuine dance...

"Play me your number ninety-two!..."

It beats me what ninety-two was... He reminds me.

"CLACK! clack! clack! clack! CLACK!..."

I step back up on the sidewalk. I'm not going to play him a damn thing! He's caused enough of a scene! He's gesticulating, flailing about... pose ninety-two... now I recognize it... he's throwing his arms around... contorting his body... working his face, everything... Pretzelman!... a real workout... he's not exactly a graceful guy... he pours it on... all right in his little chink of space?... the cars are practically on top of him... Roaring, growling something horrendous right up against him... All the bellowing end to end on Regent Street blurs the buildings in front of my eyes, the sidewalks start spinning that's how bad the air is roaring with rage from every cop as far away as Marble Arch rolling in on their bicycles, a rising storm of whistles drowning the echoing din, sweeps away the voices, the racket of engines, your eyes, your sight, your head, the whole shebang.

I can see the cop up there in his little raised platform, how he's yelling his head off, red as a beet, hopping up and down trying to signal, exploding with anger. He bellows at Sosthène: "Go away!... Go away!... Fool! Scum!"

But Sosthène can't hear him... He's jubilating, signals me that he's in the seventh heaven of power. He points to the trucks, all the buses quaking before him, all the engines oozing, spurting, leaking because they can't get going, grinding, cracking to pieces, shitting, puking. The whole huge messy herd, the monsters, spewing smoke, checked and cowed right there on the asphalt, yellow-bellied wimps. Ah! what a horrible sight... from the Empire pub all the way to the Royal it was just one big, stinking traffic jam, an eel couldn't wiggle through without getting run over, a flea wouldn't be able to find its kids. The traffic cop has had enough of wiggling his hips up on his little podium, trying to get Sosthène to clear off, he chucks the whole lot, his job, his little signal flag, his direction signs, his platform, the works, and climbs down to the cobblestones... Ah! he's all hollered out... He's a side-show giant, got the build, the shoulders, the hands...

I can see his white gloves hovering above Sosthène, right over his head, he's going to pulverize him, beat him to a pulp...

The other joker's still dancing, back and forth from one foot to the other... tossing his head around in ecstasy...

"Will you stop!" the cop yells... "Will you stop, you rascal?" You can hear his voice he's bellowing so loud... through the storm of tractors, he outshouts the lot, horns, screams, sirens, the mob of passersby yelling on the sidewalks.

Sosthène was running in front of the cop, pirouetting past his clutches between the trucks, leaps, relevés, lively glissades, more pirouettes! the cop caught up with him... peek-a-boo!... this whole scene behind the buses! quivering there, at least three thousand of them... right smack in the humongous traffic jam racket, a zillion trumpets, horns, bells, sirens, pistons, unleashed upon the road block between Charing Cross and Tottenham, a doomsday din. Death to Sosthène!

But then Sosthène, dancing like crazy, magical like nobody you've ever seen before in your life, lifted off the ground in his gown, swept up, whirling, an elf in the air, a miracle of grace, impish amid the buses, now he's here, now he's gone, a pixie, hide and seek, another smile, the Incantation Dance, all ninety-six poses from the *Vegas*, plus the cop on the warpath right on his ass, charging along, foaming with rage.

I looked on in awe, what else could I do, I wasn't going to click-clack with my fork! He wouldn't have heard me. I'd have been torn to pieces, end of story.

The huge cop rammed the buses, smashing in everything... Sosthène kept slipping between his fingers... He was light as a feather... lighter than a breeze!... And what an incredible kick the crowd got out of him! Thrilled to death! Delirious!

I decided to stay out of it, I just hollered along with everybody else. I egged on Sosthène raising hell with his copper, giving him the slip through the growling chaos, the herd of throbbing monsters. It was great sport, exciting...

"Go on, men!... Cut him off, you!..." And wah! wah! woo!... I mimicked the trumpets! What a ball! I kept my napkin ring in my pocket... and my fork... and my spoon... I didn't want to attract attention... the soldiers also were having a blast. The buses were packed with khaki-backs... they got off for a better view of the chase... they start gesticulating like Sosthène... doing a snake dance... swarm over the sidewalk... surrounding the civilians... all the soldiers hand in hand... swept by the fever... There were boozehounds mixed among them, matchstick sellers, an entire cart of violets in the crazy hoopla, plus two sea gulls and a sparrow flying right above Sosthène. I caught that last little detail. The mob left the sidewalks, invaded Piccadilly Circus, every last inch, the intersections, absolutely unstoppable, knocking the cops flat, the traffic bogging down, bringing everything to a halt, forcing the buses back, roaring like this... Brrroom!... Brroom!... Brroooo!...

Sosthène was ringmaster of the madness, he'd ripped open his gown, giving his whole heart and soul! Looking around to spot me! I ducked out of sight... The huge cop was bobbing along, caught up in the rollicking swirl. He didn't know which way to turn... He was trapped, sucked, snatched, swept away by the snake dance... winding around the buildings and right out amid the cars... It slipped along everywhere like in a dream between the thundering buses, the raging herd of mastodons... Complete pandemonium smack in the center of London, with nobody to blame but Sosthène! Ah! and there'd be hell to pay too, I was dead sure... Ah! I could already see the consequences to come, the retaliation would be something else!... I have a mind to fade out of the picture real quietly, thread my way toward Tottenham. But I couldn't budge an inch backwards, the mob was way too thick, or move forward for that fact... I was boxed in.

And the cop was whistling!... whistling his head off! Help! Emergency! He was done in! Crawling under the buses, dashing onto the double-deckers after catch-me-if-you-can Sosthène who was twirling everywhere, leaping from roof to roof, bounding twelve yards into the air just like that, a mountain goat, a chamois, a fairy. Constantly bumping and denting his noggin was driving the cop nuts, he was roaring under the wheels, a lion-man! who'd take these running pounces, smash his face in, he'd torn off his trousers, his tunic, his uniform belt, charging around in the raw, on all fours after Sosthène...

"He's thirsty," this girl was saying, "he's barking, he's got rabies."

I had seen just about my fill...

Right then came the clang of fire engine bells in the distance... "Fire!

Fire!..." Reverberating echoing through the crowd...

Bong! Bong! Bong!

Sosthène starts dancing to that melody too... from one foot to the other... doing arabesques... each and every one joyous... loopy... and as energetic as the last!... with his hand... conducting the hullabaloo...

Bong! Bong! Bong!

This whips the dancers along like bats out of hell, the tail of the line slams into the walls, smashes up, squealing sharply...

The firemen move off into the distance... their bell dies away...

Just then there bursts onto the scene a huge swarm of cops, you could see them ganged up at the other end of the Circus, on Haymarket, a hundred at least, coppers in blue... I'm not going nuts, this is just what I figured... And ferocious, I'm telling you! A damburst! Stampeding like a herd of cattle! That cop knew what he was doing with that whistle of his!...

They charge into the ruckus, come barreling, ploughing blindly, smashing the jig with their fists, jostling, pummeling the circle of dancers, treading right on top of them, thrashing, trampling. The carcasses scream and holler, smashed to a pulp, gasping under the blows, heads reel, slam together, burst, there's blood all over the place... Another swarm of cops rushes onto the scene. I slip away by the skin of my teeth! They miss me! I run! Quick wits! The buffaloes in capes are battering everything to death! Then it hits me all of a sudden—Sosthène, I don't want him to croak! Shit, here we go again! Perfect!... Another bout of his sighing! What sort of excuse could I come up with? I hunt for him... call him... run out in front of the line of buses... spot him flat out on the sidewalk, with two huge suckers whaling away at him, finishing him off, one whacking with a nightstick, the other kicking with his boots.

"Over there! Over there!" I yell... I point to the other side of the street... as though there was some extraordinary sight to see... "Fire! Fire!" I shout to incite them!... It turns the heads of those two buffaloes... They head off in that direction growling in their lead-weighted capes!

"Ah! Master," I go to Sosthène, "from the looks of your head you don't have long to live... you've got blood running all over the place!..." He's gasping in the gutter... His head's trickling. I yank off his tattered gown... No way he'll be recognized... people are still fighting in all corners, the excitement hasn't flagged, the cops are clubbing everything in front of Lyon's pub. We're going to have a chance to disappear. I try to lift Sosthène, stand him on his feet.

He's really been through hell, and how, his eyes are like jelly, his nose so swollen he's got a couple extra nostrils. And he's oozing blood from every pore.

They really worked him over.

"Your luck just doesn't quit, dear master! Your show of power didn't go over too well!..."

Right then an explosion of panic knocks us back on the sidewalk, and then the crowd pulls us along, we're bobbing in the mob. In one way it's a terrific break. He'd never have been able to stand up on his own two feet! His mouth's full of muck, blood, hair, teeth, drool...

Little by little he spits it out on the people all around. Nobody notices. He wants to talk to me, instead he pukes. Coats me in chocolate. He gets yanked farther off... At last I catch him. In the chaos he manages to get out: "So, didn't it go over?"

The news seems to surprise him.

"You're going to catch cold," I shout back.

The crowd pulls us along. A torrent moving toward Shaftesbury...

One second we're choking, the next catching a breath of fresh air, back and forth, in fits and starts, depending... It's skeleton-scrunching time. I'm getting stuck with bones all down my sides. I'm squished flat against a shop. I spot Sosthène's ugly mug, the blood dripping from his nostrils. He's even lighter than me, bobbing on top of the mob. Luckily he looks almost handsome. He's in just his shirt and briefs, both dirty and soaked through. He's had a roll in the gutter...

At last we break free of the panic... the mob's still howling as it leaves us behind. I stand off to the side with him, we duck into a small entrance. Now he can stand on his own two feet. He's pretty much back to his old self, except for the blood running all over everywhere, from his ears too.

He asks me: "Want to go have a drink?"

I didn't want to see him plastered again.

"No," I go, "we're heading back!"

We hop on a 114 bus, from Marble Arch we didn't have far... they must have still been massacring each other over on Piccadilly Circus. My thoughts were still back there. All the rioting and ruckus couldn't have been anywhere near over!

"I swear you made a fucking shambles of everything, master!"

The guy had to get it through his head that I wasn't blind...

No answer... He kept dabbing his nostrils... Anyway I didn't want to needle him. The main point was for us to get where we were going. I was antsy to see Virginia, find out what'd happened. While Sosthène's blocking up his nostrils, pinching them to stop the bleeding, just like that on the upper deck of the bus I bring up what's on my mind, rehash this latest scandal, his recklessness, how he had laid himself wide open... and how I had snatched him away from death and the blood-crazed cops...

This riles him up, he insults me, says I'm all to blame, that my cowardice made the spirits take off, especially Goâ, that I had sabotaged everything, didn't even venture a single click-clack at the fatal moment! So where was my napkin ring? My fork? I'd fallen short in every single respect! and it was a disgrace!...

He was sore as hell at me for not coming through with his click-clack. But hadn't I saved his life? Look here, didn't that count for a little something?...

He was bleeding badly from his beak, bruised around his eyes, the blood was dripping all over his body, filling his mouth, but he kept bullshitting through his clots, spraying the people sitting near us... the front of his jacket solid red...

"Let's go," I shout, "this is our stop!"

True, we weren't far. I wanted to avoid any more big scenes. A short walk. We're back in front of the house. His nose and eyes are still bleeding. I don't want us to be seen like this. We slip down the lane, and then through the garden, the kitchen...

We had a lucky break. Uncle had just stepped out. He wouldn't be back before evening. He was spending the whole day out shopping. He'd left for Ascot or some other racecourse at the crack of dawn.

I called up from the garden...

"Virginia! Virginia!"

She answered me right away, she was awfully happy, but hadn't been worrying, just waiting for us, never once had she thought: "They won't come back anymore." She trusted me. It was real sweet. It tickled me so much I kissed her right in front of Sosthène, I didn't care... She asked me where we were coming from. She was curious even so. Plus Sosthène stuck out like a sore thumb looking the way he did, shirt in tatters, blood everywhere, black eyes. He'd lost three teeth, leaving a big gap in his mouth.

"He got run over by a bus" is what I told her right away to cut short any explanations. "We went to see his wife, she was under the weather, but she feels better now."

He backed up my story.

We cleaned up a bit, splashed some water on our faces, put some food in our bellies. Feeling better at last. For me the whole thing was a joke.

"So hey, what about Goâ? You got him up your ass? Ah! whoah, not so fast!" I start from the top! I want to give Virginia a little laugh. I run through the whole episode for her, how he had made out in his battle with the buses. How he'd been worked over by the yobs from Scotland Yard.

"Ah! what a sight, ma'am! They really let loose on him! Oh, my lord! Ah! the magic ordeal! Ah! just hold your horses now! Ah! I won't fall for that trick next time around! It was one hell of a workout!"

He gives a little laugh too, had to force it though, then snaps back that I left him high and dry, that I didn't click-clack for him with my fork and napkin ring as I'd promised... that I'd been scared stiff of the cops... blown the whole business... that the power had really come to him... and we had it all in our hands... but that I had made it bugger off with my attitude... otherwise we'd have turned London topsy-turvy... sent all the cops scurrying like rats into the gutters... even as it was, the buses were completely broken down... and if that wasn't proof enough for me, it was all because I had a chip on my shoulder and was even dumber than I was yellow-bellied, and that if I hadn't thrown in the towel, and instead fished my napkin ring and fork out of my pocket, and accompanied him with my click-clacking, as we'd agreed... you would have seen such power gushing like a spring smack in the center of Piccadilly Circus, overturning buses, an earthquaking transformation the likes of which had never been seen back in Bengal where Goâ Gwendor had nevertheless worked wonders, where the lamas of Ofrefonde concocted cataclysms for the whole world over, cosmic conflagrations that split the Himalayas asunder... and shook India down to Ceylon, and threw dark clouds on the moon, which you could see through a telescope... We might have seen all this in Piccadilly if I hadn't chickened out at the moment of action... And after he had given it his best shot... in short, I had betrayed him...

"Some stuff the fighting troops are made of!" That was his conclusion... "Scared of buses!"

That's what he'd come up with. To rile me in front of Virginia.

"Cyclones! That's right, cyclones! That's what I had under my feet... I could feel them in my dance... They were whirling in my butt... if you had given me a little clack-clack right then... I'd have sent Parliament up in smoke, and the constables, and Westminster... They were enveloped. But you saw for yourself in the *Vegas*! No click-clack, no rhythm! No guts! the magic vibrations dry up! I could keep dancing until tomorrow, wear my feet down to the bone! You don't give a damn!"

We'd been within a hairsbreadth, Sosthène had felt it the whole time long, we'd been this far from witnessing something like a cosmic wonder, the overthrow of all religions, right smack in Piccadilly Circus, heaven literally on earth, with a tremendous message, he swore the magical power was simmering under the street, right under his shoes, Geon's tellurium! No sooner he executed the sixteenth dance pose... The proof being all the buses started backing up, and the mob acclaiming the miracle the first glimmers of which were already visible out over the Thames and Trafalgar Square.

I hadn't seen any of that myself, just a horrendous snarl-up, a godawful nasty free-for-all, and Sosthène beaten within an inch of his life under a mob of cops... he still had the black eyes, but that didn't matter, apparently... I was the lousy son of a bitch, the fuck-up, the saboteur, you name it... That took some nerve!

"You dumb ass," I came back at him, "let's get one thing straight, if I hadn't been around, and kept my magnificent cool, the fuzz would have torn you limb from limb, I was the one who pulled you out of the gutter, the cops would have torn you limb from limb, so you keep your rotten trap shut! That's what your saboteur's got to say to you! It makes me sick to hear all your bull—magician my ass!..."

He'd been warned once and for all... He'd lost his tongue.

"Take care of your black eyes!..."

I coddled Virginia, who was stretched out on the sofa. Our absence had given her a scare all the same. We weren't worried at all, the old man wasn't due back until dinner, and only just. He himself wasn't sure when he left.

"All right! All right! Complete rest!"

Sosthène the sorcerer was placing damp towels all over his body, he had huge black-and-blue bruises, especially on his head. A heel had ground his nape so badly it shaved his skin clean off. He was still bleeding, and a lot too, so Virginia and I kept dabbing at it...

"Ah! I'm telling you!... Ah! no kidding, I won't fall for that trick next time! That's one for the record books! Ah! it mustn't be forgotten!"

He'd gotten under my skin.

"When you going off to the war? You'll turn the cannons into slag if you dance in front of them!"

He didn't appreciate my jokes. But we started seeing eye-to-eye again when it came to feeding our faces. We both were partial to jam. And now was the chance to treat ourselves.

We had ourselves served up a really out-of-this-world tea, with five kinds of jam and toast with maple syrup and sandwiches and caramel-topped pastries stuffed with cream, plus a chocolate bombe. Just to bust the servants' balls, get them moving their asses. We were nice and cozy in the salon, lords of the manor. We started up the gramophone. All the tart, bouncy tunes, the herky-jerky beats, ragtime melodies, the songs reaching this side from New York with the Sammies, full of pizzazz and razzle-dazzle, naughty and infectious... The whole repertoire of the Empire, the newfangled vice, the wriggle-and-whine. Sosthène loved the stuff, from the first note he wanted to dance with Virginia. So what that he was still woozy, beaten black and blue, all aches and pains, he blissed out anyway when he heard the music, profane though it was. He was a genuine fanatic.

"Aren't you fed up with tripping the light fantastic? Geez, you're screwy!"

He wanted me to dance with Virginia, do the fox-trot, the one-step, the cakewalk, a memory of America. He'd danced them all with Pépé...

"Yes sir, back in San Francisco, me decked out like Uncle Sam, and she dolled up like the Statue of Liberty, a French dame with a torch! That was for the grand finale! what a smash! I'm telling you!"

We messed around a little, but not poor Virginia who didn't really feel up to much. And she was usually so playful, so mischievous.

"The cat's away so the mice'll play!"

That was Sosthène's refrain.

Even so in front of Virginia it was a thoughtless comment. Anyway, that's how I saw it. On the pretext of catering to our needs the lackies kept poking their heads in to check whether we were ripping up the joint. But we were just living it up because we had the house to ourselves, the Colonel was out, and we were the masters.

Truth is, the Colonel was a killjoy, the crafty crackpot type, wheels always turning, plus those wild outbursts over trifles. I never knew how to take old twinkle-toes. I was still waiting for him to bring up the mercury business again. When he wasn't in the picture I felt better, even physically, my headaches went away. I felt out of sorts at the mere sight of that ugly mug stuck with a monocle, and that phony smile, creasing just half of his face. Ah! I wished he'd never come back. We played a few more records. I made Virginia dance. Sosthène also made her do a polka mazurka.

All of a sudden, she feels upset, turns pale, leans on a chair. She sits down, almost faints... She feels queasy...

"I don't know..." she says out loud...

"Honey," I go, "stay still, lie down, darling, lie down..."

I kiss her... I make her stretch out full-length... Playing it safe, understandably. I calm her, set her at ease.

Poor little Virginia, it was inevitable after all her problems, and then us making her dance on top of that, it gave her a headache, a tummy-ache too, her head's spinning.

"You see, you've got to play it safe."

Ah! I've stopped feeling self-conscious in front of Sosthène. We're thick as thieves. This's our situation, so we just accept it, and have a little more tea. All at once from down the street a burst of music, blaring OOM-pah-pahs, a Barbary organ.

"Hey, listen," I go, "that's 'The Dark Waltz'... The Knights of the Moon... That's the song they used to sing at Cascade's, morning, noon and night!..."

It was grinding out in our street, right there in front of the garden. I step over to the window, take a peek...

Ah! my eyes pop open... Can't be!... Oh, yes it can!... I walk away, go back... I'm nuts, fuck, it isn't them! Oh, yes it is!... It is!... it's them all right!... I'm not seeing things at all!... I cling to the curtains... my legs like rubber... I sit down... walk back over to the window... yeah, it's them! no mistake! they even spotted me... they're waving...

There's Nelson lugging the instrument, Centipede turning the crank... Nelson's having a grand old time... he points over at me... I recognize him all right... and Curlers is out there too... Ah! the lousy pest... they're all out there with the instrument... they're driving me crazy. How they'd wind up out there?... all three of them just like that?... Who tipped them off?... This is just one more piece of funny business!... Who sent them over?... Centipede... Nelson... Curlers! Ah! such godawful, hell-bent... such vicious persecution... I'm their pigeon... I'm keeping this from Sosthène... He'd throw another fit. From the girl too... I stay cool. I step out for a breath of fresh air... I walk over to the door... down the front steps... make a dash... reach the gate... It really is them!... Plopped there... laughing their asses off... they greet me like savages.

"Ah! look who's here, you silly dumb fart! Well, well, Ferdinand, you fathead! You've got la-dee-da airs! Not a single worry in the world, you faggot! Not a worry! You've moved up now! How about that, you dumb ox! You're on the make, right, dickhead! Belly always stuffed! Ah! the pimp! Ah! you're some piece of work!"

"Ah," I throw back at them, "it's none of your business!"

Right off they give me lip.

"None of our business! None of our business! Well, how about that, so what more do you need? Ah! what bullshit, damn! Ah! you dumb prick! You cocky bastard!..."

I owed it all to them, apparently. They went on grinding away at the organ, kept up the racket... playing "The Dark Waltz" over and over... A little more and they'd have knocked me over... gesticulating so wildly in order to get it through my skull what a lousy bastard I was, ungrateful, not a nice guy.

"What the hell are you doing out here?"

Centipede was still green around the gills and all, with that little glow of his underneath... so it was in his nature, but he didn't stink so bad anymore. And Nelson was still his gimpy self, the man just couldn't stop laughing. Curlers burst out at the sight of me standing there panic-stricken... I could see all her teeth shaking in her big fat mouth... smeared with lipstick... up to her nose like a clown, practically ear to ear... Like a mask over her face... plastered with makeup and red lipstick... all weepy-eyed from laughing... plus those wobbly teeth...

I try to get them to leave... But no way... they want in... they want to visit the house... they're pushy... they don't want to stand out there in the rain... they let me know about it pronto.

"You've got a sweet setup, you're all comfy! You joker! You just wait and see! Hey, now, you never showed up at the standing gallery? Is that the way you keep your word?!"

I was waiting for that... the bad blood I'd stirred the other day, she was sore cause I stood her up.

"Ah!" she guffaws, "what a terrific pimp, not even able to deliver his girl! You'll always be good for a laugh..."

Curlers was a depraved old bitch, she had a reputation throughout the entire red-light district, she was always having fights with her man over all the time it cost her... But that's not why he'd left, he didn't have a jealous bone in his body, let's not get carried away. He'd left like some dumb jerk, she repeated loud enough, so he could come back a general! Intelligent cracks of this sort kept them laughing out there in the rain. All three soaked to the bone. I just reached out and felt their clothes, I wanted to make sure I wasn't dreaming... they were dripping wet, that's a fact... In one way it made me happy that they were absolutely real, concrete, and not some hallucination, that they were made of flesh and blood... Inevitably I had my doubts...

"Where'd you come from?" I ask.

"From hell! What about your ass?"

"Clear out of here, go to the devil!" I snap.

"No way we're going to the devil!" the trio comes back at me in unison! "We're just so very glad to be setting eyes on your gorgeous kisser! We're not going to go away just like that! After all the trouble we went through! Ah! you're kidding yourself, old buddy! Can't you see us standing here? Ah! well then, you've got some gall!"

Centipede is wailing cantankerously! Almost like back at the Tweet-Tweet Club. Ah! I still can't believe my eyes. Ah! I pissed him off. Curlers too. As for Nelson, he's not nasty, he doesn't give a shit, thinks it's all one big joke!

"You're not being straight with us, Ferdinand! Your honor's not worth tuppence! To send us packing like that! Aren't you going to give us a tour of your joint? Ah! it's just appalling! And here we come wearing our hearts on our sleeves! Just take a look at this instrument!... We've lugged it over from the Leicester... On loan from Jérôme..."

" 'I'm looking for a man in Willesden,' I said to him. 'Lend me your instrument... I don't know his address... I'll need to go door to door... ask all over for the Colonel... but I don't want to kick up a fuss, ruffle his feathers, be taken for the fuzz... once you start nosing around you can't help it...'

"So off we went, all three of us—wait till you hear the next part—we even collected two shillings six from door to door... we're happy we've hooked up with you again... and this is how you jerk us around!... You don't know when to quit! Ah! you're pressing your luck, pal!..."

None of this put a damper on Curlers...

The Knights of the Moon...
Bring you good fortune!

She was belting out the song on the sidewalk... Windows were already flying open in the houses across the street. The trio had already knocked back a few... they must have stopped for breaks along the way...

"You've been on the road since this morning?"

"You said it, buster!"

"Come in!" I say. What choice did I have, they were raising hell again. I lead the way.

Curlers is all dolled up for turning tricks... but she got rained on... her ostrich feather boa is dripping wet... her Chantilly hat veil is faded... her violet Liberty fabric dress, her cockatoo elegance... the huge handbag hanging from her shoulder down to the ground... sloppily slung! The whole mess goes tramping into the house... with Centipede and Nelson taking up the rear. The entrance hall wows them, the thick pile wool carpet, the lackeys.

I snap at them: "What about the organ? You just leaving it?"

"We'll play it for you a little later, you don't deserve to hear anything right away!" Just like that they dish it back, mischievously.

Sosthène was clueless. He'd never set eyes on them before... But they recognized him right away...

"Ah! so there he is, your Triboulet! hey, now, he was in Chink drag, we saw him with you this morning. Yeah, that's right, we were on the sidewalk. What the hell were you up to? Yeah, that guy was one crazy son of a bitch!..."

Curlers slapped her thighs, remembering what a kick he'd given her! The old geezer in his gown was a scream!

"Ah! You didn't see him, Centipede! he had all of Piccadilly, every bus stopped dead! Just like that cause he felt like imitating a butterfly! a dancing girl! Ah! kicking up hammer and tongs! the way he cavorted! Ah! what a weirdo! And then the coppers, what a stink! Racing after him, I'll say! Piccadilly was a sight! And he made like the angel in the center of the fountain, like the Eros."

Curlers aped him! picking up her skirts. She was wearing sequined stockings...

"I was over at Lyon's getting my hair done... So I had a front row seat! All hell broke loose with that mob of cops! And the buses! Ah! what a fucking mess! The cars all piled on top of each other! That's what it'd turned into! Ah! what a zoo! The old fogy! He really cracked me up! I was pissing my panties! Gaby the hairdresser goes to me: 'Honey, you're gonna hurt yourself!' And so, you're the hell-raiser! Ah! you old joker! Where'd you learn to dance like that? Ah! you old rascal! His lips are sealed! Come on, teach me your jungle jive! So I can scare buses too! Ah! Teach me your whole bag of tricks..."

They slapped him real hard on the back! All three thought he was this super-duper hero, after the way he'd stopped all traffic in Piccadilly! by writhing around in his slant suit!

"Ah! he's one of a kind!"

Sosthène was a featherweight, the backslaps sent him reeling!

"Let's have a peek at what you've got underneath..."

They were crazy about battle scars. He's glad to oblige, undoes his buttons, pretty proud. Try as he might to be a fakir, he got banged up anyway...

Not just those two black eyes and the gash on his nape, but his ribs punched raw!

"Hey, look at this, tattoos!"

Now that had them marveling... A rose, a female snake charmer, and a squirrel... all in blue and yellow, from collarbone to crotch, very delicately crafted with cabalistic significance apparently, it looked like lace it was so finely wrought. It had a metaphysical meaning, but he was forbidden from revealing it to the uninitiated under penalty of the worst sorts of disasters. Another one of his cock-and-bulls... The three rotters blew a gut they were laughing so hard...

"That guy'll always make me piss myself," Curlers gasped out.

They hadn't spotted Virginia stretched out on the sofa in front of the fireplace. They were laughing so much they'd overlooked her.

"Ah! well, I'll be!..." Curlers spots her.

She rushes over... kisses the girl.

"Ah! does this ever make me happy. Look how cute this kid is..."

She shows her to the two hooligans.

"Isn't she pretty now! Look what he's got his hands on... The guy's a real pro!"

Planted in front of the sofa, Curlers gazed in admiration... with the eyes of an expert... a connoisseur.

"But what's wrong with you? You're pale as death! Ah! my poor darling, this guy didn't hurt you, did he? He's an animal, an ignoramus."

She drops back to her knees, kisses her again...

"You're still beautiful, my precious!"

She cuddles, coddles her. Showers her with affection.

"Well, since you're here," I ask, "what the fuck you come for?"

My little crack really sends them rolling in the aisles! I'm not plastered, they're the ones who've been drinking, not me. They reek of liquor. Especially Nelson, he's zonked, rocking back and forth in front of my eyes. Now they're splitting their sides.

"Ah! That's a hot one! Ah! Really is!"

Curlers is laughing herself hoarse, she's lost her voice. She doubles up, rattling her necklace chains, has at least five-six flopping against her belly, all made of gold no less... and inset with small sparklers. She's rich, everybody knows it, she didn't work herself to death for her old men, ever since her younger days she always had a bank account, snitching just so much from her pimp each week, simple as that, she thrived all on her own, she's a businesswoman, even put two or three tarts to work for her.

"My weakness, you know, is for young girls! That's the honest truth! I adore them when they're in the bloom of youth. I could lay one every morning... Say, Ferdinand! like her! your blossom! Ah! I've got to say you know how to pick them! I just love her! I love her, she's a treasure!"

She dropped to her knees to woo the girl. She entreated her like that right against the sofa, drenched boa in tow, she'd taken off her shoes because they were sopping wet.

"Come off it! get up, Curlers, leave her alone, she's not feeling well..."

"Shit!" she snaps back, "I'm going to sing something, look, just for her... 'When we're two!'... You're a pain in our ass... 'Things aren't the same!'..."

She couldn't go on, too hoarse...

"Hey, pour us a little glass of cordial! Your boss's got some... She'll have a drink with me!..."

"She shouldn't, she's ill..."

I put my foot down.

"Ah! what a dumb jerk!"

She won't quit.

I slap her down brutally.

"You're jealous, you lousy bastard! You're jealous! Shit, just use your eyes! I love both of you!"

She kisses her again, she wants to kiss me too.

Virginia has no idea what to do. She's wondering whether I'm going to get mad. I don't. I rack my brains, trying to think of a way to shove them out the door. If I give them the boot, they'd raise a stink outside... it'd bring the cops around, a crowd would flock in the street.

I feel like such a dumb jerk I stand there helpless. I ask my question again.

"What do you want here, you ugly creeps?"

"Give me a little something to drink, then I'll tell you."

Curlers is more palsy-walsy, the other two are standoffish. I take the whiskey out of the cabinet. They pour themselves a straight shot. Then have another. Sosthène drinks to our health.

I tell him: "We don't own the place, the Colonel can walk back in any minute!..."

The truth is we're acting like total boors. Ever since that mercury business I'm leery...

This tickles their funny bone again. They double over like hunchbacks in hysterics, my note of caution's the most hilarious thing they've ever heard. All three are laughing up a storm... lined up along the top of the sofa, I've got them right in front of my nose, they look like a trio of funny-faced masks. They lean down for a better look at me. What are they really after?

I press Virginia against me, hold her tight in my arms. I can see they're hatching some nasty piece of business.

"Where'd you come from? Why you in such hysterics?"

They're driving me up the wall... Enough's enough.

"This is no time of day to come here... to a respectable home."

I'd rather they leave on their own.

"Respectable! Respectable! Oh! man! Get a load of that! The gentleman's taking dancing lessons."

That's Nelson snapping out a crack.

"My, my, how handsome he looks in his handsome suit. Ah! lover boy's fresh as a daisy! When he first arrived in London he was naked as the day he was born! pinned with his medal!"

The trio nod "yes, yes," they back him up... Still leaning down right over us... Virginia's shivering from the cold...

Bim! Bum! Bells!

They sing in chorus out of the blue, bellowing at the top of their lungs. They're cuckoo.

Bing! Bang! Bong!
Bong! Bing! Bonk—rz!

They're doing chimes.

She knocks back a small shot... then a big one... She straightens up, heaves a "Whew!" because she's on fire! Thrilled!

"That's right, Mademoiselle! 'Bum!' "

She points at me...

"Crawling with crabs! When he got here he was a total scuzzball! Kind-heartedness! That's what saved his ass! everybody's nobility of soul! and now the louse doesn't know anybody but colonels! Yeah, you heard me right! Ah! shit! he's sitting pretty, the twit! a gigolo living off my loss! terrific deal, right? He'd lick his plates clean, the pathetic bag of bones. 'A penny, ladies-gents!' He scraped by on handouts. And now he shits in his pals' hands! Doesn't recognize anybody anymore! Just salutes colonels! Yeah, you've got that straight! wiseguy! Ah! damn! what a savory character! Ah! prize con artist! He's got a comfy setup, ladies-gents! A comfy setup! Rocking his baby doll beddy-bye!"

She aped me...

"She feels sick to her stomach! It was bound to happen with a repulsive slob like that! Come on, my precious, sing along with me!"

She wanted Virginia to get up, stand on her feet a spell, she'd been prone long enough... she wanted her to play the piano...

"It's prettier than the Barbary organ! it takes in less money, and how! Nelson, so tell me how much you took in along our way from Trafalgar! Ah! what a fabulous trip! what a whopping repertoire, huh! I did the pushing! so let's hear the grand total!"

"Twelve bob fifty! I already told you..."

"That's my dowry, darling! That's my dowry! Aren't you happy?"

She takes Virginia's hand. She jams her hat on her head, veil, the works.

"I love your baby doll! do I ever! I don't want her to be unhappy!"

She whimpers...

"Drink with me, you rotten louse! So you'll find out what's what! You don't have a clue!..."

She's choked up over Virginia.

"Ah! you're a first-class scumbag."

Centipede and Sosthène and the other guy all want to play some cards. But Curlers is blubbery, nixes the idea. She hangs onto Virginia, calls me a heartless pimp.

All right already.

"Curlers, be careful, you're not at Cascade's now."

She jumps up. She takes me at my word.

"Cascade! Cascade! You let him be! You should be shining his shoes! Now there's a man who saved you. He's worth a million of you, scuzzball!"

That was the opinion of Nelson and Centipede too, they OK'd her crack.

Great shot, right on target... Ah! I had it coming to me!... I could see their three ugly mugs.

"Oh, yes sir, it really makes a person sick!" the trio said just like that, in unison, disgusted.

I'd hit my limit. They were all nodding. Where'd they get such balls? And Centipede, what rock did that acrobat crawl out from under? standing there sniggering his ass off? I'd bumped off at least one of him, I thought to myself, but was this the real guy or some impostor? Was I seeing double, triple, centuple? Maybe I should end all this and find out? Maybe I should grab him by the pecker? Just looking at me cracked him up, he stood there over the sofa like that razzing his head off, stooping a little to give me a closer look, and a chance to figure out an answer... Ah! he was really a sly, depraved bastard! and incredibly amused over his little maneuver... over my reaction to the whole business.

"Look, dicklick, he's ready to blow."

He was warning Curlers that I was about to flip back into my idiot act, my wacko wildman number... that was the whole reason they'd come... But I was absolutely on the ball... I didn't let Virginia out of my clutches, my sweetheart, my precious everything... I looked hard at her... kissed her... she kissed me... I held on... my hope, my determination...

"Honey..." I went to her... "Honey..." I didn't want to flip into any more hallucinations... I knew the way they came over me... I was familiar with the experience by now... just a teeny sip of liquor... just one small glass was all it took... and then I'd get to flapping my lips... somebody would contradict me... I'd get fired up... and the rest is history... Always because of my head, it was written down on my discharge papers!...

"Cephalalgia, faulty memory, epileptic hebephrenia, post-shock post-traumatic syndrome..."

What it meant was that at the drop of a hat I took off, my mind started wandering... over the smallest wrinkle.

So I really had to stay on my toes, I could never be wary enough. I'd paid a high price for my experience, I was an easy mark for people who wanted to pull my strings. Even so I wanted some clear answers, to find out why they'd come. How they'd found me. But Curlers was the only one doing the talking. The others kept pretty much clammed up, waiting for a little fun, the time of their lives, meaning for me to start acting like a raving lunatic, and put on one of my big performances... But they showed up too late, I wasn't budging! I played their game, toying back with them. Just popping out a question here and there! Ah! something smelled damn fishy!... Ah! I didn't like these wily shady jackal games! it must have been second nature for them...

They sucked the booze back without waiting for an invitation, greedily, and she held her own with the men... Gin bitter, calvados, peppermint schnapps... Colonel O'Collogham owned one hell of a liquor cabinet... there was enough for a pope's funeral... at least a dozen labels of whiskey... brandy like you hardly ever taste... sherry and port like you can't imagine... genuine elixirs! An entire wall stocked with row after row of small casks... just had to serve yourself... turn open the small taps... they weren't shy...

I was the one who sat back and waited. Playing cat and mouse... I wasn't going to be the guy to blow it... they were hitting the bottle... And they'd keep hitting it for a long time to come... whiskey, brandy... a full selection of ports... Sosthène did his share... and he wasn't much of a drinker.

The huge choice made Curlers realize something.

"Say, kid, this guy puts it away!"

"Ah! It's for guests," I answer, "go right ahead!"

She pours out another glass for herself, a genuine cocktail of Pernod and sherry. It was her man's favorite mix.

"He doesn't deserve for me to still love him... and to drink to his health! You're the one I love, lambkins!" She pounces on Centipede, kisses him...

"Give me a smooch!" she says to me, "Make it wet and sloppy!"

Then she has second thoughts, eyes me from head to toe, wants to put me through another round of insults, but can't, she's staggering, reeling, she's got to sit down, feels queasy.

"Pass me a cigar, that'll do me good..."

There are top-class smokes, a whole box full, fat jobs all covered with gold sparkles, really huge suckers.

"Wow, this is terrific!"

They all help themselves! She kisses Nelson.

"Give me a light, buddy! Give me a light!"

"Don't you think our friend Ferdinand over there is feeling sorry for himself, look how down in the mouth he is, a young man like that! a young man! And that other jerk who made me come here, that rotten jerk! Centipede! 'Wait, you'll see what a funny guy he is! You never laughed so hard in your life! You should have seen him at the Tweet-Tweet Club! You'd have died pissing yourself! Going through his acrobatic act for us! The whole audience was crazy about him! he called me his little ghost! Ah! what a weirdo, a complete freak show!... You should have seen him soaring around! shooting from the dance floor up into the air like a real frog! He was all alone up there in the chandeliers!' Centipede had never laughed so much! Well, fuck you then! I turn the guy's stomach! Just my luck to have come! I never saw a gloomier-looking loser in my life! Your injuries the reason? Your head spinning? Didn't I sell you on anything? Or is your darling what's bugging you, you jealous all over again?

"Now you're not jealous, are you, my beauty? Here, take a puff on my cigar with me... It'll do you good too... women ought to smoke... You don't look well... you fretting yourself sick?... is that guy making you unhappy?"

I've had enough.

I feel I'm at the end of my rope.

"Go on! Get the hell out of here!" I shout... "Haven't you drunk enough?"

"No! No!" Nelson and the other one go... "No! not enough! No! No way..."

They're comfortably slouched... stretched out... about to doze off any minute now...

"A bite to eat you said!... A bite to eat! We'll be on our way after we have some food... A light snack! Your boss hasn't come back!... Come on! don't worry, sweetie! You've got hours to spare! Hey, Nelson, he hasn't come back yet, right? And he's not about to any time soon, also right? Your boss's tied up!"

They seemed to be mighty sure of themselves...

"Who do you mean? Who's not going to come back?"

"Your colonel, who else, my poor little fellow! Ah! this guy's thick as a brick, geez! dumb as they come! the adorable little thing!"

They're making a laughingstock of me.

Sosthène was sort of lost, he inclined his head toward me as if to ask: "Well?... What's the meaning of all this?..."

They patted him on the back over his splendid show of force, his mind-blowing hullabaloo over on Piccadilly, the entire Circus in an uproar! They'd never seen anything like that before in their lives!... plus that gown of his with the gold dragon!... was it a publicity stunt?... Did he work for a store? For Selfridges? Harrods?... they wanted to know! Plus that flair of his! what a fighter! Raising holy hell smack in the mob of heavies from Scotland Yard! the shock beefsteaks! Ah! hell yes! such class! ah! what a tough guy!

They were blown away.

Music to Sosthène's ears.

"Three cheers for Sosthène! The tiger! The Chinaman!"

They'd christened him right off the bat... Another round to his health! We were whooping it up in the salon... lost in clouds what's more... every last cigar puffed away into smoke. He wanted to make a little speech in kind thanks: "Gentlemen," he began, "Ladies and gentlemen I am most thrilled by your magnificent praise!... thrilled! thrilled!..."

He repeated it three times... Wow! he couldn't get over it! The hardest of all *ths*... and he did it from the get-go! thrilled! thrilled! Ah! Ah! Ah! oooh!... he was roaring with pride...

"Show-off! Show-off!" he called me. "You see... I got down your *th*... I can do it!... I can do it!..."

It was an honest-to-goodness miracle.

"You see, you brat!... You see, you dummy! Tell me that won't do the trick!..."

"Thrilled! Thrilled!" he booms out the word, doesn't skip a single letter!... and he kept repeating it over and over. He'd licked the damn thing!

He's pooped out, plops back down. He just sits there like a dumb lump, in a total daze, google-eyed.

Curlers was bamboozled, couldn't do like him, she gave it a shot and hurt her mouth, practically popped out her teeth.

"I butcher my English!" she confessed over her defeat. "I've been in London for twenty-five years, but the thing is I'm just too French, the longer I stay the less I talk... I'm going backwards! All my tricks want to make conversation! Especially since the war! with me they get what they ask for! Ah, yes, pussycat!

The Queen of England!
Fell on her fanny!

"But say, I do know how to count in pounds! twenty-one shillings in a guinea! I'm right on the nose, you can be sure of that! I've got the knack down. Hello, yes, pussycat!... Say, baby doll, I'm going to eat you up!..."

This was starting to give her new ideas. She pounces back on Virginia... even though she was right up against me so I could protect her from these outpourings.

"Hold on!" I stop her, "you haven't said anything... What're you doing around here?"

"Ah! the little fox's curious! This little fellow's curious, isn't he, huh? He wants to know everything! Ah! she's going to be unhappy all right! with a lunkhead like that! Ah! I'm telling you! what a rotten mess! I'd ring your chimes, sweetie! it'd be pure paradise! You'd have everything you needed, baby doll!..."

She snuggled up against her.

"Aren't you going to say good-bye to her?" she hits me with... Real nerve.

"Good-bye, you tramp? You come out with some real bull, bitch!"

That rubs her the wrong way, she gets sore.

"Look here, you think that'd be the first time something like that ever happened, you brat? think you'll be twiddling your thumbs all hunky-dory until hell freezes over? With your baby doll? think nobody's going to come after you? And move you out into a place of your own?"

"Why not?" I go...

"Just wait and see! London's not like back home!"

What was behind that crack? Where'd she learn to talk like that? I stood there like a jerk, she was making a fool of me and knew a little too much for my liking. They got a wicked kick out of seeing me flounder around.

I didn't want to leave Virginia, that was one thing for damn sure.

"I beg your pardon, Curlers, but I'm staying with her... This is between us..."

Now they're back laughing hysterically!

"Ah! This guy's too much... a joke a minute!... this crazy character just won't quit! Ah! listen to him! unbelievable! the police wagons won't stop him either! Ah! they're going to have their hands full down at the Yard!"

Ah! I didn't know what the hell they were going on about! They were talking in riddles, teasing me with puzzles. At bottom they were a bunch of degenerates... They'd tanked up, toasted, stuffed themselves to the gills, now they were gorged, upbeat, out for some fun. They kicked back their heels in the salon, right at home!

"Come on! Play me 'The Blue Danube,' " Curlers called out.

Da dum dum da da!
Da dum dum da da!

"How about this one, my titmouse! How about this, my cutie pie!"

It's a long way to Tipperary

"You'll play that one for his truly."

She wanted a complete repertoire... and wouldn't take no for an answer. The butler walked in. Time to set the table.

"I'm going to do a card reading," Nelson goes, "scram, busboy! beat it! you're jumping the gun! Your master's not back yet! And he won't be back any time soon! Ah! I'll say! You tell him! You over there, go on and tell him!"

A sure bet they'd cooked up some dirty trick together... Why were they even here in the first place?

When we are two...
Things aren't the same...

"Play me that one, sweetheart... Come on, I'll give you my arm... We'll sing a duet!"

She won't quit... Virginia rises... They walk over to the piano. Virginia plays a little... She starts "The Blue Danube"... But her head starts spinning. She needs to go back to the sofa. Reason for insults to start flying—at me.

"What'd you do to her, you lousy son of a bitch? You're the one making her sick."

"Here, my angel, a drop of brandy..."

I won't have any of that... I forbid it... I knock the glass out of Curlers' hand. A turn for the worse.

"Shit!" she screams, "such high-class liquor! Ah! it's just about time we run this guy in! a pain in everybody's ass, that's what he is!..."

"Hey, are you talking to me?"

"You bet, you dirty little shit-ass! you got snot hanging from your nose! You lousy phony! I'm telling you, it's about time you start sewing linen sacks! at least you'll be good for something! with your poor useless fingers!"

Her blood was boiling. And such a scowl, she was so sick to her stomach.

"Cop!" I yell back just like that right in her face, "cop! cop!"

She starts gasping and choking... She spilled too much in her rage...

"Cop? Cop?" she stutters... "Hey, I'm not the one who squealed... Not me..."

The other two down in the mouth... she's landing them in deep shit.

"Don't talk in riddles! spit it out! go on!" I give her an order, right there with her back to the wall... she turns red... she trips over her tongue...

"Wait, you're wrong... You're wrong!... You don't get it."

"I don't get it? Shit! For the past hour you've been talking in riddles! Ah! you old sow! You're rotten to the core, that's what you mean! You've got to think hard! You don't have a clue! You'd like to squeal on me, end of story! You're a stoolie, you bitch! You're a stoolie, out with it!..."

I'd hooked her with live bait. Such a big show-off, she was getting her back up, especially in front of Virginia. But she wound up looking like a jerk.

"Fish around! Fish around! You hooker!"

I had the upper hand.

"Say, Centipede," she was bouncing back... "Say, why don't you clue him in... tell him who came to get me... Ah! get on with it, I want him to hear right away... Go ahead, tell him... Quit stalling!"

She plants herself in the middle of the salon, working her feather boa like a kite...

"Go ahead, tell him, screw the bastard!"

She didn't want to be beaten. But the other guy wasn't in the mood to talk.

"Well, Matthew, that's who, you little chump! If you want to know. Now you know what you're running away from? Now do you have just a wee little idea of the tight squeeze you're in? Sink in, huh, does it? Really? Centipede, tell him whether I'm lying!..."

"No, it's right on the money... it's true..."

"You can see the writing on the wall, shit yes! You can see you don't stand a chance in hell!"

Centipede backed up her story... A person could swear by it...

"You're bluffing, lovey-dovey... You're bluffing, go on..."

I was getting her dander up...

"Ah! If you'd seen how happy Matthew was... 'OK,' he goes to me, 'I understand, they're together, the pair of them, him and the Chink'..."

"How'd he know?"

"You can ask him that one yourself... He makes me come down, he does, he sends me over his mutt Mollesbam, the guy with the Cinzano-red hair... I had a little chat with Pretty Peach, Jong-kind's old lady, the Dutchman, you've met Pretty Peach, right? Mollesbam too, with his pince-nez... He goes to me: 'Curlers! Room 115!'... He doesn't explain why or what... The guy's a brute... can't expect him to show any manners... Deputy Constable's what he goes by... So you better believe I obeyed!... in my situation... they've known me over at the Yard for twenty years. 'Did you get your VD shot?' That's how they talk to me... 'I'm going to run you in...' 'Fine, Mr. Constable, sir...' Never an extra word... my pound... my two pounds on the table... my payoff... 'Good-bye!... Madame Curlers! you're still a knockout!...' I know them, that's their private joke... Hello!... Good-bye! So long!... Go to hell! I don't like them, they don't like me either... I fork over... And we're quits!

"Now I'm not too hot about room 115, that's where they ask their questions. I've never had any trouble myself... Just listen to this, I once had three pimps, and let me tell you they were thugs... I didn't squeal on a single one... not over at Scotland Yard anymore than back home at police headquarters in Paris, and I really had reason to... I switched houses four-five times... switched sidewalks... towns too... even respected the pub owners, although they're lousy bastards one and all!... So a slob like you putting me down really bugs the hell out of me!... follow me? The idea that I'd go shooting my mouth off to the cops!... You've got a screw loose up there, you dumb shit! I really think you're nuts talking such crap! It's damn true! You're right, Centipede!... Now if they call me, of course I go, I'm not about to keep them hanging around! It's nothing at all for them to wake me up! 'Get your ass down here, tramp!' I run! Otherwise I'm behind bars! And in a snap! A woman on her own! Just try it! But I'm not nuts about room 115! I know what I'm talking about! and I don't like Matthew either!... He comes on like an old pal. I prefer lousy SOBs! I prefer his constable, the brute!... I walk in... he lays into me point-blank...

" 'Do you know the Colonel? Don't lie, Curlers!...'

"I know colonels, and in every shape and size too, you better believe it! Some are phonies, some the real thing! I've had whole slews of them! cocks of the walk! cons! cards! I don't remember each and every one... A few slipped my mind... and majors too, and lieutenants, at your service! and the privates, I go to him, 'With all due respect, I've stopped counting!...' And he thinks to himself... 'She takes me for some idiot...' I know how his mind works... You've got to give him a straight answer... You know he speaks good French... 'Yes, but I mean, the Colonel... the one who dabbles in inventions... doesn't that ring a bell, Curlers?' He lets me think it over... 'Run through your mind... the one who's with Ferdinand out in Willesden...' He didn't have to say it twice. Now you know I'm never one to ask questions. 'Nope, doesn't ring a bell, Inspector, sir.'

"'What about Sosthène de Rodiencourt? Don't you know that guy? You were standing curbside this morning when he was doing his Chinaman act in Piccadilly!... You're not going to deny it, are you?'

"'Yes, I was there, Inspector, sir, I had a good laugh, I admit, but I don't know the man...'

"'Be careful, Curlers,' he then says to me real serious... He motions me closer... because this is some big secret... I can say no more.. Ah! you can see that it's true! Hand me the big glass of brandy! I'm doing too much talking! And you're not doing any at all!... I don't know the Colonel, can you imagine! The Chinaman neither. And you call me a liar! And the other guy over there calls me a liar too! But I'm the only one not lying! the only one who loves you! You also, my love blossom! I'm just crazy about you!..."

She went back to pawing up the girl.

"Fuck off," I go to her! "It's all over your face, you're lying. He's the one who sent you!..."

"Ah! you sap, the things that come out of your mouth! You're really sticking it to me! You're making me so sick I won't be able to stand the sight of you anymore!... And here I defended you! I answered back, 'Inspector, sir, you've got to be putting me on... Ferdinand mixed up in espionage? That's really too wild and I don't believe a word! A lummox like him, a butterfingers who's goofy in the head because he's been trepanned they say, a guy who can fall on his face just by walking down a street and needs to be scraped off the sidewalk—I really can't picture him as a spy. I can't vouch for the Chink. I don't know what he's up to. But your Ferdinand's bonkers! His time's running out, he's a poor devil, on the skids... the pimps over at Cascade's felt sorry for him... He landed here dead broke, still convalescing... everybody'll tell you the same... piss-poor... a down-and-out nutcase... Fantomas in person! Take the word of a woman of experience!... If he's a spy, then I'm a cardinal...' You can see how I stuck up for you... 'He's freaky... sort of nuts, because of his head... he's still got a bullet lodged inside... maybe two...' I threw in... 'He gets these attacks... All the men'll tell you the same... the women too... they know him down at the Leicester...' Didn't I do right?"

"Yeah! Yeah! You did right!..."

"I couldn't push it too far... otherwise he'd have said: 'She's got her finger in the pie!...' 'He was in the hospital in Hazebrouck back in France with Roger, Cascade's brother, the guy who was executed by firing squad...' Didn't I do right to mention all that?"

"Yeah, you did right, a terrific job..."

All three turned their eyes on me. They weren't so sure. Virginia was trying to keep up... she was mostly confused... Too much slang for her... But she was pretty scared... She suspected this was pretty awful news for us... Seeing them so close up gave her the jitters, that trio of faces, all three riveting us with their stares...

"Go on! Clear off! You heard me!... I'm calling the police..."

"Don't bother, they'll come on their own! Come on! Let's beat it! get a move on!..."

They got up... this time they do leave, they don't fight the issue... It's dark outside now. They've drunk the bottles dry, downed every last drop of whiskey... they hold it pretty well... they walk out on their own feet more or less!

Close your lovely eyes...
For the hours are short!...
Close your lovely eyes!...

Curlers is a ball of fire... when she stops singing, she starts spouting...

I want your heart!... I want your heart...

And so doing she walks out onto the front steps... wailing into the night...

I want your heart!... I want your heart...

They walk down the steps. They don't say good-bye... They don't care about us anymore... they're arguing... I can hear them through the darkness... who'll be the one to push the cart, who won't... At last it's settled, they're off... you can hear the creaking...

Then they don't give a shit, they start cranking away...

It's the dark waltz!...

You can still hear them off in the distance... crystal clear... and then it's over...

Ah! I tell myself things'll work out! Unsettling impressions... all the nailbiting, the exhaustion... they shake up your head in the end... and your spirits... you don't know what's happening to you anymore... you start thinking all kinds of crap, that's all there is to it... Best get some shut-eye, that's absolutely for sure... My mind's made up... I take charge...

"Let's call it a night!... up to bed, kids! Let's forget about those trouble-makers! They came over to get smashed, that's all! Stinking hell-raisers! Small-time hoods! Let's get some rest!"

I kiss Virginia again! I help her up the stairs.

"He won't be back," I go.

I meant the Colonel...

"He won't be back till tomorrow morning..."

Another one of my impressions.

Poor Virginia, she couldn't take anymore... that trio had rattled her something terrible with their malarkey...

"Darling!..." she called me... "Darling!..."

Poor little dove... Pale, too, and queasy... on practically every step she felt sick to her stomach...

Sosthène says to her: "Suck some ice! with a drop of crème de menthe!..."

That was one solution.

"Oh! no! Oh! no!"

Didn't want to...

I kiss her, undress her, she was ill, limp and lifeless... a child.

"There!" she goes... "There!"

Along her ribs... stabbing pains. She wasn't real swollen, you noticed it just a little bit. And that's all. No mistake, it seems. The doctor she'd gone to see on Sternwell Road nearby had been totally positive on that score.

"Come back and see me in a month, and don't do anything reckless, no bicycle-riding, no tennis!"

She wasn't exactly jumping around. She felt better on her back. I kept glancing at her belly. Ah! All the rotten breaks came my way! It bummed me out.

"Poor Ferdinand! Poor Ferdinand!"

She was the one who felt sorry for me, but all in fun, seeing the down-in-the-mouth look on my face... Ah! what a mess I was in! Ah! I'd botched things up good! I kiss her again a couple-three times. I tuck her in, kiss her.

"Good night! Good night!..."

She looked like a kid herself to me! old she wasn't, with a room still full of dolls, teeny cutesy cradles thick with streaming ribbons... Ah! it felt so strange seeing Virginia like that, I kept watching and watching her... I'd never have believed this before... She didn't have the same effect on me... but my love for her was mighty strong all the same... I loved her almost more than before... We couldn't stay together like this all night long. What if the old man walked in suddenly! I kiss her one more time... "Good night!" And then I go up to our room with the twin beds.

The other wiseguy's been in bed for an hour already!... I barge in, spunky/perky as hell, all confidence.

"So tell me now, Sosthène! No bad dreams? Did you kiss the blues good-bye?"

I wanted to clear up a few things.

"Stop worrying yourself sick! Curlers is a booze-soaked carcass! who spouts total crap! Ain't worth a hoot, dear Sosthène! a big fat zero! Kiss her good-bye!"

All of a sudden I was upbeat. Feeling responsible for a lot of people's welfare! I had to take a stand! Straighten out the situation! get everybody out of this jam! Turn this back into the cushy setup it once was, with room for Sosthène too! I owed my life to the guy! So he said anyway! Let's put our rotten luck behind us! Let's all get out of this mess together! I didn't want life to bug him anymore! I wanted him to take advantage of this chance! The days of pain and sorrow were history! Now we were going to have some fun! Whoop it up! Get a terrific bang out of the good life! I could see a bright future ahead of us! Wonderful! Just like that, off the top of my head for no reason, my mood had flipped around because I'd had enough, that's all, and all things must come to an end! When you're young you're flaky, like a spoiled little birdie you flitter back and forth between gloom and sunshine, between laughter and tears, you can always see patches of blue through the blackest twisters.

All right! Now to bed, I'm full of laughs, tell him a few jokes to cheer him up a little in advance, so that he'll eat up our brand new chance, and snatch a little taste right now.

No go. He keeps scowling, burrows his head in his pillow! And here I am, busting my butt, going all out, whipping myself up. I even tune out the humming in my head, all my energy poured into puns, madly hopping from subject to subject. I pump myself up, put on a happy face, stifle the voice of gloom and doom. He balks, turns thumbs down, doesn't even want to crack a smile. He thinks the fact the Colonel's still out is a bad omen.

"Is not! Is not!" I reassure him. "He's at his club, that's all. He's out on a binge, he's got the right... he's bored stiff at home constantly surrounded by his family... banging away at his gas masks... He wants a little breath of fresh air. He'll come back one of these days... on a binge, so look out! I can see him right this second, plastered, drunk as a skunk over at the Kit-Cat Club... at the Windmill Theatre... a couple-three clubs, a piece of ass... pussy and poker!... British-style... 'Champagne! Champagne!...' Sly and slick in his dinner jacket... He'll come back by cab... just open your eyes every morning... maybe with a soldier boy... a Tommy tops! Maybe he's getting plugged... Can't rule it out! There's a war on! And how! there's a war on!... Sure, you can see it in the fact he's depraved."

I was thinking about the scene with his niece, the servants...

"One hell of a sex maniac if you ask me!"

Ah! I wasn't crazy about the guy.

So we kept chatting on like that about him until we finally fell asleep... All the same we were pooped... It must have been going on one o'clock! Tick-tock... Tick-tock... I wake up... it wasn't anything special... just the clock's plain old tick-tock... I've put up with lots of other kinds of noise. My nerves no doubt probably.

"Hey!" I yell... "You going to give it a rest?"

I was really ticked off, my own voice made me jump... Ah! I'm screwy, I swear! But Sosthène wasn't asleep... I found him sitting up, he couldn't breathe right, gasping for air, smothering!

"You sick too?" I ask him.

In a foul mood I was, he was getting under my skin with his fits, and now they were coming on him at night to boot! We had enough work cut out for us during the day... I was already tying myself in knots to steer clear of catastrophe... The least we could do is get a little sleep...

I ask him: "Don't you want me to open the window?"

"If you like, I can't take it anymore."

"Can't take what anymore?"

"When will you understand!..."

Big sigh! He was down in the dumps, that was all.

"You're stubborn," he adds.

"Stubborn about what?"

He starts bawling, the whole routine, head in his hands... a grand performance. He sobs away.

"Ah! what a fine mess! Aren't you ashamed? You're falling to pieces! You're scared, say it! Say that you're scared!"

I head straight for the jugular!...

"No, I am not afraid!" he protests.

"Are too! You're scared shitless! Admit it!..."

"I am not scared shitless!"

I was riling him on purpose... I kept at it: "That lama of yours is really terrific! As terrific as my balls!"

This rubs him the wrong way.

"You've got it easy, you little slob!"

I knew his game.

"OK, that's enough, you going to drop it? You want out, right? You want out? You're going to go cry to the Colonel! Ah! You're really too rotten for words!"

"Send me off to my death right now!"

I was putting him in a huff. He was hopping up and down on his mattress, hammering away at it with his fists!

"I do what I want, damn! I do what I want!"

"But I'm not sending you off to do anything at all!"

"You are so! You are! You're the one! You're crafty! You want to see me dead... You want revenge for the mercury!"

"Ah! Unbelievable! You slay me, you bastard! I'm already in a tight enough spot as it is without going around killing more people!..."

"You will so! You will! I can see you... I can see right through you!"

Some insinuations...

He was bitching and moaning, refused to get anything through his thick skull...

"I'm not the one who woke you up, am I, you rotten blabbermouth! That shows you right there! Clear as day! You're the instigator! You know I'm in enough of a mess with Virginia... cause she might be pregnant..."

"That's no reason... that's no reason..."

Such a numbskulled son of a bitch!...

"You're a stupid ass!... A stupid ass... you just don't get it!"

"Get what?"

He wound up rattling me with his something's-cooking routine!

"So what is it? Spit it out... What's the big deal?"

"The big deal is that we've been had!" he snaps back. "Isn't that good enough for you, sweetheart?"

"Not in my book we aren't! You're talking crap! You just want some attention! Wake me up some other day!"

"You too blind to see the moon? Too blind to see that this is all one big plot? that we're dead and buried! we're history! a dream! No? This is all news to you?"

"You're full of bull, bonehead! Full of bull!"

I stayed upbeat as long as possible, I didn't get in such moods often... I was bringing him down, real down.

"I don't know whether she's pregnant, but you're dumb as they come!"

He rattled his bed, literally going ape in his hysterics. I was pushing him over the edge.

"Go ahead! Turn on the light! Let's hear it! Start babbling! This way you won't have woken me up for nothing! Come on! I'm all ears!"

I wanted to know the whole story, see just how interesting it was.

"Look how late it is! Two o'clock! Do you always get your fits this time of night? Can't you do your blubbering in the afternoon? Don't you ever feel like dancing every once in a while? You want your gown? You want me to do some click-clacks for you! You want to shoot more of your bull? You want me to go out for some ice cream?"

I was trying to pick a fight with him.

He could just barely slit his eyes open, they were practically sealed, swollen twice their size with red and blue shiners. He kept fiddling at them with his fingers, and they were bleeding. He'd been messed up pretty badly. I get up, moisten a towel for him, and take it back over...

"Go ahead! Come on... did you have a bad dream?"

All said and done, I just wanted him to make up his mind, dump his load of crap and be done with it! Considering it bugged him so badly he couldn't sleep.

"Ah! You don't know! Ah! you don't know!"

It looked like everything he had on his little brain overwhelmed him. Legs crossed, he rocked back and forth, dabbing at his eyes.

"Well?... Well?..."

At last he starts getting it out.

"I'm certain he's ratting on us to the cops!"

So that's what was eating away at him so much, he'd thought it all through!

"Well, now," I go to him... "you're one hell of a clever devil! so where'd you come up with that one, you sly fox?"

Myself, I couldn't have cared less one way or the other.

"That's the reason you woke me up, you bum? Ah! Cripes, you've got some nerve!"

Fuck, he gave me a laugh sitting over there on his bed... a scrawny bag of bones... belly matted with hair... brick red... so skinny you could count all his ribs... He looked like Gandhi in a way... but minus the hook nose, his was more of a trumpet job...

Ah! he was positive the Colonel, with all his weird wacky ways, was selling us out to the fuzz... one of Sosthène's brainstorms... it came to him during the night just like that, pow, and he couldn't sleep anymore...

"So why's he ratting on us?"

Ah! he thought I was such a damn pain in the neck with my brainless questions!

"Does Mr. Twit speak English?" It aggravates him that I spoke English... "Now I don't speak English!... But I know my England! since 1870, mister! And the Indies too! And Baluchistan and Bengal! and Egypt! and Palestine! I've been places, young man! The Moluccas! and the Falklands! So that just goes to show you that I know lots of people and the Crown Colonies of the British throne! Plus big-time entertainers! Sharing the same bill! Little Tich! And Barrymore! Senior! And lords and prime ministers! And Thornycroft! yes, Thornycroft! I've said the name! yes, the engineer! And General Booth! That's right, mister, take it from me! this Colonel of yours is a vampire! He's sucking our blood at this very moment! Tomorrow he'll dump us right in the hands of the cops!"

"Just hold on there, he's not mine! You're the one who picked him up from the paper!"

Ah! I was pissed! Now he was linking me to the Colonel!

"Come on, you worship the guy, don't deny it, he's your daddy-in-law!"

"Chink, you're soft in the head! Where'd you come up with him squealing on us? In dreamland?"

"Could be, pimp! But since you're such a smart aleck... where is Colonel O'Collogham right this second? Take a little guess, Mr. Funnyman?"

"I'd say he's out on the town, I've already told you, the guy's having a good time... taking his mind off things... he'll take a taxi home... Right now he's under the table... enjoying life... he'll come back with the milkman... in his little truck... Giddy-up horsey!..."

"Ah! a sly one you are, you little sap! Let me explain where things really stand. Even as we speak the Colonel is having a good time, oh yes indeed! But not how you think! And in a way you won't find so funny! He's feeding his face, fair enough! But with the Inspector! He's telling him terrific stories! Choice gossip! Ah! you haven't heard the last of it, my fearless wonder! My courageous Tommy! Ah! one terrific tale! He's unloading himself, all right, the cuckold! He's pulling some rotten trick on us! The gall of the man! What nerve! he's letting us really have it! I'm telling you, he's bad news! He plays it close to the chest! And for keeps! In one sneaky slippery move, wham! he lands us behind bars!... If you had my experience you'd see things my way... Don't have to have second sight, or know English... That's the way it is, and no other! The Inspector's not bored!..."

But I did see things another way. I saw the Colonel out on some wild bender, trying to forget his worries, to buck himself up a little before the trials... he wasn't as screwy as people thought... he was scared shitless like everybody else...

"No, you've got it wrong... it's Scotland Yard. The others showed up to rub it in... stoolie and friends!... Don't you get the deal?"

My stupidity was driving him up the wall!

"You make love, sure! But don't stick your nose in serious business! You can get it up! And that's all you know! It's a rotten shame when a person's caught with his pants down! I can smell their plans! I don't have my head in a pussy!"

"So I'll call the girl then..."

"You want to turn our lives into a living hell! Watch your step, you poor son of a bitch! You're heading for disaster!..."

"OK, but why's he snitching on us?..."

I just wanted to know once and for all.

"Ah! geez, you're slow, you poor kid! Ah! Really! you're damaged all over! it wiped out your smarts! You never worked for them!... You're not wise to their ways! No! But I have worked for them! and not for a year, but for ten, for twenty. I always went without. 'Monsieur Sosthène de Rodiencourt's a crook!' That's what they called me if you want to know! I raked in fortunes for them! with my feet and my head! I've roamed deserts for those gentlemen, dug so damn deep down I thought I'd never come back up, all for those chowderheads! Had to have worked for them to understand! I'd have so many treasures I wouldn't know what the hell to do with them if they hadn't cleaned me out! like robbers on a dark night! and each and every time! In the Indies I left millions behind! Whether drumming up business! Or in the music hall! Everywhere the same old Royal Army Service Corps! You get rooked and you can't say a word! They sell you down the river! after squeezing out every last drop! as soon as you make their profit! Refund, my balls! Open and shut! You're not a member of the club! Bring it here, boy! Bring it here! You're a dog in their eyes! Rover! Pow! A swift kick right in the kisser! That's your cut! back in the doghouse! Scram! You show up and laze around! Plop! Your ass's behind bars! 'He's a raving lunatic!' They're positive! 'He's a foreigner! He's mad!' That's the line they'd take once they owed you dough! They start hassling the hell out of you over the pettiest crap, so you'll charge around like crazy! You never got anything to show for it! And when the time comes to divvy up the take, you wind up empty-handed! You're dead broke! Robbed blind! You wake up on a pile of damp wet straw! with a police record on your ass! cause the fruits of your labor have turned into a heap of dung on you! you're afraid to look yourself in the mirror anymore! they let you have a wooden pitcher!... That's Jackal and Company!... I know what I'm talking about! I know them! From here to Westminster I have my sneaking suspicions about their game! Birds of a feather! Our Colonel's got just one obsession—feeding his face on disaster! His kind've already given me a taste of the way they operate, you know! And keep in mind, same difference all over! Whether you deal with them in Pondicherry, Soho, or in Plymouth!... th! th!... as you pronounce so well! they're all double-crossing bloodsuckers! you jump to it, gentlemen! They skin you alive! That's what a foreigner means to them, a hide for their boots! I've been through the mill! I've paid the price! I can see the whole thing coming! It's a crying shame!"

"So what's this dough he wants to keep all for himself? the subsidy for the masks? The guy's loaded!"

"He never wants to set eyes on us ever again, that's all! He's sick to death of your crazy cock!... He's jealous, don't forget it! He knows how to cover up, he's a genuine Fregoli. You think he's an iceberg! wham, you're handing him just what he wants! a nice big scalpel! And he'll drink your blood! He's got deep dark secrets to his personality, and I know all about them!... Remember the riding crop! What he dished out to the kid! It shapes their character! The taste runs in their family!"

"What do you mean by that?"

"Don't look for answers! It's sheer perversion! Keep your eyes open! You're laying yourself open, on top of everything else! You're barreling along! Plowing his niece! Wait till you see what he's got up his sleeve! Your nostrils'll pop inside out! You've no idea how underhanded a person he can be!"

I was starting to get a funny feeling, I have to admit...

"The second he's fed up, he'll have a thousand and one opportunities to be up to his tricks! Go on, out! you bums! So many ways to choose! Haul off these prowlers! I've no idea where they came from! The Yard never asks questions when it comes to foreigners! Get out! Throw this riffraff in the clink!...

" 'Spies, you say?'

" 'Just think about it for a minute! You bet they are! People fussing around with inventions!... Lurking around patents! Scum from hell!' They've abused the Colonel's trust! He's delighted! And how! He hams it up! He's the one who wheeled and dealed the whole thing. Like that just at the right time! All for him, all in his bag, glory and cold hard cash! 'How about this war! A horrid business, isn't it? Washing up villains from every corner of the earth! Get rid of them, dear constable! I hand them over to you in person! All for the defense of the Empire! And the victory of King George! Go on! Let them hang!'

"And this really gets their mouths watering! It's the latest craze, the latest madness! who doesn't have his own little spy! or big one! In a mask! In black from head to toe! Ah! I ask you now! The cops don't give a shit about some pimp! some old jailbird! But two spies in one swoop! Now that's a prize package! Nowadays that puts a cop a cut above the rest! It beats pickpocketing by a long shot! Don't you have even a tiny little idea?..."

Yeah, a tiny one, but still he had to be hallucinating! He always put the blackest spin on everything! His big shortcoming... Plus, Curlers and gang had totally rattled him. All their mysterious mumbo-jumbo had given him the willies. I can say for myself that seeing Centipede again had given me a turn too! But I knew what I was dealing with... I was a victim of mirages!

"I've got to fill in Virginia!" is what I decide. "If something bad happens to us she's got to be told."

But Sosthène was against the idea: "I'm telling you they're in cahoots, you jerk!"

His great fear!...

He woke me up over it, so I'd shit my pants too!

"So just come right out and tell him you're dumping the whole thing!... Come up with some excuse!..."

No answer.

"You're not going over to Wickers, are you? let's hear it, you skunk!"

He was chickening out. He didn't answer yes or no. Just sat there with his legs crossed on his bed. Just kept nodding his head like a Buddha, an ape...

"What the hell do you take me for! Out with it, right now!"

I'd been pushed to the limit at last.

"What kind of mess did you land us in? You just wait and see the Colonel's reaction!"

"Hold on! Hold on! You're a lucky SOB! What risk are you running, my good-for-nothing bum! If it doesn't work, you don't give a damn! You've got your cushy setup! You're not out there sniffing! I'm the one who kicks the bucket! Not you! And if it works, all the better! Either way you win! Ah! you're pretty damn cynical! The war's screwing up your life! But you've got every reason to be thrilled! I'm the one who's the victim here!"

That makes him start bawling again, his whole body racked by sobs, he soaked his sheets.

"So what about the *Vegas*? Stop believing in them, or something? The whole Goâ song and dance was just a load of crap, is that it?"

I was galling him. I wanted him to snap out of it and stop his sniveling, to buck up just a little.

"So you admit it then, it was a bunch of bull? You wanted me to sniff too? that was the trick? own up, come on! Let's hear it!..."

He didn't answer a word.

"Ah! When it comes to first-class bums, you're one for the books! You led us into a mess! You string us along and then dump us at the first sign of trouble! Ah! it's the most stinking rotten thing I've ever heard of! You can be proud! You look like a total idiot!"

True, when you got down to it, he was the one who'd engineered the whole scheme, we'd wheeled and dealed with that screwball, collected all the equipment, this unholy shambles, the masks and the rest, and the only way we'd get out of it now would be with a trip behind bars, the situation was so damned complicated, things were taking a turn for the worse... Matthew, Wickers... the fuzz!... Curlers... the spies... the Consulate... too much all at once! and on top of everything else, the Ghosts! We might just as well throw in the towel! and on top of everything, my poor darling knocked up right at that very moment... All the shit hitting the fan at the same second! Ah! perfect timing!... what a coincidence!... we were really racking up our run of rotten jinxes! Ah! I was proud of my successes! Romeo the screw-up! I didn't have a thing to brag about... It was my fault, and then again it wasn't... I'd given in to my impulses... Normally I wouldn't have laid a finger on her, when all calm and in control... right from the start I loved her too much... I admired her beauty... starry-eyed, I respected her... happy under her spell... her kindness... her cheerfulness... I wouldn't have hurt a hair on her head with all my carryings-on... What it had taken was the Tweet-Tweet Club! the drunken binge! the circumstances, exhaustion... I got the whole picture now... it was my head especially that had whacked out on me... a fit of panic, and I'd pounced on her... Now I got the whole picture... I wasn't a hundred percent to blame... Didn't matter, I was still responsible... I didn't try to wriggle out of it... I said as much to Sosthène again...

"My head's a little fuzzy... but I'm responsible! No argument! It's written in black and white on my discharge forms. 'Trepanned, mental spasms, but responsible.' I won't deny it. Honor and conscience! It runs in the family."

He gazed at me with his totally blank, weepy eyes.

"Yes, that's right, I'm still proclaiming it! You woke me up, and don't you forget it! I'll never abandon her! You woke me up, listen to me! I'm not made of the same stuff as you! I'm no fiasco, I keep my word! Wounded! Trepanned! Dead or alive! That's the way we are, the men called up in '14!"

That shut him up but good.

"I'm no quitter. I'll be the child's father! That's the way I am!"

That crack made me proud...

"Poor brat! You're a child yourself! what are you babbling about?"

Ah! I'd riled him up.

"I'm not ditching anything, for Christ's sake!"

He was rattling the bed to pieces in his wild fury.

"Ah! you've gone too far! I'm not going to sit here and be insulted! Watch your words! You snot-nose! You little squirt!"

He snaps to, beside himself, rolling his eyes!

"Ah! You've stopped your tears now!" Ah! I'm splitting my sides! "Temper, temper, temper!"

But he wasn't laughing along.

"Repeat that! Repeat that! I didn't quit on anything! You're a lying son of a bitch!"

He's beside himself.

"Mister, your *Vegas*'re a load of crapola! Your Chinese gown! Your jig! Your wriggly nose! You're a chickenshit lama! Nyah! Nyah! Nyah! Nothing but a swindler. You didn't pull anything over on me! with your lousy masquerade! Bungler! Digging up a bigger jerk than you would be some job!"

Ah! I was deeply wounding him, he was giving me his dead-fish stare. Sly devil!

"Young man! Young man! You're mad! You're raving on like a lunatic! I'm listening to you! It's demented! You're sick in the body! You've suffered! That might be one excuse! Your mind's not worth much! But your sickness runs deeper! Your heart's not in the right place!"

"Not in the right place! Ah! Not in the right place!"

I jump back.

"Take that back, or you're history! I'll smash you right in the face with this pisspot!"

If he keeps it up, I'll slam him with the chamberpot!

"Big chicken! Slouch! Lazy bum!"

He springs over to the clock, grabs it, he's going to defend himself...

"Just try it again!" he goes to me... "Just try!"

I look, he's holding it out arm's length over his head, it's twenty after three. He's going to catapult it at me. I don't wait around... KEE-RASH! Smack in the mirror! The glass explodes! into smithereens! He comes through unscathed, cackling.

"Ah! You rotten bastard!" I lunge for his neck.

"Son of a bitch! Son of a bitch! You'll pay for everything!"

"Wah! Wah!" He's hollering, I squeeze hard, he's bawling his head off!... "Wah! Wah!" I'm kneeling on top of him, bouncing up and down, his body's my trampoline...

"Let it out! Let it out! Yell, you bastard! Ain't nobody around!"

Knock! Knock! Knock! Somebody's at the door...

"Please!... Please!" a voice calls... It's Virginia...

She walks in, wearing a nightgown.

"Look!" I go... "There, look!..."

Don't have much else to say. The other guy under me's an awful sight. I've messed him up a little more with my one arm, whacking away with my elbow. I split open his shiners. They were bleeding, we sop them up, the carpet's all splattered with blood. Virginia goes down to the pantry, it's four in the morning. She's going to make us some coffee.

Sosthène's moaning, he pukes, I punched his belly one too many times. He socked me in the head. My mind just keeps on reeling.

At long last we wind up going to bed. I apologize to Virginia when she comes back up from the kitchen.

She's not pleased.

"Sleep!..." she goes to me. "Sleep! you're no good!"

I want to shake Sosthène's hand.

He's already snoring away, dead to the world. I think I really got him sore. Still no word from the Colonel.

Meanwhile one thing for sure was that he still hadn't come back... One day... two... no word... We stopped talking about him... It was a touchy subject with Virginia anyway... She might have been pretty worried... He was her uncle, her only relative... lousy bastard that he was, he was her bread-and-butter despite everything.

I flipped through the *Mirror* and the *Daily Mail*, especially under the "Personals"... Not even the smallest item... It was really extraordinary. The servants were clueless. Apparently it'd been years since anything like this had happened to him... He'd already run away on occasion... The last time was in 1908... Shrim, the head butler, remembered that in 1905 he'd flown the coop for two months in exactly the same way, without letting either him or anyone else know. Just like that, on the spur of the moment, boom! out of there! Nobody had even found out why, or what he'd been up to outside. One fine evening he'd come back, grungy and flea-ridden, his trousers in tatters. Shrim had put him to bed himself. Three straight days sacked out. Then he picked up his life where he left off as though nothing had happened. Nobody had asked any questions. Maybe this was the same sort of deal. Maybe he'd be back in a couple-three months, maybe a couple-three days!

Maybe he'd joined up again! re-enlisted in the service of the Royal Pioneers? And he'd be dropping us a line from the front? Maybe it was the same wind that was blowing over Cascade's pimps? The wind of heroes! He'd be back, fuck it, whenever he felt like. He hadn't left any orders. The suppliers kept up their deliveries all the same. His bank took care of the bills.

Virginia felt a little better. It was just that she got tired so easily. She went white over the pettiest trifle. Pregnancy wasn't her cup of tea. Now her back was killing her. And she used to be so always on the go. An impish, bouncy kid... Ah! I was as gentle as a lamb! We went back out to play with the little birdies in the garden... Virginia was an old friend, especially for the chaffinches, their beady eyes very curious, they'd fly over to peck crumbs from her hand. Birds are the most adorable creatures. Funny little pompons with tricks for looking bigger, puffing themselves up in their feathers. Crafty devils. In your hand a bird's nothing at all, a sprite of the air. "Tweetwee!" a wee flake of wind. Ah! To be a bird! With the pure sky to pass your life in! Shit, just not the same! I pointed this out to Virginia, as nicely as could be, of course... Little darling, little friend... she was a bird herself in a way... And wild man that I was, I'd played a nasty trick on her... Yet even sitting down this way, she'd get a little queasy and tuckered out... she had to stretch out on her back. I waited on her hand and foot, I can assure you. I played the daddy, and she the mommy, it made her laugh, but too hard! A little tear rolled down her cheek... I kissed her quickly... What I thought was: a child!... I sat there dumbfounded... Without moving a muscle.

"It's raining, dear!"

So it was. Had to go back inside. She had a little cough too... still and all she was robust, with a sturdy build for a little girl, muscular, springy, you name it...

Fine, we go indoors. I phone a couple-three places... I still wanted to get some idea what'd become of that clown! Where he might have holed up! In the Jellicot Bar? where they had these special canteen-style barmaids who talked dirty to the little geezers? Might have appealed to the queer bird. A hangout for old fogy veterans—just his type—who played poker. Or maybe at the Squadron Club? where his mail was sent, where Shrim would take his suitcase whenever he'd go to the theater and stay out all night? No sight of him there either. I tell myself: I don't know what's cooking but it doesn't smell good. Sosthène just sat there. He quit putting himself out. He didn't want to lift a finger for any reason. He was waiting for his prophecy to be fulfilled, for those cops to show up and haul us in. Everybody behind bars. He was betting on it in front of the servants. A sure thing.

Virginia just laughed off his ideas, his buffoonish outbursts, his "Oh! dear! Oh my!"s over every little thing... plus those sighs he heaved... Whenever he talked a little fast she made him repeat every word...

"Say it again, Captain!"

She'd nicknamed him Captain. But he refused to learn English, he fought against it tooth and nail, not to mention his *th*'s and *thous*...

"I'll give you a lesson right away if you slip your robe back on! and dance the way you did the other day!" He had to do another Piccadilly for us! But he was the only one who was against it! No more Piccadillys, no more nothing! he wasn't in a magic mood, the Goâ trance and battle had pooped him out so much he couldn't even foresee when the supernatural powers would seize him again. During the brawl with the cops he'd put out so much, his energy had sunk so far below any potential "Fourth Sphere" that now he was burned out, no joke, probably for the next several years. And naturally it was all my fault. Because if I'd played my little napkin ring the way I should have clack-clack, if I hadn't sabotaged the whole thing, etc. etc. He kept trying to pick a fight with me. Nasty bickering to get his mind off the present situation... and he still had a way to go with the masks... he had to get back to the experiments... He wanted to quit! I blew his big chance for him!... If only I'd played my little drumsticks on Piccadilly... absolutely as agreed... kept up the rhythm clack-clack... clack-clackkk... events would have taken a wonderful turn... the great miracle would have occurred... His visions of glory were carrying him away again. I kept my mouth shut. It was pointless... plain dishonesty, that's all... I didn't dare think about the future! My hands were damn full! I thought: Tough, the die's cast, whatever happens will happen! meanwhile, we've got bed, board and heat... Catastrophe for catastrophe, it's less trouble just to stay put... What's magical is that we never leave each other's side, not even for a second, Virginia and I, that we never end up apart, neither on good nor bad days, and that this may hold true for the rest of our lives...

In a way I was turning into a responsible guy, as least as far as emotions went... All the same there was still a bill we had to settle, complications... Feelings don't patch up everything... I hashed the situation over with Sosthène. We were having a nice chat...

Brrrring! the telephone...

"Hello! Hello! Who is it?"

"St. Paul's Cathedral..."

Those very words just like that...

"What did you say?"

We're surprised...

"Call Mr. Sosthène to the phone! We want to talk with him..."

A rather hoarse voice.

"Mr. Sosthène isn't here!"

My quick wits.

"He is so! He is so there!"

They're insistent.

"And so who are you?"

"I'm the Good Lord."

Click! we hang up... Joker.

Who was it?

We start wondering.

Who could be in the know?

"Sosthène," I lay into him... "You opened your mouth!... You blabbed to the servants! You've been acting like a dirty pig!"

He swears to me up and down. Not much of a guarantee. OK, so it gave us a smile, but I'm in no mood for a repeat.

I take the phone off the hook.

Rap! Rap! Rap! now it's the door...

A policeman. I say: "This is it!" No.

"Mr. Sosthène de Rodiencourt? Miss Virginia O'Collogham?"

He hands over two cards, spins on his heels, leaves. Two summonses, the same for both.

Will call at Room 912
Friday 6th, 3 P.M.
Scotland Yard 1.

I'm first to read, then Virginia, then Sosthène.

I decide: "Well, gang! No way you're going... I'm sure this is fake."

I don't beat around the bush... the way I explain it gives Virginia the shakes... I'm just so sure... that it's some horrible ambush... Not that she's one bit scared... couldn't be more energetic, brazen... but she gets another weak spell, it's her condition... We're forced to stretch her out on her back, her teeth chattering. She looks at me... I'm a big blur... don't look like myself... She's a little dizzy... I pat her hands... They're ice cold... I kiss her... I kiss her... I see her lifeless... stop seeing her... stop seeing anything.

Her smile returns... brings me back to life... I belong to her like a bird... I'm in the cage of her happiness... she can take me any place she wants... I don't want her to go away anymore... I don't want to leave her for a single second... I'll forget about all my woes, my arm, even my head, the perpetual noise inside, the aches and pains all over my body, the Consulate, the summons—all just by seeing her happy... I want her to be utterly happy... For the moment that's complicated... the road's sort of bumpy. The proof is the summons... Mustn't show up, it's a trap... Our minds are made up.

But if we don't go, they'll come here! That's no solution!

Moral: get the hell out of here! Make tracks! For a week or two! go off for a spin! the rest of us, off for a spin too! a terrific binge! the Colonel had buzzed off, and so if he came back unexpectedly it shouldn't be too big a surprise to see that we went out for a little fresh air ourselves...

That was one approach!

"And anyway, damn, we got nothing to lose! Come on, let's hit the road!"

Virginia was all for it. But what about being down to our last penny! You had to allow for out-of-pocket expenses... A jaunt for three doesn't come free! So Virginia gets this bright idea. I don't make any suggestions. She goes up to the third floor, into her uncle's study. Not a moment's hesitation. She opens a couple-three-four drawers... we can hear her shaking out the bureau... she brings us down seven pounds fifty... Pretty piddling, we wouldn't travel too far on that... Even so, two weeks... maybe three... time enough for the cops to think we're miles from anywhere... or out of the country... We played out our scheme pretty well... didn't sound the alarm... behaved completely normal, like the Colonel... informed the lackeys that we'd be back for dinner... we were going out for a stroll around town...

Maybe it wasn't the cleverest strategy, maybe it didn't fool anybody. We were caught with our pants down, and had to think fast. A pretty strange sight we must have looked.

Here we are out on the street.

Ah! Heads up! Keep on your toes! Mustn't be spotted again in Tottenham! or Piccadilly! Run away! Run away! from the wolf's jaws! Ah! oddballs get picked out in a snap!

I think: We'll blend in better on streets mobbed with people. Let's head east... Poplar!... we hop a 116 bus... Come to think of it, even more tempting... down by Greenwich, the docks, the pubs... Still and all I had some unsettled business in that neck of the woods... Ah! but that's the spot that draws me... we have our favorite neighborhoods... not to mention the London pub, the Hospital, the long raspberry-and-black bastionlike building where Clodovitz was on staff, the doctor buddy of my friends. It took balls to show my face in those parts... Tough! I was hooked! So we hop a bus. The route, the colorful shops, seen from the upper deck while being rattled around, cheerfully bouncing back and forth, the whole world is dancing. Virginia was starting to feel more confident. I'd brought along her fur. She was glad to have it. I kept a close eye on her. She felt better out in the open.

Now that we were on our way, escaping from that Willesden prison, I felt perky... I shouted out to the passersby... "Hello! Hello!" in a burst of joy...

"Aren't we having the time of our lives?"

Sosthène was out of it...

"Hi there, little fellow! we're free!"

Life was looking great to me... I kissed Virginia while bumping around... rounding corners... the bus sent us flying into each other... it's intoxicating, the wind whipping our faces... this freedom... It sends Sosthène to sleep... his head bouncing around at every twist and turn... From Willesden to the Elephant is a pretty long ride, a good hour... The Strand, Cheapside... the crush of cars... swarms, mobs every which way... bumper to bumper, higgledy-piggledy, sideways, forward and backward... a snarl-up the world has never seen since... I'm talking about the winter of 1916. You had to see the thoroughfare, vehicles tearing apart, smashing up, exploding London's huge streets. From America torrents of grub and gear, a huge jumble of weapons, cannons, cannon fodder, landaus, trains of equipment, omnibuses, the last hansoms, whole columns on the march, Tipperary, steam engines smack in the middle of the street, gigantic cooking pots, the whole mess all heaped on top of each other, player pianos, pontoon bridges in sections, or partially assembled, tricky maneuvers from one intersection to the next, the outlets, the sidewalk in upheaval, cracking apart, the whole wooden walkway splintering under the thud of traffic, ramming/plowing up the curbsides in its rush toward Victoria, the grand embarkation for Flanders, the continent in commotion, kingdoms in turmoil...

It was a truly magical carousel, a thousand times more fun than some old merry-go-round. Our 116 bus was riding out far, we were getting our dough's worth... Ah! traffic's so pleasant, it soothes many a setback...

I hugged my Virginia tightly, I bellowed my love to her, the bus drowned my words in its roar... its vibration...

"You're an angel, Virginia! You appear and the sun comes out!"

More delicate, more sensitive than an angel by a long shot, a thousand times over! in the state she was in! Poor little baby doll, so fragile! What gentle valor!

"Virginia, you're an angel!"

Sosthène couldn't really make up his mind whether leaving Willesden was such a hot idea... Now he was starting to second-guess himself... with every bump, misgivings... "What if the Colonel doesn't find us? What if the police come back to see us?... What if the servants telephone?... To the Engineers Club?..." an endless litany of "what-ifs"!...

I say: "Why don't you put on a happy face, it's a beautiful day, spring is in the air, and new offensives! I'd put all the gloom behind me now!"

It hadn't rained for two or three days, the sun actually peeked out from time to time. Having a March that's not too soggy might actually be cause for celebrations, processions of gratitude... In London downpours are the norm, spring opens the floodgates.

Sosthène wasn't thrilled, or feeling festive, his mind was on Scotland Yard.

"Look, Sosthène, look at all the soldier boys." I point out the sidewalk for him to admire, the war-ready companies rolling in huge waves toward Victoria, an endless sea of khaki...

"Look at their faces, they're not crying, yet they're off to that son of a bitching front... by tonight they'll be lined up in the trenches! Young, bursting with health! Sosthène, you're just a selfish bum! You just think about your own belly! Not a pretty sight at your age!"

No answer.

"Maybe you miss dancing?"

I was teasing him.

"You can see we're out for a ride, can't you?"

He just bumped along, in a total fog.

The bus rumblegrumbles, smokes, backfires, spews all the way up Fleet Street, the Press hub, magazines, marble walls, huffing and puffing herky-jerky higher and higher, bingo! top of the hill, and one last bump to a stop... Rrrring! the bell! Full speed ahead! Charge, short bursts, barrel along! Watch out, bikes! Nose dips, rears, on our way up again! Ludgate Hill! the big Dome right in front of us! Immense! Gigantic St. Paul's Cathedral! our telephone call! We have a chuckle... The spot's not exactly pleasant, but right after the small square the river comes up fast, Blackfriars Bridge, a vista opens out. Below on the water the stream of yellow, pale pink fog, ebbing in sunlight.

The bus turns onto the bridge, starts across. The mists envelop it, the double-decker sails through midair. We can't see a thing anymore. It's absolutely impenetrable. I suggest we get off, that we take in the view from the parapet, the boats, the banks, the activity.

But maybe Virginia's tired?... No! No! she wants to go for a walk too!...

In one way the neighborhood's safe and clear... no danger of running into anybody we shouldn't... guys like Matthew... or snoops... these parts are just for work... people on the job, in a hurry... without wandering eyes... just racing along... they're not nosy. We lean our elbows on the ledge... don't see much... everything veiled in mist. We can make out the ships, hear their heavy heaving, the lapping water... the current breaking against the arch... whirling in the huge hole... the ships digging, furrowing, roaring, churning up the foam, gliding along... *shouuuu*.

The sea gulls graze past us, dive into the eddies, hover over the mist, cry, twirl around... The sun's rays shine brighter, strike the two banks, the giant wall of docks, the enormous brick rows, glisten in yellows, mauves, blaze on the windowpanes, cascade, trickle down along the shores, the sludge, flow back into the current, scatter in a brilliantly shimmering trail...

Ah! it's fairy magic, pure and simple! Nobody'll deny it! I ask Sosthène what he thinks. He didn't want to go into it. It was too cold on the parapet for him, and I was too worked up, he was shivering, his nose solid mauve. Virginia was shivery too... Ah! now big rivers give me a thrill! they fire my imagination... I go into ecstasies at the sight of flowing water...

Still, I was cold too, damn it!

"A grog!" I propose... "A grog!"

I knew a small saloon in Blackfriars, real close, a hopskipjump.

"Do you want to ruin my stomach completely?"

Pigheaded jerk.

We head up to Fenchurch Street... I find my pub, I can still see it, just opposite the Belle Sauvage, the small courtyard with the sign. You see the "belle sauvage" in question, stark naked and nicely stacked, dancing with sprays of feathers all over her body, on her ass, her head, her tits... A period piece. Sort of like the Colonel with his kooky thing for masks... It gets me to thinking. What kind of shape is our future taking?... Some prospect!... Now that it occurs to me, where's that goofy bastard farting around these days?... what's he cooking up?... Why didn't he come back? I run through it all in my mind!... What about his plan?... And that phone call? And the note from the Yard?... Maybe he was the instigator?... What the hell was this all about in the end?... a nasty business... I was guessing myself to death... I had to keep my trap shut... otherwise I'd worry the girl some more... plus it was too delicate, her relative, her uncle... who was naturally a lousy creep... a geezer with the hots... a filthy human being... She couldn't deny it, could she, my fragile precious darling. I kissed her again a little... I kept kissing her more and more... Such things aren't done in public bars. I couldn't snap out of my muddle, didn't know what tack to take. A whole slew of problems on top of my shattered nerves, plus my personal troubles with the Consulate and others... Ah! shit, enough already! I give Virginia another kiss... Ah! not a damn thing was working out at all! Rough going at every turn. And she, my poor precious! knocked up! my fairy! my affection! And me the father! Some father! A champ! Sosthène let me stew over our rotten lot, he felt real comfortable in the pub! He poured himself tea with rum, one small carafe after another... and he wasn't much of a drunkard either... he was acquiring a taste for the hard stuff... ever since his awful fright.

"I thought you didn't like liquor!"

"You upset me, that's the only reason!"

A tear wells in his eye. The quick-to-cry type. So I was the one causing him grief... Oh! the nerve of the guy!... the heartless son of a bitch!

A big act.

"You going to drink everything?" I ask, "the whole seven pounds fifty?"

He's miffed. We leave.

Back on the sidewalk.

A bolt from the blue.

"Hey, Prospero Jim! That's the guy we ought to look up!"

Curlers mentioned him the other day on the bench in front of the Leicester... He'd opened up another joint according to Curlers... on the other side of the Thames... with his insurance dough... a "saloon" for workers, a dockers' snack bar, just a simple canteen, who'd have ever thought!... not even close to a full-service inn... that bomb business didn't go over too well with the insurance company... they hadn't reimbursed the total costs, just a small fraction... But old Prospero Jim was a sweet talker, he had a real way with words, plus useful connections in every quarter, in all the docks, workshops, with practically every single crew that traveled the coast as well as overseas, and in customs—he knew a big shot! Ah! if he wanted to get involved! He'd get us out of our jam in no time. This sudden idea gave me a new burst of hope.

"What if he had some little trick—hey, listen to this, it's great—for getting us over to Ireland? Completely on the hush-hush, top secret, you name it? Something down in the hold for us three? Wouldn't you like that, Virginia?"

You bet she went for that right away! The idea was to wander the world. She couldn't ask for more. Adventure didn't scare her. Sosthène neither. But how were we going to go about it? What angle would we take for starters? where'd we get the dough? the papers? He was worrying himself sick over piddling details.

No sooner said... then off! Fucking hell! Let's hunt up this Prospero! track down this acrobat! Got to cross back over the entire bridge! First things first, it might be located out that way... past the elevator factory, past Blackfriars and the Depot, the dry dock, right after the reservoirs where the shore rises, where the narrow streets twist and turn, the skewered rows of cottages, the thousands upon thousands of doors with knockers, geraniums as far as the eye can see, the whole jumble of bricked-in dead ends, Holborn Commons, Jelly Gates, gray mazes crawling with bratbroods, constantly darting between your legs, commotion, stray junk, hoops, pots, racket, kids worming in everywhere, cheeping as they hop along on one foot, thumbing noses, somersaulting, boom! leapfrogging! girls, boys, head over heels! plunk! in the gutter! the sudden explosion of life sweeps you off your feet! splatters you with such lively joy! the sunshine strikes you full force, burns your heart with delight, the slimy walls, the magic alleyways, girls with hitched-up skirts, tawny-haired misses, tow-topped urchins! youth in all its rough-and-tumble rambunctiousness, frenzy! frenzy! Gamboling for all eternity! To die like this, totally swept away by youth, joy, swarms of children! complete happiness! the crowning joy of England! so pure, so bright-eyed and bushy-tailed, so divine! titillating daisies and roses! Ah! I'm elated! Ah! I'm intoxicated! I forget what I'm after! I lose my way! Prospero! Prospero! Your canteen! We'll find you! Even if you're hidden under the shores, huddled down in a sewer, with the rats, and contraband! You won't get away anymore! Quick, ask for directions! From this passerby... that other one... at that house... around the whole neighborhood... Excuse me? Nobody knows! Here's the Dingby... the ruins... still left as is... mud, ashes, beams. At last we find a chatterbox... actually happy to remember, that he just might have heard something about Prospero being back on the opposite shore... another trip across the bridge!... a wooden building supposedly... The Moor and Cheese was its name... We're off again... Tooley Street... A quick ferry... Here we are... Jamaica, the large outer dock... twenty yards to the right we run into it... It's as big as an honest-to-God warehouse, immense, ugly, black, awful, an enormous building at the end of the towpath, right opposite the water... There's the sign with the words "The Moor and Cheese, Prospero proprietor"... No mistake, this is the place all right. I push open the door. No surprise. He saw us coming. He must have been watching from his counter.

"Hi, how you doing?" No explanations...

"So," I go, "back on your feet?"

"Oh," he answers, "sort of..."

Playing it safe.

I don't press.

"This here's Sosthène," I introduce him, "a true friend! and this is Miss O'Collogham... Can you serve us up something hot? This river of yours is an icebox!..."

It was real drafty inside his place too, not sealed too tight, the north wind gusted through every wall... Just some patched-up warehouse. In the middle, a huge black wooden chest, with the counter on top. Kerosene lamps on the tables. Duckboard covering every square inch of the floor as on a ship. It could hold quite a crowd, enough chairs for a regiment.

"Say, you've got more elbow room than at the Dingby! fact is, you've expanded! You must be having quite a time, huh?"

I act friendly.

"Oh! it comes and goes!" he confesses... "I don't turn away customers. But every once in a while, you know how it is, there are bombs!..."

I think to myself: He's going right at it!

I thought he meant Boro... no, he was talking about the zeppelin bombs that had fallen on Cabbell Street... the night before last... A low-flying zeppelin... Floating very quietly over London... in full glare of the lighthouses... Targeting the St. Katharine Docks... the complete rundown was in the *Mirror*...

"Hey, you can take out insurance!"

An off-the-cuff comment, no harm intended.

Rubs him the wrong way.

"Insurance against crime is what I need! Nobody's insured against crime!"

"You saying that for my benefit, Prospero?"

"Oh! For everybody's..."

Digging up the past.

I don't press, back off, didn't want any trouble.

We came on other business. His canteen was vacant... a couple-three customers at one end... the big rush would be later on in the day, he explains to me even so, when the crowd rolled up from the docks, the stevedores, the entire work force at the big four o'clock break in the action... Then the place turned into an instant mob scene. Right now they were on the job, slogging away, bats out of hell in the holds, working at lightning war speed, the crews slaving on top of each other! every which way with full dump trucks, with cranes, ships drawn along the quays, whistles blowing, steam shooting, the crews hauling ass, pivoting, swarming, crawling, streaming into the holds, hordes of rats, rummaging, shouldering, digging their hooks into the goods, starboarding, tipping up trunks, dizzy whirl of hoists, charging along, stowing on tenders, hauling the ropes taut! Ready! Set! Go! The locomotive lets out a whine, carries off... Two-three cargos to unload along a couple-three rows plus two-three others with each ebb tide, two-three thirty-five-man crews in six-eight-hour shifts, what a circus, what an earsplitting din!... Smoking day and night!... And the word for the pace is ferocious! No lazy slugs around there! At killer speed! not a dry hair from the St. Katharine Docks to London Pier. No thumb-twiddling! all the stops pulled out! the mob lavished with tuppence an hour. You could see the docks from Prospero's place, a full view from his fanlight, the activity, the winches.

"No snoozing down on your wharf, I'll say! You're not kidding you pack them in... They must come up from the wharf thirsty as hell! You're going to be able to buy yourself a pub big as this!..." sweeping my arms wide as the Thames... "when this is all over!..."

Never had I seen so many guys slamming around so much stuff, crates, barrels, scrap metal, grain meal, caravaning from every side, charging down into the black holes of the holds, clanking against ballast tanks, catching with winches, murderers! grinding the winch up something awful! breaking off all its teeth! the chain snaps! whips out! the whole thing comes crashing down! Brraang! the old tub lets out a gasp! its huge paunch thunders! Boom! the nasty accident knocks through the belly, the entire skeleton... Prospero's joint quakes...

Maybe this doesn't interest you... please accept my apologies... So anyway, I was on the part where I was feeling out Prospero...

"They blow in from all over, look at that! Did you see that?... Brisbane? Australia?"

The very boat right under his window just sitting there, you could see the name: Brisbane Australia. A cargo of wool and frozen meat. He sighs, gives a vague answer.

"Oh! Australia's tho nithe! They got othtriches! theep! Ithn't that right, Mademoithelle?..."

He had a lisp.

Another sigh...

"There're people from all over... people who never come back..."

Giving us a routine.

"Well!" I go, the guy's getting on my nerves, "so you don't know of anything?"

I get right to the point.

"Anything what?"

"A trip, damn it! For getting the hell out of here!"
I spelled it out.
"You a detherter?"
"No! No! I'm not! Discharged!"
"Mixed up in anything?"
"Sort of... but nothing too bad..."
If only he knew all the ways.
"And the old man and her? Taking them with you?"
"It's not what you think..."
I know what he's thinking.
"Where do you want to go?..."
"Where there's no Matthew..."
"Don't like him?"
"No..."
"Makes two of us..."
At least we have one thing in common.
"Got a passport? how about the geezer? the kid?"
"There're ways to find them..."
"The kid got any relatives?"
He was wary of me, my fly-by-night ways...
"Where you off to, friend?"
True, it was a snap decision, but there wasn't any time for hemming and hawing... He was an all-right guy!
"Well?" I ask.
"Well, you've got a few screws loose!"
Exactly.
"You plunge ahead! charge right along! You don't give a damn! Don't you know there's a war on, lamebrain? that you just don't go traipsing around the world like that? wherever you take a fancy? that it's prohibited everywhere? Haven't you heard?"
Ah! I knew that! Old news! He was wiggling off the hook, that's all.
"My congrats, Mademoiselle! Bravo! An explorer! You're going to take in a country or two! Passepartout! The King of the Road!"
He was pulling my leg, just his style, picking fights in front of the ladies, grabbing the spotlight as always, his old habit...
I hold my tongue... Now's not the time... I want to keep him talking.
"All right, you don't like doing favors!..."
"Me, do favors?"
He jumps back. A conceited peacock...
"Ah! now just hold on! Listen up, Mr. Fancy Pants, Prospero has done more huge favors than you've got mustache hairs! A skillion more! Only you show up and take him for a fucking idiot with your harebrained scheme! Like it's as easy as taking a piss! Leave the country! Leave the country! Epilepsy

on the brain! Il signor is packing off with minors! plus grandpops! Plus what else?"

I pushed him to the boiling point. He was lisping angrily.

"Would you like me to give you a round of applause?"

He was playing dumb.

"Course not! Course not! You know damn well! I'm asking you for a ship! not the moon!... you know, headed to Australia, for instance!... any ships like that around?... no?... Are they so incredibly extraspecial?"

"A journey! A journey! listen to that, Christ Almighty! and what about dough! You expecting a free ride now?"

Ah! good point! That shut me up! I'd forgotten! Scatterbrain! Completely slipped my mind! Clean out! That's a fact! Well, just those seven pounds fifty! what the girl swiped! A drop in the bucket for Australia!...

"Ferdinand! Eeeyouu are marvelous! Marvelllous! A prizewinner! Signor Escampetta! Clandestina! nulle peso! thee leeemeeet!"

He laughed so hard he started coughing... wiggling his eyebrows... winking... applauding.

"Unbelievable!... Unbelievable!... The girlfriend! The acquaintance! Customer! The whole gang! Off we go! Signor! Pougadinos! Signor Pougadinos! Signor Penniless Zero!"

He saw Sosthène as our mark. Pretty far off the mark, I'd say...

"Mademoiselle çou bambino, he's got a bad case of Fourgnioule! Fourgnioule! In love! Burning up in the oven!"

He screwed his head around like that...

"Sicko, my boy! Sicko!"

He wasn't putting me off the track, his two-faced posturing wasn't bluffing me... meanwhile he said nothing...

"Dish us up a little broth if you don't have any java ready. Don't you have better things to do than holler at us? What's the matter, beef stew off the menu?"

I knew what came out of his kitchen... quick meals at any time, broth with a pinch of salt, pickles, tripe. He had everything in his scullery at the other side of the small courtyard. We went over for a look at his grub, his cold cuts, sandwiches, sausages, simmering Irish stew... We all paid our compliments, and from the heart too, our mouths watering. Honored to have a taste. Prospero was a louse, but not a cheapskate, his friends had free rein. Back in those days it was the done thing, an openhearted come-one-come-all attitude. From the first mouthful you never stopped till the pots were licked clean. A plate for every man, and down with the pigs! Nobility, in its own way. Never any questions. I'd have croaked twenty-five times over, and in a snap, a dog-hungry derelict, if not for the pimps of St. John's, their helping hand in the nick of time! So now at some thirty plus years distance I'm just paying them their due, giving them a generous bow, I would have gone belly up ages ago, I wouldn't be the writer I am today, with a sentimental streak, if I hadn't found them so palsy-walsy and all back when. It'd be a shame. I'd have gotten done in by the fog, coughed myself to death. I held on by sponging off them, forever and ever. Back in those days, like at the Leicester for instance, we ate potluck, whatever was put in front of us round-the-clock service, morning, noon and night. No song and dance about setting fifteen-twenty extra places, give or take a few... A nice crowd would always show up, around noon, just roll in, who knows from where, a motley crew, starving to death... hookers, cousins, some relatives or other, some stray pimp, or street survivor, a bookie, a mystery man, a manicurist, and in the wee hours for a light supper even an entertainer, the stocking seller, somebody's sister's john, a couple-three sloshed characters who dozed off right on top of the table, and tarts between tricks, in and out, one last quick bite, to plug in the gaps. From Upper Soho to Tilbury, from Albert Gate to the Leicester, and in every knock shop in between, the grub-slingers never had a minute's rest. An endless procession of legs of lamb, fattened chickens, Chester hams! No stinting over chow. Only the very best! Plus you had to see the atmosphere! sheer agonies of appetites, ravenous enough to scoff down a dog. Women who'd been streetwalking for hours on end, pacing around in the icy fog, would walk in pale as ghosts, dead famished. They needed to put something in their bellies. A simple stroll through the damp air was all it took to set our heads spinning. Prospero understood perfectly, we made a slap-up meal of his sausages, followed by minced pork in mustard sauce.

Our spirits perked back up. Virginia didn't feel queasy anymore. We just kept sitting there for a spell, chatting about this and that, taking in the panorama, quite a view, you get a pretty good look, through the picture window, the tiny box houses, the facing docks, the lock, the bridge, the hill... Immediately after comes the ruins of his former pub, the Dingby, the one that blew up. Nothing left but sections of beam, rubble, a heap of trash. He hadn't cleared anything out yet. It'd gone down like a ship, collapsed into the mud and the drink. The Thames is a good three or four hundred yards deep in that spot. A splendid stretch of water! I feel like I'm off on another round, yapping yet again about this sumptuous spectacle out on the river, the port traffic, the steamers, the cargo ships toiling, spewing their mists, huff-puffing their way upriver, right alongside the banks, dodging the beacons, grazing the buoys, spiffy monsters, all decked out, circling with birds, sea gulls and curlews, spinning out their souls, diving here, there, petals from the sky in the lapping wake. And the whole swarm of boats, the toiling small fry, dories, skiffs, officers' dinghies, marine floats, pulling hard on the oars, sails hauling on, fancydancing, tossed from one eddy to another, butts slapping the water, charging to the moorings, the locks, rowing like mad, hopping, doing polkas, pirouetting! dropping anchor and whirling, sparrows of the surf! The raw life of rivers! From my story you'll guess that I'm not talking about some fragile little spell but awesome water-faring magic... And don't go thinking in any way—how low it'd be—that I want to hex you, to blow pixie dust in your eyes, razzle-dazzle you in order to pull some double-cross... cook up some treacherous dizzy spell... hoodwink you... dimwit of the deeps... with visions of you floating down toward the sandy shores... whisking way out there, all bloated, on the Southend jetties... where dawn breaks... and the sea unfurls its waves... its long green hills... roars, swells, swoons... and sweeps everything away!

O memories too poignant by half! All the grandeur, misery, cargos of the open sea! Dundee schooners! Cutters in the sea spray! The trade winds are dead! Dead, the magic! Into thin air the cavalry of surf! the carpet of tall, roaring waves! Farewell, rich pitch-coated Cardiffs, coal shovels boring through the foam! Farewell, mad jibs and spanker sails! Farewell, free wind-whipped wandering!... Let's wail at the sea! Curl up! Ludicrous predicament! crippled word-dog! Back to sleep! Back to your room! Everything's fine this way! Each to his own riffraff! Let's wail over our hand compasses! over the Sham Island quay, over the lost pub, where the fleet moors, over the deserted ships being refitted, over the rusty lockgates, one-eyed semaphores, downed masts! The race is run! Our predicaments, dead! Dead, the captain! Let's kiss our service papers good-bye! Registered ghosts! Dockmaster of the port, at your service! Sea gull, carry those roving souls off into the sky! Clouds, blot them out!...

Ah! I'm off the deep end! Ah! I'm going to the dogs! Ah! I quiverquake at the memories! Narcissus and those tendencies of his! cast a longing gaze, you louse! touch! touch! speak your heart! Making the most of the silence!

Now where were we... the streetwalkers' turf, our red-light pages...

As I was saying, in a sort of mixed-up kind of way I'll admit, we weren't exactly hitting it off with Prospero...

He thought I was a troublemaker with my plans, my crazy idea about picking up and sailing away! with the family! without papers! or a penny to my name! plus an underage kid to boot!

"Ah! you know what? You're talking crime here!"

His big conclusion.

"Aren't you the least little bit aware of that?"

True, it was damn brave of me.

"You mean you don't see anything wrong?"

Tough! Just tough! I kept hammering away. Finally he saw it my way all the same...

"Well, look, if you had thirty-forty pounds... I'd tell you to go on over and see the Skipper... Jovil... on Cannon Street... sometimes he's got a small transport... but not with your measly handful of change! gramps and baby! what a chump! You're not well! Don't tell me you're leaving granny behind?"

I keep my cool. I'm not going to start bickering. We've all got to emigrate together. That was our agreement, end of story... Swear/cross our hearts/a deal. Sosthène stood behind me one hundred percent. It suited him just great for us to beat it the hell out of here as far away as we could go.

He wasn't anxious to see the Colonel again... nor the workshop... nor the masks... It was just he wasn't for slinking off like a pair of crooks. He wanted us to stop by Scotland Yard... polite and proper to the last... He wanted us to report to the summons. A real sucker's idea. I make no secret of what I think, the suggestion's outrageous. While I raked him over the coals, he acted dumb as a bunny, kept blinking his eyes.

"You've got a screwy way of looking at things, sweetie!"

Fact is his eyes were all gummed up... The daylight hurt him, that's for sure... He wanted to eat more tripe, another helping, a plate with cabbage...

The whole trip long, Virginia was the one having the best time. She had almost started to look herself again, laughing hard over the way we kept getting our signals crossed.

"Ferdinand is awfully darling! He wants a boat for a penny!"

I wanted a boat for a penny! a golliwog crew! that's what sense she'd made out of this rigmarole!

Rrrrreeee! Right that second! Sirens on the docks! A break! Three-thirty! Come and get it! Ten twelve twenty more sirens ripping across both banks... screaming! Come and get it! Here they are in a flash! the mob! charging! chugging... youngsters out in front... oldsters grousing... hobbling... hacking... spitting... a mad rush... Chinamen first... Then Malaysians... passing through the door, piling in seats... British dockworkers in bowler hats... nonchalant sorts... blackened with coal dust... hairy torsos... tattooed hulks up from the mines, spitting in the open wind... First come first served... the huge stew pot! Three men shouldering it in on poles, hoist it onto the counter. Pieces from the bottom all rich succulent! Dig around! In no time, the huge joint is slurping gurgling from wall to wall, men sloshing back soup, choking with hunger. The young bucks holler out for more... The geezers grumble through their coughs, surly, spitting out curses...

"Damned Prospero! Rascal! Dog! Man-eater! Thief!"

He didn't want to bring on the chow. All for a penny, complete with tea and every comfort. It didn't take much. The slightest little thing lit their fuses, not just their ferocious appetites, who gets seconds first, but any reason at all, you name it. The least little ray of sunshine, the least little patch of blue was like the end of the world, firing their thoughts with visions of crime. Since normally they never got a good look at each other deep down in their fogs of coal dust, all of a sudden each man could see his buddy's face... in the raw daylight... and saw a hideous, ugly mug... the sight made them yell square in each other's noses.

"Oh yeah! Look at your face! Christ! what a mess you got!"

They found each other incredibly gross and grungy. They couldn't stand each other in the sunlight... After two seconds, fists flew, blood spilled...

"Man-eater! Man-eater! Cash! the check! Greedy!" The whistle exploding from every direction! Sirens! Back to work! Everybody down in the holds! Mad hustle! Charging back! Rally to the winches! Boom! Bottleneck at the door! The mob gives way, oozes out, mashed between the flaps! the hard-luck cases, the oldest old-timers collapse... roll around, lie at the bottom of the ballast tank... snaking across the floor... puking up their grub... can't get away with that in the ranks! The boatswain has his eye on you... and to the last straggler:

"Shilling! Out! Move it! Lard-ass! Off the rosters!"

Wasn't fun and games as careers go. Sosthène had his own opinion.

"I could never endure it! I couldn't be a docker! I couldn't get shoved around!"

But then if you think for a second about the cops the other day, they treated him a whole lot worse. He's just putting on airs.

Prospero pops back in from the kitchen.

"Tho then, everything OK?"

"How much?"

"One and thix!"

He points to the waiter: "For him!"

From us he doesn't accept a penny. He sits down, we have a chat. The waiter leaves. The joint's deserted. Right away I bring up the Dingby again, talk about the buildup to the big Ka-Boom! that unforgettable night! of the fire! How had it exploded? I recalled the details. Boro hadn't messed around! Just tossed it in, wham! How we'd all hotfooted it out of there! Ah! what a fast getaway! and Carmen, the old gal! the way she howled! the knife in her ass! Prospero had a laugh, or rather he forced one out. Didn't dig my joke.

"So it didn't work out well?"

I meant the insurance.

"Did too! Did too! Just shut your face!..."

I was being an ass on purpose... wouldn't give up... the whole rigmarole... the buildup... the mad dash into the streets... Ah! he didn't think I was funny!... Come on, laugh hard! ah! he'll open up a little, the stinking louse!... Where'd the men hole up? More questions... Jim Tickett the bookie?... who got injured if I recall... and Gorgeous Jérôme, Mr. Accordion?... and Slim Cossack? where'd they all fly to? "Ah! those odd birds, my old boy! Ah! galloping gunpowder! they wouldn't run any faster over there with three hundred thousand krauts on their asses! take it from me! the truth! the war, Prospero! the war!"

I was lording it over him. I wanted to push him over the edge. He'd refused to give me any hot leads, now I'd make him sweat his guts out. Sosthène opened his trap. He didn't have a clue. And here I'd already filled him in about the Dingby business, the explosion, the bomb... over and over again!... But he didn't believe a single word I said. He took me for a bullshit artist!... Now he stood there with his jaw on the floor because it was an absolute fact. If he'd known Claben, Delphine, the magical cigarettes, the catastrophe in his shop, well then, he would have felt like a real jerk, he would have gotten some small idea of what a real-live hex is all about, a real scary whammy, a genuine out-of-this-world event! nothing to do with Goâ grimaces, his Hindubious Brahmin shimmytwist. We weren't all that far from Greenwich, about a mile or so down the river. I say "river" in English! the way other Frenchmen throw around their English *yous*!... It's classier... I say "you" to you... It all ends in flames anyway, "tu," "vous," "you," one day or another, it ends in ash or air, for you and "thee," for he and we... when the evil whammy sweeps us all off, down the hatch, into the drink, into the fire... That's the way the script was written, no getting away from it!

I explained this all to Prospero. Sosthène lent an ear too. I told them both about the way magic works. A big boom!... blowup! And everything goes flying! That's all that matters! the slightest excuse! Ba-boom!... Everything explodes! Lightning! the skies are loaded with it! Black magic is at work! I'd seen Prospero explode! I'd seen Claben explode! And there was more on the way! There'd be others! Still in full swing! Flanders was exploding like crazy! and a zillion skillion times harder! So that's the whole story! Prospero's joint, the Dingby, blew sky high with the counter, all four walls! because of a small little grenade, an egg! the entire dump had been totaled...

"Ah! geez, talk about funny! Don't tell me you didn't buy a new Pleyel?"

I didn't see any piano.

"Have you seen Borokom again?"

"Oh! I'm not looking for that guy!"

It was his business after all... It was his joint Boro had totaled.

In short, he clammed up.

"Well!" I wrap up... "Shall we be on our way? You are going to let us leave?"

"As you like..."

Yet he was in the know... At least two men from the Leicester had shipped out thanks to him... stowaways... Before he joined up Victor had vouched for it himself... on a Greek freighter... Greek freighters were his special line... sailboats too... La Plata... depending on the season... But for us it was no-go... he was dead set against! He even arranged leave-now-pay-later deals to America, I had the word, he advanced the thirty-five pounds, and you refunded him the sum once you got on your feet, plus his piece of the action, 150 guineas... Never got stiffed even once, he was always paid back pronto... Meaning that he knew how to pick his people. But we didn't interest him. A personal mental block, that's all. We rubbed him the wrong way...

"So you really don't know of anything?"

I took another shot, I wanted him to clue me in, was it yes or no, damn it! let's get this over with...
"For all three of you, you mean?"
"Of course!"
"Right off the street, with no dough? No passport? You're crazy, Ferdy!"
"Looks to me you got the jitters!"
"You cracked?"
He points to my head...
"Don't you have any idea? not even the tiniest little hint?"
"Drop it!... Just drop it!... You're a big baby, that's what this is all about! You're scared of the police!"
Ah! the police...
"Me, scared of the police?"
What a cheap shot!
"You little lamebrain! Show-off! War hero my balls! Zatz wight! Zatz wight!"
He was starting to lisp... he was losing it...
"Nyah! Nyah! Nyah!..."
"You won't make it past Tilbury! not even Tilbury! Take zat from me! They scour everywhere! Zatz wight! everywhere! the hold! the upper deck! dinghies! you won't ethcape! the compath! the shitholthz! Get me? They even check out the rats!"
I was keen on the idea anyway. I couldn't care less about his excuses.
"We've got to leave, I'm telling you! We've got to! You've got to give us a name!..."
"Ah! Forget it! Eeeyouu! Eeeyouu clown!"
He looks at the clock.
"Jesus Christ! Jesus Christ! the patrol! Five o'clock! the patrol!"
He snaps to... A distraction.
"Don't eeeyouuu know I've got to *fermer*! Go on, everybody, get the hell out of here!"
"Ah! hey now, you call this polite! Now you're insulting young ladies! Some manners!"
"Shit! Shit! Shit!" he replies. Hopped up, at the boiling point!
"Tough," I go...
We sit back down.
But Virginia was motioning to me. She didn't like arguments. Sosthène didn't know how to act... I sat riveted to the spot... I took it all calmly.
"We're not leaving! tra-la-la! we're not leaving... You're going to tell us where to find that pretty boat! Ho ho! Where your fine friends are loading their ship! me! me! me!"
Just like that, dumb as they come! Thick as a brick!
"Shit! That's my answer! Shit! Eeeyouuu get me, snot-nose! bum! bed-

wetter..."

"We're still not going anywhere! Not! Not! Not!"

I bounce up and down on my butt, having a blast, bumping the bench, I won't budge!... I pat myself on the back! Nyah! Nyah! I go...

"Your patrol won't eat us!"

He saw I meant business.

He sizes up the situation. Looks at us, then at the waterway out past the windowpanes... flowing along... the broad Thames... he looks at each of us in turn... distrustful... wondering whether he'll be first to blink. He looks at the floor!... and then at my fists... he's a squeaky customer, I'm on guard.

My hands go to my pockets... feeling around... I act like I'm fishing for something... a charade...

"Watch out for the bomb!" I shout...

Horsing around!

He jumps back... he's nuts!

"Fer... Fer... Ferdinand!" he stammers...

Eyes as big as saucers... frozen to the spot... choking on his words... I open my fists for him... empty...

"In your seat, sucker..."

Everybody laughs. I set his mind at rest... He makes an effort...

"Get the hell out!..."

He sits down, his legs turned to putty! Such a fit! the idiot! Shit-scared real bad! Over nothing!

"OK, OK!" I go, "we'll clear out! just tell us which ship... and we'll beat it!..."

I'm being a sport about it.

If he says nothing I'll start up again, concoct some new trick, I'll turn his life into a living hell!...

"Knock off the mule act! the name of a ship! You know plenty, damn it! So out with it!"

He hems and haws! He nods!

"Come on! Open up! Don't play with yourself!... Talk! it's five o'clock!"

"Out! Out! You bastards!"

He's throwing us out the door again.

"No! No! Prospero! Don't be mean! I'll throw a real bomb! It doesn't do you any good!"

I pretend to search myself again.

He's beside himself.

"Out! Out!"

"Slip us a name! And we'll disappear!... we'll never set eyes on you again! So there, a deal?"

He splutters... sniffles... doesn't know what to do...

"But you don't have a red cent! Where you going?"

"America!"

"Just like that?"

"You said it!"

Nothing's stopping us.

"Didn't Jujube leave just like that? And Lulu Puce? And Villemombe? So don't go saying it's impossible! Monsieur Prospero! You're completely in the know! It's just that you don't want to cough up! Signor Prospero! You're holding out on us!"

I work him over like Matthew, I give him the third degree. He's all confused. He gets up... plops back down... splutters some crap... clams up... suddenly snaps to! frantic! Then he cuts the cheese... an enormous fart... reverberating... echoing... he just sits there like a dumb jerk... out of it... on the bench... staring at all of us... hard...

I'm embarrassed in front of Virginia... the filthy pig...

Sosthène busts out laughing. Weird reaction!

I'll make this stinking bastard talk!

He hunches on the bench, riveted to the spot. Hardheaded.

"Beat it!" he grumbles... "Beat it! Shit!"

"Nobody's beating it! Start talking!"

I stay put.

He fidgets in place, wriggling his ass over toward the counter. I won't have any of that.

"Keep still, Prospero!"

A fraction of an inch! I whack him across the face with the siphon.

Good! He got the message.

"Well?"

"Well, OK, here it is then! You asked for it! Don't come crying to me later!"

In a sweat, he makes up his mind.

"No, nobody's crying here... we're all ears!"

"OK, Jovil's your man... Cannon Dock... Tell him I sent you... Cannon Dock..."

"Sure about that? For certain? Jovil? Cannon?"

I didn't want any snags!

"Don't worry... You're coming from Prospero's... At customs keep your lips buttoned... play it safe... Maybe he's still taking people on..."

"Where to?"

"La Plata!"

"Hot damn!"

"Like that, all three of you?"

"Let's have a look!"

I wanted him to show us where to go through the window... so we could find it outside.

"The masts sticking out! oh! what a pain in the ass!"
I was giving him a rough time.
"Out there on the Millwall... the masts..."
It was Cannon Dock...
"Sticking out..."
I had twenty-twenty!
"Ask for Jovil! Prospero! He'll know right off."
"So, anyway, tell me, is it some sailboat?"
"You expecting the *Lusitania* or something?"
"What'll we do on board?"
"Play cards!"
I wanted details.
"What's the name of this boat of yours?"
"*Kong Hamsün*!..."
"Skipper Jovil... *Kong Hamsün*..."
I repeated the info myself.
"Hey, what if we get thrown out?"
"You'll see!"
"No, you're the one who'll see—us again, duckie!"
I didn't let up.
"Ah! you're a pain in the ass!"
I was disgusting him.
"OK! OK! Don't get miffed! We'll race over!"
I make the girl walk ahead of us... I slip out on the qt, shuffling sidelong. Then slam the door, we're outside.
"Hop to it! Cannon Dock!"
First, we've got to find the ferry, the one that crosses the locks... we run smack into it! Chug! Chug! Chug!... Heading to the other shore! We hit the ground running... five minutes straight... like mad!...
Virginia's a little short of breath... Sosthène's having a hard time because of his workout the other day!... Cursing everything... scuttling like a crab... his ass sideways... his bumps, black-and-blue bruises, scabs all over his body... the horrible Piccadilly shellacking! He's bitching... moaning!...
"Go back!" I yell... "Go take a rest!..."
"There they are, son! Hey! There they are!..."
It's true! I hadn't seen them!... We're standing underneath!
Ah! You bet! Ah! such superduper vessels! What stems! What sides! What magic! Ah! the wonderful ships! Lined up down the dock two, three, four, sitting pretty, gigantic, stem to stern!
They take up almost the whole expanse of water, all Cannon Dock, from jib to prow, towering hulks, with soaring yards, from sky to stern, from one side to the other, trembling silhouettes in the mirror of the basin, immense branches, jutting bowsprits, topsails of adventure, grazing the rooftops,

looming high above the warehouses.

We walk down along the dock, wind our way from one mooring to the next...

Under the shadow of a prow, everything grovels, burrows down in its ugliness, withers, nothing stands in comparison, it shrivels, water rat, man-rat, nothing competes, amazed sorry-looking, peters out, disappears, little rat.

The magnificently soaring stems! Mercy on us!

We roamed around a little more, touching the ropes, the anchors, a giant's earrings, charm bracelets, colossal stoppers, lacework of algae, green, blue, red, at the end of the chain, finery of the deep, gods of terror, wigs.

We went over to read the names, in gold yellow and red on the shields... The *Draggar*, the *Norodosky*... Ah! the *Kong Hamsün*!... Ah! Immediately I'm all admiration! I'm thrilled! What a piece of work! I touch it! The vastness, the power of the huge side! Rough! Brown! Wood and salt! Sea spray foams! The side rises... higher... higher still... exhilarating! Let's dash to the prow! What defiant bravado! The prow! What majesty! Carved design! The enormous bearded guy in his crown towered over the stem! In a breastplate! the works! Sword in fist! He orders, commands! the waves! It's him! King Hamsün! Curly haired! Ringlets! beard! green eyes! all freshly painted! A magnificent ship poised to glide across the sea! Cast off! cast off! Not yet? What a throng! What toil! The bridges mobbed! On every level! climbing, plummeting! a hundred... a thousand sweaty shipmates... Zooming around, whipping all over the place... A flood of dockers... spilling over the gangways between cabins... lugging barrels and casks! cotton, huge enormous bobbins, three, six at a time... jam-packing their holds... whiskey brandy for the tropics... wire for down under... I nab a crotchety geezer sitting on a stone post... He gives me a foggy look... I shake him...

"Jovil? Skipper Jovil?..."

"Jovil!" he goes to me. "There!" Pointing. Then he spits. The guardrail above us... the man standing there leaning over... in the cap... beet red face... the hollering hole... that's him! He points him out again! That's him all right! He's yelling, screaming his head off at that very moment... at the crane... wants it to start up... get "unhunged"... That's Jovil the skipper, all right, that raving madman!

"There! There!" the old man keeps insisting! That's him!

The roaring skipper booms so loudly that his voice echoes way back in the warehouses... and the whole wharf reverberates, all Cannon Dock is set quaking! The way he howls to his men... He's a raging beast! Insults for all around! Great Satan! What on earth! Whorehouse! Christ in heaven! dogs!... all hell's breaking loose something horrible!

And yet the whole area round about is hopping with activity, no slacking off on the job, swiveling, hoisting in the bulwarks, from every line, stuff pouring down in every direction, sweating and slaving from upper deck to stern, oh heave that bail! this way! Turn around! There! Torrents of curses sweeping down into the holds! The small trucks at dock level jam-crushed! racing like mad! Metal crunch! Smashup! More laborers gathering, pouring out of every crevice, yellow, black, pale as ghosts, in frock coats, stark naked, without a stitch, hunting for jobs, under umbrellas, straw hats, start today, for one and six an hour, a real working over, up and down the ship! whoever hangs toughest wins! from every side street, Prospero's customers turning up for work.

The saddest thing in the world is all the lines holding down the ship at both ends—huge as it is, paunch bulging, it's still light as air and would soar off, a bird, despite the heavy-duty cargo in its wooden belly, crammed to bursting, the wind singing in the topmasts would whisk it away by its boughs, even just as is, in dry dock, without sails, it'd be off if the men weren't hell-bent on holding it down with a hundred thousand lines, pulling hard till they're red in the face, it'd pull away from the docks, bare as a bone, and take to the heights, sail off sailing through the clouds, rising to the very top of the sky, a harp come alive in the oceans of azure, that's the way it'd set sail, the spirit of travel, absolutely indecent, just shut your eyes and you'd be swept off for a long time, off into the vast open space of a magical life free of care, a passenger of the world's dreams!

It's the lines, the cables binding, holding the ship down all over, that's what's fouling up all the traffic on the dock, tripping everybody up, makes them fall flat on their faces, and Skipper Jovil hollering his lungs out. They wait till the very last second to cast off, the ship tests the wind, sails away smoothly... If this isn't a miracle, what is?

Ah! I'm happy only when I'm around ships, it's in my blood, and I ask for nothing more.

I was bellowing all this over at Sosthène, giving the skipper a run for his money. I wanted Sosthène to share my enthusiasm. At moments when I least expect it, these fits of enthusiasm sweep over me, I listen to myself in surprise shooting my mouth off. I was forgetting the reason we'd come... namely, to skip the country...

It goes right to your head, you can't resist it, the smell for starters, the smell of hemp and caulking.

"Come on now, call him!"

He shook me. My eyes had gone blurry under the influence of the spell, the place, the situation... embarking for Fantasy Land! I couldn't bring myself back down to earth, use the fraction of common sense at my disposal. I just stood there goo-goo eyed against the hull, I really felt like kissing the planking, the whole big reeking scuttle, its coal tar, its halyard, its creaking pulleys, you name it, its colossal cauldron on the coals, I'd have gulped down the whole concoction, the rat stew and the dancing babble, the lapping current, farandoling around the hull, steady rush of ripples from every corner of the dock, heading toward its big rough belly, I'd have drunk that down too! Oh! such huge love! I was absolutely crazy about its whistling song, breezes seized in the upper strings, more and more fragile, rigging needles, lace, from topsail yard to topsail yard, boldly gusting, from azure to azure!...

It's all too much! Your soul veers up and away...

But Sosthène snaps me back to reality.

"Yoo-hoo! Go ahead!"

He yanks me out of the spell.

I bawl in turn: "Jovil! Skipper Jovil!"

I call over to him: "Is it you, man?"

"Yeah, my dear! Yeah! wah! wah!"

He burped out his answer.

He leans over the planking, thrusts his body down so far his mug's sticking right in our faces.

"Yeah?"

He's got just three teeth left in his kisser.

He cranes down a little more to get a better gander at us... stretches out his ostrich neck...

"Jovil? Jovil?" I repeat.

"Yeah! Yeah!"

Rich vocabulary. Another guy pokes up over the planking, another red mug right above us... But this one keeps his trap shut... Our man's running the show... Now they're both spitting... all around us... humongous gobs... I step back... they go into fits over the way I dodge the spray. They jabber in gobbledygook, their speech starting down in their throats, gurgling up in small hiccups, singsonging, then running out their noses. It's Swedish, according to Sosthène, from time to time they talk in bubbles, it's the fish side of language... it's like English, but not so bouncy, so frisky, more quack than chirp...

Roar! Roar! two blasts! they burp together... Two minds at work...

"What do you want?" he finally asks.

I motion that we want to come aboard... to sail away, all three of us... One! Two! Three!

That tickles his funny bone, he's hysterical again, and everybody around him, the whole crew. They're hardy-har-haring so hard their backslaps could kill a bull.

"Come on!"

I'm a laugh a minute for them! I stumble, slog away, what an obstacle course! Just approaching the ladder is a hectic whirl, a grueling feat. I nearly topple fifteen-twenty times under the torrents of girders, hovering and waltzing everywhere you look, teetering, bousing, hallucinating, a raft's beams! jutting bowsprits, huge hammocks of stuff, crates floating through the air, prodigious playthings, a flying bazaar, grand pianos for the tropics, the whole shebang screeching, veering down into the storerooms, pitching, plummeting, crashbanging into the holds. Boom! I worm my way amid the insults. I reach Jovil.

I'm standing right in front of him, he totally ignores me. He climbs on top of a barrel, from which vantage he towers over the scene. He thunders orders, roars into the masts, the capstans, his voice echoing through the clouds, raging at the sailors heave-hoing, tautening coils, dangling from lines, whisking through empty air, on pulleys, grazing past, snatching in midflight, yaw sail! Brailing up sail in the sunshine!

"Down halyard... And one!... And two... Halyard down!..."

The sail goes limp! snaps! flagwaves! The wind kicks in! A work gang ten-twelve strong fastens the yard, pulls down hard, sweating like horses as they explode in one titanic uuh! the large royal sail gives way, pivots on one wing... hauls on! the other! Collapses! Relieved! crumples in a heap on the bridge, oozes flat... an enormous pancake!... The men grumble charge something horrible... a ferocious racket... the whole crew pounces on top... belly-flopping, rolling around, squeezing out the last drop at the command: "Kiop! Kiop! Kiop! Kiop!" Jovil up on his barrel keeping time, "Kiop! Kiop!" Thirty-five strong hell-bent on twisting up the tough fabric... on wrestling under control the gigantic folds, kneading, coiling...

"Heave ho! Heave ho!" a furious effort! They all yell at every "Kiop! Kiop!" to make it shrink, wrap tighter than before... roll itself into a monster cigarette... just like that dazzling on the bridge... white... Ah! got it!... Ah! solid job! Jovil's proud as hell! He locks his hands over his head like a winning champ!

"Come on!" he calls me... "Come on!... What you want?"

What do I want?

His mind's back on me.

"To go to La Plata!"

I snap at the opportunity. Lay my cards right on the table. I'd like to set sail pronto, Sosthène, Virginia and me. Not a minute to waste. I want to spell it out to him up real close. I stand on tiptoe. He bends down, does his best. I want to whisper in his ear. We have some trouble catching each other's drift because of the din all around, plus the broken English we're jabbering, especially him, take it from me, I'm not just trying to blow my own horn... he's impossible to understand, every word's a hiccup, he snorts, spit-gobs, starts over from the top... We're going nowhere fast... He pulls his pipe out of his mouth.

Up real close like this, my nose in his mug, he's a whole lot more gruesome-looking, missing all his upper teeth, which is what makes him splutter so badly. Two scars on his left cheek, crosswise, and one hell of a cross it is. His dangling sleeve is a wooden arm that ends in a metal hook. I show him my hand too, the way it dangles lifelessly, we've both gotten our share of knocks. In his case it wasn't the war, but a yard, he explains, acting out the accident, how it crushed his arm just above his elbow. This detail brings us closer. We can really open up to each other. He lets me understand how strong he is with his hook... how he can lift anything he wants... how I ought to get one put on... just like his... it'd do me more good than a flabby arm... which I really ought to get chopped off... it'd make my life a whole lot easier... To drive home the point he leans over, hooks... a cannonball that weighs a good 220 pounds... just whisks it up whoosh! light as a feather! It knocks my socks off! What a Hercules! We trade compliments... I marvel. I congratulate him... But I'd like him to drop me a wee hint about my scheme... like whether he'll take us on as extra hands?

"Prospero!" I whisper... "Prospero!"

My tipster... I point toward the canteen out there... on the other side of the river...

"Prospero says we can... go... with you!... America!"

I made motions, far! far! farther still! forever! Oh! geez! just takes those few words to send him back into hysterics. This works Sosthène up... "Voyage! Voyage!" He gesticulates, wants to help me... he shouts in his falsetto...

"Ocean cruise!... Long course!..."

And then the ship out at sea... the sound of the waves... swoosh! swoosh!... he does an imitation... he rolls... pitches... paints a picture of the voyage for Jovil... clues him in on what we're after... "Voyash!... Voyash!..." He caught on! Old beet-face! Red cap!... It fires up the pair of them! "Voyash! Voyash!" They're hee-hawing like jackasses... Why?... Plain morons. They show me the hold down below... running crosswise to the bridge... a vast gaping hole... an enormous pit... "Voyash!... Voyash!..." They're whacking each other's sides laughing so hard, everybody's just so damn funny! Right then a billow of flour explodes from the dark depths... a hurricane!... A group achoo!...

"Voyash! Voyash!" The animals bark, chuckle, stomp up a storm. A hardee-har-har jig. Jovil's in hysterics more than anybody... His fit of laughter spills over into song, mouth wide open... wide... our "Voyash" craze! What clowns we are, real comedians.

"There! There!..." He shows us again... the hold down so deep. He does a little jig up on his barrel, he's laughing so uncontrollably. He tap-dances through his moans... in real pain... one more second he'll burst... He calls everybody over to see us! Featherbrains, unbelievable creatures! It's too much for one man! He booms out to all quarters, from the top of the masts to the bottom of the holds! Everybody back on deck! Hustle over on the double! The crew trundles along, drags their feet, grumbles and groans, and then the rush is on... from cables, from gangways, a steady stream, caulkers, gofers, cabin boys, coolies...

From the rigging, the wind sails, they come dropping, tumbling down, a mob at the loudmouth's feet... the deafening din breaks off, all the slamming and banging, the storm deep down in the hull... war hammers... You couldn't hear yourself think...

They keep piling in, blacks, slopes, hairy things, hanging from every spar, dangling in bunches from the foresails, monkeys. From the dock in waves... heave ho! A gurgling ooze! men floating along, clinging to rafts, hoisting themselves up on the bridge, the repair caulkers... gripping the planks, crawling up close for a laugh, flocking around that big fat bastard... up there on his barrel jabbering, treating us like total assholes! When he does his ludicrous rendition of us begging, everybody shits themselves... nearly pass out... staggering into each other they're guffawing so hard... It's too funny! Too witty!... At this point the scrawny carrot-top stumbles into us... wobbly on his feet... reeling... choking on his laughter... holding his sides... slips... overboard! the drink sweeps him away! the screwy rotten jerk-off! swings level to a cask... Whack!... his face in smithereens... bleeding everywhere... a sheet of red spreading... Ah! all just too hilarious! I've got to laugh too... the stinking bum's still at it... another round of gags... About how we want to go to America, fearless globe-trotters that we are! and brave the sea and waves for two shillings fifty! He points out to them how shrewd we are... They hee-haw, bop up and down on their butts they're so crazy in stitches. Ah! they're having a ball at our expense. They shout over to me, meowing... barking... how about going down into the hold with the darling?... mimicking... Meanwhile Jovil's still a ball of fire up there on his barrel, a real hit, gesticulating, throwing out his arms, whirling his hook stump right above our heads. I think that he wants to see all three of us hang... that they're sick and tired of looking at us... Bam! he stops dead. He starts humming... awaiting the verdict. The jury is the mob of sailors around us... squatting on their heels... the crew who'll give thumbs up or down... they grumble, roll, reel on their asses... Deadlocked. I catch on that what they're deciding is not whether to hang us, but to take us on or not... They spit, bitch, can't be bothered...

The big ape gets pissed off, jumps down from the barrel, climbs back up, calls them every horrible name in the book! He nabs me with his fist, drags me off, wants to have a one-on-one.

We go all the way to the back, dash behind the helm into this little hut.

Once he's inside there's room for nothing else... his huge body packs the place full. He shuts the door after us. I'm squished up against the wall... He barks right into my face.

"Money? Money? How much?"

He really wants to know just exactly how much I got on me. I don't want to lie.

"No money!"

But I've got my resources, plenty to fall back on, have to keep that in mind.

"Prospero! Prospero! Money!"

That's the honest truth. He promised.

He shakes his head. He doesn't believe me.

"Papers? Papers? You got papers?"

Ah! papers! Sure we got them! of every kind and country! little ones, big ones, and not just the ones we'll need!... Always the same!... Real passports, real visas... They don't fool around at emigration... Those cops are the pickiest SOBs... real sticklers over IDs! especially us with the little girl... My little Virginia, so young... pure stowaway stuff... Ah! such a tall order!

"Papers! Papers!... Ah!"

I chatted him up a little... tried to clue him in on the delicacy of the situation... said we'd be getting hitched as soon as possible... first thing after we landed... it was thumbs up all decided... I want to warm his heart...

"Yop! Yop! Yop!" he brushes me off. "No females! Body! No females on board!..." He's blunt, the filthy slob! His refusal stabs me like a knife... I'm not going to leave my Virginia! Ah! no way in hell! He gets a kick out of my distress!

Glug! Glug! he goes right in front of my face... a loud noise against the roof of his mouth... an enormous gurgle... just like that, the fish... doesn't give a damn about anybody...

Glug! Glug!

That means I ought to laugh, too. Don't feel like...

"No passport?" He doubles up, howls, haws. "Passport!... Glug! Glug!..."

He ogles me up real close... practically touches me with his fat kisser. He rolls his eyes. He thinks I'm some off-the-wall kook with this family trip of mine.

"No? No? No money? Impossible!"

"Why impossible?"

I press hard, damn it!

"Women, no! Old fogey, no!..."

Real cruel terms. Glug! Glug! That's what I think.

But as for me alone, well now, he's all for that!

"You!..." He accepts me. He signs me on!

"With other guys! Come on! Crew! Crew!"

I see what he means. I've got all the luck. He taps out a bouncy number up on his little table... whistling... thrilled... absolutely delighted... but he bangs his head against the deadlight... the little room rattles, the ceiling's too low for him... he arches over, keeps up his jig anyway... Clip clop bam!... I can see he's signing me on cheerfully. He's glad, I belong to him... he can see me even now up in the masts... busy striking the foresails... a headcase recruit!... Better than nothing... anything is... I'm hired. But no Virginia! no Sosthène! Ah! no ifs ands or buts about that! Ah! I still felt sore at him. I show him my arm again, up real close right under his nose, scars and all, so that he won't get any wrong ideas, a limp gimp, a stump worse than his own, with no hook, a totally bum flipper.

Never mind! Never mind! No problem! I should just come! by myself, mind you! He took me as I was. In La Plata, in South America, he'd get me fitted out with a hook. He swore, a done deal! He promised me clear sailing.

"The war!" he bellowed! "The war!" while fingering my scar! Just like that standing there against each other! "The war! Glug! Glug!"

He hurt me something excruciating. Jammed in the way I was, I couldn't get away. I howled even louder than he did. His fun kept growing. He worked me over passionately. I screamed bloody murder. He stamped his feet, a little lunatic at the sight of me writhing in agony. I was about to sink my teeth in his jowls, the hell with his strength! He wants to razzle-dazzle me again. Plop! He throws me to the foot of the small table... Pling! He nabs me by my undershorts! Plunk! he hoists me pop! up by my joined feet, in a flash!... I'm astounded! I congratulate him! I go into raptures! I kiss him...

"Everything OK?" I ask... "Everything fine?"

I want to wrap this up. We'd been hashing it out in his tiny storeroom for an eternity. Back outside they must really have been wondering what we were kicking around. I could see real clearly that he was thinking hard. He burped right in my face.

He's still turning it over.

"Aren't you a cook?" The idea pops into his head. "All Frenchmen are cooks!"

A brilliant stroke.

"Oh! yes! Oh! yes!" I reply...

What do I have to lose?

"Good! Ah! Good! Fine!"

He whacks me on my back so hard he practically knocks my limbs loose. We weren't exactly talking gourmet ship's fare here, I'd manage just fine. Ah! the perfect solution to my problems.

"Voyash! Voyash!" he repeats...

"You said it, Henri! I adore you!"

"Yup! Yup! Certainly!" Three cheers for me! Whatever it takes to speed up the deal... We'd be sitting pretty! I'd turn into a mouse on the *Hamsün*!... It was our one chance in a thousand! Once I'd transshipped, I'd deal with America just fine... Just let me at those new chances and resources! Here it wasn't worth the trouble! There was too much nasty business brewing... never knew what was around the next corner... We had to get the hell out... End of story, period. Hoist sails! You can say that again! An absolutely perfect opportunity! Ah! I wasn't about to drag my feet!

"All right, let's go! Goddamn! Sherry! Oh, Frenchy!"

"I'll be there! Skip! I'll be there!"

A promise! a deal! We shake on it! One hell of a sailor! I'll be there at 8:15! That's when we set sail! Cross my heart! On the dot o'clock and all that jazz! Hurray! A new life! Now that's not all! Mademoiselle, the geezer, disappear! To hell with those drags! Forget about them! Screw the old man! Screw the little girl! They can go fuck each other! A new life! A clean break! Piss and vinegar! all settled!

I'm embarking by myself! Signed on, fuck it all! A free man! Let's shoot the works! No backing out! They brought me bad luck! To hell with that dead weight! I understand my destiny! So long! I'm not a victim of my good heart anymore!... Long live the future!... Freewheeling youth! Good-bye! I'm out of here! See you tonight!

I was ready to dash off... He nabbed me. Ready to charge off and buy a shirt. He holds me back by my stump... He shows me the gang gathered around, squatting there, the entire crew, all the dockers in a circle around the barrel waiting for word... More mugs sticking up from the hold, out from the gangways... acrobats in the masts... everybody awaiting the decision...

Then he booms into the heights, so that everybody on board can hear the news.

"Froggy on his way! Froggy on the list! Ooh! Ooh!"

Hurrahs, monster cheers from the depths to the mast tips, an explosion so fierce that the old tub shudders the water far and wide, sends waves sweeping across the whole dock, rippling all the way to the river.

"Froggy on the list!"

They're slayed with hysterics, think I'm such a stitch, from the poles high in the sky down to the water's surface, two topple over into the drink, convulsed with laughter. Never in their lives did they ever see a funnier bird than me on the list! From black to yellow, brown to green, they're all trying to outroar each other with their guffawing. The whole crew razzing me! Doesn't really get under my skin. Could be a hell of a lot worse, as situations go. They even flash me smiles sort of. Maybe they think that'll embarrass me... Ah! You've got another thing coming! Ah! Suckers! Ah! Go ahead and laugh! Ah! I'm in a laughing mood myself! He who laughs last laughs loudest! Keep those faces smiling! Smiling! Boneheads! Dumb idiots! You haven't seen anything! Miserable storm-tossed galley slaves! I'll feed your faces, chow down my cooking! I'm sure you'll just love it! I have visions of special treats, rats in shallot sauce! Rat croquettes! Just wait and see, my hardies! I've got great stuff! That's what was going on behind my eyes, that's what those fatheads were doing to me! I'll get my turn! Booaahh! I bellow back... damn them!... aping right back into their mugs. "Goons! Froggy tells you all to fuck off! Every last one!" That was no bull. Don't worry! I'll get my own back tonight! A promise was a promise. Goddamn smart-ass bastards! If you want fireworks, I'm your man! Laying into each other, you stinking oafs... The Skip and his roughnecks can all go and get stuffed!

That's what was running through my mind!... So they thought I was so wet behind the ears, well, they'd have a nice little surprise in store for them! They weren't the first tattooed gang I'd run into in my life! I'd been around the block, and more than once! Ah! it was really getting my dander up! I could barely see straight for a second! Oh! geez! the hooligans! I'd like to see them under barrage fire! Who'd be shit-scared then? Booah! Booah! I bellow back once more! Be seeing you! Fuckups! They don't have what it takes to pull anything over on me! Chickenshit toughies! I'd have liked to see them try! I'd be going, you bet! America, here I come! La Plata tooty-too! Yeah! I'd leave my crummy luck right here behind! This isn't some little school kid's dare-ya!...

"I'll shock you into shape!" I shot back at them! "I'll make you pirouette through the air, that's the kind of wallop my cooking'll pack!" Primo chili pepper! I show them the hot hard-on!... "You'll jump right onto the moon! Your mouth'll sea gull you off and away! Bye-bye, swellheads!"

With that I clam up. The skipper is gurgling himself to death... He never saw me lose my temper before. It's the most hilarious thing in the world.

Tough-guy routines turn me off...

"See you tonight! Thugs! So long!"

Now, on to the hard part! The touchiest... ditching the kid and the old fart... coming up with the right cover story... solid reasons... my devotion... my great hopes... the chief reasons... first, I go on ahead as a sailor... then they follow after... later on down the line... later on...

They were waiting for me at the foot of the ladder. They were pacing back and forth... two hours long they'd been waiting... they'd had a real hard time with the sailors. Two of the cockiest drunks wanted to kiss Virginia... They had to make a run for it under a rain of jeers... Catcalls and curses poured down on them from every mast, plus humongous gobs of spit, green, yellow, huge loogies... In the end they escaped, huddled back in a warehouse. They were just coming out. Virginia totally shattered... my darling!... my tender heart... my lovely beauty!... The disgusting behavior of those monsters! She was becoming quite delicate, inevitably so in her condition, fragile and sensitive! I did my best to console her!

"Dear! They don't know! Drunken dogs!"

That was both true and not true. Men don't need to be boozed up in order to ravage heaven and earth. Carnage's in their blood! It's a miracle they're still going strong, given how long they've been trying to wipe each other off the face of the earth. Just got one thing on the brain—the Void! Nasty customers, born to crime! They see red wherever they look. Mustn't keep hammering away at this, it'd spell the end of all poetry.

This bias against us put Sosthène back in the dumps. The hatred of the crew, drowning us in their spit, without the slightest provocation.

"The bias of seafarers!" I explain right away. "They're prejudiced! And it'd mean nothing at all, pops! nothing! if they wanted to lay their hands on you out on the high seas! I mean, without a blink! they'd sack you right then and there!"

I just tell him straight out.

"Plus your age!"

"Ah! Plus my age!"

Damn! that dumbfounded him.

"Say, you know, there are some guys on there, gnarled wrecks who're three-four times older than me!"

He was positive.

"They don't want the girl either..."

"What about you?"

"I'm in... well, as an extra hand... in the galley."

"Right! You're taking off, no problem! You're ditching us!..."

That was the size of it.

The news sort of dampened his mood, and he'd already been pretty much in a funk.

"He's going away!" he says to the girl.

They both look at me... they don't believe their ears right away... they look at the ship sitting over there... the painters out there caulking away...

"He's going away..."

They're crestfallen. They'd never imagined...

"You're right... you're right... it's a fine ship... And so, miss, what are we going to do?"

That was the question.

Virginia was looking away... into the distance over toward the other side... the other bank... just like that a blank gaze... Without a peep... nothing negative... she turns back toward me... darling face free of anger... even with a sweet smile... I can still see her through the mauve mist... just standing there pale as a ghost, staring at us... the wind in her hair... whipping along in shifting gusts... smearing everything... the few rays of sunshine... the mist... the rain... the mauve smoke... she had a dab on the tip of her nose... her tiny impish nose... like a cat's... Ah! I can see it all again sharp as a picture... standing there on the dock... right against the ship... her smile... I'll see it again, I do believe, once I cross over to the other side... to the other shore at the end of it all... pure magic... she didn't utter a word against me... still ready to laugh off everything... but still and all, tired pale as a ghost... because of the state she was in, no getting around it...

I take charge.

"Come on, let's hit the road!"

My thoughts were on something hot to drink.

"That's what you both need! You can barely stand on your own two feet! Something to warm the cockles of the lady and gentleman! A grog! They've been conned!"

I take them by the arm, haul them off. Yours truly is hell on wheels! A ball of fire! I wanted to make them swallow the hard part... explain to them affectionately that if I was going to leave just like that all by myself, sail off to La Plata in America, it was because I was setting up our future, I'd have it nailed down in no time... and I'd send for them immediately... you see, absolutely ideal perfecto... and you had to admit my way was shrewder than all three of us landing like bums without a penny to our names... down-and-out emigrants... with three pounds fifty to our names!...

No response.

We were walking along arm in arm, through the blind alleys among the docks. They were pretty much against the idea... I could tell by their faces... they were real kind, enough to keep quiet about it, but underneath they felt upset. I wasn't giving them any consolation whatsoever... But it just made plain sense, because if we landed together like that all at once we wouldn't last long... it was absolutely crazy... they didn't argue back... Just kept saying "yes"... "yes"... but I could see by their faces... they were thinking "no"... "no"...

It was painful, how else could it be? Still and all, I wanted them to realize...

She wound up crying, what with me yakking away right and left... my poor sweet little girl... too cruel for her to cope with... especially under these circumstances... staying behind alone with her relative in the big house in Willesden... with the masks, the carrying-on, plus his special thing for riding crops... not to mention the other character, Sosthène, who had come onto the scene... who was on his magic kick... that whole mess, plus being knocked up to boot... You bet it was no joke! but still and all you had to react some way somehow...

"Come on! It's not the end of the world!"

I reacted.

But supposing things don't turn out so hot... and some surprise bad breaks come my way... supposing I flop... vanish without a trace... and nobody ever sees me again?... Just because you say "America" doesn't mean it's all going to work out! They were worrying me sick as hell with this little act of theirs, coming across like it was really all up to me to make up my own mind... So, sure, I was thinking hard.

We were looking for our way... the little back streets that would lead us out of the docks... It was a rat's nest... mazes... buildings tall as any cliffs... brick top to bottom, with clefts, fissures... We thread our way along... At the bottom it's all dark and gloomy... miles of zigzagging alleys... nothing but bricks, warehouses... all the west docks up to East Ham... Gives you something to chew over in your mind... As labyrinths go, this one is pretty awesome... I tried to get them to open up a little... They just kept saying "yes

yes," period. They agreed with my plan... not a word against me... not a single peep... Down in dead-end streets of this sort, walled in so tightly, so deep, the sunlight pokes through patches of mist... flickering between mauve and blue... a soft inviting glow... which has you singing the blues, no denying it... and you listen to your moans sadly... I myself could start singing the blues after all... I could be all heartsick... I had my mournful reasons... I just kept them to myself, that's all... I was discreet... but I could sing the blues... Plus my leg hurt... as much as the old fart's did... and I had a hell of a time chugging along... plus my head and ear were killing me like usual... I start to hobble so they'll notice... They don't notice a thing... selfish jerks... I say so out loud... I try to pry some kind of reaction out of them... We're walking around in circles from one street to the next... I say it again, louder this time... I deserve a pat on the back, when all's said and done, for going off like that all by my lonesome!

Zero response...

But the truth was the truth... some sailor out there bouncing around, my life hanging in the balance! on the raging seas!... A hero yet one more time! to be blunt about it... Ah! their sorry-looking mugs were driving me up the wall... I found the pair of them disgusting, ungrateful... they had no inkling about what sort of risks I was running... how I was sacrificing myself for everybody's sake... ready to go off and play the fool in the yards... me with my neuritis, my bum arm... my slowpoke peg... my spinning head... I was running huge risks... all out of courageous kindness... But since it wasn't worth the trouble... and nothing touched their hearts of stone... I'd lost my reason to exist... I might as well let myself be snatched away by a tornado... throw myself in the drink, that's all... be swept off by a storm...

"You'll be sorry!"

There, I said it.

They weren't particularly moved... They just kept walking along, pitiful as hell from one sidewalk to the next... goddamn it! they were really getting to be a pain in my ass!...

Plain and simple pigheads!...

They could drop dead for all I cared! Distinguished sulkers! They were getting on my nerves! I couldn't stand the sight of them anymore! Selfish jerks! they were bugging the hell out of me! Lying low, sitting pretty, lucky devils in short, they weren't running my big risks! They had it easy, just sit back and wait for me!... I'd be up there high-flying in the masts!... I'd be braving the hurricanes! It'd be me down there cooking through the storms! they would be living high on the hog! spared the blows of fate! they just had to worry about showing the old man a good time, playing nice-nice with his masks, dragging out the tests, slowpoking around, every little rigmarole they could think of in order to keep stalling... to kill time... until I could send them word, set myself up in the pampas... bring them over, and save the whole situation. It was a valorous plan of action. Just let me show you my triumphs of courage! I was going to outdo myself like never before! Swear/cross my heart it'd happen in no time! They'd be following me in a few short weeks. I'd reserve two cabins for them on a Plutus Company liner, touted for its ritziness, nonstop for La Plata. Famous superduper comforts, not some sub-ass-wetter with torpedoes like the *Kong Hamsün*... a picturesque bucket with halyard and sails, docked here all nice and cushy, but you can bet your life once cast off she'd turn into the crummiest slave ship around, all hands hard on the oars, prow plowing storm-whipped waves, foam up her ass. Damned both north and south, a floating hell.

The skipper must have really let loose once he was out at sea! You could tell just by seeing him up there on his barrel! Already roaring mad! He must have turned into a whirligig once he revved up, whipping the riffraff along with his tongue lashings, from stem to stern! Ah! So think about that one minute, why don't you?!

Plus, talking about my courage, you really had to keep in mind that an old tub like the *Kong* is big as life out at sea, all decked rigged out in white, a gust-blown cathedral, harum-scarum in the waves, a sitting target for all pirates. A powder keg, this huge billowing pirouette down into the deep.

I painted a nice picture of the danger for my confederates... explained how fragile a ship really is!...

It was all lost on them... I was looking for a pub, a bar, a tea room, any place at all with a roof over it, so I could spell it out for them a little clearer... A hot drink, black coffee, maybe a Bovril with a spot of rum... so we'd be able to sit down at least... and not have to keep on the move... What's more, the time was going by... it was starting to get dark... There was a strict air-raid curfew in effect ever since the zeppelins entered the war. It wouldn't have taken much for us to lose our way between Millwall and Romney Dock. Nothing but dead-end streets and detours... brick cliffs everywhere... warehouse fortresses... and not a single pub!... In the end we had no idea where we were... We kept running up against the backs of courtyards... I didn't want to knock on a door... The English don't need a reason to start fretting as soon as they see somebody lurking around like that in the twilight, especially Frenchmen.... and with a little girl, to boot... in a short skirt... they sure as hell must have been flapping their lips in this neck of the woods, the hospital was around the corner, the black and raspberry building where we met Clodo that time... gossip travels fast... news of rapes... screwups... from pubs to dead-end streets... whether true or false... One thing you never do is ring somebody's bell at twilight...

"Bear left!" I shout... "Bear left! Hey, what about Prospero? What about Prospero?"

The guy'd slipped my mind! I was beat from all the walking! Oh! yeah, great idea! There'd be some java there!

"Let's go, gang! Don't just stand there!"

We cross back over where we came! on our way! I wasn't thinking about Prospero anymore. We had some business to settle, and how! Ah! I'm going to whip up a little taste for them! Prospero's Loffeekee!

"Take it from me! Nice and hot, bubbling away! Genuine mocha java!"

I was firing them up.

I want to extend him my congratulations! Two pennies! two pennies! for the cashier! Just to be nice! House of hot tips! Ah! what a first-class way to set sail! I just want a chance to pay him back! That mug on Jovil! A real distinguished gentleman!

They're back smiling.

They're taking things better. Truth is, it got to me too, all of a sudden, the way that gang of scumballs puked all over us, treated us worse than dogs, plastered us with ridicule. OK, so Prospero didn't have anything to do with it, that was crystal clear, he hadn't misled, cheated, lied to me... all well and good... his info was right on the money, proved by the fact that I'd be setting sail at 8:15!... and on the spur of the moment... on his word! without a red cent!... that was nothing to sneeze at!... a rock-solid recommendation... a result!... It was just that maybe if I sweet-talked him... pressed hard... pestered him to death... I'd manage to convince him to take the little one too... plus even old gramps... First, I had to go back on the attack, act horribly offended, damn unhappy, my friends insulted that way, what a total disgrace!

Fair enough, the Port Authorities were keeping an iron grip on the boatswains, really hunting down smugglers, so that you might think twice... and on top of that, the boat was so crammed... so packed to the gills for the crews... squashed in their quarters like sardines... that it was inevitable three extra boneheads... wouldn't be welcomed with open arms... the Ministry of Munitions didn't fool around... Any cut in your roll... means the skipper's pulled in... the tub impounded! No ifs ands or buts!

That was all the out-and-out thugs in the crew needed to hear... Fires were child's play. A splitting hull, a hole in the waves, a cross mark over at Lloyd's, cut the applause!

Ah! I was feeling sorry for myself! for my bag of bones ready to set sail! I was thinking it over hard! A victim, that's what I was, nothing less, at the mercy, tossed by the perverse quirks of fate!... Ah! my personal destiny! And these friends of mine, what louts! They saw me on a bed of roses! The monsters! Never in my life dealt with characters more deaf! more blind! grousing under my breath while groping our way along the Albert Embankment... the dock opposite Prospero's place... Ah! my personal fate! Ah! and how! Pains! Sacrifices! Who from? Me from, that's who! Fucking hell!...

I couldn't stand any more tears! Ah! It was too damn unfair! Ah! I was sick and tired of their faces! Ah! The smug jerks! I told them off as we walked along... enough already with the sighs!

"I'm the one who's going to be the acrobat up there in the *Kong Hamsün*'s shrouds! My ass is on the line! My bones! I'm the one who's going to be somersaulting around fifty yards up in the atmosphere, above the raging elements! Cheers to you all! Tirralirra! I'm the dumb jerk every time something needs to get done! Ah! you've got zero self-respect, feeling sorry for yourselves and all that! I'm the one you should be feeling tremendously sorry for! I'm the one coping with emergencies! Ah! your cool-customer act stinks!"

My ranting didn't disturb them in the least!

At one spot the bank turned treacherous... You could slip right into the drink just like that... Splash!... straight off the deck of the footbridge... plus there was the rigging that kept tripping you up... Sosthène tangles his foot, stumbles, sprawls!... sits on an anchor!... howls... he hurt himself... Got banged up pretty bad... Fortunately it's a good omen... running into an anchor!... it brings instant luck... Got to admit it, that's all. Chance runs the show. He said so himself.

"Move your ass, you loafer! Move it! Look where it is!"

We were going to come back out on Prospero's place... We could make out the dim glow at the end of the pebble path... the canteen... the fanlight... We walk up to it. Enter. It's already full of customers. Swirling with smoke so thick it was like a mauve aquarium! The sea green fellows were drifting under the ceiling lamps! Garlands of tiny red lights around the tables, their pipes. I jostle two ornery characters... threats fly back and forth... I move along my way, stepping quick... I want to break the news to Prospero... that fine friend of mine!... good as gold!... tell him I'm off... he'll never see me again!... that it's all signed and sealed for America!

Such a racket at the counter, got to scream to make myself heard. I bellow at the top of my lungs.

"Hey! Prospero! It's OK! Boom! Dee-aaa!..."

My rallying cry. He can see me wending my way... through the mauve pipe smoke... so thick you could cut it with a knife... I think I'm catching him by surprise... Wrong. He's rinsing glasses... and just keeps on... He's chatting with a greaseball, a chauffeur from the Majorio.

He introduces me: "José de Majorque."

"Hey, you know what?" I break the news. "I'm shipping out!"

"Shipping out on what?

"Why, on that old tub of yours!"

"What old tub of mine?"

"Why, on the *Hamsün*, you dolt!"

Gets a snigger from him.

"Must have been dreaming, fella," he goes to me...

"Dreaming? What do you mean? It's a done deal!"

"Come off it now!"

"You can fuck off, Prospero, that's all I got to say! I set sail at eight o'clock, that good enough for you?"

Felt like killing him the way he kept shrugging.

"Tonight? You imbecile, tonight's your party!"

What a comeback!

"My party? Party for what?"

"Saint Ferdinand, sweetheart!"

"Ferdinand?"

It didn't make any sense to me.

"Sure is!" he responds emphatically... "Didn't you know anything about it?..."

What the hell did my party have to do with anything?

"Come off it, everybody wants to give you the bash you deserve! You don't leave on the day of your bash! Just unheard of!"

Of course his buddy was in total agreement, José de Majorque.

They were both rolling their eyes in horror over how I could even think about leaving on such a day! The day of my party! Unbelievable!

I didn't have a calendar, he neither of course!

Smelled fishy...

So then, he starts talking to me about Cascade, working girls, friends, who all wanted to offer me special wishes, and how they'd be offended to death if I just upped and left without so much as a ta-ta because they were all gearing up for a terrific blowout, this would be everybody's chance to drown their blues in rivers of champagne, wash them away once and for all, it would be one hell of a victory celebration! For the speedy homecoming of our fighting men! So I just couldn't skip out. Jesus Christ Almighty, an out-of-this-world wild binge, big bash, asshole, the whole shebang! A hookers' holiday, the whole houseful! All for Saint Ferdinand! You don't leave on the day of your party!... Even so it took me aback... I didn't want to come across like too big an ignoramus... What if it was true... I'd be able to see what they were about... whether they honestly meant to be friendly...

I wanted to stand him to a drink... He's a step ahead of me.

"My round!"

He foists himself on our little group.

"Miss? A glass of Banyul's? And what about you, granddad?"

Drinks all around.

He was pulling the rug out from under me.

Ah! I wondered what was going on... I'd never before seen anybody so concerned about my name-day party... Saint Ferdinand...

They all start kissing me... the round of drinks gets their juices flowing... Prospero... the driver... Sosthène... the girl... exploding in merriment... They wish me all the happiness in the world... I ask how the old gang's been doing... back at the boardinghouse... asked about those who'd been called up... two dead already...

"Ah! Cascade phoned." It suddenly comes back to him!

He catches me up on a few others... this one... that one... on Carmen with the stitches in her ass... He was in a chatty mood... So what was the big deal about this party of mine? I wanted to ask him, it was a screwy idea. Funny how it happened to come up just now... I didn't really get it... What was this palsy-walsy business all about? I hadn't seen anybody for months... I'd beat it the hell away from them... Why were they coming back to bug me? Curlers was to blame. She'd spread tales, worked up the gang... My skipping out didn't exactly thrill them... They had something up their sleeve... Right, my bash!... best wishes?... wishes that... that... that... the whole thing stinks to high heaven!... I'd find out what their game was!... or should I throw in a monkey wrench right now?... tear out of here?... But what if it was all a con back at the ship? And signing me on was just a big bunch of bull!... just for laughs too?... and I'd got diddled everywhere?... Ah! fucking hell!... enough was enough... At ease! Start over again from the top! A seat! Let's tough it out! Maybe I should clear the hell off again?... They wouldn't take me in... They all wound up making me laugh! Tough guys my ass! Reason enough for me! I get sloshed! I tell Sosthène: "Do like me! the little one too! Sit down!..."

We take Prospero up on his offer! Let him fill 'er up! on the house! Since it's my name-day party! Cheers! And here's one to all the blabbermouths at the bar! to all the blabbermouths in the world! Let them all spit, jabber, and swear, God be damned! burp and burn their tongues! Bah! breathe fire it packs such a punch! a knockout wallop of alcohol. To my name day! Saint Ferdinand! Let the good times roll! Let's celebrate! My act bowls Prospero over, he thought I was going to skip out! run off with my tail between my legs under the nasty digs! No way! Full of piss and vinegar, and that's that! All drinks on the house! He introduces me to another friend, an ice-cream man from Soho, who was likewise angling for a way out of the country, some gimmick for getting over to Argentina... From what I could make out he'd jumped ship a year and a half ago already... the *Regina Marina*...

He wasn't too bad on guitar... he even had a permit to give concerts in Soho... Now you don't just pick up a music permit from under some cop's foot... in fact, it's a pretty damn difficult piece of paper to get your hands on... the sort of thing that's passed down in the family... which goes to say it was a golden goose you'd never swap for anything... This gets us onto the topic of permits... The thousand and one ways of faking them... how you can turn one into three or four... in short, all the crooked ins and outs of the business...

We got to chatting about Boro, how he'd finagled his own permit for playing piano in pubs from a peddler, then sold it to Guédon for two pounds fifty to pay off the fine for disturbing the peace that'd been dogging him... But Guédon was a real screwup, a few days later he gets lured into a raid over at the La Reale bar... Trying to escape, he tears along, charging ahead of the cops, the strain makes him see blurry, he falls right over into the water at the foot of the bridge, at the Embankment, he sinks to the bottom, the river traffic, the crabs devour him in less than a week, the permit along with him, those are the kind of crabs they got down by Victoria Embankment, not a shred left behind, the most voracious along the entire bank, "walking sewers" they call them, a special species, in with the tide, scads and scads, such huge heaping layers, so dense so compact they look like part of the real embankment, you can actually walk across them unawares... Those are the kind of crabs they were.

Virginia closed her eyes, the whirl of talk had really tuckered her out... plus all the hustle and bustle... she fell fast asleep...

"Beddy-bye!..." I cradle her, my darling... "Beddy-bye!..."

True, she was as little as could be, especially like this in my arms, a teeny tiny little kid who'd been way too bouncy.

"That floozie of yours isn't too friendly!" Prospero observes. "She's asleep on the night of your name-day party!"

A crack to get under my skin.

"Ah! You're a pain in the ass with this party of mine!"

I was being too patient.

"See ya!"

I got up... They were boring the hell out of me with this party of mine!

"You just wait and see what we've got planned for you!"

Bunch of stubborn pricks!

"Shit!" I say to them all, "Shit! And shit again!"

They were pushing me over the edge.

"Got to run, I just told you, right? I got to be back there by eight! At eight he ships out! at eight."

"You don't have any idea what a boat's all about!"

The Neapolitan, plus the other one, Majorque, bust out in crazy laughter!

"He doesn't know what it's like! One week, take it from me, that's all I give you!... And a week's a long time! you'll drop dead! They'll make soup from your bones! that's what you'll be cooking up!"

Oh! Geez! Oh! Geez! That was a hot one!

"String bean soup! happy peasants you are!"

I felt sorry for them...

"We'll talk about this again, kid!"

What louts! I preferred keeping my trap shut!

The guy from Naples, the music man, wanted to roll me for drinks, give me my just desserts. I didn't bet much, two pennies three sets. Still and all, I preferred using three dice. I'd spotted another pair in the back, but it was dark as an asshole! with just the light from a small wall lamp. Before anything, I wanted the kid off her feet, wanted to set her up nice and comfy on a couple of chairs, or a bench if I could find one. Right then somebody asks for Prospero, two men at the door, and then this small gang. I can see what's up, street peddlers, messengers, handymen from all over, Maltese, Chinks, dagos, Papuans... roving bands that slink around the docks bartering, fobbing off cheap junk, at dusk, small-time fencing. Hushed voices, dickering in the dark, without a glance at the customers, coming and going just the way they'd arrived... The sort of merchandise that's a snap to hide, a wad of silk, the real stuff, a cloud nabbed in a fist, poppy juice, just a few drops, essence of rose... Easy warehouse pickings. Hand quicker than the eye. Across from the Dingby before the fire, the same scene would always spring up just after dark, a spate of finagling, of shadowy trafficking in the doorway. On this side of the river, ditto.

"Prospero!..." somebody whispers...

He's disturbed another three four times, has to go to the door in person!

No great shakes at billiards, I wasn't exactly racking up the points. They spotted me twelve points because of my arm, time was ticking away, I had to step on it!

"I'm off, Prospero! Bye, buddy! Have a nice and happy one!"

Mind made up.

He steps in front of me.

"Don't go!... Don't go!... Come on! Look around! Everybody's gone!"

Right he was! A fact! I'm surprised myself... Everybody was gone! He plants himself in front of me, absolutely blocks my way.

"Come on, old pal! These ideas of yours! where're you going? It's your party!"

The joint stands empty now, the tables cleared, not a living soul, all the customers into thin air, nothing left but the smoke swirling, drifting under the ceiling lamps and the smell of cabbage, rancid grease, tobacco and liquor.

The stink turned your stomach. I sat back down.

"It's moving!" I say to him. "This canteen of yours! It's moving!"

All swaying up above, all the ceiling lanterns, right down the line... not just one... all of them... just like that, all the rows attached to the rafters, so that my head started rocking too... real crummy sensation...

Prospero wouldn't stop jabbering, the damned pest.

"You can't be leaving, Ferdinand! You can't!..."

"Fuck!" I answer back... "Fuck and shit!"

I couldn't stand up... a queasiness...

"You won't be leaving today!"

The bull was fixated on the idea!

I was pretty pigheaded myself.

"I will too! Will too! Laddie!"

"Just open your eyes a little!" he says to me... "Open them good!... You haven't seen the best... You didn't look closely..."

He points over at the corner, all the way back in the darkness... I couldn't see shit.

"You can too!... You can too!... Look hard!"

I stare wide-eyed... Ah! over there!... look at that!... the hat... the feathers... arms crossed... somebody asleep... on the table...

"So what?" I ask.

He calls out: "Delphine! Hey!... Delphine!..."

The lump stirs... the topper... it's her! it's her! that hair! She rubs her eyes. She looks to see where the voice is coming from...

"Delphine! Delphine! It's us! Here's a kiss!"

I'm affectionate. I've got no reason to play Hide and Seek.

"Ah! darling! Ah! treasure!"

She dashes to her feet... hitches up her skirts, her train. Here she is!... She flings her arms around my neck...

"I knew, darling! I knew! I knew you'd be back!"

Now that's a surprise...

"How did you know?"

For my own information...

"Oh! a little bird told me!"

"You sure keep your ears open, don't you now, sweetie pie!"

No doubt about it, it was all the rage... throwing up a smoke screen... Even the old whore was in on the act! Guessing games... big fuss!...

They both lay into me. Teamwork.

"Stay, oh come on! You're going to have a ball! Your little girl too! And your handsome old geezer! your weirdo! Is he leaving us?"

They both agree it's a crime. She takes pity on me, solemnly...

"Worried young man! Oh my, oh my!"

The hag wants to wheedle me. I'm her fancy. She declares her feelings... "My fancy! My fancy!..." She throws her arms around my neck again. Virginia's not too jealous, luckily, for God's sake!... It's my name-day party, for one thing! Every heart glad! The good cheer even infects Delphine, Saint Ferdinand is my special day.

"A long life to Ferdinand! Long happiness!"

I'm thrilled. Bliss! Health! Fortune! All that for me!

I wound up having a good laugh too.

I took the joke well.

Now that she'd been shaken out of her sleep, Delphine was all wound up. She was yelping away hoarse and shrill. People could probably hear her for blocks around... She got the bug to a toast right away, to raise her glass to Victory! So we had to fill her glass, and all the way to the brim. She'd planted herself in front of the sideboard, turned toward us, her hat askew, skirts, train, all hitched up, show time...

For us! For us! The announcement is made. In our honor. Guests of honor in the audience! She's about to start: "Honorable Company!"

Perk up your ears! A song has been selected! Warm-up time! She'll act out a few lines from *The Merry Wives of Windsor*. Raise your glasses high! All at once, the passion seizes her, she screws up her mouth, rolls her left eye into her hair, throwing herself body and soul into her performance.

Fie on sinful fantasy!
Fie on lust and luxury!
Lust is but a bloody fire!

With a cry she's off singing... her voice hits too high a note... cracks, swings off pitch, dissolves into a fit of hacking... once she starts coughing she can't stop... she's hooting so hard the glass she just downed comes trickling back out her nostrils... she's not upset... We sit her back down... she wants to have another go... Ah! anything but that!... I congratulate her... We chat a little more... I didn't want to ask her any questions... though I really was tempted... like about what had been happening since that time back at Van Claben's... and whether she'd read the papers... or had any run-ins... or about how she'd disappeared... and nobody'd spotted her anywhere? and now she turns up here? Ah! I still couldn't get over suddenly seeing her again... The sight of her gave me quite a turn... she popped right up out of some dream, bam... veil fingerless gloves the works... as though nothing had happened... the same fired-up screwy chatterbox as always... and this was only the beginning... That's how I saw it... I thought I was dreaming with my eyes wide open... yet it really was her all right... Delphine in frills and bone, wide-eyed, yapping away, the whole shebang... her and nobody else!... I wasn't drunk now, hadn't puffed anything... Plus Greenwich wasn't far... just across the way... No!... on the same side of the river! two minutes away... shit!...

I look at that face of hers again... white as a sheet! plastered with powder and makeup... shit I'm sweating...

"Sweet little kisser!" I say to her... "Sweet little kisser!"

I'm about to yell! shit... I grab hold of myself... give it everything they got... She asks me who Virginia is... doesn't know her... Have to introduce her... Yet here she just sang from *The Merry Wives of Windsor* in front of her!... Ah! my oh my!... what could she have been thinking!

"Darling! Darling pet!"

I make the introductions... We couldn't hear ourselves talking in the joint anymore... it was starting to fill up, people arriving... hollering loud enough to wake the dead... I had to scream my lungs out in order to get the intros right...

"Mrs. Delphine!..." my voice was drowned out... "Mrs. Delphine!"

A big curtsy from the artiste to the gathering... the boys at the bar! A right proper introduction... I mustn't skip anything, had to mention every detail... her finery... the pretty feathers... the lorgnette, her old standards! the artiste she once... and still was! Goddamn! I had to run right down the list! and explain and translate for Sosthène... the moron didn't get it.

"Delphine Vane! Sosthène! Artiste!"

She corrects me, gets sore: "Yes... Artist... certainly! A theater actress! Many parts, young man! Many souls! And then some!"

She thinks my intro needs more pizzazz.

This gets a roar! from the whole joint!... from every table front to back!...

Just with a glimpse at that topper of hers, the two veils, the yellow and red ostrich plumes, the lorgnette, real laugh-getters, even in London!...

Now she's defiant, bawls them out...

"Asses! Asses! Despicable asses!"

Brang!... Bang!... Bomf!... Explosions outside! Right at that second! The whole sky it seems... the ground quakes... Boom! Boom! Bombs dropping on Poplar... Everything's rattling, the shack, the tables, the works... A savage bombardment... from zeppelins?... We still can't see yet... the whole sky is flickering red... the lapping water... the darkness burns bright... with searchlights... we can hear the firemen's bells going hell for leather... their water tanks whizzing past... racing into the night... the whole opposite bank a shimmering red mirror...

Ba-da-boom!... Crash!... Another barrage... the clouds are echoing with the thunder... It isn't grim or frightening, instead it has the feel of a country fair, and ba-da-boom!... fireworks!...

"Hurray! Hurray!"

Sharp crackle... heavy boom, all hell's breaking loose in deafening thunder... Delphine's completely carried away:

"Hurray!... Hurray!... Celebration!... Long live Mary!... Long live the king!"

She hops, prances about, grabs her hat, veils, she wants to whip up the crowd... She raises her glass three times to the king's health...

Whoah, lookee there! The river superintendent! The one from the police upriver. Just slipped in on us, we were too wrapped up in our fireworks show... He calls out to us... stepped out of an open boat...

"Gentlemen! Gentlemen! A child is lost!..."

He's looking for him.

He sweeps us with the beam of his flashlight...

"No, sir!... No, sir!..." in unison.

"Good!..."

"Good night!"

He disappears.

The shit was really flying something fantastic at the top of the sky, kabooming loudly every which way in the atmosphere!... baskets of flaming flowers spilling over the city, with dizzily whirling stems, blue, yellow, red foliage...

Ah! They really knew how to put on one magnificent show! Ah! Altogether different from the son of a bitching front lines! here the bombs burst up among the stars, streaking detonating in the heavens! They didn't come shooting down into your hair! You could kick back and enjoy the spectacle! The view through the dump's small windowpanes could have been better. They all piled back outside for a better gawk at the sights.

I grab Sosthène, now was the time... I dash off...

"Hey! Nutcase! I'm late... the boat's leaving! Eight fifteen."

"Ah! You bastard!" is all he can shout. "What're you going to do, ditch the little one, you rat?... Is that what you're going to do?"

"And what about you?" I answer. "You're here, aren't you, you creep? Can't you take care of her? Go through a little trouble by any wild chance? While I'm off making my way for you!... setting things up over there? Can't you keep the uncle entertained? Can't you help him out?... You're a real deadbeat, damn, I can't believe my ears!..."

What a look, what a face, he was lolling back and forth.

"Ah! The things you say!... Ah! such things!..."

Stubborn! He thought I was a low-life because I was leaving, a quitter, a lousy bum! He didn't want to hang around London. He wanted to leave at the same time, right away... didn't want to wait... He knew America... He'd make out even better than I would... That's how he saw it...

"You're too old, you geezer... you're too old..."

He told me to fuck off.

"You stay with her! That's your role! She's pregnant. You said so yourself!..."

Now it was finger-pointing time... I had to holler myself hoarse. The blasts outside were so loud we couldn't hear ourselves talking. Bombs whizzing, sizzling above Kingsbury, Brompton, Millbridge... even farther out... toward Newport... the whole sky flaring with explosions, in hails, in bouquets whistling everywhere, all the echoes crackling rumbling, every pane a mirror of flames.

It was the great zeppelin hunt, everybody outside had their socks knocked off, all shouting on the embankment, hey, they weren't zeppelins up there, they were airplanes, Taubes, the latest model. The Germans had announced they were going to reduce London to smithereens! That remained to be seen. The customers weren't afraid, they wanted ringside seats.

I went out with the girl. Got to admit it was an exciting show... Bets were on... All the stevedores had a stake... The first to spot the zeppelin takes the pot! The searchlights were searching the sky... Whenever they turned up empty the crowd ahhed and awhed... miffed... a barrage of catcalls... Go ahead, boo the fireworks!... they were tripping each other up, what a big joke... All of a sudden you hear people going "Ooo! Ooo!"... I thought they'd spotted something... false alarm!... It was some other group on the embankment... closing in... shouting!

Prospero boomed loudest: "Over here!... Hey! Hey! Over here!..."

And then, for me: "Ferdinand! Ferdy!"

"What's up?"

"Hey! Here, over here!" A real racket between cannon blasts. Those arriving would answer: "Oooh! Oooh!" A slaphappy crew!... a shouting match... to see whose voice could sound the loudest... Boom! Boom! Oooh! Oooh! from earth to sky. What a terrific time! I wish I could have seen the expression on those newcomers... turning up so late... Because we were all hollering our lungs out for them...

"Hey! hey! Guys!... Over here! Here! Come on over so we can give you a kiss!..."

The new group chuckles, stumbles, gropes... hangs on wherever... swears... plants smooches on cheeks... I'm all for... I start groping too... Somebody calls me... my name... So I finally ask who it is... Can't place the faces in the glimmer from up above... Shit!

"Long live Ferdinand! Long live Ferdinand!"

One person yelling...

"There he is! There he is!..."

It's a mob scene... I'm on my guard... I look for Virginia... grab her... don't want to leave her side...

"There he is! There! Hey! Hey!"

The entire embankment is mobbed... all the customers have filed outside, plopping down wherever, on top of each other... I grope the new arrivals.... Everybody laughs... Ah! I do recognize them...

"It's Renée!... Ah! wow, and who's that?... It's Finette!... Ah! geez, it's the whole cathouse!..."

All the women! and big Angèle! And how they're laughing their asses off down there on the ground like that, shoving each other across the gravel, a bunch of kids, having a ball, crazy ladies... I'm floundering around them... don't know where I am anymore... Where's Cascade? The whole Leicester gang's here! An outing! A spree! Loony ladies on the loose! One hell of a party for me, I'm telling you!

They make me out in the dark!

"There you go, you little fart! You rotten brat! You bed-wetter! Peek-a-boo!"

I'm pawed, knocked on my ass... they all climb on top of me, trampling me, just for laughs, right down against the gravel... I bellow, beg for mercy!

"Your party, Ferdinand! Your party!"

Mustn't put up a fight, they'd eat me alive, hilarious harpies.

"Your party! Your party!..."

The bug up their ass... They came down from the center of town just for that reason, to wish me all the best, in unison, the whole cathouse, young bitches and old bats. A long bus trek, then hoofing it a good way, in whorehouse heels across gravel!

All just for me!...

The bombardment's fun for them, they laugh like hyenas over the sprays of sparks, but even so some bombs do hit the ground... we're sitting in a hail of debris... ricocheting all across the stones...

"I got something in my eye!" Curlers shouts.

Can't be!... Still and all it's scary... Everybody piles back inside... There, by the canteen lamplight, I can see their faces, don't recognize each and every one... Little Nestor is fluttering his lids, dazzled by the brightness... Curlers is pissed, she twisted her foot but good... Flyswatter doesn't want to lend her a hand, he's more in a mood to chew her out. They all jostle in at the doorway, the girls feel each other up, start flipping out, the bombardment's overexciting them... Right away they're hot to play Blindman's Bluff with the sailors, they blindfold the men... Right off, lascivious pawing... the ladies walked over along the embankment, a good strip of shore from the Wapping tube stop... they take off their shoes, their feet are burning. I introduce Virginia.

"Don't bother," they answer. "We know who your little darling is."

Curlers blabbed the whole story with a thousand and one details about our last run-in. My little girl's so beautiful... such lovely calves, such lovely eyes, you name it... and I'm an oaf... That's unanimous... a boor... a lout...

Ka-boom!... it's starting up again outside... big time... we go back onto the doorstep, mustn't miss a trick... Hustling and bustling... mad laughter...

"Tuhwheep! Tuhwheep! Hoo! Hoo!"

Curlers hoots... calling into the darkness... Still others are answering from up along the embankment... from out toward the docks... the rest of the gang... the whole Leicester pub's on the way... Gertrude's back, Girouette, Carmen... They came the Tower Bridge way... They wanted a look at the fire... Then they finally rolled in. Without Cascade... He'd be around a little later... He didn't stroll around with the women. He'd meet up with them again somewhere or other... back at the bar or over at the racetrack... but never in the street together. It's the way things were done... Inevitably we wound up talking about him, what he thought about my behavior...

"I miss the old guy! I do! I'm sure he's making a mess of things!..." A quote.

"Ah! You'd better believe you're the apple of his eye! He wouldn't have carried on a hundredth as much about any other guy, what a hullabaloo! Your sorry ass!"

How had things been going since I left? The fuzz? Matthew? Maybe they'd come around asking about me?

Yeah, seemed so... a little... And the guys at the front?... Any word? Yeah, three dead... The others in tip-top... And the ladies?... Rirette and the rest of the gang?... hard at work? frills and flounces?... Such laziness... pigheadedness... the Tommies made them drink way too much... they'd get sloshed such a disgrace... Getting them up out of the sack was one hell of a chore... at four in the afternoon... A girl without a pimp has no professional pride... still snoring away at dinnertime... when all was said and done, they were a pack of stinking bitches... Angèle could swear and threaten and blow her top all she wanted, no good... uppity attitudes... rebellion in the ranks... No pimp no respect... Cascade did all he could but he didn't want to smack them around... They were his just for safekeeping! They took advantage of his promise... Come Saturdays they were so smashed they puked up and down the hallways... they lived on nothing but whiskey, on pure ether in Ninette's case... She even got her dog drunk... They had even worked the vice out of their systems... just snored their lives away... the whole thing, apparently, because they were distressed and worried, waiting for word...

The war! The war! always the war! The only thing that sort of roused them was all the ker-booming... and it had to be thundering something godawful, rattling heaven and earth, to crack open their eyelids a wee bit... A whore without a man loses her fizz.

Judging by the sirens, we had a huge bombing raid on our hands this time around...

And it was heading our way...

Rumor put at least a dozen zeppelins up in the sky... but we were still waiting for our first glimpse of one... nothing but showering shrapnel... ricocheting all over the roof, the entire shack was shaking/quaking...

Everybody raised a glass to my health, then to those absent, to those present, to the ladies, to Miss Virginia, to the Chinaman... I picked up the details from stray comments... about those who had fallen in Flanders, Raymond La Comptée... Bobby Drug... plus Lulu Brême in the Vosges... Carmen was the gossip queen, not so sloshed, not as silly a cunt as the others, she got a kick out of scuttlebutt...

The crashbanging had been going on again for quite some time now... the door rattles open... a pack of loudmouths... another fresh load... tousled tarts, Mario's stable, five or six girls also showing their faces at my party... Out on a binge... And seriously stewed... horsing around, drunk as skunks... I see Curlers pounce on them, big wet smooches for one and all... endless lovey-dovey, what a show. Dédé Accordion is also along for the ride, right away he climbs on the table, sets himself up, plays us "La Marseillaise" to the sound of the cannon fire... and then immediately breaks into "The Blue Danube"... the waltz... the lovely waltz... mince around!...

"Start mincing! Start mincing! Waltz! Start mincing!"

He invites everyone to dance...

I didn't want to waltz or anything... I wanted to clear out... Mince around my balls! For one thing, how'd they all get here? how'd they find me? I pop the question to Mona Lisa again, she holds out on me.

"Search me! Search me! Go shit! I'm out of here, my friends! Off and running! I'm taking Virginia, get a good look! Virginia, the girl I love!"

Take it or leave it!

This gets them all up on their feet, such a din! a horrible racket! They won't have this at all!... Such an uproar, it drowns out the music, the accordion, the cannon fire outside, the sirens, the dock alarm. Won't have it! absolutely no way! They grab hold of me... force me back into my seat... Ah! I plow into the mob... throw a few uppercuts, with what's left in my left, they collar me, I'm down for the count. Three-four keep me pinned to the floor... All because they're so thrilled to lay eyes on me again... I'm outraged in front of Virginia... I work myself free... call them every name in the book...

"But we'd lost touch with you, you big lug!"

I've got to get it through my head we're talking about genuine fondness. I'd had it with talk! Dédé Accordion, a real comedian that one, wanted to razz the sailors a little, he clambers up onto their table, does a jig... Doesn't go over too well with them...

"Jump, Froggy! Get the hell out!"

They were admiring the cannonade, they didn't want any distractions! But one of them, the tall skinny one, gets all worked up...

"Go on, Dédé!... Go on, me love! Love you, Dédé! Boom! Boom! Love you!"

He rises from his bench... staggers... wants to nab him by his trousers... give Dédé a kiss... a sure bet he's a flaming queen...

Ping! Bing! Bang!... Right in the kisser! A hail of fists! His pals let him have it! He crumples to the floor. Bleeds. Back to his seat, crying, wiping himself off, dripping all over the table, puking, bright red, he's led away...

Outside the big event is still going strong... the whole atmosphere's ignited... the firemen are clanging, galloping full tilt... You can hear them stampeding on the opposite shore... charging after the fires... the flames must be raging in Wapping... Honest, this is an all-out attack, not just a lot of noise, or some drill...

Another voice calling for me... from the back of the joint...

"Where's the little ass... where's the sweetheart?"

Curlers is after me. Screaming her lungs out. A hoarse holler, bad vocal chords! "I've got bad vocal chords!" Her badge of honor. "Ever since my first communion!" She thumped her chest... Aaargh! Aaargh! while hacking... she sounded like a dog choking... her proof...

"It's spread to my wind bags! Since my first communion!... I caught cold in the church! In Sacré Cœur in Montmartre! Never shook it!

"Little ass! Little ass! Where are you?"

She gropes around in the dark. Stumbling. I try to duck her... and run smack into her instead...

"Here you are, sweetheart!"

She'd circled the place three times... She wants us to go back to the bistro, the little girl too...

"You are pretty, Miss Virginia! You are pretty, darling, a wonder!"

She gazed in admiration at Virginia under the ceiling lamp. She held the girl by the shoulders, right in front of her, very tenderly.

All the customers and tarts were outside yelling at every thunderclap.

"Hello, boys! Hit him! Bang!"

They were cheering them on. Tracking the battle in the clouds... the volley of blasts kept the place rattling, quivering in every joint, such a heavy bombardment, even the embankment was dancing. A big turn-on for Curlers, watching Virginia up real close, her eyes glued to the girl... She didn't give a shit about outside...

"You're pretty," she repeated... and then coaxingly: "Darling, darling... are you ill?..."

She asked me, worried.

"What're you doing to her? The little pumpkin's pale as a ghost! You son of a bitch, go on, get out of here! Are you beating her?"

"Of course I'm not beating her!"

Outside the cannon fire breaks off, could it be the air raid's over? the audience discusses/jabbers, and then everything quiets down. The embankment empties out, it's late, Big Ben bongs 3:30. No sound but the lapping of the river and noises from the distance, the port, the wind from Tilbury, the boats towing, haling each other... Ah! I'd love to be setting sail too... Maybe I had another minute left?... Maybe they were already there?... But I'd run myself too ragged, on top of the buzzing in my head... Plus the fight with those crazy ladies... I came out of it dead tired... not to mention Delphine, her dirty cracks... What should I do? Wait another half hour, that's my decision. I sit down, Virginia, Curlers, the Napo across the table, Dédé at my side with a couple-three women. Got to wait, we chat... the topic always goes back to brawls and muggings. The women knew quite a thing or two about muggers. The poor gals've been their victims for several weeks running, extraordinary muggings by unbelievable thugs, the ballsiest pickpockets anybody's ever seen... That was the word going around. From Bond Street to Tottenham, they clean you out in a snap, your whole day's take, your wad of dough, papers, they frisk you, whisk past like arrows, before you even notice they're gone. They melt back into the darkness. That explains the ladies' woes, why their lives are one big mess, and they're scraping bottom, rolling in dead broke from turning tricks, after eight ten hours of doing their damnedest, in the pits, sick, grungy. Those cash/stash vampires... the pitch-black to blame.

Angèle wasn't buying any of this hoo-haa.

"Crapola, my lovelies! You're stewed to the gills! You guzzled your dough, and that's that!"

Ah! they explode in protest! how shocking! The very mention of such crimes! How insulting! What filthy suspicions! Ah! too much to take! The innocents rise up! Blubber, choke on their sobs! It's the honest-to-God absolute truth! night wolves, the culprits! They all sing the same song! The whole town knows it! Vampires, a gang of Fantomas! They belonged to Consuelo's gang, the pimp over at the Madrid Follies, the slot machine guy... Didn't need to rack your brains, pull your hair out. He was the criminal mastermind! The boom had already been lowered on him because of his telltale MO... It cost him an ear back in 1909... It was Jean-Jean who'd lopped it off one Christmas night... Jean-Jean the Parisian always used to settle his scores on Christmas night...

Curlers had seen the whole thing with her own eyes. She could dredge up memories, yes she could... Twenty-two years she'd been in London... "My first abortion..." she started to rattle them off... "I might have had an English girl, how about that! older than yours!..." A smooch for Virginia!... "Pretty miss!"

Her memories rolled out helter-skelter... in dribs and drabs...

"Back in those days!... hackhack... the pimps were shown respect!... hackhack!... their ladies too... hackhack!... on the sidewalks of London! plus the work, I think! hackhack! they didn't go off to war to get buggered! hackhack!"

But Angèle put up an argument, she wasn't falling for that hogwash, ghosts, vampires, etc. It was all just a bunch of bunk as far as she was concerned... cock-and-bull cooked up by dishonest, lying perverts who didn't take their jobs seriously anymore, who drank away their take in bars!

Ah! well, you've never heard such a flare-up... "You big fat shit! You dirty bitch! You're rotten!" That screwball could really flap her gums! liar! Ah! enough already! what gall! flinging lies smack into your face!

They're exploding! choking!

"Ah! the big whore! Your ass!..."

Virginia didn't catch every word... Too much slang for her ears... But she was having a good time all the same... the greatest, in fact!... sleep was the last thing on her mind... this henhouse of hell-raisers was something new... a lot more fun than her uncle's...

Curlers starts up again: "Say, she's pale as a ghost, this kid of yours..."

"Is that any of your business?"

"You bet, you bum! It sure is!... Your little cutie pie's so delicate!... Come on, will you leave her with me?... Go on, buzz off!... beat it to America!..."

She was kicking me out.

Ah! real witty! The whores were pissing themselves laughing at the sight of me being treated like such a royal sucker! Marrying off my girl to Curlers! And sailing off as a little cabin boy!... all by myself!...

With a breeze in your sails...
Go, little cabin boy...

All together now!... the whole café, the tables, the bar! even Sosthène! even big Angèle!...

Cracking up a gang of tarts is a snap... they laugh at every little fart... one drowning fly sets off wild fits... the really awful thing, and I do mean awful, was that my tenderest most delicate darling was getting just as big a bang... laughing her little head off just like the others... the dumbest pranks, brainless hyenas. I'd never seen her have a grander time... over the worst dumbass puns... over everything and nothing... over me, in the end... such a pretty picture I made with my travel craze, my bug to be a seafaring cook!

Now there was something to die yukking over, they all thought I was such a damn funny clown... A scream! A laugh riot! The hookers' big hoot!

"You've got ants in your pants! Let's toast! Don't go and drown yourself! You've got it good here, you sap!..."

That's what they thought... They start ragging me about Virginia.

"Aren't you taking her to school? They'll snatch her away from you! Get a gander at those ankle socks!..."

They come over to feel up her calves...

"Let us have your baby doll... Give her to us! You're not using her... You're dumping her!"

With that they swoop upon Virginia, smooch away at her from every which way.

Curlers won't have it, she's boiling.

"Beat it! Beat it! sex maniacs!..."

"Oooh! Oooh! Grandma! To hell with your crotchety crotch! She belongs to us! The dolly's ours! Little Red Riding Hood!"

More outpourings of affection, endless pecks! Everybody kisses my little honey bun! Even Prospero gets in his smooch, it's his little cousin so he claims.

Sosthène blows kisses over the table. He can barely move a muscle. He didn't turn down one single glass, toasted every time. Normally the guy never touched the stuff, so this hits him hard, knocks him for a loop right where he's sitting... He has just about enough strength to lift his glass for refills... and then smiles all around... Prospero opens another bottle of brandy... dumps it all into the mulled wine, a big bowlful, gin too, plus some lemon zest... "The special house punch of the Moor and Cheese," so he announces... It packs enough of a punch to wipe out a regiment. I make like I'm drinking... but I'm not... It gives me such an awful headache... I don't have too much upstairs as it is... I can talk/go wacky just fine without any help...

the fact remains the booze keeps on gurgling away... then the question pops into my head... what about the tab? Real fast it scares the pants off me... I let Prospero know...

"Watch it, pal! Not a red cent from me!..."

"It'll be taken care of!" he replies.

"Fine! Fine!"

I drop it.

After all, what's right is right... I paid on my end, damn it! They can pay theirs! They're doing me the honors! it's perfectly natural! is it my party, or isn't it, damn it! I'm 80 percent disabled! they might just get that through their heads! And about time too!

A point of honor.

But what about my party? This whole thing is one big mystery!...

All so confusing... I ask again...

"So what about my party, Prospero?"

"Bottoms up! You're talking with your mouth full..."

Pointless for me to keep pressing. All of a sudden they're crazy/hysterical.

"A song!" They jump on my case! "A song! Sing! Sing! Encore! Encore! Encore! Sing, Ferdy! Or pay up! Goddamn it!..."

Nasty of them!

Quickly I take the floor... belt out...

Your lovely eyes!...

from my repertoire in the Twelfth...

For the hours are sh-o-ort!

etc..., and then break right into

Fairy Queen...

by poplar request, in English... The big hit of Gaby Deslys, the star of the Empire in those days...

I brought the house down, especially because of my accent, I had a knack for impersonations.

Virginia now! her turn!

"Come on, Miss! In French! In French!"

Virginia was laughing so much she couldn't sing... She was having a grand old time with this crowd. The mulled wine was perking her up. A new sensation for the kid. Even so, after a minute she found her voice.

"In French! In French!..."

A solo, please!...

The Swallow!

replete with all the lights and shades, winding away, then prettily back, soaring flights, peeling trills... graceful in her song as in her smiles and laughter... all three rippling...

Ah, swallow, come back to us!

What a smash hit! The ladies were drinking her up with their eyes! "Good God, she's darling! That's the truth! An angel..."

Curlers the wildest of the bunch...

"An angel!... A voice from heaven!..."

Ecstasy!

Delphine was the only one who didn't fall for it, she didn't care for the song, or the darling, or anything at all... She's all steamed up, bitching, screaming, clambers on a table, belts out:

It's a long way to Tipperary...

A monkey wrench in the works... They grab her, yank her off... Right then another row, more banging at the door... some guys knocking... Prospero dashes to the wicket... Voices asking: "Are they in there?"

I recognize one... Cascade!

Then the whole joint explodes in shouting... All the girls squealing at him! "Over here! Over here! Hello!" The whole joint is jumping! What a real happy reunion!

"He's over there! He's over there!" they yell...

They're talking about me...

"Ah! great! ah! great! the little ass..."

Now it hits me... just as I suspected... they're springing their trap... an ambush... in their clutches lamb to the slaughter! This big show all for my benefit! What crapola! Saint Ferdinand! And the other bullshit! A damn lot of trouble they put themselves through! Kid's stuff when you're dealing with a dumb sucker like me! We should have gotten the hell out of here! at dawn! run for it... The first idea, the right idea!... All the lovey-dovey fooled us... They must have brought along the cops... I don't see them yet... But I smell a rat... It's the scalp dance!... "Revenge!..." They said to each other!... "Ferdinand's double-crossing us!" And so here they are! Just breezing in on us! A piece of cake! Candy from a baby! Ah! fuck! I jump to my feet, square off!...

"That you, Ferdy?"

I can see him walking toward me... his gray bowler... his slicked forelock...

"Come on! What's your game?" I pop the question...

"Why, nothing, my boy, nothing at all!..."

He looks real surprised to see me so worried, brutal!

"Feeling sick?..." he asks... "Feeling sick? You mean you're not glad to run into me again?... anyhow, sit down... sit down!..."

He's calm.

I want to chew him out but I lose my nerve.

"Monsieur is visiting London, I hear?"

He's the one who goes on the attack... He glances over at the bench... toward Sosthène... a little smile for Virginia...

The girls are chuckling, they're in seventh heaven... over the way he's treating me, like some kid... some excitable nut...

At this Prospero starts laying it on thick... fills out a few details.

"Cascade, hell, you don't know the half of it! Monsieur is going away! Monsieur's off on a journey!... Monsieur has seen enough of us all!... There's the news! Ah! None too soon! *Oltremare!* America! with the chick! And Monsieur Sosthène sitting right here! an ethpedition!..."

"Oh man, oh man! Ferdinand, so fast! Just like that with no luggage? No farewells?"

I surprised Cascade. He knocks back his bowler, a flick of the fingers... straightens it out, the whole time studying me...

I look at him too...

It must have been four months more or less since I'd left the Leicester... The time had taken its toll on Cascade, he'd aged, his forehead curl had gone gray, his kiss curl, slicked down in place... His whole face had gone dark... crow's-feet... just like that, pow! he had worn himself to a frazzle!... Even his African Battalion Cross, his "Bat d'Af," the tattoo in the corner of his eyelid, had deepened a shade...

He shakes his head a little for no reason... some private joke... then he stops... passes his hand across his face as though to wipe away a world of worry... lost in thought again...

"So, sonny, that your suitcase?"

He drawls the question.

"Nice job packing!"

He looks at Virginia...

"The baby doll?"

He studies her...

"Huh! well, well! I say, little man!... Will you take a look at that... Darling... Darling!..."

He's checking her out.

"Why don't you show her wares? Look at me, I show what my ladies got!"

Ah! That's an understatement... He's ribbing me...

Those ladies of his bust out laughing, choking, moaning... they're in stitches...

Ah! I'm an absolute riot!... Ah! geez, no kidding! Ah! I'm unbelievable!...

I don't know why...

Delphine's the only one not having a good time, sipping real slowly from her grog, closed in on herself, grumbling under her breath, teary-eyed... She pours herself another shot of rum... Her makeup's plastered on thicker than Curlers'... Since she's crying it starts dissolving... in streaks... her cheeks running with blue and red rivulets... She gets up, walks off to another table... she can't listen to another word from this crew... she throws her head into her mitts... hunches up... boo-hoos... big sobs... she's a pain in everybody's ass... blubbering something awful...

Putting on a big pout...

"What's wrong, Delphine?"

No answer.

They ask me to sing again.

I'm ready and willing, but it'll be "Little Sailor Boy"!...

At that they yell at me, no, not that one... So I get pissed! They want a love song... I refuse...

So Cascade performs... He's back in the swing. Just one of those tired spells...

Boom! Boo! Boo! Boom!
Here comes our Town Mayor!
Three steps forward!
Three steps back!

A big guffaw... He's merrier in his seat than on his feet... Heart trouble, I found out later, his age. It made him look like hell...

The song started with the chorus:

Three steps forward!...

And then the trombone imitation!... The guy who screwed up had to pay the consequences... By downing three glasses in a row... Screwing up was all the fun! Was I leaving or wasn't I? Some lush wanted to know... He came over and sniffed right under my nose...

"Going? Going, lad?"

Curlers joined in, too... with her own song...

Give me your girl
Pétronurl!...

And then the chorus at the top of her lungs...

Give me! Give me!
Your girl...
I'm crazy 'bout her...
Madame Cantaloupe!...
Oupe! Oupe! Oupe!

Stamping loudly with the beat.

"He's comfy here! He's staying put!"

That was the decision! My fate from everyone's lips... Cascade was the most flat-out...

"He won't be leaving!..."

It took some real nerve, in a way... although their intentions were friendly...

"Monsieur Sosthène's staying with us, too! Isn't this all terrific, Monsieur Sosthène?"

By then Sosthène was seeing double, gibbering... Playing patty cake with Mona Lisa... they kept finding ten-twelve hands!... Which meant they kept walloping each other good and hard... first one, then the other, just for fun... Whack! Whack! Whack! They were having a grand old time! the *mariniero* from La Reale felt in the mood to dance the *matchiche*... So he wraps Mimi in his arms, keeps her hopping with his lovey-dovey pawing. But Prospero wanted to call it a night... close up shop... it was past time, supposedly. Hector works the gramophone despite being forbidden... one of those morning glory-shaped jobs that screaked something horrible!... Prospero wanted an end to the hoof-stomping... to call it quits right then and there!

Bram! Brang! The shutters jangling... Police again! Lucky it wasn't the real thing!... only the night watchman from just down the way, over at Poplar Dock...

We let them in... those guys weren't nasty sorts... it was just their throats were always parched, they were real sponges... It was their turn to stand watch, so they'd popped in to check what all the singing was about... they sat down among the ladies... Cascade told the story of Jérôme the Flute! who on a sudden whim to strut his stuff had bet one of his dames that he could walk across the roof of the Crystal Palace without breaking anything... A phenomenal feat, just imagine for a minute! Practically fifty yards up off the ground... crossing the entire glass dome with nothing for balance but little iron rods... you might as well be walking on air... a Tara-Tohé tightrope trick!... nothing less than a miracle!... On the big day everybody had come to watch, the whole gang from the Leicester, the Royal... Right when he gets to the top! Scared shitless! Just came over him, plop! A wreck! He chickens out!... He motions he's on his way back down!... not pressing on... Ah! You should have heard the hell breaking loose!... "Cocksucker! Big zero! Blockhead! Limpdick! greaseball quitter!" They wanted him dead! Their insults echoed under the glass roof! The entire Crystal Palace was in an uproar! He saved his ass just in the nick of time, they were ready to string him up! Like greased lightning he was out of there, flew through the turnstile... And nobody ever laid eyes on him again, nowhere, knocked off his high horse... a beeline for America! Lost!... vanished off the face of the earth!... So went Jérôme's story...

"You're a different situation, kiddo, you've got no reason to clear out!"

The ladies were still laughing at what a goofy jerk Jérôme looked like up on the roof of the Crystal Palace! Oh! Oh! Oh!

One thing leads to another, good cheer all around, I catch up on the news about practically everybody... the crowd at the Monaco... Victor's... the Aztec... in Soho!... in short, all my buddies' hangouts... the Eiffel Tower... all over the place, guys leaving, ladies left behind... the Consulate was sending out calls... "Everybody's asking for you!" Right. I knew what he was after...

"Look, you see, perfect togetherness!..."

He laughs!... He shows me Angèle and Mona Lisa drinking from the same glass...

"You see... not a nasty peep... they've made up!... If they start scrapping again I told them: 'I'm joining up pronto! My haversack!' See the effect it has?... doves! And I wouldn't think twice!... I've warned them! War or peace! I want some damn peace and quiet!... You know how I feel about it, right?... Noise is a real pain in my ass... You've got noise up there, don't you, in your head? Told me so yourself, right? Right?..."

"Ah! A little, for sure!... Just a little..."

I didn't want to gripe.

So he's back talking to me about the war... about my wounds... and then back to my head... Wondering whether it still hurts me... He treated me nice... We return to the topic of women... Fact is, the hatchet's been buried... everything's hunky-dory...

"If they start scrapping again, they know what to expect!... I'm clearing off, I'm enlisting! I'll do just like everybody else!... The haversack! at the first word!... Ah, kiddo, it's love!... And I wouldn't think twice about it, you know me... I'm not the kind of guy who says one thing and does another! But you know how I feel too... it'll cost me dearly, and how! Very dearly..."

He rivets me...

"Does liquor mess up your head?"

It had no effect at all on him... He never went crazy because of booze... What's more, he didn't overdo it... Solid as a rock... We're back on the war again... my wounds... my head... he wonders whether I'm still in much pain...

"Ah! How about that! Ah! how about those big fairies!..."

He was stuck on that idea about military types... He starts fuming just at the thought. Couldn't let go...

He slicks his palm over his creamed curl...

He had hard, heavy mitts, the thick thumbs of a strangler. Gruesome hands, tougher than mine, even compared to my left! my one good paw... But there was nothing nasty about his face, always looked ready for a good laugh, always hankering for some fun... a good joke. London hadn't gotten him down at all... It was the war that stuck in his craw... And then fuck it all tough shit let's go!... He was off again! Pulled his bowler down over his curl and Ta-ra-ra-BOOM-dee-ay! let's get this show on the road!... the first dance! the biddie and the kiddie into the whirl... mad youth! Even so he'd aged in the not quite three months since we'd last seen each other. The girls didn't lift a finger to make life easier for him, gave him a real run for his money with all the dumb shit they pulled... constant hassles, day-in day-out disasters, over nothing and everything! He had eleven on his back... René's girls! Jojo's! Baldie Tatave's, Shithouse Jack's, and so on, plus Périgot's backup stable, and Vison's, and Grendemer's... a whole jointful... plus two or three besides... From everybody who'd cleared out, got sent to the front, joined up to the beat of marching bands! ordinary guys who'd caught the fever, others who'd got nabbed, he'd taken on all their women, for safekeeping, like a brother they could rely on, until their speedy return! So long! What a godawful mess! He had one hell of a zoo on his hands! No heart! No feeling! Angèle told me about it. A devil of a job to get the girls to hand over their take to the pimps... They bawled... forgot everything... sloppy, grungy, sneaky, yakking themselves to death, plus being soused to the gills worse than ever... the climate sure had a hell of a lot to do with it... They were dead flat-out bored. Plus their doctor visits... A song and dance every time over needles... They didn't give a damn about their rotting asses... as long as they could slip into new duds, boa feathers, kooky hats... plus knock back a few Pernods... they blew all their dough on crap, were in hock everywhere, even at the shoemaker's! They drank the pennies meant for repairs, traipsed through puddles, coughing their heads off... That's the sort of scene it was, and such jealousy, they'd put on a face for days on end, they wanted to spend the rest of their lives in the sack.

Cascade came back to his seat, pooped, sweaty. He watched his fillies dancing, all lighthearted laughing.

"They look so sweet when they're like this, kid! I'd have to beat them black and blue only once a day!..."

One hitch, he wasn't a violent man, the idea of handing out lumps turned him off...

"I want to make them feel just the way you see them now! I'll wind up killing them!"

He had to fight to get a word in edgewise. They thumbed their noses at him just for the hell of it. They acted up on purpose out on the street... standing the dagos to drinks, making crude passes, vampire ghosts weren't their only problem!... Another situation on his hands... he had to put up his dukes with little whippersnappers at the drop of a hat... and even wogs who came sniffing around the henhouse... Plenty to shave years off a guy... Plus this war that just wouldn't end...

"And here I was going to make way for the next guy!... How long do you think it can last?..."

Another couple-three years, I thought.

"You don't say, Christ, we'll all be six feet under!"

With that we returned to the topic of business... the quality of the customers... about this and that... Meanwhile, everybody's boozing it up like mad all around us, blabbing helter-skelter, screaming, smashing every and anything... throwing glasses at each other whole stacks at a time!...

Had to yell up against each other's ears. Angèle shouted her lungs out to add her two cents. And Jacasse, well the gal was in conniptions, one pissed hellcat... she hollered your ear off...

Cascade was sick and tired of her loud mouth...

"Will you shut the hell up!"

But the story about Raoul had hooked Cascade, just that and no other...

He went back to it again. He couldn't get it out of his head. I could see where he was going.

"Ah! How about that now!... Ah! How about that!..."

He wanted me to tell him one more time... rocking back and forth in his seat... his eyes glued on me... to be sure I wasn't putting one over on him... hadn't concocted any of it... and that it really had happened the way I said...

"You're positive now?... You're not mixed up? When they came he was asleep? Positive? That's the story?"

"Give me a break, come on... I was there!..." What more could I say?... "I was in the bed across from his... Number 14!..."

Nothing does the trick like details. I could see the story touched him... He was clinging to one wee doubt...

"They took him away at four o'clock? It was light out, you say?"

"Not yet."

"Was he limping?"

"Sure was, I'm telling you!"

He wanted to know about the firing squad... How big was it?

I'd missed that!...

"Ah! See now! You see!..."

He held on to his doubt... Not a big one... he didn't entirely believe me... But it was true.

"Did he give you my address?"

"I told you he did. Give me a break! The night before! How else would I've come?"

I'd gone over it a hundred times... I couldn't add any more to what I'd already said... But he felt a gnawing doubt... I had to tell the story one more time... Raoul's last words... when he'd told me: "Don't go there! Make yourself scarce!" and other stuff... I didn't remember everything. Anyway the address stuck in my mind. In the end I just clammed up. I was tired of repeating the same story over and over...

I couldn't tell him any more than I had...

He was worrying himself sick, that's a fact. Putting himself through hell over nothing... Eating his heart out with doubt... wondering whether Raoul had really been executed... He didn't believe me entirely... But it was true...

He just sat there, rocking... straddling his seat... Suddenly he felt real down in the dumps... just sat there like that... on the bench... stopped talking... didn't look at anything or anybody... didn't hear the uproar... the hell-raising all around... just kept grumbling the same thing...

"Fuck it all! Shit, that's tough..."

He wouldn't let up... patted his curl again... smoothed it down... one swipe of his palm... dead set, grousing... dogging his idea in his own mind... without a thought for the people around us...

Got to say, the party was going full swing... the girls had forced Prospero to get his ocarina back out... or else they'd break every last glass in the house... They start calling each other hysterics because of the tango... that's the dance that drives them nuts! and right into each other!... There goes Angèle, a bug up her ass, she wants to pounce on Carmen... The armistice is over!... "Nya! Nya! Nya!!" The battle flares! Insults fly! One camp for, another against... A circle forms, inside they can massacre each other... Cascade's looking but not seeing... his eyes fixed straight ahead... lost in thought... he puts his bowler back on... takes it off... dogging his idea...

He grabs me by the sleeve, leads me away, leaves the ladies to slap each other around...

"You understand!" he goes to me... "You understand... his mother... anyhow it's none of your business... I'm the one who brought him up, right... Right, huh?... that's what's important!"

He was calling on me as a witness... All I saw was some guy carrying on like a fanatic... making his life miserable with his obsession...

When you're young you're in a hurry, even hard knocks don't teach you a thing, you need to put on a few years, you need booze to start putting two and two together... and so you don't louse everything up as soon as you stick your nose in... Youth is a bitch... Cascade was boring the pants off me with this Raoul rigmarole. I had completely forgotten about Raoul myself... But he didn't. There's a load of reasons for tears. Loads for laughs, too! That was my take on life back in those days!...

I tell him: "Enough already, Cascade! You've got to come to grips! Think about something else! Look at Curlers, she's not all in a flap."

As a matter of fact, she was stripping. Getting ready for bed right there in front of everybody on top of the billiard table... she'd taken off her blouse, her camisole, her slip. She stretched out on top. That was the idea... Vigils tickled her, she was chuckling away, in seventh heaven... Cascade couldn't have cared less...

"So, kiddo!" he goes, then asks: "You're staying with us then? Where'd you want to make off to?..."

"To La Plata aboard the *Hamsün*!... the *Kong Hamsün*... with Jovil the boatswain..."

"Who dug that one up for you? Prospero?"

Then he darts him this look, real nasty...

I kind of straighten things out... talk fast... patch up...

"It was all my idea, I really pushed the guy..."

I don't want any run-ins with Prospero...

"He was dead set against it!"

I assert... assure... wouldn't want Prospero to take the rap... I'm on the level...

"Well, that's all right then!... That's more like it..."

He rests easier... it mustn't have been part of the plan for me to take such liberties... sail away across the seas! He was going to have a nice little chat with Prospero! I had to stay, end of discussion.

I looked at Cascade again... his topper yanked down over his eyes... his cigarette butt back and forth... to and from his mouth... he's on edge... All of a sudden the whole scene got to him... He was staring at the girls... They were having a high old time!...

Everybody cakewalk!... Cancan!... wagging... rocking... it really rubbed Cascade the wrong way... I could see he was about to jump right in the middle, slap around three or four of them... They were making noise on purpose... He held himself in check... chewed his tobacco... I could see his jaws...

"Will you take a look at this sideshow!..."

They were drunk on their asses... They'd put away more than the men, more than the sailors...

"Why'd you make them come?..."

I ask him, after all.

"Aw, knock it off, you know it's your party!..."

Here we go again! He's back on that kick!... This is as much a party as crepes suzette up my ass!... He was pushing me to my limit!

"Is so a party! is so! You'll see!"

He was absolutely insistent. He had a thing for riddles...

"OK, great!..."

He starts back up with his bitching... hunches down in his seat... Bang! Bang! Bang! Somebody's at the door, knocking hard this time...

"Cut the music!" Prospero orders...

The girls snuff/blow out the lights, Cascade won't have it, they're relit...

Prospero cracks open the door. Two men barge inside. It's Trafalgar Nelson and Centipede... All out of breath and sweaty. They see Cascade, dash over to him...

"They got here!" he wheezes, "they got here!..."

"And so? So? Let 'em come in!..."

He doesn't like shouting.

"Where are they?"

"In the hansom!..."

"Where are they, I'm asking you..."
"Jermyn Street..."
"And so then?"
"They're coming via the dock..."
"They're carrying it? Just like that?"
He motions... Is it heavy?...
They nod yes.
"Centipede, you go show them the way... They won't know... Tell them it's OK. Nelson, you keep an eye on the door! Make sure you stay put! They're on the way!"
All of a sudden there's commotion outside... people calling... more Twee-eets! Twee-eets!...
A crunch of gravel... footsteps...
"Prospero! Prospero! The roast beef!"
Cascade gets the show on the road.
"Girls, chow time!" he orders...
"More on the way," Prospero grumbles...
"More? Oh! crap! cripes! Will you get a move on? And don't forget the gravy! Nice and hot! Got it?..."
Prospero walks out, leaves the door open...
Dead quiet outside... nobody talking... no nothing... just the lapping on the embankment... Prospero's mill busy grinding away... way back... in the kitchen... the ding... ding... ding... of the tram very far off... on the other side... the other bank!... Wapping...
Sosthène draws close to me... asks...
"What's up?... D'you hear?"
He's not as soused as all that...
Cascade hears him...
"Your ass!" He shuts him up.
Now's no time to rub Cascade the wrong way.... But I'd been wondering myself... Tobacco?... Hot merchandise?... A bag of poppies?... opium?... or else carpets?... weapons?... some secret shipment, whatever the case... funny business, for sure... I ask Cascade...
"Is it big?..."
I'd seen his gesture...
"You'll see! You'll see! Stay put!..."
"Ah, the hell with this, I'm out of here! Geez, they're waiting for me down at the old tub!"
"No, they're not! They're not! They aren't waiting for you."
I'm rubbing him the wrong way...
"Are so," I go, "are so waiting for me..."
They were getting on my nerves all of a sudden, the whole pack of them... all together again just like that at Prospero's place!... perfect timing! a

miracle... Just what the hell was going on?... that little son of a bitch Nelson, that lousy bastard Centipede!... and all these drunks?... and that dyke over there!... and Cascade!... and maybe Jovil along with the rest?... all in cahoots!... An ambush in the bag!...

"Hey, wait!" I ask him flat out, "did you all plan to meet up here?"

"Another ladle" he answers me back... "mulled wine for your chest. You're going to catch cholera! Drafts are just terrible, you know! Cholera!"

The door stood wide open... The girls were coughing, sniggering, nudging each other with their elbows...

Crunch of gravel... a crowd's on the way... getting closer at last... Cascade grabs the lamp, blows it out... The girls start bitching...

"Knock it off!"

He goes outside. Talks. Comes back in. There's three of them... carrying what?... I can see their silhouettes in the black door frame... whatever they're bringing, it's heavy...

Virginia whispers to me: "They're carrying someone..."

I didn't want to guess. They pulled the door shut. Prospero relights the lamp. Now you can see. I can see the porters. Clodovitz and Boro. I had the feeling... They set down their package on the floor... It's heavy, huge, reeks to high heaven... Right off it takes one and all by surprise... spreading... Everybody catches a whiff... keeps mum... all eyes on me... creosote... tar... it packs a wallop...

Clodo... his big banana ears... the old rat-face is standing there right in front of me... sweating, dripping... glad to have arrived...

"Hello, Doctor!" I go to him...

"Howth tricks, pal?... How you doing?..."

They must have come a long ways... he takes off his glasses... sits... they had quite a time of it... I see he's in a frock coat... Black from head to toe with a white tie... gussied up in a tux...

"Doctor!" I ask him... "Doctor! What are you bringing us?..."

I'd rather talk to him than Boro... I can't stand the sight of Boro... brutal, fast-talking con artist... I can't stomach the guy... whereas Clodovitz is an all right sort... you can still talk to him...

Boro had a load on his mind... circling all around the package... going, coming, rocking back and forth... like some bear... looks to me he's put on a few pounds since we last saw each other... around his shoulders... his ass... his hands... he's busting out of his jacket...

He answers for Clodo...

"Oooh! Oooh! You'll see, whippersnapper!..."

He chuckles to himself, shaking his big huge head, his chest, a barrel!... Ooh!... Ooh!... Ooh!...

"You'll see, whiz kid!"

"Whiiizzzzz!" he goes.

"Drrrrinks! Goddamn it! Drrrrinks!..."

Always parched!...

Sosthène sniffs, sneezes... for good reason... the dust particles in the air, seems to me... All at once everybody's sneezing... And then we break out laughing... our spirits high! Yes, indeedy, it's my party! Good cheer all around! music and dancing! Ever so much! A real wild time! Tra-la! Yippee! Dee-ay! The ladies want what they want! No letup, not even for a minute! they climb onto Boro, smooch/fiddlediddle him every which way! Squeals! Making whoopee! Clodo's also getting his jollies, yukking it up, real down in the dumps when he walked in, but now look at him, practically saucy, trying to suck Nénette's tittie! The two have a little tussle...

"Doctor, you're such a kidder!"

A rip-roaring wild old time all around!... Everybody pawing each other, a no-holds-barred smooch fest! The sailors take liberties... the watchmen can't see straight anymore... They've been celebrating so hard, chugging down mug after mug! toasting me! They can't believe their eyes anymore!... They rub/tug at them...

"Long life! Happy Ferdinand! Long live France! Long live sailors!..."

But, geez, the stink is something vile... Don't they have noses?... They couldn't give a shit... It's coming from the bundle... in back... I'd like a look... It's giving off this odor... a stench... looks like it doesn't bother anybody... they sniff the air a few times... but that's all...

I'd like to go over for a peek... Carmen's got her eye on me... she didn't have any drinks, not her... I ask Boro... He doesn't understand a word... too absorbed... He's got four girls hollering after him... trying to rip his pants off... With one jerk of his body, wham, he breaks free... leaps away... he's light on his feet when he makes the effort... his huge noggin weighs nothing at all... he grabs little Elise, and they're off on the dance floor... A whirlwind... Everybody's swept up... Three lamps are lit... The party's back in full swing wilder than ever! Spirits so high! the girls are having a contest to see who can spin faster! faster, faster still!... spinning tops! Bats out of hell! twisters! Bzing! Bing! Backwards! on your ass... Bang! smithereens! Curlers is the wildest of the bunch, she's spinning with Lulu Mouche... their arms and legs in a tangle... whirling... grazing their knees... flat on their faces they both blubber... Now the band strikes up... all the fifes... the sailors on ocarinas... Prospero on guitar, the dago too... Dédé's too sloshed!... Centipede invites Virginia... he won't take no for an answer... Cascade's got new life in him... hot to trot... he leads the *matchiche*... sends Carmen flying from one end of the room to the other... Brown Sugar has hitched her skirt up over her head... she sticks her comb in her mouth, play-fangs... solid green... she wants to show us her belly dance... She hollers she's got the most beautiful beaver... That pisses off Angèle... who struts over to show what she thinks about that... whether that's the proper way to dress for a dance! they're going to mess it up... But there's no more grog in the bowl... the battle breaks off... Got to light another punch... What an incredible rigmarole... No flames no spirits!... At last, got it going!... back in business!... This is an honest-to-goodness party!... No mistake about that! I say so to Boro myself... One hitch, the bundle they brought, sitting over there... In a tarpaulin... I ask him again... No answer... The stink's honest-to-god awful... looks like it doesn't bother anybody... They take a sniff, and that's all... They kick up their heels, wave their arms, flap their jaws... as though nothing were wrong... The chorus is all the rage:

Watch your step!
Watch your step!

The girls belt it out, and again from the top... they don't even know what's coming out of their mouths... one's bawling out "The Pampolaine"... the vino's hot now...

Vouash your step!
Vouash your step!

Frenchified...

"Ah! Terrific job! Ah! terrific!..." Each her own personal fan club... such great singers one and all.

Sosthène, who had really been put through hell, been worked over up and down every inch of his body, who had taken so many horrible whacks and now couldn't walk anymore, whom the cops had roughed up so badly, punched black-and-blue, huge bruises all over his body, all of a sudden he's feeling up for some fun, a kid again with Mireille, he latches on to the ceiling lamps, starts leapfrogging... Everybody's fun just kept growing and growing... Cascade sends me over his old lady, Angèle...

"Ferdinand's bored!..."

She invites me... I can't say no... And we're off!... I'm not too crazy about the *matchiche*... It's too complicated for me... I get all screwed up... I prefer a new step...

"Polka!" I request... "A polka!..."

"All right!"

Prospero changes tunes... rats! it's a waltz... Never mind!... OK!...

Yeeiikkes!... right then... an awful screech!... From in back... from the darkness!... a stuck pig...

Everything stops...

Yeeooowww!... all over again!...

It's Delphine, I'll be damned...

I call her: "Delphine!... Delphine..."

I recognized her voice... Is somebody hurting her?... I can't see a thing... all the ladies in the place are yelling... a free-for-all!... pandemonium!... That banshee scream has flipped them out... They're totally berserk... bawling, frantic, in a panic, huddling up against each other... I let go of Angèle, she drops right to her knees... She just kneels there, freaked, squealing, staring into space where she fell, reciting in a quavering voice:

Saint Beard! Saint Flower!
Hope of our Savior!
All who pray to you
Will never perish!

Three-four times in a row like that. She stands up, flings herself on Carmen, into her arms... They sob, mumble together, moan...

"Virginia! Virginia!..." I call.

She comes running... I kiss her...

Well?... Well?... What's the big catastrophe?

"Cascade! Cascade!" I holler for him... That's no way to behave! He's in back, looking into the business... He took the lamp... He's bending over along with the others. They're absorbed. Delphine is on her knees... They give her a push... uh-uh... she wants to stay there... they start yanking tugging her... they want her out!... Such a howl of protest! You'd think they were slitting her throat!... Back to screaming!... They don't want her messing around with the sack, they want to stop her.

She claws back, bites, clings...

They pound her, she lets out horrendous howls, breaks free, escapes, scurries, reaches the other end of the room, stands up, threatens us...

"Hear Macbeth! Hear! Infirm of purpose!..."

She's wound up again, accuses us, her threatening finger, bug-eyed, horror, you name it.

Her back against the wall...

"Give me the dagger! The sleeping and the dead..."

She commands us. She rants, chokes, pants! She charges back into the mob, at the package, hurls herself on top again, locks it in a body clutch.

"Darling! Darling!" she calls. "Forget me not!"

The whole joint yells, baits her, a screaming match. Got to get her out of here! Enough already! Up close the reek is truly foul... Rotting meat, putrid flesh, plus with those dust particles in the air... a combo that gives you the heaves... Of course I'm familiar with it... real familiar...

While they're scrapping with Delphine—they're trying to pry her away, she's fighting back—I bend down... take a look... the lamp's right here... I can see up close... first the head... a real mishmash... steeping inside... And with them whaling away like that! oatmeal! It's no dream!... The head!... The head!... it's a head all right! well, a huge hunk anyway!... it's Claben... his mug all right... but minus his eyes!... and just a mishmash attached... neck shreds... the whole thing scorched real bad... in the canvas sack... sitting in its ooze... This is what they lugged over?... with all that big song and dance... the sack... rotting flesh... Ah! I was starting to catch on... one hell of a job... damn!... Where'd they get their hands on it?... That was the first question that popped into my mind... the sight of the corpse didn't get to me, I'd seen my share, and then some!... Ah! what a business!... I see... I see... I take another close look... they're not concerned about me... they're at each other's throats over Delphine... Prospero doesn't want her thrown out... so she can kick up a fuss outside! They're going to slug it out over her...

"No scenes! I don't want a scene!"

Prospero's shouting at the top of his lungs...

Sosthène looks along with me... leans down likewise... holding the lamp for me... I don't want Virginia coming near... I sit her down... I bend over, just me... take an even closer look... trying to find the hole... in the skull... where Boro came out and attacked him... knocked him flat... And Bang! and Ping!... I was there... You bet I want a look-see!... But Delphine with the others over there, she spots me looking, touching her corpse... Ah! she's off again... charges back at me... pounces on top... a she-tiger!...

"You witch! you devil!" she screams... "You killed that angel!"

I'm not going to hash it out with her, I've got a situation on my hands.

"Bullshit!" I shout, "That's out of line!"

Ah! I'm defending myself, fuck this! Ah! And how!

"I didn't kill anybody or anything! You sleazy slob! You've got some nerve, you liar!

"Yes! Yes! You did!" she insists...

The other jerks're splitting their sides... they don't know their asses from their elbows, too sloshed!... She comes up close, tries to hypnotize me just like that... burps right in my face! Bowah! I stay cool...

"Bowah!..." I answer back... And then I literally bowl her over!... her ass smack in the mishmash... Squish!... flat out... She's stuck now... laughing... she splattered us all over... the girls are letting out such screams... Carmen's blouse is dripping... real gross move... Everybody's got a whiff... Big guffaw!

For my part, I chew out Delphine right there on the floor... I'm on her case... I'm dead set she know the score... and not get any wrong ideas!...

"It was the cigarettes! Remember? The cigarettes!..."

I myself sure do remember! I do recall!... She's the one who brought them... she'd gone out on purpose just to pick them up who knows where! Ah! this isn't just a bunch of crap!... such things do exist! it's the truth!... I say so in front of the others... What's right is right! She should tell the whole story! Her fault! Yes! Her fault! A waste of time trying to pin it on me!...

I bawl, I bellow it out! She's sitting there her ass in the head-stew. I shout to the world that she's the one! Everybody knows! And so drop it! Loud enough for all to hear!

Nobody's listening to me... they're rolling on the benches laughing so hard... they don't understand a word. The watchmen are busting their guts too. They've lost their tunics, their shoes. They've drunk themselves stark naked, all except for their uniform belts, crawling on all fours under the women. Just barking away in delight.

"You big pain in the ass! You dirty rotten bitch!..." I was thinking!... About Delphine! Be just like her to finger me!... And Boro over there, lips buttoned...

"There's a murderer among us!"

That's what I shout loud and clear! Nobody gives a shit.

"Drink up, kiddo," Cascade tries reasoning with me. "Drink up, this is bad for the old bean!"

The others watch me thinking... bust out laughing, those sons of bitches!

"You big fat hypocrite!" I insult her... "You broken-down jade! Silly old fart! Ugly creep!..."

I'll teach them how to behave! she's a murderer ten times over like me! I say it! right to Delphine! Even repeat it... I'm not hiding!... I shout over the commotion...

Now Curlers is putting in her two cents worth... I didn't ask anything from her! She walks over, grabs me by the neck, screams loud enough for all ears!

"Hey, know what? A train ran over him!"

She busts a gut over that one.

"Who?" I go...

"Our lucky surprise package here! right over his mug!"

She points to the stinking package.

"No, it didn't! Lightning struck him!"

I turn around. Prospero tossed out that crack. Wise-ass...

I didn't ask that asshole anything either! One nasty dig! two big laughs! and then everybody joins in! An all-around knee-slapper! They'd never seen anything so funny!

"Lightning! Lightning!" they repeated...

"Well, fuck you then! Fuck you all!"

I couldn't take any more of their bullshit.

Now Delphine revved back up, after sitting on her ass in the oatmeal, she clambers back up on her feet and starts chewing me out... a stinking mess she is... oozing all over... her slip's thick with corpse-slime...

"Wash your hands! Off to bed! To bed!"

She's sending me to bed... cursing me...

"Damn you! Damn you!" she declaims...

Prospero walks off with our lamp...

"All right! Let's go! That's enough!"

The women stop him... they want to be able to see...

"Shh! Shh!" Delphine's not finished! "Listen! There's knocking at the gate! Shh! Child!..."

She makes like she's listening.

"A shutter!"

She sniffs the air: "A smell of blood!"

Here we go!

She reels... grabs her skirt... heaves sighs... paces back, forth, revving up...

A group "Shh! Shh!..."

She's going to give us a little number.

"A smell of blood! A smell of blood!"

She declaims like that inspired... freezes... finger in the air.

Her pet pose.

She looks at the audience. If she starts in on me again, I'll smash this chair in her face.

First off, there's no smell of blood... She's talking dumb... I know what blood smells like! It smells like something scorched, rotten... Not quite the same thing! plus with a sort of whiff of creosote... Just needed one look at the dead meat, the head... I'd seen plenty corpses, heads... That's not going to fool me... No way!...

I didn't want to talk to Boro, but I light into him anyway... I ask again: "Hey, where'd you pick this up from?..."

Hadn't the body been pulled out yet? I meant, dug out from the debris. I could still see him down in that cellar... I hadn't dreamed it up either. How we'd shunted him around!... and the fire that caught right afterward... the junk heap... the pigsty!...

He ignores my question.

"Come on!" I go... "You deaf or what? Where'd it come from?"

He grumbles, that's all.

"The hell with this! Quack! Quack!..." I holler.

"From the hospital!..." He comes out and says.

He acts sore with me. I wonder over what? Fuck him!... I'm the one who'd have good reasons! If I must say so myself! I do. To him. He yanks down his bowler... fixes a scowl...

"I've got a stomachache," he growls, "those string beans!..."

"So where'd you carry it from?" I start back up... "The hospital? from far away?..."

"From London!" he goes.

I don't get it.

So, he'd been pulled up? already exhumed?

"From the morgue, that's where he comes from, you dumb little jerk!... Can you picture him in a bed looking that way, or what? Well, can you?... From the London morgue! There! Satisfied, mister?..."

I put him on edge.

"But I didn't have a clue!"

"You never have a clue about anything, you dumb bastard! Monsieur clears off, end of story... Monsieur shits and is off! Monsieur doesn't like trouble! let his pals go and fend for themselves!..."

Him with that accent of his, rolling the *r*s of his "clearrrs" and "bastarrrd" and "trrrouble"...

I was starting to figure it out...

Clodo was the one who'd pulled him out... taken advantage of his post... his duties at the hospital... It must have been one hell of a mess...

"How'd you manage it?"

"Just had to come yourself!... You'd've seen!..."

Delphine was bellowing full blast... she'd worked herself back to fever pitch... caught a second wind... bellowing in front of the wall... the tragedy was rattling every inch of her body... her arms... her head... her eyes... her belly... she was throwing herself around spastically... shredding her flowers... her train... rrrip!... another convulsion!... rrrip! bounding wildly around her stage!...

She plants herself in one spot!... Apostrophizes us: "Macbeth! Macbeth! what's the business? Such a hideous trumpet calls to parley!"

She makes like she's listening in the distance!...

She imitates: "Taa-dee!... Taa-dee!..." the sound of the hunting horn... calling her... strident shrill!... "Taa-dee!... Taa-dee!..."

"Yoo-hoo, Macbeth!... Yoo-hoo!..."

The joint explodes in an uproar! A chorus of cries! Taa-dee... Taa-dee... Total bedlam!...

Truth was, more people had shown up at the door...

Two three guys rattling the knocker...

Centipede goes over...

Forceful thumps... The door's pushed open... Two policemen... They run their flashlight over us...

"What are you scoundrels up to? What's all this light?"

They thought we had too many lights on. They go out again... bring back in a nigger... dragging him... some loudmouth... a petty thief... a tank room nigger... They caught him stealing red-handed... boring a hole into a cask of rum... to suck it down right from the opening... with those lips of theirs it's easy... everybody knows about the "kiss" trick... they tug him by the ears... he whines... protests... that makes three more who're thirsty... cops're always parched...

They go over and sit down with the others. They can see the steaming grog. They stop talking... plan to hunker down among the girls... It was past closing time, that's a fact, they're tired, take a whiff... the nigger's stopped crying, he wants a drink, to be treated like one of the guests... Before you know, it's going to be three in the morning... Cascade offers cigars... They refuse... then they accept—not the nigger, the policemen...

Delphine's having a little snooze right where she's sitting against the wall, she overdid it with all her antics. But I've got something to tell her. It can wait a while. I start smoking. This cigar is a hefty job, not some dinky cigarillo, it's got a band and place of origin, a Coronaro... It's my party! Big Ben strikes a quarter-to... its echo reverberates loud and long over the river... up into the clouds... soft cannon fire... Why this big shindig? I'd like an explanation...

Ah! The question pops up again... "Why ain't you closed?..." It's bugging the cops... So they ask nice and easy...

"It's Ferdinand's party!" Everybody responds in unison... I'm not going to show them the mess on the floor... That would give them some idea what kind of party this really is!... Delphine is getting some shut-eye practically right on top of it... Maybe that'd get a rise out of them!... Oh, brother, how I'd give anything to see that!... So much tobacco smoke right now... a murky haze through the whole joint... kind of covers the rotten meat reek... might give them the idea the place is full of shit holes... a kitchen in back...

The wheels in my head are turning...

Boom!... Bang!... right then everything starts shaking again... all the cannons going off...

A salvo of sirens... Still more to come!... That was just an intermission... Kerboom!... A huge blast over Poplar... Got to be a zeppelin this time around... They all dash to the door... I stay put, my ears are humming too loud... each cannon boom echoes inside me... rattles my whole head... I see stars... I sure the hell am fed up with these earsplitting fireworks... some people are going back out for another look... I want some peace and quiet, Christ!... I want to go way in back! I bump into Boro... He's on his knees... I didn't see him... He's in the pitch-dark... redoing the package... tying up the bundle... you've never whiffed such a stinko knockout reek!... No problem for him... He slogs away at the sack... Centipede holds one end... "Hmph!... Uuh!..." Two... three ropes... and then knots... Heave! ho!... They move up off the floor... Legs slings it across his back... they walk out... threading their way... the back door... not the one on the dock... through the small courtyard... Nobody the wiser... They let in a draft, which rouses Delphine, a chilly blast... She didn't see a thing... rubs her eyes a little... perks back up... Right away she starts bellowing... haranguing... Nobody pays her any mind... Everybody's interested in what's outside... all eyes peeled for the zeppelins...

"There!... There!..."

Some spot them!... Or claim to!... Hurray for the searchlights!...

Delphine stands back up!...

"Infectious minds!" she shouts out... right off the insults start flying... "To their deaf pillows will discharge their secrets!..."

It's aggravating the hell out of her that nobody's listening... She's moving heaven and earth in the back of the joint... bellowing louder and louder... she wants to bring everybody back inside... to create a sensation... Cascade creeps up from behind, gives her a good swift kick in that ass that sends her flying ten feet in the air. She lands, lets out a yell that drowns everything, the noise of the cannon fire!

"Out damned spot!" she rages... "Get the fuck out!"

She's all up in arms something awful, one ornery mood. We're the ones she wants the fuck out the door... Cascade grabs her, rolls her under his arm, and off he goes. He's strong. She claws, scratches, yanks, howls horribly!... By coincidence the others are coming back inside... Too much thundering out there... Bombs are exploding and whizzing past at ground level now... the entire embankment is ricocheting with shrapnel... The roofs are rattling... This is Delphine's big moment... she gets all the more worked up. At every blast, she hops, boom! boom! Hops right out the door!

"Lady Macbeth!" she calls... "Lady Macbeth! There we are!"

Lady Macbeth! That's her all right!...

She's all alone out there at present. She's hollering through the hail of shrapnel. The zeppelin's turning right above the warehouse... the shrapnel ricocheting all over the sheet metal roofs! No more going outside.

The gang's not afraid, they're ready to whoop it up. Everybody toasts me, all the best on my party... To Delphine too, outside! "Hurray, Delphine! Hurray, good girl!" The policemen shut the door, they don't want the rest of us going out. It's strictly forbidden! All the same there's one hell of a racket out there. The shack's shaking. It even wakes up the watchmen, who'd dozed off under the tables. The women yank them by their feet...

"No! No! It's Saint Patrick's Day!"

They're not crazy about Saint Ferdinand!... they're both Irish! Saint Ferdinand means nothing to the Irish... Everybody starts back with the smooching!

Outside Boom! Boom! faster and faster... The power of cannon blasts!... the nigger digs the boom! booming! thrilled with terror! he grovels on his knees... rolls marbles... Boom! Boom! Scaring the ladies with his huge mouth... Boom! Boom!...

My poor little Virginia's the only one dozing nice and pretty... all snuggled up on the bench... a little angel... soundly... for the past hour... I watch over her sleep... The animals didn't wake her up... the cannon neither... she needs sleep in the state she's in... I sure love her, I really do... I say so to Gertrude who's right there...

"I sure love you too," she answers.

Straightaway everybody likes everybody in the place... It's the warm glow of my party... Too bad there's this reek... "In love! in love!" they're wailing just like that, all lovey-dovey with the policemen, and then to each other... wiggling around a little... but no more dancing, too smashed, too pooped, right off they start flapping about helplessly, crumple, in twosomes... foursomes... in heaps... snoring away... they need a shot of booze, a pick-me-up!... the gang's dozed off! We try to rustle up some... some bottles, I mean... Ping! Ping! Pong!... here we go again... A bomb blew up, direct hit in the river! A gust... a violent blast... a whirlwind... water splattering... everything in the joint is jolted out of place... knocked around, toppled, the glasses... flasks... drawers... the walls of the shack buckle crack... the boomboom! drives the ladies wacko! they start whaling away at each other's asses! doing their own rendition of the force, the violence... Blam! Wham! Wham!... hard enough to break their butts! A trio pounces on Renée, turns her over, tans her fanny bright red... I too want to spank her... it'll bring me luck, they say. Well, this makes the whole place slaphappy! The police are having a great time, crawling around, writhing in hysterics so badly two start choking, puke, turn bright crimson, they can't take anymore...

"Oh! my! my!" they gasp out...

Renée's getting spanked, everybody taking a whack, and she's gesticulating, howling, flailing around, croaking in wild delight, kroar! kroar! like a cat ready to kick the bucket with each slap on her ass. It's so goddamn hilarious people are going bonkers, they're in stitches pissing everywhere, rolling barfing burping through the whole place all on top of each other!

I'm not going to puke on my little girl sleeping there like an angel... Ah! no way! Ah! what a stinking thing to do!...

But all of a sudden, wham! I jump up with a start. Where'd they get to? I can't see Boro or Clodovitz anymore. It's true! A fact! I'm completely nailed to the spot! terror!... I'm convinced!... I can't contain myself.

They've gone off to pull some double cross! "Traitors here! Traitors!" I shout, assert... Nobody'll stop me!

Ah! I want to look for Delphine... I want to declaim along with her. Ah! I'm no louse! I want her to know! I stumble into her outside on the gravel. She insults me, she doesn't want to get up on her feet... wants to sleep just the way she is nice and peaceful... just like that under the awful shells!... She's courageous! scoffs at me!... I'm just a coward! I argue endlessly, throw in the towel, shit! The hell with her!...

The girls in the pub are sloshed so bad, paddling Renée so hard she's bleeding like crazy, streaming with thick rivulets... the nigger comes over to lap it all up... another wild fit of laughter... Now on to me. They're going to spank me, they insist, it's my turn.... they run after me... I fight them off, calm them down a bit... So now they're going to go over and give Virginia a shake, they're so berserk over the whole business... They want to teach her the *matchiche*!... I teach them a few good stamps of my heel... Whomp! on their feet!... they've all got corns! they jump... eeeee!

Plop back down on the cops!... Yikes!... You! You! Hey!

I have another go at Cascade, whisper up against his ear: "Where'd they get to?..."

The question's bugging me... I want to know where they carried the mess....

If it was supposed to be all in fun, I didn't find it funny, supposed to be some big clever stunt, for my money they were a couple of lunkheaded jerks, two godawful scumbags! Corpses aren't supposed to be paraded around, you'd have to be a kid to get a kick out of that stuff, a couple of not-so-smart smart alecks of their sort, people who aren't going off to war, puny pathetic wimpy pimps! clowns my balls! I spell out a few things in his ear, so they don't go thinking I'm impressed!... poor pathetic moron maggots!...

Plus that technique of theirs! Ah! let's not get started!...

They strut outside right in the middle of an air-raid alert! Such perfect timing! When every cop in creation has his eyes on the embankment! Ah! they had a knack for doing exactly the right thing!...

I congratulate them!...

"Couldn't they leave him here?..."

It looked like a little smarter thing to do...

"Why, did you want to turn him into croquettes, or what?" he asks, smart-mouthed.

"What the hell are they going to do with him?" I ask again, "beside making croquettes?..."

That was the question.

"They're going to dump him into the drink, sugarpuss! Since you want to know! The crabs'll gobble him up, end of story!... Satisfied, sonny?... Since you wanted the details! Can't burn him up any more than he's already been! Am I right? Did you get a look at his head? Ever feel like snacking on him yourself sometimes?... Somebody's got to take care of the job! Since you couldn't give a hoot!... Mr. Hot Lips!... Mr. Leaves-His-Work-Half-Finished! Mr. Got-Other-Plans!... We've got to get cracking, move our asses for him! Got to whisk his slop away! Deal with his little you-know-whats! There, Mr. Fine-Young-Man! Fantastic hero, and all that jazz! Mr. Got-Nothing-But-Love-on-His-Mind!"

Now I had my answer... something to chew over... so they were having a go at me, in short... More than one person had a score to settle with me... this crew here or some other!... Just about everybody, to tell the truth... Starting with my family... with my father... my mother... Then with the cops... with Centipede, others... and now with the pimps... the French Consulate... how about the Sixteenth Armored Cavalry Division?... Wasn't too sure about that one... with Totor, Titune, Curlers, Girouette, the Colonel, and Tartempion... I already had too much hanging over my head for one more score to change much of anything! they could all go fuck themselves! That's how I saw it!... They just stirred up a lot of nasty memories!... Pure jealousy on their part!... That's all!...

Ah! I was forgetting about my pregnant girl, my angel, my cherub, my life... Ah! I don't want them to lay a finger on her!... I'll kill them all, damn it!... they could all take a shot at her, in a single file that stretches from earth to heaven... it wouldn't change a damn thing about nothing, and then they could end by polishing me off! since that's how things were done! I wouldn't budge an inch, I'd stand my ground, give my last drop of blood to defend my idol.

That was my attitude! Fighting words! I chewed his ass out, laid it on the line! Ah! I sit him down! He makes a move!... Studies me a second... says to himself: "Just look at this little animal!..."

I use the opportunity to strike. I grab him, I want the upper hand. I want to hear him say to himself: "Really, this guy's not somebody to mess around with!"

"They'll hang me!" I proclaim... "And how! they'll hang me! High! That's right! They've got tons of reasons..."

But I was fed up to my eyebrows! No more Hide and Seek! I've won! Hands down! I'm not pushing too hard! I want respect. That's all. I drag Virginia to her feet! I want her to dance... We don't give a hoot about the boomdaboom! We've seen our share of total godawful messes! This one here doesn't add up to more than a couple-three little farts!

Cascade nabs me by the sleeve: "Hey, didn't you see Matthew again?"

"Not yet."

"Because the investigation's still going on... maybe you're not up on the latest?..."

"You know damn well I've been busy, we were at the Colonel's... in Willesden... You know that!..."

"Yes, but it's ongoing all the same... Willesden or not..."

Right in my face. Dished it right back at me.

"That's the score, dickhead! Now you've got the info. What've you got to say? Still leaving tonight?"

"No! No! Course not!..."

All eyes on me.

"You're staying then?"

"What's it look like?"

I don't bat an eyelid, face them head on.

"Hurray, old buddy! Now that's guts for you!"

Congrats from all around!

"And your little lady?"

He points to my little angel lying asleep there.

"She's British... I told you, it's for her uncle..."

I wanted them to get the story straight... she wasn't some slut...

"Well, if you're going to put her to work, why'd you want to go so far away?... isn't she happy here with us?"

"That's not it, you know... not so fast..."
He didn't really get it.
She woke up nice and gently.
"Hello, miss!"
He looks at her. He hadn't taken a real good gander before. Now he sticks his face up close. "Say, she's got beautiful eyes!"
He was acting gallant, which was unusual for him. Hardly ever smiled at the ladies.
"Good-bye, miss!"
"Good-bye, sir!"
Not scared off, my little sweetheart.
He thought hard.
"You ought to stick her in longer dresses... She looks like jailbait..."
He was already picturing the standing gallery where his own tarts worked...
"Ah! but you know, she's cute!..."
He was confident.
"One problem though, look out for the dagos! A word of advice. They're wild about this type, they're nuts... A crazy thing about blondes! they'll snatch her off! Gone in a gust! A whirl! Wildmen, take it from me. *Italgos! Fumiero!* Isn't that right, Prospero?... that's how they train them down there! Right, Signor Prospero?..."
He hawks up a huge loogie. Memories... still sort of taking their toll on him... One more time he says just like that: "Hell, miss." A wink. Then he glances off to the side, his mind elsewhere...
Meantime the girls are wiggling around, climbing and clambering on top of the cops! sliding off, kissing cuddling them for all they're worth!... Can't let up a single second, can't let the cops worry about anything, they're nice and comfy here, and here's right where they should stay... Kiss!... Kiss!... Kiss!... Furious pawing and mauling. The girls pop off the men's helmets, make as if they're pissing inside. I don't even crack a smile. The way I see it, there's something fishy about the watchmen, they came on purpose like it was no big deal, with these out-of-it expressions, all confused/sloshed on their last legs, but really they're having a grand old time, eyes peeled... they're setting us up... We're the suckers in this game!... All of a sudden the truth hits me... turns me inside out floors me!... I think about it! and tremble!... splutter!... shiver from head to toe... Virginia sees me, takes my hands, I go white, red, don't know which end is up anymore... Terror stabbing through me... Just my imagination... No, not some figment! I feel myself with my hands... It's me!... Me and nobody else!... No mistake... No way I'm dreaming at all! Shit! Hilarious! Knocked for a loop by a headache! the ache in his head, I mean, holy smoke! His stew! Not mine! His! Oh! You You-oouu! "I'm trembling! Trembling!..." Always the same! I go red! Em-

barrassment!...

"Shit! Shit! He's back!"

I shout over to Delphine!

"Can you hear me, lady?" I want a look at her! "Hey, Butt-blister? He left! And he's come back!"

She can't hear me, she's outside.

"Reduced to mush, catch that? Cream cheese! He's revolting! reeks worse than you three hundred miles off!"

My grand announcement.

"Now that's a man! a sausage!..."

I don't give a shit whether they're listening to me! I don't give a shit about their song and dance! I don't give a shit about anything! Swept away with terror! Nobody can stand up to me! I'm thunder! Boom! Boom! I can do it all by myself like the nigger! I drop bombs! I've seen my share of cannonades... Five and a hundred thousand times more than all of you put together! And you can all go take a flying fuck!

This makes me feel good! I'm making my presence felt... I'm proud... I'm somebody. I kiss Virginia! I've trounced my fear. They realize it. I'm getting a round of applause.

That wakes up Delphine, she shouts at me from the outside, screaming nasty cracks upwind...

"Little man! Stupid little man!" she calls me...

She's brave enough in the dark.

Ah! in the end I laugh it off, the hell with it all!... Scared at first, and then it's OK... Got to grin and bear it! Ghoulish clowns! little jokers, I'm going to lay something on you, listen up!

Be good oh my beautiful stranger!
For whom so many songs I have sung!

I belt it out cold without a single sour note! That gets the whole gang back into their seats. Nobody knew I had such stage talent! I'm a big smash. I sort of play it down.

"Hey, Cascade!" I go back on the attack, "so what about this investigation? Got nothing more to add on the subject?"

"Go on! Go on! Keep singing! We'll get back to that later!"

No kind of answer.

A few more bombs are falling again, not on Wapping, farther east, toward Chelsea... the sea...

Little Renée and big Angèle are tearing at each other tooth and nail over the helmets... each saying they look better on herself... they try them on brimming with piss... splattering it all over... And then they break back into their cakewalk... a pretty woozy-wobbly version... all under the pink ceiling lamps. That's where everybody's crammed in on top of each other between the four tables... Can't let one copper out... the matter's settled that's the trick... can't let even a single one go sniffing around outside... the clowns've got to come back... meet up in front of the door... Ah! then look out, big trouble!... sure, the bulls are slugging it back like there's no tomorrow, but still they might have some sneaking suspicions... for example, that stink a while back... Got to show them a little more fun... always more... the way I see it, we haven't won yet by a long shot... the ladies are hitching their dresses up to their ears... really kicking their heels!... Cascade and Prospero clap along... They're cranking the bash back up... Hit it, ladies! Leap through the air... the cancan, the good old BOOM-Dee-ay! Ta-ra-ra-BOOM! Dee-ay... Then the farandole... the cops've got quite a lot to keep them entertained... knickers wherever they look... thick clumps of hair through lace... pussies bouncing around... Ta-ra-ra-BOOM-de-ay! Right up against their peepers!... Through the boozy haze a mind-boggling blur... actually their eyes are starting to blink... they're nodding off fast!... can't see shit... collapse on the table, heads on folded arms, they burp, they've had their fill...

Fair enough, these cops are loaded to the gills with gin, but even so the wheels in my head are turning... I think they've seen suspected something... they're just putting on an act like they're plastered... they've keeled over, that'd be too much to hope for...

I do a little polka with Virginia. Then we sit back down. I want to talk to Cascade again... about what's nagging me...

"So how'd it all happen that you got him out of the morgue?... in pieces, such a mishmash?... on your backs?... in a cab?... a cart?... Wasn't he happy at the morgue?..."

I pop the question. I ask him... for the tenth time at least...

"Why start parading him around town?... dump him in the drink?... What's the point?..."

He readjusts his bowler... with a flick of his fingers... looks me up and down... I disgust him.

"Don't you know the first thing about this place here? Don't you know how the system works?"

Sorry-ass jerk that I was...

I exasperate him, oh that's a fact!

"The dummy speaks English! The dummy knows it all! The dummy knows shit! Doesn't know about EXHIBITS FOR THE PROSECUTION!... PROSECUSHEEUN!"

He crammed his mouth full... and spit out capital letters... just like that! PROSECUSHEEUN!

"Mean nothing to you? It's not just hot air, you know!... Such things do exist! Take it from me!..."

Then he starts shaking his head, so sorry I'm thick as a brick.

"Once they get an exhibit for the PROSECUSHEEUN on you! You're swinging from the end of a rope! That's where it lands you! That's how things work around here! Do you get me now, yes or no, damn it?... Didn't you learn back in the regiment? about exhibits for the PROSECUSHEEUN? That's the only thing that exists! But you over there, you lie low, don't give a shit! rush off! rush off! The pretty young woman runs along for some fun! He still thinks he's fighting the war! Oh yes he does, Madame! he ditches his exhibit for the PROSECUSHEEUN! The others have just got to dump it somewhere!... Ah! you're a darling little runt! We won't forget you next time around!"

He was glad for the chance to rake me over the coals...

"Exhibit for the PROSECUSHEEUN, angel-face, that's how things work! The dead meat's what I'm talking about, get it? Your friends are working for you, yes they are! Of course it means zero to you! Those boys are sacrificing themselves! giving one hundred percent! You don't have it in you! They're erasing your crimes! Covering up for you, Mister Goof-Off! Skid Row Romeo! Ferdinand the Disgrace!"

He was lashing out in anger.

"Hanged? You're asking yourself? Hanged? You better believe it! Don't think twice! exhibit for the PROSECUSHEEUN! You know how to speak English! Say good-bye to your miss! my dear old Récamier!..."

Happy with his tirade.

Where he'd dig up "Récamier," can somebody tell me? A name that meant nothing... just for effect!...

But where'd that piece of meat get to? in the river? in its canvas sack? the whole bundle?... That's where it must be right now... I could see the open boat... the river traffic... the drink... exhibit for the PROSECUSHEEUN! Ah! Scared shitless again! Ah! a horrible mixed-up mess, and getting worse by the minute... Ah! heading toward a total fiasco!... Ah! I was shaking, kissing the little girl... she was clueless... hadn't seen a thing... happened while she was asleep... I ask Cascade one more time:

"So it's over? They tossed it out? hell, that's great! We won't bring it up anymore!..."

I wanted to put an end to this business once and for all.

"Won't bring it up?... Won't bring it up?... we'll see!"

He still needed convincing.

"Pet, you just keep talking... makes life easy... drags things out, it does! drags them out... I can't say another word..."

"Ah! shit, will you listen, I had nothing to do with it!..."

I'm getting aggravated too. He's egging me on.

"You crack me up! Look, it's my party!"

I do like them, act happy-go-lucky. I grab Virginia, whisk her off, we tear into a farandole, the fact she's knocked up doesn't keep her from dancing! I chug down some bubbly right from the bottle... to the last drop... waltzing the whole time... glug-glug! glug-glug!

Here comes the lady of Paris...

In a flash the bubbly sets all my ideas boiling... my whole head balloons... I'm twice my size... pow! I explode! Christ Almighty, it's thunder!... It's love!... Can't hear myself think!... Boom! Boom! and Boom! Boom! This has nothing to do with that Claben business, damn it to hell! "Bombed-out dive! Stinking rotten!" I yell at everybody! The hyenas all cackle! "Heartless! Heartless!" I shout at them! even the fuzz think I'm a stitch! even Virginia is wriggling in delight at the ridiculous spectacle I'm making! Everybody dancing together, in one big long line, on two feet, on all fours, on their haunches, toads, kicking up their feet Russian-style, wriggling their whole bodies... Gisèle's got that Russian kick down pat, Madame Gisèle they call her. She lived in Russia for eighteen years, a hooker. Nothing to sneeze at.

Yop! Yop! you ought to see the way she leaps, springs, yelps, all around the floor. A real live witch in a whirl once she got going... she can breathe fire too, right from her mouth, long terrific flames, from gasoline, that's her other talent.

"Pépé can do the same thing too, plus dance Russian-style."

Sosthène makes sure I'm informed.

"Too bad she's not here now. We'd have a great time."

Such talents are hard to come by. Sosthène cries over his Pépé, the sudden memory of her, his dear absent love. His chest heaves with huge sobs... Ah! they give him a shake... None of that now... they drag him back into the *matchiche*... No gloomy Guses at my party! Virginia feels a whole lot better... she's wide awake, doesn't feel at all queasy anymore. The ladies come over for some lovey-dovey, she gives them a kick in that skimpy outfit of hers... schoolgirl skirt... And now Sosthène's raring to go, he drags my angel away into the dance, and they're both off together...

Virginia's the more graceful of the two, no doubt about it... a sorceress... She moves to the music as light as air... Everybody looks on in admiration... she's exquisite... the pixie of the whirlwind... swept along by the dance it's a dream... with a driving beat... turn glide kittenish... twirl away one two three a waltz... baby doll...

Admiration from one and all, and some predictable jealousy... Especially Carmen had an attitude about it, the girl came on too strong for her taste, she kept making eyes at Cascade.

"Peek-a-boo! Peek-a-boo! Take a look!" she blurts out at me...

Just then the band was sour-noting something horrible, plus the ocarina. Curlers was on cornet. She had to keep herself busy... The half-crocked lushes choired along, each to his own tune. It must have sounded horrendous out on the dock. If the night patrol enters, barges in for a look-see, we're going to get hauled away... The night patrol doesn't fool around like our watchmen friends over there, our boozers, outlandish but easygoing. The night patrol's a bunch of roughnecks, pigheaded scum, cut no breaks.

I warn Cascade.

"Careful! They're yelling too loud!"

No answer.

"And what the hell are the boaters up to?"

They're taking their own good time, if you ask me.

"All you had to do was go along and then you'd know."

"Are they sending it far away?"

"I'll say!"

A joke.

"You know, out to sea!... not in front of the Chamber of Commerce!... As far out as possible... Did you ever row a boat before?" he asks.

Oh! so it's dirty cracks he's after! I can dish out my share! I give him a demonstration real fast.

"When it comes to corpses, dear sir, let me tell you I've seen shitloads!... More than you'll ever see in your lifetime!... soldiers, brave men! worthy, decorated! not filthy pigs! dung-covered jerks! lousy rotten Clabens! So here's to you! Remember who you're talking to! Just save it!"

I put him back in his place.

I was getting riled, I was this close to whacking him, the guy was bugging me so bad! relief with a wallop! Mr. Expert Pimp!...

He sees I'm going through the roof!... Acknowledges the fact!... Sort of realizes... quite willing to admit I've got my reasons...

"Discuss without losing your temper... You're not behind bars yet! But I'm telling you! Watch out! There's that exhibit for the PROSECUSHEEUN!"

Here we go again with the PROSECUSHEEUN!

"I told you! You deaf or what?... This isn't the Epinettes here! You're in London, get me? In London!"

My laid-back attitude was getting to him.

"In London! it's the exhibit for the PROSECUSHEEUN! There, did you get it? No exhibit for the PROSECUSHEEUN no guilty verdict! You understand English: Guilty! And so who's ditching your exhibit for the PROSECUSHEEUN right now even as we speak! I'm not talking about John Bull's exhibit! But yours! Your exhibit for the PROSECUSHEEUN! Not you, big talker! Not John Bull! Your pals, that's who! Yeah, sweetheart, your pals! Not the pope! Don't you realize? Huh? Here's how they say the word here: REE-AH-LAEEZZZ!... now that's English! the real spoken stuff! REE-AH-LAEEZZZ!" Pigheaded on that point, saying I should have left with them, got personally involved, I must be feeling pretty damn ashamed now!

"You're one lucky devil! Got to say it! You're one lucky devil!..."

It turned his stomach.

Outside, it was thundering again, over the western part of the city. Through the window, the panes, you could see the bouquets of shrapnel bursting in the clouds... and even farther out toward Chelsea... plus the pencil beams of the searchlights scurrying after the flecks... like some kid's game.

The ladies were dancing among themselves, whomping each other on the rump, a whack at each cannon burst... they let up a terrible howl, but nobody was really afraid. It was happening too far away.

Delphine was bellowing out on the embankment... giving her performance... she didn't want to be disturbed...

"Knights! Knights!" she was calling... she wanted the knights to come running.

Inside, there was no intermission. Bottles were being popped faster and faster... Pop! Bang! Pop! The waltz of the corks! a flood of bubbly! The Scottish polka was the big dance of the moment, a titillating step, with sharp squeals...

I was watching Virginia dance with Little Sweetheart. I wasn't too crazy about Little Sweetheart, crafty, syrupy, two-faced... but I wasn't going to go into a snit! Cascade snaps out of his thinking mood. He too is watching the dancers...

"So tell me now," he asks me, "she keeping it?"

"She keeping what?" I wasn't following...

"The kid!"

"We'll see..."

Wasn't his business.

Another moment of silence, then he pops out just like that point-blank: "What you scraping by on right now? You flat broke? Or are you holing up somewhere?..."

He fishes around, pulls out of his pocket a wad of pounds, big bills, five-pound notes!

"Take it!" he goes... gives it to me.

Kind of sudden.

I'd rather not. But do.

"I'll pay you back!" I act dignified...

"It's OK."

I'll have to pay him pretty soon, I'm thinking... even with this supposed party of mine... champagne and the works... I don't want to be in Prospero's debt, I prefer borrowing from Cascade.

"I'll pay you back!" I repeat...

"Whatever! but what about your Chink over there, he flat broke?"

He has to shout this right into my ear, the noise of the cannons is drowning out everything.

"Yeah, but you know what, he's an inventor! an explorer! he comes from India!"

Sosthène's a big shot, and I want Cascade to know about it, not get any wrong idea on the subject, a first-class fellow. I give him the details.

He laughs, doesn't believe me.

He's watching Virginia, the way she's dancing, such a young slip, so perky and bright...

"So tell me, Little-Miss-Knocked-Up over there, you going to put her to work when she's big as a house, or what?... since you're making her keep it... she's going to need to take it easy..."

That's what was on his mind.

I glanced over, it was nice of him in a way...

"You want another girl?" he proposes. "While she's taking a break?"

A kindhearted offer.

"How about a couple?"

He pointed over to the ladies. I just had to take my pick. They were writhing under the ceiling lamps. Right away his mind jumped to my emergency needs, he saw I was hard up, his first thought, hookers. Nothing nasty or brutal, he just wanted to lend a helping hand because he knew how life works, keeping the wolf from the door was serious business, and grub doesn't fall from heaven...

"Whatever you decide, you know... You just say the word..."

It remained to be seen, of course... No need for me to be shy.

Cascade had a good ten or twelve just in his own Leicester stable... I could have taken one of them in as a member of the family... even two or three... so that Virginia could have a nice quiet rest, we'd be on easy street, and everything would all fall fantastically into place... Ah! I was tempted... I kept listening... It'd make my whole life simpler...

He could see I was in a bind.

And then wham! Matthew pops into my mind! Oh! look out! panic! Enough daydreaming! Short little memory of mine! I grab hold of myself! Ah! that thought slammed the door!

"Cut the snow job, pal, OK?... Quick, we're out of here! Geez, oh brother, where was my head at!"

He eyeballs me, I'm making him sore!

Boom! Bang! Bing! Over our heads the action's heating up... raging in every corner of the sky! All hell's breaking loose something terrible! Wapping! Ping! Bang! Whoosh! Explosions everywhere!

He asks me again, pigheaded...

"Don't you want another girl? you sure?"

He hollers loud into my ear.

"No! No!" I shout back... "it'll be OK!"

"You don't want Little Sweetheart?"
"Ah! no way!"
He laughs, knows I can't stomach her...
Broom!... Bra-boom!... Pots and pans!
There goes the nigger, the petty thief the cops dragged in, back to his dumb-ass tricks.
He belly flops to the floor...
"Broum! Broum!" he apes... just like that on all fours... at every shell burst... he bounces up and down... rattling the whole joint, he's strong, sends everything flying... the tables, the benches... the bottles... everything around him... he's a hellcat... announces he wants to pray to God... so he starts bellowing... bawling God out... threatening... yelling even louder than Delphine... with raised arm, threatening God!... "God! God! you're no good!" he shouts... He leaps, pounces on the ladies, grabs Carmen, then Flyswatter... he trips... all three go rolling... across the floor, tooth and nail... he pulls up Carmen's dress... wants to plant her with a kiss...
"Mommy! Mommy!..." he calls her...
She screams rape. All the girls come running, can't pass up this golden opportunity... they all yank up their dresses so he can see their cracks... Just like that, a mess of knickers... frills... flouncy silk lingerie... Ah! he's in raptures... he does a Mohammed number... bends over... bows low pops up like that fast fast fast all at once... arms in the air!... "Zou! Zou! Zou!" he shouts each time... Geez, he's one weird character! We dump all the beer on top of him, empty our mugs, our bottles... our grogs... he downs everything, head tilted backwards... Glug! Glug! Glug!... And then the party's off again wilder than ever! the farandole's in full swing, they knock the nigger over, roll him around, trample him. He lets out a wail under their feet, can't breathe... even so he hollers out his "cheers" to the pub keeper, the young ladies, the men! and the Good Lord! Goddamn it! All of a sudden he forgives him! "I forgive you!" he roars... Climbs back up on his knees. Meditates, collects his thoughts again... Mug dripping, eyes popping, he roars:
"I forgive you, Heavenly Father!..."
All is forgiven!
Got to take over from the musicians, they're frazzled. Dédé's a deadbeat. Léonie picks up the guitar—she's Prospero's maid, from Brittany, she learned how to play in Rio. The girls are in ecstasies, tumbling on top of each other, it's the absinth-champagne combo that's got them squealing... They flaunt every stitch of their batistes and their big openings... Whoops-a-daisy! A hullabaloo of hysterical laughter... The shack's coming apart at the seams, quaking from the echo, rumbling like a drum.
"Here's to King George! To victory over the Krauts!"
They're going as far as that! Cascade is toastmaster!
In the midst of the enthusiasm, the hurrays, the sailors in turn slip off

their duds, start roughhousing as much as the cops. Stark naked you can see their tattoos. The biggest belly's got the most tattoos. "Rule Victoria" etched in green letters, with the Queen Mother straddling a magnificent dolphin. The girls gawk in admiration, a break in the action, you don't come across a tattoo of this caliber every day...

Right away it sparks a battle of one-upmanship. Hairy chests vs. hairy asses. Opinion is split. Each shows his doodads. There are lots of tattoos, the women got as many as the men, especially on their tits. The contest is organized. The most popular tattoos are hearts pierced by daggers. But the finest is hands down the cop with his queen and dolphin... a genuine monument. The folds of fat around his belly fill in for waves, he gives us a demonstration. Everybody's jealous. Cascade offers him some bubbly, he's crowned champ. Little Renée passes the bottles around. She's got the jitters, spills one. The cannon terrifies her...

"Is it all getting to you?" people ask.

"I... I... don't know... I... I... don't know..." she stammers...

She's in a dither... the only one, plus the nigger... echoing the blasts, rolling his eyeballs, booming from his huge mouth. Boom!... Boom!... Boom!... Without letup...

"Long live the Russians!... Long live Tibet!..."

Sosthène's getting excited... He wants people to listen up.

"Long live Tibet!..."

Nobody asked him anything...

This air raid just won't quit... another round's starting... out toward Lambeth... the others still aren't back... nothing's working... Try my best to distract myself from my worries... I realize...

Maybe they drowned too?... It'd be best if they never came back... And what if they were all in cahoots?... that fires my suspicions again... My heart starts racing at the mere thought... I sit down.

"You think so, Virginia? Do you?..."

I ask her, she can't understand me. Incapable of suspicion. Even so I'm sure as hell. It's a trap, a scheme. That's why he's been fussing over me, Mr. Swindler over there, turning my head with girls, etc... goddamned pimp! I can see what you're up to! my party and all that jazz! I know you like a book! Ah! it blows me away! You bet it's one nice piece of work! Just think for a second about the coincidence, today of all days is my name-day party! They're dead set on doing me in! That's what's behind all this! Big as life! I get the picture! The end of my rope! The others are never coming back! They're out there ratting on me! A big act! And it's the cops who're going to come knocking! Not the locals either! But the others from the Yard, Matthew's gang, the eager beaver's on the job. I can see them stepping out of the darkness... no, it's not them! Just some sailors... what an absolutely terrific haul... In you go, rabbits! Shut the trap! Jump! Into the fryer! Your ass is cooked! As sure as I'm sitting here I can see what's coming!... Right on cue! boom! Serve hot and crisp! Ah! moron that I am! Ah! my party! Exactly what's coming to me! Oh! terrific con! In cahoots one and all!

I'm beating it! And this time for good! I grab Virginia! I tug her!

"Come on, we're off! Let's hit the road, missy!..."

One bound! Two! Halt! Cascade's there! Barring the door! He was ready for us!

Back off! I sit down again. Everybody's splitting their sides, I'm an absolute scream! What a sap! his party! my party! Oh, geez! Just too rich! "Sing us another!" Don't want to. They insult me. This one cop, the skinny guy, wants to sing, nobody's entertained, they boo him off, he thinks they're calling for an encore, takes another shot. This triggered such an uproar, an ugly stink, they squirt his head with the siphons. "Show some manners, please!" I step in. "Respect the law!" I'm booed, lambasted, hounded off. I huddle in a corner with Virginia, keep mum, collect my wits. I hold Virginia by the arm. I talk to myself. "Careful, kid! Take a powder!..." I'm determined!... Got to take advantage of the hubbub... On tiptoe... Beat it out of here! On the qt! Terrific!... Terrific!... Nobody'll suspect! The coast isn't clear just yet... There's a cop over there with his eye on us... I can see him monitoring us while pretending to look the other way... Ah! I've got a bad feeling... Let's wait just a little bit longer... But the others are going to show up... No doubt about it... Matthew's bullies... proud as peacocks... birds of a feather, sons of bitches every one of 'em... Ah! If that investigation is really starting up again!... That's all I need, geez!... I won't wiggle out of it this time around... it's my ass!... It'll make it into the *Mirror*... I can see my photo! The Greenwich affair back in the news!... Oh! hell! my bright ideas! I thought the story was dead! Tough luck, chump! It was all in my dreams! Head in the clouds!... Ah! my heart's racing again, thumping loud, faster and faster, a drum stuck in my throat, my belly's throbbing, my guts... I'm sagging at the knees, caving in, what great shape I'm in!... my ears are whistling, drumrolling, trumpeting so loud I can't hear a thing outside. My whole world's in a spin... I stretch out... afraid to move a muscle... It'll be back in the news! I'm spluttering... sweating ha... hard... Back in the news!... One of those roundups!... Ah! handcuffs... handcuffs everywhere!... on wrists... on ankles!... Got to get out of here!... That's it, simple solution!... Hotfoot it!... Glued to the spot quivering so bad, I'm really flying out of whack... Ah!... brr... brr... brrr!... I'm shivering!... I can hear the ocarinas... roaring like organs... I don't want to leave Virginia... I squeeze her against my heart... chatter away at her... very affectionately...

"Virginia, I don't feel well..."

She can see for herself... I'm not just carrying on...

"Let's step outside, OK? for a second?..."

"But that's not allowed... the air raid!..."

"Yes, but I can't take it anymore, I'm suffocating..."

Sosthène's not feeling well either... he's waving to me frantically... he also would like a breath of fresh air... We'll need some alibi...

Bingo! We have to go out and get Delphine! I shout real loud...

"Will everybody just listen how she's yelling! That can't go on like that outside! She'll bring a mob of cops to our door! It's got to stop! She absolutely has to come back inside! We've got to go get her!"

Such quick wits I have.

"Go fetch the bitch!" comes the answer.

So now we're outside. Better already! Phew! We can breathe! The air's nippy! The night swallows us up, pleasant feeling. It's booming away over our heads, and how... Ricocheting all over the gravel, the shrapnel of antiaircraft fire... No big deal...

We sit down, do some thinking, size up our situation now that we're out of the Ta-ra-ra-boom! not to mention the smoke, the reek of booze, but the worst part was the way they kept bellowing in your ears, pounding your brain to pulp, I prefer cannon fire. But this is no time to philosophize. I shake Sosthène. "We've got to make a dash for it!"

"Think so?"

He's not so sure. He'd like to rest a while... just like that, with his back against the shack... taking advantage of the pitch-dark...

"OK, all right, but look, just for a minute! no more... You're not going to have a snooze."

That'd be a dumb move.

I sort of watch the to-and-fro... the water... continuing along... gliding through the darkness... there're lanterns in every which direction... boat traffic... crisscrossing... disappearing... red... yellow... green... A siren's echo... plus the heavy chuff of bellows real close... right on top of me pfoo... pfoo!... from some machine... a freighter chugging along... grazing by... alongside us... we can see its huge side... shadow upon shadow... passing... Fires are blazing throughout the city... Enough bombs hit their mark despite everything... and I'm not talking small bonfires... but three... four separate ones... conflagrations... enormous things... flames licking the clouds... smoke streaming in plumes along the rooftops... wreaths so long so immense that they blanket all of London, the whole breadth and stretch, the entire northern edge... wafting as far as Big Ben, enveloping the Clock Tower, the Tower of London, the House of Commons, the Palace, you name it... Ah! what a spectacle! gigantic! I'd never have believed anything could have been so beautiful!... You couldn't see a thing from inside that dump! Ah! we did right to step outside...

"Come on, let's move it! The fun and games are over! Forward march, gang! Let's melt back into the city! disappear into the streets again!..."

Those are the orders... we've got to take advantage of the darkness while it lasts... keep an eye open along the towpath... the footpath for tramps and cops... avoid running into anybody via the little twist in the road and then the docks and then Millwall... Hop a transport ferry... Once on the other side we're home free... Poplar's just a maze of small back streets... zigzagging up to the tube... less than three hundred yards out in the open... The tube's our only chance... unless they've thought of everything... scattered cops around the station... but mustn't let my imagination run away with me...

I was good at reconnaissance, approach maneuvers... I had all the army tricks down pat... the proof is that Mr. Magician Sosthène had taken me on for that very purpose, hired me right off the street for his caravan, his Tibet, his Tara-Tohé, his mirages! Damn it all! To hell with pipe dreams! Back to work!...

I was guiding Virginia by the arm, making sure she didn't twist her foot, the stones were awful, she'd got dizzy on coming out of the joint, leaving the smoky den, the hollering, plus she'd danced too much, drunk too hard just to keep everybody happy, clinking glasses with all the ladies... and hopping, dancing on top of that! I was worried! And all through the evening, all through the night! Where was my head at? I was genuinely nuts! Hadn't it dawned on me? Maybe she hurt herself? bumped something? her belly? And that's why she wasn't feeling well!... plus she'd given out a couple-three times... practically fainted... she'd been a bad girl jumping all over the place like that... understandable at her age... But what about me, I should have thought about it!... It was the obvious thing to do... Come on, I was older than her... I ought to have looked out for the kid... I was twenty-two... she just fifteen... well, almost... I upbraided her gently... ah! no harsh words... sweetness and light... saying it was nothing serious...

Sosthène was slogging along behind us... moaning because of his corns... Little Sweetheart had tread on top for a couple-three dances... He was going to take off his shoes, continue barefoot... he informed us:

"Just like in Benares!..." he announces... "like in Benares..."

In Benares walking barefoot was sacred... he explains to us... the way of the fakirs...

We stop for Benares, so he can fall in with the ritual...

"You going to go back to your ballet act?"

He wasn't anxious to.

The first light of dawn was spreading about the docks, not bright, lost in the fog... It sheds a dim glow on our embankment...

The large Tower Bridge in the distance gradually looms out of the mist, very slowly baring its keep, raising high into the air the gigantic arms of its arches, sitting in the middle of the river like that, for the ships to enter... the huge steamships steaming, puff! puff! puff! in big furbelows... shuddering chugging forward... in black columns of smoke... huge plumes blue, mauve, pink puffs of steam... Pavane on the river... in broad daylight... bulwark in fanciest finery... the shores to the east shimmering with a thousand and one lanterns, winking, trembling... the work crews congregating... flocking... vaulting up the rungs... black on gray... A great commotion sweeping the area... the crew rejoining their ships at daybreak... pouring down to the docks... changing hands... quitting time for the graveyard shift... two-three winches screak, grind horrendously... the noise the knocking... a grating screech... high into the sky... and then it all snaps into gear again, chug! chug! chug! small puffs of steam... The giant *Portland*, the crane bellows a savage blast... Rise and shine.

The river quivering, crisscrossed, whipped up every which way... A hundred small open boats rush out, charge into the traffic... sculling... with a splash! splash! splash!... pulling hard at the oars... streaming in from all corners... into the wakes... onto the stems... the sterns... slipping around the laggard stems... corks of foam... grazing past everything... arches... propeller blades... churning furiously!... fervent halyards seized in flight... from one end to the other... bellying cargos... overwhelming monsters... a small fry of pilot fish in the first light of day from crest to crest of foam nimbly scudding free... splashing up farther away... even more lively... spinning tops rocking from wave to wave... sending up sprays...

I've painted you a small picture of the farandole out on the lapping waves... But there's more to life than sights to see! We've got to hurry along... Sitting around's no good for us... Sosthène was ready. He goes back on his plan. Doesn't want to barefoot it anymore... slips his clodhoppers back on, he's a contrary character...

"Come on! Let's go, Benares!"

I hustle him along.

Virginia could use a break, I see... The darling's sort of struggling to keep up... And she's not the dillydallying sort.

"I could use some sleep!..." she confesses...

"But you already got some!..."

It comes over her... closes her eyes...

"Virginia, we have to go!..."

We were too close to the canteen... if there was going to be a roundup... which I was sure was due any minute now... It was dead certain settled... sitting there on our asses like good little boys and girls in the brisk morning air... Oh! holy Christ! As clear as two plus two. I could see it all coming, just mind-boggling! Ah! the worthless bums! the cannibals!... Ah! I can't control myself anymore! Ah! I flare back up! Roaring mad! Ah! first-class shits! Ah! I shout: "Fuck you, assholes!"

I warn them, I'm pissed off... A sure bet they put the finger on us! sold us out straight to the fuzz! Ah! the bunch of bastards! I work myself into a lather! I rebel! Rise up! I see indignities everywhere! challenges! slimy devils crawling out from under every stone... right there through the fog I can make them out... careful! I warn my friends... I want them to see the shadows... In the grip of emotion myself... I can see freakish shapes in the fog... of people, and that's a fact... light as air, that's all... on the barge... on the companion hatch... around the small mast, the tackle... dancing/jigging/fluttering about... hand in hand a big long line... No denying it... a farandole... circling spinning... skimming the waves... then rising... people in the air... disappearing... The circle dance above the Thames!... I tell the wizard right away, whisper against his ear. He's got to know...

"Careful, you poor sucker! Very great danger!..."

Ah! I'd bet my life on it!...

"You hallucinating?" he responds.

"Hallucinating? You rotten little jerk! Can't you hear the music?"

Not a note.

Dumb as a post, what a disgrace.

"Well then, how do you expect to see the delicate, bewitching circle dance? You can't see anything hear anything! End of discussion!"

I felt sorry for the guy...

"Come on, you old has-been! Let's get going! I see people, and that's the end of that! I can't spell it out for you any clearer! We're being watched! That's the news I've got for you! Goddamn it!"

I bawl them out one more time... saying I'll give all I've got to save them! my last breath! so they had to listen to me! I insist!

"Great danger! Treacherous mists from the glaucous river! intertwining, coiling, Love! Love!" I work myself up! "Flocks! Flocks! You hear me?... They're moving forward! Dancing! Circling back on us! Dodging! Skirting around! Shore! Shh! Phew! Circling back! No more Millwall! Treacherous haze! No more transshipments! Muddle up! Muddleheaded! Muddymist me loves! Muddled our ways! He who muddles best muddles muddiest! Wheeouuh! I understand myself!"

They're terrified... looking hard at me... I'm still the same guy! Exploding with energy!

"Ladies of the fog, I bow to you! You first, please! Daydream! Your servant! Your page!"

I draw them to me, the kid and Sosthène, slip in their ears hush-hush...

"Let's head out for Limehouse! Poplar! Gung ho! I'm rescuing you!..."

My quick wits!

My idea made for a long detour. So much the better! the worse!...

"Come on, let's go! get a move on! Let's go back to the city on the beam, my ballooning toads!"

A well-hatched plan! Via the small slime path... the yokels' lane, below the towpath... where you slip on everything from sludge to kelp... tidal pools... lucky thing I sort of knew the way... I'd been over to "Samarland," the fruit-sellers dock... with Little Paul... for a Spanish chick... that was our way out...

Ah! we mustn't wind back up at the canteen!... Another zigzag... a right after that, the semaphore... a grayish mauve-streaked mass... the same color sky, river, houses... Against the fence... far in the distance I can spot two shapes, two people stooping... I peer hard... all a haze... the fog moving in wrapping them in a dense shroud... Streaming in fast from up river... a stampede... huge flocks... smothering everything...

Ah! Got to find out!... Spooked!... The cops! It's them! No! Wrong! Phew! Oh, no! Delphine on the ground, the nigger beside her...

"Delphine! Delphine!..."

I'm glad. I call her... They're arm in arm, kissing, caressing, keeping each other warm, tonguey-tonguey... loads of lovey-dovey... they found each other in the darkness, the cold...

She spots me. Right away starts shouting:

"Ah! It's you, my little bloodsucker!"

And she's shuddering, gesticulating!... Her hat flies off... her red veil flapping like crazy... swept off by a gust... her hair down over her face...

Clambers back on her feet.

Starts raving. I bring it out in the gal. The nigger, scared shitless, throws himself on his belly... asks forgiveness... Thinks I'm with the police...

"Police!" he pleads... "Police! Not me! Not me!..."

Just like me, hallucinating... Sees cops wherever he looks. The guy cracks me up, about time I had a turn.

"So tell me," I ask the beauty, "so tell me, honey, is this your black man?"

I was making a joke about the guy from way back when, the guy from the Greenwich, the one from the night we smoked the magic cigarettes who supposedly had run into her, the black guy she met on the railroad bridge while looking for the doctor that fateful night...

In short, the whole awful mess. I didn't give a shit about her!

"Ah! The thug! The boor!"

She bounds up, a she-lion! she insults me! Wild-eyed on her feet! Ah! how dare I! Low-down! spluttering in rage... in total disgust!...

"Oh! Oh! Go! Gosh! Oh! You!... you!... Wretch!..." she's reached her limit. "You!... dare recall!... thug! miserable wreck! Silence, memories! Saee!-lence!"

Splatt!... she spits in my face...

"Murderer! Murderer!" she shouts herself hoarse... "Barbarian!"

She doesn't give a damn whether she's raising a ruckus... that'll bring the bulls down on us... I'll teach her! this scares the nigger so bad he starts circling around on all fours... shaking so hard he can't think... "Be! Be! Be! Be!..." he splutters... rolls on the ground... wants to hide under Delphine... climb into her petticoats... dives in... rummages around underneath...

"Jesus!" he wails!... "Pity! Pity!"

She's in an ornery mood, gives him a few whomps with her feet, her arms, pummels his head... wham! wham! wham! wham! breaks her umbrella!... Oh! Christ Almighty, what a clobbering!

"Little mother!" he cries at each whack... "I love you!"

And then Oooh! He explodes in guffaws... an enormous bass boom! Ooooh! Oooooh! echoing along the whole river.

She's whaling... whaling away... plus him laughing... Oooh! flat on the ground, collapsed, belly in the pebbles... his skull taking the full brunt! wham! wham! wham! wham!...

She climbs on top... the final assault!... Gee up! Delphine's not laughing, she's on the warpath, so roaring mad she's fit to be tied... She wants to beat me too, makes a charge for me when she sees me laughing my silly-ass head off. I snatch her umbrella away. Disarmed, she bellows twice as loud.

"Kill me! Kill me then!"

She recuperates her topper, pops it back on her head, plus the veil and gloves. There now, in position for me to kill her! She absolutely insists:

"There! There!..."

She shows me her heart, points to the exact spot! right here and nowhere else! she rips away everything! rrrip! over the spot where I'm supposed to strike her!...

If the cops show up it's going to look just dandy!... On purpose she howls at me at the top of her lungs... I'm sure you can hear her on the opposite shore...

"Lady Macbeth speaks to you!"

"Shut the hell up! Shut the hell up!"

I've had it.

If I lay a finger on her she'll howl bloody murder.

"You stinking weasel!" she lashes out... "Get your face out of my sight!..."

She's sending me packing.

"No! No!" she changes her mind, confident. "Listen!" she whispers in my ear... "Seyton! I must disappear!... Kill me!... Seyton! kill me!... Wretch! as you killed so well the others!"

Now I'm Seyton, that's the way it is, some new nickname, my party's over. She's turned on by the idea of me killing her as I killed so well the others!...

She looks at me, rolls her peepers, I've got to make up my mind to do it.

"Seyton! Seyton!" she's got a one-track mind. I'm Seyton! That's what she's hot on, pop-eyed at the bright idea.

"Macbeth! Macbeth!" she howls into the wind... now she's calling that guy too... She's got something to tell him. She grabs me, gives me a smooch, a taste of witchcraft. I'm smothered in caresses. Pure passion. She spills her heart. Whispering up against my face. She desires me. She's got to ravage me supposedly... She paws me, turns on the charm... I'm clasped in her embrace... entwined's more like it... then abruptly, in a snap, she yanks herself away... walks off... clambers back onto the embankment way high up against the fence. We're in for another tirade... I spring after her, want to talk some sense into her: "Come on, Delphine, enough's enough! You're not this crazy! Listen to me! you're going to bring the cops!..."

"Fuck off!" She's not interested.

"What have you done with poor Claben?"

That's the bug up her ass.

"He's in the river, you dumb cunt!"

Now there's an answer for you! She doesn't get it... It's her big hang-up... the nigger's howling the same time she is, he wants me to murder her as she says... He leaps back down to the gravel... fidgety on all fours:

"Kill me! Kill me!" he barks. Back to his doggie routine by the riverside... He's possessed. Pretty state of affairs.

"Let's go! We're leaving!"

I beat it.

She throws herself on me, clinging.

"The dawn!" she exclaims!... "the dawn! Boys, the dawn! Salute the dawn! What joy!" She's beside herself! She flings her arms up into the sky, shrieking.

I'd just love to bump her off!

A barge is moving past our spot... sailing out of the fog... maneuvering toward us... alongside the pebbly shore...

She shouts over to the bargeman...

"At once the benefit of sleep! And do the effects of watching! What a weird business... Oh! the clamor! All the benefit of sleep! Yet with eyes that see clearly! Watch out, boys! Watch out!"

The ship hands stampede on deck... wave their poles... passing into the clouds... the boat grazes past... glides along... disappears...

She shouts after them, warns them about the worst sort of perils!

"Don't be deceived, young men!.."

They didn't notice her at all. And here she was shouting her head off! She's not sore. Ah! no way! no way! She knows what it's all about!

"They know me there!"

She points to the stretch of endless mists!... That never occurred to me... they're buddies! Oh! geez! what a ninny! She's jumping for joy.

"Oh! boys! boys!..."

It hits me. Everything falls into place! All the spells, eyes wide open!... She brings it all home to me... Ah! splendid tricks! I'm ecstatic... I won't fly in her face...

She's back on my case again... I've got to hear the whole story... She still has a few more real zingers to lay on me...

"All the dangerous leaps of the cat! of the elf! lying down! Understand? Young man? Miracle! Beddy-bye! Understand! get to bed! Dream! Dream!

Little man!"

That's an order.

I'm not dreaming, no way. My problem is coming up with some way to put an end to this, then skedaddle without her screaming bloody murder... I wanted to avoid that... Oh heck! Tough nuts!

I motion to Sosthène... and the girl... for them to run along ahead of me... I'll catch up... no need to wait cause I'll be right behind...

"Take a right!... A right!..."

The gravel path continues on the right... then the lock then the Peninsula Shipping Company Dock... I let them leave... and zip!... I clear out!...

I limp, still able to run despite all... Ah! she sends up a howl, oh brother! Roaring after me literally up into the sky!... the water carries sound... in a huge way... you can hear her trap thundering from every corner... echoing everywhere... on every breeze... suddenly shifting... gusting... put-downs roaring from every direction!...

"Ferdinand! Beast! Frog! Monkey!" A long list of names for me...

"Ferdinand! Dog! Heartless dog!..."

I turn onto the parapet of the lock... It's mobbed up there... the workers' fairway... they're wondering why there's all this brouhaha...

"She's bonkers!" I explain.

I give another try at getting her to shut up... Motioning to her from up where I am.

"Shush! Shush! Shush!"

Fuck off, and a hell of a lot worse than before! Stridently shrieking, she booms ten times louder than me!

"Give me the dagger! Coward! Macbeth has murdered sleep!"

She's absolutely dead set. She'll never shut up.

Screw you! Bye-bye!

"Let's cast off! Step it up, gang!..."

But my little gang of jokers is worn to a frazzle! Especially the girl, she's falling off her feet!... Hit by another dizzy spell... but we need to keep moving forward all the same!... this is no neck of the woods to screw around in... Right away the small side streets... from the dock on the right... inside... shadowy... after the Insulinde silos... and then more back alleyways... tricky turns and zigzags... Dungow... Bermondsey... Hercule Commons... fast as our legs can carry us... almost as far as Lambeth Bridge... once there, a breather, a break... Intermission, we deserve it!... We were able to catch our breath. My darling Virginia was fluttering her lids... blinking her sleepy eyes... I upbraided her gently...

"You danced too much, honey!..."

"Oh, but it was so amusing!..."

She had no regrets... Her pug nose such impertinence... always in a flutter over every trifle, a smile, a laugh, a small suggestion, now the fog was turning to drizzle, beading upon her beautiful hair, her divine curls, with every wet gust...

Ah! I kissed her once more... twice... three times... as we ran along... just like that double-quick!... sweetheart darling!... We'd stopped worrying about Sosthène... Who was talking to himself behind us...

"Where are we going?" he shouts at me suddenlike!...

"Get there! Then you'll see!"

True, I had to pick a spot.

"Well?"

I was leaning toward returning to her uncle's. Things had to be patched up quickly because I was leaving... Maybe I could stall a little longer?... Maybe phone him up first?... Now that was wise sensible... I was looking at Sosthène, the girl... they were waiting for me to decide...

The weather was clearing up a little... it wasn't coming down so hard... it might just turn out to be a beautiful day... maybe we could wait until evening?... Bop around a bit longer... Take advantage of the time we had left?...

"Aren't you cold, Virginia?"

"Chilly! Chilly!..." she laughs back.

Complaining wasn't her style... even in downpours... There was the matter of her short skirt... It had rubbed Cascade the wrong way... Maybe it was even shorter now that it was drenched...

You could already see her legs, strong and delicate, muscular, tanned, feline... oh, the wonderful arc from thigh to ankle!... taut with the bloom of youth, with joy!... blazing leaping with light!

Ah! my eyes played tricks on me every time! Oh! hell! Oh! man! I can still see that skimpy little skirt... charming/amusing... with pleats... tartan...

Oh! that's a fact, the hem was high, even for England!... Plus on top of that... a bun in the oven... well, only I knew... But still! Still! Oh! knock it off! Your eyes aren't playing tricks, you've got to take action! Should we go back?... Or not?... Ah! I splither, splatter, splutter... I quiver... don't know my ass from my elbow... I can see this is all going to come to an awful end...

"I got it!" I shout... "I got it!"

That's all.

I wasn't writing novels yet. I didn't know how to doodle out seven hundred pages like that in crazy quilt patterns... I was choking with excitement...

Sosthène throws in the towel, plops down right on the sidewalk... waiting for me to make up my mind...

"Whenever you're ready!..."

He's freezing, shaking. I see he's a miserable wreck...

I ask: "Not feeling good, huh?"

"Oh! I'll get over it!..." he reassures me... "it's my heart... skipping a beat..."

I give him a chance to rest up... the bus is better than the tube... I thought it over... The tube's crawling with cops... I announce to Sosthène: "The bus!"

"Go ahead! Go ahead! You're in charge!..."

Well all right then! I'm determined!...

"London Bridge, OK, we'll cross it... the bus from the Monument... Number 113... York Square stop! You phone up!..."

"No! Not me, you!"

"If you like..."

"Your way's the only way, monsieur!... Come on, we'll be right behind..."

I hold out my hands, pull him up to his feet, we start off again nice and slowly. London Bridge isn't right around the corner, there's still a ways to go, we ran ourselves ragged with all our zigzagging, crisscrossing to cover our tracks, from one back street to another... we're done in... At last there it is... It's high, from where we are down on Tooley Street I mean... A real climb... But then from the handrail we have this lookout! We can see almost clear to Woolrich, the entire vista, the whole river up to Manor Way... King Docks... It's a wonderful view...

I tell him: "Now's the time to catch our breath! Just get a lungful of that air..." It's true, a sea breeze... it sweeps past you up on the parapet... blasts you in shifting gusts... washes your face clean...

From up there we can see the boats... all the activity of the wharfs... all the grand goings-on... dropping anchor... crews... the whole racket... the whole carousel... fat ones... skinny ones... long and tapered... camouflaged... the flat stockades... the whole works towed steered among the swirling eddies... a whistle blast! the decks explode in commotion!... hard on the oars veering out making fast... gripping the seamarks... the buoys bobbing... impudent dinghies oh everywhere... racing past, pivoting, splashing... whipping up a froth... ten, a hundred, a thousand... everything plays tricks with your eyes... you've got to love it... It sure does fascinate me... No secret there... I gaze on in wonder... I want them to experience it... I want my two little pets to go just as crazy over it... I draw their attention, Sosthène's and the girl's, to the deftness, the winning way the boats draw in, drift, ship oars... smoothly down the length of the river... It's going to fascinate them too, but they're cold, they let me know... The sea gulls are crisscrossing the sky, to and fro, hovering, swooping down on the beacons... tenderly perching...

The great current roars under the arches way down below, swelling, furrowing, frothing... nasty, must say... knocking about roughing up the small dinghies... driving them back into the wind! the big steamer *Cardiff* loaded down starting out on its way belting, plowing, plugging, driving toward the pylons... chug! chug! chug!... the entire machine... pale churning wild... gives up moors... Ker-bang plunk!... the enormous heap of metal... a thundering racket!... ship at anchor!

That snaps me out of it... whew!... "Just get a load of that," I point out to them... "Tell me it isn't terrific! The skill in maneuvering... the dangers..."
They get the picture, but they're cold. They're cold, period.
"Fine! All right then! On our way!..."
I'll drop it.
It's still sort of dark out... The electric Wrigley sign, huge sucker, is still lit, we can just about make it out through the fog even though we're practically on top of it, off to our right above the Orpington factory... It's going to be a cloudy day, now I'm scared. I thought it'd be sunny.
The gusts of wind stink of soot, we linger on the parapet until I make up my mind once and for all, off to the Colonel's or not, and then this pungent, deep yellow smoke, from a fire still visible out toward East Ham, flickering glows, with huge licks of flame off and on.
The zeppelins really did come. The old geezer can't see shit, but Virginia's got good eyes. She can see out there in the distance... I show her... right by Cannon Dock... That's where we were just now...
"Hey, they've left!" I notice... "Sosthène!" I wake him up.
"Left whozits?"
"The *Kong Hamsün*! Dummy!"
It was a fact, not a single mast, and you can spot sailing ships all the way to kingdom come... sticking out over the rooftops...
No argument from him.
"Yes!... Yes!... Right you are!..."
He was coming to terms with it.
Sharp northern blasts whipped us full in the face. Sosthène was all shivery, jiggling like crazy from the chill.
"You sick or what, huh? You sick?"
"You... you... you got... eyes!"
"OK, let's get going!"
Another at least three-four hundred yards across the rest of the bridge. I lay my hooks into them. Virginia in one arm... him in the other...
"Off we go! my little scamps! On the double!... Can you both hear me?..."
I repeat the orders.
"So, on to the Monument, via the 113! At York Square, everybody off! It's not hard! You, miss, phone up!"
There now, that's terrific!
"Yes, but what do you say to maybe getting a cup of java!"
He got the idea in his head.
"A cup of java where? A cup of java, that's easy to say! It's still too early..."
"Some mocha, mister!"
He won't let go.
"Where you going to dig it up?"
"Right nearby!" He points to the opposite shore...

I knew he had a thing for java.

"At the Calabar! Ever been?"

Never.

"In Twickenham, you oaf! Take it from me! After the station... Victor Saloon!..."

"At this time of morning?"

"You bet!"

"How'd you know?"

"A little bird told me..."

Ah! I know this flimflam artist like a book! He's giving us the come-on...

For the kid too, it was a good idea! a hot cup of coffee is just what she needed.

Regardless, this was a moment's weakness... we should have picked up and left pronto straightaway just the way we were and gone over to her uncle's, and not keep roving traipsing around... from one coffee house to another... just excuses... not the thing to do, not responsible. I realized this... but the pair led me astray...

"Mocha is life!"

The prospect bucks him back up... puts him in a totally clownish/prankish mood...

Standing in the middle of the bridge on a windy day gives you a force to reckon with, the gusts turn you around sweep you off... Got to fight your way through...

It was giving them the biggest kick in the world, grand old practical jokers now, friends, making like they were flying away, whisked off into empty air, with me running after them, latching on...

Two little loonies...

"Come on!" I lose my temper... "Knock it off!"

They pretended to kick the bucket. The old geezer hammed it up the worst.

I tackle the kid, arm in arm... now, forward march!

I'm fighting the gusts with her. Ah! this is a genuine tempest, make no mistake about that! She's laughing! Laughing! She's happy!...

"Ah! what a pretty sight!" I shout. "Youth!..."

Sosthène comes up from behind. He's acting the rake, the rogue...

Is that you little lady?
From the other afternoon?

He sings in his falsest falsetto...

Up against me in the tube...

He's jigging, turning himself on... a sudden gust catches him... carries him off. He goes slamming into the parapet... doesn't give a damn, he's cracking up too hard! The pair are laughing themselves silly...

Another squall, a real violent blast... we wobble... zigzag... stopped short, pushed back, we forge ahead once more... all three of us pushing forward...

Hurray! The end! We've done it! Crossed the bridge! Whew!... Ah! some fun!... They're in seventh heaven, splitting their sides, never been through anything so hilarious!

I smooth her skirt down, the wind had blasted it up to her chin. They'd have walked back into the city looking like that... They didn't give a hoot about anything anymore... Now they want to play Hide and Seek... They're impossible!... I'm the only one not chuckling... They're not one bit tired anymore... I have a genius for making people laugh. They want me to give them a demo of my bitching and moaning routine. They refuse to budge an inch until I start making my face, knotting my brows.

"Ferdinand, dear! make your face!..."

"Come on, let's go! Hit the road!"

I've had it.

Now I'm the clown. That beats everything!

Me of all people, always one to watch his step, and his tongue!

DALKEY ARCHIVE PAPERBACKS

HARRY MATHEWS, *Cigarettes.*
The Conversions.
The Journalist.
The Sinking of the Odradek Stadium.
Singular Pleasures.
Tlooth.
20 Lines a Day.
JOSEPH MCELROY, *Women and Men.*
ROBERT L. MCLAUGHLIN, ED.,
Innovations: An Anthology of Modern & Contemporary Fiction.
JAMES MERRILL, *The (Diblos) Notebook.*
STEVEN MILLHAUSER, *The Barnum Museum.*
In the Penny Arcade.
OLIVE MOORE, *Spleen.*
STEVEN MOORE, *Ronald Firbank: An Annotated Bibliography.*
NICHOLAS MOSLEY, *Accident.*
Assassins.
Children of Darkness and Light.
Impossible Object.
Judith.
Natalie Natalia.
WARREN F. MOTTE, JR., *Oulipo.*
YVES NAVARRE, *Our Share of Time.*
WILFRIDO D. NOLLEDO, *But for the Lovers.*
FLANN O'BRIEN, *At Swim-Two-Birds.*
The Best of Myles.
The Dalkey Archive.
The Hard Life.
The Poor Mouth.
The Third Policeman.
CLAUDE OLLIER, *The Mise-en-Scène.*
FERNANDO DEL PASO, *Palinuro of Mexico.*
RAYMOND QUENEAU, *The Last Days.*
Pierrot Mon Ami.
Saint Glinglin.
ISHMAEL REED, *The Free-Lance Pallbearers.*
The Terrible Twos.
The Terrible Threes.
REYOUNG, *Unbabbling.*
JULIÁN RÍOS, *Poundemonium.*
JACQUES ROUBAUD, *Some Thing Black.*
The Great Fire of London.
The Plurality of Worlds of Lewis.
The Princess Hoppy.
LEON S. ROUDIEZ, *French Fiction Revisited.*
SEVERO SARDUY, *Cobra* and *Maitreya.*
ARNO SCHMIDT, *Collected Stories.*
Nobodaddy's Children.
JUNE AKERS SEESE,
Is This What Other Women Feel Too?
What Waiting Really Means.
VIKTOR SHKLOVSKY, *Theory of Prose.*
JOSEF SKVORECKY,
The Engineer of Human Souls.
CLAUDE SIMON, *The Invitation.*
GILBERT SORRENTINO, *Aberration of Starlight.*
Crystal Vision.
Imaginative Qualities of Actual Things.
Mulligan Stew.
Pack of Lies.
The Sky Changes.
Splendide-Hôtel.
Steelwork.
Under the Shadow.
W. M. SPACKMAN, *The Complete Fiction.*
GERTRUDE STEIN, *The Making of Americans.*
A Novel of Thank You.
PIOTR SZEWC, *Annihilation.*
ALEXANDER THEROUX, *The Lollipop Trollops.*
ESTHER TUSQUETS, *Stranded.*
LUISA VALENZUELA, *He Who Searches.*
PAUL WEST,
Words for a Deaf Daughter and *Gala.*
CURTIS WHITE,
Memories of My Father Watching TV.
Monstrous Possibility.
DIANE WILLIAMS,
Excitability: Selected Stories.
DOUGLAS WOOLF, *Wall to Wall.*
PHILIP WYLIE, *Generation of Vipers.*
MARGUERITE YOUNG, *Angel in the Forest.*
Miss MacIntosh, My Darling.
LOUIS ZUKOFSKY, *Collected Fiction.*
SCOTT ZWIREN, *God Head.*

Printed in the USA
CPSIA information can be obtained
at www.ICGtesting.com
JSHW022236181123
52294JS00003B/4